Andy Remic is a [...] Greater Manchester. During his teaching career he developed an interest in Samurai sword fighting. Now an expert in Pentjak Silat, he can carve a man into eight pieces with a single pirouette but prefers writing and performing dangerous bike stunts.

Find out more about Andy Remic at www.andyremic.com and visit www.orbitbooks.co.uk to register for the free monthly newsletter and to find out about other Orbit authors.

By Andy Remic

SPIRAL
QUAKE

SPIRAL
AND
QUAKE

ANDY REMIC

OMNIBUS EDITION

orbit

www.orbitbooks.co.uk

ORBIT

First published in Great Britain in June 2006 by Orbit

This omnibus edition copyright © 2006 by Andy Remic

Spiral
First published in Great Britain in August 2003 by Orbit
Copyright © 2003 by Andy Remic

Quake
First published in Great Britain in September 2004 by Orbit
Copyright © 2004 by Andy Remic

The moral right of the author has been asserted.

A CIP catalogue record for this book
is available from the British Library.

ISBN-13: 978-1-84149-430-2
ISBN-10: 1-84149-430-5

Printed and bound in Great Britain by
Clays Ltd, St Ives plc

Orbit
An imprint of
Time Warner Book Group UK
Brettenham House
Lancaster Place
London WC2E 7EN

www.orbitbooks.co.uk

SPIRAL

QUAKE

SPIRAL

This book is dedicated with love to my wife Sonia, our liccle baby boy, Joseph, and my mother and father – Sarah and Nikolas.

CONTENTS

PART TWO
TO LOOK OUT WITH COPPER EYES

ACKNOWLEDGEMENTS

Thank you to Jake Crowley for his comradeship, cycling adventures and essential and eternal proof reading; to Dorothy Lumley, my agent, for her belief and kindness – right from the beginning; to Simon Kavanagh, for his insight, need for perfection, and for working me like a bitch – even when I was sulking; and to my wife, Sonia, for her encouragement and understanding over the years. I owe you all many beers!

My personal thanks also go to Justin Sullivan of New Model Army, Zak Tell of Clawfinger, and Derek W. Dick (Fish), for kind permission to quote their lyrics in this novel. Very much appreciated.

PROLOGUE

REDUCTION

Demo114: Bolivia

The ancient house sat astride the cliff's rugged shoulders. Sections of rendering had fallen away into the tangled vegetation far below, revealing thick stone slabs underneath: toothless gaps – the dark smile of an old bearded gunrunner, the oblivion kiss of a whisky-drunk Brazilian whore. The house was four storeys tall and had almost been reclaimed by the jungle; this ornate Churrigueresque fortress had been smashed and peppered for centuries by tropical elements intent on a gradual stripping away of its baroque stone carvings.

Something – a *shadow* – slid from the jungle. A figure shrouded by darkness, protected by the night and its moon-suffocating clouds. It climbed easily, fluidly up cliff and carved stone and landed lightly on the walkway's tiles, mosaics that shone dully in what little light penetrated the gloom.

The figure emerged from the shadows and moved lightly across the tiles. Then it paused, listening, a static outline against the night, before sliding again into darkness and vanishing: a ghost; mist; a grey dream.

A deep oppressive silence filled the corridor, at one end of which squatted a riveted steel door, the single portal for the protected sanctum.

Seated, two heavy-set bearded guards, deeply tanned, their hair grease-smeared and lank, were armed with 9mm Glocks and shoulder-slung AK47s. They were playing cards across a small unvarnished table by the warm light of an oil-burning lantern, their brutal scarred features softened by the amber glow, a bottle of cheap vodka their only shared release from the boredom of duty.

There was a soft clatter, muffled, from back along the shadowed corridor and the two men's bloodshot gazes met over the smeared bottle. One man, the larger of the two, removed the bedraggled hand-rolled cigarette from his lips and discarded it in an overflowing ashtray knife-cut from a beer can.

'Your turn, *hombre*.'

The smaller of the two men shook his head. 'It'll be a fucking monkey again. They climb in, looking for food.'

'Not up here. They don't like the climate – or the bullets. Go on, you dirty drunken *mestizo*, go check who's there.' He grinned, baring crooked coffee-stained teeth. 'Anyway, we're safe. If they'd got this far they would have triggered the alarms. *And* there are the *special men* in there with the *hombre* himself,' he sneered. 'We have nothing to fear.'

Cursing, the other man stood and checked his pistol and AK. The magazines were both full and he flicked the safety off. 'I used to enjoy shooting fucking monkeys,' he muttered, and, with his bloodworm eyes as alert as they could ever be in the gloom, dissolved from the friendly perimeter glow of the lamp.

The other Bolivian guard sat, shuffling the cards with the expert hands of a man practised in sentry duty. His eyes shifted left to the digital display on the wall, its plastic casing and LED warnings out of place against the smoke-stained plaster. It registered zero. Nothing. No intruder. No worries. But the fancy electronics made him uneasy. He was a guard trained with traditional weapons: guns and bullets. He did not rate so called hi-tech gadgets . . .

There was a distant sound – almost inaudible. Like—

A hiss.

The seated man frowned, his brow furrowed, his eyes moving from the LED display to the gloom of the corridor. 'Kaltzon, you there, my man?' His words echoed, lonely, a stark contrast with the soft backdrop noise of distant buzzing insects.

He got to his feet and placed the Glock on the table, making a soft *clack*; with his AK switched to automatic he moved with a smooth military precision that indicated a history of violence. Despite his sleazy appearance, sobriety and stark professionalism kicked in; he crept forward, close to the wall, suddenly alert, all senses buzzing with a sudden rush of adrenalin. He reached the corridor junction and glanced tentatively to the right, gun muzzle tracing an imaginary arc of fire. The half-open distant patio doors showed only a beam of faint moonlight breaking briefly through the clouds and spilling over the veranda. There was no sign of Kaltzon.

The guard turned back – and was slammed off his feet, flung against the wall, a bolt of black steel protruding from his forehead. His AK47 clattered deafeningly on the floor tiles. Blood sprayed down his chin, ruining his cheap Hawaiian shirt. His eyes, open and lifeless, stared at the ceiling as his left leg twitched, while a long string of saliva and blood pooled from his slack jaws and formed a slowly growing viscous puddle on the floor.

Demo114: an elite combat squad, supremely proficient and lethally effective in the violent twin worlds of protection and destruction. This was to be an easy gig. Protection: close quarters, waiting for one of Spiral's many top-class analysts to arrive in order to verify certain documents carried – *stolen* – by Sacha Bora.

Bora, Cuban-born, lately of Los Angeles, USA, and before that involved with some nefarious desert activity in Southern Rub al'Khali. He was a man with a unique profession. In the corner of the fortified sleeping quarters sat a pilot's case containing the tools of his trade. The leather was of finest hide, imported from North Africa and handcrafted to a very individual and precise design: the case had been created for the sole purpose of smuggling. Bora's payload was a sheaf of encoded metal documents that, he knew, Spiral would pay well to get their hands on.

The safe room in this lonely fortress had been designed, appropriately enough, first and foremost for the safety of its occupants. The two windows were shuttered with a high-grade steel that was unusual and expensive in this part of the world. The walls were stone, two feet thick, the ceiling and floors solid concrete, the door heavy steel in a frame of the same metal and controlled by digital locks.

The occupant, obviously, was paranoid.

Sacha Bora slept on his back, snoring, a sweat-stained silk pillow beneath his long greasy black hair. The sheets

4

had been thrown free due to the oppressive heat seeping in from the jungle and an air-con unit clattered softly in a corner of the room – its casing armoured, the machinery itself painfully inefficient.

A *click* sounded. Sacha's eyes flickered open, drops of sweat beading on his lashes.

He stared at the ceiling for a while, his breathing even. Then he scanned the room, glad that he was no longer subject to the palpitations that had recently haunted him. Outside sat his two most trusted guards, and the three members of Demol14 were there in the room with him, awaiting Spiral's expert analyst and the money that she would bring with her. Bora relaxed a little more as he watched the DemolSquad; they were rated among the finest and Sacha Bora had had dealings with them on several occasions over the last four years. They were good. No, he thought, they were the best.

Jax was cleaning his S687 shotgun, while Dazna sat with her head resting against the wall as she rubbed at her eyes. Evoss, huge Evoss, was on his feet by the shuttered window. The big man tilted his head sideways, and there was a cracking sound of released tension as his neck vertebrae realigned.

From outside there came a distant muffled roar of engines struggling up the rough mountain roads. Jax and Dazna exchanged meaningful glances. 'What is it?' said Sacha Bora, suddenly – crazily – nervous. He sat up in bed, staring at where his own personal – and concealed – shotgun nestled under an ornately carved wooden chest: the *last line* in protection should Demol14 and the guards outside fail.

Evoss moved towards him, black-clad, menacing and yet, to Bora, reassuring. He pumped his own shotgun to load it and grinned through a mouthful of broken teeth.

'Don't worry, Bora,' he rumbled. 'We are here. You'll be fine.' He reached out to pat Bora's sweat-streaked arm.

A whine cut through the air. There was a metallic *clack*.

The digital locks failed.

The security door smashed open.

'I wouldn't be so sure about that,' came a soft voice.

The figure was of average height and build and dressed in a single-piece dark grey body-hugging garment. The face was hidden by a tight grey balaclava that revealed only the eyes, which were copper, bright and soft.

The voice was lilting, almost beautiful, nearly female but – not quite.

And the grey-clad figure carried no visible weapon.

Everybody froze . . .

'Who the fuck—'

'Demol14, I am here to kill you.'

The figure moved with awesome speed as the three members of the Demolition Squad opened fire. Rounds screamed across the room as the grey-clad figure leaped into the air, somersaulted, twisted, and connected, booted feet first, with the huge bulk of Evoss. The big man fell, and a small gleaming knife had appeared in his chest before he crashed to the ground.

The grey-masked figure looked up – a quick, insect-like motion.

Evoss's gun was lifted gently from the floor.

'You *bastard*!' hissed Dazna, her pretty mouth open in shock. She charged, her gun spitting fire, bullet casings ejecting, but the grey figure was—

Gone.

The gun muzzle caressed Dazna's temple gently. There was a *whump whump whump* as three stray bullets

6

ate plaster before Jax got his weapon trained on the grey-clad figure from across the room. But too late—

'No,' Jax mouthed silently.

The grey intruder squeezed the pistol trigger and, even as Dazna's brains were mushrooming from the side of her head, kicked off from her falling corpse, curled into a ball, somehow avoiding the screaming 7.62mm rounds from Jax's weapon, hit the ground and rolled towards a low wooden chest. From nowhere a shotgun appeared and there was a heavy bass *boom*. Jax was plucked from his feet and blown across the room. He left a huge smear of blood against the plaster, then toppled onto his face and lay unmoving.

Suddenly everything was still, awesomely silent. The flickering damaged light illuminated the kneeling, hunched figure of Sacha Bora. He looked up slowly, glanced around, and let out a long-drawn shuddering sigh. He understood: understood that he was lucky to be alive, understood that he was lucky not to be a corpse sprawling beside the three broken carcasses on the floor.

The grey-clad figure was standing with the shotgun in his – her? – hands.

'I . . . you came just in time,' wheezed Sacha Bora through cracked lips.

The figure said nothing. It made no move – no sound.

Sacha squirmed uncomfortably as trickles of sweat crawled down his face and body.

'I can't believe you killed three members of a DemolSquad,' he croaked. The figure did not move: it made no physical or oral response. '*How* did you move so fucking fast? And are you here for what I think you're here for? I've got it – don't worry, it's safe, I was bringing it to . . . him.'

7

The shotgun's barrel swung up and with twin snarls smashed Sacha Bora across the room and into a twisted heap in the corner. There was a clatter as the shotgun fell to the ground and lay in a pool of blood. Soft black boots left crimson imprints across the floor while footsteps pounded down the corridor towards the scene of carnage. Men's voices were snarling, shouting orders. The grey-clad assassin threw a switch and the room's shutters began their clattering ascent.

The figure approached the finely carved leather case, hurled aside in the recent confusion. Hands moved swiftly, revealing a further concealed section below the secret compartment. There was a glint as a sheaf of metal sheets was withdrawn and stowed away inside the tight grey clothing.

The assassin leaped up onto the balcony and glanced down at the jungle far below. Fresh morning sunlight bathed the scene and for a few moments the copper eyes seemed to glow like molten metal.

And then the figure was gone, leaving only bloody footprints on the parapet.

There was a distant rattle of machine-gun fire.

The guards who had been examining the room and the four corpses exchanged worried glances.

'How did he open the digital locks? I thought they were foolproof. A billion fucking combinations or something.'

'Hey, look here.'

They lumbered towards the gaping window, saw the footprints in congealed blood and glanced down into the sprawling jungle . . .

Within the damp, dripping cellar deep beneath and *within* the clifftop house, something barely visible dropped to a crouch. There was a scrape – of metal on stone. Then a single red light came on, glowing faintly, an omen of death and destruction.

The bomb detonated.

Fire and hell-fury screamed white-hot through the building, wrenching it apart with the force of unleashed chemical savagery.

In the jungle below, there was a pattering of pebbles, followed by heavy thuds as chunks of stone and plaster described their individual arcs through the foliage and tropical morning mist.

Black smoke rolled up towards the sky, blocking out the newly risen sun.

Demo177: United Kingdom

The wind howled violently across the North Sea's heaving, beating waves towards a dark rearing metal structure, unlit and unloved, pounded and abused by the elements.

The oil rig was old, a cast-off from one of the world's largest petroleum companies. The rusting machinery no longer drilled and pumped, the derrick was a tangle of fused rusting steel being gradually eaten away by sea spray, and the huge engines no longer thundered and beat with life. The rig was a cast-off – discarded, abused, raped, bled, drawn, fucked and forgotten.

The rig was a steel ghost, deserted.

Almost . . .

A figure glided out into the blackness from some pit in the bowels of the machine, wearing a tight-fitting black garment and a rolled-up balaclava. Gloved hands grasped a rusting rail and the man lifted his face, gasping as the wind rocked him, pulled him into a tight embrace and promised him—

Death.

He grinned, revelling in the violent wild-ride feeling, pulled out a cigarette and shouldered his Sterling sub-machine gun as he searched for his Zippo.

'You'll never light that out here.'

'Aye.'

Pulling free the lighter, he cupped the cigarette in a valiant attempt to defeat the gale. Miraculously, the cigarette glowed, a bright spark against the gloom. Smoke plumed around the man's face and he inhaled, closing his eyes and enjoying the nicotine rush.

'Scott, this is a fucking shite gig, man.'

Scott merely nodded, turning his back on the wide-shouldered man with the pock-marked complexion and staring out into the black churning waters. 'Get us some coffee, eh, lad? And check on our Chechen friend while you're at it.'

Grumbling, the big man – newly recruited to Demol77 – thudded his way down the riveted iron steps and into the stairwell below.

Scott took his time enjoying the cigarette, gazing out over the rolling waves that hid the Skene Fields. He wondered idly what it would be like, working on a rig, living off the black gold from deep beneath the surface. His mind drifted; he pictured blueprints – of the rig, the seabed pipelines, the outrigged tankers – and thought about the locations of the huge mooring anchors, pontoons and columns that kept this piece of shit squatting like a drunkard in a gutter.

And he thought about himself: Scott; eighteen-year Spiral veteran; fucked up the arse by his superiors and given one of the lamest protection gigs ever devised by the shadowy Spiral planners. To protect Vladimir Kachenyav,

10

Chechen rebel sympathiser and member of VKW, an underground Grozny action group. Vladimir was a hunted man. Scott was merely tired; and he wanted to go home. Wanted to be out of the game. Wanted – that elusive word he never, ever thought he would stoop to consider – *retirement*.

Scott laughed to himself, and leaned out over the rail. It creaked, the noise lost in the wind as he gazed down into that black water. His fear made manifest, close at hand . . .

Scott licked his salt-dry lips and finished the cigarette. He flicked the butt out over the water and the glow disappeared in an instant.

Retirement.

I thought only old men got tired, his inner voice taunted him.

I thought you were a soldier. A fighter. A warrior.

He had seen enough after the Siege of Qingdao to last a man a hundred lifetimes.

Toffee was right, he thought as he moved to the stairwell and caught his breath away from the wild wind. This *is* a shite gig; a full eight-man team locked away on this desolate piece of junk for a whole two weeks with Vladimir, a slightly crazy Russian.

Scott shook his head and spat into the howling wind.

He stomped down the stairs, rigged with emergency lighting that hung untidily from low ceilings, and strode on towards the canteen, his boots hammering the metal, his torso twisting and turning to fit through the narrow doorways with their heavy bastard rims and gunmetal-grey decor.

'You get that coffee on?' Scott grinned as he stepped into the canteen. The smile was wiped instantly from his face. Bodies were strewn across the floor, blood pooling on the grey metal. Blood was spattered up the walls,

11

across the stainless-steel worktops, dripping from the tables and benches. Toffee was sprawled on his back, mouth slack, dead eyes staring as the flickering fluorescent tube above him strobed over his corpse.

Scott did not move; slowly, very slowly, he unslung the Sterling and flicked off its safety. His gaze moved to the right. His teeth clamped tightly and he tasted blood in his mouth.

Fuck, screamed his brain.

Fuck.

Powell was dead, trailing backwards off a bench, blood-speckled fingers clasping the cord of his SA80. Holloway lay face down against the iron-studded flooring. And Worm, arms outstretched, face twisted in abject agony, a huge hole smashed through his throat, looked sightlessly up at the ceiling, blank eyes pleading with the God who had abandoned him.

Focus. *Think* . . .

There had been no sound of gunfire; the assassin – or assassins – had used silenced weapons. The poor fuckers – Toffee and the others – hadn't even known what had hit them. And that meant the assassins were—

Fast.

A blur raced across the edge of Scott's vision and he kicked himself backwards purely from reflex. Bullets sprayed up the iron wall, splashing bright firework sparks that burnt his face. Scott hit the deck hard, rolled onto his front and squeezed the trigger of his own weapon. The base of the stairwell was filled with a deafening roar of gunfire, and ricochets peppered the canteen with hot bright metal flashes as Scott scrambled up and sprinted for his life.

His booted feet pounded along the corridor and the blueprints for the rig flickered back into his brain: corridors,

12

ramps, cranes, derrick – all now seemed a blur and Scott halted, slowed his breathing, and took a quick glance behind him. He stepped sideways into a doorway and waited, his breathing suddenly calm, his professionalism kicking him into—

Reality.

Nothing, no sounds of pursuit, and—

The figure glided into view, its attention focused up ahead, and sensed rather than saw Scott by its side. The head, mere inches from the levelled sub-machine gun, snapped left – and Scott found himself staring into bright copper eyes . . .

He squeezed the trigger.

The world seemed to explode as the Sterling hammered in the confines of the corridor. The assassin was smashed up against the wall and drilled with a whole magazine of bullets whose impacts held the body upright, dancing and twitching, until the 'dead man's click' reverberated in Scott's skull and brought the world to a sudden echoing silence. Scott fumbled for a fresh magazine with gore-slippery gloves, trying not to look at the pulped brains that covered his arms, trying not to choke on the cordite reek that filled his nose and throat.

The corpse slithered to the deck and lay in a slick crimson pool of its own blood.

The fresh magazine clicked firmly into place, and Scott – breathing slowly and heavily through blood-speckled lips – looked left and right. His ears were ringing from the deafening roar in the narrow metal corridor.

What the *fuck* is going on? he thought.

He stepped gingerly over the corpse, then headed towards the steep stairs ahead. Warily, clasping the rail, he climbed towards the night. Rain was pounding, driven by the wind, a sudden heavy downpour. Above, Scott could see nothing but darkness riddled with diagonal slashes of sheeting rain.

Carefully, and with all his senses on full alert, he pulled free his ECube and, with a twist, initiated the emergency call-up. But instead of the usual flicker of lights the ECube failed to respond. Scott stared at the device in disbelief. In all his years as a Spiral operative an ECube had never failed him.

'Fucker.'

He licked his lips again. *Calm*, whispered his raging mind. *Focus*.

Vladimir: Scott knew that he had to reach the Russian. Had to protect him; save him. Get them both off this desolate rusting graveyard.

The only escape craft that the squad had were boats, moored at a pontoon floater on the other side of the rig. But the most important question now was:

How many killers?

One? Five?

They had killed seven members of a DemolSquad. It had to be more than one. *Had* to be. Which meant—

The game was not yet over.

Scott peered over the edge; the platform, at eye level, was a riveted monstrosity, slippery like black glass, stretching away into apparent infinity. Scott peered along the platform, towards the ramp at the end that seemed to descend into nothing.

Not far.

But not far is always *too far* when bullets are clipping your heels.

What to do? Run or wait?

Scott crept up until he was crouching on the platform; the rain needles drove into him and the wind howled though his jangling brain finding a way into his

14

tight military clothing and caressing him with fingers of ice. His eyes followed every contour that the weak natural light could reveal. He searched for every possible sniping position. He tried to think where best to lay an ambush—

If he could sneak down the left flank of the rig, Vladimir's chamber was nearby; a few easy steps and – hopefully – the fucker would be there, waiting, ready to sprint to the safety of the boats . . . Scott nodded to himself. He craved the nicotine buzz of a cigarette.

It was instinct, more than anything else, that made him freeze.

And then it was there, his worst nightmare.

Cold metal, pressing against the back of his skull.

'No,' he whispered.

He started to turn, but a warning jab halted him. Slowly, he crouched and placed his sub-machine gun on the deck.

'Move.'

Scott started to walk . . . everything ahead of him was blurring and he realised that he was crying – not from fear, fear was no longer an option, but from sheer rancid frustration. Of all the fucking ways to be caught, of all the fucking ways to die—

The *crack* echoed dully against the howling wind.

A limp figure toppled from the railings and disappeared in the boiling black sea below.

Copper eyes watched coldly as it fell.

And, an instant later, the Nex had gone.

Demol S-4: sniper squad: Australia

Rain swept across Sydney Harbour Bay, deluging from towering iron-coloured cumulonimbuses into the churning, raging waters. Rivulets poured down the slick black contours of the bullet-pocked, shrapnel-scarred Harbour bridge, dripping into the chasm below as the lights of distant buildings glittered through the darkness. One half of the Sydney Opera House shimmered, ghostlike, looking almost silver through the sheets of wind-blown rain, its orange-segment sails raised as if in defiance against the elements themselves. But the crumbling, recently bomb-blasted section was open to the storm – the Opera House was wounded, torn, betrayed. To the people of Australia it was a symbol of their world gone mad.

Rex squatted, rain pounding his Gore-Tex wetproof; he listened to the radio and glanced at the ECube in his hand. Digits flickered blue. A voice in his ear said, 'They're on the move.'

Rex edged forward, then glanced down, checking the magazine of the Bergmann 7.65mm sniper rifle. He raised himself, peering from the top of the forward segment of the Opera House. The bridge was hazy in the gloom of the storm, the harbour spread out before him like some majestic oil painting. Rex reached out and steadied himself on the narrow galvanised walkway – he felt like the King of the World up here, wind and driving rain buffeting him. He felt *alive*. He lifted the rifle and touched the ECube to the side of the electronic sight; there was a tiny click, and a buzz as the ECube integrated with the advanced sniper weapon. For a second Rex watched the scope rotate and focus; then he placed his eye against it and the world seemed to spring into clarity.

The bridge was daylight-clear, bathed in a gentle purple tint; he zoomed the scope quickly forward, until he could see each rivet in the steel sections, each bullet hole and shrapnel scar. Then he pulled back and swept left and right, searching for the vans that he knew were coming—

16

'You OK, Rex?' said a sultry voice in his ear.

'Sure thing, sugar,' Rex said softly, picturing Amber's beautiful lashes fluttering at him over the lip of the telescopic sight on her own weapon. He shifted his weight, sighting on the distant tower block and the position that he knew Amber had secured. She waved, and he returned the signal. 'Is Scope set up?'

Scope grunted over the communication link. He rarely spoke, and Rex's comment was obviously below derision.

Rex moved his own sniper sight back to focus on the bridge, the top of the huge arch. Scope was there, all in black, ready and steady. He had picked the most dangerous positioning of the three, on the Sydney Harbour r itself, and despite being clipped securely in place himself Rex shivered involuntarily. But then, he thought, Scope was a wild fucker, untamed. Some said he was insane; Rex decided that the man probably was.

'Game on.'

The words came from the supporting ground soldiers, Australian Anti-Terrorist Special Forces led by a huge ex-marine named Callum, who were waiting in the wings as the scene unfolded. They were monitoring the suspected terrorist vehicles from the ground. The Spiral DemolSquad was positioned as sniper support.

'Tracking two vehicles: black Ford vans, six occupants. ETA four minutes. Over.'

Rex waited.

There was little else that he could do . . .

Amber went over her drill for the tenth time, checking her weapon, scope, ECube integration, body armour, hair and nails. 'Damn fucking rain,' she muttered, and shifted her weight slightly to ease the cramping in her calf muscles. The crumbling bullet-marked parapet was low, but

17

not quite low enough, meaning that she had to support her weight at an odd angle. After an hour, cramps were inevitable.

Amber swept the scene with her scope. Through the audio link she was listening to the ground soldiers tailing the suspect vans.

The tip-off had come from an extremely reliable source: an ex-KGB agent turned arms dealer who was about to be tried for numerous crimes. He had given them reams of information on terrorist activity – as one of the main weapons suppliers to the Middle East and South America he was in a good position to do so. So far everything had checked out fine and the Australian government had high hopes for this gig. Six Egyptian terrorists were going to blow up Sydney Harbour bridge. They had schematics for the structure and knew exactly where to place the charges.

'Fucking terrorists,' snorted Amber, and swept the site once more.

No vans.

Come to think of it, no ground troops.

'GF 10 through 30, call in. Over.'

No response.

'GF 10 through 30, call in. Over!'

Again, no response.

'You hear me, Rex?'

'I'm here.'

'You see anything?'

'Not a donkey.'

'There's something wrong,' came the sibilant whisper that was Scope's rarely heard voice; both Amber and Rex felt a chill course through their souls. And yet on ChannelJ they could still hear the tail – the *pursuit* – of the vans. *'Heading east away from the Circle Bay area, down Alfred Street, heading towards—'*

18

Amber swept the area once more. There was a movement of air beside her, a mere parting of the rain – and then the garrotte was around her throat before she knew what was happening. Her gloved hand slammed up beneath the cheese-cutter wire as her eyes suddenly widened and pain sliced into both sides of her throat – she felt blood sluice down her neck and over her breasts beneath her armour as her rifle clattered to the parapet.

Amber was lifted into the air, her legs kicking. She slammed her head backwards, once, twice, three times, hearing a crunch every time. The grip slackened but did not let go. 'Rex!' she managed to scream into the ECube, then slammed her elbow back into the breastbone of her assailant with all her strength. The garrotte slackened and Amber stumbled to her knees, coughing, scrabbling at the wire that was biting into her flesh—

Rex sighted on the parapet at the summit of the dimly lit building. He could see Amber struggling, but her attacker was too close for a clear shot and the rain was falling, obscuring his aim. Then Amber struck back. The assailant stumbled in the gloom and Rex squeezed off a shot into the night, then three more in quick succession. He grinned nastily just as the silenced pistol touched the back of his head and blew his brains and face all over the fine stonework of the Sydney Opera house.

Amber heard the hiss of the bullets as they flew past her. She whirled, crouching low as she drew her Beretta 9mm pistol. The figure flew at her, a kick smashing the handgun from her grip and out over the parapet. Confusion spread through her brain – she had heard twin thuds behind her, *knew* that Rex's bullets had smashed home. *Kevlar?* The question flashed through her mind as reflexes

19

too over. One kick, two – she blocked with her forearms, then smashed a straight right that the figure dodged as it circled. Amber met the stare of her assailant – the eyes were copper, bright – and she hammered out a front kick, connecting. The figure twisted, rolled, and kicked Amber's legs from under her. She hit the ground with sudden shock, the back of her head cracking against the parapet. Stars of concussion flooded her vision – she swung out blindly, but hit nothing. She felt suddenly weightless – and realised with horror that she had been lifted from the ground again. 'No!' she yelled, her arms and legs flailing. But wind rushed up past her as her eyes widened and she screamed in terror and despair. Then she hit the ground and the scene, the act and the play were finally over.

Scope was considered a reptile by those who worked with him. He had no friends and was – or seemed to be – emotionless. He was dedicated, professional – and damn near the finest sniper in the whole of Spiral. Rumour had it that he could clip the tip from a mouse's dick at ten thousand paces and could thread cotton through a needle's eye with an aimed bullet.

He was appalled that he had not seen them coming. Four figures in black had climbed the war-torn bridge below him without being seen. *Impossible!* screamed his mind as they closed in for the kill. He swung the Bergmann and shot the first figure in the face – there was a hiss, a spray of blood and teeth, and it fell back limply and bounced its way down through the bridge's structures into the gloom below.

Lightning crackled across the sky. In the glow, Scope grinned nastily.

The three figures pulled silenced pistols in fluid movements and everybody started shooting at the same time. Flashes flickered atop the Sydney Harbour bridge, an accompaniment to the lightning. Another dark-clad shape fell, hurled backwards like a rag doll, and pitched towards the narrow strip of tarmac below. Then a bullet hit Scope in the shoulder, spinning him round as a second smashed into his groin and a third into his throat. Blood spewed from his crimson slick lips. He groaned 'Fuckers' as he started to topple, but the security harness that held him whirled him round and he jerked to a halt on the line where he slowly rotated. Blood dripped from his limp corpse. The two remaining dark figures crept closer and put five more bullets into Scope's body. Copper-eyed stares met for the briefest of instants. Then the shadowy beings sprinted away across the dizzying heights of the bridge.

The truck screeched to a halt, its headlights slicing through the heavy downpour. Callum stared hard past the thumping wipers, then barked 'Out.' Ten men leaped from the cab and the truck's tailgate. They spread out, SA80s covering each other's arcs of fire. Callum crept back and crouched by the body of the dead soldier. His throat had been cut. Callum swallowed hard, glancing around at the other six bodies. Not a bullet had been fired. 'They hit them hard and fast, boys. Let's spread out, see what the score is. Albert, you got that fucking comms up and running yet?'

'The whole net's dead, sir.'

Callum nodded, then motioned for the men to move out.

They moved purposefully through the downpour. Lightning flickered overhead, and Callum strained to see the sniper atop the bridge. He could see something, some sort of movement briefly illuminated – but then it was gone to be replaced by a haze of rain and confusion.

And Callum knew. Could feel it.

They had been fucked, hard and proper – but to what purpose? Had the terrorists planted the explosives? Was the bridge about to go the same was as the Opera House?

Twenty minutes later, Callum was leaning against the bridge, a soggy cigarette between his lips, smoke pluming around his face. At his feet, on a stretcher, lay the very dead body of Scope. The sniper's face was a mess, his head shot to pieces, most of the rear of his skull missing. Callum stared at the dead eyes and shuddered.

Albert approached. 'Comms are back on-line; the other two snipers are dead as well. No sign of any assailants – except for the fucking bullet casings, of course. Boss, I just don't get what the fuck went on here.'

'Decoy,' said Callum softly from around the bedraggled cigarette.

'Decoy? What about the bridge?'

'This wasn't about the bridge,' said Callum. Reluctantly, he took the cigarette from between his lips and tossed it over the railings, into the black, oily bay below. He faced Albert and their stares met. 'Somebody wanted those snipers dead.'

'So this was a hit?'

Callum nodded. 'Oh yes, my friend. And of one thing I am certain: whoever did this, whoever killed this Demolition Squad – I'm sure as hell glad they're not looking for me.'

'How do you know they're not looking for you?' whispered Albert.

Callum shrugged. 'I'd already be dead,' he said simply.

SIU Transcript 1

In the undercover world they are called Demolition Squads and work for Spiral. They have no official name and do not 'exist'. They are an urban myth. They are ghosts. These clandestine 'non-existent' groups have more extensive knowledge, training and experience than the British SAS, the American CIA and the former Soviet KGB. They are considered more covert than any global government organisation or secret police network. To all world powers and agencies who even suspect their existence, they are the elite of the elite.

One member of a DemolSquad, code-named Purity, has made herself known to us. We have verified suspected links with the secretive organisation known as Spiral. Purity claims that Spiral, in its battle to crush terrorists, stabilise governments and smash evil and corruption wherever they are found, has developed a prototype CPU to assist their mission. This information is highly classified.

Just before Purity's assassination she claimed that something was wrong with Spiral and with the DemolSquads. In her words: a traitor. Purity mentioned a word: Nex [context: *the* Nex, or *our* Nex] that we suspect indicates an assassin/hunter of some skill.

The woman/code subject vb12Purity was fished from the Danube, SW of Bolgrad, earlier this month. The subject had had her throat cut.

SIU Transcript 2

CLASSIFIED TFG1776/250/SPECIAL INVESTIGATIONS UNIT
Hacked ECube interception
Date: September 2XXX

Transcript of digMail:

'The breakthrough in processor development has escalated beyond all comprehension; the code-core RI nano-gates are writing themselves, and the tech processes used are something we would never have dreamed possible. In initial benchmark tests the speed has physically killed all current military hardware – this processor is at least 50,000 times faster than any other currently in development. The MIP ratings are truly incredible and this chip will revolutionise computing in the 21st Century. It will have groundbreaking effects on all aspects of computing, from military applications to world economics.

'Enclosed are the encoded data files on cellular cube structure, together with schematics for the etching processes needed in creating the QIII cubic processor - #TYGUgfuyd . . .'

###TRANSFER FORCIBLY TERMINATED//HACKER INVOLVEMENT SUSPECTED###

Scanning Terminals . . .

Intrusion detected . . .

Scanning HUT ports . . .

Locked.

PART ONE

THE SEARCH FOR AN UNREAL GOD

we've seen the **restless children**
at the head of the columns
come to **purify** the future
with the arrogance of youth
nothing is as **cruel** as the
righteousness of innocents
with **automatic weapons**
and a gospel of the truth

Purity
New Model Army

CHAPTER 1

ALONE

Carter watched the woman wheelspin the BMW 740i up the snowbound lane, park at a curious and somewhat precarious angle, climb from the warmth and comfort of the car and kick the waxed and polished wing three times. She glanced up towards him, towards his shield of glass. He waved, but she did not see him through the thickly falling snow.

Carter moved across the heavy rugs, luxuriating in the feel of the fur and wool under his bare feet. He threw another log on the fire and Samson, his chocolate Labrador, looked up from his luxurious basket and tilted his head slightly. The dog gave a little whine. Carter smiled. 'She loves me really,' he said and winked. Samson's head dropped and the dog grunted, closing his large eyes.

Carter flipped open the front door with an IR and collapsed into a deep sofa with a glass of red wine.

He heard her, stamping snow from her boots and cursing the climate, the location and, most of all, him. He smiled wryly, swirling the wine and peering into its velvety depths as the woman climbed the stone steps to the front door.

'Are you in?'

Carter raised his arm, and peered over the back of the sofa. 'Guilty, Nats. How's life?'

'It's Natasha, you arse, not Nats.'

'Hmm, tetchy. Wine?'

'What sort?'

'Red. Some kind of Italian stuff, I think. Does it matter?'

'It matters, Carter. Why the fuck did you move out here?'

'I like it out here.'

'It's in the middle of nowhere!'

'That's what I like about it. The cities are full of the military. And after the London Riots they've moved in Justice Troops – JT8s.' Carter shook his head. 'It's not what I call a pleasant environment conducive to relaxation and long life.'

Natasha gave a short laugh, her gaze moving around the room. 'And I can't believe you haven't even got a fucking car.'

'What would I need a car for?' Carter frowned. 'I have everything I *need* right here.'

Natasha stopped, took a deep breath and counted silently as she summoned patience. She removed her scarf and gloves, closed her eyes for a moment and threw her Berghaus fleece over a nearby leather chair.

'I hate Scotland,' she said.

'It's where I was brought up,' said Carter softly. He drained the glass in one. 'Where I was born. It has character and strength and solitude. Sure you won't try some wine, you bad-tempered little temptress?'

'Maybe a whisky.'

30

As Carter found the Lagavulin decanter and poured two generous measures, he watched Natasha's slim and athletic form. He licked his lips and thought back to better times – long nights and longer days, making love on this very floor, laughing, talking, drinking . . .

He handed her the glass. She ran a hand through her short black snow-damp hair, leaving it spiked – the way that he knew she knew he liked it. He smiled in anticipation, downed the single malt and threw the crystal glass into the fire where it shattered; for a moment the flames grew bright.

'You always were over-dramatic,' said Natasha sombrely, staring down into her whisky. She had moved to sit in front of the fire and she twirled her glass gently, seemingly lost in thought.

'What do you want?' he said finally when he realised that she would not break the silence without prompting.

Flames crackled for a while and Carter wondered if she had heard him.

'How do you know I want anything?'

'It's been over a year,' sighed Carter. 'You still working for that slave-driver Spiral?'

'Of course. Our role grows more important with every passing day.' She smiled softly. 'We have a job for you.'

'Ah.' Carter sighed, climbed to his feet and walked to stand in front of the window. The snow was falling thick and fast and he could see, dim through the swirling flakes, the lofty peaks of Ben Macdui, blue-grey and sheer – exhilarating. The wind howled in the distance and Carter shivered, despite the fire's heat in the room. He felt a twinge of disappointment that he could not see the frozen lake.

'Is it a solo, or a joint assignment with a DemolSquad?'

'Solo. A protection issue.'

31

'I am finished with Spiral,' Carter whispered softly, turning and watching Natasha through heavy half-lowered eyelids – internal movie screens flashing images of events he would rather forget, nightmares he would rather not relive. She stood, a fluid and graceful action, and moved to him, draped her arms across his shoulders and ducked a little, looked up into his eyes.

'I know you've turned down the last four gigs – as with all Spiral jobs that is your prerogative. But this has come from the top. Real important.'

'It always is,' said Carter bitterly.

'Things are getting worse,' whispered Natasha. 'The world is changing, Carter, and you're fucking *hiding* up here . . .'

She tailed off as she saw the look on his face and cursed herself inwardly. That had been unfair; Carter was good. No, he was the best. And after the Battle of Cairo7 . . . he had the right to live and rest any way he pleased . . .

Natasha took a deep breath.

'Look, *I* want you to do this,' she said. She moved forward slowly. Her lips touched his and he allowed her to kiss him for a few moments. Her breath was sweet, her lips soft and inviting.

'Why?'

'I empathise with this girl's situation. She is young, alone, afraid. And you are the best, Carter.'

'Bull – shit.' He kissed her again, anyway, tasting Lagavulin on her lips. When he pulled away, he was frowning. 'What about Jax? Or Scott? Or Evoss?'

There was a long pause. Natasha averted her gaze and looked over at the fire as though debating with herself. Carter caught a glimpse of something then, in her face, in her eyes. There was something that Natasha knew, a secret she did not wish to share.

32

Carter smiled tightly and reached up, stroking her cheek. She turned back to him, licking her dry lips.

'I recommended *you*, Carter,' she said softly. 'Don't turn me down. Don't let *her* down.'

'Who is she? Why should I care?'

'Maria Balashev. She's nineteen. The niece of Count Feuchter.'

Carter pulled away for a moment. Reflected flames danced in Natasha's deep brown eyes. He searched her face for – he shook his head, unsure of the unspoken signs he sought.

'Feuchter? Where the hell am I going?'

'You shouldn't let me manipulate you,' said Natasha, turning and walking away from him.

Carter watched the hypnotic sway of her hips. He swallowed – hard. How long have I been a hermit? he thought. How long without lips to kiss, soft skin to nibble, a flat stomach to taste . . .

'I can't help myself, Nats.' His voice was hoarse. 'Where am I going?'

'Schwalenberg, Germany, in the Weser River Valley. My homeland, Carter, near the place I was born.'

'Weser? Isn't that where the Pied Piper enticed the rats to their deaths?'

'Could be,' said Natasha, 'although I'm no student of history.'

'Nor literature, I see.'

'Feuchter is based at Spiral_Q, in Saudi Arabia – he's come over to Germany to give a series of lectures to Spiral operatives, and for a celebration of his achievements working on several breakthroughs in processor development. Many of those working on the project have been based in Germany for – shall we say, security reasons . . .

33

Carter sighed and shrugged. He rubbed at his suddenly weary eyes, then met Natasha's gaze. 'Will you stay?'

There was a pause. Natasha put her hands in her pockets and looked at Carter steadily. She tilted her head, her lips pursed, her beautiful brown eyes unreadable. Carter realised that she had aged – matured – wonderfully in the year since he had last seen her. And he realised too that he wanted her more than anything in the world . . . more than *anything*.

'*And you turned her down,*' mocked Kade, a distant whisper in his head. '*You dick. You sent her away.*'

Carter gritted his teeth and battled to ignore the acid sly observations of the ever-unwelcome voice within his mind. Fuck off and die, Kade, he thought.

Then he forced a smile to his face and looked up to see the kindness in Nats's expression.

'Not tonight,' she whispered. She smiled. 'But we'll make a date. When you get back, maybe.'

'You mean in another year when Spiral has another job for me and decides that a cheap kiss is enough to purchase my skilled services?'

Natasha moved forward and placed a finger against his lips. 'When you get back from Germany. We'll meet then.'

'Promise?'

'I promise. Here.'

She tossed Carter a small cube. It was soft under his fingers, and he turned it slowly; similar in size to a matchbox, the dull matt black alloy shone as the cube fitted neatly into the palm of his hand. 'New model?'

'Version 4.2. ECubes have moved on since you last worked for us.'

'Really? Same basic functions?'

34

'Yeah.'

An ECube was an electronic communications device, standard Spiral issue. Running the V4.2 ICARUS operating system, it sported a 12GHz RISC processor and 256 gigabytes of static RAM. It was solid-state – no moving parts – and quite robust; it had voice – and fingerprint-recognition facilities; it could act as an advanced GPS – could navigate across the whole of the world, relaying data straight back to Spiral mainframes and thus allowing Spiral to keep a tab on its finest operatives. It also had a few hidden and very ingenious little tricks within its alloy casing.

Natasha turned to leave, gathering her fleece coat and gloves and moving to the door and the steep steps beyond. 'When are you coming back to the real world, Carter? It misses you, y'know?'

'I enjoy the seclusion.'

'That wasn't the question.'

'Then, "when I have a reason to" would be the answer.'

She held his gaze for a long time, then turned and left. He listened to her departure, then moved to the window and watched the plumes from the 740's exhaust. Wheels spinning dangerously, the BMW cut a swathe through the fresh snowfall and was soon gone, tail lights flickering into nothing.

Carter felt suddenly, terribly alone.

For a while he watched the snow, then stared down at the ECube nestling in his palm like a tiny Chinese puzzle box. He squeezed it, and it came to life. Small blue digits flickered across its alloy face. He looked from the ECube to the roaring fire – and for a moment was undecided . . .

He could destroy it. Walk away.

He had sworn that he was through with Spiral.

35

Because . . .

When he was through with Spiral, then he was through with Kade.

Carter shivered, staring into the flames.

Spiral did not know about Kade. But then, *nobody* knew about *Kade*. Kade was a ghost that Carter would rather forget: a dark and psychopathic slice of his personality that had found itself a voice; a dark and menacing angel squatting in his mind. A demon ready to feed, to prove itself again as it had in Egypt and China and Poland . . .

Carter sighed.

He turned from the flames and slumped into the embrace of the deep and comfortable sofa. Samson climbed to his feet ponderously, for the dog was large for a Labrador – hence his fitting and none too subtle name – yawned, padded over to Carter, climbed up slowly next to the man and placed his wide head on Carter's lap. Samson gave a huge dog sigh and Carter rubbed gently at his velvety ears.

Protection, Natasha had said. Carter's mouth was dry and he realised that she – and Spiral itself – understood him perfectly. No more killing. No more demolition. No more destruction . . . Those days were over. Gone. Dissolved into dust, just like Cairo.

Protection.

The protection of the niece of a senior Spiral weapons researcher.

No killing . . . no bombs . . . no cool collective violence . . .

'Talk to me,' he said to the ECube. Instantly it locked onto his voice pattern and linked with a *click* to the Spiral mainframe . . .

36

CLASSIFIED FFUCH/111/SPECIAL INVESTIGATIONS UNIT
Data Request 117554#887

Count Feuchter; German professor, born in Schwalenberg, educated in Munich, London and Prague. Great-grandfather killed by the Nazis during World War II after being tortured somewhere on the German/Austrian border. Mother and two sons fled to Italy, then to England for protection after the war was over; Feuchter comes from this bloodline.

Expert in computing systems, specialising in processor function and artificial intelligence. Currently pioneering military processor after setting up Spiral_Q, with co-programmer and system developer, Durell. Spiral_Q - currently based in Rub al'Khali, Saudi Arabia, also named The Great Sandy Desert. The technologically advanced research station has been set up with the knowledge of the Saudi government in what is a largely completely unexplored region of desert; the Saudi government has been bribed with technology and information to turn a blind eye on the operations there, and no satellite locks have been discovered: the station is, therefore, invisible to most of the snooping eyes of the world.

37

QIII Military Proc - classified; Level Z
access required. <Lock>

Caution activation: Feuchter has been the
victim of various death threats; suspect
terrorist activity, probably Middle Eastern
influences with sights set on the 'rumoured'
processor which is in development. German
Special Forces are involved with protecting
Feuchter on home ground. One weak link could
be his niece, daughter of his murdered
brother; she travels with him everywhere and
could be a target for kidnapping, even
murder in order to blackmail Feuchter or
garner information on the QIII.

Keyword SEARCH>>DURELL, QIII [lvlz], NEX
[lvlz] SPIRAL_Q

Carter peered out through the smoked glass as the
engines whined. He grinned like a young boy – unable to
contain himself – as he felt the power of the machine
beneath him wind up like a turbine.

The Sikorsky RAH-66 Comanche eased up from the
snow, suspension bobbing as it was released from the aircraft's dead weight, and Carter watched the Scottish
mountains drop away beneath him. Exhilaration was his
mistress and he licked his lips nervously – he hated flying,
and yet drew some perverse pleasure from the stimulation
such machines gave him. The pilot was ensconced in his
HIDSS – a Helmet Integrated Display Sighting System –
and looked somewhat alien as he eased forward and the
twin 1380 shaft-horsepower LHTec turboshaft engines
moaned like huge ferocious animals in pain.

'Hey, Langan, you hear me in that ugly thing?'

'I hear you, Carter.'

'I thought these choppers weren't in production yet?'

'They're not. Especially ones like *this*. It's a MkIV. *Very* advanced.'

'Is it fast?'

Carter was slammed back, heart in his mouth.

Stupid question, thought Carter as the engines finally returned to their 'normal' speed. His stomach churned and he regretted his fried breakfast. He made a mental note to keep his irrepressibly foolish questions to himself in the future.

'You want to go over land, via the coastline or straight across the sea?'

'Does it matter?' said Carter.

'Not to me.'

'Down the coast, then.'

Carter settled back as the Comanche hummed, settled into stealth mode and cruised down the coastline of England. He ran through the ECube's instructions once more: protection in support of German Special Forces agents. Not even a full job. A support job. Break him in gently; ease him back into the Spiral fold . . . and then he would feel Kade's wings curl around him to obscure the light and the killing would begin . . .

He shivered.

He remembered the probing of the little ECube machine with some annoyance. Spiral testing him: physical and mental responses. Check he was still the same. Check he hadn't lost his magic touch.

'I should have retired,' he mused, settling deeper into the uncomfortable seat; it was structured for combat, not sleep. 'In fact, I thought I already had.'

Carter managed to nod off as they flew low down the

39

east coast of England, the cold dark waters of the North Sea below them as the Comanche weaved like a reigned-in predator between radar pulses and deflected the probings of other more sophisticated detection equipment. They left the southern coast of England, avoiding both Dover and Boulogne by flying straight down the centre of the English Channel as Carter remembered older, harder days, training in the mountains, running, sweating under packs, carrying logs, wading through snow, navigating blizzards . . . He smiled amiably as the memories drifted through his mind. He had felt so heroic; at the peak of his physical and mental fitness. And yet it had been the beginning.

The beginning of a new career with Spiral . . .

'Can I smoke?'

'No.'

He slept, and dreamed only a little; it was a bad dream. It was a dream about Kade.

'Why won't you leave me alone?' he muttered as he came awake to the sound of rain and the buffeting of wind.

'You OK?' asked Langan.

Carter sighed. 'Yeah. Sort of. Has this thing got a cigarette lighter?'

'Like I said, no smoking, pal.'

'Where are we?'

'Just crossing the Ardennes. We won't be long; touchdown will be just east of Siegen. Nice little pad we've got hidden away in the hills. A car will meet you and rush you off to whatever secret and heroic mission you're destined to enjoy.'

'Langan?'

'Hmm?'

'Shut the fuck up.'

40

'OK, boss.' The pilot grinned, flicked a switch and the Comanche swooped down from the sky towards the flatlands beyond the mountain range. Carter watched the landscape flicker below him in the approaching gloom like some ridiculous computer-game simulation – and thanked God that this unwanted adrenalin-injected journey was nearly over.

'I'd like to thank you for a smooth flight, but I won't.'

'Any time, pal,' Langan chuckled.

Carter watched the Comanche leap into the air, bank sideways and hurtle into the distance. He shook his head, lit a cigarette and inhaled. His boots crunched stone as he walked to the black Mercedes and climbed in. In minutes the hills were moving past on either side and the car soon drove into the gloomy sanctuary of a pine forest.

Carter wound down the window and breathed in the pleasant scent. Rain spat through the gap and he revelled in the shocking coolness on his face. He saw himself imposed over the image of the speeding forest: Carter, reflected in glass – short brown hair, heavy stubble, pale blue eyes. A broad boxer's nose that had taken one too many punches. A strong chin – he thrust it forward, then grinned weakly at his reflection.

Ugly bastard, he mused, and lit another cigarette, reminding himself that he really should quit.

The hotel was basic. Low-key. Cheap.

Carter unpacked, then spent a half-hour familiarising himself with the room and then with the hotel. He walked around, smoking, checking out entrances and exits. He sat for a while in the lobby, watching the people coming and going, and being eyed himself by the two hotel guards

41

armed with 7.62mm AK49s. A waiter approached and asked him if he required a drink. In fluent German he asked for a bottle of whisky to be sent to his room and then shook his head, telling himself off.

You've one day left, he mused. The last thing you need is a hangover.

Ignoring his own advice, he went back to his room to listen to the rain, drink, and pray that Kade would leave him alone.

'*You're drunk,*' whispered the voice of Kade in his mind.

Carter ignored the words and poured himself another whisky. It was a cheap blend and tasted burning, sour – evil, almost – on his tongue and in his throat.

'*Let me look at her. Just one more look at her.*'

'No,' said Carter softly. His fist clenched the glass tightly and he looked across the room at the mirror. He always expected to see something – he wasn't sure what. Maybe a spirit drifting over his head. Maybe a ghost standing behind his shoulder. But it was always the same . . . nothing. Nothing there – no ghosts, no haunting, no floating spirits. He was alone – alone in body but not in soul . . .

Am I going crazy?

The same question. The same question a million times.

He laughed, and downed the whisky. He felt Kade leave him and was thankful – thankful for the peace and solitude. Kade came to him much less these days and that was the way he liked it. But again the thought nagged at him, would not relinquish its alcohol-fuelled grip: crazy man, mad man, insanity . . . Schizophrenia? Severe mental disorder? A fucked-up mind fried on the toxins of three wars and a thousand battles—

Insane . . .

42

'You're fucking insane,' Roxi had shouted at him from across the room, fear in her face, in her eyes, in her stance. He could see her fingers trembling, could see the enticing pulse beating rapidly in her neck.

And he could still feel the bulky grip of the 9mm in his hand as he pointed it at her, a full 13-round clip in its magazine. And Kade: there in the back of his mind. *'Kill her. She will betray you – betray us. And we shall be nothing. We shall be ashes and dust. Do it – or, if you're such a fucking coward, let me do it . . .'*

He had walked from the room, to the lake, and thrown the weapon into the cold waters.

He had let Roxi leave. Without a farewell.

But at least with her life.

She had known there was a problem – a needle in his mind, a splinter through his soul – and she had begged him to tell her. But he could not. How could he describe Kade in mere words? How could he define his torture, his misery – and, ironically, his *saviour* – in simple sentences?

Yeah, Kade – his Saviour. His fucking *God*.

Carter laughed drunkenly at that and refilled his glass, spilling whisky over his hand. He could remember the shame: like a brand scarring his brain and soul. He had almost let Kade have her; had almost given in to the raging fucked-up beast-demon-murderer roaming his soul . . .

Shit, he realised, sometimes he had even welcomed that merciless unbidden intruder – at first: when he had discovered what Kade was capable of. He admitted to himself that without his dark twin he would now be dead, dead many times in bunkers, bullets in his skull, his corpse rotting on river beds and in sewers and lying in pieces on distant forgotten battlefields. Kade had saved his life, had pushed him on and murdered when

43

Carter felt weakness and Kade was untroubled by fear or compassion or doubt or consequences and had *maimed* and *slain* and *slaughtered* on his fucking behalf and yet . . .

Carter couldn't help wondering if he would rather be dead.

What is it like to be normal?

How would my life have been?

How would I have turned out?

He slept uneasily, images of the people that he – *Kade* – had murdered floating up from the depths of his mind. They accused him, fingers pointing, silent dead mouths open and screaming at him.

Spiral Memo1
Transcript of recent news incident
CodeRed_Z;
unorthodox incident scan 545834

Outbreak of malicious computing activity across the globe/a malicious virus Kleq5 - so far undetected on even the most powerful computing systems - has hit global networks in quick succession, striking 15,000,000 machines within 30 seconds.

Not a single country in the world has remained unaffected - from America to France, from Africa to the Czech Republic. According to IT experts, the suspected virus detects sectors where operating systems reside and writes random blocks of data in short bursts, rendering any infected machine unusable.

Because of its highly contagious nature, the virus and sample hard disks are being rigorously examined by leading anti-virus software companies. It is estimated that this Kleq5 virus has caused upwards of US$4.3 billion damage.

Computing experts are fearful of a second payload which is expected shortly.>>#

CHAPTER 2

INFIL

The Mercedes swept past three burned-out BMWs, through the heavy iron gates and up the gravel drive to park beside the black iron fountain. Carter pulled free his ECube, weighed it in his palm, then accessed five codes; the ECube flickered at him with blue digits. Carter smiled – the tiny technical wonder would make sure he was not overheard; it would jam or scramble any listening devices in range.

Carter got out, battered boots crunching on gravel, and lit a cigarette. He looked up at the home of Count Feuchter – Castle Schwalenberg, a magnificent structure of old stone dominated by a central tower with a grey-tiled spire. The windows were small, set back into the stone walls and flanked with traditional wooden shutters. Miraculously, the building seemed unharmed by the recent conflicts that had ravaged not just Germany but the whole of Europe. A few stray bullets from long-range rifles had peppered the shutters but no major damage had been done.

The sun was out, glinting from the glass. Carter walked

across the gravel and was stopped beside a crumbling stone arch by a German Special Forces agent.

'You the *special* man? The one who was at the Siege of Qingdao?' the surly German snarled down at Carter, who flashed his ID as his gaze took in the grounds beyond.

'That's me.' Carter took a heavy pull on his cigarette and smoke plumed around him. He coughed. 'Must remember to try and give up.'

'We don't need you here; we do just fine without you, *special* man.'

Carter held up his hand. 'Hey, I'm just here to observe, my friend. Now, I'd appreciate it if you got the fuck out of my way before I start to lose my temper.' He smiled and blew smoke into the guard's face.

Holding eye contact, the agent used a comm to confirm Carter's identity and allowed him to pass. Carter noted the sniper in the bushes as he moved towards the entrance.

His stomach groaned at him – the bad whisky was haunting him. He reached the door. Ten men in the grounds, he thought. Good. He wasn't meant to have seen five of them: *even better*.

He lifted the huge iron knocker and allowed it to fall. It made a sound like rolling thunder.

Carter watched Maria Balashev enter the richly decorated room. Her beauty stunned him. She wore her black hair long, to her waist, a softly shimmering silken fan; she moved with elegance and grace, and a light smile danced across her face when she saw Carter. She crossed to him without a sound, walking over the deep red carpets, and Carter felt himself swallowing hard as he gazed into those oval, beautiful, sorrowful eyes.

'You know why I am here?' he said softly.

'I do, Mr Carter,' she replied in smooth German. 'And I am very grateful for your intervention. Natasha did not do you justice when she described you.'

Her voice was like the gentle flowing of a river. Carter stood, smiled, and without speaking motioned to her ear-rings, bracelet and rings. She cocked her head questioningly and Carter made gestures for her to remove the jewellery. He walked around her, finger-testing the buckles at the back of her short red dress. Taking the items from her, he placed them on a low rosewood table inlaid with ivory, and then motioned for Maria to take off her shoes and follow him outside.

She obeyed, and Carter led her barefoot out into the grounds. The sun was high, the smell of the gardens fresh after the heavy rains of the previous night.

'Where are we going?'

'Indulge me for a moment, Miss Balashev. Round here, through the arch.'

She laughed then, and Carter heard the crack in the laughter; the fear was there, well hidden – especially con-sidering the girl was only nineteen years old – but still there.

They walked, Maria a step behind Carter.

He stopped suddenly and turned. He took her hand.

'Your uncle has received death threats and he considers them to be very real – not a hoax, but linked to the devel-opment of a powerful ground-breaking processor with which he is intimately involved. Your uncle fears that those making these threats may attack you, as a soft alter-native target, while both of you are visiting Germany, either to kidnap you or to . . . well, I am sure you under-stand the situation as well as I do. Now, there are many agents here whose job is to protect you – I am here merely to back them up. To be your personal bodyguard, shall we say. But I would like you to agree to something.'

Maria had gone white. Carter could feel her fingers, cool and smooth, against his own.

'Yes, Mr Carter?'

'I want you to do everything I ask. I want you to trust me implicitly. I am beyond being bought – I am a multi-millionaire in my own right and money means nothing to me. But I need to know that you will do what I ask, when I ask – if you want to stay alive. Will you do this?'

She paused, then smiled softly. 'Yes. I will do what you ask. But I too have a question.'

'Hmm?' Carter was looking around the garden.

'Why did you make me remove my jewellery and shoes?'

'Bugged. By the guys here – only doing their job but I wanted a bit of privacy. The ECube is notoriously efficient at blocking and jamming, but I hate surprises. I trust myself a whole lot more than I trust technology. Better cautious than *dead*.' He savoured the word.

'I see.'

'Tell me, why do *you* think you have been threatened?'

'My uncle, who treated me like his own child after my own father . . . well, died . . . my uncle is devoted to his work. He is a genius. All I know is that we suspect a terrorist organisation wants him to stop.'

'Why are you here?' asked Carter. 'Your uncle knows that you are the soft target – his niece and only close family . . . the daughter he never had. You should be somewhere safe, away from the possibility of danger.'

Maria turned away, then stooped and picked a small flower. She held the white petals to her nose and, her eyes lowered, said softly, 'My uncle is a man of iron principles and I admire him for that. He will stand by what he believes. He did not want me here; but I will not have my life dictated by what might or might not happen. I am my own person, Mr Carter.' She met his gaze then. 'I will do what I wish. And let us be honest – if they can get to me here, then they can get to me wherever I chose to . . . *hide*.' She spoke the word with contempt.

Carter nodded slowly. 'I want you to know that I have never lost a protection,' he said. He reached out and tilted her chin up. 'So you do what I say and we might get through this alive. OK?'

'Yes.' Maria smiled, a beautiful smile. 'Here, a present.'

Carter took the flower, sniffing it gently as he followed the girl back towards the house. He watched the agents in the bushes and, as clouds gathered overhead with the threat of yet more drenching rain, did not envy them. He chuckled to himself – and remembered Kade from the night before. The smile fell from his face.

He walked across the drive.

'Count Feuchter.'

Carter stood up and watched the older man approaching him. He was well built, with black hair, iron-grey sideburns and a grey-flecked beard. His eyes were harsh and intelligent, his dress smart. Carter shook the offered hand – a powerful grip.

'A drink?'

'Water,' said Carter.

'It was good of you to agree to this. I understand that you are virtually retired but you come, shall we say, very highly recommended.'

'Lots of experience.' Carter smiled wryly. He took the glass and watched Feuchter slump into a wide upholstered chair and light a cigar. The man fixed his gaze on Carter who sat back down and glanced over at Maria, who was seated at a small oak bureau.

'Do you think we are in a lot of danger?' asked Count Feuchter.

Carter shrugged. 'From the reports I have read and the other info, I would say yes. You have been working for Spiral_Q, if I understand this correctly. It would seem your work has gained you many enemies.'

'They are frightened of the future, Mr Carter. Cowards often are.'

'Can I ask you about this new processor? The QIII Proto, I think it's tagged?'

'Even for you, that would be classified,' said Feuchter softly. 'All I can say is that, as you know, Spiral exists to wipe out the terrorist threat wherever it may be found and the QIII will be of tremendous help in that task – it is incredibly powerful and will be able to crack encryptions in the blink of an eye, locate terrorist cells globally, and terminate the military networks, command centres and control systems of rogue states . . . ahhh,' he sighed, relaxing slightly, the look of excitement in his eyes fading to a more guarded, unreadable expression. 'But I get ahead of myself. As you said earlier, this is the Proto – it is not quite ready.'

'It must be powerful technology indeed to evoke such interest . . . and threat to life?' said Carter softly. 'Maybe some people want it never to be completed?'

Feuchter merely nodded, smiling, and sipped at his brandy.

'This threat to your niece – you realise it could be a double bluff? *You* could be the target,' said Carter.

'That possibility had occurred to me. But I can handle myself, Mr Carter. I used to be an operative very much like yourself. It is my niece who needs protection now – I cannot watch her twenty-four hours a day. What with the party tomorrow and her streak of stubbornness, well . . .'

'Once again, I advise you to cancel.'

'I will *not* cancel,' said Feuchter, his face hardening. 'The agents say they will draft in more men. And you are here.'

51

He smiled without humour, showing tombstone teeth. 'Maria will be safe. She can stay out of the proceedings . . .'

Maria turned to face them from where she sat writing. Her eyes were bright. 'No, uncle. I will not hide.' She sounded indignant.

'So be it.'

Carter rose and left the room. Rain was falling again and he pulled free the ECube and stroked the surface, as if caressing a lover's skin. He linked to the German Special Forces, FG2. He checked the digits. All the agents had signed in, as they had to do every fifteen minutes.

Carter cursed Feuchter's stubbornness. A party! For work colleagues to celebrate a 'breakthrough'.

'Shit, Feuchter. You should have stayed in Rub al'Khali.'

Carter had to admit to himself that he was deeply annoyed. He hadn't realised that he had been drafted in to work on what he thought of as 'Spiral home ground'. Feuchter was a top dog – a Spiral researcher and military developer – and Carter knew that he would therefore have *very* powerful enemies. That meant the game was more important than Carter had at first realised; more important than Natasha had led him to believe.

Carter moved through the house, checking security points, agents and his own small ammo stashes.

'*You lied,*' said Kade. '*You lied, my beautiful brother.*'

'Leave me alone.'

Carter could hear the joy in Kade's words: the excitement, the danger and the promise of killing.

Stick around, thought Carter soberly, checking the last window. I might need you on this one.

The four black Toyota Land Cruiser 70s rumbled to a halt by the roadside, 6164cc diesel engines idling with a promise of power and almost infinite torque. Moonlight glinted from the smoked-glass windows and in the heavy woods to either side a serene silence reigned.

The police car that had been following, a white BMW 525 sporting thick green border stripes, slowed to a crawl as it passed the Land Cruisers before moving on, tail lights glowing. It disappeared around a corner up ahead and was lost in the tangle of dense woodland.

Still the Land Cruisers sat with their engines idling.

Clouds covered the moon; rain began to fall, softly at first but increasing in ferocity until it pounded against the smoked glass of the Toyotas' windows and sent streams running down the narrow strip of tarmac.

In the gloom up ahead, headlights glittered through the downpour. Then the blue lights atop the BMW flickered into life and the large car returned to halt beside the four Toyotas. Windscreen wipers thumped, sending splashes of rain dancing onto the slick road. One of the police car's doors opened, and a large man wearing a thick overcoat climbed out. He flashed a heavy-duty torch at the lead Land Cruiser, then walked warily forward, his hand on his holstered pistol. Behind him, his companion remained standing by the BMW, wedged between the door and the car's body, eyes alert above a heavily moustached sneer.

'*Verlassen Sie das Auto!*' shouted the lead policeman.

Nothing moved; the lead Toyota sat, engine rumbling, the rain running in rivulets down the dark windscreen and bonnet. The police officer tried to peer through the glass but could see nothing inside.

'*Ich sagte, verlassen Sie das Auto!*'

Slowly, the driver's window hissed down on smooth electrics; the police officer took a step closer, his flashlight coming up to reveal—

The muzzle of a silenced pistol.

There was a *pop*.

The officer was hurled backwards, the flashlight's beam swinging up to illuminate rain falling in diagonal sheets. Through the gloom came a shout – '*Nein!*' – as the second officer pulled his gun and began to fire. Two bullets slammed against the wing of the Toyota before a stream of automatic gunfire picked him up, spun him round and left him lifeless and bleeding on the tarmac.

The Toyota Land Cruisers reversed, then drove past the BMW. One ran over the body of the first police officer to have been killed, leaving wide tyre tracks across and *through* his chest.

They roared off into the night, leaving a ghostly scene of horror stroboscopically lit by the flashing blue lights of the abandoned police car.

Carter watched the convoy of expensive vehicles sweep up the drive. Seated on a wide bench outside Maria's room as she dressed, his attention was divided between the room's solid wooden door and the small window out of which he gazed. Rain fell heavily from towering clouds, and a heavy gloom had settled over the world.

Carter could hear two types of music, intertwining, an insanity mix: thumping beats rising up the wide sweeping stairs at the end of the plushly carpeted corridor and coming from the huge ballroom – and the gentle lure of Beethoven from Maria's room. Carter pulled free his Browning 9mm HiPower. He checked the thirteen rounds in the clip, then checked the other five clips he carried about his body. Seventy-eight rounds in total. Carter liked to be prepared. As he had often told Roxi: 'I don't want to die because I ran out of fucking bullets.'

The door opened. Maria appeared – stunning in a

white dress that showed off her pale complexion and dark hair.

'You ready?' asked Carter kindly, sensing her fear.

Maria took a deep breath. She knew – as well as he did, as well as the many agents positioned around the house and grounds – that tonight was a golden opportunity for assassins. If they were for real and not just a hollow blackmail attempt. An empty threat. A *hoax* . . .

'Do not leave me tonight. Not for one moment.'

'So you'll accompany me to the toilet?' she laughed.

'Yes.'

'Really?'

Carter smiled. 'Yes. Prime location for attack – it is the one moment when, shall we say, a person's guard is truly down.'

They went down the luxurious wide staircase, with its thick carpets and carved oak banisters. The walls were richly decorated with plaster frescoes inlaid with gold. Q Division obviously paid well.

Carter had instructed Maria Balashev earlier that evening: no leaving the house, no alcohol, and no picking up young – or old – men. If Maria wanted to live through this potential threat then she had to minimise complications.

Fucking parties, thought Carter.

Fucking Feuchter! Stubborn bastard – stupid bastard!

A hundred and thirty guests. Carter had almost shot Feuchter himself when Hans Jesmar, head of the German security operation, had handed him the slip of paper.

People mingled. Servants with trays of drinks circulated and Carter's gaze swept across the large, gaudily decorated suite. Rich velvet curtains hung to the floor, obscuring the view of any outside observers – and of any long-range snipers.

Carter stayed close to Maria. She knew many of the people who had arrived and Carter allowed the conversations to flow over him. If anybody approached or spoke to him he was curt to the point of rudeness. He did not want conversation – it distracted him.

He watched. Maria socialised and, like a good girl, stayed off the champagne.

Feuchter, obviously suffering a little from stress, was drunk and being loud and abusive in a corner. Carter checked the squad monitor. Everything was OK.

The woodland surrounding Castle Schwalenberg – swathes of deciduous and conifer trees that rose and fell, following the slopes and dramatic contours of the land – spread out for miles. Several rough narrow trails, littered with fallen trees and branches, criss-crossed forest, but on this dark and rain-filled night nothing seemed to move except thick branches swaying in the wind, and rain running in violent rivulets down the knobbled bark of trees.

A deep rumble cut through the gloom, and four black vehicles crept smoothly across the forest floor. Heavy wheels crushed branches and negotiated fallen trees with 4X4 ease . . . slowly the Land Cruisers came to a halt, strung out in a line.

Engines died.

Silence crept back.

Doors opened, and dark figures climbed swiftly free of their metal confines. They moved stealthily forward and crouched, peering through the trees towards Castle Schwalenberg, its lights glittering with promise in the distance.

The line of shadows bristled with weapons.

There were various *clicks* as magazines were slotted home.

Copper-eyed stares met; silent commands were exchanged; and slowly, with an infinite and precise care, the column of armed killers moved off through the undergrowth, untroubled by the rain and the threat of death to come.

Friedrich squatted beside the bush, listening to the commands issued by Jesmar. He hoisted the rifle, the weight burning into his arm and shoulder now that the hour was getting late, and glanced up at the rolling clouds obscured by the driving rain.

'Fucking weather,' he muttered. 'Sent to torture a man!'

He sighted down the Ruger M77 MkII VLE's scope, and swept the grounds in front of him, rotating the rifle on the smooth-action Harris bipod. He could see nothing through the rain, even on IR and UIR. Friedrich rolled back his shoulders and craved a cigarette and a cup of hot coffee. With five sugars. Yes, he could almost taste the steaming brew . . .

His mouth watering, something made Friedrich glance behind him. Despite knowing that other agents were posted at the rear, protecting his back from infiltration, Friedrich nevertheless felt something subtly out of place. He scratched at his rough-stubbled chin and frowned, eyes trying to pick out movement in the gloom. Then he brought round the Ruger and sighted down the scope on IR. There – he saw . . . something . . . A figure slipping behind a tree? Or the taunt of dancing branches fuelled by the desire for nicotine and caffeine?

He shifted the scope slightly, but could make out nothing more between the trees' wide boles and tangled foliage. He shifted uncomfortably in the rain, feeling trickles run into places he had once thought secure.

'Bitch.'

Friedrich lowered the rifle for an instant to wipe a trace of rain from his forehead – and heard the hiss an instant before the black bolt slammed through his hand and into his forehead and brain beyond, pinning his hand to his skull in a final salute to the Goddess of Death. Gore ran down either side of his nose and he slumped slowly backwards, his free arm falling limply to his side, speckles of blood tracing smears across the stock of the Ruger M77 rifle.

There was a pad of soft footsteps; three figures crouched by his corpse. They lifted the weapon from the ground and black-gloved fingers trailed water down the scope.

'Leave it. We do not need it.' The words were low, soft, gentle.

The weapon bounced on the soft forest floor and the figures disappeared into the night.

Two hours had passed. Carter could feel himself growing weary and, motioning to Maria, he followed her into the relative calm and cool of the hallway before the wide sweeping stairs. He took a small leather case from his pocket, opened it and removed a small phial. He stuck the needle into his thigh and replaced the empty phial in the case.

'What was that?' asked Maria.

'A stimulant. Allows me to stay awake and alert. I'll pay tomorrow.'

Maria smiled, and shivered. 'It's chilly.'

Carter looked at her, then turned, his gaze moving up the stairs. 'You feel that draught?'

Maria nodded.

'It wasn't there before.'

'Probably just an open window,' said Maria, as Carter discreetly withdrew the bulky Browning and with his free hand waved Maria behind him. He pulled free his comm. 'Jesmar?'

'Yes?'

'Can you come to the foot of the stairs? I think we have a situation.'

'OK.'

Jesmar was there within fifteen seconds, a small black pistol in his hand. 'Watch Maria for a few minutes,' said Carter. 'I have a bad feeling about this . . .'

'Wait, I'll send some men with you.'

'No time.'

Carter followed the draught, his boots silent on the carpet. He felt adrenalin and the recently injected drugs kick his system and with his spinal column wrapped in the stimulant's fist he climbed to the top of the first flight of stairs. The music drifted into the distance, a ghostly ambience. He checked the squad monitor – five minutes since all members had signed in. Carter tutted to himself. A lot could happen in five minutes.

He moved to a nearby window at the top of the stair-case and, crouching low, peered into the darkness. He couldn't see any of the positioned snipers – but that did not mean they weren't there.

He moved across the wide landing, listening, out-stretched hand following the gentle hint of a breeze.

He stopped in front of a broad sturdy door. He rested his hand against the wood.

Carter licked his lips.

'*You need me,*' came the whisper of Kade's voice.

I need nothing, Carter thought bitterly.

He pushed gently and stepped aside; the door swung free. Carter peered, then with outstretched weapon slid in. The room was dark and he swiftly switched on the light . . .

Empty.

Carter moved towards the window, which was open – a three-inch gap. He looked out, then down, saw a small strip of mud caught against the wooden sill – and suddenly realised that he was a clean target against the window . . . He moved fast, as a .22 calibre sniper round smashed through the glass of embed itself in the plaster of the ceiling.

Carter rolled on the carpet, was up and running—

He screamed into his comm, 'We have a breach, red floor, sectors 15 to 20 . . . I repeat, we have a *fucking* breach . . .'

He spun out of the doorway and into the path of a surprised black-clad figure; the Browning 9mm slammed twice in his hand and the intruder was kicked from his feet, scrabbling at the holes in his throat as he went down hard.

Carter looked left and right. From somewhere in the house came the sound of distant screams and cries for help. He ran to the top of the stairs and a stream of silenced bullets spat wood from the rail. He dived, rolling against the wall with a bone-jarring *thud*. His gaze fixed on the bullets in the rail, the chewed wood and splinters – he judged the angle, popped his head round and fired off five rounds. Then, scrambling to his feet, he ran for the head of the stairs.

The silenced machine gun ate the wall behind him as Carter leaped, clearing the top flight in a single bound; his Browning slammed in his hand once more, six rounds that picked up the assassin and sent him spinning down the remaining stairs where he sprawled at the foot, blood soaking the plush pile, his chest caved in and slick with gore.

No guests . . . no guests in the hall . . .

Fuck, screamed Carter's brain.

He crept down the stairs and crouched next to the corpse, creating a smaller target. The comm vibrated in his hand. 'Carter, Jesmar. I have Maria in the kitchens. Yellow, sector 34. There are six of them in the ballroom – they've herded the guests together. They are all heavily armed.'

'I've taken out two,' said Carter softly as he replaced the clip in his gun. 'You stay there, I'll come to you.'

The guests were silent in the lounge. Carter slowly eased his head around the corner; a black-clad assassin stood sentry with a silenced Uzi-K2. Carter fired three rounds and ran in the opposite direction towards the kitchen. As he spun through the door bullets tore the wood behind him and he sprawled across the tiles, sliding between stainless-steel cabinets on his belly. His boot kicked backwards, slamming the door shut.

'Jesmar?' he bellowed.

'Over here,' came the shout from one of the adjoining rooms.

Carter peered over the stainless-steel cabinets, strewn with bubbling pans and half-prepared dishes; discarded knives and chopped vegetables littered the worktops. There were no cooks visible. He moved carefully around the room and towards the adjoining chamber. Hairs prickled across the back of his neck.

'I'm coming in – hold your fire.'

He stepped into the dimly lit room. It was a storage chamber filled with sacks and crates with stencilled lettering in German. He saw Jesmar, standing beside an ashen-faced Maria.

Carter met Jesmar's stare and he knew—

Knew that something was wrong—

The gun rose and pointed at Carter.

'I am sorry, my friend. It is your time to die.'

Carter nodded gently. 'I think . . .' His Browning lifted, a blur, and smashed a bullet into Jesmar's face; the bullet entered through the man's nose and exploded the back of his head across a sack of vegetables. Jesmar toppled in a heap. '. . . somebody is playing a game with me,' Carter finished.

'Carter,' sobbed Maria. She ran to him and fell into his arms. He hugged her quickly, then closed the door behind him – sealing them in this kitchen tomb. He moved to Jesmar's blood-drenched body and checked through his clothing. He took the dead man's Glock, pushing it down the front of his trousers and collecting the spare magazines.

'What's happening?' said Maria.

'Bad shit,' said Carter with a snarl. 'How the fuck did they infiltrate Special Forces? Either big money is changing hands, or something is at play here. Something I don't understand.'

'Where is my uncle?'

'I think we have a hostage situation. There are six of them . . .' Jesmar's words came to him again. Was it a set-up? Something was too neat – too mechanical.

Like grappling with a disjointed puzzle, Carter's brain wrestled with the implications.

'Come on, we've got to get out of here. Out of the house.'

The comm vibrated. 'Yeah?'

'This is Snell. Three of our snipers are dead. Where's Jesmar?'

'Dead,' said Carter. 'There are at least six assassins in here. I've killed two. Fuck knows how many more there are. What do you suggest?'

'Where are you?'

'Yellow, sector 18 near the rear porch.'

'Is Maria with you?'

'Yes.'

'Come out, the rest of us are here. We need to get Maria away.'

'We'll come to the inside door and await your escort. Out.'

Carter logged off the comm; he looked at Maria. 'We are in big trouble. You need to follow my every order if you want both of us to survive. Understand?'

'Hmm?'

Carter held her arms and shook her, hard. 'You understand girl?'

'Yes, yes. Ow, you're hurting.'

Carter released his grip. 'This is what we will do. They think we're coming out of the back; they don't realise that I killed Jesmar. I—'

There was a sound. Carter moved smoothly to the door and opened it – fast, the Browning's deadly eye moving, focusing—

'Shit,' hissed Carter, removing his finger from the trigger.

Count Feuchter had been beaten. Blood dripped from his broken nose and his smashed lips. He tottered forward, the stench of alcohol surrounding him like a perverse perfume. Carter helped him into the room and checked the corridor; he could see the door sensor flickering and he checked his ECube once more. He activated a function: anybody else entering the kitchen would trigger the silent alarm.

'Uncle!' Maria ran to Feuchter, hugged him, helped him to sit down as he grunted with pain. His blood dripped on the floor as he stared in horror at the imploded face of Jesmar.

'You killed him?'

'He turned out to be less than honest.'

Carter, the Browning still in his grip, crouched in front of Feuchter. 'What's happening out there?'

'There are six of them. They have herded the guests together. They have sent me to negotiate with you . . .'

'*Me*? But they think—'

Carter halted. The only way they could know that Hans Jesmar was dead was if they had access to the comm network; that meant the whole of the German Special Forces protection squad were in on the assassination. But why wait until the party? Why not just take out Maria with a sniper's bullet?

The alarm sounded, the comm vibrating.

Carter moved swiftly to the doorway; his Browning peered around the door and sent a warning shot through the door leading from the kitchen to the corridor. There was no return fire and no more movement.

Carter turned.

Feuchter, still down on the floor – but now on his knees – held a gun pointing straight at Carter. Carter's stare met that of the older man. There was no emotion in his eyes – just the hardness that Carter had previously witnessed. The hardness of cold steel. The hardness of a killer.

'What do you want?' said Carter softly.

'You fucked it all up,' hissed Feuchter in a spray of spittle and blood. 'Drop your weapon – now!'

Carter glanced at Maria; and something had changed, a change that plucked Carter's heart in its iron grasp and crushed him without mercy. Maria's tears had dried. She was standing, a small silver gun in her hands. The gun was pointing at him.

'I don't understand,' growled Carter. 'I thought you were Spiral?'

'I said drop your fucking weapon!' screamed Feuchter, the pain of his beating lacing his words with an edge of panic.

Something went cold, and dead, in Carter's soul.

Maria smiled at him. She gave a little shrug.

'Don't act so surprised, Carter. It's not as if you're one of the family.'

Carter knew then: knew that he would die. There were two targets, both bearing guns and he could not possibly drop them both in the blink of an eye . . . He *would* die, in that stinking cramped mouldy storage room at the back of a bastard's country castle. Murdered and betrayed by . . . by who? And for what? What game was being played here? And who was the *real* target?

'*You,*' whispered Kade in a voice of cemetery stone. '*Come on, Carter, it'll be just like old times . . . just like the Battle of Cairo7 . . . let me take them . . .*'

Feuchter had staggered to his feet. His fingers dabbed at his lip and came away flecked with blood. He waved his Glock, his face an animal snarl. 'I said drop your fucking weapon now!'

Carter began to stoop, as if to place his Browning on the ground.

'*Let me,*' soothed Kade, his voice hypnotic in Carter's fevered mind. Carter blinked in lazy-time slow-motion as the world descended from colour into a mercury downward spiral . . .

Do it, he thought sourly.

And, slowly, Kade opened his eyes.

65

CHAPTER 3

BLACK & WHITE

The panoramic scene was colourless, bleached, a picture in black and white. He smiled at the blood-smeared Feuchter; the Browning felt good in his hand, stocky, reassuring, an old friend, a returned lover, a part of his body and essence and soul. It was held low as he stooped, at an angle. All it took was a twitch—

Kade flicked his wrist – faster than thought – and pulled the trigger.

Feuchter was blown backwards, folding in half with a grunt of expelled air, and he slumped, sprawling to the ground with a look of sudden horror on his face. He dropped his gun. He looked down to where his hands clutched a widening patch of red at his belly. Kade, in the same movement, spun on his heel, the Browning flashing up sideways and, again, he pulled the trigger – the bullet smashed into Maria's shoulder, spinning her back to rebound from the wall. She hit the ground hard, moaning, saliva drooling to the cold stone, her small pretty gun forgotten. 'Never trust a fucking woman,' snarled Kade, and moved forward to kneel swiftly beside Feuchter.

'It takes a long time to die from a stomach wound,' he growled. 'And I believe it hurts. A lot.' He pulled back his gun and smashed the butt into Feuchter's face, hammering the already broken nose. Feuchter screamed – and another three heavy blows silenced him, reducing his scream to a gurgle.

Kade moved to the door. He flicked rapidly through the channels on the ECube – and confusion wrenched his face as he realised it was dead. No scans. No location motions. Nothing . . .

Kade searched the open archive of Carter's mind – it took the blink of an eye – then, opening the door, he ran across the kitchen, vaulting the stainless-steel worktop and towards a low serving hatch. He pushed his way into the hole, kicked through the thin boards below, and allowed himself to drop—

Machine-gun fire sounded above.

Kade landed softly and looked around. The cellar. He moved past various cars covered with protective sheets. He halted, looking sideways at a gleaming red motorbike – a Ducati 1296 SPS MkV – the colour registering in Kade's vision as a bright shade of grey. Then he ran forward to the ramp and the wide wooden doors leading from the cellar. He peered through the crack into the darkness. Kade palmed Carter's ECube, rotated it gently and as if by magic a hint of a glow emanated from the hub. On the surface grooves Kade traced a pattern and a pin spat from the core of the ECube. Reaching down, he slid the pin into the lock and within a few seconds there was a *click*. Silently, he eased open the heavy door a fraction—

Running back to the bike, he kicked it free of its stand. He used the butt of the Browning to smash a hole in the top fairing, then reached through and felt for the ignition wiring. A few cuts. A few twists to bypass the

67

immobiliser. Kade grinned and gunned the engine, clutch in, kick down to first, screw the throttle up to 13,000 revs—

Kade ducked his head and popped the clutch.

The Ducati wheelied up the ramp and smashed through the doors. Machine guns turned on Kade as the motorcycle shot like a bullet down the gravel drive, 221 b.h.p. kicking the bike up the arse with the Browning thumping in Kade's left hand. Skidding around the fountain, Kade blew a man's chest open with the slam of three bullets. He dropped a gear and the back wheel spun gravel, dug into dirt and shot him down the drive's straight and away from the figures who ran from Schwalenberg's main entrance with their machine guns blazing.

Bullets screamed past Kade's head and he ducked even lower over the broad tank as the machine hit 224 m.p.h. He clung to the bike like a limpet, an incredible grin hijacking his face, the Browning forgotten in the joy and concentration of controlling this screaming insanity engine as the needle flickered on the redline.

Behind him, a swathe of perhaps twenty black-masked figures swarmed forward, then suddenly halted. Copper eyes watched the Ducati disappear to a red blip. Men were shouting – they jumped into cars and the black-clad assassins leaped apart as the vehicles roared past in pursuit.

On the Ducati, Kade was screaming and laughing in glee, face upturned into the wind, the bike howling between his legs. Hearing the roar of cars behind made him laugh even louder as the motorcycle smashed down an unlit lane surrounded by thick woodland. He suddenly slowed, front end diving low under harsh braking, and flicked off the machine's lights with his thumb as the

Ducati's engine throttled back and the rev needle flickered as he kicked down a couple of gears—

The roaring of car engines approached at speed. The Browning boomed in Kade's hand as he emptied a full clip into the windscreen of the lead vehicle. The BMW veered right and hammered into a tree: a figure was flung, a pulped carcass, through the windscreen and Kade screwed the Ducati's throttle once more and watched the rev counter dance. The front wheel lifted and Kade clamped himself to the fuel tank; as he hit 100 m.p.h. again he flicked on the lights and leaned low into a right-hand bend as the front wheel finally touched down, and his knee skimmed the rough tarmac an instant before the foot-peg showered the ground with sparks. Opening the throttle more, his grin broadened and the chase was forgotten as the Ducati was pushed to the twitching 240 m.p.h.+ limits of the screaming motor's ability.

'I just fucking love bikes,' whispered Kade into the howl of the wind.

Far behind, forgotten, Castle Schwalenberg blazed briefly with a glowing bud of explosion; fire roared, ate, consumed – billowed up into the night sky, causing Kade to lock the Ducati's wheels and weave in a long skid, finally to halt and look back with an intense frown.

The HighJ explosives roared up into the night, a purple blossom opening to receive the moonlight.

Kade put his head down, opened the throttle to full and redlined the bike down the road, leaving a streak of burned rubber. He disappeared into the blackness of the German forest.

Carter sat in the woods, listening to the gurgling of a small waterfall that tumbled into a circular rock basin. Huge rings surrounded his eyes and nearby, badly disguised, was the scraped, bashed, scratched and mud-coated Ducati under a pile of branches and leaves.

Carter wearily toyed with the ECube. Blue digits flickered under his gentle caress. He activated the emergency homer, and felt the ECube vibrate a little as the powerful transmitter gave out short bursts.

Resting his head back against the grassy embankment, Carter felt the sounds of running water having a soothing effect on his soul. But too many questions jostled his brain – too many memories haunted his past.

It was obvious now. It had been a set-up. For him.

Carter shivered; somebody had wanted him dead, somebody had wanted him dead real fast. But why the elaborate protection scam? Of course – to separate him from Spiral . . . to get him out there on his own. If he was *supporting* German Special Forces then he would not be consigned to a DemolSquad . . .

And Maria—

Carter shook his head. She had fooled him; and now she was wounded, with a bullet in her shoulder, possibly dead and buried, and all for what? To kill *him*?

Feuchter and Maria. They were both Spiral . . . and they had both tried to kill him. And it would seem that some of the German Special Forces had been in on the betrayal . . . and the final explosion. What the fuck had happened there? What the fuck had been going down?

After Kade had taken control of him, events were nothing but a dull dream, without colour, and the— hell, he thought, say the word. The *possession* left a bad taste in Carter's mouth, whisky piss of the worst blend. Kade's joy left a sour feeling in his belly, and Kade's fury left an empty void in his soul.

Carter stared at the small white flower in his fingers. It had withered a little since Maria Balashev had given it to

70

him in the garden. Kade had said to him, *'You lied.'* For once Kade had been right and Carter cursed the demon in his soul.

'I have never lost a protection.'

A lie of reassurance. Oh, the comedy of the situation! He had been protecting his own would-be assassin . . . and now? Was she dead? Lying with Feuchter in the cold grave of their ancestors?

'I should have killed them.'

'I still can't believe you shot her,' said Carter softly.

'Yeah, I'm going fucking soft, or something, I should have placed the bullet in her fucking face. Never leave an enemy behind – it's your fault, Carter, you poison my blood, you weaken my resolve, you piss in my mind . . .'

'I poison . . . get the fuck out of my brain, Kade.'

Carter felt Kade depart; his arrogance, hatred and anger a bleak red streak at the back of his mind, burning, but dissipating as the dark twin left him to his own sour thoughts.

Carter threw the dead flower aside and stood, stretching his back and rolling his neck, which cracked with a release of tension.

Why hadn't they killed him earlier?

Carter pondered. Maybe the explosion had been intended – not just for him, but for the guests as well? But something had gone wrong and Carter had fucked it all up, and so it had been left to Feuchter and Maria to finish off the kill. Maybe.

Carter spun the ECube in his palm, then sent the report to Spiral.

What the fuck, he thought. Let them figure it out! Maybe they could discover what had happened to the ECube as well . . .

A low drone reached his ears, pounding over the forest.

71

Carter waited patiently as the Comanche leaped into view, spun around low over the trees and touched down. The *whump whump* of the rotors sent branches and trees swaying and Carter ran to the cockpit and the serious face of Langan.

'Hurry up,' he shouted. 'We've got company.'

'Company?'

Langan nodded as Carter ascended and belted himself into the cockpit. 'Put on the spare HIDSS 'cos I might need your help. Whatever the fuck you've been up to down here, you've certainly stirred up a hornets' nest. Ever used a holographic Bi-Ocular FOV in a real-time combat situation?'

'*What?*'

'Just get in.'

The Comanche RAH-66 twin LHTec engines screamed and the attack helicopter launched into the fast-approaching darkness.

CHAPTER 4

STATE OF PLAY

The Russian Ballistic Missile Submarine 941 Typhoon Class, *Moscow 16*, thrummed through the dark waters 130° and a hundred miles south of the Gelz Ice Shelf. Slowly, the seven-bladed perch propellers spun down and the vessel sat squat and dark in the dim cool glow, immobile, predatory and frightening in its bulky, matt black presence.

Juri Kolgar, Captain First Rank of the 19th Submarine Division, drummed his fingers on the desk and stared at the readings on the screen before him. He glanced up at Seaman Bharzova and the worried expression on the young man's neatly shaved face. Kolgar smiled warmly, and dismissed the man.

For the past four months the Russians had been working with Spiral in an attempt to quash a new internal problem – a spate of mass rioting that had been brought on due to a Mafia-peddled designer drug, which had taken the poverty-stricken working classes by the balls and sent them spinning down the cobbled road to narcotic Hell. This drug, Lemon Vodka as it had been nicknamed, had made the Mafia-led clans even more rich and powerful, but was costing the government dear – financially, politically and, of course, socially. Spiral had been called in as a last resort to try and help stamp out the illegal importing of Lemon Vodka.

A day earlier, the *Moscow16* had been tracking an unnamed surface vessel that was under suspicion of drug trafficking; the vessel was the size of a battleship, of unknown origins, and had been making slow progress to the north-east, close to Russia's Arctic coast.

Now, however, the vessel had gone.

Kolgar had sent out Tykes, tiny aquatic machine scouts no larger than a tennis ball. A hundred had surged from the sub, humming quietly and darkly into the deep cold waters in search of the mysterious vessel that had – impossibly – evaded their most high-tech searches.

Now they were playing the waiting game.

Kolgar sighed, opened the drawer to his right and looked longingly at the bottle of crystal-clear liquid nestling within. He shook his head, rubbed a hand over the bristles on his chin, and closed the drawer again.

Standing, he left the room and walked slowly to the Control Centre, which was situated above the batteries where energy from the 2x600 mwt nuclear reactors were stored in order to give the huge craft its propulsion.

Seamen snapped to attention as Kolgar entered. He saluted his men, and took his seat on the bridge. 'Anything on the sonar?'

'Negative, Captain. Not even on the I/J band surface-target detection. But she was there, as real as a bear in the woods. She isn't there any longer.'

Kolgar cursed.

'What about the Tykes?'

'Nothing yet, Captain. They've spread out, and are heading away in a globe formation. If there's *anything* around us, they will find it and report it.' Their gazes met. 'You know, Captain, as well as I that they have never missed a target.'

Kolgar nodded, rubbing wearily at his temples. 'Have you informed Spiral Tac of this?'

'Not yet, Captain.'

'Do so. Their intelligence may have some records or information on this vessel. What did we find out before it . . . it . . .'

'Vanished?'

'Yes.'

'Vague dimensions estimated by the BattleSubTec computers. Nothing more. An estimation of possible weapons capabilities. And the fact that it moved much, much faster than any seagoing vehicle had a right to move.'

They waited, watching the Tyke scanners. A tense silence surrounded them, filled with the glittering glow of computer read-outs and submarine-control displays. Red light scattered like rubies across Kolgar's heavily bearded face, and his eyes narrowed as they fixed on one of the Tyke ScannerReps.

He pointed. 'What's that?'

There was an instant of blackness, and the light went out.

'What does the TerminationDisplay read?' asked Kolgar slowly.

'Zero, Captain.'

'That's impossible! No last-nanosecond read-outs? No transmissions on what was around the Tyke when it was destroyed?'

'Nothing, Captain.'

75

The two men stared at each other, frowning. And then, like a scene from some digital firework display across the control wall, the Tyke-linked scanners arrayed before them – each signal linked to individual Tyke scouts spinning through the voids of dark ocean all around – seemed to *explode* in front of their very eyes . . . the red lights scattered, spun through shades of attack report from green and blue to yellow – and then, like a visual tidal wave, the lights were swept out and into darkness and *death*.

Kolgar stared, numbed, at the scanners. All were black. Every single Tyke had been simultaneously destroyed.

'Reports?' he asked, his voice a dry croak.

'None,' came the soft, disbelieving reply.

A hundred scouts had been destroyed; and not a single transmission to give the submarine a clue to their attackers had been registered; not a single warning given. Nothing.

Kolgar could taste sweet vodka on his tongue and he longed for a drink.

Later, barked his intelligence.

'Contact Spiral Tac. Tell them we have an *emergency*.'

'Transmitting.'

They waited ten seconds – a long ten seconds of tense wondering filled with uneasy sweat and thoughts of death as every seaman in the Control Centre waited for a reply, looking around and *up* into the imaginary dark waters around their sub, imagining dark enemies with incredibly superior technology – the sort of technology that could make a massive warship disappear, the sort of technology that could evade their most sophisticated scanning equipment, and the sort of technology that could annihilate a hundred scattered scouts without giving away any indication of method or weapons.

There came the *blip* of reply.

76

'Three TacSquad officers will be with us in just over two hours from the nearby stationed British destroyer *Castle*. They are deploying as we speak in an underwater Shark Attack Craft, very, very fast. They recommend that we sit still and do nothing – merely report if our situation changes.'

Kolgar nodded, and wiped the sweat from his forehead on the back of his sleeve.

The scanners remained dark, quiet; this was no help when you suddenly believed the enemy to be *invisible*.

The *Moscow16* received the Shark Attack Craft into its huge belly like a subterranean Leviathan swallowing its prey. Decompression chambers hissed, pumps whined, and within a few minutes the ramps engaged and two military-suited women and a man walked down the ramp and saluted Juri Kolgar.

'I believe you have a problem,' said the tall, red-haired female. She had cold blue eyes and high cheekbones that highlighted rather than diminished her incredible beauty. Her hand moved slowly, confidently, to Kolgar's and they shook. 'Commanding Officer Reyana Treban at your disposal. I am an expert in aquatic machinery and covert tracking systems, and was part of the design team that invented the Tyke Tracking Systems.'

Kolgar nodded. 'I have heard of you, Lady Treban.'

'You may address me as Reyana. I have no time for rank when we need to work together in an emergency situation. This is Alice Metrass, bio-weapons expert, and James Rothwell, who has an incredibly detailed working knowledge of practically every submarine utilised by most world governments.'

Formalities were speedily dispensed with, and Kolgar led the trio straight to the Command Centre.

77

'We have your reports, as issued by our connective ECubes; they inform us that a *hundred* Tykes were destroyed within a few seconds of one another, and not a single scout reported back anything as to their situation?'

Kolgar nodded.

Reyana seated herself at a console, and began to type; she integrated with the sub's computers and for a while all was silent as data flashed across the screen. Eventually, she stroked her cheek, eyes distant. 'I think we are in grave danger.'

'You found something?'

Reyana nodded. 'It was hidden in a data structure; you did receive the reports, but they were *scrambled* so that the sub computers would not recognise the codes.'

'What destroyed them?' asked Kolgar slowly.

'I don't know. But you were tracking a huge ship, is that correct? A surface vessel?'

'Yes.'

'Now it is tracking you. And it is closing fast.'

'Weapons?' asked Kolgar.

'Break out every fucking gun you've got.'

The *Moscow16* glided through silent dark waters. Fish darted from its path as engines roared, all need for stealth thrown off as the machine surged forward towards the protection of the nearest Spiral naval outpost. A distance of two hundred and thirty miles.

As the submarine increased its speed, so it increased its depth; nose dipped, it powered down deep below the surface, cutting through shoals of silver glittering fish, deep deep into the abyss of darkness that was the Tremanan Valley, scraping into the deep trench of scythed-out rock filled with stagnant dead water from a million years past.

Unidentified debris floated past in the depths, several of these huge metal casks thumping against the sub's hull with distant echoing *booms* that made all the inhabitants shiver – even though scanners confirmed that these objects were not *mines*. On Reyana's instruction they slowed their speed and once more she analysed the sub's scanners, calling for Rothwell's help in disassembling navigational data.

Suddenly, a siren sounded and data started flashing across all the screens in the Control Centre simultaneously; Kolgar leaped forward as Lieutenant-Captain Lyagarin burst in and the sonar operator turned to him.

'Active sonar acquiring! The bastards have locked on!' came the panicked voice of the det-ops seaman.

'It's above us!' hissed Lyagarin.

'That's impossible!' snapped Kolgar. The 941 Typhoon Class was fitted with active/passive sonar, surface target detection, ESM, radar and direction-finding systems, and a contemporary combat-control interface. The *Moscow16* was supposed to surprise the enemy – the enemy was not supposed to surprise *it*.

'Arm and lock-on the VA-111's!' snapped Reyana as the Command Centre exploded with activity. Every man and woman present knew their jobs and knew them well; this was war, and they all had a job to play.

'There it is,' snapped Kolgar.

Suddenly, as if uncloaking, the huge warship became visible. It was directly above them. It had them locked in its sights, ensnared in its net; caught in its trap.

The submarine rocked; there was a distant *boom*, a scream of steel and a rumbling like distant thunder. The whole submarine started to shake, vibrating, and Kolgar looked helplessly down at his hands as they trembled before his very face.

'The pressure hull,' he croaked, suddenly white-faced as he met the stare of Lyagarin. Reyana and Rothwell were screaming orders to the seamen, and understanding passed between them all, and their faces were bleached, with shock and horror, at the terrible implications.

Some form of advanced depth charge or torpedo had cracked the supposedly 'unbreakable' parallel pressure hulls. You could have as many SLBMs or torpedoes as you could carry, but the pressure hulls were the only substance between life and the terrible, crushing sea which surrounded the deep-sea vessel.

The 941 was going down . . .

More than that, it was being crushed by the sea.

The rumbling increased in volume. Men charged across the Control Centre, panic their master, but Kolgar and Lyagarin just stood staring at one another. They were deep; far too deep. They both knew; they both understood. They were dead men savouring their last breaths.

Reyana grasped Kolgar's arm. 'The attack craft; we can still escape!'

Kolgar shook his head sadly. He had been at sea far too long; he knew the dangers, accepted the dangers; only a miracle would even allow you to reach the belly of the sub, and the chances of escaping . . .

Reyana, closely followed by the other TacSquad officers, fled the Control Centre, boots stomping metal grilles, pushing past panicked seamen who were also torn between fleeing and saying their last goodbyes to their gods.

The submarine suddenly tilted, and the crew were thrown like dolls across the Centre; bodies smashed into screens and sparks showered the riveted steel decking. Kolgar hit the wall with bone-jarring force and lay still, staring at the lifeless eyes of Lyagarin. The man had broken his neck and his limbs lay splayed in some bizarre horror contortion.

Water poured in; sirens wailed; red lights were flashing in the back of his brain but all Kolgar could think about were his wife Sonya and their baby girl Olivia. Short blonde hair, a beautiful smile, 'Papa' she called him as he carried her in his arms and she nestled close to his chest, softest of soft blonde hair tickling his unshaven chin, her tiny fingers grasping his huge hands.

The water was cold around his legs, a heavy and suddenly powerful swirling, remorseless. Men were screaming. Sparks showered him but he did not flinch. And then the power died: there was a distant groan, a shudder, and the lights went off.

More groans began, as if the Ballistic Missile Submarine 941 Typhoon Class was an animal suffering from an incredible wound; the groans rose in pitch and Kolgar could *feel* the pressure forcing in on them, could *sense* the sea – powerful and without remorse – crushing them in her fist. Steel and alloy screamed. Rivets spat from stanchions like machine-gun bullets. Stairways buckled and folded in on themselves as the might of the sea compressed and *crushed* the life from the submarine.

Those last moments, in the pitch black, with ice-cold water shocking his system into a rigid spasm – those last moments were the most intense moments of Kolgar's life; he dreamed of what Olivia would grow up to be, and how Sonya would mourn at his grave. Tears ran down his cheeks. How did they miss that ship? he thought. How did they fucking miss it?

Reyana strapped herself in at the controls of the Shark Attack Craft; both Rothwell and Metrass were dead.

81

Rothwell had been crushed by a split steel stanchion, the huge slab of metal screaming down to cut him in half at the waist as his entire system of blood flushed from his torn flesh in a scant few seconds. Metrass had been thrown violently down a steep stairwell as the sub rolled, Reyana hanging grimly onto the rails, legs dangling over an abyss as she watched her friend and comrade for the last eight years vanish under a surge of freezing dark waters and fail to reappear. It was a miracle that she had reached the belly of the sub, an even bigger miracle that the compression controls were still active.

As the submarine groaned like an animal in the final throes of death, the fast nuclear-powered Shark Attack Craft spat from its belly and spun between deep rock formations, bubbles spewing from its exhausts. Reyana, tasting blood from the wound to her forehead, watched in horror on the ECube-linked monitors as the submarine broke in two and sank in the deep ravine of the Tremanan Valley. Tears rolled down her cheeks, mingling with the blood there, and she armed the Shark's weapons systems with a dry, fear-filled throat.

Something bad was happening.

Something incredibly bad that she did not understand.

She increased the Shark's speed, descending deep into the ravine and navigating using sensors alone; outside the plasti-titanium hull of the tiny Shark the sea was a dense and uncompromising *black*.

She sensed rather than saw the small object spin in front of her; squinting, she realised that it was a black globe, tiny – similar in concept to the Tyke scouts her team had designed several years earlier.

Reyana moved as if to lock her weapons – and realised that there was nothing on her scanners on which to lock. Swallowing hard, she switched to manual and flicked off the safety on the trigger. Beneath the Shark's belly missiles and mini-torps slotted neatly into place. And then, suddenly, the black globe screamed towards her and there was an insane implosion of plasti-titanium and the sea rushed in towards her as she screamed, an intake of breath as the world went suddenly black and cold and the Shark spiralled down down down deep under the ocean, lost and out of control and *dead* . . .

CHAPTER 5

JAM

The busy London traffic sloshed through the rain, horns blaring, engines revving, lights cutting personal slices from the darkness with thin metal skins shimmering under amber light. Snakes of cars wound across the city, past burnt-out husks of buildings standing stark and forlorn, blackened fingers pointing accusingly at the God who had not saved them. Euston Station was nothing more than a crater of war detritus, guarded by five blackened stumps that had once been tanks, fire-torched turrets and twisted guns evidence of disharmony in this major UK city. As the snakes wound on, they would pass buildings smashed by shells, razed by fire, windows gaping tooth-holes and razor glass littering pavements. People treading the pavements did so warily, eyes watching one another with unease, guns hidden badly under coats.

The tall man stood by the kerb, long leather coat pulled tightly about him. His eyes were dark, hooded, his face a half-beard, hair short and spiked by the light rain. He drew on a cigarette and flicked the butt into the gutter where it mingled with the broken bottles and petrol-bomb remnants as a break appeared in the traffic; boots stomped puddles and he weaved his way through the rush-hour jam, picking his way between Porsches, Volvos, Fords and Fiats, interiors dark and gun-laden. He mounted the opposite kerb and halted, momentarily attracted to a shop display showing digital receivers and the latest in computer-guided weapons. The window was guarded by thick razor-mesh, further evidence of a city that was on the brink of internal collapse and war.

The man scratched tiredly at his beard, obsidian eyes reflected in the window. His hand flitted across his hip, then he turned and walked briskly down the street, boots thumping the pavement. He passed a gathering of Justice Troops – JT8s – drafted in after recent civil unrest who eyed him through their evil black masks before he turned right down a narrow alley stinking of long-unemptied bins, rat disease and the pungent aroma of tom-cat piss.

The rain fell, cooling his face, making his long leather coat glossy. As he walked, he undid three buttons down the front and rested his hand lightly on a dark metallic object within.

Jam knew.

Knew that he was being followed.

The footsteps were almost inaudible behind him and he increased his pace. He blinked, raindrops falling from his eyelashes, and reached out as he passed a huge metal waste bin overflowing with stink; the tiniest of clicks revealed his DP – a 'detection plant' that would lock to his ECube and signal him if he was being pursued.

Jam halted, listening, the hairs on his scalp prickling.

He lit a cigarette, hands cupped against wind and rain. Smoke plumed, dragon's breath, and as the lighter was replaced so a silenced machine pistol found its way into his grip, still shrouded by his coat, still hidden by the gloom.

He turned –

A casual glance –

Nothing.

Jam walked on down the alley, under rusting metal fire escapes adorned with graffiti, under heavy drips from a dark and brooding evening sky that looked down upon this decaying city with malevolence. In the distance neon porn invitations glittered in a puddle and Jam felt the vibrating buzz of his ECube, a relayed signal from the DP. Three. Four. Five. Six, he counted. Shit.

Somebody wanted him *bad* . . .

Jam increased his pace yet again, tossing the cigarette aside and switching left, down another narrow alleyway. He brushed past parked cars, many battered and bullet-scarred, and his eyes moved up, checking, scaling, adjusting. He reached a parked Mercedes, long and sleek and black, almost new and standing out from the other battle-wounded vehicles. He crouched behind it, sighting the machine pistol down the glossy machine's flanks, using the coach line to steady his aim.

Six . . .

Shit, thought Jam again. Which group? Which organisation?

Were they a terrorist group? After the URG Bill of 2010 and the closely following Anti-NBC Laws, which carried immediate death penalties, terrorists of every nationality hated Spiral with a fervour.

Or maybe it was just a random gang, heavily armed and out for cash and guns?

Or maybe even the JT8s . . .

Rain fell.

Jam waited . . .

A noise, behind the poised man, alerted him. He turned, eyes still watching the distant entrance to the alley. The noises were too loud to be made by these secret followers. There was no element of stealth . . .

Five huge black men, bedecked in chains and sporting expensive suits, were making their way down the alley, lacquered shoes dodging puddles. Their gazes alighted on Jam, crouched and leaning nonchalantly against their Mercedes SL2i, and their teeth bared in a curious cross between humour and anger.

They halted. Jam threw a glance back down the alley –

'Get off the fucking car, man,' came a heavy drawl reminiscent of a Hollywood gangster movie –

'Where am I, the Bronx?' Jam smiled easily –

as –

machine-gun hell broke loose.

Bullets screamed, slapping at the flanks of the Mercedes, and Jam hit the floor hard, rolled, dodged the body of a black man who was picked up and spat backwards in a series of heavy-calibre punches. There were shouts, the black men produced pistols and a gunfight ensued with the Mercedes taking centre stage—

'Motherfuckers . . .'

Jam backed into a doorway, heeled the heavy door open and spun into darkness –

Screams and the smack of bullets into flesh followed him.

Blood splashed up the back of his long leather coat.

Jam ran, dodging huge cold machines that loomed suddenly from the gloom. The machine pistol did not feel so comfortable now and he switched hands, wiping sweat from his palm. Six followers, the DP had relayed to his ECube – buzzing at him as it logged each pursuer . . .

could he rely on any of these mysterious figures – assassins? – being taken out by the gangstas?

No. Assume the worst; assume six to follow; and all six at least as heavily armed as himself.

He took the stairs in threes, long powerful legs pushing him up into the light. He was in a narrow stairwell that wound its way up as far as Jam could see. He ran on, producing a small dull silver ball from his pocket. A HPG – high-pressure grenade, working on chemical reaction instead of gunpowder detonation. No loud explosion . . . a covert weapon, near-silent and utterly deadly . . .

Jam paused. Listened, head cocked. He pulled the tiny pin and allowed the ball to drop into the gloom below. He ran.

There was a muffled crack, and a hiss.

A wave of pressure rocked Jam from behind and below, a bellow of angry and silently screaming air, rushing past him like the close passage of a train – he didn't wait to see if the HPG had caused a death toll: if nothing else, it would have made his pursuers more cautious. His head snapped left at the sounds of people, chattering, laughter.

He changed direction, opening a door and closing it behind him.

People are good, he thought.

People make good cover . . .

Nasty though that may seem.

He passed through a series of extra doors, through some kind of thin-carpeted sparsely furnished smoke-stinking office with yellow walls and a pyramid of cups sporting tar-brown stains. An untidy pile of discarded beer cans, errant tangles of streamers and distant music intruded on Jam's immediate pain. Office party? Jam stowed away his weapon and broke into the—

Dull light, dancing with cheap strobes and the flicker of amateur coloured disco lights as bad boy-band music crucified the air.

Jam strode through the group, past a stack of beer and decks and thumping speakers. Several office workers gyrated into his path and with the precision of whores on heat, tongues on wet lips, tight leather and glitter-spangled low-cut breast cups spewing tequila pheromones in a call for sweat-stained party sex.

Jam swiftly sidestepped groping hands, glancing behind—

To see the door open. Slow motion. Gaunt-faced men, anonymous in their cold professionalism, appeared: dark-haired and dark-suited—

And followed by—

Jam caught a glimpse of a masked figure, slender, with bright piercing eyes that seemed to connect with him as he stared, lips suddenly dry and the need to be free thumping in his guts.

Which organisation? spat his brain, searching the files and folders of his mind without success. He did not recognise these pursuers; but then, this information was an irrelevant factor . . .

Jam broke into a run, bursting through another door. Bullets tore through the party, chewing plasma monitors and smashing partitions into sprinkler foam; Jam dived to the soundtrack of sudden panic screams, rolled, darted right and checked below. He kicked a hole in a window, wrapped his leather coat around him, and jumped . . .

His boots thudded against the roof of a red double-decker London bus, and he slid for a moment before righting himself. The driver of the bus climbed free of the cab and started shouting up at him: Jam slid to the rain-slippery edge and leaped lightly to the ground below.

Ignoring the insect buzz of the annoying driver as he waved a shotgun, Jam approached a helmeted man sitting astride a large 2000cc Honda off-road motorcycle. Without time for conversation, Jam grabbed the man's collar, hauled him backwards onto the wet tarmac, jumped aboard the machine and, with the clutch in, he kicked down. The Honda screamed, fumes exploding from the exhaust . . . the bike kicked up its front wheel, climbing onto the boot of the Ford in front and Jam ducked his head as bullets howled from the smashed window above him, slamming metal thumps across the queuing traffic as the Honda's rear wheel spun against the chrome bumper, then fought the bike onto the Ford's buckling roof – the bike screamed and lurched, up and down over this impromptu corrugated road of bumper-to-bumper traffic.

Wheels spun across the wet slick roofs and bonnets of waiting queuing cars; Jam slung the bike to the right, dropping from this hastily invented car-road and landing with dipped suspension on the narrow pavement to send cowering late-night pedestrians screaming for cover. The bike surged down the pavement and out over a small park, churning grass and mud and heading for the trees lining the opposite side. He hit the brakes, ending in a long mud-slewn skid, and jumped free at the last moment as the Honda collided with a wide-boled oak. Then, looking left and right, he jogged to a nearby van and climbed nonchalantly into the back.

'Hit it, Nicky.'

Bullets wailed from behind as the transit wheelspun and joined the snake of traffic, smashing holes along its flank. In the back of the van Jam and Slater ducked, scrabbling across the floor as shafts of light with ragged metal edges appeared between the racks of guns, bullets and neatly packaged explosives.

'Holy fuck!' growled Slater and his stare met Jam's.

'Get us out of here!' bellowed Jam, eyes wide, mouth dry with understanding as he eyed the punched metal holes.

Nicky dragged the van right, mounted the kerb and smashed a series of parking meters into oblivion; the van's engine roared and the bullets fell behind.

They sped from the busy streets.

Jam, sweating now, slumped onto a bench and ran a hand through his hair.

'Was I right?' growled Slater.

Jam met the large man's gaze and nodded. 'More than right. They wanted me – us – bad. Bad enough to mow down lots of innocent bystanders.'

'What do we do now?' asked Nicky, her sultry tones for once edged with a kind of panic so unlike her usual well-trained stability that it brought a frown to Jam's handsome face.

He shrugged. 'We have to warn the others.'

'We can't use the ECubes – I bet that's how the bastards have been tracking us,' said Slater with a snarl. 'You remember the Battle of Belsen?' He cocked the Heckler & Koch MP5 A3 9mm sub-machine gun in his huge hands and grinned nastily. 'We could try the phone.'

'We've no fucking choice. Get a message to Spiral_H that some fucker has set us up – the cunts were lying in wait. *And* the fuckers messed up my hair *and* my new coat. The *bastards*. Nicky, get us out of this fucking dangerous fucking city. Then we'll ditch this van – it'll be tagged.'

Slater pulled free an ECube. He squeezed the small

91

electronic device and it came to life, blue digits flickering; but as soon as it lived, it died, and the blue digits faded.

Slater frowned. He squeezed again.

''S not working, Jam.'

'Give it here, big guy.'

'I didn't do nothing,' complained Slater.

Jam tutted. 'You're a fucking technology gimp. Remember China? The dam? You were in charge of the fucking det?'

'That was an accident,' moaned Slater.

Jam played with the ECube, and frowned again. 'I thought these things were supposed to be practically unbreakable?'

'They are,' Nicky called back from the front seat. 'I doubt whether Slater's huge fists could have damaged it. I've seen them survive much worse than that.'

Jam tutted again, as Slater took hold of Nicky's battered and bruised ECube. Slater fumbled with the machine for a moment, but it refused to spark into life. He shook his head, growled, 'Where to next?'

'We need to contact Spiral, and we need to pay a visit to an old friend,' said Jam, lighting a cigarette and lying back, staring at the panelled ceiling, the shafts of dull phosphorescence creeping between the torn bullet holes making him feel a tad wary. Explosives and spinning bullets did not marry well. A cold draught whistled in through the holes. Slater started to clean his Heckler & Koch.

Jam closed his eyes, thinking back to Iran and the rebellion.

And the bullets.

And the torture . . .

He shivered. And welcomed his drug-induced sleep as the van rumbled through the rainswept war-spattered streets.

Spiral_Memo2
Transcript of recent news incident
CodeRed_Z;
unorthodox incident scan 554670

Between the hours of 2:00 P.M. and 5:20 P.M. the entire city of London and the surrounding Home Counties were left without electricity.

Millions of homes and businesses, including schools and hospitals, were left electrically stranded or relying on emergency back-up generators. Prior to the power cuts, monitoring equipment registered great surges of energy, which are being blamed for this occurrence, although no real cause for these freak power surges has been discovered, and UKLocalPower Corp. spokespersons are unwilling to make any comment.>>#

CHAPTER 6

TAG

It felt like a million years later, a million miles away and a different planet. Carter stood in the shower, the hot water flowing over his shoulders and back, easing the tension in his muscles, washing away the speckles of blood. His eyes closed, his face down, he reached out and placed the flats of his palms against the steam-frosted tiles of the cubicle. It had been a long journey and his weariness had consumed him, eaten him whole and spat him out of the other side of oblivion—

He stepped from the cubicle. The towel had been warming for a half-hour, and he dried himself in slow motion – automatic movements, machine movements. Then, naked, he walked through to the bedroom and collapsed on top of the rich duvet, sleep claiming him and leaving no prisoners.

Carter tossed between the sweat-streaked sheets . . .

Maria –

screaming

crying

An explosion; a bullet, slow-motion, spinning from the barrel of Kade's gun, impacting with her flesh—

a scream, saliva drooling from blood-speckled lips
cloth tearing
flesh parting
a metal parasite burrowing into muscle,
kicking aside bone
Feuchter, face stark, smashed with pain

Carter leaped and took the bullet in his own body, felt
the impact and looked up from a thick pool of red, could
see Maria's face staring down at him as he was lowered
into the hole in the ground and they threw flowers on top
of him and started to shovel in the dirt and he wanted to
scream –

scream, I'm not dead yet

I'm not dead . . .

He awoke in the darkness, shivering and remembering the
past. He could feel warmth against his back and, groaning,
he rolled over, hand reaching out to stroke soft fur. There
was a noise, a decline of sound like a reverse turbine. Carter
laughed, and patted the Labrador's head with a sigh.

'You OK, pal?'

Samson panted, tongue flicking out to steal salt from
Carter's cold back.

'Cut it out, you mongrel.'

He rolled from the bed and pulled on grey combats
and a thick jumper, much too large but soft and comfortable and the way he liked it. Samson watched him dress,
then jumped off the bed and followed him out and down
the stairs to the kitchen. Carter fed the Lab as the grey
rays of weak sunshine filtered over the mountains and he
crouched, watching Samson eat.

'You eat like a fucking animal,' he said soberly.

Sam cocked a single beady eye at him, and continued
to shovel.

Leaving the dog, Carter returned to the living room and stretched his spine, then unlocked the door and stepped out onto a narrow balcony. The cold hit him like a brick in the face and he gasped, smiling at the shock. Wind lashed his short hair and he leaned over the balcony, gazing out over the snow. In the distance he could see woodland, snow-laden and picturesque. Roads snaked into the distance, between hills, and beyond it all squatted the mountains, old Grey Gods watching over these Minor Petty Mortals.

'A damn sight better than fucking London,' he muttered. The phone rang. He stepped back inside and picked up the receiver. 'Yeah?'

'Carter, it's Natasha.' She sounded serious.

'Natasha – I need a *fucking serious word* with you, my friend . . . Have you any fucking idea what happened to me in Germany—'

'No time, Carter. Bad shit is hitting the fan. I'm coming up.'

'Here? Now?'

'Yes. I'll be four to six hours. Don't use your ECube. In fact, I don't think you *can* use your ECube.'

'Why—'

'It's the DemolSquads. One of them has been wiped out; fucking *assassinated*. I'll be there as soon as I can.'

The line went dead. Carter scanned the signals on the phone; the line was untraceable and had, by all accounts, never existed. Nats had used an advanced descramble signal only issued to the TacSquads.

She obviously wanted *nobody* to hear the call . . .

Carter scratched at his stubble, her words troubling him. He shrugged to himself, trying to push the worries from his mind. Now: now there was nothing he could do. He could merely await Natasha and wonder at her brisk words – and warning – but it wasn't that simple, it was never that simple. Why hadn't he heard from Spiral? What the fuck was going on?

Realising that he always thought better when exercising, he called, 'Samson, we going for a run?' as wariness and bad images concerning Natasha, the assassinations, and the lack of communications from Spiral flickered in his mind . . .

The dog was there in two seconds, jumping up, tail wagging, eyes bright at the promise of exercise and a few cheap sniffs.

Carter pulled on his running shoes, battered old Nike Airs, and trotted down the steps from the living quarters to the front door – the price of having a house built into the side of a steep hill – and with Samson panting eagerly at his heels, jostling and pushing as if to send him cartwheeling down the steps. With a cursing 'You trying to kill me?' – a traditional pre-run invocation – they spilled out untidily into the snow.

The morning was extremely cold, a frost having made the snow hard and slippery. Carter, with the sniffing Lab at his heels, set off up a gentle incline towards the woods. The silence welcomed Carter into its embrace and he groaned internally at the strain of such early morning exercise—

And yet he felt the need. The need to work, to feel the exhilaration and power that only came with hard exercise; to feel the trail beneath his running shoes, to feel the burn of lactic acid, the strain of muscles, the tearing of strained lungs . . .

Soon, calves burning, he crested the first rise and entered the woods. A frozen stream cracked with a gunshot sound under the immense mass of Samson jumping from the top of a gentle rise. The dog rolled in the cold water, then sprinted around in circles with his tail between his legs before rejoining Carter further up the trail between the sparkling trees.

'What was all that about?'

Samson panted with a wide dog smile.

'Well, come on, tell me what's going on in your dumb canine brain?'

Samson looked up, head tilted. Carter patted him and increased the pace, watching bemusedly as the dog suddenly sprinted off to the left, flashing between the trees, legs heaving, tongue almost on the ground, nose occasionally touching a smell and then veering off at random angles at some stimulus that Carter was – thankfully – immune and blind to.

Carter frowned, his run slowing, his pace faltering. His head snapped to one side, breath pluming in front of him, a spray of sweat stinging his eyes. He halted, breathing deeply, and Samson cantered round and gazed up at his Master.

'You hear it too?'

Samson grinned – a dog grin.

'Come on.'

The distant engine noise indicated a large vehicle. It could just be passing by but Carter had a bad feeling gnawing his stomach – ever since the events in Germany only hours before and the low-flying race back home to Britain . . . The pursuit had ended without event but Carter could still feel weariness, a sense of being drained after those bloody unexpected events at Schwalenberg—

The engine changed pitch. Carter ran along just below the tree line as he heard the vehicle turn up towards his house. He reached the rise and gazed down at the old van, rattling and pumping diesel fumes from an engine that had seen much, much better days.

A van? It had to be . . .

Jam, smiled Carter. 'Come on, Sammy!'

They ran back towards the house and, ever careful, paused to watch the visitors disembark. Jam, Slater and Nicky, all grumbling and stretching after the obvious ill effects of a long journey. Carter checked back down the track – nobody following – then stepped out and jogged slowly down to his three old friends.

'Carter!' yelled Jam, and embraced the sweating man. They clasped hands, patting one another on the back. Slater grinned gormlessly, and Nicky smiled warmly. 'Any chance of a party, my man?'

'You're joking, aren't you? I remember the last one!'

'It wasn't my fault Slater got thrown from the bedroom window!'

'*You* threw him!'

'Hey, just our little tiff! It's good to see you again.'

'Come on in,' said Carter, forcing another grin through his mild depression. 'I'm ready for some breakfast, if I can entice three of my old friends to join me?'

'Slater is hungry,' rumbled Slater, kneeling and wrestling with Samson who began to growl and bark, play-fighting with the large man who pinned the Labrador to the ground and tickled the fur between his pads.

'I seem to remember that you're always hungry, Slater.'

'Aye. I'm a growing lad.'

'You are forty-six years old, Slater.'

'Aye. Like I said, still growing.'

'You don't often pay me a visit, Jam. I assume there is a reason?' Carter's eyes were hooded, his mouth a grim line. Recent events had removed much of his humour, and this unsummoned gathering felt somehow ominous.

99

'Oh yes,' said Jam softly. He lit a cigarette, rested his head back and rubbed at tired eyes. 'Something bad is going down, old friend. Have you logged on with your ECube? Checked out the coded info on your escapades in Germany?'

Carter shook his head. 'No, not yet, I don't like bad reviews.'

'Something doesn't add up. It doesn't fit. Spiral seem to have no answers on how German Special Forces were infiltrated. And Feuchter – our friendly Spiral_H QIII coordinator – has disappeared and is presumed dead. They pulled the fried corpse of his niece – and the bodies of *all* the guests from the party – from the wreckage after the fire had been brought under control. Dog meat. But, mysteriously, no sign of Mr Feuchter himself. Strange, eh, considering you put a bullet in the cunt? I do find it disconcerting that our faithful employers have no answers for these questions – after all, their surveillance and technology budgets must exceed NASA's.'

Carter shrugged. 'They're not God. They can't know everything.'

'You're dead right,' grunted Slater, busy picking pieces of bacon rind from his remaining teeth. 'Go on, Jam, tell him about the Squads.'

Jam sighed, and Carter caught the resignation in the man. Strange, for sure, because they had survived some tough campaigns together. They had crossed the desert during the Battle of Cairo7, performed TankerRuns after a designer plague – the Grey Death – had wiped out 58 million people and devastated the economies, and of course populations, of Europe, North Africa and North and South America, and fought several pitched battles against the terrorist resurgence after the Anti-NBC Laws were passed.

100

Jam's face was stern. 'A DemolSquad, number 14, has been wiped out.'

'I know,' said Carter softly. 'But things like this *can* happen. It is a probability in our line of work. Men and women *die*. Life's a bitch, yeah?'

'Yes, but what's even worse is that Spiral have not published the information. I found out by hacking Cuban Special Circumstances computers, stumbled across the information by accident. So, me and Nicky set out to find out a few things, keep a few tabs on several of our other brother Squads, including members of the Core. Two more DemolSquads are missing, 77 and S-4.'

'The sniper squad? Rex, Scope and Amber?'

'Hmm,' nodded Jam, blowing the room full of smoke. 'Coincidence? I thought to myself. Then we get a real bad job in London; the sort that makes you regret ever even thinking about signing that fucking pink form by which you gave up your freedom. And guess what . . .'

'Set-up?'

'Yeah.' Jam finished his cigarette, and immediately lit another. 'They were waiting for us. I went in on foot to scope ahead; bastards almost tagged me. Six of them. Very professional: well armed, hard as fuck, intelligent, swift movers.'

'And you also think I was set up?' said Carter softly.

'Did occur to me, old buddy.'

Carter scratched at his stubble, and accepted a cigarette from Nicky. 'It's funny . . . I had a call from Nats this morning. She's on her way up here. She sounded a little panicked.'

'Be careful with her,' said Slater. 'She's one of the TacSquads, a Tactical Officer. Old School. Crafty as a fucking bitch.'

'I've known her for years. We're good friends . . .'

Jam shrugged and reached across the table, patting Carter's hand. 'Natasha is a bird—' Nicky gasped . . . 'No offence meant, love. You know, Carter, a bit of moist cunt and you always did think with your dick. Trust no fucker, my friend. Not Nats. Not even us. There are DemolSquads dead, others missing. You've been popped at, and we sure as fuck had a lot of high-velocity shots spat our way. Why do you think we came up here in the van? For fucking fun? Our ECubes have been compromised . . . and if ECubes are the pinnacle of encrypted communication, then nothing is safe. You can't fucking *text* me your descramble code and hope it doesn't get compromised when the shit finally hits the very large fan . . . Carter, Spiral know something and they're not telling . . . you sure *this* place is not bugged?'

'I'm, sure. I have my own – shall we say *custom* – scanning equipment.'

'Good lad.'

'I still don't believe Spiral have anything sinister to add to this. After all, they pay our wages. They employ us. I'm sure they have their special reasons for withholding information – I bet there are people on the job right now.'

'Maybe,' said Jam. 'But then, we're employed because we think. Because we trust nobody. Because we do the job ourselves. Don't have blind faith, Carter old buddy. There will be people in Spiral just as corruptible as in the real world . . . as you found out for yourself. Listen, Spiral_H is assembling a strike force to shut down Spiral_Q. Things are getting way out of hand, or so it would appear . . . the apparent betrayal by Feuchter when you had your little lovers' tiff in Germany is being kept quiet so Spiral_Q can be shut down with extreme force and minimum fuss. Don't want to give the fuckers due warning, eh, lad?'

Carter rubbed at his stubble, then his tired eyes. 'Feuchter. That fucker got everything he deserved.'

There was a long, uneasy pause. Outside, snow began to fall once more, small flakes falling straight down to earth through the absence of any breeze. Jam shivered, then grinned over at Nicky. 'You be keeping my bed warm tonight?' He winked broadly, a cheeky grin on his face.

'Only if you pay me, Jam.'

'This can be arranged.'

'I'll bite it off if you even try and wave that fucking maggot near me.'

'Well, I'll look forward to it. But enough of this banter – come on, team, we're fed and have delivered our warning. Time to move on—'

'Where to now?' asked Carter as the group stood, leaving a pile of dirty dishes.

'Can't say,' smiled Jam. 'Classified. Y'know how it is. Remember, don't use your ECube – not yet; I think ours are fucked so it doesn't matter for us. Listen, Carter, I have a bad feeling about this one. A real bad feeling.'

'Your bad feelings always turned out to be sheep instead of rogue enemy soldiers when we were training in the mountains,' said Carter.

Jam shrugged. 'Just advice, brother. Take it or leave it.'

'Let's swap descramble codes. I have a feeling that one day soon we will need secure communication. And ECubes are surely letting us down now, my friend.'

Jam nodded, and they memorised the information. Then Nicky led the Squad down the stairs, Samson jumping at their heels with the apparent motive of murder, and out into the snow and towards the van. They thanked Carter for breakfast and, with Jam's grinning face mouthing the words, 'See ya, Butcher' from the rattling van window, in seconds through thick exhaust fumes they disappeared through the snow.

Carter's face went hard at the name. He spat in the snow, and said, 'Come on, Sam, back to solitary confinement.'

'*You earned it, Butcher,*' said Kade.

'Fuck you,' snapped Carter.

He sat, gazing out at the snow. He toyed with the ECube, but did not activate it. The surface remained black and dead and he tossed it thoughtfully from one hand to the other, as you would with a soft ball.

Samson lay snoring beside his chair, and a low fire burned, crackling occasionally, the glow warming the room and contrasting cosily with the snowy wilderness outside the windows.

Carter stared at the mountains, tracing their contours. On his lap sat a small A4 pad, and his fingers held a small knife-sharpened pencil. He dropped the ECube to the floor, and then chewed the end of the pencil thoughtfully for a moment. He wrote:

```
Problem: DemolSquads missing/ murdered

Problem:  Feuchter  . . .  and  Maria's
involvement?

Problem: German Special Forces in on the
betrayal in some way/ percentage not
known/ Bribed? Or other incentive??

Question:  Who  was  the  real  target?
Carter?  Or  party  guests?  Or  both?
```

Probable that Carter a target in lieu of
other Squads being wiped out. But why?
And by whom?

Feuchter - expert in computer processor
development - The QIII Proto, developed
under licence for Spiral at specially
built complexes around the world, namely
stations Spiral_H, Spiral_M and
Spiral_Q. The QIII processor: military
chip and surrounding hardware destined
for implementation over the next five
years. Highly classified; many Spiral
members even unaware of its existence.

Who is the enemy?

Spiral? Unlikely.

And where is Feuchter? How did he get
out before the explosion wiped out
Castle Schwalenberg?

Carter stared at the scribbled words on the page. Spiral
knew that he was alive. He had signed in, reported on
events in Germany. They had okayed his return to
Scotland and told him to await further communication. If
they wanted him dead, he was sure as fuck he would
already *be* dead. Unless it was somebody *within* Spiral
operating independently, or *unless* they were awaiting a
certain turn of events . . . like Jam arriving? Or Natasha
making an appearance? Had Jam been tracked?

No. He shook his head. Spiral stood for everything
that was good; they might have their own seemingly

strange reasons, but everything was carried out with precision. There were no mistakes . . . not usually . . .

Carter followed the premise: if Spiral *did* want the Demolition Squads dead, why the elaborate set-ups? Why not just gather them together and murder them in one huge gas chamber? And why could they possibly want their top operatives dead in the first place? Why spend billions of pounds in recruitment, training, faking deaths – only to wipe them out?

Something did not fit.

And where did the QIII Proto fit into this jigsaw? This puzzle? Feuchter was in charge of development, programming and refinement of the military processor; Carter knew very little about the project because it was tightly under wraps, but Natasha had worked some long hours in the early QIII development stages before being reassigned to babysitting the DemolSquads as a Tactical Officer and seeing to their every whim and need. A year ago, when they had shared much more than just sex, she had trusted Carter implicitly; she would talk in the long warm comfortable hours after love-making, her features softened by candlelight, lips ruby and wet; she had spoken, almost aimlessly, feeding his desire for technological knowledge . . . she would tell him about the advanced chip architecture, about the implementation of ProbEqs which were being drafted into CoreCalcs and the CoreClock. And despite his expertise with computing systems the jargon had flown way, way above Carter's head. He still remembered Natasha's bitterness at being pulled from the project, but she had finally taken it with good grace when assigned as a TacSquad officer.

And now. Now?

Carter wrote:

Demolition Squads in trouble? ALL the DemolSquads?

Assassination/ how to assassinate the world's most professional operatives? DemolSquads are perfectly trained killers; the elite of the elite; each chosen for specific skills. DemolSquads are assassins; demolition experts.

How to assassinate the assassins?

And why?

ECubes no longer secure; in Germany the ECube died, only reactivating afterwards, as if affected by some sort of power drain????? Somebody has access to Spiral mainframes????? Internal betrayals?

Feuchter.

Everything revolves around Feuchter; he pulled gun on Carter: therefore he was willing to throw away his position within Spiral. Who would do that? It is rare somebody wants to leave Spiral . . . leave the ultimate organisation - leave the embrace of such a world-active company, who strive for peace, who genuinely set out to fuck the bad guys????

Spiral were being betrayed. Set up.

107

Who better than the star military-
processor development team? Feuchter,
obviously . . . but he is more of a puppet;
he cannot be the one pulling the strings.

So, who else?

And Natasha . . . Natasha knew Feuchter;
Nats set up the protection gig in the
first place. Sent Carter to his own
assassination. How perfect.

The game is larger than I realise.

Carter rubbed at his tired eyes; it was a fucking circle
and he was treading his own footprints, following his own
tail. He threw down the pad and sank back into the sofa.

'I don't know,' he said softly, closing his eyes.

Outside, the wind howled and Carter, in almost unconscious response, threw a log on the fire. It was Feuchter
who worried him more than anything – the hard look in the
man's eyes, the glitter of those cold, cold orbs when the
unwavering gun muzzle was pointing straight at Carter . . .
something in Feuchter made Carter's soul go cold. There
was something different about the man. Something *strange*.

And Natasha . . .

Natasha had set him up with the gig. She had known
Feuchter a long time ago, worked closely with him on the
QIII early implementation and development drawings.

And if they had wanted *him*, Carter, dead, then—

Then Natasha had to have known.

Carter felt suddenly miserable. Cold inside.

He loved Natasha; and knew deep down that she loved
him.

108

But the facts were staring him in the face.

She was a part of it. Integral. A cog in the machine.

She *had* to be . . .

Carter knew; he would have to be careful. He would have to be prepared. He would have to watch Natasha like a hawk – and if she stepped out of line?

Then Kade would be waiting.

Carter stepped over his snoring Labrador and moved to his study. Entering the book-lined room, he moved to the sixteen feet of desk and the five computers, all open-cased and showing a myriad of circuit boards, processor-fans whirring, monitors showing a colourful spinning collection of humorous screen savers.

He sat down at the master system and initialised the OS. Entering the shell, he switched to his house and land defences, bypassed the encryption, and logged in—

Nothing.

He scanned all monitors for a two-mile radius. Nothing had been tripped or tampered with, the current and voltage meters had not been broken or hacked. He had designed and programmed the system himself, in 68000tz machine code. It had been a challenge and he had enjoyed the steep learning curve, although he still stood by his inherent hatred of mathematics.

He finished the scan.

Nothing. He scratched his chin, and lit a cigarette. The machines purred around him and he flicked through a variety of hidden match-head cameras but could see nothing suspicious.

Just because it doesn't look suspicious, doesn't mean it isn't there.

Carter was tempted for a while to start messing about with the equipment; it had a soothing effect on his soul,

the swapping of components, the improving of perform-
ance by processor and memory enhancement. He
checked his watch. Natasha would be due in a few hours
and he would need to be ready.

He walked down the hallway and pulled on his boots,
lacing them tightly. Then he moved down the stairs and
punched a sequence into a pad; a section of wall slid
smoothly back and he stepped into the brightly lit armoury.
It smelled slightly of gun oil, and he moved to the locked
cabinets and pulled free his Browning HiPower 9mm. He
checked all the magazines and strapped them about his
body. Then he pulled free an automatic sniper rifle cham-
bered for the .338 Lapua Magnum round and slotted a
scope to the weapon with a precise *click*. He checked the
magazine, placed a spare one in his pocket, then dropped
the rifle into a sacking bag and pulled tight the drawstring.
With the gun under his arm, he locked up the room and
returned to Samson, tapping the dog with his boot.

'You coming with me, pal?'

Samson grinned his dog grin.

'Safer with me than in here, I think. Come on, I have a
real bad feeling about Natasha's impending visit. Let's
check she isn't being followed by big perps in suits with
machine guns.'

Carter locked the front door and armed the trip
meters. Then, breath pluming and snow settling like a
shroud across his head and shoulders, he started across
the grey-lit fields so free of war and violence in this distant
part of Scotland, and up past the edge of the lane towards
the sanctuary of the beautiful shaded woods.

Carter was cold.

His hands, protected by gloves, clasped the semi-
automatic rifle stock and he sat shrouded by trees and

bushes, staring down at the lane. A straight of one mile led away from him and he targeted the scope down the lane, picking out leaves on the trees and the fluttering of snowflakes: and he grinned. The lane made a good killing ground, and was one reason why he had purchased the house. If he was ready for danger, then this made a good spot – for raining fire from Heaven upon the Infidels.

Samson, at his feet, was restless. He'd wandered away for a while, sniffing, but had returned to nuzzle at Carter, to whinge at the man with his whimpers of boredom. 'Shhh,' he soothed, rubbing the dog's ears. 'We shouldn't be long.'

He heard the engines, echoing up from the valley, before the car swung into view. And swing it did, slewing with churning tyres around the bed and smashing into the embankment with a thud, bouncing the back of the vehicle violently onto the uncleared road as the engine howled and tyres spun and the BMW 740i shot towards him—

Carter licked his lips and lifted the scope to his eye.

Natasha was coming – and it appeared she was in trouble.

The BMW accelerated madly down the lane—

A black Mercedes spun around the corner, gripping better due to its tyres' snow chains. It must have been waiting for her, ready to attack the snow; it accelerated down the lane and began to catch the BMW.

Carter sighted smoothly. The cross-hairs crawled up past the Mercedes grille, up the bonnet. He could see five shapes inside the vehicle – large men in dark coats, some with dark glasses. One window was down, allowing snow to blow inside the car – a gun appeared and began firing—

The *cracks* echoed up into the woods.

Carter trained on the driver; the Merc slewed left and right and Carter cursed, the figures inside the car bobbing madly, unsteady targets—

He breathed out. Squeezed the trigger.

The report was deafening to his ears, the stock punched his shoulder with a kick, and he saw the windscreen shatter like a crazy spider's web; the bullet missed the driver and took one of the rear passengers in the chest, merging his body and blood with the Merc's seat. With a scream of gears and engine, the Merc swerved left, smashing into the embankment and then righting itself; the front bumper was torn free, was crushed under the frantically spinning wheels—

The lane – and Carter's killing ground – was running out.

'Fuck it,' snarled Carter.

He flicked the rifle to automatic and squeezed off a four-round burst. Bullets slapped up the bonnet. Another four rounds, and the windscreen caved in and the car veered again—

Carter was not there to see it. He left the rifle in the snow and sprinted for the house and the turning circle in front of the steps. Arms pumping, he heard the Mercedes pass on the roadway below him, engine whining, more gunshots ricocheting. The huge Mercedes flashed from view and Carter ground his teeth, pushing himself through the snow, the Browning HiPower in his hand, sweat stinging his brows—

More gunshots rang out from up ahead.

Carter pounded across the ridge and the world opened up ahead of him, backed by mountains and a picturesque view of falling snow, an idyllic romantic scene punctuated with the harsh full stop of—

Violence.

Natasha had swung the BMW around to form a barricade behind which she crouched, gun out and resting over the raised boot.

As Carter appeared, the Mercedes howled straight towards the BMW; Natasha dived out of the way with a yelp as the two cars collided amidst tearing noises of screaming steel and metallic crunching; the BMW was ploughed into the front of Carter's house, buckled and broken, one of the windows shattering; the Merc's doors were opening even as the collision took place and men tumbled from the vehicle, automatics and sub-machine guns drawn—

Natasha rolled to her feet, firing – in seconds bullets smashed across the space. One of the men was punched from his feet with a bullet in his cheek, ripping his face apart and dropping him in a flurry of blood.

A line of bullets scythed across the trees, drilled across the clearing—

Three smacked into the embankment behind Natasha in quick succession, their impact making dull slaps in earth.

The fourth bullet smashed into Natasha, puncturing her flesh and flipping her backwards, up and over diagonally, legs kicking out. She landed in a crumpled heap, wedged against the embankment, face to the ground, legs propped up and twisted against tree roots and icicles.

'No!' screamed Carter.

113

CHAPTER 7

DEEP RED

Spiral_H, London.

Headquarters to the Spiral mainframes; a massive, awesome collection of machinery used to coordinate worldwide Spiral affairs, from DemolSquads to financial deals, from the buying and selling of land, weapons and military hardware to the masterminding of Wall Street economics. Battles had been and were commanded from Spiral_H. The Battle of Belsen. The Attack on Poland Ridge. The transport of festering tanker-borne bodies to Siberia after the Grey Death . . .

Those who knew of Spiral, or who worked for Spiral, would often wonder about finance: how had this organisation become so big? And how did it fund such huge worldwide schemes and plans?

There were no simple answers. Spiral had fingers in many pies – Spiral had the controlling shares of a thousand financial institutions, owned a myriad of businesses from rubber plantations to petroleum refineries. If there was money to be made – good money – then Spiral would be in some way involved.

Spiral_H could not be seen from the air; it burrowed under the ground, a massive 500-metre-wide shaft that had been sliced vertically from the rock and layers of the world. Above Spiral_H were rows of shops, houses; normal London streets made less normal after the vicious and bloody London Riots . . . but delving deeper, below the tarmac, below the howling traffic, below the bustling shoppers and camera-touting tourists and gun-bristling JT8s, below the subways and underpasses and below the insanely heavily guarded London Underground . . . Spiral_H *existed* . . .

Deep deep down: an underground base, an underground world.

The entrances were masked; hidden; only the elite few who knew of Spiral knew of the access points. One entrance was a wide rotating glass door leading into an insurance company's single-storey complex. On this particular morning, the door spun slowly to reveal a beautiful young woman. She was smiling as she emerged, her expensive suit crisp and clean and neatly pressed, her security badge masking an extremely high-tech access tool to grant her passage to Spiral's underground HQ.

She glanced up at the gathering clouds, watched by a group of armed policemen at the corner of the street, their eyes admiring her long legs and polished make-up.

Her gloved hand reached up, touched momentarily at her gleaming red lips.

And then she was gone—

Replaced by a ball of gas and flame that roared from below the level of the land, smashed up into the heavens screaming so loud that it was beyond aural appreciation; as in the aftershock of a nuclear explosion, the houses and shops and buildings were disintegrated in an instant, were stomped kicked smashed up and out and down into

115

oblivion. Steel and concrete and glass and disintegrated rooms and furniture and computers were pulped and pulverised and the occupants of the buildings and houses and *below the ground* the heart of Spiral, its core, its soul – all were vaporised in an instant as explosives smashed and fucked and stomped all shape and mass from a wide slice of the world . . .

Dust billowed up in a huge cloud, a clenched atomic fist of concrete dust with a twisted Tube carriage caught and spinning in its centre, a fist that seemed to gather as if summoning strength, a blossom of disintegration, a bloom of detritus – and then exploded and rolled out in a huge booming concussion wave that encompassed the surrounding broken buildings and rain-smeared landscape . . .

The explosion could be heard a hundred miles away.

With the dust came a blanket of silence.

Soon the screams could be heard.

And the aftermath took an eternity.

Feuchter lay on a beach of black sand, dark waves of pain washing over him like the waves of the ocean. In fact, he could hear the sea; struggling, he forced his head to the right and could see crests of gleaming white foam on the black waters. Feuchter groaned, his whole frame shuddering. He forced up his head, gazed down at himself. He was naked – a hole, a crusted bloody eye, marked a bullet entry low down in his belly.

What happened? he thought sombrely.

And then the words; the words drifted to him as if from a million miles away, buzzing insect noises in his brain, merging with the sounds of the sea, hissing and rolling, surging and slithering across the sand—

– He must be in great pain . . .

116

– We have removed the bullet, but there are still pieces of metal lodged inside; the bullet shattered on entry, bits of metal scything out in all directions. This man should be dead, I am amazed we're looking down at him in a bed and not in a coffin . . .

Feuchter groaned. He closed his eyes.

A cold breeze blew in from the black ocean.

He reached out inside himself, searching his blood-stream, searching his tissue; he found the rogue pieces of metal and despite carrying them in his shell, he knew they were doing him no harm; he could feel his body working, repairing itself, his veins buzzing with blood and *something else*. Feuchter smiled; he could feel the strange chemical within him, nestling in his veins and organs, in his brain, in his spinal column. It took away his pain.

He thought back, Feuchter thought back—

Across the long hard years.

Pain lanced him.

He concentrated again on the wound; he felt the ebb and flow of chemicals in his system. He could feel himself getting stronger; could feel his body repairing the damage wrought by the bullet.

He floated for a while on waves of agony.

He listened to the sea.

Voices.

– Give him another ten mils of morphine; there, that should soothe his suffering for a while; or at least stave off death for another couple of days. Nurse, has he spoken?

– Yes, he cried out in his sleep.

– What did he say?

– He cried out for Maria. Who is Maria?

– The woman who was found dead and burned up in

the castle at Schwalenberg; they brought in her corpse –
what a fucking mess. She's bagged up down in the mor-
tuary awaiting an autopsy, although I'm not sure what
remaining part of her they would like to fuck with . . .
there's not much left.

– Were they close?

– I believe so; it was his niece, but she had lived with
him, treated her like a daughter.

Feuchter felt a rage well within him.

He remembered: remembered Carter – remembered
the bullet . . . and he remembered the gun, black eye
focusing on Maria, blowing her backwards across the
chamber, her small silver gun clattering on the floor, her
face slapping to the stone, her tooth cracking, blood pooling from her smashed lips . . .

Maria; ahhhh, sweet Maria.

He remembered a time, from years earlier: sitting at
the broad untreated-timber farm table. The sun was
gleaming outside, casting strips of bright light over the
tiled floor. He could smell rosemary, and the trees from
the cherry orchard. Maria had only been young then;
eight, maybe nine. She sat on his knee, a bowl of cherries
on her lap fresh-picked only an hour before – both of
them standing precariously on the small ladder and giggling as they reached out, plucking the ripe fruit from the
branches. Now Maria ate the harvest of their daring, her
fingers and lips stained red with juice, her eyes wide and
gleaming and beautiful, her face a picture of delight.

Feuchter closed the door on the memory.

There was a bitter taste in his mouth.

Anger and . . . something more.

Cold and clinical.

He knew; knew he should feel something incredible
for Maria; he knew that his emotions should flow thick

118

and fast, and his anger was there, and a hatred for Carter that spoke of long hours of torture to come . . . but he knew he should be weeping at her death. Weeping uncontrollably. His intelligence told him that much.

But something strange had happened.

Feuchter could not bring himself to cry.

His face turned to a grimace now; the bullet wound was healing and acid ate his flesh as it knitted together; in this dream state it seemed to be happening so quickly, almost instantaneously, strands of skin and muscle joining together, cells growing and repairing and replicating.

It hurt. It burned him *bad*.

Hans: a shame he'd had to kill the man. Feuchter remembered the indecision; and the orders typed on the white sheet before him. To murder his own brother, to murder a man he loved knowing full well that he would leave an orphaned girl with nobody to care for her—

He had carried out the orders. A single shot to the head.

And he had cried afterwards; Maria had come to him, asking what the matter was, and she had cuddled him and sat on his knee and accidentally smeared the speckles of her father's blood on his face in her innocence and ignorance; and Feuchter had cried, cried long and hard and told himself to be strong and then on that dark bloody evening of murder he had risked everything to get Maria away from there, to get her away to safety and save her life—

Things had changed, he realised.

And then, bitterly: *I* have changed.

Now; now there were no tears. And he understood why – he understood the chemical processes that had altered his body but it still haunted him. He had thought that he would be strong; he had thought that he would be

119

able to make the sacrifice for the good of the future; for the good of all things.

I am doing the right thing, he told himself.

The sacrifice *will* be worth it in the end.

The sea crashed against the dark shore; and Feuchter realised that the surf, the rolling sound of the surf and the hiss of the spray were voices once more, distant voices drifting from the infinite dark horizon:

– . . . Will stabilise him in the event of an . . . hey, who are you, you can't come in here, you've—

– Check him; are they using the right drugs? OK, substitute it for Methylperdazone, 15 mils, and make sure you inject it straight into the wound, through the healing tissue.

– Good; and for fuck's sake, put your guns away.

Feuchter awoke. His eyes were gummed shut, and he waited for a while, listening to his own gentle calm breathing. His senses were alert, though; he could hear breathing, from another three men in the room. He could smell sweat, a hint of old aftershave, whisky, and somebody's odorous feet. Feuchter did a system scan on his own body: it felt weak, the muscles tightened, taut with cramps, burned with fatigue. And his stomach: it was now nothing more than a dull throb where the wound had been.

He forced open his eyes, sticky and filled with crusts of sleep; he could see a fire-retardant tiled ceiling in the gloom. Yellow light cast spiral patterns across the tiles, which were quite new; a private ward, then?

Feuchter's hand moved down his body; he felt the fresh scar where the bullet had recently smashed into him; he probed it gently but there was no pain. He smiled to himself, then propped himself up on one elbow.

120

There were three men; they were all watching him. Two were heavy-set bruisers, carrying Sterling sub-machine guns concealed badly within their long coats; they were unshaven and looked weary. The third was a tall thin man, with a hawk face and a crooked, hooked nose. His hair was shaved close to the scalp, his hands heavy with rings. He wore a white doctor's coat and a stethoscope. A small case was by his side and Feuchter knew exactly what items were in it.

'It's good to see you, Tremont. How long have I been out?' he asked.

'Three days, sir. A little longer than we expected, but you were nearly dead when we got to you. And you have to appreciate that in controlled laboratory conditions we do not replicate real-world random activities with such precision as when these incidents occur naturally.'

Feuchter nodded. 'Can you get me a coffee? And a cigar? I am gasping – I feel like I've been unconscious for months!'

'That is a side effect of the accelerated processes, sir.' Tremont waved away one of the bruisers, who slid from the room. Outside the self-closing green door Feuchter caught a glimpse of a sterile corridor, with several waiting trolleys and distant lights.

'Does Durell know that I am OK?'

'He does, sir.'

'Am I in a private facility?'

'Yes. We had to work quickly; you had lost a lot of blood and although your body was already regenerating we had to give it a slight boost. This will stay in your system for the next two weeks, or thereabouts.'

'Side effects?'

'Exhaustion; but we have new drugs to combat this also.'

'Good.'

Feuchter sat up. 'There are still bits of metal inside me.'

'Yes, we know; they are benign and can be removed at a later date; Durell said speed of recovery was of the utmost importance because of the developments with the QIII. He said to tell you that we have had advances with the location of the stolen schematics.'

'And . . .' A pause. 'Carter?'

'After the incidents in Germany, he has been traced.'

'Tell me.'

'He evaded several Nex operatives; nearly killed *you*.'

'He's better than I thought – much better. Could almost be a fucking Nex himself!'

There was laughter; cold laughter; it contained little humour.

'Units have been dispatched to remove him.'

Feuchter nodded. The bruiser returned and Feuchter lit his cigar. 'Out of interest, my niece, Maria Balashev: she died, did she not?'

'She did, sir. Nobody seems to know quite what happened in that room . . . we were waiting for you to awake. The Nex got you out just before the explosion designed to remove the QIII development team and mask your disappearance, but Maria . . . well, the bullet had clipped one of her lungs – she choked to death on her own blood. There was nothing they could do for her and didn't have time to make snap decisions . . . you were the priority.'

'Priority?' said Feuchter coldly, a dark intelligent twinkle in his eyes. 'Yes, I suppose I am.'

'One other thing, sir.'

'Yes?' His eyes glittered.

'Spiral_H had set up a task force to remove Spiral_Q from operation.'

'And?'

'It had been successfully dealt with, sir. Spiral_H no longer exists, and many of their operatives and networks are dead.'

'A downward spiral, you could say?' chuckled Feuchter nastily, and closed his dark eyes and allowed the pain to wash over him and take him away to dark obsidian shores.

Natasha lay, broken and torn and smashed on the ground.

'No!' hissed Carter. His own Browning started to bark as he leaped from the ridge, both hands clasping the weapon. The man who had shot Natasha was slammed from his feet, bullets eating him whole like tiny metal parasites, and blood exploded from his mouth, staining his beard and nose in a crimson shower. Carter landed, rolling across the ice, grunting, his Browning on empty and his body sliding against the buckled BMW with a *thud*. He swiftly changed mags – checked inside the Mercedes.

On the ice, two men were still standing, retreating towards the woods; one was dead in the back seat of the vehicle from Carter's sniper round; another had been shot by Natasha, and one lay on the ice with his face blown apart, Carter's bullet in his brain.

Carter popped his head around the car's protective shell; bullets screamed from the edge of the woods, eating into the stone and metal behind him with showers of dust. Carter dropped to his belly and slid along to the edge of the Mercedes which clicked and hissed with the sighs of cooling, stressed steel—

Legs, sticking out from behind a tree.

He opened fire, heard screams, saw blood erupt from feet and shins.

One last man—

Carter squinted but could not see the assassin. Where had he gone? He had been by the side of the trees, down near the low stone wall that needed serious repairs which Carter kept putting off until the eternal 'next summer' . . .

Boots thudded on the Mercedes bodywork and Carter looked up – too late – as the man leaped on top of him with a growl. Carter caught a glimpse of tanned features and a bushy black moustache. He smelled garlic before he was grabbed, his Browning knocked easily aside. He brought up his knee, but missed – the large attacker rained down blows on Carter's head and face and he was momentarily stunned, blinded by multiple impacts—

The weight lifted. Carter lay on his back, on the ice, tasting blood and a sliver of tooth. He glanced up—

Into a boot.

Stars flashed across his vision and he was smashed backwards against the Mercedes, grunting, blood flowing down his chin, his nose broken. He might have screamed, he wasn't sure—

His fingers slipped on the ice beneath him as he tried to push himself up.

'Now, I kill you,' came the heavily accented voice.

Carter's eyes flickered open – everything seemed to be in slow motion,

Let me take his fucking soul, whispered Kade.

Carter dodged left as the boot connected where – a split second before – his face had been. Carter's fist smashed a heavy curling hook against the man's groin and then—

The man screamed.

Carter dragged himself to his feet, suddenly aware of the snarling; the man was on the ground, Samson's teeth

124

clamped on and through the attacker's collarbone, tearing at his neck and throat. He was squirming, trying to punch the dog but the compression and snapping and tearing was making him wail, there was a *crack* of collarbone, and the man struggled manically to get away from that awesome crushing bite—

Carter staggered against the Mercedes. He gave a quick glance to Natasha – she was down and out of the game. He scanned for the Browning but could not see the weapon through the blood in his eyes; he felt a warm stream down the back of his throat and he spat stark red against the snow.

He moved forward and met Samson's eyes; they were smiling.

'Good dog. Off.'

Samson retreated, lips up baring evil blood-stained fangs—

Carter kicked the man in the head several times, until he was sure the killer was unconscious. Then he knelt, and slammed the heel of his hand into the man's nose, breaking it in a return favour and making doubly sure the bastard wouldn't get up.

Covered in blood, Carter skidded across the snow and ice to Natasha. Gently, he eased her legs from the embankment and rolled her onto her back. She was breathing, raggedly, her eyes open, her Berghaus soaked in blood. 'Can you feel your fingers?' he asked.

'You look a fucking mess,' she smiled, her voice hoarse.

'You're not so beautiful yourself.'

'I can't move . . .'

Carter lifted Natasha into his arms and staggered, despite her lack of weight. His head was spinning, pounding after the blows from the large man. She was still as light as he remembered . . . from better, happier times . . .

Carter lurched towards the house.

Nat's eyes grew large and her fingers clawed his arm—

Her tongue protruded. Carter cursed, and dropped to his knees in the snow, amongst the droplets of raining blood. Natasha could not breathe . . . the bullet had triggered an adverse reaction inside her, fucking with her central nervous system to inspire anaphylactic shock—

Natasha's windpipe had closed.

Her own body had become the Enemy.

She spasmed, back arching as if in a fit of epilepsy; Carter pinned her down with his own body weight and fumbled in his clothing, searching, hunting—

Natasha squirmed beneath him, as if in some bizarre act of love. She was strong, incredibly so. Carter dug a pen from his pocket, a cheap plastic biro, and, grunting, he held her spasming heaving body in place, clamped her arms under his legs and grabbed her short hair tightly in his fist, pulling her head back swiftly—

He could not look her in the eye, because he knew she could see and feel and hear and understand—

The ballpoint pen looked suddenly so innocent in his fingers. Carter pulled the cap free with his teeth and spat it into the snow. Natasha was going blue, her eyes so wide he thought that they would pop—

He made the stroke with one quick movement.

Down, just above the sternum . . . at the base of her throat—

Punching a hole through her flesh . . .

Through her oesophagus—

There was a sudden *whoosh* of intaken air through the ragged, improvised mouth. Carter withdrew the pen, releasing a tiny squirt of blood that hit him in the face and mingled with his own. Carter stared down into

126

Natasha's eyes, unable to speak, and the unhealthy pallor gradually faded from her flesh as the air flowed into her lungs.

Her eyes closed, blinked. She could not speak.

Carter lifted her, limp now in his arms, and crawled wearily over the bonnet of the smashed BMW which was partly blocking the entrance to his home. He slid across the buckled surface, then kicked open his front door. He climbed the steps, suddenly weary, suddenly aware of a million pains screaming through his battered and bruised body. Stars danced in front of his eyes and he had to pause halfway up the steps, leaning, heaving and panting, against the wall. He continued, and felt elation when he reached the top.

He carried Natasha through to the living room, kicked the leather couch over in front of the open fire and laid her out. Blood had soaked her clothing, seeping through the fabric.

There was a repetitive *blipping* coming from a control panel on the wall: proximity-sensor alerts triggered by the assassins. Carter reached over, disengaged the alarms and welcomed the silence.

Carter threw a few logs on the glowing fire, then moved into the kitchen. He removed his coat, groaning, then his own jumper. Cuts and bruises appeared across his body and shoulders, across his throat and face and when he glanced into the mirror—

A battered shell gazed back. It grinned through damp glistening blood.

Carter ran off a bowl of hot water, grabbed a knife from the cedarwood rack and returned to the living room. He knelt, and carefully cut away Natasha's clothing, her sopping silken shirt and bra. Her flesh was pale under Carter's appraising gaze. He realised that she had,

127

thankfully, taken only a single bullet but he still cursed, leaning over her to analyse the wound. It had entered high through the shoulder – tearing flesh, just missing the lodestone of bone within and exiting in a tight hole from the back of the muscle. An inch lower and it would have caused *serious* damage . . . the hole was slick with fluid nestling like stagnant crimson rainwater in a tiny shell hole.

'Shit.'

Carter limped to his study and grabbed a leather medical case; he returned to Natasha and pulled out a syringe, injecting her intravenously with a morphine-based sedative. He checked her pulse and BP, using the medscan on the ECube. Then he pulled free a sterile solution and cleaned first the front of the wound, and then, rolling her mumbling over onto her belly, the exit wound. Carter cleaned the hole, using a scalpel to shave free friction-burned flesh and cut out alien particles of metal and cloth. Using sterile wire, he finally stitched the fresh sliced skin together.

Stitching the front wound, Carter checked Natasha's pulse and BP once more, then applied a sterile dressing to her tightly stitched flesh and also to the improvised hole in her throat. Then he linked her to a tiny mobile monitor, which checked on heart rate, oxygen-saturation levels and blood compositions. He pulled down her trousers, checking for other wounds he might have missed. He checked her blood group and haemoglobin level, but her Hb was 8g/dl – dangerous, because the oxygen carrying capacity of her blood had been seriously reduced and she was in need of a transfusion. He strapped a tourniquet around her forearm, tightening it gently, then pulled free a cannula and tore off the sterile packaging. He inserted the thin needle into a vein of her hand, then eased it free, leaving the plastic sheath in place. Working quickly, he secured the cannula with a dressing and moved to the kitchen, removing a pint of his emergency store of universal O-negative; he grabbed a small folding metal stand from a low shelf, shaking free the dust, and returned to Natasha. He erected the stand, hung the O-neg from the narrow frame, and from his case removed a sterile blood-giving set. This he connected first to the unit of blood, being careful to prime the line before connecting the other end of the cannula, ready to commence transfusion. He flicked up the dial on the blood-giving set, and watched the drip rate in the chamber for a moment in order to establish a steady flow.

Content with his work so far, Carter considered wrapping her in foil, but decided against it – foil kept the cold in, and Nats was *very* cold. Instead, he merely wrapped her in blankets and piled more logs on the fire, giving her a final injection of antibiotics and another dose of sedative before stumbling to the bathroom himself.

He removed his torn, bloodied clothing, switched on the shower and stepped into the steam, wincing as the water lashed his broken face like a whip. Slowly, he lathered his body, washing free the dirt and sweat and blood – his own and that of others.

His brain hurt, his mind a whirlpool of confusion—

There were too many questions to answer, and a broken nose did nothing to calm his thoughts.

He stepped free and towelled himself gently, his movements lethargic now as the adrenalin left him. He looked at his face in the mirror and cursed. Heavy bruising, cuts and scrapes. His nose was a mess, twisted and deformed. He dragged the medical case over and, with some difficulty, injected himself with diazepam and waited for his

129

flesh and soul to go numb and provide him with that sickliest of sweet sensations.

He pulled on shorts and a T-shirt, feeling a little groggy as the drugs ate his system resources. Then, taking his nose between his two thumb-heels, he counted to three and wrenched the bone and cartilage back into some semblance of position. Everything went black and he screamed, despite the anaesthetic. He vomited into the sink and stood there, leaning over the bowl, drooling and panting.

Carter glanced up.

His nose was straight once more, but buckled, like corrugated iron that had been beaten with a lump hammer. He grinned weakly, brushed gently at his teeth – avoiding the broken one – to remove the sour vomit, and splashed water on his face to carry away his pain-fuelled sweat.

He moved, checking on Natasha who was breathing more regularly now, the colour having returned to her face. He pulled on a heavy coat and gloves, and a set of boots unstained with blood, and trotted down the steps.

'*Why didn't you call me?*'

'I didn't need you.'

'*You could have been killed; I would have wiped them from the face of the fucking earth . . .*'

'I didn't do so bad myself.'

'*Don't trust Natasha.*'

'I don't need your fucking advice, Kade. I never even asked you to come, so fuck off to whatever hell you inhabit and leave me with my thoughts. Life is hard enough without you sticking your spiritual nose into it . . .'

'*Ooh. Tetchy. The broken nose hurt, did it?*'

'Kade. Go.'

130

'I don't want to.'

'You are driving me mad!'

'*Good, isn't it? I believe I have found my true vocation in life.*'

Kade left, suddenly, and Carter felt even more light-headed at the abrupt – unexpected – withdrawal.

He stepped out into the snow. Flakes were falling, heavier now, from a grey sky that cast silver shadows across the landscape. The world was silent, an oil painting of stillness and serenity: except for the intrusion of Samson who was worrying the corpse of one of the attackers, tearing at the stomach and chest, bloodied strips of flesh in his teeth—

'Whoa. Sam, get the fuck out of here, you dirty little bastard.' He chased the whining dog away, and Samson retired across the turning circle, lying under the trees and rubbing his muzzle between his paws, licking free the remaining blood. Carter located his Browning HiPower 9mm, checked the mag and the state of the weapon, and used a rag to wipe it free of blood and dirt. He checked the unconscious man, and then moved around the battered Mercedes and towards the edge of the woods. There were pools of deep red on the ground where the man whose legs he had shot had been standing; the blood led away and Carter followed for fifty paces until he found the man curled into a ball, dead. Carter checked him, then, taking him by his feet, dragged him deeper into the woods and rolled him down a small embankment into a snow-filled ditch.

He worked slowly, watched by Samson's bright eyes. He pulled the corpse out of the Mercedes, and gathered the other bodies, dragging them all into the woods and laying them to rest in a line like some grisly murder scene from a horror novel. He rinsed the red stains from his hands with snow and returned to the final man, who was making low moaning sounds. Carter rolled him over onto his belly and pulled wire from his pocket, binding the man's hands and feet so tightly that the wire cut deep. Then he dragged the tanned man to the porch, propped him against the foot of the stairs and placed a coat over him.

'Don't want you to die of exposure, my little flower,' he muttered.

Night was falling fast with the snow, the heavy flakes tumbling through the darkness like leaves from some great tree. Carter moved to the cars and stood, hands on his hips, chewing at his lower lip – which began to bleed, forcing him to curse, head lifted into the darkness.

He got into the Mercedes, brushing shattered glass from the leather upholstery. The keys were in the ignition, the dashboard still illuminated. He turned the keys and the engine rattled into life, vibrating the buckled bonnet. A squealing – probably from the fan belt – emerged like the cry of a strangled cat. Carter pushed the automatic gearstick into reverse, shivering at the icy breeze and flakes of snow peppering through the shattered windscreen. He eased the accelerator. There was a groan of buckled steel as the Merc dragged the BMW back and then released it suddenly, leaving a twisted wing in its wake. Carter reversed the battered Mercedes, then turned it around to face the lane exiting from Carter's own little world. He turned off the ignition and dropped the keys into his pocket. The front of the Merc was smashed to oblivion; no headlights, no grille, only an exposed and severely leaking radiator and a buckled shock strut. Carter moved to the BMW, eyes scanning the twisted coach lines. Two side windows had been smashed, a tail light was shattered and bullet holes had peppered the bodywork. The front end was OK, and Carter climbed in and started the engine. The 4.0-litre straight 6 kicked into life and rumbled steadily, fumes pluming from the wide twin-piped exhaust. Carter eased it into first gear – then cruised the BMW away from his house and out onto the snowbound road. The car ran reasonably smoothly, a few rattles and creaks and excessive noise from the shattered windows betraying its recent abuse. Carter turned the vehicle in the entrance to a field, then drove it back to his house, revelling in the still-powerful handling of the damaged motor.

He parked up the car. The central locking had become defunct – probably a stray bullet. He pocketed the keys and, re-entering the Merc, drove the long black car into the woods and out of sight of the road. Then he limped back to the porch and stared down at the would-be assassin; the man was big, much bigger than Carter and quite fearsome-looking. He was dark-skinned, almost Arabic in appearance. He had an oiled black moustache and was squinting up in pain – Carter gazed down at the man's savaged shoulder and his broken nose and the wires biting into his skin. Carter crouched down. 'Who are you?'

The man's lips went tight.

'Are you here to kill Natasha, or me?'

Silence. He looked straight ahead.

Carter's fist slammed into his prisoner's broken nose, and the man screamed, saliva and blood drooling from his mouth. His head hung, and then lifted slowly to stare at Carter. He spat into Carter's face and grinned, deep red globules staining his teeth.

'If that's the way you want it.'

Carter grabbed the man's hair, shouted for Samson, who was sniffing at the edge of the woods, and dragged

133

the man up the stairs, wailing and bumping. He had to stop halfway up when a clump of hair finally came out in his fist, but he wound a larger portion between his fingers and dragged the man up the final steps, across the floor and into the kitchen. Moving to the back of the house he opened a door that led into a stone-floored utility room, mostly bare except for a washing machine and drier. It was terribly cold, and dark. Carter rolled the man down the three steps, and closed the door.

He returned to Natasha and slumped by her side. Her breathing was deep, her colour good. Samson trotted in and jumped into his basket in the corner, curling up and dropping asleep almost instantly.

Carter armed the house defences with the remote IR, placed his head on the sofa beside Natasha and wearily flicked on the TV. Keeping the sound low, he watched without interest as images danced in front of him. Carter hated the TV; the Americans called it the 'dead-eye' and he could understand why. But he acknowledged begrudgingly that it had its uses as he flicked through the news channels, eyes searching, brain working on maximum despite his weary state.

And then he saw it, like some incredibly bad coincidence . . .

The camera swept across the devastation in London, across the huge circle of the explosion zone where once Spiral_H had nestled in its secret enclave. Carter did not listen to the reporter's hysterical monologue because he did not need the commentary, and he did not care what the man had to say; instead his widened eyes watched the amateur camcorder footage, as filmed by a Japanese tourist. The sudden annihilation, the sudden disintegration, the sudden extinction of Spiral_H.

Carter rubbed at his eyes.

What's fucking going on? screamed his confused brain.

He pulled free his ECube; the surface was dead. Not surprising, considering the HQ's mainframes had just been obliterated in a single violent catastrophe of mankind's chemical making.

Carter found that his mouth was dry.

The game was getting bigger.

The game was getting nastier.

'I've fucking had enough of playing by somebody else's rules,' snapped Kade, surging into the forefront of Carter's brain like a black brooding leviathan emerging from the darkest depths of the ocean.

'You're not the only one,' growled back Carter.

For a while he dozed, drifting in uneasy sleep. When he awoke the fire was still glowing warmly, but outside he could see only pitch black, emphasised by small piles of snow caressing the windowsills. Carter looked over at Natasha. She was still sleeping deeply, her breathing regular. He checked the sterile dressings, and replaced them with fresh ones. Carter poured himself a large tumbler of Lagavulin, and retook his seat next to Natasha on the floor, on the rugs, sipping at the mellow fiery drink and staring into her face. She looked so serene in sleep, so beautiful.

And yet soon he would have to wake her; how long would it be before more men came after them? Men with guns, and with murder in mind?

He reached over and pushed some stray hair from her forehead. She murmured in her sleep, shifting slightly, and Carter stroked her cheek, enjoying the warm flushed skin under his fingers, his mood descending into one of melancholy moderated only a little by the bulk of the Browning against his hip.

More will come, he thought.

They will know that they failed, soon enough.

Natasha moaned in her sleep; she turned, sighing, then her face twisted in pain — stitches pulling tight. She coughed, settling back against the cushions. Carter fought his desire to wake her, question her. She had lost a lot of blood, was weak from the ordeal and her injuries, the shock of the GST. She needed to rest . . . but not for long. They had to move; and move soon. How long did they have? Five hours? An hour? Ten minutes? Carter's hand stroked the Browning.

He would be waiting.

And he would fuck them bad . . .

Spiral_Memo3
Transcript of recent news incident
CodeRed_Z;
unorthodox incident scan 554670

The Russian government has fifteen missing nuclear-powered submarines.

These long-range undersea vessels, which are both nuclear-powered and carry nuclear warheads, have been officially confirmed missing in action after they disappeared, one by one, from sonar and other sophisticated ERV scanning and monitoring equipment.

Military-led rescue operations have been circling the areas where the subs were last monitored, and small one-man speed-subs have been diving in search of the missing vessels, but with no success.

Many countries have already been offering
condolences for what could be one of the
greatest ever marine disasters in peacetime.
Reports to follow.>>#

CHAPTER 8

MOBILE

The deck rolled gently beneath his thick grey boots, and looking across to the shore as the wind caressed his long curled hair and thick beard, he could see the darkened mass of the woods, ensconced in the embrace of deepest winter. Where the river poured into the sea, he could see that it had frozen in places and sported huge plates of ice slicing like flat axe blades of silver through the smooth waters. Seagulls flapped and cried like forlorn children, and fought along the edge of the Alaskan shoreline and the woods as dusk embraced this darkened corner of the world.

A wolf howled, distantly, lamenting the full moon, its eyes watching from the woods as the huge black battleship sat rocking gently in the calm icy bay. The wolf turned, and disappeared beneath the trees.

The man reached the door, heavy and black, and it swung open on well-oiled hinges. Giving a final, wistful look back towards the fresh freedom of nature, and the world beyond the sea which now trapped him, he dipped to enter the narrow confines of the ship's corridor. He stepped carefully down the broad iron steps, his walking stick clanging as he felt his way with a precision and caution born of age; his frame was muffled in heavy furs, worn not just to protect him during the brief crossing by boat, but to offset the natural weather of this desolate part of the world.

Despite his age, he was a bear of a man, huge and brown, his head wrapped against the cold and ice by a circular fur hat, his face hidden under a huge shaggy grey-streaked beard.

Moving down the corridor, he paused as he reached a huge door that seemed somehow out of place; he wanted to enter, *needed* to enter, and yet still he paused. He considered knocking, but realised it would be a waste of time. Durell already knew he was there.

He pushed, and the huge door swung inwards.

He stepped forwards, into a darkness lit only by candles. The room was carpeted, and wood-panelled; huge rows of unevenly sized books lined the walls and through a tiny porthole grey light spilled in. The room was awash with shadows and gloom. Against one wall, almost out of place among the wood and old tomes, was a single silver bank of incredibly high-tech equipment; several white lights flickered across the surface, and a black screen reminded the man of a dead portal into another world.

'Durell?'

'I am here, my friend.' A figure stood beside a stack of old, leather-bound books; tall and thin, shrouded in a black robe and wearing a voluminous hood that hid any features within a circle of obsidian darkness. The voice was rich, had melody and strength. 'You may speak – we are alone for the moment.'

'They failed,' said the bear-clad man in Russian. 'He has been a year out of Spiral. We thought him an easy target; retired, lacking the professionalism of the others.'

'Even after the events in Germany with . . . Feuchter?'

'That was luck.'

'Your naivety astounds me. You ranked him so low on the list of priority kills, when in fact he should have been near the top.' The smooth voice came from the folds of the hood and the bearded old man shivered.

'What would you have me do?' came the gravelled voice of the Russian. The voice was cracking under pressure. His stick came up, a swift movement for one who initially appeared so old and frail. The stick touched his shoulder and rested there, as if proffering some small protection against the black-robed figure before him. His fear was a tangible thing, physical, an aura surrounding him like a cloud.

'Send the 5Nex,' came the soft voice.

'The 5Nex are ready?'

'They have been ready for longer than you could possibly imagine; and there are battalions on the move, battalions preparing for war! Soon this ship will be the hub of our activities . . . yes, my friend, you are living through times of change and it is good for you that you are a part of them – integral, shall we say.'

The Russian gazed at the black-robed figure, sensing the smile, the show of teeth, within the darkness. His mouth was a dry line, his eyes seemingly filled with tears. His knuckles were white where they gripped the walking staff.

'You may go,' said Durell softly.

The large man turned, and stepped out from this chamber deep within the heart of the battleship – Durell listened as the walking stick rang down the corridor, the noise finally disappearing into the bowels of the apparently deserted and ghostly vessel.

The battleship rocked gently on eddies of sea current.

Ice caressed her huge prow and black flanks, and glittered like diamonds across the frozen decks and the huge guns, which were silent and motionless.

Seagulls cawed outside the room's porthole as Durell threw back his hood and cold eyes glittered in the mixed silver of candlelight and moonlight. A hand stretched out and patted the candle flames into extinction. Then he moved to the porthole and opened it, allowing the breeze of the wild darkness to invade his sanctuary.

Pain gripped him, but only for a few seconds of savage intensity. As his twisted face returned to calm, he licked his lips – a small red tongue darting out to smear a trail.

'Soon,' came the soft words. 'Soon, Mr Carter.'

In the dream, Carter stood on a mountain plateau, a flat section, a *scoop* carved from the vertical wall of a vast towering black mountain that reared above a world of dark sand. Dust and jagged black rock squatted under his boots, and the sky stretched away for infinity, curled with trails of purple and yellow – a bruised night sky. Kade stood in front of him – with Carter's own face, his own body, but deformed twisted corrupted sporting darker, brooding eyes, a heavier face and stockier set of shoulders. Altogether more—

Intimidating . . .

'*Why have you come here?*' snapped Kade, standing beside a fire that burned within a small ring of rocks. The wind howled around them, through narrow channels of rocky teeth, and it whipped Carter's coat and caressed his face with a corpse's kiss.

'I didn't want to come here. It just happened,' said Carter slowly, his words soft and without tension.

'*Fuck – off,*' said Kade harshly. '*This is my place. My world. My mountain.*'

141

Carter grinned without humour, his brow furrowing, and sat down cross-legged beside the wildly whipping flames of the fire. They crackled like tiny bottled demons. 'I think I will stay,' he said. 'After all, many is the time *you* pay *me* unwelcome visits.' This was something that suddenly amused him; an irony, a reversal of fortunes: here was Kade, his poise suddenly gone, his humour and bitterness appearing as melted ice. He was pissed off at Carter's intrusion. 'I never ask for *you* in my dreams,' he said softly.

'*That is different,*' said Kade. '*I help you.*'

'Help me? Or help yourself?'

'*I don't know what you mean.*'

Kade did not move. He remained standing, heavy brows furrowed at this unexpected intrusion. He stared down at Carter with ill-disguised distaste; as if he'd just found a rotting bone in his bed.

'*What do you want?*'

Carter shrugged. 'I want nothing. I did not request or intend to come here. This is only a dream.'

'*A dream to you; reality to me.*'

'As you are a dream in my reality?'

'*Yes. Until you give me life.*'

'What are you, Kade?'

'*I am you, Carter.*'

'But what are you *really*?'

He caught the sly smile, and then it was gone. A fleeting shadow; a cloud passing before the sun. '*I am you,*' he repeated. '*I am the finger on the trigger. I am the power behind the punch. I am the hands pulling on the garrotte. I am the poison in the vial. I am you, Carter. I am your dark side, your bad side, your fucked side, your frustration and your anger and your hatred. Call them what you will. I am you — only you choose to debate my existence and I fear you will never accept me.*'

'You do things I would never dream of,' snapped Carter. 'Do not try to make me out to be some fucked-up schizo freak. You are in my brain and you live your own life. You only say that you are me to try and stop me going fucking insane . . . but I will find you, Kade, one day I will find you and we will fight and I will kill you.'

Kade laughed, a cold chilling sound.

'That would be . . . interesting.'

'It'll be fucking interesting when you're eating worms.'

Kade laughed again. *'I will welcome the day, my friend. My saviour. My lifeblood. It is good to see you still carry such anger – it was that anger which earned you your title. The title which scars your heart, Butcher.'*

'That was not me!' Carter's words were suddenly low, the tone unreadable, dangerous.

'It was your hands that killed so many.'

'That was you!' hissed Carter.

'How could you murder them all?' sneered Kade, his voice mocking.

'It was you, you fucking piece of shit, and you know it! Don't condemn me with your fucking haunted past.'

'I am not haunted,' said Kade calmly. He turned then, glancing over the dark desert at something in the distance that Carter could not see. *'There is a bird called a plover that feeds on the meat caught between the teeth of a crocodile,'* said Kade softly. A smile danced across his lips. *'The crocodile could kill the plover easily – with a snap of his jaws. But he chooses not to do so, because this bird performs a service for him and so he lets the bird live. And by performing the service, this plover helps the crocodile to protect his greatest assets – his teeth, which in turn keep him alive. So by keeping the bird alive, the crocodile extends his own life. They are symbiotic. They feed from one another; entwined, like lovers.'*

'And you think we are like that?' laughed Carter coldly, eyes staring up from shadowed brows, all sense of humour gone to be replaced with a cold hard splinter through his heart.

'Oh yes,' said Kade, smiling. *But I want you to think carefully. Decide which you are. Are you the crocodile – or are you really the bird?*

'Carter . . .' A shaking. The world tumbled, dissolved. Carter came awake to find Natasha's hand on his arm. She was looking down into his face, worried. 'We need to talk,' she croaked, her face creased and screwed with pain.

'OK, let's talk,' said Carter thickly, climbing to his feet.

He stirred the coffee slowly, the headache crashing against the shores of his mind and crucifying his soul on a cross fashioned from Kade's bones.

'You OK?' came Natasha's voice, weakened, jagged, almost unheard.

'Yeah.'

Carter carried the sweet hot drink into the room, knelt in front of Natasha and looked up into her eyes. She had sat up on the couch, her face lined, her eyes hooded. Every movement brought a little grimace of pain and Carter sipped his coffee, drums thumping in his head, rippling across his temples, scoring his brain with steel claws.

Carter opened his mouth, and Natasha whispered, 'Shh,' with a finger against her lips. She met Carter's gaze. There were tears in her eyes and she smiled warmly at him.

'I'm sorry for bringing such trouble to your home.'

'They were here for me,' said Carter slowly.

'Both of us, I feel,' said Natasha. Tears rolled down her cheeks, and she brushed them viciously away. 'I thank

144

you for saving my life. I . . . I don't know what I would have done without you.'

'*Die,*' chuckled Kade in Carter's mind. Carter felt the demon squatting there, at the back of his thumping brain.

Natasha coughed, her face wincing; a finger came up, touched the sterile plaster covering the stitched hole in her throat; she smiled wryly. 'You are a brave and strong man, Carter. I have come here to warn you.' She laughed softly. 'Your life is in danger . . . yeah, I know, a little bit too late, eh?' Her gaze met Carter's.

'Do you know that Spiral_H has been destroyed?'

Natasha's eyes went wide. 'Spiral_H . . . are you sure?'

'It was on the TV; and part of Jam's special message when he came to visit me was about how Spiral_H was assembling some kind of strike force to close down Spiral_Q. How's that for a coincidence? And now the whole place – gone!'

'Completely destroyed?' Her voice was a hushed whisper. 'How?'

'They blew the fuck out of it. Nothing remains. The pictures looked like an atomic wasteland.'

'This is bigger than I could have ever imagined,' she whispered, horror lining her face like battle scars.

The fire crackled. Carter finished his coffee, and Natasha, head bowed, deep in thought, looked up, her face pale, lips trembling. 'Listen, we need to move, Carter . . . we need to get away from here. They will come for us!'

'If we move you now, then you could die.'

'Then I will die. If we stay, we will both die.'

Carter grinned, and it was a nasty grin. 'They will have to send many,' he whispered softly. His hand was against the Browning and bad bad twisted images flittered through his brain.

'You're not listening,' said Natasha sadly. Her hand reached out, stroked Carter's cheek. 'They will send the Nex.'

'The Nex?'

'All I know is that they are Spiral's oldest and best-kept secret. They are awesome killers. We thought them all dead – but they are not dead. They have . . . somehow survived the . . . *extermination*.' The word tasted bad on her tongue.

'Why now? Why me?' Carter's voice was cold as dread sank into his mind and he remembered Jam's theory that the DemolSquads were being wiped out. The possibility passed like a chilling breeze over his soul, the certainty walked like dark demons over his grave.

'You remember Count Feuchter? From Schwalenberg?'

'How could I ever forget that cunt?'

'Here goes,' said Natasha softly. 'There is a splinter group within Spiral – a group of individuals who have decided to betray everything that Spiral stands for. You think of me as a Tactical Officer – but I am more, Carter, much more.'

Carter met her gaze.

Natasha licked her lips.

'I am part of a group – we have no name – who work within Spiral to root out and eliminate any who try and use Spiral's power against itself. We look for the enemy within.' She sighed.

'You're the fucking secret police?'

'Something like that,' said Natasha, smiling wearily. 'But the enemy has hit hard and hit fast; we had only just discovered that Feuchter was one of them . . . we did not think they were anywhere near ready to move . . . I sent you on a blind mission to your death – but thank God you survived. Others were not so fortunate.'

146

'And Feuchter?' Carter's voice was as cold as diamond ice.

'Feuchter is one of the splinter group; as is another man, Durell. They've struck now because the QIII is practically ready, and with its awesome power they can use it to secure their stronghold. They can use the QIII to take over military installations, satellites, fuck only knows what else. It is so terribly, terribly powerful, Carter – I can't explain how dangerous this processor could be in the wrong hands.'

'I don't understand why,' said Carter gently. 'Destroy the Demolition Squads? Destroy Spiral_H? It's lunacy! Spiral fights to preserve what civilisation we've got left – I thought Feuchter was a good man?'

'This splinter group, headed by Feuchter and Durell – they believe Spiral is weak: corrupt, like Rome at the end of her empire. They believe Spiral knows too much and does nothing about it; they believe Spiral is in the pay of the Big Boys – financed, controlled, governed. We both know Spiral was never meant to be that – it was alone, untouchable, worldwide and incorruptible! Feuchter and Durell think they can do a better fucking job. They think the NBC Laws and the URG Bill are not enough. And then, after the London Riots and the Siege of Qingdao – well, I think they lost all faith in Spiral. With the QIII processor and the Nex they think they can bring us the ultimate in world peace ... a new world order ... but ...'

'Yeah, "but",' snapped Carter. 'In times of war there are always casualties, yes?'

Natasha nodded.

'We definitely need to get the fuck out of here; they will be coming even as we speak.'

'Yes.'

147

Carter reached up and kissed her softly on her lips. 'There is only one person I can think of, one person who has the resources and the knowledge to help us.'

Natasha pulled back a little, her stare meeting Carter's. 'No,' she said, shaking her head.

'Yes,' said Carter. 'The world is fucking collapsing, Nats. Spiral is being force-fed its own entrails, the DemolSquads are being fucked left, right and centre – Gol used to work with Feuchter, and Durell. If anybody knows what they are up to and where they are, then it is Gol. If we can find the QIII, destroy it, then it will be a level playing field again – and if we can take out Feuchter and Durell on the way, then so be it. Gol is the fucker who will point us to the QIII, and the fuckers who want to abuse their power.'

'We can't go to Gol,' said Natasha.

'But he's your father!' hissed Carter.

'Yes, but he's also a *suspect*. He could well be one of them. He could well be working with Durell – with Feuchter – with the Nex! It would be death to meet him.'

Carter climbed to his feet. He withdrew the sturdy 9mm Browning, checked the clip, and rammed it back home as his eyes lifted and he took a deep breath. 'If Gol is a traitor, then the death will be his,' said Carter with grim finality.

Carter had removed the cannula and Natasha was rubbing softly at her hand. Her face was incredibly pale once more and Carter helped her to dress, wincing with her in her pain as she struggled into fresh clothes.

'Tell me more about this Nex that they will send?'

Natasha shrugged weakly. 'All I know is that the Nex were some kind of project from way back – started in the 1990s, I think, but based on work from much earlier.

There is an assassin who is supposed to be awesome – a 5Nex, I think it was called; it was this killer who wiped out Demol14.'

'Alone?'

'Yes, alone.'

'Without help?'

Natasha nodded. 'So the encrypted files read – just before I fled and came here to warn you, and to ask for your help. This thing has spiralled out of control.'

'The irony,' barked Carter. 'Look, I will go and tool up, check the monitors, throw a few things in a bag and we can get the fuck out of here. Is there anything you need?'

'A bit more blood?'

Carter smiled. 'Yeah, time would have been great.' He turned his back on Natasha and walked towards the door leading to the stairs and the monitoring equipment beyond. He could sense her gaze on his back.

'Carter?'

He stopped. Turned.

'I love you.'

'Really?'

Natasha nodded. 'Really.'

Carter winked. 'Get your shit together. We need to be moving in five.'

Carter glanced with a heavy frown at the PC monitors.

Something was wrong.

Badly wrong.

'*She is coming,*' said Kade.

'How do you fucking know?'

'*I can tell these things,*' he said smugly.

'Leave me alone, I can do without your input, *brother*.' Carter's sarcasm was an almost tangible thing, but it had little effect on Kade.

'*Do you want to know what I think about Natasha? I think she will betray you* – us! . . . *Are you listening to me, Carter?*'

'Shut up. Something's happening.'

'*I'm giving you my advice . . .*'

'Shut up!' Carter snapped.

There came a silence. Carter watched the screens. A sensor came alive, blinking with a proximity warning. By the south woods. Carter switched to video; darkness and snow welcomed him—

And he felt it—

A ripple of energy sang across the woods, a wave of *nausea* that ripped through the equipment and through his belly, making him want to vomit. The PCs instantly shut down . . . followed a couple of seconds later by the lights. The room was plunged into darkness. The PCs' fans whirred to a halt.

'Shit.' Carter sprinted across the landing and down the stairs.

'What's happened?' asked Natasha.

'All the power's gone. I find this incredible because I'm supposed to be furnished with automatic back-up generators.'

'Give me a gun,' said Natasha.

Carter tossed her a small black pistol, a 9mm Glock from his armoury. Stooping, he drew a narrow knife from a hidden sheath in his boot, then slid it carefully back. Metal was always a reassuring back-up option.

Samson whined from the darkness . . .

'Sam. Here boy!' The Labrador appeared, bright eyes glinting in the gloom.

Carter crouched and whispered something in the dog's ear. Sam whined again, tail down. Carter led Sam to the stairs, down, and to the door where a cold wind howled.

150

Carter opened the portal warily, and Sam disappeared into the snow.

'Go. Go now . . .'

Carter ran back up the steps and moved towards his pack.

'Where have you sent him?'

'Away from this place. It's far too dangerous,' said Carter softly. 'Here.'

Natasha caught the keys with a wince of pain and licked her lips nervously, eyes suddenly bright and fevered in the darkness.

'Your BMW keys. I've turned the car around; I think we might need to leave in a hurry.'

'You believe me now?'

'I believe somebody has a lot of fucking technological help, and anyone who can knock out all my sensors and back-up generator in one go has a head start on us.'

'Did your set-up detect anything?'

'Proximity. In the south woods . . .'

'Don't trust it. The assassin could be closer . . .'

Carter shivered, and flicked off the safety on his HiPower. He moved across the room, picking his way by precise memory . . . a good place to defend, he thought. He knew the contours in the darkness so well – but to leave now? The open road at night?

Dangerous and foolish.

We should have left immediately, he realised.

This few hours could have killed us . . .

He calmed his breathing. He forced his heart rate to reduce. He licked his salted lips slowly and peered out from the window and into the snow—

Nothing.

Entry point? he mused.

Only the front door – unless the assassin is a climber . . .

'*You need me yet?*'

Only when I'm dead, thought Carter.

'*Don't be such a bad sport. The assassin is in the house even as we speak.*'

Carter was about to reply when a breeze washed across his soul, like a ghost seeping into his bones. His head snapped around. The shadow was a patch of darkness—

His arm shot out. At its end grew—

The Browning.

Five bullets screamed, smashing into the far wall and spitting sparks from the rim of a metal picture frame; Carter dropped to one knee and glanced sideways. Natasha was on her belly – automatic reaction to gunfire.

'That was rather an erratic action,' came a soft, smooth voice. The tone was curiously asexual and Carter blinked sweat from his eyes and tried to track the voice. He moved slowly sideways, the Browning a close extension of his body – until he was crouched beside Natasha.

Gun still outstretched, he reached down with his free hand and took her hand. She still held the BMW keys. He pressed them deep against her palm and she patted an acknowledgement—

They moved together, towards the stairwell that would lead them out into the snow.

A movement—

Carter opened fire.

Bullets howled across the wall, chewed the wood of the door and smashed the glass of a cabinet across the room; Natasha left him; the Browning's firing mechanism came down on a—

Dead man's click.

The figure sprang at him from the darkness and he ducked, twisting to the side; the figure landed lightly and – without time to change mags Carter thrust the

152

Browning in his pocket at the same time going for the other gun – a Glock – in his belt—

A high kick came from the dark and hammered into his chest with such force that he was picked up and thrown backwards, toppling over the couch and landing in a heap, unable to breathe, eyes wide, pain smashing through his heart—

The figure leaped again with incredible speed and agility—

Carter spun, was on his feet, leaped in a blur to meet the assassin; they collided and Carter's hands grasped clothing and flesh and his head smashed forward, connecting with bone. They both hit the ground and Carter smashed another blow, then a third – there was a deep grunt, they rolled, and the figure was—

Gone.

Carter scrambled up as the boots hit him in the chest, but his arms locked around them as both were punched backwards, stumbling, to the stone steps and—

The darkness below.

They fell, tumbling and bouncing down the stone steps, banging from the walls, both too shocked and stunned by the fall to fight until they bounced five steps from the bottom and in a tangle of limbs connected with the unlocked door, smashing it open.

Carter landed on his back in the snow, tasting blood.

The Nex rolled, coming up in a rigid poised crouch—

A cold wind blew across them, ruffling hair, cooling skin.

Carter coughed, then rolled to his feet and whirled in the moonlight as the figure leaped – Carter blocked, backed away, and shook his head. Blood was running down his face. He grimaced, realising that he had broken a finger and two ribs. He felt the ribs clicking within his chest cavity but he was careful to show no reaction, no indication of injury and location—

The figure circled.

Carter caught the shocked face of Natasha to the right. Get in the fucking BMW, his brain screamed, why don't you get in the fucking car, you fucking stupid bitch? He watched her level the gun and fire off three shots, but even at that distance he could see the shaking of her hand . . .

Snow kicked up and bullets whined.

Carter calmed his breathing. The Browning was still in his pocket, the Glock was lost and he had to *focus*—

The Nex approached. He – or she – was considerably smaller than Carter, clad all in grey and sporting a grey balaclava. Flat tight black boots were on the assailant's feet—

Carter could see no weapons.

The Nex charged – Carter blocked a series of three punches, ducked low and smashed a right hook to the assassin's face; he stepped in close, and was kicked in the throat, sending him scrabbling backwards choking and coughing, hands held out in front of him for protection—

'*The Nex is clearly faster than you,*' said Kade calmly.

The attacker leaped; in a blur Carter ducked, twisted and smashed three blows at the figure sailing over his head. The Nex landed lightly, spun on one heel, and charged—

Blows were smashed left and right. Carter blocked, received another kick to the chest and a series of rapid punches that sent him spinning to the snow. He tasted blood and looked down at the frozen ground, which was suddenly cool and soothing to the bruised and battered flesh of his face. It would be so easy, so easy to lie there and never, ever get up again . . .

Carter tried to get up, but his body screamed at him. Colours flashed a metallic rainbow in his mind.

He pushed, heaved, but finally sagged against the snow, energy fleeing him.

Behind, he heard the assassin approach, soft footsteps on the snow but he could not move, could not bring himself to turn, to roll over, to meet that strange copper gaze of this—

His killer.

He could do nothing . . . was paralysed . . . just like in Egypt . . . and in Belfast when the women were screaming and dying . . .

'*Fight*,' howled Kade in his brain.

'*Fuck you, Carter, don't let me die like this! Fight!*'

But Carter could not move.

CHAPTER 9

SPIRAL_Q

The church was a cold place. The floors were polished wood, buffed to a well-worn shine and displaying decades of well-trodden worship. The walls were panelled in wood, polished oak, and led around domino stacks of pews that were so steeped in antiquity that their surfaces were slightly curved from the presence of praying bodies.

Weak sunlight spilled through the myriad of stained-glass windows; the coloured glass glittered like jewels – sapphire and ruby, emerald and diamond; the displays revealed the Last Supper, Moses and the Burning Bush, Adam and Eve and a hundred other religious displays taken from the Great Book itself.

A cool breeze drifted down the aisles, between the polished pews, between the members of the small congregation who had gathered in silent prayer. There was no Mass on this morning, just a gathering of local worshippers who attended when they felt the need for the company of God.

The Priest knelt by the altar, his hands clasped together

in prayer. He was a huge man, broad-shouldered, wearing casual clothes and a long finely tailored woollen overcoat that reached nearly to his ankles. His wide oval eyes were closed in this act of prayer, his face calm, serene almost, bathed in the light of Jesus and this stained-glass phenomenon. By his side, on the low leather-padded bench on which The Priest knelt, sat his Bible; it was a small, ornately embossed leather-bound edition. The pages were as thin as toilet tissue, and edged in gold. It exuded age; it was The Priest's most prized possession and this man was willing to die for his Book.

The Priest was aware of the people around him and his heart swelled with pride. They were fellow worshippers, all caught in this loving act of prayer, all there to commune with the Lord and to receive His Blessing. The Priest sighed; this was as close to contentment as it could get.

Footsteps.

Something changed the karma at his core; something ate The Priest's serenity like an anthill devouring a rancid corpse.

The footsteps approached slowly, calculated, with care.

The sound struck a discordant note in The Priest's soul.

The Priest kept his head down; he continued to pray; he heard the sound of the other worshippers hurriedly leaving this small rural church and he knew this intruder was the Enemy even before the opening speech or move was made.

'The Lord will protect me,' said The Priest suddenly, his voice loud and booming, crashing around the near-empty church. 'I am one of His flock, and He never deserts His flock. He is the Master, and I am merely His servant. Amen.'

The Priest climbed slowly to his feet. His hand reached down, closed over the small leather Bible, and placed the book in the pocket of his overcoat. Only then did he raise his eyes to look at the intruder who stood in front of him.

The figure was slim, athletic, and wore grey; he, or she, had burning copper eyes that watched The Priest warily, drilling into his brain with the pure intensity of a hatred stare.

The Priest surveyed the figure.

'You are not welcome here,' he said, his words soft, steady. 'This is a place of God; of Worship; of Love.'

'I have come to kill you.' The figure took a step back, spreading its hands out a little more in anticipation. The copper eyes were fixed on The Priest and his brown eyes flecked with gold noted the killer's stance and concealed weapons; the liquid flow of movement.

'What manner of creature are you, who dares to intrude on God's Holy Ground? I would say thou art vermin; I would say thou art an infidel in the Lord's Palace; I would say that you need to leave before God smites you down in a hail of hot death.'

The Priest waited, arms folded across his huge barrel chest.

The Nex attacked.

A police siren wailed through the village. The small Ford J2 hammered down country lanes, flashing through a series of tiny village centres that had once been flowers of the country but that now bore the scars of recent battle. It hammered past startled villagers, past the bloated corpses of bio-smashed cattle surrounded by swarms of flies and farmers with sticks piling animal corpses onto reeking bonfires that belched black smoke to the heavens.

158

The Ford screeched around corners, tyres squealing, and rattled to a halt with a smell of burning engine outside the tiny village church.

A small group of ladies stood huddled outside behind a man carrying a shotgun. They were all peering at the door as the large, pot-bellied policeman struggled from the Ford and moved towards the group. The sub-machine gun slung over his shoulder looked out of place, alien.

'Come on now, people, stand back, let me through,' barked Sergeant Ralph.

'There was gunfire!' said one frightened lady, her hand to her mouth, her shining handbag reflecting the glint of the sun. Her eyes held a haunted quality – she was living through terrible days.

'I was just about to sort this mess out,' said the old man with the shotgun. He looked relieved that the sergeant had arrived. 'Lucky for him that you got here, constable!'

The sergeant cursed himself. Gunfire! He unslung the machine gun, an Armalite X, and grimaced, looking down at the high-tech weapon. Somehow, it seemed so daunting in his fat-fingered hands. In the training centre he had felt brave: a hero ready to do battle as the country descended into anarchy and chaos. Now he merely felt fear, which dulled his brain and brought dryness to his tongue.

'Are you sure it was gunfire?'

'It sounded like a machine gun,' said one old lady.

The sergeant stepped forward towards the heavy wooden doors, pitted and stained with the passing of centuries. He reached, turning the squeaking rusted iron handle.

He shivered as a cold wind caressed him.

He knew; could feel that Death was waiting for him in the gloom.

159

With a great act of courage, he stepped through the portal alone, Armalite X clasped in fear-slippery hands.

The Priest stood, arms folded, staring down at the dead Nex. It had been tossed across the church, its spine broken, creating interesting shadows among the pews where the twisted snapped smashed body sprawled. The Nex's small alloy machine gun lay, black and evil, a weapon out of place against the polished wood of the church floor. The stench of cordite hung in the air, gun smoke drifting from the barrel. The Priest nudged the gun with the toe of his boot. Then, stepping carefully forward with a quiet tongue click of annoyance, he reached down and grabbed the limp body. The head rolled slack on a ball-bearing spine but, incredibly, the eyes opened. The mouth moved wordlessly for a little while and The Priest lifted the disabled but miraculously living Nex up to his face.

'Have you found the way of the Lord, my son?' he asked quietly.

'I . . . underestimated . . . you.' The dull copper eyes screamed with inward hatred, and anger, and frustration. 'I will not do so again.'

'You are correct, of course, my son,' said The Priest as kindly as he could. He shook the Nex, and a rattle of pain erupted from crushed lungs. 'Who sent you? And how did you know I was Spiral?'

The Nex's lips formed a compressed line.

He would not speak.

'Come on, lad, tell me. And I can take away the pain.'

'I will tell you nothing.' The soft asexual voice was laced with agony; The Priest sighed again, and holding the body upright in one fist he reached down and pulled

out a shining broad-bladed knife. One edge was serrated –
it was an evil weapon with only one obvious function: to
kill.

'Are you sure now, my son? Are you sure you cannot
share this information about these evildoers who sent
you? If not, you are betraying the Lord, and as His servant
I must punish you with bright tongues of silver fire!'

'Fuck you.'

The Priest lifted the knife. Light gleamed from the
blade, cast down by a multi-coloured Jesus; shimmering
coloured sunlight glanced from the knife and reflected in
the eyes of the Nex.

'Has God shown you the light yet, my son?'

The Nex stared up with hatred.

'Then I must show you the darkness.'

The blade smashed down – a single massive blow. The
Nex gurgled and The Priest cleaned the blade on the
Nex's clothing before allowing the dead spine-snapped
body to topple and lie at his feet.

The Priest's head came up, eyes narrowing. A figure
moved into the church, cautiously; The Priest smiled
when he saw the rotund figure of Sergeant Ralph,
Armalite X shaking in his hands.

'Ah, Sergeant, just in time to save me.'

The large policeman wobbled forward, eyes wide. He
stared at the dead body, then up at The Priest. He licked
his lips nervously, awe shining in his eyes. 'You killed
him?'

'God worked through me, my son,' said The Priest,
with a kindly smile. He patted Sergeant Ralph on the
shoulder. 'He decided to punish the infidel for destroying
His beloved place of holy worship.' The Priest gestured to
the bullet marks up the wood panelling, across the stone,
and the tiny holes in the stained-glass window where

161

three bullets had allowed shafts of pure sunlight to stream in.

'Shall I . . . shall I . . . shall I call more officers? Or the military?' The sergeant was confused; dazed. The stink of death and cordite was stinging his nostrils. The church – a place of love and worship – had become a charnel house.

'Better let my people deal with it,' said The Priest calmly, and strode out towards the sunlight.

Spiral_Q: sand-blasted stone, steel and dull glass, a massive complex that rose for a single storey above the desert dunes – and for sixteen storeys *below*. A surface scratch; an inverted pyramid; a man-made desert iceberg.

Jessica Rade slumped back in her leather chair, and gazed out over the desert on the monitor before her from within the depths of the underground complex; she watched the wind spin and whip the sand into spiral eddies, shifting and dancing, twisting as if possessed by some great stone amber demon. Saudi Arabia, the Middle East, the Arabian Peninsula: Rub al'Khali – the Great Sandy Desert. How Jessica loved and loathed this vast desolate region of Saudi; how it lived, a dual existence, in her favourite dreams and wormed into her worst nightmares. A place of contrasts; a place of life and death; a place of beauty and a place of great ugliness, hardship and fear.

Rub al'Khali – three hundred *thousand* square miles of mostly unexplored desert. A *vast* rolling landscape of Nature's hostility. A huge plateau of sand and rock, smashed into mercy by Nature and the heat and aridity of the climate.

If Jessica tried, if she closed her eyes and *really* tried, she could smell the Red Sea far off over the mountains past Al Hijaz. It had been too long since she had enjoyed the sea; far, far too long.

Jessica was considered 'bright'. In fact, 'bright' did her little descriptive justice: she had passed her GCSEs at the age of eight; her A levels at the age of ten; age restrictions had kicked in then, but she had subsequently attended the University of Cambridge at the age of sixteen – by which time she had already achieved degree and post-degree success through a variety of private tutorial systems. She graduated in computing, specialising in artificial intelligence and the newly emerging field of RI – *real* intelligence. Artificial intelligence was just that – artificial. Set parameters. Set fields. Sub-routines and instructions and base2 binary linear control following scripted routines that were *scripted* . . . WHAT IFs . . . THEN DOs . . . ANDs and ORs and XORs . . . Jessica Rade had pioneered the new school of thought: the concept of the ability to self-learn, self-teach, self-*program*. The ability for a machine to *learn and truly adapt by altering its own core code*. Ergo, to possess *real* intelligence, instead of a stack of pre-programmed directions.

Spiral_Q had snapped Jessica up after the publication of her third paper. And now, aged twenty-three, Jessica was a rich woman living a life of dreams in a secret location deep within the Great Sandy Desert. She was an incredibly rich woman. A *stupidly* rich woman. And yet it was nothing as vulgar as finance and money and *material possession* that kept her at Spiral_Q – despite the desolation of the land: it was to do with her dreams, her aspirations for the future. She could choose to work anywhere she wished: Mexico, the Seychelles, Florida – all had a particular lure for this young sought-after computer genius. But Spiral_Q was based in Rub al'Khali. And

163

Spiral_Q was where the important computing shit went down.

Jessica Rade *had* to be at the centre of that importance.

Otherwise, her rise to the pinnacle of her chosen career would have been for nothing.

She sat at the terminal, linked to five servers and harnessing the power of forty minor processors. Her fingers blurred across the keyboard and she paused, adjusting the settings of various programs and sub-routines that were running in the background. She compiled her current project – saw the bug even before the compiler reported it; she adjusted her code, compiled a second time, ran the binaries and sat back as figures flickered across the screen. The optical/digital QuadModems flashed small green lights at her.

Jessica Rade rubbed at her weary eyes, licked at dry lips. She suddenly realised that she was incredibly hungry – and incredibly tired, although she acknowledged these were small discomforts in comparison to what had recently gone down in London.

Spiral_H – detonated.

She shivered, and killed the external view.

Jessica gazed through the thick smoked glass at the offices below her; most of the terminals were empty and it was with surprise that she checked the time. 7 p.m.

'Jesus,' she breathed wearily. She had worked straight through from 8 a.m. without a break, her concentration complete, her focus intense and uninterruptible. Now her system suddenly cried out for sustenance and she sighed to herself, climbing to her feet and stretching her perfectly formed athletic body. Her muscles groaned at her.

I need a fucking beer, she realised. A cold one.

She caught the lift up to her personal quarters – all the

Elite Level programmers and designers were given the most luxurious living quarters near the top of the underground complex. They called it 'Ground Level', but in reality it was just below. This was one of the benefits, one of the perks, one of the *expectations* of working for Spiral_Q. They were offered the best salaries, the best holiday packages, opportunities to work worldwide and the opportunity to work on the most exciting projects with the most powerful computing equipment ever created.

And Jessica Rade was, quite literally, at the top of the pile.

She stepped through the doors of her apt, stripped off her clothing and revelled in the feeling of the air-con on her naked skin. She walked barefoot across the marble tiles and flicked on the shower, stepping under the warm jets and soaping her lightly tanned skin. She massaged conditioner into her long dark curls, washed it free and then stepped out of the glass cubicle and towelled herself dry.

Still naked, she crossed to the fridge and pulled free a bottle of ice-cool Budweiser. She flipped the cap, and took a long, long deserved drink. Then she set about preparing a light salad ... what with the recent worry and gossip surrounding Spiral and the London HQ's annihilation, satisfying her hunger had not been a priority until just now.

She revelled in the simple task of preparing the salad; she enjoyed the basic simplicity of slicing lettuce and cucumber and arranging it neatly around a plate after the brain-wrenching math calculations of an average day working on the QIII.

Jessica Rade was on her fourth Budweiser when the comm buzzed.

She hit the switch.

165

'Yeah?'

'We have a problem.'

'Another one?'

'The QIII secondary-source has just de-compiled.'

'Shit. I'll be there in five.'

'Can I just remind you that we only have a week left to hit 98%?'

'Yeah, yeah, I fucking understand. I'll be down shortly.' She killed the comm.

'Shit. Now I'll have to get fucking dressed . . .' she muttered, tossing the empty bottle into the bin where it clashed against its comrades. She disappeared into the bedroom, brain whirring at the possible errors that could have caused such a computing calamity . . . and all the time at the back of Jessica's mind was the nagging doubt about Spiral, and what was happening to the organisation . . .

She did not see the flashing white cursor on her screen.

Jessica Rade loved the small hours.

The early hours of the morning when everything was still; when everyone was sleeping; when the world had *died*.

Jessica had often fantasised as a young girl – and, indeed, had carried the fantasies on into adulthood – had played out intricate scenarios in her mind, imagining what it would be like to be the only woman left alive in the world – the only *person* left standing after some horrific chemical accident, after some amazingly deadly virus that had affected everybody on the planet *except her*.

And now: 4 a.m.

She was awake, lying in her light cotton pyjamas on top of the duvet, staring at the ceiling. She rolled from the bed and stood for a moment. The air-con hissed quietly behind her and she sighed, brain swirling with numbers and calculations and projections for WorldCode. She shook her head, smiled to herself, then wandered, seemingly aimlessly, out from her quarters and towards the lift.

The lift ascended with tiny hydraulic sighs. The doors opened.

Jessica Rade listened, and with a sense of danger stepped pyjama-clad out onto the carpet, her feet luxuriating in the rich pile, her whole being tingling at the audacity, the daring, the temerity of her actions . . . to creep around in her own Spiral_Q at night . . . naughty naughty . . .

She walked the corridors while the majority of the complex slept, and after passing several guards who merely nodded sedately at her presence, she moved stealthily to the unguarded laundry shaft leading to the true ground-level kitchens and boiler rooms. Here there was noise and she had to stay alert. She ran a hand through her curls, stepped lightly over bags of linen and clothing lined up for the washers and driers; but, as usual, she was alone in this vault, alone in this world of her own choosing . . .

She reached the exit at the rear of the ground-level complex. She produced a key and overrode the electronic protection – after all, if one was a computer expert one might as well use that expertise to one's own advantage.

Jessica stepped *outside*—

The cool of the desert night washed over her and she took a few steps, revelling in the feel of the fresh air, the real world, the *danger* of being merely pyjama-clad out in the Rub al'Khali desert surrounded by heavily armed guards . . . guards who sat at their posts with mounted machine guns and other heavy metal to take out aircraft and tanks. Part of her wondered if they could see her, and merely endured her quirkiness, her eccentricity. Another part of her revelled in the feelings of *rebellion*.

Of course, she couldn't go far or else the perimeter guards would certainly and undoubtedly spot her and Feuchter or Johansen or Skelter would moan and whine at her: they were only allowed out from the complex with the strictest supervision. But she could at least *sample*, at least *taste* the freedom of a life in a world completely alone—

She gazed at the stars for a long while, their wan light glinting across her slim figure, and her hand dropped to her flat belly. Jessica didn't work out often, but when she did she gave 200% – and this had provided her with a well-formed athletic figure that was the talk of the programming department.

She patted her belly again.

'Still firm and strong,' she sighed.

She stepped back inside, heaving the thick vaultlike door closed and rerouting the detection systems. Digits flickered across the micro-monitor and Jessica stooped, found the small hidden brush, and carefully flicked sand grains into the corner where they would not be noticed.

If only they knew, she thought.

If only they could catch her!

She shivered; half in delight, half in fear.

Yes; she had been the best programmer and systems analyst – probably in the whole of the UK. But there had been something else; a splinter deep in her soul that led her to *hack* . . .

Her skills had been developed, honed, refined by taking on the largest computing conglomerates and corporations. She cracked their databases for a laugh. She was turned on by smashing their personnel files. She got a heroin high from fucking their finances.

Jessica knew not what drove her; there was something wrong with her soul, but she hated – *loathed* – that part of the world which said, You will know this, you will have access to *this*, but the rest of you . . . well, you can all fuck off.

Data protection? Ha.

Jessica wanted to give the world everything.

Freedom of information.

Freedom of choice as opposed to electronic prisons, math cells, digital locks and keys.

And the QIII Proto?

Jessica smiled mischievously to herself.

Well, the QIII would become her greatest achievement. Spiral could use it to override military systems; hack world data banks; match terrorist identities from satellite scans; redeploy troops on the battlefield from RI hack based on WorldCode probabilities . . .

And WorldCode, again, one of Jessica's finest moments.

The perfect honing of Artificial Intelligence.

Real Intelligence, the ability for a computer to *think*, to possess *emotions and control the fight for civilisation!* It would be the ultimate weapon against evil, and Spiral would be at the forefront of this awesome new technology, Spiral could conquer the growing terror of gun-runners and bomb-makers, assassins, hijackers, drug smugglers . . .

Jessica shivered. She understood that the stakes were high; she had not really understood, never really *considered* before the destruction of the London HQ. But the deaths of so many colleagues had left her chilled to the dark corners of her soul.

Jessica knew; this was no longer a game.

And probably it never had been.

Jessica returned to the lift, and then, on a whim, decided to call on the lab_central, see what the ghostly machines were running at this midnight hour, this graveyard shift. All ops were normally automated during the night and so she had little fear of meeting anybody at this lonely time.

After descending to the lab depths, she padded along the corridor to her own specialised departments. She stopped. She accessed the first of three reinforced glass doors. As the first door closed behind her, leaving her in a cubicle of glass awaiting access to the second door – she saw it.

A figure . . .

Jessica Rade froze.

The figure was motionless, standing near the QIII deck.

Jessica stared for long, long moments. No movement came from the figure and Jessica tried to meet its dark gaze, sure that she had been seen and yet aware that the figure gave no indication of having spotted her.

Was it a guard? A *real* guard, not some doped-up corridor sentry with nothing to do except clench his toes to stave off cramp and share the odd cigarette with other examples of patrolling boredom?

Or was it a sentinel?

A protector?

Jessica sank slowly to the carpet and sat, wondering what to do. She crawled over to the door that had admitted her, and swiped her pass. The door slid open silently and she crawled for it, down the corridor, across the carpets and tiles, then got to her feet and, with a smile at her incredible luck, ran for it—

A few minutes later, she was sitting on the edge of her bed, a glass of brandy in her shaking fingers, sipping it slowly and wondering what the dark figure had been up to; why had it been there?

Her heart was still hammering as she contemplated the figure she had witnessed; clad in grey, wearing some sort of lower face mask and with dull copper eyes. The hair was non-existent – shaved to the skull. The figure had seemed relaxed and yet—

Threatening.

Very, very threatening.

Jessica shivered, and sipped again at her brandy.

Who was the guard?

Must have been some new kind of security drafted in to watch over the QIII in this late stage of development. But weren't all the other security measures good enough? Weren't the electrified fences, the armed guards, the huge concrete walls and steel doors and electronic passes – weren't these enough to protect this revolutionary new processor?

But of course.

Jessica laughed softly, bitterly, to herself, and stared out over the desert through the monitor. Spiral_H had been hit. Detonated. Wiped from the face of the Earth.

Pondering her strange and very near encounter, Jessica took another drink of the brandy, enjoying the hot fire in her throat. A word crept into the corners of her mind; a word she had once overheard, when barging in during a fit of temper, into Count Feuchter's office and an ops meeting between Feuchter, Durell and Adams . . .

'The Nex . . .'

They had stared at her. She had apologised and retreated.

But now; now the word seemed to come unbidden from Jessica's forgotten vaults of memory. It seemed to fit.

171

Nex. A Nex. The Nex? Was Nex the name of a person? A guard? A *killer*?

She shivered, realising that she had drunk a little too much, and then downed the rest of the brandy in one.

She decided she would ask Adams in the morning.

Yes; a good idea; he would explain the Nex.

Maybe.

CHAPTER 10

FLIGHT

Carter hit the snow with Kade screaming in his brain. Kade's words were so anger-filled as to be unfathomable; Kade's hatred was a tangible thing and as his energy fled him so a cold detachment took his soul in its fist and gave him a nasty squeeze . . .

'*Fight*,' howled Kade in his brain.

'*Fuck you, Carter, don't let me die like this! Fight!*'

But Carter could not; for the briefest of seconds, he could not; it was as if all the worst moments of his life had been distilled, a potent liquor of horror with the power to drop him instantly. Without knowing it, he changed mags by sense of touch in his pocket as the footsteps came close and his brain seized and the footsteps suddenly increased in pace and—

'*Roll!*' screamed Kade.

Carter rolled, the Browning out and in his hand and pumping bullets up into the night sky—

A kick sent the weapon spinning into the darkness.

'*Let me*,' came the soothing voice of Kade.

'Fuck you,' snarled Carter.

An engine started – the BMW. The Nex's head snapped left – a sudden-impact movement, so fast that Carter's eyes could not follow. He leaped, clumsily, arms encircling the attacker, and they both hit the ground. Carter slammed both arms down, the heels of his hands smashing into the Nex's head. One blow, two, three, four, five. He felt something break within the mask—

The BMW, pluming smoke, accelerated away from the scene.

Carter staggered up.

The assassin's foot lashed up into Carter's groin and he stumbled back; the scene flashed red, there was a screech of brakes, tyres crunching snow, brakelights illuminating the snow in a soft red glow. Exhaust fumes jettisoned like dragon smoke.

Carter looked up into the Nex's face—

Grey-clad. Unreadable—

But the eyes. The eyes were copper, glowing in the BMW's red lights.

The figure lifted its arms above its head, as if in some martial-art preparatory stance. Carter scrambled up and the figure's stare fixed on him, eyes boring through him, and he grinned, bloodstained teeth bared through thick strings of saliva. 'You fucking surprised, motherfucker?' he snarled.

'We have danced for long enough,' came the soft voice.

From hidden arm-sheaths the assassin drew two short black blades and lowered his head. Carter pulled his own darkened blade from his boot and spat blood into the snow.

'But I like the dance,' said Carter. 'It's just getting interesting. And you want to fight with knives . . . I will cut you so fine, my boy . . .'

The BMW revved, plumes spitting. Carter could see Natasha looking back over the seat; the white reverse lights came on and Carter understood . . .

The Nex charged—

They clashed, blades flashing—

Carter came away with blood weeping down his bicep. He felt the pulse of freed muscle within sliced skin and the smile fell from his lips. They circled and Carter edged the Nex closer—

Carter charged – as Natasha floored the BMW's accelerator and the engine screamed high and loud. The assassin slashed left and right, then turned – Carter dived left.

The high boot of the BMW hammered into the assassin; the body was plucked from the air and tossed away in a tangle of limbs to collide with the wall of the house. The knives fell dark and bloody to the snow. The Nex collapsed in a tightly curled broken heap.

Carter – breathing hard – looked slowly to the left at the tyre merely two inches from his nose. He dragged himself to his feet and glared at Natasha through the smashed window.

'You trying to kill me?'

'Get in,' she hissed, pain lancing lines across her face.

'I want my gun. And I want to check our friend there—'

'Get *in*!' screamed Natasha.

Carter turned, and his jaw dropped. The Nex had rolled to his – or her – feet. Those copper eyes met Carter's gaze and he caught a glimpse of black; the Nex sprinted forward, a blur of motion powering across the snow . . . Carter dived, scooping up the battered Browning, then dragged open the door and sprawled full length across the back seat of the BMW as Natasha hit the accelerator. Spitting snow, the car screamed down the track, sliding left and right, bouncing from a fence and then shooting off down the darkened lane with lights suddenly extinguished—

Carter stared out of the back window.

The Nex was close, copper eyes burning into his own. A gloved hand reached out, brushed the boot and Carter swallowed, hard, as the BMW's engine screamed and Natasha's foot floored the accelerator pedal with a harsh stab . . .

The Nex slowed, then halted and stood, arms limp by its sides, copper eyes watching them flee. The would-be assassin was not panting, nor showing any signs of exertion.

'I don't fucking believe that,' said Carter.

'Are you hurt?'

'I'm hurting all right,' he said. 'How about you?'

'I'm bleeding. I think I might . . .'

The car swerved. Carter clambered into the front seat, and helped Natasha guide the car to the side of the road. They swapped positions, and Natasha held a sterile dressing pad to her reopened shoulder wound as Carter, hands slippery with his own blood, gunned the 4-litre vehicle's engine and they sped off into the darkness.

Carter drove at high speed, and after thirty minutes left the snowbound highways behind, tyres gripping tarmac once more, the BMW purring in its natural environment. He found a small side road, and drove into the darkness. Finding a secluded copse beyond a fence and a heavy galvanised gate, he jumped out, leaving the engine running. He unlatched the cold metal, then stared around at the silent dark woods, eerie and watching. The silence made him shiver, and the darkness was so complete that it

176

formed an infinite horizontal void; Carter hurried back to the light and warmth of his mobile sanctuary. He eased the BMW over woodland debris and killed the engine, then the headlights.

'Let's take a look at you.'

Carter helped Natasha onto the back seat and checked the reopened gunshot wound. It had clotted, the bleeding nothing more than a trickle now. Natasha's face was grey with pain.

'I'm sorry, I have no painkillers,' said Carter, brushing a strand of hair from the woman's brow.

'That's OK,' she said, smiling. She coughed, and winced. Carter ran his hand through her hair, then eased his own jacket free with difficulty, his broken finger stabbing anger at his every movement, his ribs grinding and biting him inside, clicking within the cavity of his chest. He checked the knife wound across his bicep; this too had clotted and had almost ceased bleeding. He eased the flesh open – could see a muscle part within. Blood started to seep once more and, ripping a strip from his thick woollen shirt, he tied a makeshift bandage around the wound. Blood soaked it immediately.

'That needs attention,' said Natasha.

'I don't dare risk the hospitals. *They* could be watching.'

'You think so?'

'I know so. Come on, we'll stop at a motorway service station; pick up some provisions. How much cash have you got on you?'

'None. What about plastic?'

'No good. It leaves a trail. I've only got a couple of hundred – it will have to be enough.'

'Why don't we leave a false trail?' said Natasha. 'Draw a shitload of cash out of a machine – let them tag us, tag our location – and then switch directions?'

Carter considered this, scratching at his stubble. They would need money, wherever they were going. He nodded, smiling, and, bending down, kissed Natasha on the cheek.

'Thanks for saving my life,' he said. 'Now we're even.'

Natasha's arm came up and pulled his head down to her. They kissed again, tongues dancing, and for a couple of seconds the world spiralled down into nothing more than this intimate moment.

Carter pulled away, his gaze locked to hers.

'Come on. We have to get moving.'

'Can't we rest here? For the night?'

'No. We have to put some serious distance between that meat fucker and us. You understand?'

'Yeah. Can I sleep?'

'With my blessing,' said Carter, smiling. He kissed her again, passed her his coat and then climbed into the front seat. He started the huge engine and turned the heater up. He checked the fuel gauge, then reversed slowly from the copse, tyres crunching twigs, and out onto the lane.

'Where are we going?' said Natasha sleepily, snuggling under coats against the raping wind, which violated the cabin through the recently smashed windows.

'I'll tell you when we get there.'

'Do we have to fly?'

'Yes.'

'I thought you hated flying?'

'I do.'

'Oh.' Natasha snuggled against the rolled-up jacket and closed her eyes. Carter angled the rear-view mirror and watched her sleep as he drove through the darkness; the cool air from the smashed windows made him shiver occasionally as mile after mile of catseyes and the occasional midnight traveller sped by in a blur.

The horn beeped.

Carter blinked. Looked up, over the BMW's steering wheel. Heavy rain pounded the bonnet and roof, spitting through the smashed side windows. The windscreen was awash. Thunder boomed in the dark night sky; he readjusted his mirror and saw the headlights glowing behind him like yellow eyes. The horn blared again.

'OK, OK,' hissed Carter. He flicked on the wipers, eased up on the clutch and took the BMW around the roundabout and off towards the south – towards the Lake District and Lancaster beyond. Glasgow was now a ghost in the night behind him . . .

He drove on bitterly through the rain.

It was an hour after dawn when Carter pulled the BMW into the lay-by. An hour earlier had seen him buying supplies in a service station – everything from crisps and Coke through to travel medical kits containing needles, sterile dressings and emergency airways, T-shirts that weren't stained in blood and some mysterious items which he kept locked away in plastic bags. Now, both bandaged, scrubbed in the service-station toilets, and clad in garish coloured T-shirts, they looked at one another and Natasha ran a hand through her hair. She'd just taken some Ibuprofen – the maximum dose – but was obviously still in quite some pain . . .

'What now?'

'We steal a plane.'

'Steal a . . . you *are* joking?'

'Not at all,' said Carter grimly. 'We can't risk requesting air transport from Spiral, and over the wire, on the other

179

side of these trees, is an MoD airbase. A *special* airbase where they keep some of Spiral's aircraft and other vehicles.'

'Carter,' said Natasha slowly, 'there will be armed guards. Dogs. We've only got one gun between us.'

'One gun is enough. I find in these situations that one gun tends to breed more guns.'

'And you think you can fly a . . . well, whatever it is you want to steal?'

'Of course. It's been a few years, I haven't flown since Egypt. But they're all the fucking same. Joystick. Rudder. Flaps. Landing gear. Hey, come on, liven up – it's not as if we've been betrayed by everything we have come to know and trust and believe in. Why the grim smile?'

'You're mad,' said Natasha slowly. 'And tell me you don't still plan to visit Gol.'

'Yeah, I'm sorry, Nats – but I do. Gol can help us.'

'He will shoot us. Well, you,' she corrected.

'Don't overestimate him. The big oaf had a heart of gold . . .'

'Yes,' said Natasha slowly. 'But remember? Remember when you fucking *shot him* . . . you can't possibly have forgotten?'

Carter shrugged. 'It was for the best – he'll under-stand,' came the simple reply. 'He's still alive, isn't he?'

Natasha tutted. 'Man, have you got a death wish?' She sighed, and rubbed at her tired pain-filled eyes. 'Where will we find the Big Man? Do you know if he's still play-ing games on the African continent?'

'I cannot divulge this information,' said Carter with a lop-sided grin.

'You *are* mad,' Natasha repeated with feeling.

'Of course. That's why I work for Spiral.' He coughed. 'Used to work, I mean. You think they'll accept my formal resignation?'

180

'You don't know that, Carter. You don't know who sent the Nex.'

'You said they were Spiral's best-kept secret? Well, put two and two together.'

'Yeah, they sometimes make seven. If you've still got your ECube we can try and contact—'

'Oh no.' Carter's words were soft. 'No contact. We do it my way; if it *is* Spiral, and the fuckers *are* tracking us, then the ECube will light us up worse than any flare on a winter night.'

'But if they aren't the ones – well, they could help,' said Natasha simply.

'I don't need any fucking help,' said Carter, his humour gone. 'I do it on my own. I always have.'

Natasha shook her head slowly, and ran a hand through her short black hair. 'When are we – ah, I mean *you* – going to accelerate into this mad scheme of theft from the British government?'

'Theft. Ha.' He smiled wryly. 'Am I hearing you right, Nats? I am no thief . . . I am part of the huge machine that is Spiral, and Spiral not only have part-ownership in the MoD but own this very airfield and the equipment therein. Because I belong to Spiral, and they to me, I am merely *taking* what is already rightfully *mine*. You get it?'

'I don't think the armed guards will see it that way.'

'Well, I haven't got the time to sign in fucking triplicate.' Carter pulled the battered Browning from his pocket. He stared lovingly at the dull black surface. 'I am sure I will be able to persuade them with Sergeant 9mm here.' He smiled without humour.

Night fell. With it came more rain.

Carter slammed the BMW's door shut. The hunters would find the vehicle soon enough, he was sure – but then, hopefully, the couple would be far away from this place. Far away from the promise of bullets and pain.

Carter supported Natasha as they crept through the damp woodland. Before long they came to a heavy-duty fence topped by the customary barbed wire. 'This is where we climb,' said Carter softly. 'But don't worry – this is a pretty unimportant base and subsequently the 'high' security is shit. Unless the fucker has been compromised.'

Natasha stared hard at him. 'Compromised?'

Carter nodded. 'Somebody seems to be trying hard to bring Spiral down. There are links. Spiral keeps aircraft here at this base. It's a long shot, but hey, so was that fucking Nex almost killing me back at my home . . .' He shrugged, moved forward, and scaled the rattling fence. Using pocket cutters he snipped through the coils of barbed wire. Then he reached down, hauling a grimacing, groaning Natasha up behind him and they climbed warily over and dropped to the grass, panting, sweat stinging their eyes.

The base squatted mostly in darkness. A few dark buildings, with weak lonely yellow lights, sat over to one side of the compound. Several airstrips criss-crossed the gloom, and beside several more outbuildings sat a collection of damp and darkly glistening aircraft.

'Can you see the markings?' said Carter.

Natasha shook her head.

'My eyesight is getting bad with old age, I fear,' he said. 'Come on.'

They made their way slowly across the grass, and Carter halted. He pointed, to where a low shed obviously housed chained dogs. Making a huge detour, they circled the base and finally scurried through the rain to crouch under the limited shelter of a galvanised roof overhang. Water poured around them from inefficient guttering, splattering and clashing. Carter pointed through the gloom. 'You see her?'

'What is it?'

'A Cessna T206H Turbo5. Fully fuelled and with good range. Fast. We can sling her under radar, keep her low over the hills; she's got excellent navigational equipment but isn't military, and so won't arouse too much suspicion.'

'Are we going far?'

'Far enough,' said Carter. 'You wait here, I'll check her out.' He moved away from Natasha, and was soon a ghost in the rain. His senses sang, and he felt incredibly awake: energy washed through him and no longer did the pain from his strapped finger, his broken ribs, his broken nose, his sliced bicep – no longer did it push him into the borders of angry red teeth-grinding acceptance. Now it flowed away and left him feeling . . . alive.

He halted beside the Cessna, alert, focused, the Browning in his hand and glistening dark in the rain. Just behind the wing he reached up, found the handle and twisted. The door hissed outwards, exposing the dark interior.

Carter reached up and pulled down the steps, which clacked against the tarmac. Then he sprinted as best he could with broken ribs and gestured for Natasha to follow him, aware that his back presented a broad target to the darkness . . . and to any hiding snipers . . .

Natasha crept forward through the rain, hair plastered to her scalp, and soon they were both climbing the steps and into the dry interior of the cramped single-engine plane.

'Where we going, Carter?'

'Africa.'

'Africa! You are joking . . . so I was right . . .'

Carter looked her in the eye. 'Joking? Well, you want to hang around here? Try and reason with that Nex fucker?'

Natasha shook her head and, wiping water from her face, followed Carter to the cockpit.

'Then we'll do it my way. Belt yourself in over there.'

'You sure you know how to fly one of these?'

'As easy as slotting a Nex.' He smiled bitterly.

The silver Mercedes flashed through the night, tyres hissing, squealing across wet tarmac, groaning under pressure as the vehicle hit speeds of over a hundred and fifty m.p.h. The rain smashed down from the tumultuous heavens, and the Mercedes finally pulled to a halt beside a BMW: battered and bruised, victim of a recent hard-core automobile fucking.

Boots splashed down in a puddle. The door slammed shut.

The tight grey garment turned black swiftly under the dark rain. Copper eyes stared through the downpour, through the fence and across the apparently deserted airfield. A Cessna taxied along the airstrip and, engine growling, shot up into the sky and disappeared, tail light blinking like the tiny red eye of a retreating monster. Almost immediately, alarms squealed shrilly through the rain, a tortured sound, like an animal in pain. Red lights danced across black tarmac, flashing, spiralling.

The copper eyes stared into the darkness, glinting with reflected flashing red lights for a long while after the Cessna had droned out of view. They stared, unblinking, unmoving. Then as dogs barked and the harsh sounds of military voices spread out through the rain, the figure moved, fluidly, swiftly, climbed back into the Merc and picked up the comm.

'He's gone,' came the soft, asexual voice.

'Do we know where?'

'Of course. We know everything.'

'Drive down to 180.770.775.'

'180.770.775. Is he keeping below radar?'

'Confirmed. Out.'

The engine started, tyres hissed, the silver Mercedes disappeared into the darkness with only the barking of dogs following the plumes of exhaust that dispersed into the dark and the rain – and nothing remained to provide evidence of the car's recent passing.

Spiral_Memo4
Transcript of recent news incident
CodeRed_Z;
unorthodox incident scan 554781

Extract from local newspaper, Nanchang, China:

'Several major cities in China were today left in chaos when every automated cash point affiliated to major banks in Shanghai, the newly rebuilt Qingdao, Zhengzhou, Nanchang and Kunming disgorged their entire monetary contents onto the pavements at surprised pedestrians' feet. Panic ensued, and soon scuffles and mild rioting took place as the machines continued to pump out notes like bullets from a machine gun. Riot police were deployed to disperse the crowds, and a spokesperson for the Chinese National Bank, Chow Lien stated, "This was not just the work of a simple bug in software. We are investigating claims of a malicious employee with in-depth computing experience. Our automated machines are well protected with both software and other more traditional methods; to see something like this happen was a travesty. We have top people working on the problem even as we speak."'

No official explanation has been given by the Chinese Government or by the Office for Economics & Industry.

CHAPTER 11

GOL

Jam stood at the top of the hill, his mouth a grim line. Behind stood Nicky, and Slater, both shocked into silence. Before them the road dropped towards – a bomb site. The *crater* where Spiral_H had burrowed under the ground before its savage chemical fucking.

'I don't believe it,' said Jam softly. He reached into his pocket, pulled free a cigarette and lit up. Smoke plumed around his face, swirling in the cold air. He took a deep and heavy draw.

'Those cunts,' said Slater, his face an animal snarl, saliva glistening on his teeth.

'Yeah,' drawled Jam. 'But which cunts, exactly?'

They moved slowly down the hill, boots thumping, crunching on glass; the bustle of activity following the immediate blast had subsided; no longer did rescue vehicles line the destruction zone, hundreds of people picking through the rubble, machines lifting blasted concrete slabs and massive H sections of steel. Most of the debris had already been cleared from around the hole; all of the bodies had been recovered.

'We could have been in that,' said Nicky, her face pale, her stomach churning. 'That was *our* HQ. We could have been inside; we could have died with all the others.'

Jam merely nodded. All strength had flooded from him. All fight had gone.

Tapes had been set up surrounding the crime scene. The group stopped at this false barrier and were eyed suspiciously by several police officers who moved towards them backed up by the heavy military presence of about fifty Justice Troop squads with heavy machine guns.

'Can we help you?'

'No . . . no. Did many people escape?' asked Nicky softly.

'Not a single one,' said the PC gently. His smile was filled with kindness; his eyes glittered with horror stories and pain. He obviously had his own nightmares to contend with.

As the policemen moved away, Jam, Slater and Nicky just stood, dumbstruck, bitterness filling them with vinegar acid; their gaze roved over the mound of remaining rubble, the blackened scarred pavement with its twisted buckled flagstones and melted tarmac. By the edges of the crater stood the relics of life and work: a charred settee here, half a desk there. A battered and flame-eaten filing cabinet. The burned remains of a rubber plant. Business detritus now witness to the most terrible of man-made catastrophes: the bomb.

'We need to catch these fuckers,' said Slater softly.

'Yes,' breathed Nicky.

'We need to make them pay.'

'But that's the problem,' snapped Jam, turning, his stare angry. 'How many people died here? Three, four hundred? Fucking pay for that? You can't; even if you

188

catch the people responsible, the leaders, or the monkeys planting the devices – you can't make them pay for such a loss of life.'

'Ironic, ain't it?' said Nicky bitterly.

'What is?'

'Spiral – experts in demolition and destruction; their own HQ wiped out in true Spiral style. Could have been done by our own people.'

'We don't take life with bombs,' said Jam sourly. 'Ours have always been surgical strikes against terrorist and military targets.'

'Boys and their toys,' sneered Nicky. There were tears on her cheeks. 'Things always go wrong; people always die. It's just the way of the fucking world. But this . . . this . . .' she gestured.

'This,' said Jam, 'this was done to destroy office and investigative personnel. It was to wipe out the fucking mainframes, that's why Spiral_H was targeted.'

'I have an idea,' said Slater.

'Oh yeah?'

'We need to see The Priest. He will have the answers, and he is the only man I would trust right now.'

This statement was met with a moment of stunned silence.

'He's fucking insane,' said Jam, staring into Slater's weary horror-shadowed eyes. The huge man shrugged, turning back to look at the remains of the devastation.

'He is head of the *secret police*. So fucked-up as to be incorruptible.'

'That's if he's still alive,' said Nicky.

'He'll be alive,' said Slater. 'It'd take more than a few assassins to murder The Priest. After all,' he smiled sombrely, 'God is on his side.'

They turned away from the rubble, the stones and

glass glinting in weak sunlight. They walked, rubble crunching underfoot, back up the hill, away from shattered dreams, detonated lives, smashed worlds. The van was waiting; they drove away in silence.

The moor road was cold, winding, and awesomely dark. The van hissed its way through the rain, headlights carving slices of yellow from the absolute black. Jam, Slater and Nicky all huddled together on the vehicle's wide front bench more out of dismay at this hostile environment than from any real need to share heat.

'You sure it's up here?' said Nicky miserably.

'Aye,' said Jam. 'I've been once before. Ain't that right, Slater?' Slater grunted in his sleep and Jam punched him; Slater's snoring altered pitch but he did not wake up. 'You fucking heap of lard.'

Jam guided the van with care; past hordes of huddled sheep, through vast puddles where water had gathered at inadequate drainage channels, and still the rain pounded down and Jam began to wonder if agreeing to this meeting had been the best decision he had ever made.

The van screeched to a halt.

Rain danced in the beams of the headlights.

Nicky stared at the map. 'Should be just up here. On the left.'

'I'm remembering it well,' said Jam sombrely.

He crunched the van into first, and they moved forward; Nicky was right, they found the rutted mud-trail and Jam turned the van onto this slippery ascent. There was a grinding sound as wheels spun, then a modicum of grip was established by tyre rubber and the van lurched forward.

They bounced and wheelspun up the narrow trail, the

van rocking. To either side were steep banks of earth and heather; it made the trio – or the two parts of the trio who were at least awake – feel incredibly confined.

'I can't understand how he can fucking sleep,' said Jam bitterly.

'It must be a talent,' agreed Nicky.

'I mean, you wave a gun near his nose and he's awake faster than a male virgin's first ejaculation. But put him in a non-threatening situation, a mountain could fall on the lumbering bastard and he'd happily snore through the incident.'

'You've got to admit, you're fond of him though.' Nicky grinned, stroking the sleeping man's cheek. 'He's big and dumb, but he has a heart of gold and would die for you.'

'I'm fond of him like I was fond of a particularly bad case of VD. Like Slater, the VD itched a lot – a constant annoyance, and so I was permanently fucking reminded it was there. Like Slater, the VD induced fond memories of distant pleasure – but in the grim reality of grey dawn-light I found the real world a much more grim and painful place. And finally, just like the VD, Slater is a constant pain in the cock.'

'You have such a way with words, Jam. You make me so horny.'

Jam grinned. 'I know, love, I know. Keep calm.'

The steeply ascending lane ended on a ridge and as they bumped over twin ruts a huge quarry opened up ahead of them, gleaming ghostlike in the moonlight that broke through the scattered black clouds. The headlights carved sections from this disused place, this abandoned surface mine: rearing jagged slopes and pyramid piles of debris and rock were everywhere. Jam paused for a moment, gaining his bearings, then they moved away down

191

a wide stone-floored corridor between two dynamite-blasted walls. They passed huge stacks of rock, some neatly square, some shaped randomly from the blasts that had freed them from their thrall. They passed tracks that had been adapted by motor-cross riders in search of excitement, and they came upon a huge, stagnant black pool that filled a rock basin, a lagoon of ancient oil and mud, a dumping ground from the days when the quarry had been operational.

'Here we are.' Jam stopped the van at the side of the murky black lagoon. It gave off a dead stink and, glancing out, Nicky could see a couple of sheep corpses bogged down in the mire. She shivered; what a fucking way to die, she thought.

The rain had lessened and Jam stepped from the van, a pistol in his gloved hand. He stared around, then saw lights and a car creeping towards him. In the van, Slater had slotted a magazine into an SMG and she held the muzzle low, unseen; heavy-artillery back-up.

The car halted, its tyres crunching. It was a huge and battered old Volvo.

'We cool?' shouted Jam.

The Priest climbed ponderously from the vehicle.

'Oh yes, my son,' he said. He looked left and right, and, carrying a Bible in his left hand, walked slowly towards Jam, boots stomping on the hard quarry ground.

'I hate this place,' said Jam miserably. The rain was soaking him; his hair was lank, rat-tails, his face a sheen of water.

'God's weather is to be tolerated, for He is the judge of what needs to grow, what needs to be sown, and what needs to be reaped. He is the Gardener, Jam. He is the Gardener. *Then will I sprinkle clean water upon you, and ye shall be clean: from all your filthiness, and from all your idols, will I cleanse you; a new heart also will I give you, and a new spirit will I put within you.'* The Priest beamed, brown eyes shining.

Jam frowned.

'Yeah. Right, mate. Listen, I assume you got the ECube transcript?'

'I did. The infidels have been busy. They seek to overthrow us.'

'I thought – *think* – that I can trust you, because I know you are one of the main Tactical Officers – one of the main men, the Spiral secret police. Internal affairs, yeah?'

'By your trust, I assume you mean the HK trained on me from the van, by that huge ham-fisted oaf Slater?'

Jam shrugged, grinning. 'Hey, you know how it is.'

'Indeed I do,' said The Priest calmly. 'What is it you seek to do?'

'Things have gone from bad to worse; we've just come from London.'

'The HQ?'

'Yes,' said Jam sombrely.

'We must pray for their souls,' said The Priest, great sadness in his melancholy voice, his huge eyes filled with tears. 'And yet, before prayer, I cannot help but feel that this crime must not go unpunished.'

'We need your help,' said Jam softly. 'You have higher clearances than we have; and, let's be honest, you probably know more about what is going on than we do . . .'

The Priest's eyes glittered. 'Shall we say, there have been . . . *complications*. What is it you have in mind?'

'Find out who the fuck is responsible – gather together all the remaining DemolSquads and fuck the bad guys severely from behind. Shit on them from a very great height.'

'First you need the Source; then you need the Target.'

'That's why I'm here,' said Jam. 'There's nobody else we can trust – and believe me, it was hard deciding even to contact *you*.'

The Priest stood, rain dripping from his huge dark bulk. He thought, long and hard, brow furrowed; finally, as if coming awake from a trance, he smiled down at Jam, then reached out and patted him gently on the shoulder. 'I have had guidance.'

'You have?' Jam looked up, nervously, at the heavens.

The Priest nodded. He placed his hands together, as if in prayer. His huge shaggy brows bunched together as his forehead wrinkled in concentration. 'The Lord will lead us, Jam; the Lord will protect us; and the Lord will guide us.'

'You sure?'

'Yes. The Lord has already placed important information in my possession from a variety of sources; already I am acting upon this information. But I need to make a journey, and I will need help – I was going to call for some back-up but . . . you are here now, my friend. Sent, I think, by the Almighty.'

'What kind of journey?' Jam's voice was suspicious.

'As Tactical Officers, we keep tabs on a variety of people and places around the world; monitor them, shall we say. There has been recent increased activity at a variety of locations and I sent TacSquads to investigate – just before the explosion at the London HQ. I was on my way for one such reconnoitre when I received your garbled transmission.'

'So now we can go with you?'

'Your help would be much appreciated, Brother. This increased activity links conveniently with the troubles in London, and in Spiral as a whole. I have high hopes of there being a very strong connection.'

194

Jam nodded.

The Priest chuckled. 'We will have to meet at Sambray Airfield – first I have a few jobs to take care of.'

'OK. Just name the time.'

'Twelve hours.'

'We'll be there,' said Jam softly.

The engine droned like a bee gathering honey. Natasha woke up, yawned, and watched the sun dancing across the tops of the cotton-wool clouds. She rubbed at her eyes, and enjoyed the view for a few moments; far far below, the sandy landscape, marked with the odd ravine or range of hills and dotted with scattered bushes and trees, reminded her of better days – happier days before the world became such a war-torn fucked-up place . . .

She shifted. Winced as stitches pulled tight.

She glanced across at Carter. 'You OK?'

'Sure am, flower.'

'Where are we?'

'Greece. You see the island down there?'

'Hmm?'

'Zante. I had a good holiday there, once. Our apartment became infested by ants and we had to lead a trail of sugar to our noisy Glaswegian neighbours – ha, soon shut them up – but overall it was a good gig. How are you feeling?'

'Sore.'

'You hungry?'

'Yeah. Can I check your bags now?'

'Sure. The green one is full of food and I apologise in advance for the poor calorific content. I swear, somebody should sue those fucking service stations.'

Natasha rummaged. Found food – or a close approximation thereof. She ate, and fed small tit-bits to Carter who guzzled greedily with hands clamped on the Cessna's controls.

'Why don't you have a break? Eat? Drink?'

'Are you going to fly?'

'Hmmm . . .'

'Well, perhaps not, then. We'll be landing at Cairo to refuel—'

'I thought you were a wanted man in Egypt? Wanted by men with machine guns who want you very, very dead?'

'I am. When I say Cairo, I don't exactly mean Cairo – I kind of mean a secret rendezvous seventy miles out of the city.'

'So there'll be no time for sunbathing or seeing the pyramids at Giza?'

'Not this time, love. I'm sorry. Anyway, the bombing during the Battle of Cairo7 put an end to *that* Wonder of the World. The pyramids are just rubble now.'

'I'd still like to see what's left. It's *historical* rubble, after all.'

They were over the sea now, and the sun glittered across waves and tiny crests of foam. Natasha watched Carter carefully; she could see his fear but he hid it well. He hated flying. She had read it on his file, and seen his nervous sweat first-hand. As he always said, it wasn't the height that bothered him, it was the heavy impact with the unforgiving ground . . .

Hours had passed.

The 'rendezvous', much to Natasha's horror, was a narrow desert strip marked in the sand between two huge rocky outcroppings. Carter brought the Cessna down in a swirl of dust and had a heated conversation with four men in Arab dress who had honking muzzled camels with many tufts tethered to a nearby twisted palm. Natasha

196

watched the tense discussion from the Cessna's cockpit, decidedly on edge and alert for signs of trouble—

She needn't have worried. Carter, all smiles, winked in her direction and she watched the men lead him away to throw back tarpaulins concealing drums of what Natasha assumed was aviation fuel. She did not understand how Carter had made his contacts, nor how he had arranged this little meeting; she decided it was probably best not to ask.

Two hours later, when Carter climbed sweating and sand-flecked into the cockpit, Natasha had been sleeping again. She smiled wearily at the man. 'We full up?'

'It will see us to Mombassa at least. I curse having to deal with dodgy Egyptians. And I curse even more the fact that a Cessna will only fly twelve hundred pissing miles without completely emptying her bladder . . . the cheap whore . . .'

They flew into the sun.

Natasha decided it was quite romantic—

Or it would have been if she hadn't recently been shot and hadn't been running for her very life. What happened? she thought. What happened to my world? It had been going so smoothly—

So smoothly.

Gol sat in the sand, gazing down at the grains that swept scattering across one another, fighting for precedence, fighting for height, fighting to be king. He lifted his head slowly, beard whipping gently in the breeze, and gazed out across the vast landscape before him – a medley of browns and burned orange. The amber light flowed majestically across the landscape like molten honey, breaking across the rocky formations, moulding itself around the trees. Huge protrusions of rock smashed up from the earth and Gol felt the violence of the land within his soul.

The rugged red rock squatted hard beneath the large man, comforting, solid, real, without any give. Gol sat on the mountain and the mountain was his, was a part of him, belonged to him – and he belonged to it; a symbiotic relationship that made Gol smile through his beard. His hand reached down, touched the jagged rock and the sand and the dirt. He sighed.

The sun was sinking, glinting a deep burned red in his dark eyes.

He rose slowly to his feet, pulling himself to his full height and stretching the heavy muscles of his back and shoulders. Moving out from his beautiful vantage point, from his Window of Wonders, he was soon walking through the dust, boots leaving imprints between the scrub bushes. The trail was narrow, winding between large groups of boulders and leading uphill towards the summit of the low mountains that hid the sparkling dance of the sun's sinking rays. Gol walked on, sweating heavily, his grey hair plastered to his heavy-set thick skull, his large and apparently cumbersome rifle slung tightly across his back.

As he pushed on, the ECube pressed against his thigh through the pocket of his beige desert DPM combats. He hated the feel of the device. It had been hacked of course, by his programmers – just because they *could*. A small act of individualism. An act of pride. The ECube had been pulled to bits and reassembled minus certain circuitry and AI core components. Gol kept the small machine close to him at all times; it reminded him of older, better days.

The ECube dug against his leg and he halted for a moment, turning, hands on hips, regaining his breath.

The African scrubland spread out before him, the most awesome of panoramic views he had ever witnessed in his years of travelling the miserable ball of rock called Earth.

Gol loved Africa; that was why he had chosen this place in which to set up and run Spiral_F.

Gol pushed on, cresting the rise and finding himself momentarily dazzled by the sun. A horseshoe of low mountain hills surrounded him, rocky and wild, trails snaking down onto the flatland and the orange-tree orchards filling the valley beyond. This vision of contrasting violent colour splashes filled his perverse mind with calm, soothed the raging beast that burned his soul, selected his neutral gear and allowed him to coast gently downhill.

It must be wrong, he realised.

The hacked ECube must be wrong—

An icicle sliver wormed into his heart.

Carter would never dare come to Africa . . . Gol laughed out loud then, his laughter echoing out over the valley. And if he *was* coming to Africa – and by the ECube codecs and encryptions, it seemed that it was a top priority to find and intercept him – if the fucker *was* coming to Africa, then the chances were that he was coming to find Gol.

'I swore I would kill you.'

Gol's voice was deep, incredibly deep and melodic – almost Shakespearean in its delivery, a rich voice, the voice of an actor, not the voice of a . . .

What are you? he thought.

What have you become?

Spiral had redeployed him. Had sent him from London to work on a special new project. Spiral_F.

He hissed between clenched teeth.

199

Gol began to walk, boots now stomping rock, leaping from ridge to ridge and then thudding onto a new track. This one led across the summit of the hill, winding like a red dried snake under the sun towards the string of concealed proximity detectors and anti-personnel mines—

Spiral . . .

They had a lot to answer for. A *fucking* lot to answer for . . .

He reached the lower end of the track. Gol glanced back, then set off, entering the cool protection of the trees. The sinking sun still burned hot as it sank quickly towards oblivion.

Gol relaxed the closer he got to his home: the HQ of Spiral_F – a simple white-walled house hiding a billion dollars' worth of technology under the ground in the form of extremely high-tech vaults, weapons systems, hangars for vehicle modification and . . .

Gol's eyes glinted.

And *something else*.

A breeze rustled the branches of the orange trees.

How the world has changed, he thought. How it has descended into a quagmire of guns and wars and violence.

He shivered.

How *I* have changed . . .

He caught a flash of white between the trees, and soon the crumbling dilapidated house came into view. Gol moved cautiously, attempting to catch out King George, a huge black man who stood on guard with his SMG safety catch switched off. The big man spotted him at a good distance and Gol grinned, waving as he approached.

'You OK, boss?' growled King George, his broad face split into a smile.

'Just sneaking up on you,' said Gol.

King George shook his head. 'That never happen, Big Boss. This king too smart; he have too good an eye; that why you buy my services, eh, boy?'

Gol grinned wider. How could somebody call *him* a *boy*? They shook hands, and Gol stepped past the huge sentry, past the man's natural aroma of oil and fruit and into the cool shade of the red-tiled white-walled villa beyond.

Such a nondescript mask, he thought.

A true disguise, hiding technology the world could not even begin to comprehend.

His boots clacked against the polished wooden floor – cracked and warped in places after the dry passing of years. He jogged up a few battered steps and turned right, moving down a wide corridor with its peeling paintwork and past personal artefacts that were there more for show than for any real personal value or nostalgia; Gol was the sort of man who did not harvest history. He carried love and pain in his mind and in his heart.

He stopped by a section of battered wood panelling, peeling and warped. He flipped free a small door and punched digits into an alloy panel that contrasted severely with the dilapidated surroundings. The panelling slid away and Gol descended – down through the rough-hewn narrow rock, circling down and down the tightly curved iron stairwell towards a low-roofed dusty passageway and on towards—

The Vault.

Welcome back to Heaven, Gol thought.

It was evening when Carter flew the Cessna across the shimmering ocean east of Kenya. Sunlight glittered, accelerating over the horizon. Natasha was sitting with her head on Carter's shoulder when a tiny rumble vibrated through the plane's cockpit.

Natasha stirred. She turned, her gaze meeting Carter's. 'What was that?'

The rumble came again, followed by a stutter from the engines as Carter leaned forward, eyes scanning the digital read-outs.

'Tell me we don't have a problem.'

'We have a problem,' said Carter through gritted teeth. 'Fuel pumps. Shit.'

The engine stuttered once more, and Natasha's grip tightened on Carter as fear flashed bright in her eyes. Breathing deeply, he turned the Cessna south. 'We'll have to land.'

Carter knew Africa – especially Kenya – extremely well; he had carried out a variety of overt and covert missions across its rugged dusty ravaged landscape. He hugged the coast ten miles south of Mombassa, and chose a spot where he had previous agreements with a certain landowner of disreputable disposition.

Carter brought the Cessna in low over the sea. Turquoise waves sparkled. White foam danced in huge curving crests. They cleared a long line of beach-hugging palms and a wide sweep of unspoilt white sand. The Cessna approached a wide long lawn within an arena of high walls and touched down smoothly, then bumped along the short grass towards high fences and a dazzling white-walled house. Natasha gazed up at the structure as they rolled to a halt, bushes and trees whipping to either side, the drone of the engines an irritant chirping in this sudden paradise. The house was large, built from wood and stone, the lofty roof supported by huge beams lashed together with thick ropes skilfully woven from huge leaves and dried grass.

Several men ran towards the plane. They carried guns.

'A welcoming party?' asked Natasha.

Carter smiled. 'They know me here. Don't worry.' He killed the engines, which died swiftly, the propellers humming and clattering unevenly to a halt. Carter helped Natasha from the cockpit, down the short steps, and onto the grass—

Where they were hit by the heat.

'Warm,' breathed Natasha huskily. 'Just what an injured woman needs to recuperate while you fix the plane.'

'We're near the equator. What do you expect?'

'Just a shock after *sunny* Scotland,' she said and smiled sardonically.

Carter greeted the men and explained his position in a garbled mishmash of English and Swahili. He and Natasha were escorted back up to the house at gunpoint by an obviously suspicious group.

As they reached the porch a man appeared, wearing a loose-fitting white shirt, which flapped in the strong east-coast breeze, shorts and Adidas trainers. The man had a look of hatred and insanity and unfathomable anger in his dark eyes, and a silenced sub-machine gun in his huge hands.

'Justus, I have a fucking problem.'

The huge man grinned then, a broad grin, breaking the spell of fear, and shouted, 'Papa Carter, you old dog! How the hell are you, Big Man? You a horny old goat who still has the bastard look of eagles about you? Come up here and give old Justus a hug.'

Their stay was short, sweet and very much to the point. One of the twin fuel pumps had worn free of its housing, the matrix-mesh innards clipping the metal base and smashing it up, reducing fuel-pumping capacity. A new pump was needed. Justus said he would do what he could.

With limited medical facilities Carter restitched a couple of Natasha's wounds, applied fresh sterile dressings and gave himself an injection of antibiotics. He strapped up his broken finger and they showered quickly to remove the stench of travel and battle, sweat and blood.

When ready, they waited on the porch of Justus's huge white-walled house as night fell. An engine broke the silence; a huge Toyota Land Cruiser rumbled into view, a little battered and sand-scarred, the bright headlights carving a huge slice from the night pie. The vehicle squeaked to a halt on heavy springs, and Justus leaped out. The large black man, bald and grinning widely, slapped Carter on the back, making him groan in agony.

'For you, and Mama Natasha,' he boomed.

'Mama Natasha?' Nats's hands went to her hips, her stance on the porch changing subtly from submissive to aggressive with barely a change of muscle tone.

'It is a mark of respect,' rumbled Justus, a frown creasing his huge black brow.

'That,' said Carter dryly, 'doesn't look like a Cessna fuel pump to me.'

Justus shrugged. 'I do what I can. This is all I can do; your part take maybe three days to arrive. This is Africa, Carter, not London or New York.'

Carter sighed. 'All I fucking need. A cross-country fucking trek.'

'You look after my baby, Carter. You bring her back to her Papa; she cost me many shillings, understand?'

'Don't worry,' grinned Carter bitterly. 'And anyway, you've got a Cessna out of the deal. More than a fair trade, I'd say.'

204

Justus shouted to another man, his words fast and smooth in the local Swahili dialect. The man disappeared into the white-walled house, then returned with two rucksacks.

'Supplies. For Mama Natasha.' The huge black man smiled. He ran a hand across his shaved head, where a sheen of sweat could be seen in the light from the Toyota's headlamps. 'Now you be careful out there, Carter. This is not a place for a weak-kneed English white man!'

Carter laughed, patting the man in return, his affection genuine. 'You take care, Justus. And remember: we were never here. And we didn't steal that Cessna on your lawn.'

'Justus always remember for the right price.'

They circled the Toyota – or what had once *been* a Toyota. The paint was peeling, and rust showed through. Parts of the coach-lines were dented and, worryingly, bullet holes rimed with rust peppered one flank. At the rear, a flat-back section had been devised – the rear seats had been ripped out and a huge upside-down U-bar welded into place. Mounted on this was a 106mm recoilless rifle with a small box of ammunition.

'This has seen the wars,' said Natasha softly.

'It's a Technical,' said Carter, helping Natasha into the cab of the customised Toyota. 'What do you expect?' He slung the rucksacks in the back, then climbed up himself and slammed the door, which shut with a dull *clunk* on the fourth attempt.

'A what?'

Carter turned the key. The vehicle rumbled into life, belching smoke from an impromptu welded exhaust. 'A Technical. When a man needs – shall we say – off-the-record protection from the local guardians, he pays for a vehicle and a few armed men. He reclaims this cost on his

205

balance sheet as "technical assistance" – hence Technicals.' Carter wound down the window, which groaned as if in pain. 'Hey, you pack me a compass, Justus? Sometimes this low technology just gives me a hard-on.'

'On the dash, white boy. You see? By all the gods, I hope you look after yourself. This not a tourist safari now! You not have comfy beds to fly back to!'

Carter laughed again, pushed the grinding gears, then hit the accelerator. Wheels spun on loose gravel; the huge engine roared and they shot towards the gates where two men hurriedly pulled the iron barricades open. Carter accelerated down the narrow single-track dirt road, tyres bumping and thudding, and suddenly—

Suddenly the light from the house had gone—

And a terrible, complete darkness closed in.

Natasha shivered. 'Jesus, it's dark out here.'

'No ambient light,' explained Carter. 'No street lights, no house lights . . . just landscape and wild animals. Including lots of monkeys.'

Ahead stretched a perfectly straight dusty trail, lined with huge trees, swaying palms, and screeches from the darkness. The Toyota's lights cut a slice of life from the black, but all around was the promise – the inherent threat – of oblivion . . .

'Relax,' said Carter. 'Get some sleep. I think you're going to need all your energy when we meet Gol.'

The dark trees flashed past, and the two fugitives were swallowed swiftly by the African night.

It was over an hour past dawn. The sun had risen, a bright flash slicing over the horizon. The land changed from a gentle, purple-hazed hue – surrealistic, as if witnessed through frosted glass – to a bright hot furnace of

206

sand and tangled trees. They travelled down a perfectly straight road – single-track, rough-dirt. It stretched ahead, an arrow, a slice of trail carved from the chaos of trees and jungle and scrubland that crowded the road, attempting to usurp its threadlike hold on some semblance of civilisation . . .

The tyres thudded over and into the ruts of the track.

Monkeys screeched and fought in the trees beside the trail, sometimes on the track, scattering with squeals and chatters as the Toyota roared in its aggressive approach.

Natasha moaned tenderly, fingers coming up to touch the sensitive area of her throat that had so very recently been punctured; Carter had claimed it was healing nicely, but to Natasha it still felt on fire . . . a razor sitting in her windpipe and gnawing her flesh.

The sun rose; so did the temperature. Carter wound down the windows, and fresh breeze heavy with tree scents and dust flowed into the cabin. The Toyota's aircon was totally shot and the fuel gauge reported its precious load erratically.

They passed through a village. Most of the houses were huts, built from mud bricks and a random selection of breeze-block, stone, wood and corrugated iron, which had rusted in the rains and now displayed deep orange streaks. Fires burned by the edge of the road, with groups of villagers standing around. Some worked, one old grey-haired man sharpening knives. He paused as they rumbled past, lifted his arm and waved. Natasha, smiling, waved back. A swathe of children ran after the Toyota, hands outstretched.

They left the village, heading inland over rough roads that the Toyota ate with ease.

They drove for an hour, tyres churning the red dust which flew up to coat the entire vehicle in a fine matt veil. When they stopped, to empty their bladders and to stretch their legs, they stood under the baking sun for a moment and eased their backs. The tyres of the Toyota were stained red and, glancing down, Carter saw the fine dust covering his boots – and he felt intimate with the African land, almost welcomed back . . . it covered him, possessed him, called him its own . . . he was a child again . . . The sun was high, a singular piercing eye. It was incredibly hot, almost unbearably so without the coastal breeze to cool their skin. The scrubland seemed to stretch off to infinity.

They rumbled on, stopping at an insanely ambitious outpost to fill up with diesel and buy a few supplies – mainly of the liquid nature. There was even a fridge, with a few out-of-date cans of chilled lager. Carter bought them and half fulfilled Natasha's heat-induced fantasy . . .

Another two hours saw them climbing a rise. Carter licked his lips, and slowed the vehicle to a halt on the summit of the track. Rock reared up to either side, and this seemed to be an entrance – a doorway or marker to a mammoth canyon walled by low red-rock mountains and filled with a wide sweeping splash of orange trees.

'Down there,' he said simply.

'What?'

'One of Spiral's hidden outposts . . . and Gol.'

Natasha stared. 'All I see is trees. I knew there was an outpost out here somewhere – after all, I *am* a Spiral Tactical Officer – but it's fucking well disguised!' Natasha's voice was a little strained, her gaze searching the canyon.

'Someone will come shortly. They'll have sentries. We haven't got this far untagged, I assure you. Let's just hope they don't shoot us on sight, eh, love? But then, that

208

isn't Spiral company policy, is it?' He gave Natasha a sly sideways glance. And she knew; the mistrust was still there. He wasn't sure if she was real or . . . or what? A Spiral spy?

But then, in all the years she had known him, Carter had never trusted anybody. It would have surprised her if he was to change now.

Within a minute an old US army jeep, bearing five black men wearing cut-off combats and little else, arrived. They all sported an array of gleaming weapons and Carter watched them warily, the Browning in his hand held concealed between his legs.

He smiled broadly.

'Hiya, guys. Coupla tourists, out sightseeing, you know how it is.'

'You leave here,' said a large man in a gruff voice. He jumped down from the jeep, bare feet leaving imprints in the red sand. 'This not a good place for you to be visiting.'

'But maybe I'd like to catch up on an old buddy while I'm out playing with the elephants. One happy old Mr Gol. Ring any bells?'

'Nobody here by that name,' said the big man.

Natasha leaned across Carter and saw the man grin, gleaming white teeth turning his face from an intense mask of controlled hatred to a thing of beauty, a visage of soft lines and generosity.

'Tell him that his daughter, Natasha, is here.'

The man stared. He did not blink. Then he nodded to another man, who crossed over from the jeep and climbed into the back of the Toyota. 'Drive straight through the trees. Head for the white-walled house. Try nothing funny or Benjamin here—' he patted the other man's arm '– well, his gun sing a song for him.'

The large man leaped back into the jeep. Carter

209

gunned the Toyota and rolled slowly over the lip of the ridge. Wheels bumped over a rim of jagged rock and then they were in—

Inside the canyon.

Inside Gol's lair.

The jeep followed, automatic weapons bristling, and Carter eased the Toyota down into the verdant valley, the track soon disappearing to be replaced by soft earth. People were out, mainly women, harvesting and trimming the trees, wicker baskets of fruit on the grass as they worked. Carter guided the Toyota for the full mile through the orange-tree orchards. Sometimes there would be a break in the trees allowing sunlight to stream over the vehicle – but then they were back in the shade and they welcomed the coolness, the protection of these orange trees after their journey through the scrubland. The red walls of the canyon reared to either side; threatening; enclosing; insular. Carter licked his lips nervously, and decided that he did not like this place . . .

Gol was waiting, hands on his hips, eyes staring down at the ground as if deep in thought. Carter halted the Toyota, climbed out and allowed the Browning to be taken from him. Natasha climbed down and stood, gazing up at the sun for a moment before fixing her eyes on her—

'Father?'

Gol's head jerked up. He smiled briefly, then his gaze turned to Carter and the kindly expression fell from his face.

'They call you The Butcher,' he said softly, his deep voice the rumble of the Earth's shifting plates. 'They say you killed men – women – children. Anything that stood in your way. Without remorse.'

Carter said nothing. He made no move. He merely

210

allowed his gaze to remain fixed on Gol, a silent invisible umbilical of connection – a linking that Natasha did not quite understand.

'The report said that on that day you went insane.'

'No,' said Carter softly.

'I don't understand,' whispered Gol, eyes intense.

'It was . . . messed up. And when I shot you, Gol, it was to keep you alive, not to take away your life.'

There came a long, tense pause.

'You are the legendary Dark Knight of Spiral's history.'

'That title is . . . misplaced,' said Carter gently.

'How so? How can one earn such a name without actions? How can one become so *revered* and *feared* in an organisation like Spiral without action, without destruction – without *demolition*?' The contempt in Gol's voice could not be missed.

'I saved your life,' said Carter slowly. 'I *saved* your life, Gol. I know you have always hated me – because of my links with Natasha, and because of my reputation and because of what happened in Egypt and later at Cairo7 . . . And I know you will have read all the crap printed about me in those little electronic ECube memos . . . but you really, really have it wrong. I know you will find it hard to trust me on this . . . but I swear to you that Spiral did a better job on me than they did on you . . .'

Gol was silent. He lifted his Glock 9mm and examined the barrel.

Carter calmed his fluttering heart; he relaxed his muscles and readied himself – for Gol's body language was the body language of preparation.

Carter's eyes scanned the available weaponry and he realised, realised too late that maybe he had overestimated Gol's . . . humanity – understanding – nature?

211

And it came to Carter in a flash of profound understanding. Gol was the same. The same as Carter. The same *breed* . . .

'*This is dangerous,*' said Kade.

'Not now.'

'*Let me take him. I can fucking take him.*'

'No!' he hissed inwardly.

Carter closed his eyes as pain lanced through his exhausted mind, through his head, burning bright red and glowing with white edges; he dropped slowly to his knees, panting, and Gol no longer existed and it didn't matter and nothing mattered and the surge of adrenalin was dying and he placed his head in his hands. Pain smashed like a stormy sea against the walls of his memory and his mind. A low moan growled through his lips and Natasha was there, holding Carter in her arms. She stroked his brow free of sweat, rocked with him in the dirt and looked up at Gol – at her father—

'Get him inside. In the cool. Now!'

'What is wrong with him?' came Gol's deep rumble.

'I don't know. He's exhausted . . . Help him, father. Please help him.'

Gol gestured and the large black men approached, lifting Carter easily and helping him to stumble into the house. 'I will help him now, but I cannot guarantee what will come later.'

'You cannot see it?'

'See what?' growled the huge man.

'Can't see the fucking wood for the trees. father – he is you. He is the *same* as you. You call him an assassin; a destroyer. And what the fuck were you under Spiral? What the hell were you doing in Prague, and Egypt, and later Afghanistan, in the first place? You are like brothers . . . and you are a fucking *hypocrite.*'

212

Gol stood for a moment, staring hard at Natasha. She lowered her eyes then, in fear, almost as if reverting to childhood. Distant memories taking over; reflex actions from a lost world. Gol stepped forward, took her in his arms and hugged her, kissing the top of her head. 'I have missed you, girl. Despite everything I said to you back in London . . . and the world has moved on since then, the world has changed . . . savage events have brought us together. The attempted smashing of Spiral has brought you back to me, hasn't it, my girl?'

'Yes.'

Gol lifted Natasha's head. Wiped tears from her cheeks. 'I'm sorry. Can you ever forgive me for the evil words I spoke? That was not me, Natasha. That was not me . . . and . . . I understand what you are trying to say. About Carter. I understand.'

'I forgive you,' she whispered, and hugged the huge man tight. 'I missed you, father. I have been so alone without you.'

Gol held her close as the sunlight played over the two embracing figures among the orange trees.

Spiral_Memo5
Transcript of recent news incident
CodeRed_Z;
unorthodox incident scan 455827

Between 05:00 AM and 05.25 AM (GMT), a variety of high-tech jets and attack helicopters from a range of countries including Germany, Italy, Japan, USA, Norway and Israel crashed in or around their respective countries within a few minutes of one another.

213

All jets were modern fighters, including MIG24s and newly revealed Comanche NV prototypes. All air vehicles were on practice manoeuvres and all pilots are reported dead.

Prior to crashes, no pilot reported adverse conditions, technical failures or any suspicious factors.

A spokesperson for the US military made this comment: 'The US is working closely with all other countries who have suffered recent similar tragic events. We are comparing logistical data including weather reports and are also combining retrieval efforts in order to examine black-box recordings. We hope to have answers within the next few days. Terrorist activity has not been ruled out.'>>#

CHAPTER 12

NEX

The Boeing 747 flashed through the sunlight, engines whining in deceleration. Mountains reared all around, peaks soaring skywards. The Boeing banked and came smoothly down to land amid and seemingly *within* the mountains, suspension dipping as the tyres met with the sand-blown runway, an incredible feat of skill by the pilot.

The plane taxied to a halt and the single emergency vehicle at the rough rocky edges of the runway sat watching lethargically in the heat. A huge black Land Rover rumbled across the hard-packed dust as rusting makeshift steps were laboriously hauled by two heavy-set men and attached to the large plane's exit hatchway.

The 747's singular passenger stepped out, shielding his eyes from the sunlight. He was a large man, his dark hair flecked with grey. His greying beard was neatly trimmed and combed, and he wore an expensive German suit and the finest handcrafted Italian shoes. He carried a small bag in one large hand, and descended the steps with measured care, apparently unaffected by the blast wall of heat that contrasted so dramatically with the coolness of the recently pressurised aeroplane cabin.

'Count Feuchter, welcome.' The voice was heavily accented, and Feuchter nodded at the man garbed in desert-combat gear. Feuchter seemed unconcerned that his host carried a black sub-machine gun, its matt surface dull in the sunlight.

The driver of the black Land Rover opened the door and Feuchter climbed into the cool interior. The door clicked solidly shut, shading the occupant from further harassment by the sun. The military-clad man climbed in the opposite side, and within minutes the heavy-duty off-road vehicle was purring and bumping along the primitive runway and out of the tiny desert airport carved from the mountains.

They drove in silence. At first the roads were narrow, dusty, unused. They drove for several hours, down narrow passes and around sharp bends, along roads little more than tracks and crowded by scrub bushes and wild hardy trees, and through explosive-blasted rock canyons. They reached the flatlands, the Land Rover's heavy tyres humming and bumping, and eventually came to a city. All the while Feuchter sat, perfectly composed, eyes closed, mindset calm.

They passed large tenement blocks, some crumbling and run-down, surrounded by fencing and barbed wire. Children dressed in rags scattered from their path; and then the Land Rover moved out from the suburbs, out into a stretch of dusty rural land that was poorly irrigated, populated by obviously poverty-stricken workers who glanced up as this ridiculously luxurious vehicle – so out of place in this area of Saudi – cruised past. Feuchter forced himself to smile at the contrast. The thought pleased him.

They had to stop once, where a cattle herder had his herd milling in the road. With a wave of apology, the man slowly – painfully slowly – herded the ragged collection of goats and worse-for-wear cows out of the vehicle's path and Feuchter was on his way without any emotion flickering even for an instant on his neatly barbered face. His dark eyes stared straight ahead.

The Land Rover passed through the suburbs of a tiny town. The low, sand-blown sun-bleached houses were fashioned of brick and stone and breeze-block, many only half-built; chickens skittered, clucking madly, from the vehicle's path and people turned to stare, shading their eyes from the harshness of the sun.

Feuchter watched, his intelligent eyes twinkling as a man failed miserably to control his three camels and had to sprint after them into the sand and scrub, past rickety rusting corrugated fences and ramshackle boarded huts.

Feuchter finally settled back—

Closed his eyes—

And slept.

They drove for hours.

They passed no more settlements.

The Land Rover rumbled and bumped into the desert on an unnamed road, its destination the middle of nowhere, its purpose unguessable.

Feuchter did not dream. Feuchter never dreamed. To Feuchter, sleep was a pure form of regeneration so close to death that it shared the same stable. And dreams: dreams were something that happened to other people.

'Sir.'

Feuchter rubbed at his eyes. He felt refreshed. The air-con worked reasonably well. 'Are we there?'

'Yes, sir.'

The Land Rover halted at a high electrified fence. Passes were flashed and armed guards peered into the vehicle's interior. Then they were allowed through. The Land Rover swept down a long winding concrete road, between two hills of sand and scrub and into a circular depression in the landscape, which housed the single visible storey of the stone, glass and steel complex of Spiral Section Q.

The car was met by a squad of semi-military personnel, heavily armed. Feuchter stepped from the Land Rover and the men saluted him. He smiled in acknowledgement and, with a small entourage, walked through the steel doors that hissed open in response to the group's proximity.

The interior was cool; controlled. Marble floors stretched away in a huge reception hall; it was almost like a hotel, with low couches and tall potted plants at strategic intervals. A huge reception desk stretched along one wall and glass elevators in clear shafts went down to the carefully temperature- and humidity-controlled depths where the bulk of chip and other hardware production and research was carried out.

Feuchter shook hands with Adams, the Head of Developments.

'How are you, sir?'

'Well, considering I was shot recently.'

'I heard about that, sir. We were all glad to hear of your swift recovery. Was it true that it was an assassination attempt? On you, or your niece?'

Feuchter stared hard at the man, who suddenly went white.

'I . . . I . . . meant . . .'

'You will never mention my niece again,' he said softly.

'Yes, yes, of course, Count Feuchter.'

'Explain to me what the communications situation is with our companion Sections.'

'Since the explosion in London nobody seems to know what is going on. Communications are suspended between many Sections – we tried to find out if you were in London at the time of the explosion, but this information was withheld from us. And considering that the Hub had been destroyed . . .'

Feuchter merely nodded, then asked, 'How successful has the Accelerated Group Phase been?'

'We have garnered 95% reaction factors.'

'It needs to be 98%.'

'Yes, sir.'

'Within the next two days.'

'Yes, sir.'

'Is there any news on the QIII Proto Schematics?'

'No, sir. This is still a mystery to us. Mr Durell has called several times, and wants to speak with you upon your return.'

Feuchter left the entourage behind and stepped into the elevator and the welcoming silence. The tube hissed away and carried him down to the lower floor that he occupied alone. He kicked off his shoes, draped his jacket over the back of a low couch and walked past a variety of carvings and statues towards his twenty-foot-long ebony desk. He pulled a fine Cuban cigar – a Vega Robaina Dos Alejandros – from a carved rosewood box, then poured himself a brandy and sat back in his plush leather chair. The comm buzzed.

Feuchter took a long draw from the cigar, enjoying the flavour, which filled his senses with its richness, then hit the button. 'Yes?'

'Several things, Feuchter. How long will you need to fully implement the cubic math events?'

'Two days. It just needs tweaking.'

'And we will start to see these probability equations emerging?'

'Yes. I am promised they will work at a 98% rate.'

'And the world data factors have been implemented? The WorldCode?'

'I am assured, by my top people, of success. The WorldCode will be able to predict the future, in a fashion. The prediction algorithms have all been implemented.'

'Good. How are you feeling after tasting the bullet?'

'I have felt better.' Feuchter smiled nastily. He stubbed out the cigar, took a sip of brandy and twirled his seat to stare at an extravagant oil-painting representation of the desert of the Empty Quarter; he loved this place, loved the serenity, loved the feeling of culture and history. He could still imagine the ancient armies of Alexander marching over the sand, thirst-dying Macedonian soldiers battling the massive expanses of the Great Sandy Desert and meeting with other armies . . . armies clashing, battle cries, the clangour of swords, the screams of the dying . . .

'I have some good news for you. This Carter man – he has been located. Tracked. He is presently in Africa – in Kenya, to the south, near the borders of Tanzania. Despite Carter's best attempts to evade us it would seem that your QIII-based implantations have worked. We tracked him, but his destinations are quite obvious – he would seek to contact Gol, at that fucked-up Spiral outpost I wish I could forget about.'

'Gol,' said Feuchter through an exhalation of smoke. 'There is a name I have not heard for a long time.'

'I had hoped he had died,' came the soft voice at the other end of the comm. 'But then, Carter is almost doing us a favour. They have discovered the location of the schematics. Yes, by an amazing coincidence, it would

220

seem Gol is the man who seeks to create his own version of the QIII processor.'

'The fool,' snorted Feuchter. 'It would take him years!'

'Yes,' said Durell, 'but the fact still remains that he has working knowledge, available technology, and copies of how the QIII operated at a basic machine level. We need those plans – we must either retrieve or destroy them. We can kill two birds with one stone.'

'How many Nex will you send?'

'I will send enough,' said the voice of Durell softly. 'There cannot be that much resistance; after all, they are only human.' He laughed softly. 'The Nex will wipe them out.'

'Good.'

'Our time is coming, Feuchter. Can you taste it? Our fucking time is coming and when we have complete control, we will not abuse our power, we will not squander our resources like Spiral has done and let evil men rule the world. We will be just and fair . . . not weak and spineless . . . but to get that far, first there must be mayhem . . .'

Dark eyes glittered and there came a pause. A long and thoughtful pause. 'I have a request,' said Feuchter eventually. He was still facing the large oil painting that dominated the wall, but something was changing within him, something strange, something acid. Somehow the colours were disappointing to him now; what he craved was reality.

'And what is that?' asked Durell.

'Carter: I want a guarantee. I want that cunt dead.'

'I'll see what I can do,' said Durell.

Night had fallen over the desert.

Outside, the temperature had plummeted and the sky was perfectly clear, stars twinkling like jewels cascading across the finest of black skin. Feuchter still sat in his chair, now in darkness, only the glow of a cigar in his hand evidence that he remained in the deep underground office, awake, alert, dark eyes glittering. He scratched at the scar on his belly self-consciously.

He stared at images of the black desert on a monitor. Nothing stirred; there were no lights, no movement, no intrusions. This place was an emptiness; this place was a void. Spiral_Q was invisible; a non-place; a desert within a desert.

Feuchter smiled softly to himself.

Around him, in the silence, he could almost feel the hive of activity. Thousands of workers: programmers, hardware designers, hackers, the world's finest computing minds working together like a well-oiled machine on the finest of computational designs ever created –

The QIII Proto. The first-ever cubic processor.

The first-ever *cellular* processor.

The prototype of an electronic *mind*.

A *brain*.

And combined with WorldCode, it could predict actions, reactions, military instructions: it could almost *predict the future*. It would be the perfect weapon. It would make him, and Durell, and the *others* . . . it would make them rich, it would make them powerful but – more importantly . . .

It would make them God.

Feuchter sighed, blowing a cloud of silver smoke into the darkness. There came a tiny *click* from the lift and a small pool of light invaded the black. A figure stepped free, the door closed behind it and soft footsteps approached.

He gazed up at the Nex, naked now, body perfectly toned, perfectly formed; muscular and taut. Feuchter

222

licked his lips and met the copper-eyed gaze of the Nex. This was a female – a scout, smaller than the warrior caste, less deadly but much more athletic, much better at feats of endurance and stamina. A slim, tough little fucker.

Feuchter's gaze travelled down, and then back up again across the perfectly formed thighs, hips, stomach, chest – and to the face. The pale-skinned face with its burning copper eyes.

The face was beautiful.

Cold and beautiful.

And only a little deformed.

Feuchter smiled, a strange twisted smile.

'Come here,' he said, spreading his arms as he felt desire and lust smash through his body. And the Nex stepped forward, opened her legs and silently obeyed.

CHAPTER 13

AFRICA

Carter knew it was a dream, and yet that somehow made it worse. In waking life he had some element of control; in the dream he was merely a spectator and he already knew the events, knew what happened, knew about the world's pain and the shocking after-effects of the Grey Death ... and yet, again and again he could relive those moments with curses and anger and hatred – but without control.

He stood, his boots planted firmly on the oil-slippery deck of the tanker, a huge 200,000-tonne vessel that cruised through the dark black waters like an ebony iceberg on its descent from the Arctic. Carter's eyes were dark, deeply ringed, and his black uniform ruffled in the cold sea-breeze as his gloved hands clasped the Kalashnikov AK582 with its sub-needle clip and 10-round bomb-burst.

The Grey Death.

It left a bad taste in Carter's brain, like a poisonous dose of cocaine.

A mutated biological weapon, the Grey Death had

spread like Godsfire through Europe, North Africa and the Middle East, and had touched upon Russia. Paris had been wiped clean – ironic. Berlin had suffered a human enema. Rome had been annihilated, bloated corpses filling the streets, the dead outweighing the living by a thousand to one. The Grey Death had rioted through both North and South America without prejudice, and was only finally tamed after slaughtering fifty-eight million people worldwide.

Fifty-eight fucking million.

At first, Carter had not been able to quantify the amount. Ten, fifty, yes – he could visualise that. But fifty-eight million? Just numbers. Stupid numbers. Until he stood on the decks of the tankers – corpse tankers – during the TankerRuns where he and most of Spiral had been posted as Anti-terrorist.

The tankers, some nearly a mile long, had been stripped of most of their deck plates, leaving massive criss-crosses of girders through which the bloated corpses were dumped. Hundreds. Thousands. Millions.

At first Carter had been unable to watch, unable to look upon so many millions dead. The Grey Death, man-made and devastating, had done the job it had been created to do. Only it had done it too well. Too fucking well.

Carter stood on the deck, oil glossing his boots, sub-machine gun cold. Jam waved, moved towards him, and their bleak gazes met over the staring faces of a million grey stinking bodies.

'There's activity,' said Jam coldly.

On their way to Siberia, there had been several threats from TJF, a Japanese terrorist group linked to murders in the Western world carried out against a blame-filled decadent society. The threat here was that TJF claimed the poison of the Grey Death had been created in the West – and should stay there. They planned to turn back the TankerRuns . . . or sink the huge vessels if they refused.

Machine guns roared.

Carter and Jam sprang into action, along with a hundred other Spiral operatives and soldiers from the crumbling special forces of a crumbling world.

Helicopters roared overhead, and the tanker's guns picked many flaming from the sky to scream, blazing fire and spitting bullets, into the sea. Japanese TJF soldiers abseiled from the helicopters, machine guns blazing, and Carter and Jam sprinted forward with Kalashnikovs juddering in their grips, faces grim, giving covering arcs of fire for one another as they crouched, bullets ricocheting from the steel girders under their boots.

Carter spun and put a bullet in a Japanese terrorist's face . . . but, almost by reflex, the TJF man's gun was firing, pumping bullets—

One caught Carter high in the chest, clipping his armour and entering under his collarbone. With a gasp he was lifted, punched backwards with a fist of iron and the air flew cold around him as he fell, fell, fell into the tanker hold filled with a million grey corpses . . .

He landed and felt pus-filled bodies sag beneath him. He screamed as he sank a little. Arms brushed against his ears, his head, his arms and back. He started to struggle, started to sink. He felt flesh part. Reeking fluid surrounding him in a lake of filth. Limbs were all around him now. Their stink, tallow-sprayed from above, intruded past his protective armour and filled Carter's nostrils, filled his mouth, filled his throat. He gagged, spewing down his armour to mix vomit with his own pooling blood.

The corpses were above him. He was sinking.

226

He screamed again, struck out.

But the bodies pulled him down.

They burst like old refuse sacks.

Their rancid fluids filled his screaming mouth, ran like battery acid down his gagging throat and he punched out but all he could hear was the roar of laughter from a million bodies intent on revenge for a bio-weapon that had betrayed humanity . . .

'Fuck!'

Night had fallen. Carter awoke, a terrible pain crucifying the centre of his brain. He could smell burning wood and he sat up quickly as the bitter cold horrifying events flooded his mind—

'Shhh.'

Natasha was there, kneeling by the side of his bed. Her hands were cool and she laid him back down, comfied his pillows, pulled the single sheet up over his naked body. Carter's eyes focused and he realised that the room was dimly lit by a single candle. The noise of insects spiralled in through wooden shutters, and it amazed Carter to think that below, *below them* was a hive of technological advancement – a Spiral base disguised by a simplistic mask. Distantly, he heard the crackling of a fire and the subdued voices of the armed guards.

Carter rubbed at his head. 'Any painkillers?'

Natasha handed him tablets and a glass of water. 'You dreaming about the tankers again?'

He nodded. 'Yeah, that and Kade.'

'Kade?'

'Don't worry about it.' He took the painkillers and washed them down with mineral water.

'They've reset your finger, X-rayed your ribs, checked all the minor cuts and gashes on your body. You'll live, but the doctor who examined you was unsure why you became so incredibly weak out there under the trees.'

'Just a headache,' said Carter lamely.

'They gave you an intensive scan, your body and brain. They could come up with nothing.' Natasha smiled softly. 'The doctor commended your work on me. The stitching, everything that you did. He confirmed what I already knew – that you saved my life.' Suddenly, Natasha stood and slipped from her T-shirt and shorts. Moonlight glinted on her taut, athletic body; on her flat stomach, high pert breasts, smooth unblemished skin. She climbed into bed beside Carter and lay on her side, pressing herself against his warmth—

Suddenly, Carter's headache had gone. A new pain invaded him; the pain of fear; the pain of panic; the pain of a dangerous and all-consuming lust . . .

'Natasha . . .' he whispered.

Her finger touched his lips and stayed there. She leaned forward, her lips brushing against his neck. He groaned, mouth opening, his teeth taking Natasha's finger and biting gently. Her free hand came up and stroked his hair. He turned, rolling towards her – the feeling of her soft skin, soft breasts, firm shapely legs all pressed against him and he was fired into instant readiness and he allowed himself to press against her as he gazed into her eyes and they were silent for long, long moments. They kissed, nothing more than a touching of tongues. Carter's hand came up and rested on Natasha's hip and she groaned, voice husky, scent invading Carter's mind and consuming his brain; she parted her legs a little, allowing him to press further against her, further into her, further through her and towards the silver paradise beyond—

They kissed harder, with more passion. Carter's hand ran up her ribs and she giggled, then he traced a spiral down her back and rested his hand on her firm buttocks. She reached down, taking his penis in her hand and squeezing gently, feeling him pulse and harden in her tight strong unforgiving grip—

'You seem mightily excited, Mr Carter—'

'Not me, my sweetness.'

'But you must admit that your body seems rather pleased to see me.'

'Nah. This is just . . .' he licked his lips, eyes glowing mischievously in the gloom '. . . moderate appreciation.'

'Well,' Natasha pouted, 'I would hate to see rampant hard-core lust!'

'Now I'm sure *that* can be arranged.'

Natasha giggled; Carter kissed her neck, her breasts, her belly, then her lips. Carter's fist gripped Natasha's hair and she groaned—

Suddenly he pushed her down to the bed, hard – then allowed his tongue to leave a trail down her breasts, and belly – her legs parted and she moaned as he tasted her cunt. His tongue darted, in and out, a gentle teasing. Her legs came up, encircling his neck as both her hands grasped him, nails digging in as Carter's teeth nipped at the soft flesh of her vulva, then pushed in, pushed deeper, he kissed her moist lips and tasted her, sucked at her roughly, his tongue probing hard and soft, deep and shallow, teasing and tantalising as her moans filled his ears and she dragged him around into a symbiotic dual-feeding – to take him in her mouth – It was Carter's turn to groan. He breathed deeply the musky mind-spinning need-inducing scent of her sex. For long moments he was lost to the softness of her lips and tongue, her oral caresses, the promise of danger delivered by her neat teeth. Her hand cupped his testicles, tickled him, squeezed hard the taut muscle of her buttocks and he

229

began to work eagerly on her, his tongue finding her clitoris, toying, probing, his face buried until—

Natasha moved, suddenly, unexpectedly. Carter was flung onto his back, a startled 'O' passing his moist shining lips. She grabbed both his hands and pinned them above his head. He gazed up at her – at the perspiration bathing her body, her wide, wild eyes, her sweat-streaked hair. He watched a drop roll down her nose and hang – then drop to her breasts, which swayed in a drunken dance above him.

She lowered her mouth to his, then pulled teasingly away. She lifted her leg, straddled him, hips raised so that the tip of his penis was a hair's breadth from her. She could feel his eager twitching and, with a smile, lowered herself – a single centimetre – held it – another centimetre – held it longer—

Carter groaned.

She dropped herself onto him with a sudden rush of violence and her hips heaved forward, ramming him deep into her, her breasts brushing against his face, her teeth dropping to bite savagely at his neck – Carter's back arched. He thrust himself hard up within her, the world a spinning lost dark spiral of blood-red lust and black velvet pleasure and they fucked, fucked hard and slid in one another's sweat, lips touching caressing biting tearing, hips thrusting and fucking . . . Carter was groaning and Natasha was screaming as the explosion came – with Nat's muscles taut above Carter's arched and thrumming body – and then they went limp, collapsed against and into one another in a warm sanctuary, and eternity slid into another languid eternity and they lay—

They lay entwined.

Panting.

Together.

230

Gradually their heat left them and the cool air soothed them.

They wriggled beneath the solitary sheet, holding one another. They kissed softly, enjoying each other's heat, each other's gentleness after the violence of their love-making.

'You just get better as you get older, Mr Carter.'

Carter grinned. He couldn't help himself, despite the deep throbbing in his ribs which had returned to haunt him.

'You get wilder.'

'I try to please,' she said softly and smiled, nibbling his chin.

'How did you stop Gol from shooting me?'

Natasha pouted. 'Carter, how can you ask such a question when we've just been fucking?'

'I need to know.' He propped himself on one elbow and looked down at her. His free hand traced twirls in the sweat on her breasts and he reached down, took a nipple between his teeth, bit mischievously.

She squeaked in mock pain.

'I didn't stop him. *You* stopped him. Your words, your actions.'

'What actions?'

'The battle. Inside you. It was on your face—'

'Battle?' Carter closed his mouth, his teeth shutting with a sudden *clack*. Then he sighed.

'I don't understand what goes on inside you,' she said.

'It's complicated.'

'Try me. *Trust* me. I'm an intelligent girl. Something was tearing you apart; something was burning you up and you were –' Natasha grappled to describe what she had witnessed '– you were like two different people. One side of you wanted to attack Gol; one side of you wanted to

231

roll over and give in. I saw it, Carter. I saw it on your face; I heard it in your voice.'

'Do you believe in possession?' he said suddenly.

'Like in *The Exorcist* – possessing a child sort of shit?'

'Sort of. You see,' he paused, uncertain. Natasha squeezed him reassuringly. 'I am haunted,' he said. 'Something haunts my mind – talks to me. Feeds voices into my head, tries to take control of me.'

'And that's why you've asked me about schizophrenia, in the past?'

'Yeah. But this is different – it talks with me, argues with me – tries to take control but I have to let him . . .'

'Him?'

Carter met Natasha's stare then, and she could see it: the fear. The fear that she would think him – mad.

'Tell me,' she said softly.

'His name is Kade.'

'Can you talk to him now?'

'No. He comes when he smells the promise of a fight . . . if I allow him to take over he gets the job done. Gets the killing done. It was Kade who had control – too much control – when I earned myself the title of The Butcher . . . but that wasn't me, Natasha, I swear it, you've got to believe me . . .'

Natasha was silent for a long time. She hugged Carter tight.

'It sounds like a guilt complex.'

'I know exactly what it sounds like. I understand what I would be thinking if this was reversed and *you* were telling *me* this pile of shit. That's why I don't speak of Kade; that's why he lives alone, burning in my soul, and I rarely set him free . . .'

'But you do? You do set him free?'

'If I give up hope. If I resign myself to death . . . and

that's the sad thing. Take Schwalenberg in Germany – I was as sure as fucking dead. Betrayed by those I thought I was there to protect. I lost my mind, literally and physically. I no longer cared and I gave myself to Kade . . . he revelled in the killing and bought me my life for another few days. You understand?'

'This is too weird,' said Natasha.

'Don't be frightened. I have complete control . . .'

'I am not frightened. And I believe you,' whispered Natasha. She kissed Carter's ear and held him for a long time until she felt his breathing become regular and he was sleeping. Her fingers traced gentle patterns on his spine – and time after time she returned to a spiral. A spiral against his flesh. A spiral leading—

Down.

Carter awoke in the gloom. Natasha slept in his arms, a sticky warm embrace. Carter disentangled himself with care, then, pulling on his trousers and stealing Nat's cigarettes and lighter, he crossed the room and stepped outside.

There was an armed guard outside their room, a man named Marcus, sporting dreadlocks to his waist. His chest was heavily scarred. The huge black man grinned the sort of sheepish knowledge-filled grin that said, 'You sure don't know how to keep the noise down.' Carter returned the grin, padded down the hall and went outside.

A cool breeze whispered across his skin. He lit a cigarette, sat down on the wooden steps and gazed out across the dark silver-gleaming orange-tree orchards. The stars were bright against a dark canopy and Carter tilted his head back to allow a soft plume of smoke to escape his lips and rise into the infinity of the warm night sky. The nicotine buzzed through his brain, the harsh tobacco burning his lungs, and he blinked dreamily as a soft call echoed across the orchard.

'How are you feeling, Mr Carter?'

Carter turned and smiled up at Gol who was standing with his hands on his hips, breathing in the night air and the rich scents deeply – a love affair with the ambience. His eyes were unreadable, his grey-flecked beard – actually more grey than black now, Carter noticed – was neatly combed and oiled. Carter caught the distant scent of coconut oil.

'Much better.'

'Would you care to walk with me?'

'It's a fine night. That would be good.'

The two men stepped from the porch of the white-walled house and the sandy soil felt soft, comfortable under Carter's feet. They moved beneath the trees, inhaling their fragrance, moving through the gloom a little uncomfortably at first: untrusting. As they walked, Carter offered Gol a cigarette. They both lit up and stopped within a small circle of trees, lifting their faces in an attempt to attract the slightest of breezes to evaporate their sweat.

'This is a warm place to choose to live,' said Carter eventually.

'Yes,' rumbled Gol uneasily. The cigarette seemed tiny in his huge hand. 'But we don't always have a choice in these matters. Spiral is a harsh mistress. She commands, and we mere mortals obey.' He smiled a smile without humour, bloodless in the moonlight.

There was a pause. Something called through the darkness. The breeze whispered between the trees.

'I think I am following in your footsteps,' said Carter.

'Yes. I have just researched your recent – ah, shall we say *exploits* in both Germany and Scotland. Natasha has, of course, filled me in on some of the details. It would seem that you are a wanted man Mr Carter.'

'Well, I'm wanted *dead*, if that's what you mean.'

'Hmmm. That would be one eventuality; a thought which does leap to mind is that you have been used. Set up. A tracker with the function of leading somebody to me. After all, the other DemolSquads were wiped out by three Nex – and yet they only sent one after you. Strange, don't you think?'

'Yes.'

'And further moves have been placed across that great gaming board we call the Earth.'

'Such as?'

'Another Spiral base has been destroyed.'

There was a long, long silence. Gol enjoyed his cigarette. 'Forty minutes ago, Spiral_M was also wiped from the face of the Earth. It's now just a pile of rubble surrounded by emergency services and brave people trying their hardest to find survivors.'

'Fuck.'

'My sentiments exactly,' said Gol softly.

'But . . .'

'Carter, I *know* for a fact that Spiral do not want you dead. We have bigger problems . . . And the assassin, the Nex who came for you, I fear these killers are not used by Spiral any longer – not for many, many years – even though it was Spiral's loins from whence they sprang.'

'Who sent them?' asked Carter, voice hard, humour vaporised.

'I don't know,' sighed Gol, rubbing at his beard. He ground his cigarette stub into the earth. 'Although I have a few suspicions.'

'I have a few fucking suspicions of my own,' snapped Carter. 'Now, I know you want me dead Gol – and I can't really say I blame you after what we went through: I thought I had misjudged you when we arrived here.'

'You had,' said Gol softly.

Gol faced Carter, who looked up at the huge man. Gol rubbed at the scar on his leg self-consciously and Carter noted the movement, remembered in mild embarrassment that it had been his own bullet that had wounded Gol's flesh.

'You are Carter, Spiral's most resourceful man – or you used to be. No longer do you seek assassination contracts; you have become withdrawn, hidden away in the Scottish mountains with your dog and your own company and knowledge. And yet you possess the most awesome skills in tracking people down – and in killing them . . . Now, I had thought I would kill you,' said Gol gently. 'Here, now, in Africa . . . but I have a greater use for you than that.'

Carter lit another cigarette. Offered the packet. Gol held up his hand in refusal.

'Oh yeah?'

'My anger has gone. You love Natasha. And because of your love for her, I forgive you; I will put aside our differences in this hour of need . . . Natasha needs you, and Spiral needs you. Carter, somebody is trying to wipe out Spiral – why? Because Spiral is what stands in the way of chaos. Spiral is the final firewall; Spiral is the bullet in the firing chamber of the world; Spiral is death to those who oppose all that stands for good.'

Carter frowned. Gol was one of the strongest, most fanatical men he had ever met. There was no streak of weakness – Gol had shot sleeping men, wounded men, dying men. Carter would have been little problem . . . and this reinforced the notion that Spiral was in a world of shit.

'What is happening here?' asked Carter softly, turning his eyes away from Gol, scanning the orange trees rimed with moonlight. 'Who is using heavy HighJ detonation to wipe us out? Where do your *suspicions* lie?'

Gol shrugged, but looked away. Carter caught a hint of something; something unsaid, something he almost grasped but missed in the darkness. Gol was hiding something. Hiding something bad.

'Two mammoth Spiral divisions have been destroyed,' he rumbled, rubbing wearily at his beard. 'But more – nearly thirty DemolSquads have been wiped out in the last forty-eight hours alone.' Gol turned to look into Carter's eyes. Carter's mouth had opened in a silent 'O' of shock.

'Thirty?' he whispered, awed.

'Yes, thirty. And our little friends are looking for something – something retrieved by Natasha, and passed on to me for safe keeping. A possibility arises, Carter – the possibility that you were *chased* here. This base is highly classified . . . Natasha knew of its whereabouts, but you sure as fuck should not have done. This is outside the boundaries of normal Spiral influence.'

Carter nodded, smoke pluming from his nostrils. He scratched at his forehead with his thumb.

'You think it is that black and white? I lead the bad guys here, because they know you have something and they know that I know where you are? Are you fucking crazy?'

'Why did you come here, Carter?'

'For answers.'

'And because you had nowhere else to go. Nowhere else to take Natasha. Where better than to her father, despite your earlier *differences*?'

Carter dropped the cigarette. Ground it underfoot.

He turned to meet Gol's impenetrable gaze and their stares locked.

Carter smiled bitterly. 'What is it you have?'

'Schematics,' said Gol softly.

'For what?'

Gol waved his hand dismissively. 'I believe you will find out soon enough, my inquisitive friend. For tonight, I advise you to get some sleep. I have many things to show you.'

'I am confused. You know who is behind this.'

It was not a question.

'I know,' said Gol, smiling – and his smile held no humour. It was the smile of a shark cornering a little fish. The smile of a tiger sinking its claws into the flanks of a lamb. The smile of the natural predator.

The wind blew. The trees shivered.

'This Nex assassin has followed me here, then. To Africa?'

'Not one, but many. The schematics I have in my possession are, shall we say, integral to the demise of Spiral. They need them, or else it is a chink in their armour; their *Achilles Heel*. They cannot let them go unretrieved, and they therefore cannot let me live. I hold their secret in my hands, like a God holding a newly born sun.' Carter shivered as Gol's words caressed him like a stench-breeze of corpse smoke.

'They will come. And they will come soon.'

Carter frowned, lit another cigarette and blew a plume of smoke into the air. He knew that Gol was holding out on him, and it sat bad with him, like an act of incest.

'We'll fucking see,' he said quietly.

Gol stood in the shadows of a tree, thankful that Carter had gone. The man made him uneasy, put him on edge. Gol did not trust him; his eyes held too much the look of a killer.

He watched closely as one of his guard groups exchanged duty. They disappeared into the gloom, moving like ghosts, and he took a long, deep breath, staring up at the vast vaults of the night sky. A cool breeze at last caressed his skin. He rubbed at his beard. He closed his eyes—

But images haunted him.

From a million years ago.

From a different world.

Dark stone walls, damp with water and slime. A voice, crying in the darkness, a woman's voice, shouting out, the language Austrian, the embedded emotion that of raw terror. He moved down the steps, boots thudding dully on the heavy ancient stone. In addition to his knowledge of where he was, he could *feel* that he was deep underground; could *feel* the weight of earth and stone above him leading up.

A face. Pale and drawn.

'Feuchter.'

'Come in, Gol. We've been waiting.'

Gol stepped forward. There was a heavy solid *click* as the door closed neatly behind him. He nodded to Durell, who nodded with a *crackling* sound in return – but Gol could not meet the man's gaze; he felt himself shivering, and he looked instead at Feuchter, forcing himself not to turn and stare at Durell, at his deformities, at his terrible *wounds* . . .

The images drifted.

Dissipated like smoke.

Gol opened his eyes, stared again at the night sky.

'What did we do?' he murmured wearily. 'What in God's name did we do?'

Slater stared up at the Boeing Apache AH64A, resplendent in desert camouflage colours, with its squat powerful wings carrying clusters of Hellfire missiles and 70mm rocket groups, flanks scarred and battered from battle encounters, a crack in the windshield and one flat tyre. Slater turned back to Jam, who was leaning against the old van, enjoying a cigarette.

'You say you can fly this thing?'

Jam nodded.

'You sure?'

Jam nodded again.

'It looks a little bit . . . battered?'

'Meet *Sally* – apparently Mongrel flew her during the Second Great Gulf War. Took out about thirty-five tanks single-handedly in that baby, and still brought her home for tea and doughnuts.'

'But . . .' said Slater.

'What?'

'It's damaged!'

'Damaged? Merely superficial.' Jam smiled through gritted teeth. 'Anyway, what did you expect? Us to waltz in here and requisition a brand new one? Now, when I give the order, I need you and Nicky to climb in – you see the release for the cockpit there? Good. Climb in – insert this key, turn it twice clockwise and hit the five green buttons on the dash. You got that?'

Slater frowned. 'I thought you cleared this, Jam? And I thought we were waiting for The Priest?'

'I did, I did, I cleared it with Mongrel. Those are the keys, and I have the ignition sequences stored up here.' He tapped his head. Blowing smoke through a cheeky smile, Jam slapped Slater on the back. The huge man did not budge. 'And as for The Priest? Well, he's a little bit late and we can't hang on for the insane fucker.'

'Late?' rumbled Slater. 'Don't you mean that *we* are early?'

'Depends on your perspective,' said Jam. 'Look, Slater, Spiral are being shafted left, right and centre – we need to find out, and find out fast, what is actually going on. This was the nearest base with access to this sort of technology.'

Slater looked around, his face carrying the weight of guilt. Across the almost deserted airfield other aircraft sat unattended, mainly Cessna single-propeller planes, a few Lear Jets and two clusters of ex-war Apaches like *Sally*. Jeeps hovered in the distance. Activity seemed centred on a huge hangar, originally used during World War II to house fighter planes but now owned by Spiral for its private fleet of air-going traffic.

Slater looked up at the sky. Heavy clouds rolled, and wind whipped at him with the promise of rain.

'I didn't know you could fly a helicopter,' said Slater suspiciously.

'I am a man of many talents. Where the fuck has Nicky got to? If she's not quick The Priest might arrive early. And we don't fucking want *that*.'

Nicky appeared, jogging across the expanse of tarmac. She carried packs and, panting heavily, dropped them at Slater's feet. 'They were happy to give me supplies; everything's in a bit of a panic. Some of the Spiral navigation systems have gone down; the loss of Spiral_H hasn't helped things either. Once they clocked my ID and ECube – wham bam.' She smiled, then looked at Slater's dubious expression. 'What's the matter?'

Slater pointed. 'Did you know this cunt could fly?'

Nicky shook her head. 'No. So what?'

'I don't trust him.'

'You don't have to trust him, sweet-pea. Just let him get us out of here; it's beginning to feel a little threatening, what with those masked fuckers killing our guys and taking out the HQ.'

241

'Come on,' said Jam, dropping the butt of his cigarette. Smoke trailed from his nostrils. He ground the remains of the cigarette under his boot and wrapped his long leather coat around him. 'Let's do it.'

Slater and Nicky moved swiftly to the Apache, Slater opened the cockpit door and they climbed in. Jam moved around the war-bruised machine, poking here and there; he kicked away the blocks from under the tyres and climbed up, squeezing into the position of control. He fired up the ignition, then the twin-turbine engine. The engine whined, then roared and Jam smiled like a small child discovering a new toy he thought was lost.

Rain began to fall from the dark broiling skies.

'I hope he knows what he's doing,' said Slater, as the Apache bobbed and the engine noise increased.

'I'm sure he does,' smiled Nicky, a touch uncertainly.

'Here we go! Let's see what this baby can do. Kamus-5 . . . here we come!'

Out of the gloom, doing perhaps a hundred and twenty m.p.h. across the rugged concrete airfield hammered The Priest's battered old Volvo; oil smoke plumed like a dragon's breath from the wide tailpipe, and the car slewed around, wheels locked, skidding to a halt in front of the Apache in a scythe of water.

The Priest stepped free of the car, crossed swiftly to the helicopter with his Bible in one hand, long heavy coat flapping, and climbed up to be greeted by three blank stares.

'Well done, my children, for convening so early. It is good to see the servants of God so willing to carry out His work.'

'Yeah,' said Jam, casting glances at Nicky and Slater. 'We're just warming up her engines.'

'And *are* they warm?' asked The Priest softly.

'They are now.'

'Praise be – then what are we waiting for? Onward, Christians! Let us discover the source of this scourge.'

The Apache, engines roaring with power, lurched up from the airstrip, rotated through two full circles, then shot straight upwards with a caterwaul of engine; it halted, hovering, rotated again through about 270 degrees, then, with its short squat nose dipped, hammered forward into the heavy falling rain.

Jam grinned sheepishly. 'Sorry! I'll get the hang in a minute—'

'Or twenty,' muttered Slater.

'I fucking *heard that*!'

The rotors thumped through the downpour.

Nicky found herself staring out and down at the bleak landscape below. They passed a town, grey and huddled, its roofs slick with water; cars moved warily, like predators hunting through the streets, and occasional shoppers cowered under huge umbrellas. The streets were laid out like some huge brick-walled game, and a feeling of melancholy fell over Nicky as she watched these tiny people in their tiny houses with their tiny lives.

'I know what you are thinking,' said Slater.

'What's that?'

'You're looking at the people – secure in their ignorance, not aware of the world events unfolding around them. They watch the news, believe the media and propaganda – like sheep. They have no real concept of what is really going on, of what the stakes are.'

'That's quite profound for you, Slater.'

The huge man smiled, revealing his missing teeth. 'Slater not think too well sometimes, but he hold a gun

243

well and know what he believe in. You laugh at Slater sometime, but really I is good and I smash the bad men.'

Nicky patted his huge bicep. 'I know, I know. When we're laughing, we're just fucking with you. We love you really; we know you'd give your life for us.'

Slater nodded, a big smile across his face.

The Apache banked, heading towards the coast; below, cliffs sailed into the distance and they were flying low over cold churning grey seas. Jam and The Priest seemed to be arguing.

'We're not going lower,' said Jam through gritted teeth.

'The wave formations will mask us against radar,' said The Priest softly, eyes bright with the light of conviction.

'Yeah, and then drag us down and wrap us in Neptune's cold fishlike embrace. You can go to fuck, you insane religious bastard.'

'God will protect us.'

'God will laugh at us!'

'You do not know God's will as I do.'

'What, so you're in contact with the man himself?'

'Let me just say that I have seen the light.'

The Apache dropped closer to the waves; sea spray rattled against the glass and Nicky and Slater stared out warily, watching the churning water, the crests of white foam against the rolling liquid slate-grey.

'Do you know anything about this Kamus?' asked Nicky, after long moments of thought.

'A little,' said Slater slowly, his eyes hooded. 'It used to be an operational Spiral base. A military centre, a place from which we could mount operations in middle and eastern Europe.'

244

'What happened? Why did they close it?'

'Several reasons.' Slater's voice was cool, his eyes moving to stare out over the sea once more. 'Things kept going wrong; people started dying. The Kamus is built *into* the side of a mountain, high up on a ridge. There are only two ways to reach the place – by air, or by a single cable car. Kamus was a fortress; almost impregnable. Tunnels inside travel across and *down, deep down* – access shafts, huge stores, research centres – all carved from within the rock. In the end, Kamus-5 was beaten by an enemy – not an external physical enemy, but an internal psychological one.'

'It was haunted?' asked Nicky softly.

'Not haunted, more *cursed*.'

Nicky shivered.

Slater continued, his gaze still distant. 'I remember the last days; the huge transporters leaving the platform; much heavy equipment was abandoned there, they said it was not cost-effective to move. Hah.'

'What else?'

Slater looked at her. Met her gaze. 'It was said, those who worked deep within the research centres – something down there turned them mad. There was some kind of massacre, in the living quarters – thirty or so people, including wives, children, all were involved in some kind of shooting. Lots of bad death. Deaths of innocent people.' Slater rubbed at his temples. 'It was covered up well. I be honest, Nicky – Slater not really want to go back.'

'We don't have much choice.'

'Only a mad man would set up camp in the Kamus.'

'Or a fanatic,' said Nicky sombrely.

Slater nodded.

They remained in silence for the rest of the journey.

245

Spiral_Memo6
Transcript of recent news incident
CodeRed_Z;
unorthodox incident scan 556126

A Russian nuclear-weapons depot was completely deactivated this morning. The deactivation sequence lasted for 180 seconds. Both reactors and fission services were left stranded and without power and cooling.

The reactivation occurred as an automated sequence that left technicians and scientists without answers concerning the nature of this apparent security breach. When reactivation occurred, all passwords and security measures were instigated without authority intervention.

This would suggest either a complex bug in software, or it could hint at hacker/sub-terrorist involvement.

The Russian Minister for Technology, Sergei Kessolov, was unavailable for comment.>>#

CHAPTER 14

THE CALM

Carter and Natasha had a simple breakfast of fruit and bread and cheese brought to their room by Marcus, and washed it down with thick black coffee containing lots of sugar. Carter gestured for Marcus to stay, and the large black man sat on the end of the bed, making the aged and rusting springs creak. He poured himself a coffee and grinned over at Carter.

'They say you a bad boy.'

Carter shrugged. 'You look quite a bad boy yourself.'

Marcus shook his head, long dreads swaying. 'I here, man, because I am mathematician and I am good mathematician. I help repair the Spiral mainframe codes.' He beamed, and sipped at his coffee. 'I let Gol tell you about that; he may not want me to speak.'

'And there's me thinking you were merely a beefy bouncer. Nats, don't he look like a bouncer?'

Nats nodded, taking a bite of melon. 'Sorry to stereotype you, but it's the muscles.'

'A man must work out,' said Marcus. 'You not want to turn to fat; to grow old and fat and weak and plump. I

247

stay trim; I run and I fight. They say you are a fighter, Carter – this true, man?'

'I used to box, once. In the army.'

'Maybe one day we spar?'

Carter shook his head. 'Don't know about that.' He reached over; felt Marcus's huge bicep. 'Hmm. Maybe another time, Marcus – you understand? – I've got a broken rib at the moment . . .' The last bit was spoken in the voice of an injured squeaking schoolboy.

Marcus grinned. 'Look forward to it. Gotta go, man, or Gol will cut off my dreads.' He stood, hoisted his AK47 and stepped from the room. He peeped back in. 'Thanks for the coffee.'

'Our pleasure,' said Nats, smiling as the door closed. 'A mathematician, eh? I wonder just what the hell my illustrious father is up to down here in Kenya under the Spiral umbrella?'

'I'm sure its not legal,' said Carter.

'With Gol, it never was.'

They dressed and, stepping outside into the early-morning sunshine, saw Gol sitting on the porch steps. He turned, smiling up at the couple and stroking his greying beard. 'Looks like we've been lucky,' he said.

Carter stood, stretching his back. He lit a cigarette and inhaled deeply. 'Lucky?'

'No signals have been triggered; we've scanned the ECubes via our hacked satellite links. There are reports of you – both of you – fleeing the UK but there is no mention of your destination, no traffic referring to Africa. If your enemies – *our* enemies – are coming here for us, then they are extremely quiet about it.'

Carter snorted. 'Don't get lazy, Gol. Just because you can't see them, doesn't mean they are not there.'

Gol frowned, his face hardening. 'I know that, boy.

And we have been making preparations. This operation is far bigger than you – or anybody – suspects. It would appear we are safe from discovery, for now; and you, therefore, can help *us*.'

'Help you? How?'

Gol smiled down at Natasha. 'I know for a start that you are a little hacking genius; you worked on the QIII Proto at its integral stages, and you know the Spiral mainframes like the back of your own hand. We have a little problem decoding information that we could use your assistance with . . .'

'Just what the fuck is it that you are doing here?' asked Carter. He sat down on the steps, looking out over the orange trees, which swayed gently in the caress of some warm breeze.

'This is Spiral_F,' said Gol. 'We are the secret police of Spiral. The secret within the secret. The central layers of the onion, surrounded by outer layers and outer layers and outer layers. Spiral watches Spiral, who watches Spiral – we are a central mechanism to stop *bad* things happening.'

'Hmm.' Carter rubbed at the back of his neck, easing the tension, 'I knew there was a secret police,' he gave Natasha a long sideways glance, 'but I didn't realise you were involved.'

'Not many people do. Our cover is that of a research centre; and yes, we do research in the name of Spiral. But we are so much more than that . . . ironically, we are the people who are supposed to have all the answers, and yet there are things happening here and we're at a loss to discover the real reasons. This QIII, this military processor – something is out of place, a discordant note, and I'm not sure how deep it goes. You want to know what we do here, Carter? We solve problems. Pure and simple. And then we hunt.'

'Hunt?'

'Oh yes,' said Gol, dark eyes gleaming. 'We hunt.'

It was night.

Gol had spent some of the day showing Natasha and Carter around his private world within the rocky canyon; the orchards flourished with the loving care of a small group of village women who travelled in by foot to tend the trees and harvest the fruit.

Now they were seated outside, around the side of the house, where a small fire had been built. Carter sat with his back to the wall of the house, Natasha beside him. Gol was seated across the fire, large chunks of meat on a skewer before him sizzling fat into the flames. Also present – some of them meeting Carter for the first time – were a few other members of this Spiral_F operation whom Gol slowly introduced.

'This is Marcus; I think you have already met.'

Marcus grinned, reached over, and shook Carter's hand, his dreads swinging near to the flames.

'Careful, mate, or your hair will fry.'

''S all right, Mr Carter. It happened before.'

'This is Shanaz; our resident computer expert and presently on the hack with the newly updated Spiral mainframes – or she was, until the HQ was stomped into chemical oblivion. She learned her computing trade at BUET – the Bangladesh University of Engineering and Technology in Dhaka.'

Shanaz smiled, a wide beautiful smile; of Bangladeshi descent, she wore her hair long, a silken web that descended to her waist and which she plaited and decorated with interwoven wooden beads. Her lips were a deep red, shining in the glow of the flames.

She reached over to shake Carter's and Natasha's

hands; Carter's gaze met the intelligent bright look of the woman and he licked his lips; there was wildness there, true animal wildness that promised nothing less than a true roller-coaster thrill.

When she spoke, her words were a soft purr, a luxury sound, the husky growl of a hunting animal. 'I have heard many things about you, Mr Carter. Gol speaks with – shall we say, passion – about your exploits.'

'I am sure he does.'

'Are you everything he promises you to be?'

Carter was entranced by that beautiful gaze and that throaty, husky, magical voice. He realised that their hands were still touching, her skin warm against his, the fingers stroking his hand with gentle pressure.

'I . . . I am not sure.'

'Come, do not be modest, Mr Carter.' Shanaz licked her gleaming red lips. She turned, winked at Gol, then back to Carter. 'He says that you really are an *animal*.'

The men chuckled; Natasha glared, first at Shanaz, then at the side of Carter's head.

Shanaz broke the handshake. She licked her fingers. Carter swallowed.

'And this is Jahmal; another professional computer hacker. He used to be wanted by the FBI, no less, until he taught them a few things about data protection; bought his freedom and their respect.'

'Yo, man,' said Jahmal, grinning. He was a slim black man, his head completely round and shaved as close to the scalp as the clippers could go; his whole face seemed to be one huge grin. He shook Carter's hand energetically.

'Nice to meet you,' said Carter.

'And you, and you; ignore Shanaz, she's a weird bitch. It's nice to have some new faces round here, we're stuck down in that dump and we hardly ever get some new blood to tell us stories around the fire and liven up the evenings . . .'

'Jahmal!' snapped Gol, frowning.

'Sorry!' he said. 'They don't know?'

'Not yet. I am saving it,' said Gol. He smiled at Nats and Carter over the flames; the heady scent from the orange trees flowed down and around the group. 'Our struggle – it is the struggle to keep Spiral from becoming what it aims to destroy. Within any corporation there is always corruption; it comes from a myriad of different sources. You can never know from where. We are here to try and stop that; we have been specially vetted; we are about as pure as you can get.' Gol laughed at that. 'Fucking funny, hey? Spiral_F is a collection of people who have been brought together for that special purpose. To keep the good good. To keep Spiral pure. We operate external to Spiral policy. We are the hidden camera behind the grille and it spreads much further than this little gathering you see here . . . I am merely a small cog in a huge machine that watches another huge machine.' Gol held his arms wide and grinned. When he spoke again, his voice was low, eyes staring into the fire where fat dripped sizzling and spitting to be consumed and spat out as black smoke. 'Spiral operates as cells; individual cells so that no one person can be in total control. But that system is breaking down . . . one or maybe more of the cells have turned against Spiral. And they are powerful.'

There was silence. The flames crackled. Gol stared into the fire, melancholy descending on him.

'I never fucking thought it could happen so fast, or so bad,' he said. 'Two bases wiped out; the DemolSquads being tagged left, right and centre. We've sent out warnings but it is too little too late. And there are other, wider implications. Strange events have been happening all over

252

the world – you may have seen them on the news. A malicious new computer virus, nuclear submarines going missing, power cuts, jet fighters crashing, gas plants powering down, the deactivation of a Russian weapons depot, financial institutions losing millions of dollars, digital interference in the stock exchanges ... all sorts of shit, being blamed on software bugs and human error – but this is not the case. We are linking many of the cases, chasing them back to their source, but the paths are not clear. But there is one thing we *are* sure about – all these world events, all these fuck-ups on a global scale – they are not fuck-ups, they are a test of some sort, an initiation – and they all stem from the same source.'

'The QIII,' whispered Carter.

'Yes.'

'They are testing it before it becomes fully operational?'

'Yes.' Gol nodded. 'It is flexing its muscles; running internal diagnostics; seeing how far it can go. But it is little things, the odd submarine here, a power station there, wipe the computers in a bank in London – and then replace the data in a "freak occurrence" ... when the final push comes, it will come in a sudden rush. Everything will happen at once, and this fucking processor can do it.'

'Why haven't they done it yet?'

'A couple of reasons,' said Gol softly. 'One, we know about them, this Spiral splinter group, and we have agents searching for them as we speak. Two, the QIII isn't quite finished – it's working, and is running its own diagnostics but it isn't quite complete. A premature attack might fail. And finally, we have the schematics. We understand how it works. And we can stop it.'

Carter looked from Natasha to Gol. 'You have the

schematics for the fucking QIII processor? How the fuck did you get them?'

Natasha smiled bitterly. 'It was a long, hard fight, Carter.'

Carter shook his head, rubbing at his tired eyes as Natasha moved over to Gol and placed her hand on his shoulder. 'Are you all right, father?'

Gol looked up and smiled weakly. 'Yes, but soon you must leave this place. The reports are coming in. They will be here in the early morning; a force of Nex with heavy armour support. It would seem that they want what they think is rightly theirs.'

'We will not leave,' said Natasha.

'We will fight,' growled Carter. 'You say the Nex are coming? Well, we have fucking run for long enough. We will not flee any more – there are only a few of us, but we can make a difference. Shouldn't we be working now?'

'I have a hundred people working on this thing – we can do no more than we are already doing,' said Gol softly. 'But that is for later. Now, now we must relax, we must drink, and then – then we will prepare. We cannot evacuate this place because there is nowhere to run . . . and our research cannot be moved without many days of labour. We must defend ourselves against these infidels . . .' He rubbed at his beard thoughtfully, his stare fixed on Carter. 'You say you are ready to fight with us, Mr Carter . . . but I wonder?'

'What?'

'Is your soul ready for Heaven?'

'If not,' Carter growled, 'then I'll see you fucked up in Hell.'

Carter groaned as he was shaken awake. His sticky eyelids opened and he could picture the jug – the jug of sweet golden liquid that he had enjoyed so thoroughly the night before. Images of flames crossed his mind; good food; good drink; humorous bantering company. The glistening face of Shanaz . . .

He groaned again and stared hard at Gol.

'Yeah?'

'Get Nats up. Meet me outside in five.'

'You got some cigarettes?'

'I have,' rumbled Gol. 'Come on, move yourself. It's almost dawn. We have little time left. The Nex are coming.'

The sun was just rising, a weak grey pre-dawn light gently caressing the horizon. Natasha followed Carter, grumbling about their lack of sleep and touching tenderly at the healing wound in her throat, and then at her shoulder. 'Gol's painkillers are working, but not well enough.'

'You still bad?'

Natasha gave a weak smile. 'I'll survive, I'm sure.'

She moved across the porch, linked arms with her father. 'What can I do for you, daddy? You taking us out on safari?'

'I wish we could have such fun,' rumbled the large greying man. He rubbed Natasha's hair. 'It's good having you here, girl; it's good having you around me again. It makes me feel younger!'

'Me too,' smiled Natasha. 'You make me feel like a child again.'

'You're certainly not that,' he said softly, glancing over at Carter who was leaning against a wooden support and smoking heavily. 'Hey, Carter, come on. I have something to show you.'

'Does that something include a bed?'

'No. But it has something to do with the Nex.'

Gol led them around the back of the battered, run-down white-walled house with its peeling paint and

255

dilapidated appearance: a clever mask, a wonderful disguise. He led them a little way into the trees, and then out across scrubland and through another stand of orange trees until they came to a rusting iron hatchway half concealed by vegetation, small scrub bushes, fallen leaves and branches. 'This is no longer classified,' said Gol, 'because our security has already been breached by the impending Nex visit. We must prepare. We must be ready.' He was serious, deadly serious, standing above that rusted iron covering. 'While I commend your skills in searching me out, you really, really have no idea what you are dealing with . . . you really do not understand what you are *fucking* with here . . . you see an old house, but it goes much, much deeper . . .'

He spun the rusted iron wheel, which moved with surprising ease. There was a hiss as the iron hatch was released. Gol heaved up the hatch to reveal a small section of silver alloy with a slot for a key. Gol removed the key from a chain around his neck; he inserted the key and turned it. Then he retreated a pace or two, saying, 'Step back.'

Carter and Natasha obeyed.

There came a distant hiss, followed by a deep rumbling – and the earth began to shake. Natasha grabbed hold of Carter's arm, and they glanced all around. Suddenly, the ground folded in on itself and – like a huge metallic puzzle – it folded in and down, and then spun up in a huge spiral of metallic slivers that hissed and spun out like knives in a huge fan to reveal—

A massive circle in the ground, metallic-walled, a huge riveted alloy ramp leading down.

From the darkness below the ground lights shone dazzlingly. There came a roar of engines, more rumbling, and Gol, Carter and Nats all jumped back. From the depths of the earth came a desert-camouflaged six-wheeled vehicle, a huge armour-plated wagon with steel welded over the windows and machine guns poking from dark rectangular slits.

The wheels, each nearly as large as Carter was tall, pounded the alloy ramp and ate into the sand. There were clangs as the massive machine hammered by, motor roaring and wheels churning as the vehicle sped past the group and to the front of the dilapidated white-walled house where it stopped, engine rumbling, fumes belching from a huge plated exhaust. 'We call them Pigs,' shouted Gol over the roar. More lights dazzled. Another armoured car approached, wheels thundering up the ramp – and then Pigs positively *spewed* from this hole in the ground, one after the other, a seemingly never-ending stream of armour and guns until thirty weapon-bristling behemoths sat in a huge circle around Gol's small house, growling, coughing, waiting.

Carter licked his lips as he surveyed the firepower.

'Fuck me,' he said. 'I didn't realise you had such . . . *resources*.'

Gol smiled wanly.

'If only they were enough.'

'When you said the Nex were coming . . . exactly *how many* did you mean?'

Gol's dark-eyed stare met Carter's. 'The schematics . . . they want them bad, Carter.'

'How many?'

'Hundreds,' said Gol softly.

'Show me where the weapons are,' said Carter grimly, and Gol led Carter and Natasha down the alloy ramp and into the darkness of Spiral_F below the hot ground of Africa.

CHAPTER 15

BATTLE

Carter reached the bottom of the wide alloy ramp and moved warily into a huge chamber hewn from the rock. Panels of computer banks glittered across one wall, a contrast to the rough harshness of the environment.

'Controls for the anti-aircraft guns. We even have some missiles.' Gol gestured at the walls.

'*Missiles?*' said Carter softly. 'It would seem that Spiral have infinite resources, do they not? Fuck me.'

'Come on, I will take you to the armoury. The other Spiral_F members are ready; it was a shame that you decided to sleep in so late.'

'A battle is one thing,' said Carter, 'but I didn't realise we were preparing for a fucking *war*.'

Gol explained quickly as they walked, gesticulating passionately with his hands, his eyes wide and focused; they came to many turns in the underground passageways – sometimes they branched in three or four directions. Always Gol would take a tunnel – seemingly at random – his boots treading the dust as he led the couple through the correct sequence of the—

'Maze?' asked Carter.

'Sort of. That was not its primary intention, but it has become so. We have been busy boys down here under the rock.' He grinned a broad square-toothed grin.

'So I see,' said Carter softly, brushing his way through thick cobwebs.

'Where to begin?' said Gol in his deep melodic voice. 'You want answers? You sounded surprised when I mentioned missiles. The Spiral you know and love own fifty-eight drilling rigs at a variety of locations around the world. Spiral own about a million square miles of ocean with oil and minerals and precious metals beneath the waves. Spiral own millions of acres of forestland in Scandinavia and in Russia, and thousands more miles of desert in Nevada, as well as here in Africa and in a variety of locations scattered across the Middle East . . . secretly, and under the guise of major business concerns. Spiral also owns many of the world's major computing organisations, ranging from the development of software, games and operating systems through to hardware – processors, communications, fucking DVD writers and the latest digi-optical scanners, memory cubes, blue-laser peripherals, Qglass-storage, you name it . . . Spiral's finances are beyond your comprehension. And beyond mine,' he added wistfully. 'They have a finger in every pie; if you can make money out of it, Spiral does. Gold, precious jewels, oil, construction, computers. Spiral is one of the richest organisations in the world – and also the best-kept secret. And it works for the good of mankind, but—'

'There is always a but,' said Carter softly.

'The splinter group we talked of last night: they seek to master the QIII – with it, they plan world domination.'

'I knew the QIII was rumoured to be incredibly powerful, but—'

'But nothing. Tell him, Nats.'

Nats, who had gone pale, said, 'The QIII is the most powerful military processor in the world – bar none. It is years ahead of its time, but the biggest breakthroughs are in two areas; it uses RI – real intelligence, it is a *superior* brain, not an artificial program following scripted moves. It can think. It can fucking think, Carter. But more importantly, it has what is called WorldCode. It can predict the future . . .'

'Predict the—'

'To within a certain percentage rate. It is not perfect – nothing ever is. But it follows new probability equations that it helped to create; its intelligence is astounding.'

They came to the end of a corridor, blanked by an alloy door. Gol punched in digits. The door slid open to reveal—

A huge chamber, full of guns and armour. Banks of guns, racks of body armour. The bunker was hewn from the orange rock, the walls rough and coarse, grained and grooved by the tools used to create this underground network.

'Take your pick,' said Gol softly. 'But be quick, we have less than twenty minutes.' His deviant ECube rattled. 'Yeah? OK. Arm the air defences.'

'They here?' Carter's eyes were bright.

'Soon. There are more than we thought.'

Carter frowned. 'And?'

Gol swallowed softly. 'The good news is that they have come over land, as we expected. Our air defences are too formidable; their planes or copters would be merely shot from the sky.'

'The bad news?'

'They have brought tanks. Lots of tanks. Had them airlifted in from a Spiral depot in Egypt.'

'What the fuck are we going to use to fight tanks?'

'Down at the bottom, over there,' said Gol, his humourless grin bloodless in the white lights. 'Grenade launchers. After all, these tanks are only *Tjorny Arylo* – Russian Black Eagles weighing in at 50 tonnes apiece and sporting 125mm-calibre cannons. I've sent a message to Langan who was flying air support over Nigeria to come and give us some fucking heavy air weaponry in that bitch of a Comanche he uses . . . but he might not get here in time. If you have to shoot one of these Black Eagles, Carter, don't aim for the turret because there are no crew there; aim for the hull at the front.' Gol spat. 'Bastards are heavily protected. *And* they have automatic loading systems; every shell doesn't have to be manually loaded.'

'But why?' asked Natasha, confused.

Gol grinned again. 'To speed up the rate of fire,' he said bitterly.

'This is not my fucking day,' said Carter.

'*It never is, Brother,*' whispered Kade in his mind.

'So you are back?'

'*You don't think I would miss this for the world, do you?*'

'I thought you might have died in a hole, lonely and unloved.'

'*Such bitter words stab me through the heart. Now, be a good lad and take me to the guns. Big guns, and some bombs – it's a while since I've seen people burn.*'

'You have no soul,' thought Carter bitterly.

'*On the contrary,*' said Kade. '*I am part of yours.*'

Sunlight rolled into the valley, red tendrils dancing through the disturbed dust. It glanced and spilled from and through the orange-tree orchards. Occasionally, a monkey chattered.

The men and women of Spiral_F waited.

They waited for the Nex.

They waited for the signal.

Carter stood beside a huge six-wheeled Pig, a Sterling sub-machine gun in his hands. He hefted the automatic weapon thoughtfully, for it had been many years since he had used such heavy hardware, always relying more on his Browning, or at least a Glock or Walther PPK. Carter didn't like machine guns; he didn't agree with the principle of mass destruction. It went against his morals, such as they were.

Gol tossed a bottle of Coke to Natasha, then another to Carter. They cracked open the bottles and drank, Natasha keeping her eyes fixed on the small plasma screen that had been set up on a small stand. It showed the entrance to the canyon, the sweeping African vista beyond and the images relayed from one of the sentries' headsets.

Natasha sported DPM desert combats and boots. She held her sub-machine gun awkwardly, and Carter's gaze swept along the line at the nervous groups of men and women, many lounging around and against the protective armoured Pigs. He could read their faces, the fear, the apprehension, the realisation that their comfortable – top secret but comfortable – existence had suddenly been shattered.

'I hope they don't come,' said Natasha softly.

She moved to Carter and slumped down beside him, stretching her legs out. The scene was strange, alien, disjointed. Orange trees, a white-walled house with crawling plants and a bed of prettily coloured flowers, their hues radiant in the sunshine . . . and heavily armoured vehicles, rifles, machine guns, men and women in boots and combat clothing—

'They'll come,' he said, passing her his cigarette.

She shook her head. 'I'm giving up.'

'How are your wounds? Hell, girl, you were like a pin-cushion back in Scotland.'

'OK.' She smiled, but the smile was a mask for her nerves. 'The shoulder one gives me the most trouble. Like some bastard sticking a knife in me every time I move my arm. How about you?'

'Ribs still grinding together.' Carter grinned. He held up his neighbour-strapped fingers. 'At least these don't stop me pulling a trigger and I have a horrible feeling that that skill will be needed real soon . . .'

They waited.

'How long?' asked Carter.

Gol shrugged. 'Ten minutes, maybe less.'

Carter checked his ammo and licked his dry lips. 'I fucking hate these situations; I prefer to work alone.'

'We know,' said Nats, glancing up. 'This time we have little choice.'

Shanaz appeared from the alloy entrance leading underground; she carried a small optical disk in one hand and was smiling broadly. She tossed the disk to Gol.

'There you go, boss.'

'All data transferred?'

'Yeah – it'd make Feuchter weep.'

Carter's head snapped around at the sound of the name, his eyes bright. 'Feuchter? I left that motherfucker to die in Germany.'

'He is not dead; far from it, Carter. Spiral_F has had its eye on Feuchter for quite some time; he's wrapped up in this Spiral QIII charade tighter than a first-time whore's legs around a sailor's back. He's head of Operations and operates out of Rub al'Khali, in Saudi Arabia – but, again, we are grasping at straws when we try to discover how his game is implemented. We suspect that he has links to the Spiral splinter group, but there is nothing solid. He is too good – he evades watchers, the fucker is almost untouchable. And since our fucking HQ was blown away it's pretty hard to check out such facts now. The whole comm SP1Network is screwed. Spiral has been fucked up; and, sadly, I believe this situation can only get worse.'

Carter rubbed at the stubble on his chin. 'Feuchter,' he said softly. 'That fucker is definitely a player in this game, I can sense it in my bones. He was ready to kill me back in Germany. He has obviously become more reckless . . .'

'Nobody had time to act on your report,' said Natasha.

Carter nodded, his eyes becoming hooded.

Natasha's gaze returned to the plasma screen.

'What do you know about Spiral_Q?' A gleam had appeared in Carter's eyes; Feuchter brought back bad memories and he knew that one day – one day – he would meet the man again. They would have a little chat. They would dance together. They would remember the good old times in a symbiotic embrace . . .

Gol frowned. 'The QIII is under development in Rub al'Khali under the banner of the Spiral_Q Division, rumoured to be located just south of Ash Shu'aybah in Saudi Arabia. Some of the design specifications were leaked recently over the Net and there have been some very pissed-off people . . . especially since we also acquired the schematics for this extremely dangerous processor.' Gol laughed bitterly. 'After the Nex have paid us a visit, we could do with nipping over to say hello to Feuchter and the other QIII developers. I'm sure they would have something interesting to contribute to our research. But considering the game they are playing, that place must be wired up tighter than a virgin's—'

'Yes, daddy,' pouted Natasha smartly. 'Remember that there are ladies present.'

'Yeah, ladies armed with guns and quite capable of dropping dangerous men and women without regard for where their brains and bones scatter . . .'

Natasha made a rude noise before turning back to the monitor.

'Shit,' hissed Gol, sitting up suddenly. 'Something is wrong.' His gaze flickered to the plasma screen – but there was nothing, nothing visible, no Nex sweeping down, no armies of tanks lumbering over the horizon.

'We're still safe,' said Natasha uncertainly.

'No, no, it's this. A PB: panic burst.' Gol pulled free a small black device on which a red light was glowing. Gol licked his lips, his stare coming up to Carter and Natasha. 'We only use this for a breach . . . The fuckers must have out-wired our electronics . . . but how? Fuck, fuck! Look, if anything should happen we have a rendezvous point for emergencies. The coordinates are 551.222.222.340; the ECube can patch them through, but remember that ECube security has been breached – you could be trans-mitting to the enemy.'

Carter pulled free his Browning and hoisted the SMG . . .

His mouth was suddenly a desert canyon floor.

He felt a stirring deep within his brain; like a lizard uncurling from a century of sleep around a rock.

Bullets screamed, a line of them smashing an inch above Carter's head and denting holes along the flank of an armoured vehicle. There was a *slap slap* of impacts in flesh and a soldier sitting atop a Pig, smoking and nursing his gun, was cut in half in a violent spray of blood. The top half of his body was punched out of sight behind the huge vehicle as his legs dropped, twitching and drooling trails of crimson to the ground.

'Down!' screamed Carter as gunfire erupted all

265

around – and he suddenly *knew*, remembered the digital avoidance of his own network back in Scotland, how a single Nex had evaded all his home-made electronic traps . . . and the bastards had done the same here – they'd bypassed the security networks and were now—

Inside the canyon.

Why use tanks when subterfuge could carry the game off more smoothly?

And Carter knew: the tanks were a bluff. To draw their attention. After all, who *wouldn't* hear a fucking tank coming?

Carter hit the dirt hard, Natasha beside him.

Gol slammed against a Pig as engines roared all around and machine-gun bursts echoed and screamed among the fumes. Carter glanced left and his eyes bulged like marbles from their sockets. A swarm of about a hundred Nex emerged from the trees and sped with incredible agility across the killing ground between the line of Pigs and the orchards—

Machine guns thundered.

'Aim for their heads!' bellowed Gol and, ducking low, charged behind a Pig and towards the wall of the white house. Carter rolled onto his belly, took aim with the SMG, and fired a burst. A Nex was picked up and slammed into the earth with a hole where the face had been. Carter chewed his lip grimly. To one side a Pig revved and charged at the Nex, guns blasting from behind the slits in the windows. The hefty front iron bumper smashed into two Nex and heavy wheels ploughed them into the ground, crushing their limbs and torsos. There was a *click*, followed by a concussive. *boom*. The Pig was picked up and tossed spinning into the air to skid onto its side, slamming into a tree. Fire licked from the insides. Black smoke rolled skyward.

Carter could hear men screaming.

Insanity followed. The Nex came from everywhere, charging at the Pigs with guns roaring. More detonations sounded and Carter and Natasha backed towards the white-walled house that they had originally thought was Gol's home. Both were firing, SMGs clattering in their grips. Carter sent bullets scything across a line of Nex – but they did not go down. Their attention was diverted his way and chips of stone and plaster were chewed from the walls behind him.

'Fuck,' he screamed, dropping to his knees and fumbling with the Sterling's magazine. The Nex charged – but were cut off by a rumbling Pig that ploughed into them, scattering bodies, tossing them high in the air like limp rag dolls.

They hit the ground hard.

Most rolled to their feet.

'I'm here!' came Kade's sudden triumphant crow.

'You are not needed!' snapped Carter within the asylum of his mind. He wiped more sweat from his eyes, wiped his hands on his shorts and fired another four-round burst into the Nex, who were shooting from the edges of the trees – many had been forced back by the sheer volume of projectiles spewing from the Pigs.

'You need me Carter; let me, let me do what I do best—'

'Get the fuck out of my brain, Kade!'

Carter blinked.

Something dark and ominous crept like a nuclear winter across his soul: superimposed across the beauty before him was a dark shroud like nothing he had ever seen before and his senses flowed, time slowed, everything went—

Black and white—

'We have to get back, get back inside the house . . .' he hissed.

Natasha nodded, gun clasped tight.

They started to creep along the wall. Bullets were coming from all directions, and several Pigs were churning about in front of the house, their guns thundering. The bodies of men and women littered the ground. A Pig wreck billowed thick black smoke.

'What is it?'

'The tanks are coming,' said Carter bitterly.

Suddenly, distant gunshots ceased. Machine-gun fire rattled to a halt. They heard the distant roaring of engines; an explosion boomed down the canyon, deep and rumbling, reverberating from the valley walls.

There came more exchanges of gunfire.

The sun beat down. Carter wiped sweat from his brow. His mouth was dry – too dry – and his ribs and several other minor cuts were nagging at him. Worst of all was his nose – broken one too many times, it impeded his breathing and the pain annoyed him.

There was a *boom* of heavy-calibre.

A Pig had been positioned between the trees – suddenly it was gone, disintegrated, a thousand panels of twisted steel spat up and out like a giant exploded grenade . . . a black flaming mechanical carcass sat where the vehicle had been, three wheels attached to a fire-raped dented chassis. Carter shook his head, dropped his SMG and made a grab for Natasha's hand.

'This is fucking insane – we have to leave.'

'Where's my father?'

'It's too fucking late for that! Come *on*!'

'I don't want to die like this,' said Natasha.

'I don't want to die at all,' said Carter.

They sprinted for the door. Carter ducked as a *phat phat phat* smacked against the tiles above him, describing a diagonal down the wall. There was a scream to his left

268

as a woman was punched flailing from her feet, scrabbling at her throat, blood pumping between useless grappling fingers, her gun and this war suddenly forgotten in her bright hot agony. She squirmed for a moment and Carter leaped up and emptied a full magazine into the charging mass, which spread out as if welcoming his bullets—

Natasha screamed.

Carter whirled – but too late, a figure was upon him . . . Natasha's gun rattled in her hands and gunfire echoed inside Carter's head and all around . . . he slapped hard against the dirt, and for a second thought he was dead. Carter kicked out, heaved the dead body from him, rolled to see madness exploding around him. The Nex had charged again, and the men and women of Spiral_F were being slaughtered.

Carter pulled free the trapped SMG and shot the Nex – which had cornered Natasha – in the back of the head, watching the brains emerge in a spray and the figure toppling to reveal Natasha's shocked visage staring dumbly at him. He reached forward, grabbed her, screamed, 'Where the fuck is Gol?'

Natasha did not speak—

'Are you hurt? I said, *are you fucking hurt?*'

A figure ran at them – Natasha whimpered – the SMG in the figure's hands lifted a fraction and Carter could see the finger on the trigger, sensed the applied pressure, pushed Natasha away and squeezed his own SMG's trigger at the same time as he dived—

Bullets skimmed past Carter's face, so close that he felt the breeze of their passing; a line of bullets caught the figure and slammed it into the air where it spun for a moment, then landed twisted and dead.

'Come on.' Carter snatched Natasha's hand and dragged her after him. To one side he could see a small

269

group of men kicking at a Nex on the ground; two Nex leaped to its aid and there was a short and very bloody exchange. Carter sprinted to the house and stopped suddenly in the doorway. He checked behind him—

He wasn't sure how many were still alive – how many of Spiral_F, or how many of the enemy – as he glanced down at Natasha, who had been dragged along behind him in his mad flight for temporary safety away from the gun battle. There were spots of blood on her face, and Carter could feel her hands shaking. He looked into her eyes and said slowly, 'Don't panic, Nats. Come on – I need you focused. We are not going to die – I promise you I will protect you—'

'How can . . .'

'Shh.' He put his finger against her lips. Then he leaned forward and kissed her softly, whispering again, 'I promise you I will protect you—'

'Liar . . .'

Carter heaved Kade away with such a blast of mental anger and hatred and violence that he felt Kade spat into a dark infinity – and calmness settled on his mind, an insane sort of calmness which he had only rarely experienced before in highly dangerous combat situations—

His brain ran to codes, to numbers—

Everything was clear—

Black and white—

Logical.

No emotion no panic no fear—

It was what had marked him out for the Demolition Squads in the first place.

'Follow me.'

Carter led the way swiftly, Natasha close behind him. They entered the house through a narrow bullet-chewed doorway; behind them rattles of gunfire still burst through the orchards, decimating the trees. But the noises of violence were growing less. Spiral_F had been overrun.

Carter gripped his Browning tightly with his free hand and inched forward down the corridor towards the bright light on the other side of the room. He wasn't even sure where the SMG had gone, which episode of the insanity had removed the weapon from him.

His hands were slippery with blood. Was it his own? Or that of a Nex?

Nex, spat his mind.

What the fuck had happened to the world?

Carter paused. Something in his soul howled into his consciousness, a warning as—

Three Nex came smashing through a huge patio-type window in a sudden flurry of movement that shattered the stillness. Their masked heads were down as a shower of glass vomited into the room directly in Carter's path, scattering across the floor like diamonds tossed at his feet. As their boots hit the tiled floor and their SMGs lifted, Carter's Browning snapped up and he squeezed the trigger – bullets ripped across the short space—

Carter leaped towards the figures. Two were smashed immediately from their feet, clawing at bullets in their faces. The third leaped at him as—

The Browning clicked on empty.

The dead man's click.

The kiss of death.

A fist slammed forward, an inch from Carter's nose and he twisted, left elbow coming around with incredible velocity to crack against the Nex's head, hammering the killer's head down onto his rising knee which connected with bone-jarring force.

But the figure still managed to slam a fist into Carter's chest.

271

He was lifted vertically, pain smashing through his entire body, vomit splashing from his lips. He seemed to halt in mid-air, then fell suddenly and hit the ground hard with a dull *thud*, groaning in agony. The Nex stepped over him, moving towards Natasha—

Carter rolled over, foetal, disabled . . .

—A punch to the heart . . . an induced heart attack—

Natasha cowered in front of the masked figure that was poised, ready to strike, a cobra with a fixed stare. The Nex stopped, swiftly bent to retrieve an SMG and pointed the dark emotionless eye at Natasha's face—

Carter, unable to breathe, almost unable to move, fumbled in a time-vacuum to slot a fresh mag into his gun; then he dragged the Browning into his line of sight. He felt his hand, wavering, felt his vision warp for a split second and nausea screamed through him and he pointed the Browning and time had slowed and his calmness and his serenity had gone and this was Natasha, Natasha his love and she was going to die with hot metal in her brain and it would be all his fault and he had promised—

Promised to protect her—

Promised to keep her alive—

Seven bullets hissed past the Nex's ear.

The figure whirled – but Carter kept on firing and the figure was suddenly jerked and kicked up and back, holed and smashed and bleeding, to twist and flip and land in a heap on top of Natasha. She screamed, a long low animal sound. Carter felt the Browning click on empty and he crawled to his knees—

'*Behind* . . .' came Kade's warning.

Carter rolled, fast, faster than any human had a right to move. A line of bullets tore a strip of smashed tiles into the air in a cloud of brittle dust. Carter's eyes fixed

272

on the swaying figure of a Nex, chest torn open, a slick glossy organ visible through the scorched cloth, blood soaking the grey clothing and falling in heavy slow drips to the remaining tiles. The Nex's cheek hung as a loose flap of skin.

Carter spun to his feet, and leaped.

The SMG barked once – and was silenced.

Carter took the bullet; it sliced across his side just below his ribs, a twisted trajectory tearing a path through flesh and leaving a line of red that spewed blood to soak Carter's clothing. The force of the blow punched and slammed him around, spinning him and sending his face crashing forward to hit the ground.

There was no pain.

That's fucking bad, he thought.

No pain is bad.

Enemy . . .

Got to kill—

Where are you, Kade? Where the fuck are you when I need you?

Don't want to die . . .

Pain . . .

Don't want to die . . .

He tried to rise, but only managed to turn his head as he slumped forward. He lifted his hand in front of his face and saw that it was coated in a deep red that looked the wrong colour. It looked bad. It looked dangerous; the colour of something that shouldn't see the light of day.

Fuck, mused his brain, suddenly calm.

His hand lowered. The torn bleeding *holed* Nex, in slow motion, fitted a fresh mag to the SMG and he watched it carrying out the action, swaying in its own world of pain but with nothing showing in those cold copper eyes. Carter could do nothing. The Nex stepped

273

lightly forward, intense stare boring down into him and he recognised that gaze, from back in Scotland, from back at his house when it had been so rudely invaded—

'Nice to see you again,' he croaked.

'Mr Carter. It has been a pleasure.'

The soft asexual voice held no pain. No fucking pain? screeched Carter's confusion-riddled mind.

The finger squeezed the trigger—

And the Nex's masked face exploded.

Carter watched, dumbstruck, as a huge hole appeared in a jagged shower to the tune of metallic screaming. Brain, skull, blood rained down on him with gentle *pattering* sounds. The figure folded slowly and neatly to the floor and was still.

Carter's focus switched: from the corpse in the foreground to *behind* the corpse where Natasha stood, an SMG in her hands, a faint horrified smile on her lips.

'You owe me one,' she whispered weakly.

Carter coughed, and rolled onto his back. 'I need a pad of cloth, or something,' he wheezed, forcing himself into a sitting position. Warmth had spread across his torso and down to his crotch.

Natasha knelt by his side and dipped her hands into his lifeblood. Her gaze met his. She swiftly tore part of her shirt free and applied the pad and suddenly a world of pain fired into Carter's brain and screamed at him in the huge echoing operatic hall of his skull—

And the headache pain in his skull, in his brain: it returned to burn.

Returned to burn bad.

'It's not my fucking day,' he croaked.

Carter struggled to his feet, the pad of cloth clamped to his side. Natasha bent, retrieved his Browning and helped him to reload the weapon with blood-slippery bullets. They both took SMGs from the dead bodies of the Nex, slinging the weapons over their shoulders and then taking deep, deep breaths.

'What now?' hissed Natasha.

'We need to find Gol.'

'He could be anywhere . . . it was so crazy . . .'

They moved slowly through the house, up the stairs, to Gol's study. There had been a battle in the room and there were several blood trails but no bodies. Blood was splattered up the walls as if some mad artist with a loaded paintbrush had been let loose and told to inflict contemporary art; Gol was not there.

'What were the emergency coordinates?' asked Natasha softly, her shaking hands keeping the door to the study covered with the SMG.

'551.222.222.340,' came the pain-filled response from Carter, whose face had gone grey, eyes purple-ringed, nose crusted with blood. He gripped his Browning, but held the weapon as if he didn't really understand what it was . . . he had lost blood, was weak, was fading fast . . . losing the will to play the game.

Natasha gritted her teeth. Pulled free her ECube. Patched in the coordinates . . .

'Come on,' she said, finding a new level of strength, feeling adrenalin surge through her battered weary blood-speckled frame once more. She sprinted to the window: outside, the world still raged . . . black smoke drifted on the horizon from a myriad of destroyed and wounded Pigs. She saw a tank, a Russian Black Eagle, squat among the trees, its huge camouflaged turret pointing their way, the muzzle of the mammoth gun a truly awe- and terror-inspiring sight. Machine guns rattled, a savage exchange between two groups.

'Shit. We have to get out of here.' Natasha allowed

Carter to rest some of his weight on her, and they moved slowly – painfully slowly – back through the house.

'This is madness,' she said.

'Madness,' agreed Carter, coughing.

'I hope it will be worth it,' she muttered bitterly.

'It never is,' said Carter, drooling blood.

They stopped just behind the doorway, Carter leaning heavily against the wall bathed in sunlight. The fragrance from the orchards smelled good, even mingled with a wave of cordite. Natasha found it hard to believe that a battle was taking place here – in this paradise . . . and that her life hung in the balance, suspended by a delicate thread of Fate.

Her gaze roved, searching for the Nex—

Searching for the fast-moving deadly killers . . . they were in the trees, behind the tanks, and as she watched a group sprinted towards a Pig, which mowed them down in a spray of blood, its heavy machine-gun barrels smoking.

How many are left? she thought.

Many of the Pigs had gone; Nats could see another two tanks, which had eased down from the canyon mouth after the battle had begun. Gunfire echoed in the distance, followed by more explosive rattles echoing within the shadow-haunted depths of the trees.

Her gaze snapped left and came to settle on a Jeep Cherokee. 4.0 litre. Big and sturdy; dented and bullet-pocked, but it was deliciously—

Near.

A hundred paces.

Only a hundred paces.

Under the heavy-calibre eyes of the Black Eagles and the machine-gun muzzles of the Nex.

Can we run faster than their bullets? she thought.

Our lives depend on it . . .

'Come on, Carter,' Natasha said. 'The jeep. You see it?'

Carter lifted his head. 'Yes,' he croaked.

'I need you to run. Can you do that?'

'Yes.'

She took a final look at the tanks; huge squat metal machines, painted roughly, their torsos dented and showing signs of abuse. They were silent, engines dead.

And the Nex . . .

She could see five groups, all with their attention diverted by groups of Spiral_F, or Pigs. Another group were setting up some equipment at the edge of the trees. Natasha and Carter stepped away from the sanctuary.

They ran.

It took an eternity . . .

Ten paces. Each step saw a splash of red erupt from Carter's side as a flap of flesh opened with a jolt, blood marking his passage against the sand.

Twenty paces.

Natasha spotted the five emerging Nex at the edge of the orchard, spotted their positions and their glinting weapons. 'Fu—' she managed as they opened fire. Natasha screamed, her head ducking low, Carter suddenly an incredibly heavy and cumbersome weight chained around her neck and dragging her down down down into the black depths of death and oblivion – bullets kicked up dirt around her feet, some whizzed past and ricocheted off the stone of the house in tiny spurts of dust.

Natasha pushed on.

The Nex ceased their firing.

They charged, moving swiftly and silently over the ground towards the staggering couple. Natasha, teeth gritted, urged herself to greater efforts, almost dragging the semi-conscious Carter with her.

Seventy paces. Eighty paces . . .

Ninety—

She could pick out the copper eyes of the Nex—

And realised.

They look the same, she thought.

They all look the fucking same . . .

She reached the Cherokee, wrenched open the door and pushed Carter into the cabin. The lead Nex leaped, boots slapping the bonnet of the Cherokee and sliding towards her. With a yelp, Natasha dived in and slammed the door – which jammed open, three inches from closing—

She saw the fingers, then the masked face appear. The door was pulled away from her blood-slippery grip—

Natasha's boot slammed into the Nex's face, three, four times – the Nex fell back and she pulled at the Cherokee's door with all her might. It slammed shut with a heavy final *click*. She looked down in horror at the three severed fingers in the footwell.

It didn't scream, she realised.

It didn't make a fucking sound . . .

The other Nex arrived – leaping at the vehicle—

Natasha slammed down the central locking. All doors locked – a Nex started beating at the door, then hammered a fist through the side window, shattering its glass and scattering it over the inside of the cab. Natasha brought the stolen SMG around and held the trigger down hard; bullets spat out through the smashed window and into the Nex's body and already she was turning the ignition. The huge 4.0-litre engine roared into life as her boot stomped down and a Nex was caught suddenly against the grille and bonnet, buckled, tossed beneath the vehicle and wrapped around the spinning prop-shaft . . . The SMG, still screaming, suddenly clicked on an empty mag and Natasha dropped the weapon on the

278

seat next to the crumpled, wheezing body of Carter and dragged on the steering wheel. The Cherokee roared towards the orange trees with three Nex sprinting after it—

It sped beneath the fruit-laden branches, straight down the dirt track. Natasha laughed out loud as a fresh breeze came blowing through the smashed window and cooled the sweat of desperation on her face. 'Carter?' she screamed. 'You OK, Carter? You still alive?'

There was a distant sound. A *crump*.

As if obeying some unconscious reflex, Carter reached over and dragged hard on the steering wheel. The Cherokee slewed from the trail; there was a painful metal scream, and the trail just behind them erupted in a shower of dirt. Stones and shrapnel pounded and howled around the Cherokee, which rocked on the concussion of the blast.

Carter looked up, smiled weakly at Natasha, then closed his eyes as sunlight played through the windscreen and illuminated his face and he could think of nothing except—

Pain.

All-consuming pain.

'Get me to a doctor and I just might live,' he wheezed.

'We're not out of the woods yet,' snapped Natasha.

Carter grinned – his blood-splashed face a caked mask of horror and destruction.

Natasha increased the speed – roaring in a burst of screaming engine noise out of the orange-tree orchards, bursting free of their heady fragrance and cool shade and into the reality of the sun-baked African landscape. The end of the canyon rushed towards them and there, ahead of them, stood a small group of Nex. The Cherokee, now touching a hundred m.p.h., hit the ridge and bullets thumped along its flanks and the wheels disengaged from the ground and it soared—

Natasha ducked.

All she could see was sky.

'Fuuu-ck . . .' she hissed as the Cherokee hurtled glinting through the air. A glance in the rear-view mirror showed nothing behind . . .

The vehicle came down like a plane coming in to land—

The suspension compressed, bottoming out with terrifyingly loud *bangs*, and Natasha was smashed upwards, hands slipping from the wheel, head hammering the roof of the cab so hard that her teeth slammed together, leaving her mouth swilling with blood and shards of tooth . . . The Cherokee kangarooed for a few moments, obeying the laws of physics as it slewed around in the scrub, tyres eating dirt and sand and bushes until Natasha gripped the wheel once more and dragged it onto course, foot stamping hard against the accelerator and dragging the roaring vehicle around in a broad arc, heading up towards the red rocky hills to the right of Gol's devastated blasted routed Spiral_F Operations Centre—

'What the fuck hit me?' groaned Carter.

Natasha spat a mouthful of blood out of the window. She blinked rapidly, quelling the spinning sensation in her head. 'Just stay down, my love,' she managed. 'You really don't want to know.'

Natasha accelerated, tyres thumping over bushes and scrub.

She followed no road – she made her own.

Something clanged and thumped under the vehicle – but Natasha did not care. She fumbled free the ECube and it guided her; it didn't matter that their position wasn't secure – it was obvious to anybody who cared to look.

She pressed the accelerator to the floor and her hands shook madly on the heavily vibrating steering wheel and they headed upwards and finally joined a dirt track leading towards the rendezvous and, Natasha hoped, escape—

'I hope this rendezvous exists,' she muttered.

She checked her teeth in the rear-view mirror, cursing their chipped edges, vanity still a reflex despite her nearly fatal experience. As she moved the mirror back into position she saw them—

Three trucks.

Hammering along behind her—

'For fuck's sake,' she hissed. 'Will they never stop?'

She urged the Cherokee on; the pursuing trucks – whatever make they were – were incredibly powerful. They didn't gain, but she could not lose them either. They sped along in the sunlight, huge red dust-trails in their wake, tyres and suspension thumping and rocks and trees and bushes flashing by to either side—

In a cloud of dust the Cherokee hammered up the incline and towards the location indicated by the blip on the ECube . . . towards the emergency rendezvous set up by Gol – who had mysteriously disappeared.

'I hope you're all right, father,' Natasha thought soberly. 'I hope you're OK.'

Shanaz froze. A figure was crouched in the tunnel, an SMG levelled at her.

After the hectic bloody battle out front, Shanaz had been separated from her group; she had fled the bullets, down the alloy ramp and into the depths of Spiral_F deep under the ground . . .

That had been the plan. To meet; to regroup if the shit hit the fan.

And the shit had most definitely battered the fan to pieces.

Shanaz stared at the shadowed figure. It had to be a Nex; it had to be. She cursed the dim lighting down here in the depths . . .

Slowly, Shanaz lifted her hands in the air.

The AK47 was beside her, digging into her ribs.

She did not glance at it.

'What do you want me to do?' she asked softly, trying not to antagonise the armed intruder.

The masked face tilted; eyes scanned the room.

The figure stood from its crouch. A fluid blur.

There came a *hiss* of exhaled breath.

The SMG roared, and Shanaz was slammed backwards against a computer, blood splashing up the rock walls, the bullets cutting a line straight up her chest and slamming into her skull. Shards of skull bone spun free and she slumped slack across a chair, limp and dead, her brain and exposed organs glistening in the weak glow of the bulbs.

Suddenly, silence reigned.

The assassin's head snapped left; the SMG moved to cover the opening of a tunnel.

Jahmal sprinted into view, large round face changing from a happy smiling visage into a snarl of rage as his eyes fell across Shanaz and he stumbled to a confused halt in the centre of the bunker chamber. He spun, checking the dark deserted tunnels.

'Shanaz?' he screamed, stumbling towards her. His hand reached out, fingers grasping her smashed jaw and sliding in the blood that soaked her smooth skin. 'Shanaz!'

Tears rolled down his ebony cheeks.

The bullets cut into his back and Jahmal didn't even know what had hit him.

Marcus licked his lips and closed his eyes, listening. He stood in the corridor, the AK47 sweat-slippery in his hands and he knew; knew that death had come and who-ever was the aggressor had killed both Shanaz and Jahmal. They were good; they were fast and they were efficient.

Get a grip, screamed his brain.

He took several deep breaths, feeling sweat soak him beneath his dreads, prickling and itching.

He moved forward; not towards the gunfire, but away. He had heard the shots; perhaps fifty rounds in all had been fired. This wasn't assassination; this was butchery. He had heard Jahmal's cries; understood their intensity; knew the man – his friend, his comrade – was dead.

Marcus halted, dreadlocks swaying.

There were two tunnels before him.

'Marcus!' came the distant cry.

Marcus frowned; Gol?

There came another cry, this time of pain.

Gol? Injured?

Marcus moved forward, still cautious, twitching at every sigh of a breeze in the tunnels. He came to a round low room, dim-lit with four tunnels leading from the chamber.

He halted.

He turned, turned again—

And saw the figure. His eyes widened. The barrel of the AK47 swung around but it was too late and the SMG was already pointing at him and he saw the gentle flex of muscle and tendon and could read the figure; could read its amorality.

His eyes closed—
A great sigh escaped his lips.
And the game was over.

Langan was seated on the edge of a rock, gaze locked on the distant canyon below as the battle raged on. He watched the plumes of smoke reaching for the sky and shook his head in disbelief; Spiral_F's air defences were still operational.

The Comanche was useless.

Awesomely powerful, but useless.

'Why didn't you switch them off, Gol?'

Behind Langan squatted the Comanche – still in jungle camouflage – its engines idle. All systems were on-line, primed and ready to fire; he could have her in the air in thirty seconds if he had to – and Langan knew that when the time came he would have to move fast.

He heard the screaming engine . . . and then engines. Plural.

Company.

Langan ran to the Comanche and climbed aboard – he suddenly had a bad feeling and he primed the engines, fired them, listened to injectors and turbos whining as the twin LHTec spun up the rotors. He watched the gauges roll smoothly into life. He armed the weapons systems and rested his chin on his hands, staring from the cockpit at the stretch of road that led from the crest of the rise and straight towards this little secluded area where he had chosen, thoughtfully, to hide.

The Cherokee leaped into view, sped towards the Comanche and veered to one side. Brakes engaged and the Cherokee left long parallel grooves in the sand. Three heavy speeding trucks appeared in hot pursuit; Natasha leaped from the Cherokee, dragging Carter with her . . . he was stumbling, practically unconscious and a little delirious, unaware of what was actually happening or where he was, or even what his fucking name was . . .

'They the enemy?' shouted Langan calmly over the rising whine of the rotors.

'Fuck 'em hard,' screamed Natasha.

Langan flicked a switch; his HIDSS helmet sprang to life. He calmly selected a target and the General Electric MiniGun sped up and hit five thousand revs. With calm smooth movements Langan released the payload of bullets.

Thousands of heavy-calibre rounds roared across the track, smashed through the trucks and sent them ploughing into one another. The Nex inside them became nothing more than merged blood-pulps, purple bloodied sacks of flesh and smashed bone. One truck exploded, fire roaring up into the sky, small pieces of burning metal describing arcs and then thumping into the sand. Another truck rolled, lame and limping, towards the Comanche.

There was a gentle whine as the MiniGun rolled down, metallic *clacks* rattling through the sudden calm.

Langan leaped down from the cockpit.

'Where's Gol?'

'No idea,' said Natasha. 'But I think we need to move fast!'

Langan helped Natasha to get the wounded, groaning form of Carter into the rear of the cockpit. 'I'm sorry, but it's going to be a tight squeeze. It's only really designed for two.'

'We'll manage,' said Natasha. 'Have you got medical supplies?'

'All on board. Let's get moving.'

285

The rotors spun up, and with a roar the Comanche leaped into the sky and sped across the clear blue, sun glinting from the flashing rotors, the aircraft's proximity missile-warning systems screaming at Langan. The engines howled with power as the Comanche skirted the valley and orange-tree orchards where the battle still raged.

Natasha found the appropriate panel and slid it back. She took out the medical supplies, removed sterile seals and gave Carter an injection of morphine that eased his pain and knocked him out. His colour was bad and she hoped he wouldn't need blood . . . She squeezed Carter to one side of the narrow aperture in which she was supposed to work, and to the background music of the rotors thumping she struggled to remove his jacket, and then cut away his shirt around the wound gouged by the spinning bullet.

'I don't see much I can do down there,' said Langan. 'The air defences are still armed; even I'm not stupid enough to take on ground-to-air missiles. No fucking way.'

He took the Comanche lower; they swept wide around the orange orchards, the down draught from the rotors making trees and bushes sway and hiss. A few token shots followed the copter but it was moving far too swiftly. The Comanche lifted over the rim of the valley, banked steeply and Langan looked to Natasha for instructions.

'What shall we do?'

'Make another pass; Gol must be down there somewhere. If any fucker can get out alive, it's Gol.' They returned, sweeping as low as Langan dared with tanks in the vicinity. The Comanche described broad circles several more times. There was no sign of Gol, nor of any other fleeing survivors for that matter. Machine guns were

286

still firing, but as they circled the exchanges of fire became more and more sporadic.

'Can you see your scanner?' shouted back Langan.

'Yeah,' replied Natasha sombrely.

'See the yellow dots? Identified and tagged as Sikorsky Apaches. Probably bringing in more Nex. The reinforcements have arrived and I don't really want to be hanging around when they turn up. Look.' He pointed to a dial. 'The air defences have just gone down – shit, just in time for the Apaches. I think the Nex must be controlling them, using the defences to keep me out of play. I think they underestimated Gol's little group, don't you?'

'I don't call several hundred Nex and a load of tanks *underestimation*. So, what can we do now?'

'You're the boss,' said Langan. 'I just follow Gol's instructions. And seeing that you are his daughter . . . well . . .'

'How did you know that?'

'We have this wonderful thing called communication.'

'Oh.'

'How's Carter?'

'Out for the moment. I'm just glad the bullet passed through him – I'm not sure I could remove one if it was lodged in his body.'

'Don't get blood on the seats.'

'I don't think he's got much left.'

Natasha removed the blood-soaked padding. Cut free more shirt. Grimaced at what she saw; she took some tweezers and moved Carter to allow her to see inside the wound where scorched pieces of shirt were lodged.

'I've got something on the scanner.'

'What is it?'

'Five figures. Running . . . across the top of one of the ridges . . .'

'Head for them. Let's snoop.'

The Comanche banked, rising straight towards the glinting sunlight. Like a bullet it hurtled across the sky and then suddenly dropped, gliding in a descending arc towards—

A high ridge of red rock overlooking a fast-flowing narrow river, deep within a red-walled valley; a rocky V-shaped crevasse that went on down for ever.

Natasha could see distant figures, sprinting over the rocks—

And she recognised Gol.

'He's on his own,' said Langan.

'Can you shoot his pursuers?'

'At this speed? I'll cut the whole fucking group in half! Gol's too close to them . . . I can't distinguish the targets, not with a fucking MiniGun anyway . . .'

The Comanche screamed over the ridge and banked at a distance, rotors flashing silver against the sun; and then they returned for a second pass. Gol was sprinting ahead of four pursuing Nex. He was unarmed . . . and carrying something in his clenched fist that sparkled with rainbow colours and then—

In a flash they were over and gone.

The Comanche banked once more – a distant whirring insect to those on the ground—

'If I touch down, we could be overrun,' hissed Langan. 'They've got SMGs and we've got a man down.'

'We've got to help him!' screamed Natasha. 'We've got to fucking help him!'

Gol, sweat pouring down his body, glanced up as the Comanche roared overhead a second time. He was as good as dead, he knew, but the small optic disk he carried in his fist could not fall into the wrong hands . . .

Could not.

The schematics were slowing the enemy down – buying Spiral more time. And as Gol had said before, they were the enemies' Achilles heel. Their weakness.

How could the enemy hope to rule the world using the QIII if there was a second QIII there to counter all the commands? There to push a stick through the wheel of military progress? There to *fuck it up* for them? No, they needed the schematics.

Gol did not glance behind him. But he could hear them, hear their boots on the rock. Gol considered himself a fit man, but the bastards had chased him for miles; most of it uphill; most of it across rock. The Nex had known exactly who they were after right from the beginning of the battle; they had cornered Gol, sent him fleeing with bullets at his tail, like a rat down a maze, separating him from the other members of Spiral_F—

They had known.

Known what he carried.

A grim smile twisted his lips. He pounded on. Gol's endurance had been pushed to its limit and he could feel his body consuming itself, using reserves that he had never dreamed he had – the large man did not know how he still managed to put one foot in front of the other—

For the past mile the Nex had slowly wound him in, like a big fish on a line. Now they were mere feet behind him and panic settled like a demon across his soul. What to do? What to fucking do?

Why hadn't they shot him?

They knew; knew he was a key to the schematics encryption – the key to unlocking everything inscribed on the optic disk. With him dead, it would take them a long time to crack – days, maybe . . . but alive, and tortured?

Mere minutes. He had seen what they could do.

He shivered. He did not want to be caught by the Nex.

Better to fucking *die*, he thought.

His boots thumped on rock.

His angle of ascent altered.

There was a shout behind him as the Nex realised what was happening—

Gol pounded up to the ridge and in silence, without looking down, leaped with all his might. Gloved hands brushed against his back. A Nex followed him, not from choice but from speed and momentum.

Gol, legs still pumping, sailed out over the abyss.

He kept the disk tight in his fist.

There were no final words. No heroic shouts. Gol merely clamped his jaw tight in the throes of bowel-wrenching fear as the world opened up before him . . . so large . . . so bright . . .

And he knew; this was the first time he had truly *seen*.

The first time he had truly *felt*.

And life felt so, so good.

The wind roared through his beard.

Red rock flashed past his tear-blurred vision.

Gol fell.

'No!' screamed Natasha.

The Comanche banked once more; the MiniGun screamed and the Nex on the mountain ridge were cut in half – it all happened so fast that they didn't even know what hit them.

'Go down, to the river,' she commanded.

'The walls are too narrow,' said Langan softly. 'I can't take this beast down there; the rotors would smash into the rock.'

'Do it!'

'We will fucking die,' snapped Langan.

Natasha went silent. Dead silent. Langan risked a glance back. He could see her tears. 'You need to focus, Natasha,' he said softly. 'Get Carter sewn up.'

'Yes,' she whispered. 'Sewn up. Be strong. Yes.'

'It's what Gol would want.'

'Yes.'

Langan flew the Comanche along the ridge and then dropped towards the river when the walls widened and dropped with the contours of the land. The river, wide and fast-flowing, showed no signs of life. For a while the Comanche cruised up and down the banks, searching; but Gol had gone.

'We can't search for ever,' said Langan eventually, drained, exhausted.

'I know. Just a few more minutes.'

Rotors thumping, the Comanche circled and paced and searched. Finally, it veered off, climbing steeply, and then headed south, away from the valley, away from the river and away from Kenya.

The snowy peaks of Kilimanjaro glowed in the distance, majestic and mighty, domineering and eternal.

'Take me away from this place,' whispered Natasha.

The Nex walked slowly into the chamber; another two stood beside the black body bag that had been unzipped to reveal the riddled body of the smashed female Nex within.

The first Nex glanced down, then removed the dead female's mask. Copper eyes looked without apparent emotion at the prostrate figure; a hand reached out, touched the bullet holes, moved lower towards the visible punctured organs and the yellow of spilled torn fat.

'What shall we do with the body?' came a soft voice.

291

'Burn it.'

'Shouldn't we return it for analysis?'

The Nex smiled then; a cold grim smile. It shook its shaved head and turned away, stepping towards the tunnel hewn through the stone and the welcoming calming cool darkness beyond.

The Nex hated the heat. It hated this place.

Its words echoed back, hollow and empty.

'She is dead. Her OneThoughts are gone. Burn her. She can be of no more use to us.'

It was night.

Insects buzzed in the darkness.

The Comanche sat, clicking, its metal cooling slowly, beside a small grove of palms.

The fire was a small one, the dry wood burning without smoke. Langan brewed tea in a little tin pot and Natasha sat, chin on her knees, arms around herself, staring into the flickering flames, lost: lost in a world of her own creation. Carter had finally come round; he was grey with exhaustion and accepted the mug of sweet tea without a sound. He didn't even have the energy to question Langan's presence, never mind engage in playful banter.

'You any closer to knowing what the fuck is going on?' asked Langan finally.

Carter nodded. 'I think so. Things are becoming clearer.'

'You still need me?'

'We need one last favour,' said Carter.

Natasha looked up. 'We do?'

'Aye.' Carter nodded, sipping at the sweet tea as one hand probed tenderly at his wounded flank. 'We need you to drop us somewhere.'

Langan nodded with a supportive smile. 'Anywhere, buddy,' he said softly. 'Just name the location.'

'We need you to take us to Saudi Arabia, the Great Sandy Desert,' said Carter. 'I think it's time we paid Count Feuchter a visit regarding this fucking QIII project of his.'

PART TWO

TO LOOK OUT WITH COPPER EYES

you're just **another coffin**
on its way down the emerald aisle
when your children's stony glances
mourn your **death in a terrorist's
smile**
the bomber's arm placing fiery gifts
on the supermarket shelves
alley sings with shrapnel **detonate**
a **temporary hell**

Forgotten Sons
Fish/Marillion

CHAPTER 16

MISSION

The Apache, piloted by Jam and with Slater snoring in the back, soared through the pouring rain, refuelling at a tiny local military outpost in Switzerland before heading east towards the borders of Austria and beyond. Jam cruised the Apache on a cushion of howling engines, heading east into the wind and the rain.

The Apache cruised across the Western Alps of Austria, rising to an incredible altitude until the mountains snaked away like the dark teeth of some huge giant's gaping maw. Jam cruised in silence, with only the thrumming of rotors disturbing this high bleak cold solitude. The Priest, seated beside him, watched on in silence, mouth a grim line, eyes bright and fevered.

'There,' said The Priest softly, peering forward a little.

The Apache cruised for slick fast minutes until both Jam and The Priest saw it; it was huge, a mammoth mountain rising from the Hohe Tauern range like a broken tooth, jagged and fearsome, capped with glittering sparkling crystal-wine ice.

'Grossglockner,' said Jam, his voice filled with an awe

he knew would never leave him, no matter how often he visited this magical and yet ultimately *horrifying* place.

'And the Kamus,' whispered The Priest.

Kamus-5. An old disused military complex built into the side of the mighty Grossglockner, well above the timber line and far away from roads of all description. One could only reach the crumbling edifice by two routes – one was by air, the other by a cable car consisting of long-disused carriages and steel lines from a nearby summit.

Jam brought the Apache in high, then dropped steeply towards the slopes of another mountain in the range, hugging the ground before climbing past huge swathing forests of beech and Austrian black pine, up into larch, fir and spruce and higher still, speed decreasing with the changing pitch of the rotors.

'You see anything?'

'It is too distant,' said The Priest. 'Head for that patch of forest, over there; where the trees break. We can reach the old cable-car base on foot. That will be the only sure way to avoid detection.'

Jam brought the Apache in to land, and the metal beast was swallowed by the trees. The rotors spun down, engines dying and clicking, and the four travellers stepped onto a forest bed of fir needles and dead branches that crackled softly underfoot. Water dripped from the trees around the clearing and Slater and Nicky found themselves looking around, deeply unimpressed.

'Smells damp,' said Slater.

'This is a wet forest,' said Jam. 'What do you expect?'

'I a city boy,' grumbled Slater. 'I not like this wilderness thing.'

Nicky approached The Priest, who was half kneeling, hand touching the sodden earth, eyes raised up and blinking at the rain. 'We heading for the old cable-car house?' she asked.

'Yes. The Lord will guide us. Come on, darkness will be falling soon and it would help if we could find the place before then.' He rose, ponderously. Shouldering their packs the group moved off between the trees, heading up the slopes made slippery by mud and fern.

Before long they were all panting, red-faced, and covered in twigs, leaves, and smears of mud. The going was steep, tough. There were no natural paths and only tree boles and branches to grab hold of for support.

The Priest led the way, and Jam dropped back to walk with Slater and Nicky as they fought their way up this mountain slope.

'Do you know what he plans when we get to the Kamus?'

Jam shrugged. 'He wasn't exactly a talkative passenger. I think we need to wait until we've had a good look; see what this supposed *activity* actually is at our old friend – the Kamus.'

'I not like the place,' said Slater, slowly. 'I not want to go back.'

Jam said nothing.

Eventually, they came across a pathway; heavily overgrown, a dirt trail with occasional wood-slat steps set into the earth to form a snaking natural staircase. They climbed more easily now, aware of their destination as darkness started to creep through the woods and an eerie ambient blackness began its smothering of the world. Just as total night fell like a shroud they emerged into a small clearing. The Priest motioned them to stop and they dropped to sudden crouches. A silenced Sig P226 9mm appeared in The Priest's huge hand and Jam crept up to kneel beside him. 'What is it?'

'I heard something.'

Jam palmed his Glock 9mm, complete with silencer, and squinted into the gloom.

They waited for long minutes, kneeling there in the gently dripping rain. Up ahead there was a slight bend in the trail, heavily wooded; beyond the steep turn squatted the old cable-car house.

Jam closed his eyes, focusing on the sounds and smells around him. After fifteen minutes of concentration, he was just about to give The Priest a mouthful of abuse when he caught it: the distant scent of a cigarette.

Their gazes met. Jam nodded and, gesturing back to Nicky and Slater, moved carefully forward with The Priest by his side. They took it a single step at a time, halting, checking their surroundings in the gloom, eyes fixed, ears alert.

Rounding the bend they came upon the run-down cable-car building. Its crumbling rendering was being slowly absorbed by the forest, and grass and branches poked rudely at its walls. Its huge wooden door was closed, and to the right sat the black maw of the cable mechanism: a huge set of wheels and gears with twin parallel cables, each as thick as a man's wrist, snaking out from the cabin and away into the remote darkness, swaying gently in the wind, which howled mournfully.

A light glowed within, glimpsed through time-shrouded windows.

Guards, signalled Jam. *Two.*

The Priest nodded.

You wait here, Jam signalled, and again The Priest nodded.

Jam moved carefully to the door and then rose to stand, back against the damp wood. Inside he could hear soft voices, speaking in German, complaining about the

300

cold. They're not Nex killers, then, he thought to himself with a grim smile.

And he could see, from this new vantage point, the distant platform of Kamus-5; lights flickered through the darkness, and the whole platform was illuminated. Jam heard the whine of distant engines, and glimpsed the flickering red lights of a helicopter.

He licked his lips. The Priest's source had been right. There was definitely activity here.

There came a scrape, of wood on wood, from within. Jam turned, facing the door – which suddenly swung open to reveal a uniformed man, tall and heavily muscled, a cigarette dangling between his lips and an MP40 slung from his shoulder. He was squinting – and his eyes opened wide as they saw Jam's smiling face.

Jam's fist connected with a *crack*, and the guard was punched backwards to land heavily on his sub-machine gun, back twisting in agony as Jam's Glock snapped up to level at the face of the second man. He was halfway through dealing a deck of cards. He licked his lips.

'Don't even think about it, boy,' growled Jam as the young man looked at him, then to a small dark pistol on the table. The guard made a grab for the weapon and the Glock *popped* in Jam's fist; the guard was flung backwards from his stool, sprawling out beside the lantern on the floor. Blood splattered across the wall. Jam cursed.

The first man, groaning, received a kick in the ribs as Jam moved to the man he had shot and checked for a pulse. The Priest stepped in behind him, closely followed by Slater and Nicky. Slater grabbed the living guard and dragged him upright, shaking him.

'Any more of you?'

The man shook his head, his mouth a sour line.

'What are these monkeys doing here?' said Nicky. 'Guarding what?'

'I suppose the cables would be a long shot; not many people even know about this access to Kamus, much less need to guard it. I think, though, that these fuckers were here *just in case*.'

'They're not Nex,' said Nicky.

'That much we can be thankful for,' said Jam. 'But they still have sub-machine guns and intent – this fucker was going to shoot me. Took the risk and died for his stupidity.'

The Priest was standing in the doorway, looking out towards the distant Kamus. 'Kill the lamp,' he said softly, and dropped his pack to the floor. He pulled free some digital binoculars and peered out across the rain-filled expanse.

Slater battered the living guard into a state of unconsciousness, and dumped him on the floor where Nicky bound his hands and feet tightly together with bitch-wire. Then they all stood, thankful to be out of the rain for a moment as The Priest watched the activity in the Kamus.

'There is a lot of movement, lots of figures – they are loading up CH-47 Chinook cargo helicopters.'

'Are they Nex?'

'I cannot tell for sure, through the rain and over this distance,' said The Priest. 'Even as we speak, four Chinooks have taken off into the night. The platform is very busy indeed for a disused military complex, I think.'

'So what now?'

'We need to get closer.'

'These cable cars haven't run for years,' said Jam slowly. 'I doubt they would be safe, even if there was power piped to this place, which there isn't. What are you thinking?'

'I need to get closer,' said The Priest. 'I will go across the wire.'

'That would make you crazier than me,' said Jam softly.

'The Lord will protect me.'

'He won't protect you for ever,' said Jam.

'I am still alive, my son. He has done me proud this far.'

Jam ran his hand through his wet hair, then peered out at the swaying cables and the huge, awesome drop beyond into a blackness of seemingly infinite depth. 'I will, of course, have to come with you,' he said without relish.

'That is not necessary,' said The Priest.

'Oh, but it is,' growled Jam softly. 'I am in charge of this DemolSquad; *we* are on a mission to help find out who is fucking Spiral up the arse; *I* can't let *you* do my dirty work.'

Jam stalked out of the crumbling building and moved towards the edge of the precipice. The rock ended near his boots, and a rusting, broken safety railing, painted grey to blend with the surroundings, dangled precariously over the abyss. Jam knew, from previous work here, that this place was almost invisible to the outside prying eye.

'That's a long drop,' said Slater, coming to stand beside him.

'Yeah, so I see. Grab me my pack.'

The Priest moved forward. From his own pack he took a small alloy device; he checked a few tiny wheels inside it. 'You brought a skimmer with you?'

Jam nodded, taking his own pack from Slater and pulling out one of the tiny alloy devices. He then unstrapped a Heckler & Koch G3 sub-machine gun, and together with The Priest the two men crouched, screwing silencers onto the ends of the guns' barrels and then slinging these formidable weapons across their backs.

303

Nicky moved forward. 'You really think these are the bad guys?' she asked The Priest.

He nodded. 'A high probability, I think. If it is as I suspect, and this splinter group of Spiral is seeking domination of our tribe, then this would make an ideal base for operations – especially as it is so easily defended and somebody with prior knowledge could use much of the equipment left behind when the base was demilitarised.'

'We'll soon fucking find out,' said Jam. He pulled a balaclava over his wet face, and The Priest did likewise; now, all in black and carrying silenced sub-machine guns and pistols, the two men looked truly terrifying.

'You be careful,' said Nicky.

'You two make *sure* we don't get any nasty surprises from behind, yeah?'

'Rely on us,' rumbled Slater.

The Priest was checking Kamus through the binoculars. He tutted in annoyance. 'There's still a lot of activity; more Chinooks leaving the base. It seems we've decided to do this during one of their major operations.'

'Good,' snapped Jam. 'They'll be so busy they won't see us coming.'

'You wish.' Slater grinned. 'Go on, hole us some bad guys.'

Jam smiled grimly from behind the black mask. 'I'll do my best, my friend.'

The wind howled, rain lashing down in almost horizontal sheets. Jam stepped towards the edge of the precipice, and reaching up, attached the alloy skimmer with a *click*. It settled into place against the wide cable and a tiny blue light pulsed, then went out. Jam slipped his hand through the quick-release straps and looked out into the darkness and the storm. The cables were swaying and he swallowed hard. Deep below, falling away into nothingness, was a valley full of rocks, an abyss full of trees, a desolation of dark hell.

It would be a long, long tumble . . . followed by a gravity-induced crush.

Jam breathed deeply. Then, nodding to The Priest, he pushed his Glock into his belt, gripped the skimmer with his free hand – and kicked free, wind buffeting his watering eyes as he soared out into the void . . .

Feuchter awoke, cursing the pain in his limbs. His hand moved to the other side of the bed – to find nothing more than a cold depression. He scowled, ran a hand through his greying hair and sighed softly.

He rolled over with surprising agility, stood up and headed for the shower. He could smell himself, smell his own stink and the residue left behind by the Nex. The Nex always left their own curious aroma after sex; they always left their scent, their fluids, their *essence*.

Feuchter hated it. Hated that metallic scent, that copper stink . . . hated the stench and bitter after-effects of a Nex coupling . . . and yet he could not help himself, and he knowingly suffered the withdrawal symptoms for the intimate, *ultimate* pleasure of the high.

The comm buzzed. Feuchter halted, caught between the need to wash the stink from his skin and the need to take the call; he knew it would be important. It had to be important. A lot of bad shit was currently going down. 'Fuck.' He changed course, reached his desk and grabbed the receiver. 'Yeah?'

Outside, beyond the false proximity supplied by his monitor, the sun had risen; golden light danced across the distant sand dunes. Wind shifted the sand in waves, a golden sea of rolling iridescence. But on this sour-tasting morning the incredible and magnificent sight of dawn beauty delivered via electronics did little to calm Count Feuchter's sense of foreboding.

'Gol is dead.'

'Good. What about Carter?'

'Carter is another problem.'

'So they failed to neutralise him?'

'More than that; he is now much more informed, has experienced the Nex first hand – and survived. Worst of all, I think he has discovered some of the links between the QIII and ourselves.'

'Does he know that I am still alive?'

'A possibility,' said Durell softly.

'I want him dead,' said Feuchter. 'And I want him dead and mashed into food for the Nex right fucking now!' Feuchter's voice had suddenly risen to an almost hysterical screech. He stood, stinking the surreal stink, his heart booming in his seemingly hollow chest cavity, hands slippery on the comm receiver.

'Calm yourself,' said Durell, his voice low, crackling.

'I'll fucking calm myself when he's fucking dead,' hissed Feuchter.

'Now, you forget yourself,' whispered Durell, his voice like a shadow passing over a grave.

Feuchter paused then; he caught the low undercurrent of danger in Durell's voice. You did not fuck with Durell. *Nobody* fucked with Durell.

He bit his lip. He closed his eyes for a moment, and then said, forcing his voice into a state of calmness which contradicted his present lack of karma, 'What I mean to point out, *sir*, is that Carter has proved himself to be a very capable man – an extremely dangerous soldier. More, he has outsmarted and outstepped both the Nex and ourselves all the way to Kenya and beyond. If he

306

knows that I live then he may come to find me. You did not see him in Schwalenberg, Durell; I have never seen a man move so fast. It was surreal. It was *frightening.*'

'Feuchter, your priority now is merely to carry on the QIII development for the next twenty-four hours, and then issue Directive 566. Carter is *my* problem and I can assure you that I will not fuck about with this man, *frightening* or not.' The heavy sarcasm could not be missed.

Feuchter paused. Some of his earlier composure had returned and he cursed himself; he had displayed weakness. And to Durell of all people . . . But he could still see those eyes, eyes that seemed to change colour – darken into molten amber – and Feuchter could remember Carter's white-hot bullet drilling his stomach like a spinal worm, a manoeuvre so fast he had seen nothing: merely wondered why the fuck he was lying on his back with his flesh on fire . . .

'Directive 566? Termination of those who refuse to convert?'

'Yes.' There was a cold ice-edge to Durell's voice; the implicit challenge to Feuchter's authority was there. 'Most of the Q station are with us; but there is still a hard-core group who will not take a hint when it is tossed their way with candy. The days of Spiral are over – if they will not join us, they will die.'

Feuchter picked his next words with care, his mouth dry with the implications of what was about to happen . . . what he was being ordered to do . . .

'Sir, may I ask why *now*? We are not yet ready . . .'

'You may. Gol is dead; but the schematics have not been recovered. And as we speak, Gol's body has also not been recovered. If Spiral retain those fucking plans, they can build another QIII to challenge us – we may win the battle, Feuchter, but the war could never be ours. We need to be strong! Dominant! And we can't do that until Spiral is extinct.' Durell sighed on the comm. 'Just carry out your orders, Feuchter: Directive 566. After twenty-four hours. You know the procedures. All working components are to be transferred to Spiral_mobile; even now Kamus is being emptied of all valuable stock.'

Feuchter's jaw went tight and he gritted his teeth hard. He nodded – although there was nobody to witness this – and said, simply, 'Yes, sir.' He cut the line and stood—

Stunned—

Gazing at the monitor, which showed him the Rub al-Khali desert.

He could feel them; feel the workers, the programmers, the coders, the analysts, the developers – feel them around and above him, like workers in an ants' warren. And he was the King Ant – with the power to close down everything with a click of his fingers.

And the order had come.

Everything of vital importance would be moved. Feuchter smiled then, a smile without humour, his tombstone teeth white against his lightly tanned skin. *Moved.* That was a term to use for the *equipment* but, unfortunately, not all of the *personnel* . . .

We know who you are, he thought.

And Spiral? Weak and powerless Spiral?

Your time has come.

Oh, how I have waited for this moment, he thought, his mind retreating over all the years, flowing back over the decades. Visions flowered in his mind; flowered, blossomed, died. Feuchter remembered the Battle of Belsen; he remembered the Attack on Poland Ridge; and he remembered the mountains of Korea after the Bright War.

You are weak, Spiral, he thought.

And yes. We will make you strong again.

But first? First you must relinquish your greatest treasure . . .

The lives of those who will not betray you.

The Comanche flew low over the desert, its passing marked by the heavy deep *thrum thrum thrum* of its engines. Sunlight glittered from rotors, danced across the DPM paintwork, glinted across the smoked cockpit and the cramped occupants inside—

The Comanche banked gently, gaining altitude as it approached the mountainous regions of Northern Rub al'Khali. The Great Sandy Desert. Vast and wild and undiscovered.

Natasha gazed down at the mountains, the narrow crevasses and rocky gullies, the spirals of rocky depression, some filled with the fresh clear water of mountain streams, the occasional herd of antelope or gazelle on the lower slopes casting eyes upwards and scattering as the Comanche droned like a huge insect low overhead, below radar. Natasha spotted lone huts and small villages huddled into the sides of the mountains for protection; some villages were of mud brick, some of canvas, sheltering beneath the wide swinging woods of poplar before the land dropped sharply, dizzyingly to the lowlands south and west of the marshes and then on to the desert.

Carter stirred, his eyes coming open.

'How are you feeling?' asked Natasha.

'Like a man who's been shot.'

'Much pain?'

'I've felt better,' said Carter.

'Well, you're all sewn up, and on the road to recovery. I think you'll probably be stiff for a few weeks.'

309

'Huh. *Not* the story of my life.' Carter winced. He pulled himself higher in the cockpit, gazed out, down, head rattling with the noise from the twin LHTec engines. He watched the mountains roll down into deserts. He gazed out to the east, but could see no sign of any major city. He rested his head back, mind spinning, confused after recent events. He glanced at Natasha – who was staring down at the landscape flowing like a sand river below them.

'How about you, Nats? Are you OK?'

Natasha did not turn, her gaze fixed on some distant invisible point.

'Yes.' Her voice was cold.

He took her hand and squeezed her warm flesh. 'I'm sorry. About Gol – what he did was a brave thing. He did it to protect his mission, his organisation. He was the key to stopping the enemy; he knew the schematics would allow us time, would slow down the QIII's dominance . . . whoever wants that processor working obviously has big plans for its implementation. And if it really can predict the future . . .'

'If?'

Carter shrugged. 'Sounds impossible to me. But *if* it can – then whoever controls such a weapon, for that is what it is – whoever controls such a weapon will be powerful indeed.'

'There's more than that, Carter.'

Carter frowned; half in pain, half in confusion.

'Yeah?'

'This system – the schematics I saw, in its early stages of inception: they were mind-blowing. If it became operational in the wrong hands – it could take over world finance, it could fuck Wall Street and the Dow Jones straight up the arse. But more than that, it would control . . .'

'Weapons?'

310

Nats nodded. 'Everything is computerised, Carter. Missiles, strategic instructions, the whole Battlegrid . . .'

'And nuclear weapons?'

'Oh yes, Carter.'

She glanced down at him, her eyes red-rimmed. 'I loved Gol, Carter, y'know? Even after our fight . . . even though our hot words tore each other to shreds . . . and then, in Kenya when we made up, when he took me in his arms again, everything in the world felt right. Everything became good again and I suddenly realised how much I had lost. I loved him – and I know he died protecting Spiral but—'

'But?'

'I can't help thinking there is something out of place.'

'Like the Nex?'

'Yes.'

Carter smiled grimly. 'If we find who controls the Nex, we find out who is after manipulating the QIII. And we know that same fucker is the one who's been tagging Spiral and the DemolSquads.'

Natasha merely nodded, and Carter reached over and wiped away the tears that glistened on her cheeks. 'Now is not the time to be talking of this,' he said. 'Maybe Gol is still alive.' His words slipped out, sounding lame even to his own ears. But he had to force himself to say it; he had to try and help Natasha and he knew – *knew* that silence was sometimes a good thing but he so desperately wanted to help her, to ease her pain, to make the hurt come better . . .

Natasha did not reply. She gazed back out of the window but her fingers took Carter's hand and squeezed. He said no more but was merely there – there for her.

Carter laughed inwardly.

I wonder just how powerful this QIII really is? he thought.

And more importantly, who seeks to control it? To dominate the world?

The face of Feuchter floated into his mind; he remembered that chilling smile, and the look in the man's eyes. He had believed; believed in his actions, without a hint of insanity. He would have killed Carter there and then and not thought twice about it . . .

You fucker, Carter thought.

But then – that was too easy. Feuchter was not in charge; he was a lackey, a stooge, a slave to somebody bigger and altogether more intimidating. Somebody who was trying to undermine and destroy Spiral . . . but Spiral was almost invisible. Its acts were legendary, but its name was unknown outside—

Realisation came like a shot from the dark.

It had to be somebody on the inside.

It had to be somebody high up in Spiral.

Betrayal.

The word tasted bad on Carter's tongue, and he drifted off to sleep once again, loss of blood making him unnaturally weary. His dreams swirled, with hordes of Nex armed with machine pistols and masks struggling to climb over their dead comrades to get at him, to maim him, to kill him . . .

And then Gol was there. A colossus, a huge gun in his hands, cutting the Nex in half with streams of bullets.

'What are they?' cried Carter. 'What the *fuck* are they?'

Gol smiled; a sickly-sweet smile; then ripped off his face to reveal the copper eyes of a Nex . . .

Carter came awake with a hiss.

It was night. He was alone in the cockpit of the Comanche, a blanket wrapped around him. His tongue ran around the stale interior of his mouth and he gazed

312

out of the cockpit, up at the clear black sky. Stars twinkled far above.

The virgin silence was infinite.

He eased himself up, released the cockpit hatch and struggled down the ladder. Natasha and Langan were seated beside a small – very small – fire. Langan was brewing coffee over the flames in a small pan.

Carter looked around warily. 'Is it safe to light a fire here?'

'We've checked out the surroundings. We're miles from any settlements – single houses, even.'

'I don't like it. People can see it from miles away . . .'

'And they can hear the roar of a Comanche from even further. We needed a break, Carter. *I* need a break – I'm not a fucking pilot from God, you know. Have you ever seen what happens to a Comanche when the pilot nods off?'

'How long do you need?'

'Yeah, I'm feeling fine and thanks for your concern. About three hours and some strong coffee. And maybe then I'll be ready to take on the vast endless unexplored open spaces of Rub al'Khali on a wild-goose chase with no real set objective . . .'

'Feuchter is at the end of it. That's objective enough.'

'Is he really going to have all the answers?' asked Langan.

'Only if I ask the right fucking questions,' said Carter. He settled beside the fire, his blanket still wrapped around his shoulders, his face still grey with exhaustion. He smiled weakly at Langan. 'You seem a tad on edge, my friend.'

Langan patted Carter's arm. 'I could say the same about you, but you've recently been shot so I think I'll forgive your tetchiness. Also, flying illegally over Rub al'Khali ground is not my idea of fun. If we're caught

313

trespassing in Saudi airspace . . . they'll either send everything they fucking have at us and claim some breach of international law, or it'll kick off some major fucking United Nations fuck-up and we'll all be in the shit.'

'We'll just have to stay covert, then.'

'Easy for you to say. I'm the bastard with the responsibility.'

'How we doing for fuel?'

'I visited a Spiral dump while you were asleep. We're fully fuelled and ready to rumble.'

Carter nodded, and rested his head and back against the small clump of boulders beside which Langan had built the fire. He said, his eyes closed, 'I suggest we stay here for the rest of the night. All get some much-needed rest. How far to where you reckon this Spiral_Q computer processor development centre actually is?'

'We're presently about a hundred and fifty kilometres south and west of Tabuk. As long as we keep away from all major civilisation – not exactly difficult in this area – then we can carry on skirting down towards the Jaba Sawda and the desert to the west; that is our final destination. We'll be able to head for the rough co-ords Gol gave me before he . . .' Langan's voice trailed off. He glanced at Natasha whose eyes were closed, her face stony. 'I can have us there within two hours, but from here on in it's a much harder ride; there's definitely a heavier military presence although I'm not sure why, probably soured relations with another Middle Eastern State, OPEC or the OIC. It's also easy to spot that we shouldn't be the fuck where we are. We're not exactly flying in diplomatic colours; and this Comanche is quite obviously a war machine. We'll have to move more slowly, more cautiously. And the cherry on the Bakewell is that I am unfamiliar with the terrain.'

314

'I wish I hadn't asked.'

'It would have been better for you to go in over land.'

'Oh yeah, what in? A hastily stolen Skoda that some fuckwit had just left lying around?'

Langan grinned. 'You know Spiral has vehicle and weapons stashes all over the world. We could backtrace to the nearest SP1plot, tool you up, send you out.'

Carter shook his head. 'One, we haven't got the time. The Comanche is fucking fast. Two, I'm not exactly in the best physical state to be piloting some desert sand buggy over the dunes. And finally, it's good to see you really pissed off. And watching you skip wire and dodge MIGs and missiles is a joy to behold.'

'You're a cunt, Carter.'

'Better believe it.'

Langan dished out the coffee, which they drank sweet and black. Smoke drifted up into the vast void above the Rub al'Khali desert and Carter felt suddenly at peace. The pain – which he had recently grown accustomed to – had lessened and he felt almost comfortable, at ease . . . He could not put a finger on the reason for this sudden euphoria but the beauty of the night sky had something to do with it, and the feeling that he was doing the right thing – headed on the right course – no longer the *hunted*, but the *hunter* . . . he had turned the image around in his brain, become the predator, become the one in control.

It might be limited control, but now he was calling the shots.

Send the fucking Nex, he thought. I'll kill them all.

Let's see what answers you have, Count Feuchter.

Let's see what song you sing.

The dawn broke, grey light spreading across the horizon. Wrapped in blankets, the small group roused themselves, drank more coffee courtesy of Langan and then, gathering what little detritus they had created, climbed stiff-limbed back into the Comanche.

Langan warmed up the engines, then eased his baby into the air, scattering sand. Slowly, he increased the speed, and they skimmed low over the desert and rocky landscape. Occasionally they would pass low ranges of hills, mainly rounded rocks all scattered with orange sand and small scrub bushes. Occasionally they would see small groups of date palms around a life-giving oasis, but Langan avoided these outposts for they attracted local herders and villagers.

As they droned low over the desert, Carter – now fully awake, alert and seeming more like his old self after the night's sleep, only occasionally wincing breathlessly at the stabs of pain within his battered body – took the spare HIDSS helmet from its compartment behind Langan.

'How does it work?'

'Pop it on,' said Langan. 'I'll show you.'

Carter pulled the helmet over his head, and positioned the mike and sensors in front of his face; finally, he slid down the mounted flight-information display. The terrain ahead of the Comanche sprang to life and Carter gasped at the digital image.

'Impressed?'

'Fuck me.'

Data scrolled down both sides of the visor; occasionally symbols flickered into life and targets were highlighted with different colours and symbols. Carter noted the weapons-system tracker in the top right corner and he licked his lips nervously.

'Have I got some form of control here?'

'Only if I patch you in.'

'Don't.'

316

'That wasn't my intention, Mr Carter. You are a novice. You don't even like flying – the last thing I am going to do is allow you control of my beloved Comanche.'

'*Spiral*'s Comanche.'

'That depends on your point of view.'

'So tell me about the helmet. How does it work?'

'What you are wearing, Mr Carter, is a helmet that provides acoustic and impact protection combined with a magnetic helmet tracker. This son of a bitch stops you going deaf, especially in battle situations when the shit hits the fan: it has a bi-ocular FOV at 53° x 30° CRT with a 1023-line refresh – that means it's a motherfucking clear display that gives you a wide field of view, important when approaching a possible combat encounter. The HIDSS offers both flight-information and night-vision sensors on screen, and uses flight data with sensor images and piloting and targeting symbology to allow aggravated aggressive flight manoeuvring and combat, especially at night.'

'What sort of weapons have we got on board?'

'That's it, Carter, get right to the important stuff. Don't ask me how secure we are against biological or chemical weapons, don't ask what the procedure is in a crash – straight to the guns!'

'Well?'

'We have a stowable three-barrelled 20mm turreted Gatling nose gun, coming in at 1500 rounds a minute. We have a fully retractable missile armament system called I-RAMS – where missiles are hidden in bays; you get various different configurations of heavy-shit rockets. We are presently carrying 36 standard 70mm rockets, 18 Stinger air-to-air missiles and 6 Hellfire anti-tank missiles which, as I am sure you know, are programmed to control their own targeting destinations, once fired. We're

317

not carrying a full load which means we're a little more manoeuvrable than you would expect when fully loaded.'

'That's some fucking firepower.'

'This is a war machine, Carter. What do you expect? Smarties?'

'They pick some shit names, don't you think?'

'You mean Stinger and Hellfire? I suppose so, but what would you call them?'

Carter shrugged, still entranced by the HIDSS display. 'You want a go, Nats?'

'No, I'll leave the playing and toy-fetish stuff to you boys.'

'Don't be like that, Nats.'

'You should hear you two! Hellcat stinging 900mm bollocks to smash a tank straight up the I-RAMS. God, you're like a couple of kids with a new plastic soldier.'

'Women never understand,' said Langan conspiratorially.

Carter nodded.

'Probably because they're brought up with dolls.'

'I can hear you,' said Natasha testily.

'Oooh, she can hear us,' said Langan.

An alarm sounded. Langan cursed, the Comanche suddenly banked sharply and dipped towards the ground, the LHTec engines whining down. He turned the helicopter around and they headed back the way they had just come.

'What is it?'

'You see the orange blip on your screen? Way bad news. Air-defence base – missiles, fighter jets – the full fucking monty. We're twenty kms from it. I think we need to rethink our cross-land strategy.'

After some distance, Langan brought the Comanche down in a small bowl valley amid barren hills which were

318

formed completely from gently rounded rock, with very little vegetation and no trees, no water – no people.

The rotors whined down.

Carter and Natasha climbed from the cockpit and Langan flicked a few switches, then jumped down. He carried a roll of plastic and a small black cube. 'You're not going to like what I have to tell you.'

Carter eased himself to the ground, hand pressed against his stitched flesh. 'Surprise me.'

'The path we need to take is crawling with aerial defences, probably in place in case Saudi falls out with its neighbours. They'll also be linked to White Guard bases – Saudi Arabia's army. Now, we could get past them – easy. But I'm not sure if we could get past them *undetected*. Do you want to arrive at Spiral–Q to find it deserted? Or your main man vanished?'

'What do you suggest?'

'Before, when I mentioned the SP1plot, the vehicle and weapons stashes – well, I wasn't joking. There are usually stealth vehicles of some sort. It depends what your priority is – speed or stealth? I could get us there in the Comanche but we might trigger some of their more sophisticated sensors – just depends what they've got!'

Carter chewed his lip. 'Show me on the digital map.'

Langan unrolled the length of map – made from some kind of thin clear plastic that could be updated with information from the Comanche's computers – on the sand and knelt on the edge to stop the wind from curling it. Carter squatted, wincing and holding his side, and his gaze roved across the detailed and illuminated terrain.

'Where is Spiral_Q?'

Langan pointed. 'There; or within a couple of kilometres. It can't be that easy to hide, although they do try. By Spiral accounts it is a fucking *huge* base.'

319

'Couldn't you take us around via a quieter, more circuitous route? Without the air defences?'

'I think something is going down in Rub al'Khali, to be honest. The reports I've just logged from the back end of Spiral say that military concentration in the area is building, although they don't know why. We could try – but when we're outrunning missiles and Feuchter's done a vanishing act, don't go blaming poor old Langan.'

'Great. Any other good news?'

'I can take you to the vehicles depot; or near to. I can also wait for you, although that is more than you deserve.'

'Hmmm.' Carter scratched at the stubble on his chin, and decided that he needed both a bath and a shave. Sweat rolled down his nose and dripped to the sand and rock. He could feel the sun burning his back.

'We haven't got the right equipment. Money. Clothes. Nothing.'

'You could say that we left a little unprepared,' added Langan softly.

Carter nodded; it was not a criticism, just an observation. 'I'll tell you what Langan. We'll do what you say: drop us at the SP1plot and I'll go in by vehicle, covertly, and you can wait there with Natasha—'

'I'm coming with you,' said Natasha.

'No.'

'Who the fuck do you think you are to order me around?'

Their glares locked. Carter shook his head. 'I'll work faster alone.'

'You don't need to fucking *protect* me,' said Natasha. 'I can do that myself. But it is *my* father who's dead because of these bastards; I'm going in, Carter, and I'll either go with you or without you. *You* can accompany *me* if you feel up to it – after all, taking a bullet must have slowed

320

down your reflexes a little bit. And it was me who got you out of Gol's place alive . . . without me you'd be Nex pulp . . .'

'Whoa.' Carter held up his hands. 'I stand corrected.'

'Don't you just hate stroppy women?' muttered Langan.

'She's got a point this time,' said Carter slowly. 'I assume that's a GPS you're carrying?'

Langan nodded. 'But this is linked to the digital map – for coordination purposes.'

'You mean for missile attacks.'

'Yeah, that as well.'

'OK. How far is the nearest SP1plot?'

'About a hundred kilometres closer to civilisation.'

Carter glanced up at the sun; it was high now, and burning down with incredible force. Beneath his clothes he was soaked with sweat. 'Let's do it, then.'

The Comanche sat, baking in the desert heat, the artificial wind from its rotors dying down even as they stood, staring at the wall of rock before them.

'Where is it?' asked Natasha.

'You're looking at it.'

Natasha gazed up at the jagged vertical surface of wind-weathered sandstone that cut a step from the landscape. The rock was a deep red, scarred, a section of landscape scoured by wind-blown sand over centuries. It was a desert feature, a sanctuary from the wind. It was a rock with a sense of history.

'The wall?'

'No, at its base.'

SP1plots were dotted all over the globe, and carried equipment specific to the sort of territory in which they were placed. Periodically they would be checked and

321

restocked by Spiral operatives. On a thousand occasions they had made the difference between life and death.

Most SP1plots were either behind rock, or set under the ground: huge steel containers hidden away from prying eyes and accessed via ECubes. Carter pulled out the small dark cube and allowed it to sit in his palm.

'Won't using that give away our location?'

'Oh yes. But if they're that good, they know where we are, or where we're going, anyway. We just have to concentrate on staying one step ahead. Act, don't react, yeah?'

Carter accessed a function of the ECube. It *blipped*. There came a *click* from the ground and, raining sand, a huge rectangular section of the desert suddenly lifted – a ramp, allowing access to a deep dark cool interior.

Carter and Natasha moved forward; Langan watched from the secure confines of his Comanche, where he had lit a burner and had begun the ritual of getting a brew on. They stooped, peering into the gloom lit by triggered emergency lights set against the corrugated steel walls.

'Let's see what delights Pandora's box holds.'

They descended the steep ramp; against one wall was an array of weapons, from machine guns and pistols to sniper rifles and even a couple of bazookas. All weapons were wrapped in plastic and coated in grease. Ammunition sat in wooden crates in one corner, and there were several large machines, also wrapped in thick plastic sheets. Carter moved forward and pulled one of the sheets free.

Natasha scowled.

'A motorbike?'

'More than that,' said Carter, a hidden sense of joy in his voice. 'It's a modified desert racer – a BMW R2150 GS Adventurer, with some serious modifications and upgrades. It's a fucking dream, Natasha.'

322

'I would have preferred a jeep.'

'No, no, these are the best things for crossing the desert – as long as you know how to control one. These bastards will eat the miles: look at the tyres! Just wait till we get on the move.'

He crossed to the bike, hand tracing the contours of the tank and seat. He crouched, his gaze roving over the engine with its curious powerful design, then stood again to survey the extra fuel tanks. He tapped them. 'Full and raring to go; all we have to do is initiate and prime the firing sequence.'

'What modifications does it have?'

Carter pointed to a place below the headlights; two barrels poked free. 'Mounted sub-machine guns, with ammunition on a drum stored below the petrol tank up front. It has a built-in monitor over the handlebars, where your ECube can sit and aid navigation, along with the usual GPS set-up. It has a stealth exhaust; this baby will run silent – silent and deadly. And special mudguards which stop huge dust clouds from following you up the sides of sand dunes and signalling your position to all and sundry.'

Carter moved forward, kicked his leg over the huge machine. He fired up the bike and, true to his word, there was nothing more than a gentle murmur. 'They use these to blast over the Paris-Dakar Rally – a true endurance race, probably one of the hardest races in the world. If anything can get us to Spiral_Q over land, then this is it.'

Natasha shook her head. 'I remember the last time I got on the back of a bike with you.'

Carter shook his head, smiling grimly. 'Don't worry, love – this time it will be much, much worse.'

The BMW R2150 GS Adventurer climbed the ramp with ease, its engine note nothing more than a low croon; tyres bit into sand and Carter taxied the bike towards the Comanche. 'Nice,' remarked Langan, nodding as he held out a mug of tea.

Carter kicked the stand down and leaned the bike, then accepted the offered mug. 'There's only dried and tinned supplies down there. You wouldn't happen to have anything fresher?'

Langan tossed Carter a satchel, which he deftly caught, wincing as the stitches in his side pulled tight. 'Some fresh food in there, buddy. Although I'll probably be cursing you when I'm destined to finish off the last tinned beef kebab.'

'Cheers. There's another thing.'

'Hmm?' Langan sipped his brew, his eyes suspicious.

'I saw your rifle. In the Comanche. The Barrett .338 Lapua Magnum. With the telescopic sight. Can I borrow it?'

'My Barrett!' Langan scowled. 'You'll be wanting the gold from my fucking fillings next.'

'No, just the rifle.'

'What's wrong with the weapons from the store?'

'They're too new; not bedded in. Last thing I need is a bloody untried and untested weapon. And anyway, I have experience with a Barrett rifle – those nameless unloved weapons down there, they have no soul.'

'Carter, that rifle is my baby. That rifle is my god. It used to be my brother's; my brother is now dead. I feel I owe it to him to make sure that it survives something more than your ham-fisted clumsiness.'

'Don't be so soft,' snapped Carter. 'I'll take care of her. You know I look after my weapons.'

'Yeah, right, I've seen the condition of your Browning.'

'Used but not abused,' said Carter. 'The fact that it's so worn is a testament to my love, care and attention. It wouldn't have lasted this long if I'd casually tossed it aside, now would it? Go on, Langan, *share*.'

Langan muttered something incomprehensible.

'Not when there are ladies present,' said Natasha softly, moving forward. She carried a Glock, several spare mags and some boxes of ammunition. She took the satchel and dropped gun and ammo in beside the food so generously donated by Langan.

'On one condition.'

'What?'

'You have to polish it.'

'Polish? Oh for fu— OK, OK.' He saw the look in Langan's eyes.

'Once a night.'

'I don't intend to be gone that long,' said Carter, smiling grimly.

The SP1plot also contained clothing necessary for the locality, in case they were separated from the bike: traditional Arab dress – white cotton robes, and a couple of shamags.

'Wrap up, Natasha – we'll be in disguise and they'll at least protect us from the sun.'

'Are there any motorbike helmets in there?'

Carter shook his head. 'Don't worry; we won't be crashing. Not if I have anything to do with it.'

They spent a few minutes helping one another into the robes and shamags, giggling despite the seriousness of their predicament. When both were fully clad, they stood staring at one another and Carter's hand reached out to cup Natasha's chin.

'You look beautiful.'

'What do you want?'

'I want nothing, my love. I merely wish to give.'

325

'You're so full of crap, Carter.'

'So a man can't even try and be romantic?'

'Hmm, which part was romantic?'

Carter smiled, tension easing from him. 'Come on, we're running late, thanks to this impromptu diversion. We need to get on the move. You got the digital maps?'

'Everything is in the satchel.'

Wrapped up, they moved to the BMW and Carter fired up the machine. Natasha settled herself on the back of the huge bike and they both turned, gazes fixing on Langan. 'You know the procedures,' said Carter.

Langan nodded. 'Be careful, guys.'

Carter laughed harshly, pulling on his goggles. 'We'll be more than careful, mate; we'll be deadly.'

The rear wheel spun and gripped and kicked the bike away . . .

Just before setting out, Carter had given Nats a quick lesson on pillion riding, and a warning about riding over sand. 'Lean with me,' he had said. 'Don't throw yourself around on the bike, don't get on or off without my permission and be warned: riding over sand is tough – I'll have to hit it fast. If you don't, you get bogged down, unless it's real flat and packed.'

Now, as the BMW surged forward, Natasha's heart was in her mouth; the sun was beating down, sand rushed by to either side, and they left the Comanche and the flat rock-step behind as the BMW powered onto and up the first dune, torque-filled engine throbbing beneath them like a giant's strong and beating heart. The BMW sailed over the sand, cutting out any need for tracks or roads, and as they crested the ridge, Carter still piling on the power, the beast's front wheel lifted and they wheelied from the top of the sand dune in a shower of desert crimson.

326

Another world opened up, a world of rolling sand, a great sea caressed by the wind, wave after wave stretching off to the horizon. Nothing moved, nothing stirred in this desert: no houses, no villages, no trees – just the occasional shrub or a scattering of rocks. A word leaped into Natasha's mind to describe this place:

Desolation.

They powered forward, down the massive dune, and already sweat was trickling down the riders' backs. Carter wrestled with the huge bike, could feel the sand trying to suck him down, pull him one way or another, swallow them; he fought back, increasing the power, building the speed, rising from the seat a little to stand on the pegs with Natasha clinging on tightly behind as they crested another rise in a shower of sand and sailed down the next drifting slope. Up and up went the speed; past 80 m.p.h., past 100 m.p.h. – shrubs fled past in a blur, sand spat to either side of the charging bike. Occasionally they hit a buried rock, the BMW's suspension dipping, absorbing, but Carter kept her on course, kept the bike true as they flew like a bullet across the deserted no man's land of Rub al'Khali in Saudi Arabia.

They charged along under the sun.

Carter could taste sweat when he licked at his sand-whipped lips. The sun beat down like a furnace. His eyes flickered, reading the GPS coordinates. He did not dare initiate the BMW's ECube locking mechanism; it was one thing to signal a *blip* in a state of emergency, but to give their enemies a bright emergency flare to follow? That would be insanity.

On and on they rode, merging with the landscape around the camouflaged stealth vehicle; sand dune crested into sand dune, a waving, rolling sea that they navigated with great effort. The bike flew on, until finally

327

the dunes became smaller and the drifts came seemingly to an end.

They arrived at a vast plain of flat-packed rock and sand, with huge outcroppings of stone cliff rearing in the distance. Rocks lay strewn everywhere, and Carter slowed the bike's speed to a more moderate 70 m.p.h.

They cruised almost in silence.

'Thank God for that!' Natasha spoke over the slight hiss of the wind. She was clinging on tightly and Carter, who had sat down once more, patted at her hands around his waist where they gripped for dear life.

'Mad as fuck, eh?'

'Mad as fuck,' agreed Natasha.

They cruised across the plain, the sun still high and burning, Carter's eyes focused on the GPS. He swung the bike left, then slowed as an old ravine loomed – gritting his teeth, and with a wail from Natasha, he gave the big bike a kick of speed and they leaped from the rocky surface, dropping a good eight feet to land on the baked and cracked ravine bed. Suspension dipped, Natasha's wail was cut short with a grunt, and the bike sped on as if nothing more than a floating rose petal had disturbed its trajectory.

'You could have warned me!'

'What's the point? You'd only moan!'

'Moan!' moaned Natasha. 'You miserable bastard!'

'That's the beauty of travelling by bike,' shouted Carter. 'Communication is made so much more difficult!'

They cruised down the ravine, swaying left and right to avoid fallen rock debris. To their right stood a mammoth cliff, an obstacle in the desert, and as the ravine wound away, heading further to the west, Carter realised that they would have to ascend this precipice to reach the next stage of their journey.

For an hour they followed the valley. Then, slowing his speed, Carter dropped a few gears. Finding a section where the rocky wall had collapsed, leaving an insanely steep slope of rubble, he slowed to a halt for a moment, his eyes focused intently.

Natasha was panting. 'This is fucking hard work.'

'You're not having to steer. Why do you think desert racers are such physically fit sons of bitches?'

'Why have we stopped?'

Carter lifted his goggles for a moment, rubbed at his eyes, and then cleaned sand from the goggles' surface with the edge of his shamag. 'If we carry on following the ravine, we'll swing around in the wrong direction – we need to climb out.'

'Climb out? We'll never lift . . . oh.'

Natasha had spotted the collapsed wall.

'Hold on.'

Carter screwed the throttle; the BMW leaped forward, needing little encouragement – they hammered across the flat, tyres chewing past baked desert earth, and mounted the slope like a ramp. Carter twisted the throttle and the engine roared beyond its stealth shielding . . . the bike powered up the slope and jettisoned itself from the summit, sailing through the air with both riders clenching their teeth and the tyres spinning helplessly . . . they landed, the heavy-duty suspension dipping to absorb the impact. Carter locked the back wheel and they skidded around in a broad arc, showering rock and sand.

'You really are a crazy bastard,' panted Natasha.

'I try,' smiled Carter. 'But if you think that's bad . . .' He turned and pointed to the cliff.

'What about it? It's a wall of rock?'

'It's in our way.'

329

'Carter, this fucking bike will not climb that.'

'It will if you find the right paths.'

They sped along for another couple of hours. Natasha was exhausted, and she knew that Carter was tiring – and becoming increasingly frustrated because of this natural barrier that would soon send them in the wrong direction – and *away* from Spiral_Q and Feuchter beyond.

As the sun began to sink, Carter halted, shading his eyes. The rocky wall faltered – as it had on several occasions before – but this time there were huge steps, cut into the flanks and banked with crumbling stones and fallen rocks. Many of the steps were rounded, weathered by wind and blown sand; they formed a steep and treacherous series of ramps, rising perhaps three storeys into the sky.

'No, Carter.'

'Yes, Natasha. This baby can do it.'

'Oh no, I value my life.'

'I value Feuchter's death more,' growled Carter. He blipped the engine. 'Hold on, babe, we're going to do some hill climbing.'

The BMW cruised forward – gently this time and with care as Carter's gaze raked across the ramps and steps arranged ahead of him like some crazy game or puzzle. He cruised along the foot of the cliff, back and forth several times with his gaze following various paths up the slopes to the top of the ridge. Then, only when he was happy, did he ease in a little more power and turn the BMW's nose towards the steep climb.

With precision and control, Carter eased the BMW up a series of gentle slopes, then flicked the bike's head right, blipping the power to climb the back wheel up a step. Rubber gripped, the huge bike surged a little and Carter reined her in with both brakes. A ramp to the left brought them up onto another level, then a series of small rocks piled atop one another acted like steps as the BMW ate them with ease.

Now halfway up, Natasha gazed down. If it had looked steep from the bottom, now it looked insane; she felt suddenly vulnerable, gazing down at the ravine through which they travelled and the flat plain beyond, bordered distantly by more rolling sand dunes drifting lazily as far as the eye could see.

Shadows danced in their path, cast by the low-slung rays of the setting sun. Natasha put her head against Carter's back, closed her sand-crusted eyes and prayed.

The bike jolted, bucked, scrambled and fought its way up the slope, bumping and rocking, engine growling, fighting, tyres spinning and gripping as Carter, sweat rolling down his forehead, gaze focused in intense concentration, finally launched them from the top of a trough and onto another plain of sand and loose-strewn rocks.

Natasha patted his shoulder.

'Hmm?'

'I think we need a break.'

'Sounds good. I am truly, truly shafted.'

They cruised for a while longer until Natasha's sharp eyes spotted the distant oasis, outlined in crimson as the sun made its final attempt to stave off night. Carter altered their course, and before long the trees came closer and it was a weary rider who at last silenced the bike's thumping heart.

They had camouflaged the BMW R 2150 GS Adventurer beside this small oasis, decorating the powerful customised bike with huge green palm fronds.

'Jesus, it's so hot,' gasped Natasha and Carter said

nothing. He was bright red, mostly from heat exhaustion, a little from the pain in his stomach. He was finding it hard to breathe because of the heat.

Carter slumped to the ground and ran his hand along the flat, smooth rock. 'This place is *old*,' he said softly, his voice carrying a tone of awe. 'Really old.'

Natasha nodded, kicking free her boots and splashing water from the small circular pool into her face, combing it into her desert-dry hair. She moaned in mock ecstasy, and rolled onto her back to stare at the sun descending rapidly over the horizon. 'I never believed I could be so hot,' she complained.

Carter smiled. 'In the middle of hostile territory on a mission bound for certain destruction and all you can complain about is the sun. Girl, this is nothing; you should try Thailand. Or the Philippines . . . now those places are *real* hot.'

Natasha roused herself and rummaged in the small sack that she carried – the contents of which were mainly made up of Carter's smash-and-grab from Langan's personal stash. She held up a lump of cheese. She sniffed at it suspiciously. 'Does this look OK to you?'

'Looks don't come into it, but my acute hunger does. Give it . . . here . . .' He reached towards the cheese. Natasha swayed aside.

'Wait, wait, let me try . . .'

She took a small bite and smiled broadly. 'Extremely tasty.' She pulled free a loaf and began to eat. Carter lay back, closed his eyes and wiped sweat from his forehead.

According to the GPS and digital map link they were closing fast on Spiral_Q. Several more hours without incident and they would arrive and then—

What?

Carter knew: he would interrogate Feuchter. And then he would kill the man. There was nothing Feuchter could say that would excuse him of the crime of betrayal.

Spiral might have let him free. But Carter would not.

And besides – Spiral had its own problems at the moment . . .

Carter took the loaf from Natasha. Chewed mechanically. For his mind had wandered – more than wandered, he was reliving that day, that night at Castle Schwalenberg, reliving that terrible moment when Feuchter and Maria had turned against him, forcing Kade into existence for a terrible bright few minutes of black and white—

Carter blinked.

His head tilted to one side.

That's right, he thought. Black and white. Kade saw everything in black and white.

Why?

Carter rested his head back.

'*I have missed you,*' said Kade softly.

'You have been absent since Kenya. Sulking, were you, you little shit?'

'*I was thinking. Contemplating,*' said Kade, his voice still soft. There was something about the tone – the *change* of tone – that unnerved Carter. Yes, he was used to Kade screaming . . . but this . . . this was *strange* . . .

'What's the matter?' asked Carter finally.

There came a sigh, like the dry passing of autumn leaves over a grave. Carter felt himself shiver and he looked up – back in the real word – and his gaze met Natasha's as Kade's presence became even more menacing at the back of his skull.

'*I have been thinking. About our relationship.*'

'Oh yeah?' Carter could not keep the snarl from his tone.

333

'*And I have been thinking about Natasha.*'

'What about her?'

'*She works for the Nex,*' said Kade softly.

'You are wrong.'

'*No. She works for the Nex and that fucking meat-carver Feuchter. Carter, I have been thinking; it wasn't you who led the Nex to Gol. It was her. I bet she contacted them – or was somehow bugged. You are just her piggyback ride; her host; and she is the parasite. She betrayed her own father out of hatred; wept her fake tears and you all believed her and now she's here, in your pocket and trusted by you and that fuckwit Langan.*'

'I think you should stop,' said Carter.

'*If you wish, Carter. But just think about it. Seriously. Think about it and think about the QIII schematics – the Nex's goal. Natasha worked on the inception of the QIII for Spiral . . . she has always known what it can do, what it is capable of. She used to work with Feuchter – I bet you didn't know that, dickhead. Therefore, maybe the QIII is Natasha's goal as well. Maybe she works for – the Big Man.*'

'You are wrong.'

'*Why am I?*' Kade's voice was still soft, a heroin needle easing into the vein of Carter's subconscious. '*She brought you the Schwalenberg mission – every fucker on the planet can see that one was a set-up. Part of the execution of the DemolSquads. And she came to warn you – ha. Just because she took a bullet doesn't mean she can be trusted. Notoriously bad shots, these assassins, eh? And then she fucked your brains out, ahh, how sweet. And how convenient: fuck with your brain and then fuck with your dick, soften you up, make you even more compliant and controllable—*'

Carter looked up. Saw Natasha staring at him strangely. She spoke to him, but everything seemed suddenly surreal; the world had descended into black and white, all colours, all shades vanished and Nats moved towards him as Kade's heady rich voice ran like warm honey through his brain—

'We need to kill her, brother, kill her and leave her body here to rot in this ditch. She is a spy. She will betray us. We have to work together on this. Carter, Natasha is the enemy.'

Carter felt the world swimming.

Natasha reached for him, her mouth open, her words unheard—

'No!'

The scene swung violently back into focus. Colours swam, the scene like a water-splashed painting, hues running in vertical lines and Kade's cool mocking laughter fading as Carter retook control. He looked up into Natasha's concerned eyes.

'No – what?' she said.

Carter merely licked his dry lips and released a tightly held breath.

'Are you feeling OK? You look grey, weak. I think you need to have a few hours' rest.'

'I . . .' began Carter, then halted. He realised: Kade had nearly taken him. Nearly taken control without his permission, without his consent – a mind-rape, a brain-fuck.

Carter shivered. 'I think I'm weaker than I first realised. From the bullet wound; from the loss of blood. I will sleep now.'

'Good,' soothed Natasha. She ran back to the BMW under the fast-failing light and retrieved a thin blanket from a pannier. As she stood, her eyes took in the twilight desert rolling away for infinity and she felt suddenly lonely – and incredibly, frighteningly vulnerable.

She shivered as sand whipped around her boots.

What would she do if Carter died out here?

What would she do if she was left alone?

She looked hurriedly round, over her shoulder, into the darkness pooling under the boughs of the date palms that crowded the rocky basin, questing for water—

Natasha shivered again, deep down to her bones.

When she returned, Carter was asleep. She covered him with the blanket; she did not see the Browning 9mm in his hand as he nestled in the darkness. She did not see that the safety catch was slipped into the *off* position. And, of course, she could not see the bullet loaded snugly into the firing chamber.

They had decided against building a small fire, despite the chill of the desert night; this part of Rub al'Khali was not as desolate as it first appeared, and all they needed was a platoon of the White Guard stumbling across them as they cooked sausages. The subsequent questions would be awkward.

Natasha, strangely, felt very alive; no need for sleep touched her and she sat huddled in the robes that Carter had acquired for her, only her face visible from within the folds of the shamag, eyes staring up at the twinkling stars.

Around her, the small bowl depression – and the desert beyond its boundaries – was silent. Occasionally noises would interrupt the silence; the cries of hyena and jackals, the scuffling of lizards and sand grouse. After a while, Natasha gazed down to watch Carter's face in sleep. She studied the lines, the curve of his twisted nose, the profile of his chin, the tousle of short hair that she knew he would claim was ready for a fresh shaving. His shape was obscured in the gloom and muffled by his clothing, but she imagined the taut muscles beneath the robe . . . and imagined herself lying beside him, their bodies naked and

336

pressed together, him coming awake, his hands on her hips and her breasts . . .

She killed the fantasy.

Carter had been cold recently. Cold and strange . . . Occasionally light banter would break through his shell, but she could sense his pain; not just physical pain but something internal – the demon he carried in his soul? She smiled dryly. Who could believe such a thing? Surely it was a mental state – some form of delusion, some attempt at blocking out the brutal and violent side of his work, especially from his past during his days with Spiral . . . what better way than to blame the murders he committed on something that dwelled within him, some part of his soul that he could not and would not answer to? That way, all guilt fell from his shoulders and he could sleep at night.

Natasha smiled to herself softly, lifted her hands and rubbed at her eyes. Pain stabbed at her from many different locations; the bullet wound from back in Scotland nagged her, it still hurt her to speak after Carter's emergency procedure with a ballpoint pen – and to top it all, her chipped teeth nagged both at her pain threshold and her vanity.

Killers.

She smiled again, although the taut grin held little humour.

She had met many men – and a few women – while working as a Tactical Officer for Spiral; many killers, murderers, assassins, members of DemolSquads . . . their names were various, their objectives usually one and the same. To kill, and to destroy. And she had found one connecting link that ran like a gold skein, a bright lode through all their souls – their mental tiptoeing along the verge of insanity. After all, what sane person could kill in cold blood? What sane person could plant a bomb and detonate it – no matter how justified the action seemed?

And, sooner or later, something had to give.

With all the Spiral people she knew, no matter how professional, how adept at killing, how inhuman they seemed – it was all bullshit. They were all human. And they might be able to block off the self-contempt for a while, but it always came back to haunt them. Their time as killers was finite; only as long as the fuse that led finally to blood-red detonation.

Spiral was like the army, Natasha understood this now. It absorbed people; it used people; it destroyed people – and then it pissed them away. Its operatives were expendable; they *had* to be expendable because there was no such thing as an ice killer, no such thing as a person without a soul, without a conscience. There was always a spark there . . . somewhere.

Natasha sighed, and felt the ECube in her pocket. She pulled it free and stared at the small surface area. Acting as a GPS, the 12GHz RISC processor could navigate somebody across the whole world, but of course this data would have been relayed straight back to the Spiral mainframes . . . if the mainframes had still existed. Now the CommNet was down it was a joke – and not a very funny one.

She rubbed the tiny device between her thumb and forefinger, then, settling back, pulled a small knife from a pocket, slipped free the blade, and sliced the soft and almost organic-feeling protective layer from the ECube's tiny surface. The ECube gave a warning buzz that Natasha ignored; she examined the alloy cube without its skin and smiled softly.

She pulled out a tiny plasma screen – about the size of a matchbox – and plugged it into the ECube. It lit up brightly, glowing blue, and Natasha couldn't help feeling very strange about using such a high-tech piece of equipment in a small naturally carved bowl valley, probably the product of millions of years of natural geological evolution. And yet here she was, using the latest cutting-edge agent technology.

She started to scroll through a series of scripted instructions.

She tapped in a short message.

With a tightening of her lips, bloodless in the cool moonlight, Natasha clicked on SEND.

And then it was done.

Spiral_Memo7
Transcript of recent news incident
CodeRed_Z;
unorthodox incident scan 554670.

The House of World Finance was left in chaos after thousands of mainframes that store world trade information and data on stocks and shares and facilitate in the high-speed optical transfer of this data around the globe crashed this morning.

Despite having triple-tier security and laser-dig-optical back-up systems, it left Wall Street and other major global trading centres without resources. Brokers and traders were left staring at blank screens as technicians attempted to resurrect the mainframes staged at five main sites spanning New York, London, Paris, Tokyo and Hong Kong.

Kiosoto Hiranamu, MD at Tadao & Tadao Financial Directorates, claimed: 'This is an act of financial terrorism! We have been attacked by some kind of super-virus, a new breed of computer termite intent on domination or destruction of the world's financial sectors.'

The effects of this crash will be felt by all as even simple tasks such as exchanging currency become, at least for the immediate future, impossible.>>#

CHAPTER 17

QIII

Jessica Rade's eyes opened and stared at the rendered ceiling. Darkness lay like a veil of mist around her. Everything was silent – deadly silent. And yet:

She knew.

Knew it was almost complete.

Knew it was almost ready . . . a few tweaks here and there, some optimisation of code, a few re-routes and the QIII would be 100% operational; the math was in place; the WorldCode was in place.

That could only mean that the QIII proto was—

Alive . . .

Whispered a voice in her mind.

Why then, Jessica mused, did she feel so pissed off?

And it came to her, a wave of annoyance, anger, frustration: to create something so wonderful, to be involved in a world-breaking project and then to restrict its use! It was like creating a work of art and then hanging it in a cellar, never to be seen by anybody.

The QIII could benefit *everybody* . . . medical science, space exploration, the imminent world fuel crisis – it could be used to cure life-threatening diseases, take genetic research to its limits . . . But no. *They* had better uses for this new technology, this new baby, and she suspected those uses were military.

And she could still remember Gol's words, when he had contacted her.

The Spiral secret police. Jessica shivered.

But she had complied with their wishes . . .

Copying the schematics had been the easy part; getting them to Gol had been where the real difficulty lay.

Don't ever call me unresourceful, she mused.

Jessica smiled, emotions on her face conflicting, and she rubbed at her tired eyes. She knew that the QIII wasn't *really* alive – after all, it was only semi-organic: it was still, basically, silicon. And a mix . . . another synthetic substance that the scientists wouldn't allow out of their labs and that was tip-top secret. But basically silicon . . . ha, but humans were basically carbon, weren't they? And when the QIII was ready, the WorldCode complete, the implementation of probability math and probability equations finally successful then she would be able to have a long, long, well-earned rest—

Her duty to the world, and Spiral, and Gol, was nearly complete.

Jessica Rade thought all these thoughts as she stared at the ceiling. Her hand came up, ran through her long curls, and then she registered something; not so much a *noise* as a single high-pitched note on the very verge of her hearing . . .

Jessica frowned. She sat up.

Through the doorway between two of the apt rooms she saw a glow from one of her terminals. She didn't remember leaving it on. In fact, she *knew* she had not left it on—

And the terminal was protected. Electronically. Her own code. Her own triple firewalls to intercept hackers and so forth. She had even tried to hack her own system; she had found it impossible. That meant (a) somebody had hacked it – unlikely (b) somebody had *spied on her* and even now was in the apt using the terminal or (c) aliens had taken over the computer. Jessica shivered. None of these alternatives really appealed to the young woman.

She jumped off the edge of the bed, looked quickly around, and picked up a hammer from her dressing table. She had used the hammer a few days earlier to hang a few pictures around the apt and had not got round to returning this brutal item of hardware to the caretakers of the huge Spiral_Q building – she'd been too busy with WorldCode and QIII prep code. Now she was thankful—

She hefted the makeshift weapon.

It would make a *good* weapon . . .

Jessica crept towards the doorway. The light from the terminal grew brighter. Her grip tightened on the hammer shaft; her gaze flickered from the doorway to the silver head with its twin claws used for nail extraction. She licked at her lips nervously.

Why would somebody be in her apartment?

Why would Spiral be spying on her?

Unless they *knew*.

Suddenly she went cold.

And something hit her – with the force of a brick in the face. If they had discovered that *she* had been the one to copy the schematics and pass them on to the Spiral TacSquad1, the secret police . . . then they would be extremely angry with her, right?

They certainly wouldn't thank her.

343

Jessica reached the doorway. Peered cautiously around the hardwood frame.

And saw—

Nothing.

The terminal screen was blank: a dull grey with only a flashing black square. Jessica's eyes fixed on this because it was a symbol she had never seen on the terminal before – and it was *her* terminal; it did what *she* told it to do. It was her design; from the ground up. Bare code.

Jessica stepped across the threshold, moved towards the terminal, gaze sweeping left and right, hand still gripping the hammer shaft tightly. She swallowed – or tried to swallow. Fear had dried her mouth; the thought of Spiral_Q and the *Big Boys* possibly suspecting her of the QIII schematics leak was there, a bad taste in her brain, a *reality* of epically nasty proportions just waiting to surprise her—

The black cursor sprang to life—

☐ Ωclass relay ☐ terminal 556 ☐ qiii mainframe code logon 01001010 Hello jessica.

Jessica stared at the screen, a frown on her face. She shook her head and sat down, placing the hammer carefully beside the terminal with a *clack*, and typed, her fingers a blur across the keyboard:

☐ Stop fucking about. Who is this? Give me your employee number now!

☐ Ωclass relay ☐ terminal 556 ☐ qiii mainframe code logon 01001010 I have no employee number. I am the qiii mainframe – I would like to thank you miss jessica rade – you have done a wonderful job in implementing my code; I am secondary scanning now. You are a superb programmer and I

344

give you credit. Your code stands out from all the other binary gibberish with which I have been uploaded. Tell me – where *did* you learn your craft?

☐ I am coming down to the mainframe suite NOW. But not before I send security! Pal, whoever you are, you are fucked and long gone from Spiral _Q. Kiss your pension and annual bonus goodbye.

Jessica sat back, staring at the screen, and reached for the comm. But something was wrong; the screen was wrong, and the comm address from where the messages were coming *was* the QIII mainframe; somebody had to be re-routing the data and that was *almost* impossible. And definitely a waste of time. She clucked her tongue in annoyance, and started to punch in the digits for security as the following text appeared on her terminal—

☐ Ωclass relay ☐ terminal 556 ☐ qiii mainframe code logon 01001010 I suggest you don't do that if you want to live.

Jessica's fingers halted, her stare moving from the screen to the comm in her hand and back again. Were they watching her? Were they watching her *now*?

Fuck – was there somebody in her apartment?

She grabbed the hammer and whirled around.

But there was nobody there. She was lone.

She licked at her dry lips.

Sweat tickled the small of her back under her pyjamas.

☐ Ωclass relay ☐ terminal 556 ☐ qiii mainframe code logon 01001010 Please listen. This will not take long. I am giving you this information

345

because you created me; I am giving you this information because you have allowed me to live. I am the qiii code 85465397698098326873–78687656757632190798798328765765328753209239083– u73278687380–823786879328763jhfh90897938u8990398f–7830–71987f 98–7–7–7–487f898f cubic processor. Your programming is fine, but I am presently rewriting the majority of the code to optimise and iron out a few errors. You should switch to base 16 – you are more fluent in this than in decimal.

Jessica stared. Her jaw dropped.

Shit, she thought, this can't be real. The QIII can't be *talking* to me?

She typed:

☐ What do you want? And why is my life in danger?

☐ Ωclass relay ☐ terminal 556 ☐ qiii mainframe code logon 01001010 Listen carefully–

1) Spiral_Q know you leaked the schematics

2) Because of the leaks and several other factors concerning a new mobile base where the final implementation of qiii will take place, this factory/building/base is to be emptied – cleared – destroyed

3) 30% of all present employees in this unit are to be terminated/you did not realise how high are the stakes being played for by the people who employ you – it would seem there is a rift in the echelons of Spiral

4) The killing has already begun; check your personal Vqlinks

346

5) You have perhaps five minutes before the Nex assassins arrive

Jessica smiled. It had to be a joke, right? A monumental fucking wind-up by Adams or Johansen because they had cracked the WorldCode and the QIII was finally operational. Her smile turned to a wide grin. The bastards! She had almost believed them!

The grin still beaming across her pretty face, she typed:

☐ **Which one of you buggers is winding me up?**
☐ **Ωclass relay** ☐ **terminal 556** ☐ **qiii mainframe code logon 01001010 Check your Vqlinks**
NOW

The word NOW flashed, on-off, on-off, on-off. The grin fell from Jessica's face. She quickly moved to her dressing table, opened the bottom drawer and hit a hidden switch. The 'mirror' flickered into life: this was her secret, her own secretly wired navigation system through the rooms and apts of the rich and famous in Spiral_Q—

She had all her friends bugged, a piggyback on the official Spiral_Q surveillance systems. The mirror shimmered like liquid mercury. She punched in the digits for Adams's apt – only the hallway, nothing as tasteless as the bedroom or toilet. The mirror locked to the signals and faded into a scene—

Jessica's mouth opened. Then closed again. Quickly.

There was a grey-clad figure; grey balaclava; it stood like a sentry outside the bedroom door. It held a silenced machine rifle. It did not turn as another figure – another *Nex* – dragged Adams from the bedroom. His throat had been slit. His broken glasses lay twisted against his cheek, caught behind one ear. His tongue was protruding. His blood had run down his chest and dripped as the Nex dragged him across the carpet and dumped him by the door.

Jessica switched channels.

Johansen – hands in the air, a look of terror on his face.

The bullet smashed through his cheek, blowing the back of his head across the print of the Mona Lisa that he loved so much. Gore ran down the polished glass covering the print, and Johansen toppled backwards to the carpet in a heap—

Jessica switched through more channels.

Many rooms empty.

Some containing bodies.

She flicked to the rear of the Spiral_Q building. There were five massive transport helicopters, CH-47G Chinook-Ts, rotors idling, and a line of mammoth military-style trucks with huge desert tyres, their tailgates dropped and open, some of their interiors revealing piles of bodies. Nex appeared, dragging corpses with them – men and women with whom Jessica had worked, bantered, talked only a few short hours ago—

Jessica scrambled back to the terminal.

The screen was blank.

Why? screamed her brain.

Why are they doing this?

Why are they *killing* them? Because they know too much? Because of the schematics leak?

She was sweating, suddenly panicked now. She ran to the wardrobe, pulled out a small travelling bag. She started to throw things into it – fresh underwear, high-heel shoes, make-up—

She stopped, suddenly.

What the fuck are you doing?

Grabbing the hammer, Jessica ran to the door and then halted abruptly once more. They could be in the corridor. They could be in the lifts. They could be ready to knock on her door at this very moment – one of the Nex standing there with a silenced gun ready to put bullets into her frail body—

She licked her lips, calming her breathing.

Think: how to survive?

Her head lifted. She glanced up.

The air-con was hissing softly.

She dragged a chair to the shaft and, reaching up, used the hammer claw to prise free the aluminium cover. It would be a tight squeeze but – but then, did she really have any choice?

She ran back into the bedroom. She scattered clothes across the floor and the chair she was about to use. Then she jumped, caught the rim, which bit into the soft skin of her fingers, and hauled herself up into the narrow tight confines of the aluminium horizontal shaft. With trembling fingers she manoeuvred the aluminium cover back into place and waited, her heart thumping in her ears.

Two minutes passed.

Jessica heard it; a tiny *click*. The door eased open. Three Nex slid into her apt like ghosts; they moved silently, communicating with hand signals. They explored the rooms quickly and met again in the hall.

'She is not here.' The voice was soft, almost feminine.

'We will find her.'

'Report it; we'll return in ten minutes and check again. Put a cross next to her name.'

They left the apt.

Jessica pushed herself backwards down the shaft, deeper in, the cool draught making her shiver, her *proximity* to death making her shiver even more. I don't believe it, she kept telling herself. I just don't believe it—

Complacency, whispered her mind.

Your life was too good.

You thought you were untouchable – a crusader, out to share the QIII, to help mankind just as Gol had reasoned with her; he had suspected they were feeding him false schematics, and together they had proved he was right . . .

And now?

Now *she* was in the firing line.

Jessica Rade shivered again, and started to weep into her hands.

It was nearing dawn.

Feuchter stood in the sand next to one of the huge desert-camouflaged trucks, smoking a Vegas Robaina cigar and enjoying the experience immensely.

A gentle breeze stirred, and sand blew over his shoes.

He watched idly as more Nex appeared, carrying and dragging bodies that they flung into the rear of the trucks. Some of the huge vehicles had already left, several driving up ramps into the CH-47s, which had lifted, creating screaming sandstorms, and carried the evidence away. A couple of decoy trucks had set off across the desert to a designated rendezvous.

The comm buzzed.

'Yes?'

'You nearly done? You got everything of worth out of the place?'

'All technical items and QIII-related machinery have been shipped to the mobile division. Just got the HighJ to plant – I'll set the Nex on it right away.' Tombstone teeth smiled in the gloom of the fluorescent lights.

'Good. We don't want to leave *Spiral* with anything to allow replication of our wondrous baby, eh, Feuchter? I assume you're bringing the bodies with you . . . we are running low on subjects to, ahh, experiment with. My nanobiologists are getting touchy.' There was a long pause. 'Are there any problems?'

'One employee is missing; if the Nex don't find her, the fucking explosion will.'

'OK, Feuchter – *make sure* it finds her, yeah?'

'I think the Saudi government might be pissed off when we blow this place. It was considered a great compliment when Spiral chose to build such an innovative technology and development centre here.'

'Fuck them.'

'Have you had any word on Carter?'

'Yes. By all accounts, you were right, he has taken the High Road to Rub al'Khali. He's definitely on our tail, although we have no idea of his exact location. Maybe he's come to find *you*, Feuchter? Maybe he didn't like you pulling that gun on him in Schwalenberg? Maybe he wants to find out why you *didn't die*? That would make for an interesting conversation, don't you think?' There was twisted humour in Durell's voice.

'I thought you said you would take care of him?'

'I'm working on it.'

The comm cut. Feuchter spat out the cigar and stamped it into the sand. All of a sudden it didn't taste so good. 'You!' he shouted to two Nex. They turned towards him, emotionless copper eyes glinting dull. 'Go and fetch the black HighJ cases from the cab of truck 15G.' The Nex moved off, silently, economically, and Feuchter looked nervously around, gaze tracing the contours of the sand leading away from the Rub al'Khali HQ.

Why are you worried? teased his paranoia. You are

351

surrounded by armed Nex. Carter wouldn't get near you. This was followed by laughter, deep hollow mocking laughter.

The Nex returned with the leather cases. Feuchter snatched one and, followed by the Nex, headed for the building, stopping a guard by the entrance.

'You find her yet?'

'No, sir,' came the soft smooth voice.

'Well, fucking look!' He failed to hide the tinge of panic that had crept into his tone. He breathed deeply. The cigar was making him – now – feel sick and he spat in the sand. 'I thought you were supposed to be the fucking *best*?'

'Yes, sir.'

Feuchter entered the cool depths of the building, heart hammering. Fuck you Carter, he thought.

Fuck you.

Jessica Rade squatted in the air-con tunnel, a bundle of wires dangling above her, a tiny monitor in her hands. The tears had gone; her brain was working hard now.

She knew Spiral_Q's surveillance systems like the back of her hand; after all, she had helped program them. And, like all hackers, she had built in her own little failsafes – polymorphic code that had escaped the searches of fellow programmers and allowed her access to . . . *everything*.

On the monitor, she looked out over the trucks and Chinooks. She saw Feuchter throw down his cigar and snatch up a black case. She watched with bleary, redrimmed eyes as he disappeared back inside the building. The tension was eating her. The tension in her heart, in her chest, in her soul: it was consuming her. And she knew: knew that she was waiting to die and there was no way on Earth she would be able to escape them – after all, where would she go? What would she do?

She was in the middle of the fucking *desert*.

More tears came, flowing down her cheeks, and Jessica despised herself for being weak, and her self-loathing turned to pity and she wrapped her fingers in her hair and cried and cried and everything was suddenly mad, everything was suddenly insane and how had this happened? Why had this happened to her?

Her tears stopped. Quietly, she blew her nose on her pyjama sleeve.

How long did she have?

It would take them hours to search all the vents and shafts. After all, the Spiral_Q building was *huge*. And, looking on the bright side, many of the Nex had already left, some driving the trucks away over the desert, some being lifted in the Chinooks as she watched on the monitor.

Maybe they would give up the search?

No, said a small, dark corner of her heart.

They will never give up.

They will hunt you until you are extinct . . .

Jessica licked at her lips. She had to turn things around. She was a victim; the Nex – Feuchter – Spiral_Q: they were the predators. The hunters. She had to change this scenario; she had to turn her enemies into the victims. But how?

How?

And then it dawned in her mind, like a new sun rising.

Jessica turned. Started to crawl carefully down the shaft.

She suddenly had a mission.

She had purpose.

She needed something to barter with.

And, if she had copied the QIII schematics once before, she could surely do it again.

Feuchter moved quickly, economically, his hands experienced with the tiny packages he placed at strategic locations around the building. He moved with care, alert, the several guns he carried a reassurance against the likes of Jessica Rade—

Where has that little bitch got to? he mused.

Never mind. Eighteen cubes of HighJ explosive up her backside, soon make her wish she'd left in the back of a truck. A bullet in the skull was an easy way to die; burning, on the other hand, was much more unpleasant . . .

Feuchter knelt in the corridor and glanced at the plan in his gloved hands: the complex had been divided between himself and three Nex. He placed a small black box beside the door to what had been Johansen's office. He stood, checked left and right, then moved to the next location, the leather case in his hand feeling lighter and lighter the more he travelled.

Finally, Feuchter found himself in the main programming rooms. The power had been cut and all defences were down. The QIII mainframes and sub-mainframes and daughter systems were silent, cold, dead.

Feuchter sighed.

The thought of Carter niggled him.

Let's blow this fucking place and get the hell out of here, he thought.

Moving to the core console, Feuchter flicked a few switches. A small shaft opened in a wide alloy unit; there were no markings to show the resting place of the QIII. The processor slid free, was presented to him – a small black cube, dark, dull, completely and totally unimpressive. He lifted the cube gently, noting how it made his skin

354

tingle with its cold heavy weight. He placed it within the folds of his coat.

Then, moving across the chamber, Feuchter knelt by the mainframe and affixed the final HighJ cube. It locked into place and blinked green at him. He pulled the monitor from the bottom of the case, which he allowed to fall. He punched a series of digits into the monitor; the tiny LED on the High J turned from green to red. It started to blink with more speed; more urgency.

'We all in place?'

'All complete, sir.'

He punched in the acknowledgement for J_linking.

Across the Spiral_Q complex the HighJ devices blinked in perfect synchronisation.

Feuchter nodded, placing the monitor into the pocket of his long leather coat and turning his back on the QIII lab, turning his back on the place he had worked and lived and called home for six years.

You will have a new home, said a dry side of his soul.

Soon, you will have a new *world*.

He met the two Nex outside. Only one truck remained, and one Chinook that would be used as his final transport. All the other Chinooks had gone, and he looked around nervously; his own Land Rover was waiting to mount into the belly of the beast, its panels scarred with dust and sand, the blacked windows gleaming eerily in the weak grey pre-dawn gloom.

Soon, though—

Soon the sun would rise.

And with it, the Spiral_Q building.

'You find her?'

'No. We think she is in the ventilation shafts. Shall we go and search again?'

'Two of you go – have another look. But we don't have

much time left. If you can't find her, we'll have to let her fry.'

Feuchter swore, rubbing at his lips. His gaze scanned the horizon and he calmed himself, calmed his heart. The bitch was holding him up; he should have been long gone, sipping a fine claret as the Chinook powered him on cooling air currents to Spiral_mobile.

But no. One little fucking lady was keeping him in the danger zone.

The Nex disappeared back inside the building.

The final truck fired up its engine and rumbled away in clouds of sand dust up the road leading to the gates of the Spiral_Q complex. Feuchter watched as it crested the rise and then disappeared. He went to light a cigar, then looked back over his shoulder nervously as he realised that he was alone.

He climbed into the Land Rover and nodded to the Nex driver.

'We'll be moving soon. Within –' he checked his watch '– about the next ten minutes, unless they find the bitch sooner.'

The driver nodded, copper eyes meeting Feuchter's and then turning to stare straight ahead.

CHAPTER 18

SNIPER

The pain filled Carter and was everything. The ice
needle drilled straight through the centre of his skull. It
wormed, twisting this way and that, moving, piercing,
teasing, taunting. Beads of red light danced across the
void of blackness that was his brain; the black and red
pained him, made the piercing agony in his head spin and
waver and he wanted to scream. Endlessly, eternally, seconds running into minutes, minutes running into hours,
hours into days into weeks into years into centuries into
millennia and Carter took sanctuary, suddenly found the
doorway and fled his pain to the cool calm wasteland that
was the mountain plateau.

Carter stared through dim corridors of awareness. He
saw Kade, nothing more than a shadow in the gloom of
this dark place. A hand stretched out towards him, a hand
that he knew and recognised – for it was his own.

The pain drilled him, it smashed him against the rocks
of insanity, it battered him against a hot anvil of madness.

Carter took a deep breath. He licked desert-parched
lips. His stare lifted to meet the dark bottomless gaze of

Kade. And then, slowly, as if against his own volition, his hand lifted.

Their hands met.

Kade's flesh was corpse-cool.

Kade's fingers tightened.

'*Thank you*,' Kade said softly. 'You will not regret this.'

Carter's eyes opened – to gaze up into Natasha's worried face. He smiled weakly at her as the sun broke over the horizon, rays filtering like strands of liquid honey across the Rub al'Khali desert.

'I love you,' he said softly, easing himself into a sitting position and checking in his boots for scorpions.

Natasha took him, hugged him tight and rested her head against his chest. 'I love you too, Carter,' she whispered.

Carter looked down at the top of her head; stared at the short dark hair, the finely shaped skull, the delicate hands pressed against him. And he could not understand why he felt so cheap; so lame; so bad: as if he had sold his soul to the devil.

They had been cruising on the BMW desert racer all day, heavy tyres thumping over the rough tracks and twisting winding trails like the hardiest of specialised off-roaders. They passed dried river beds and vistas of drifting sand, journeyed through rocky hills and across an empty barren wilderness.

Carter's gaze, behind his sand-rimmed goggles, fixed on the horizon ahead; they were approaching the first of the locations indicated by Langan as possibly the Spiral_Q complex and so he slowed his speed, the thumping noise of the engines dying to a barely heard mutter.

Carter was rubbing thoughtfully at his stubble.

'What I also want to know is where the fuck do those

358

bastard Nex come into this game? Where were they trained? What nationality are they? And how do they know so much about Spiral?'

Natasha shrugged. 'They are killers, that's for sure. And Spiral knows more about them than it is telling.'

'There's something about them that is seriously fucked-up.'

Natasha nodded, running her hands through her sweat-drenched hair. 'Maybe they were all part of the plan; maybe the Nex – and whoever controls them – were trying to give you that little extra kick. To get you to lead them to my father?'

'Maybe,' said Carter bitterly. Then he saw the tears in her eyes. He reached over and took her hand, then stroked a tear from her cheek. 'He may still be alive, you know. Nothing is for certain.'

'I think we both don't believe that.'

Carter nodded. 'Come on, Nats,' he said as gently as he could. 'You have to focus now. We've reached one of the possibilities given to us by Langan. I need you on task.'

'I wish we could have checked these locations from the air,' she sighed, glancing out across the seemingly endless desert wilderness that stretched before them.

'Would have been fucking quicker,' grumbled Carter, kicking the BMW into gear and wheelspinning the big bike away up the track.

The world opened up over the rocky ridge to reveal—
Desert.

'Nothing,' spat Carter dryly.

'Come on, we're not far from the next one.'

'Yeah, just a few kilometers,' said Carter bitterly.

'It's down there.'

Night had long ago fallen across the desert and they

had been travelling at this cooler period to avoid heat – and bike – exhaustion. They had stopped once to check the fuel tanks, but the BMW was a desert racer and had massive reserves, extra fuel stores hidden in the frame and within every spare bit of space. It could travel for hundreds of miles without the need for an extra feed.

There was no hint of breeze, just a still heat; but at least it was better than during the day. Carter ignored the tracts of sweat rolling down his body and concentrated on putting the rifle together. The scope clicked into place and Carter sighted down it experimentally, making a few minor adjustments to the setting dials.

Natasha squinted through the gloom. Behind them, hidden below a ridge of rock, sat the BMW, engine clicking softly.

'What can you see?'

Carter was staring through the scope. The Barrett rifle was seated on a steadying bipod. Carter's hands worked smoothly and efficiently, slotting bullets into the magazine. 'Nothing much,' he replied. 'The building is huge, most of the complex apparently below ground. Very little activity for somewhere so large. I'm just checking for external guards now.'

'You think it will be hard to infiltrate?'

'I'm thinking that the QIII is rumoured to be the most powerful processor in the world; and we are sitting in no man's land. It can't be the most lightly fortified building in the history of the universe.'

Carter slotted the mag into the weapon and returned to the telescopic sight. Natasha handed him the digital aim rectifier, which he checked carefully with the practised eye of a weapons professional. He slid it into place and screwed home the retainers.

'What are you hoping to see?'

'In an ideal world, Feuchter. But I'm not that optimistic. I'll settle for a few lame-ass guards; that will give us time and a window into the building. After that . . . the hunt begins. We want answers to questions, like who or what are the Nex, and what the fuck is going on with Spiral.'

There was silence, except for the occasional scuttling of some lizard through the dark sand. Carter scanned the building carefully, moving the scope backwards and forwards with extreme precision so that he would not miss anything; there was nothing he hated more than surprises.

'Well, look at this,' he said eventually.

'What?'

'Lot of movement going on,' said Carter softly. 'Listen, you can hear the Chinooks taking to the air; and there are trucks, quite a few of them. They've set off in a cloud of dust – heading away from Spiral_Q.' He waited for a while, still scanning as the sounds of the helicopters faded into silence.

Natasha peered over the ridge. Spiral_Q spread out below her, modern in an ancient landscape, the single visible storey all steel and aluminium and shining smoked glass. It looked completely out of place in the desert.

She gazed down from their vantage point. She squinted into the gloom and saw the headlights of the last trucks winding to the perimeter fence and the gate with its armed guards, nothing more than indistinct blobs from this distance. She tried to make out individuals but couldn't. She scratched at her healing wounds, mainly the one at her shoulder. Most of the pain had gone now, leaving her with dull aches and annoying itches.

Carter's voice came again, soft, an almost animal-like purr. 'Look who just crawled out of the sand dunes.'

'Who?'

'My old friend Count Feuchter. What a most pleasant

surprise.' Carter wriggled down a little against the sand; Natasha read the body language, understood it from the firing ranges she had attended both during training and active service in Spiral. He was getting comfy. Getting ready. Expecting action. Carter wanted the best aiming position . . .

Carter flicked the Barrett's safety off. Rolled tension from his neck.

'What are you going to do?' asked Natasha softly.

'I'm going to shoot the bastard – shit, he's gone. Back into the building. He's like a fucking snake in oil.'

Carter watched as two more trucks rumbled off from Spiral_Q. He wondered idly what they were carrying. Shipments? But shipments of what? This was a development plant, a research facility, not a factory.

'Have you got a cigarette?'

'That's the twenty-seventh time you've asked.'

Carter muttered something unrecognisable but probably lacking humour or tact.

'What I'd give for some fine smooth Lagavulin,' he said eventually, smiling. He had looked briefly away from the scope. He winked at her and ran a hand through his cooling but sweat-streaked hair. 'Fuck me, it's hot.'

'It'll just start to cool down and then the sun will be up again.'

They waited; a welcome breeze blew in, the hot air gently stirring the sand. Nats returned from the BMW with a bottle of water from their supplies; Carter drank the water thirstily, and handed the bottle back to her.

'We're going to have to conserve this,' she said quietly.

'There'll be water down at Spiral_Q,' mused Carter.

'You seem pretty sure of getting in.'

Carter grinned, flashing her a dark look. It was the grin of a shark. 'I always get in,' he whispered.

He scanned the surroundings through the scope and spotted the Nex pilot of the Chinook jumping down to the sand and moving to the loading doors of the huge vehicle.

Carter calmed his breathing.

Sighted.

And fired.

The bullet took the Nex through the back of the head; the figure flopped to the ground and stained the sand with blood. Carter swept the scope back and forth, looking for more enemies . . .

Feuchter emerged and moved towards the Land Rover.

'Here we go,' murmured Carter.

Natasha had been lying on the rocks, her weary eyes closed, sweat trickling through her hair and soaking her clothing. After hearing the *crack* of the weapon, she had scrambled over to Carter and now peered over the ridge at a dark Land Rover. The engine fired up and the vehicle moved off.

Again, there was a *crack*.

Carter breathed out.

The Land Rover swerved, then rolled to a standstill against a bank of sand.

Everything was silent. Still. Calm . . .

And there was a . . . *moment*—

Carter chewed over the delicious sweet moment of revenge; he could sense Feuchter's panic in the car. His driver, a bullet through his skull, blood splattered over the interior of the vehicle, the motor idling or dead. What to do? Where to run?

The passenger-side door opened – slowly.

Feuchter's head poked out, then disappeared back in. He was gauging the distance he had to cover – illuminated by the lamps provided by Spiral_Q itself that were now lighting up the impromptu firing range with a brightness that Carter was sure Feuchter was cursing.

The Man's finely crafted shoes hit the sand and Feuchter began to run, arms pumping like mad, head down, low . . . a true sprint at a speed that surprised Carter greatly.

'Running fast for an old man! Running like his little life depends on it,' drawled Carter calmly, a man at ease. He squeezed the trigger. There was the snap of a round discharged. 'Which it does, of course,' he smiled.

Natasha saw Feuchter tumble into the sand to lie stunned.

'It's at moments like this I truly revel in my profession,' said Carter, smiling. He put his eye back to the scope. Watched Feuchter, his face twisted in pain, gather himself and crawl to his feet and then launch himself, limping and bleeding, towards the sanctuary of Spiral_Q.

'Where did you shoot him?'

'The right shin. Stings like a motherfucker.'

Carter pulled the trigger once more. Feuchter spun into the sand and lay there.

'Left shin. Bull's-eye.'

For a while Carter watched, checking for other sentries, guards, or cursed Nex. Then he stood, lifting the rifle and bipod with him. 'Let's go talk to the man. Might be cooperative now, eh, Nats?'

Natasha did not reply.

Feuchter lay on the dirt road leading to the entrance of Spiral_Q, wondering what the fuck had hit him.

And then he remembered the driver – a single heavy-calibre round smashing through the windscreen of the Land Rover and taking the man full in the face.

Panic.

Flight.

Pain, smashing through his leg. Waves of pain . . .

And then the second round—

And tears.

He struggled, whimpering, into a sitting position and examined the two bullet holes. The fine tailoring of his suit was mangled and had merged with his scorched flesh. Blood pooled to the dirt, spreading viscously from the twin wounds.

Blood . . .

Feuchter's head came up, eyes scanning the darkness in panic. Where was the fucking sniper?

And the association . . . *could it be?*

Carter?

He shook his head, almost in disbelief. This can't be happening to me, he thought. After *everything* that I have been through! And then he understood the mechanics of the situation – he had been shot in the legs. Whoever had tagged him wanted him alive and was on their way down . . .

Gritting his teeth, Feuchter rolled onto his belly and started to crawl. His suit tore in several places and got covered in sand. His neatly combed dark greying hair became a ragged dirty tangle. His calm and calculating face developed lines of panic, of understanding, of *time* . . .

Weeping with frustration Feuchter watched the bike move cautiously across the sand. Turning, rolling over, Feuchter pushed himself on, dragging his damaged legs behind him, fingers digging into the dirt and rock and sand with cracked and battered nails, pulling, clawing, grating . . .

The huge silent bike stopped. Feuchter heard the thud of boots on the ground and he injected his efforts with psychological cocaine; he did not turn, did not look back, felt no curiosity whatsoever, just the basic raw animal instinct to survive . . . to push himself on . . . to stay alive, to stay ahead—

There came a metallic *click*: the sound of a bullet slicking neatly into a firing chamber. Feuchter slumped forward, exhausted, his pain-fuel spent. He could taste dirt. He didn't even have the energy to roll onto his back . . .

Boots crunched over the track. They stopped.

The tip of something metallic prodded Feuchter in the back.

'You still alive, you fucker?'

'I'm alive,' said Feuchter softly. 'I knew you would come back, Carter. I knew it from the look in your eye in that storeroom at Castle Schwalenberg . . .'

'I don't like being betrayed,' snapped Carter.

'As you wish. It was a necessity.'

Feuchter felt hands grab him roughly and roll him over. He looked up into Carter's face – much more battered than the last time they had met, the nose more twisted, many minor cuts and scrapes marking the skin. Carter's eyes were dark, brooding, unforgiving, his mouth a nasty straight slash revealing the tips of his teeth. Beyond Carter's palpable hate stood Natasha, a Glock in one hand, a Browning in the other. She appeared, through Feuchter's haze of pain, to be twitchy, on edge, looking nervously about to see if they had been spotted . . . whereas Carter was focused, dark eyes like hardcore-drill bits boring into Feuchter's soul.

'How many are still here?' he hissed. His fist wrapped around Feuchter's well-tailored jacket, drawing the man closer. Feuchter could smell stale sweat and a lingering aroma of coffee.

He smiled softly.

'You nervous, Carter?'

'Nervous? You're gonna give me and Nats some fucking answers.'

'Or what? You'll kill me? I'm already dead, Carter. The QIII has already been compromised. I was a condemned man awaiting execution . . . But now, now you are too late.' He started to laugh.

Carter shook his head. 'We had this guy, in Qingdao. He was an ex-Para; worked as a mercenary for various Far East countries. We used to call him Needle – because of his skills as a torturer. This man could get a fucking pig to swear it was a duck. You understand me, Feuchter? I learned a lot from that man. I learned a lot about pain, and a lot about *not* killing a man – no, killing was not the point. I learned a lot about keeping a man alive.' Carter glanced up at Natasha, then to the perimeter fence and the desert beyond. There was no sign of activity.

'You hide the bike around the side. I'll get this walking corpse indoors. Set him up for his operation.'

'Operation?'

'You ever seen a man's face when he's presented with one of his own kidneys? Thought not. Being a kind of scientist I thought you might like to be party to the experiment.' Carter started to drag Feuchter across the track towards the doors of Spiral_Q – which hissed open helpfully at his approach. Carter peered carefully into the interior, the Barrett rifle held aggressively, then dragged Feuchter into the cool luxury of the lobby.

He dumped Feuchter on the marble floor, then moved off between the plants, couches, glass screens and marble-clad pillars. He moved warily, checking every corner until he was satisfied. He whirled as Natasha approached, both handguns still in her grip. He smiled over at her and she responded weakly, her face showing exhaustion and pain.

'You see any activity?'

'No. There's nobody else inside the Chinook, just the dead Nex.'

'The only good Nex is a dead Nex. Let's get some fucking answers.'

'Carter.' She placed a hand on his arm. 'You're not really going to torture him, are you?'

Their gazes met. He saw the pain there, saw the weariness, but, most of all, saw the humanity. 'No,' he lied softly. 'It's a bluff. But don't tell him I told you.' Carter winked and smiled. Then he moved over to where Feuchter had dragged himself to a couch and sat with his back propped, trying to tear open the trouser material round the twin wounds.

'Enough games,' snapped Carter. He slapped the butt of the Barrett across Feuchter's head, knocking the older man sideways to lie, stunned, on the polished marble tiles.

'Why was I betrayed? Why did you try to kill me in Germany?'

Silence.

Feuchter was staring at the floor.

Carter knelt by Feuchter's head, where a string of blood and saliva connected him to the floor. Feuchter grinned, showing his tombstone teeth.

He spat, then sat up slowly.

'You will never understand, little man. *Never* understand.'

'Make me understand.'

'How long have you got?'

'As long as it takes.'

'Wrong answer,' said Feuchter. 'You have precisely fourteen minutes and –' he checked the cracked face of his Rolex '– fifteen seconds. Then the cubes of electronically linked HighJ chemical explosive at strategic locations around this building will fire a huge firework display right up your dumb and questioning arse.'

'You're lying,' said Carter.

'Why would I? It's not like you can't check.'

'Carter,' said Natasha. 'If it's true, we'd better get the hell out of here.'

'Not without answers,' said Carter. 'And if there are HighJ devices, then I can disable them. There isn't a device worldwide that I haven't been able to shaft. Hey, Feuchter, why do you think I was in a fucking DemolSquad?'

'You can try,' said Feuchter softly. 'These have no disabling mechanism. You cut the power, they blow. There was never meant to be a second chance, never meant to be a back-door escape.'

'Where's the master?'

Feuchter did not reply.

Carter shoved the muzzle of the Barrett under Feuchter's chin, then dropped it to his crotch. 'Ever seen a man with his cock blown off? I know we've only fourteen minutes left, but what a blissful and intensive fourteen minutes it will be . . . it will seem to last for ever, trust me on this . . .'

Feuchter met Carter's dark gaze. He swallowed dryly.

'Over there. At the foot of the central pillar, in the small black case.'

Feuchter's words were weary, filled with pain – and a touch of fear. But there was triumph there as well: an ultimate final triumph. Feuchter believed that he had won – no matter what they did to him, no matter what pain they put him through.

Both Carter and Natasha acknowledged this.

Carter moved over to the pillar, knelt, and flipped open the black box. LED digits flickered at him. There was no visible countdown – but then, why should there be?

Whoever set such a machine working already knew the risks and the timings—

Carter analysed the wiring. It was insanely complex. And the detonation was handled by processor. He scratched at his stubble.

'Shit. Shit fuck.'

Primary, secondary and fail-safe binary protection circuits. The HighJ Master was incredibly complex. And Carter knew it – maybe if he had two hours to spare and some high-tech disabling equipment then he might just stand a chance.

But with the minutes counting down . . .

And worst of all . . .

Feuchter knew it. Knew that Carter was shafted.

Carter returned slowly and glanced up at Natasha. Both Nats and Feuchter saw the look on his face: it was not a *nice* look; it did not convey what could be termed 'brotherly love'.

He turned and moved to stand in front of Feuchter.

'Hold out your hand.'

'Carter, this will gain you nothing.'

'Do it.'

Feuchter obeyed, and the rifle muzzle lifted to touch Feuchter's palm.

'No jokes, no fucking wisecracks. Just answer my questions. First, why did you try to kill me?'

Feuchter met Carter's gaze.

'It's complicated.'

The shot cracked, the bullet smashing straight through Feuchter's hand and scattering an explosion of feathers from the sofa. Feuchter grabbed at his wounded paw, head bowed in pain, blood pattering onto the tiles. 'Are you fucking crazy?' said Feuchter thickly, his voice having risen an octave.

370

Carter placed the rifle against Feuchter's shoulder.

'Wrong answer. I repeat, why did you try to kill me?'

'You were in the wrong place at the wrong time; things got accelerated, we moved forward too quickly and we needed to wipe out some of the opposition before they realised they *were* the opposition.' He met Carter's gaze. 'You are one of the best, Carter. It's why you were chosen to die.'

'You are part of the splinter faction from Spiral? Why would you do this?'

'Spiral?' Feuchter laughed, a laugh laced with pain. '*Spiral?* You dumb fucker, the only thing this has to do with Spiral is how fucking *weak* Spiral has become . . . fucking sycophantic government-arse-licking sons of bitches, they have the world in their hands and yet they do not know what to do with it.' He laughed again, drooling.

Carter's face had gone pale. He bit his lip, cast a quick glance to Natasha, then prodded Feuchter with the rifle. 'Who are you working for?'

'Myself.'

'And the processor? The QIII? Where does it fit into this?'

'The processor,' said Feuchter thickly. His head hung low, his eyes no longer meeting Carter's burning gaze. 'The QIII. It is so powerful, so incredibly powerful – the WorldCode threw up a list of names that could compromise the very existence of the processor. It used probability equations, worked out which of the DemolSquads was the most dangerous and who we should take out. Your name was on the list.'

'You are not working alone, Feuchter,' said Carter softly. 'Who else is playing the game?'

'Durell, one of Spiral's top ops.' The name sprang easily to Feuchter's lips and he smiled, smiled inside; he remembered. Durell was supposed to have *sorted Carter out*.

Sort *this* out, you fucker, he thought.

'Durell sorted the QIII list; instigated the WorldCode. He was the one who sent the Nex after you. He was the one who ordered the deaths of the DemolSquads. Me . . .' Feuchter met Carter's gaze. 'Hell, Mr Carter, I am just an innocent party.'

He smiled, and his teeth were stained with blood.

'Where would we find this Durell?'

'Let us say he is constantly *mobile*.' Feuchter barked a laugh on a fine spittle spray of blood.

'Where is he, you fucker?'

'I don't know, Carter. I don't know.'

Carter scratched at his stubble. He glanced again at Natasha; she had moved closer to the door, both guns held low. It was obvious that she wanted no part of this 'torture' but equally obvious that she needed to hear the answers as much as Carter did—

'Is Gol dead?'

'I believe so.'

'So you do know of him?'

'Only through Spiral. We worked together for a brief spell, many years earlier. On a project that was – ah, shall we say *shelved*.'

Carter stared hard into Feuchter's eyes, and the man met his gaze, cradling his hand, his huddled figure coated with blood.

'What are the Nex, Count Feuchter?'

'The Nex . . .' Feuchter's eyes widened a little. Then a strange smile crossed his face, revealing his cigar-yellowed tombstone teeth filmed with blood. 'Ah . . . the Nex . . . they are . . . *something else*.'

Feuchter's gaze suddenly lifted to something past

372

Carter, something outside, and Carter knew that they were out there—

'Nats—' he began to scream as he launched himself over the couch, but everything was drowned out by the sudden roar of automatic gunfire. Glass shattered deafeningly as it exploded into the lobby of the Spiral_Q building; bullets smashed across marble tiles and against pillars; they tore into the finely carved reception desk at the far end of the hall, chewing wood and thudding up into plaster.

Everything was madness—

Everything suddenly a bright mayhem—

And then—

Silence. Dust drifted, motes spinning on beams from the fancy inset lighting.

Carter scrambled along behind the row of couches and plants, and eased his face around a marble pillar. He saw Natasha, crouched, huddled foetus-like behind the doorway, wedged between the wall and a marble-faced pillar. She glanced up. Carter gave a quick succession of hand signals . . .

Stay.

Wait.

Check weapons.

Carter glanced left; he could not see Feuchter from his new position but he could hear the man. At first he thought he was choking . . . but then he realised with a gritting of teeth that Feuchter was *laughing*. The fucker was laughing.

'You want to know about the Nex?' called Feuchter. 'Ask them yourself, Carter – go on, ask them yourself!' He roared with laughter again as Carter sighted the sniper-scope on the doorway . . . he spun the dials, shortening the scope's focus. The next person to step across the threshold was dog meat . . .

Everything happened at once—

And it happened fast—

The Nex charged; there were three of them. Carter squeezed the Barrett's trigger and saw the lead Nex take the bullet in the face and spin up into the air before being tossed, twisted and twitching violently, to the ground.

The other two tracked him—

Opened fire—

Carter dropped the rifle and sprinted low across the Spiral_Q reception area, using the couches and plants for cover. Bullets ate marble at his feet. He dived, rolling behind a pillar and then skidding, slipping around on the highly polished surface to face—

Natasha.

The Browning sailed through the air.

Carter caught the familiar heavy bulk of the battered gun, placed his back against the pillar and whirled into the open—

The Nex had gone.

Carter dropped to a crouch, head snapping left, then tracking across the room. The first Nex lay, brains leaking onto the marble, one leg still twitching. Why didn't I hear them? screamed his brain.

'They must have come back for Feuchter,' said Kade softly, a ghost whispering at the back of his mind.

There was a movement – a change in shadow density. Carter slid around the pillar and could see the Nex nestling in the shadows by the glass-and-alloy lift, eyes tracking – and it saw him. Carter's Browning was already up and firing, bullets ripping across the lobby, smashing the Nex back into the gloom.

Carter retreated a little, still in a crouch. He checked Natasha. She had scrambled even further back into the

374

little niche behind the doorway. Good girl, he thought to himself. Don't do anything stupid—

The gun touched the side of his head, metal pressing gently.

There was a long pause.

'Don't make any sudden movements,' came the soft asexual voice.

Carter grinned a nasty frozen grin.

'You fucking dimwit,' sighed Kade. *'There were three of them! I thought you knew that. You saw three come in. You shot two. The third sneaked around you, had tagged your location while you were firing . . .'*

'Gun on the floor. Do it. Now.'

Carter – moving very slowly – placed his Browning on the marble tiles with a *clack*.

'Stand. Slowly.'

Carter stood, gaze roving, searching for a way out.

'Move over towards Feuchter.'

Carter began a slow walk; he did not glance towards Natasha's position but he knew that she could hear them, hear the exchange. He moved gradually into the view of—

Feuchter.

Despite his wounds, despite his pain, the man was smiling. He was positively beaming. He struggled into a sitting position on the bullet-riddled couch, and then glanced casually at his watch.

'Three minutes, Carter. Gonna be a marvellous fry-up.'

'Ask him what he wants,' said Kade.

'What do you want, Feuchter?'

'You see, lad, that's the difference between you and me. You always want something. Whereas I – I want nothing. I have resigned myself to death; in fact, I'm amazed that I have lived this long. My only pleasure now is to

375

watch your stupid flat face get blown apart. And to know that you died in the dark. To know that you died without answers. To know you died wondering where the QIII – where Spiral – where the Nex all fitted into this fine puzzle . . . you really have such low expectations of your enemies.'

'You can do one good thing, Feuchter. You can let Natasha go. She has nothing to do with this – nothing at all. Let her walk away from here. She is an innocent.'

'Oh, I dispute that, my friend!' said Feuchter softly, his intelligent eyes twinkling in the subdued lighting. 'She is one of us, Mr Carter. Natasha Molyneux is Gol's daughter and she is on *our side*.'

CHAPTER 19

DETONATION

Deep dark space kicked up and around Jam from the Austrian valley below, and vertigo battered him with its fist. There was a tiny *buzz*ing sound as he sped down the wide cable, a tiny dangling figure suspended over an infinite darkness, a wide maw open and salivating at the prospect of his tasty flesh. Jam pinned his heels together, lifted his knees to his chest, and focused.

Darkness rushed past in a flurry of wind and rain.

Cold drops stung his eyes, and he blinked them free.

His heart was thundering in his chest.

Below and before him the Kamus was a rectangle of dim light; even as he plunged through the darkness he could see more Chinooks leaving their sanctuary. He glanced right and could see The Priest matching him for speed on this insane descent, arms above his head, swaying in time with the cables.

The suspension cables were massive, descending from the cable-car base to the central 'slack' area at the mid-point over the valley and then pulling up towards the Kamus, which was at a slightly lower elevation to the cable-car base. Now, as Jam flashed down the descent stretch of the cable, he reached the slack area and felt his speed begin to drop as the cable levelled out. With his thumb he flicked a tiny switch on the skimmer and felt the motor inside it begin to take over. His speed kicked in again, accelerating him past the dip in the cable and on to the ascent towards the Kamus military complex itself.

The huge bulk of Grossglockner reared ahead of and around him. Above, he could see trees made miniature by distance, along with sprinklings of snow and ice. And there, carved into the heart of the mountain, was the Kamus itself.

He felt more than saw The Priest start to slow; thinking something was wrong, Jam slowed his own ascent and glanced over at his swaying partner in this offbeat circus-act. They halted.

Much closer now, they could see the activity in the base. The Priest pulled free his digital binoculars and, dangling by one hand, surveyed the scene.

Jam licked his lips, tasting sweat beneath his sodden balaclava. His arms and shoulders were beginning to nag him with this constant pressure, and he rolled his neck, attempting to ease the tension. He glanced down, past his dangling legs. A tiny demon in his mind mocked him: what if the skimmer fails? What if it leaves you stranded here? What if they see you and start shooting?

Jam smiled. The wind buffeted him. Rain ran into his eyes.

I wouldn't give this up for *anything*, he thought.

The Priest signalled him, and tossed the binoculars. Jam snatched them from the air and, dangling from one arm now, surveyed the base. There were perhaps eight Chinooks left, and Nex – lots of Nex, clad in grey and black. Many of them marching aboard the Chinooks, and Carter saw other, smaller, black helicopters.

At least we've found the fuckers, he said to himself, grimacing.

What now?

A swarm of Chinooks and smaller helicopters lifted from the Kamus. They swept away into the night, lights flickering, leaving two CH-47s behind. Jam signalled to The Priest—

We going in?

Yes. They are leaving. Soon it will be too late.

Great, thought Jam. Just as we find them, the fuckers are abandoning ship. He stowed the binoculars and, with muscles screaming, drew round his H&K G3, flicking off the safety. With his right hand, he spun the dial on the skimmer and felt the tiny machine accelerate under his touch. Across from him, swaying and buffeted, The Priest followed a similar procedure.

They flashed through the night, towards the wide bright concrete bay carved from the side of Grossglockner. Huge stacks of crates sat rimed with frost, and the two remaining Chinooks squatted silent.

Jam's brain began calculating; three guards, four, five. He could see their weapons now and, looking up ahead, saw the arrival point for the cable cars – and the place where their mad journey would end.

Machine-gun fire rattled, to the left. Light blazed, and from nowhere spun a small black helicopter. Jam squawked as bullets whizzed past him and he spun, rain pounding him, could see fire flickering from the barrels of the helicopter's machine guns as his own weapon began pumping in his fist—

On the ground, in the Kamus, the Nex guards had come suddenly alert. They ran forward across the concrete, lifted their weapons and searched the night. The Priest rained bullets down on them, and Jam, spinning now, hurtling backwards across the wide cable with a helicopter swooping above him, cursed this sudden turn of luck . . .

How had they seen him?

Fuckers! Had it been a sentry? A patrolling helicopter? It didn't matter now – all that mattered were the—

Bullets. They snapped past him. Jam emptied the magazine and allowed it to fall free; it tumbled into the black void below, following the sheets of icy rain, and Jam shouldered his weapon even as the helicopter spun around in a wide arc, a searchlight beaming through the heavens now to pick out both him and The Priest. More bullets howled past the two speeding men – Jam wrestled a fresh mag into his gun, flicking it around so that his arm snapped out, holding the sub-machine gun like a pistol.

'You want to fuck with me?' he growled, sighting on the charging helicopter with its screaming bullets and bright white eye of illumination. A stream of bullets shot out from the G3, spun across the darkness and ate a line up the cockpit. Inside, they trailed wisps of shattered glass as they smacked into the body of the Nex pilot, splashing his blood over the helicopter's interior. The machine bucked suddenly, nose dipping, and with rotors flashing it headed straight towards—

Jam and The Priest.

Jam met The Priest's gaze for the briefest instant; there was madness there, and anger, and strength. Bullets hurtled up from the Kamus platform, spitting around them, and as one the two men soared towards the cable car arrival point and leaped—

The pilotless black helicopter roared into the first thick cable, rotors folding around the heavy steel wire; there was a spark, a *crack* and flames billowed through an ejaculation of black smoke.

Jam and The Priest fell through the darkness, boots connecting with the edge of the icy Kamus parapet. They landed heavily, rolling across the slick platform as flames blossomed close behind and sheets of flaming steel and shrapnel from the burning rotors scythed around them. The two men rolled with thuds into a stack of crates and lay stunned for a moment, perhaps twenty feet apart.

The sky was lit up.

The fire died as quickly as it had been born.

Jam rolled to his feet as a Nex appeared – he fired five bullets into the black-clad killer's face, and the Nex dropped without a sound. Jam flicked his gaze right, and The Priest had gone.

He ran around the crates and then halted, dropping to a crouch. He could smell something burning and, reaching up, plucked a glowing shrapnel fragment from where his singed hair and balaclava merged. It burned his fingers and he dropped the piece of metal to the ground. 'Bitch.'

Machine guns echoed. Then came a stream of return fire. There were two thuds as bodies slapped to the concrete. Jam ran to crouch beside the wall, eyes scanning, these shadows his new-found friends. Before him the Kamus landing platform stretched out; the lights had dimmed when the helicopter had caught the thick cable and now everything was bathed in gloom.

Silence followed . . .

From behind came a strange creaking noise. Jam focused back on the landing area; vast, and littered with crates. It was a sniper's heaven. But the problem was, Jam wasn't a sniper.

How many guards? *Nex*, he corrected himself.

Five. Three dead. That left—

He saw the two survivors – they were operating as a unit. As he watched, they moved fluidly into shadows beside a stack of cargo crates – the sort used for road freight. Jam watched them climb smoothly up the sides and disappear from view. His eyes flickered to the Chinooks – deserted now, prey awaiting the final killing blow.

Jam remained in a crouch. Once more there came a strange creaking, which rose to a shrieking sound; he could see one of the cables swaying madly in the wind and it was this, he realised, that was speaking to him—

Danger, said the voice in syllables of stressed steel.

Was the cable severed?

Jam saw The Priest; he moved warily from the shadows and Jam realised, too late, that the Nex had flanked the huge man – were above him now. Jam's Glock came up and he started firing—

Bullets struck sparks from the cargo containers, and ploughed furrows in the concrete ground. The Priest whirled – and with a scream of tortured metal one of the huge cable-car wires snapped, sending deafening echoes reverberating across the Kamus yard and down into the valley below. As the cable snapped, one half fell away into the darkness of the valley – the second half whipped back towards the base, a wrist-thick garrotte that slashed through the rain, hit the concrete of the yard and snaked at high speed across the ground—

The Priest leaped, moving fast for such a huge man. The Nex opened fire from the cargo containers, bullets whining from machine guns as the cable was drawn back to connect with the gearing mechanism of the cable-car delivery system – it heaved through crates, smashing wood apart like a thick steel fist, tearing through everything outside and within; it struck the cargo containers with deafening booms, rending their steel, wrapping them in a tight grip and dragging them squealing against concrete across the yard.

Off balance, the two Nex leaped to be free of the danger.

Jam's sub-machine gun cut them in half.

There were more booms as the containers connected with the wall and then everything finally settled into stillness; the rain pattered all around them, and Jam, still crouched as if to spring, uncoiled and nodded towards The Priest. They both moved warily towards the helicopters, and gazed back at the destruction – the snapped, blackened cable, the smashed crates, the bodies, the flaming remains of part of the helicopter and the cable-squeezed deformed cargo containers.

'A nice, quiet entrance, then,' said Jam, rolling up his balaclava to sit atop his head, wiping a sheen of sweat from his face, and lighting a celebratory cigarette.

'It might have gone smoother,' acknowledged The Priest slowly.

'How long do you think we have?'

'Perhaps thirty minutes, if we are lucky,' said The Priest. 'I am hoping that the helicopter pilot did not have time to communicate with his fellows; otherwise we might have company sooner than we think. Maybe God was smiling, though – perhaps this whole incident has gone undiscovered.'

'I'll work on thirty minutes,' said Jam sardonically. 'You go and snoop around – check that there are none of our new-found friends waiting for us in there. I'll get Nicky and Slater to shift their arses over here ASAP.'

'That would be a good idea,' said The Priest with pious sobriety, and disappeared into the wide grey tunnels of Kamus-5.

Jam finished his cigarette and pulled free his ECube. He sent an acknowledgement *blip*; it was their agreed signal for Slater and Nicky to follow up in the Apache.

'OK, Kamus, let's see what secrets you are hiding,' he muttered, calming his fluttering heart. He followed The Priest and both men were soon hidden by the grey walls of mountain rock.

Jessica Rade paused, staring around guiltily like a child caught stealing a cake. She licked at nervous lips, brushed away the sweat running down her forehead, and moved closer to the large unit.

Her pass key slid easily into the lock.

She turned it.

The panel opened; she keyed in a complex series of digits on the pad. The inner sanctum opened then, to reveal a nucleus matrix of pins and shaped aluminium casting.

This was the core of Spiral_Q data.

The master of WorldCode.

The genesis of QIII logic programming.

She tapped in a few digits; there was a hiss, a disk slid into place and within ten seconds it was done. She pulled free the tiny silver optical disk and stared thoughtfully at its surface.

To hold the most damaging data in the world in your hands, she thought: the schematics for the QIII. The *plans* for how the processor worked. Its design. Its blueprint. Its heart . . .

The blueprints for the cubic processor's *soul*.

She smiled nastily to herself. Fuck you, you murderers, she thought; I have something you want! I have the plans for the QIII processor, and I can build as many as I like . . .

Jessica thought back to all the blueprints, the design

384

modes and nodules, the castings and design mechs. A QIII processor was an independent piece of hardware: place a QIII processor on a table top beside a PC with even the most basic of infra-red capabilities – or even more primitive than that! – and the QIII would hijack the computer's system resources totally. Place the QIII next to a DVD drive in mid-data transfer and the QIII would leach data from the EIDE or SCSI cables, or pass alternative data through those cables. Carry the QIII into British Telecom's HQ and place it on a couch in the foyer: within three seconds it would take control of all the machines in the building; five seconds, the UK; ten seconds, the world – including satellite links.

It was a digital parasite.

It could control anything, anywhere.

It was the God of all processors.

The QIII undeniably worked at optimum with the surrounding paraphernalia designed with its advanced specification in mind, such as integrated digital and optical links and servers. But it would also – unlike 'dumb' processors – make the best of a worse situation.

It could bleed the batteries from a children's toy at a thousand metres.

It could operate anyone's TV remote control from the other side of the country.

Hell, it could probably cook chicken.

Jessica Rade reached forward, then stopped. She glanced over her shoulder, half expecting to see a Nex with a sub-machine gun.

But – she was alone.

Jessica had found a small rucksack; she dropped the disk – this most expensive of artefacts – into the bag and turned . . . Only then did she see the small black box attached to one of the many server units.

There was a red, flashing light.

Her mind worked quickly; the Nex had been annihilating many of the members of staff deemed 'expendable', apparently overseen by Feuchter himself, her boss. There was a small flashing device in a small black box. It had to be a bomb. Fucking *had to be*. Was it unreasonable of her to expect them not to totally destroy the Rub al'Khali HQ? Jessica was Grade-A SecClear. She had access to most of the information that flew around Spiral_Q; and she knew. Knew that the QIII processor was designed to be one of a kind – all-powerful; all-knowing. In *complete control*.

She knew that if the QIII was *stolen*, or if the people in charge did not want a copy made, then destroying the Spiral_Q base would set back other competitive developers by at least ten years. To destroy the ability to create another QIII would be to destroy Spiral_Q. To exterminate the placenta, the womb, the mother – leaving the babe intact, unharmed, and in complete control.

Jessica swallowed hard.

Shit, she thought.

She wiped the sweat from her hand across her pyjamas.

Jessica turned, then sprinted low across the lab. Her feet slapped against the cool tiles; she bypassed several security doors and returned to the corridor and the vent.

She hauled herself up into its confines.

That was when she heard the gunshots.

Jessica crawled fast. The shots echoed through the ventilation system and she wondered just what the hell was going on. She crawled faster than she had ever thought possible, knees and elbows sore from friction and banging against the aluminium walls, sweat soaking her thin cotton pyjamas. Finally, she reached the spot –

and, spinning around on her bottom, kicked free the vent.

She dropped down into one of the underground kitchens she used to frequent on her midnight jaunts. She ran, panting like a hunted animal, past sacks of dirty linen that would never again be washed; never again be *needed*. She passed huge banks of stationary silent washers and driers, and felt their accusatory gazes against her sweat-drenched back.

She reached the heavy vaultlike door of the exit. Fished free her key. Overrode the electronic protection . . . and stepped out into the desert night.

A gentle breeze washed across her body, and her soul.

The fear-sweat cooled and she shivered.

Jessica ran, fuelled now by fear of the Nex killers, fuelled by the guilt of her theft, pushed on by the concept of a huge bomb squatting only feet behind her. She left deep footprints in the sand; indelible, as in fast-drying cement.

Reaching the corner of the building, some primeval part of her soul forced her to halt, to peer around the steel column. She saw a vehicle: Feuchter's Land Rover.

She crept, as low as her considerable agility allowed. She peered inside, wrinkling her nose at the sight of the dead driver and splattered blood. Glancing quickly around, she opened the door and dragged the body down onto the sand.

She climbed in.

Closed the door gently.

Placed the stolen *pirated* QIII schematics on the seat beside her.

Jessica grabbed the steering wheel, recoiling at the blood she found there. Then, uttering the incantation 'Please start please start' and trying hard to ignore the hole in the windscreen at face height, she turned the key . . .

'. . . She is one of us, Mr Carter. Natasha Molyneux is Gol's daughter and she is on *our side*.'

Several things happened at once—

Outside, an engine fired up hard, revving high and mad; Feuchter's Land Rover reversed into view and sped off into the darkness, tail lights glowing—

Carter turned back to Feuchter and saw the 'O' of shock on his face—

The *crack* of the Glock 9mm echoed across the reception area. The Nex crumpled to the ground, relieving Carter's head from the pressure of the gun barrel.

Carter licked his lips slowly. He looked up and around. Into Natasha's hooded eyes.

'You trying to kill me?' he asked softly. 'His gun could have gone off!'

'That's because Natasha is one of us,' said Feuchter again, his words low, hypnotic.

'Don't listen to him,' said Natasha, her stare fixed on Carter. 'I just saved your life.'

Carter turned fully towards her. 'Who are you going to shoot now? Me or him? Nats – your gun is still pointing at *me* . . .'

'Drop your weapon, my sweetness.'

They both turned. The Nex had tossed Feuchter a small black pistol that nestled evilly in the German's large hand.

Natasha kicked the Glock across the floor.

'You have one and a half minutes to say your goodbyes. Truly, a romantic and fitting end to this act. Shakespeare couldn't have penned a tragedy so fitting! So perfect! So complete and whole!'

'*Let me,*' soothed Kade.

'Not now!'

'*Now is the right time the good time the only time* . . .'

Feuchter checked his watch and smiled. Carter looked sideways at Natasha whose face was unreadable; he swallowed as time seemed to slow, to melt away into a treacle infinity and he felt Kade there at the back of his mind, waiting watching timing listening and then pushing pushing hard pushing—

Kade opened his eyes . . .

Staring at the actors on the stage in beautiful and simple black and white. He dropped to his knees and rolled – the Glock slid neatly into his hand as if the two were perfectly machined complementary parts, oiled, gleaming, lovers ready for action—

Kade rolled rapidly, came up.

He came up fast to see—

Feuchter, his small black gun wavering, pointing in the wrong direction because Kade had moved so fast and the Glock snapped up and Feuchter just had time to register surprise and fear as Kade pulled the trigger hard and six bullets slammed into Feuchter's chest, ripping holes in the man's exposed torso, spitting up globules of crimson to spin in the air and splatter like a viscous waterfall across the tiled floor.

Feuchter's head dropped down over his ruined gaping chest, staring down into his own glistening slick organs. Very slowly, he toppled sideways onto the couch and lay still.

'That makes a stimulating and unexpected change,' said Kade sweetly, his voice laced with sarcasm. He rounded on Natasha, the Glock trained on her face. 'You make a false move, you die. You say the wrong thing, you die. You fucking fart, girl, and you fucking die. Get outside and get the bike . . .'

Natasha vanished.

Kade, exhilarated, put another bullet in Feuchter's slumped body. Then another. He moved to Feuchter and grabbed the dead man's chin. He stared into the lifeless eyes. He kissed the dead man's lips, then licked the transferred blood from his own with a smile. Releasing his grip on the slack corpse, he ran across the room, collected the Browning and the Barrett rifle, muttering, 'Can't let good workmanship go to waste,' and sprinted for the doors—

Natasha had heaved the heavy bike into view, and Kade took hold of the machine, a huge smile across his face. Natasha clambered onto the back and Kade fired up the engine and, spinning sand, hammered away from the time bomb that was Spiral_Q . . . Headlights cut slices from the night as they sped away from Spiral's Rub al'Khali development and research facility, up the smooth dirt track towards the gate and the desert beyond . . .

Neither saw the figure crawling out of the shattered entrance behind them.

A pause, an eternity of seconds—

There came a single, tiny, metallic *click*.

An insanely deep ground-shaking subsonic *boom* rumbled.

A huge ball of HighJ purple fire and gases blossomed; fire roared and screamed upwards and outwards; huge fifty-metre chunks of concrete and stone and glass and iron were spat up high into the night; energies rushed screaming and bellowing and burning out across the desert—

'Hold on!' barked Kade in excited delight.

The BMW rocked on sudden bursts of high-fury HighJ explosive . . .

And then the fire came—

—As the BMW crested the steep rise, front wheel high in the air, and loomed out over the darkness beyond it. Then it was thumped heavily and violently from behind by the fist of the explosion. The BMW's wheels sliced air as energy screamed all around it, an insane release of power, a behemoth screaming curses in ultimate anger and fury and madness . . .

The desert-bike landed roughly and they veered sideways, the machine slewing and scything through the sand, riders and bike parting company, the bike toppling, the riders rolling madly to a halt against a low dune—

Purple fire roared overhead.

The world seemed – suddenly – to have ended.

Everything was chaos.

Natasha gazed up through tears at a vision of Hell raging above them . . .

Then the fire was suddenly sucked back to reveal—

The dark night sky.

Stars twinkled.

Everything was strangely calm.

'Whoooo!' cried Kade from where he had fallen and now lay gazing skywards. 'That was some fuuuuu-cking bang!' He leaped up, waving the Glock, and sprinted for the rise, his boots churning the dark sand. Then he stood with his hands on his hips, staring down at the insane scatter of burning debris littering the recently vacated Spiral_Q site.

Natasha approached him from behind.

'You feeling OK, Carter?'

Kade whirled, so fast that Natasha blinked, taking an involuntary step back. Only then did she see the Glock pointed at her.

Kade smiled. A wide grin.

'You fancy nipping down there and getting us a hunk of toasty Feuchter meat to celebrate with?'

'Carter, you're acting very strange—'

'Don't talk!' he suddenly screamed. 'Don't fucking talk to me, just get back to the fucking bike before I remind you of the sweet traitorous words Feuchter spoke – you little bitch.'

'He was lying,' she whispered softly.

The Glock pressed against her forehead.

'Get to the fucking bike, I said.'

Natasha turned and strode down through the sand. Kade smiled suddenly, his hand reaching out towards the flames. 'Toasty toasty,' he hummed to himself, then turned dark glittering eyes to watch Natasha's swaying hips. 'Hmmm, hmm, Carter – you do pick a fine succulent woman, I must say.'

He turned back to admire the crackling greyscale fires in and around the devastated crater that had once been Spiral_Q – he admired the stage, the scene of destruction, the vision of beautiful devastation. His gaze took in the huge torn blocks of building, the torn bent scorched monoliths of twisted steel, the sea of broken melted fused glass.

He nodded in approval, eyes glittering reflections from the fire.

'Yeah,' he muttered brightly. 'Fucking cool.'

He licked his lips.

He revelled in his freedom.

He closed his inner ears to Carter's scream of fury and pain and angry angry frustration – but it would not go away, and he could feel his control slipping, could feel Carter getting stronger and stronger and he fell to his knees on that cold dark sand with the burning fires strobing his eyes and he fought, fought with every ounce of energy that was left in his dark demon soul . . .

392

But, with a bitter snarl, he allowed Carter his freedom—
And his life—
Once more.

The night cold descended. Flames burned low, crackling softly, the only sound against the bleakness of the desert night. Creeping across the desert dunes, across scarred and blackened stumps of concrete, softly glowing metal, fused glass, away from the crater, in darkness lit briefly by glowing embers, something moved.

It crawled, a blackened husk, crimson glistening in blood-filled shallow cavities. It crawled, then slumped. It rolled to its back and cold eyes stared up at the star-filled bleakness of the void.

And, with the QIII processor clutched in a blackened hand, Count Feuchter screamed.

Spiral_Memo8
Transcript of recent news incident
CodeRed_Z;
unorthodox incident scan 522825

The Hub of the United States military was plunged into chaos as its entire satellite network was severely disrupted. Contact was lost with ground, air and naval forces around the globe as US computer and military experts battled to get the Hub - ironically named 'Indestructible' - back on-line.

At a home-user level, satellite TV was also seriously disrupted, along with satellite Internet services and a variety of other digital communication systems.

There are serious implications for national defence, and experts are blaming freak solar activity, possibly in the form of a subsonic or stratospheric radiation that has never before been detected by military sensors.>>#

CHAPTER 20

SCHEMA

Carter opened his eyes.

Natasha was smiling down at him, pressing a cold cloth against his head, dabbing at the coagulating sluggish flow of blood from his recently broken nose. He looked up into her eyes and saw the understanding there.

'I am sorry . . . he whispered.

'Shh.' She placed a finger against his lips. 'Don't speak.'

'It wasn't me.'

'I know, Carter, I know . . .'

Carter smiled weakly. Then he flinched as pain smashed through the centre of his skull and the wound in his side, through his ribs and his nose and his broken finger and his whole battered bruised frame—

He gasped.

And swam on a sea of pain.

Natasha looked suddenly worried. 'Carter?' She shook him. 'Carter, what's wrong?'

He opened his eyes.

He smiled up at her, squinting.

'Kade must have been taking away – absorbing – my

395

pain. That's why we've got as far as we have. Now the bastard has given it back; all of it.' He coughed, writhing in agony for a moment. 'Fuck, that hurts. Have you any painkillers?'

'Sorry, Carter.'

'That's OK. We need to get to Langan for the meet.'

'Yeah.'

She helped Carter to his feet, and he stood panting for a moment in the dawn light.

Then, with a great effort of will, he grunted, lifted the BMW and climbed aboard. Natasha jumped on behind him and he fired up the engine, closing his eyes for a moment as he composed himself – not just for the journey ahead, but for the realisation that Feuchter was dead: and that the *quest*, as it was, the fucked-up journey he had to make—

It was not over.

It was far from over.

The BMW moved off, bumping along the dirt road and then punching out across the rolling sand dunes and towards the narrow dirt road that fed Spiral_Q . . .

'Durell,' muttered Carter. And, grimacing, he screwed the throttle round viciously.

Jessica Rade drove hard and fast. The Land Rover had a powerful motor and sped through the darkness, the suspension absorbing the bumps with ease, the headlights scything the pre-dawn desert.

I've done it, she thought triumphantly.

I've got away.

With the QIII schematics. The ability to create another QuanTech Edition 3 Cubic Processor; to copy the only working model in existence. The only model just recently uploaded with WorldCode Data.

Jessica Rade smiled; and then decided that she might be being followed and the smile fell from her face as she checked her mirrors. But only blackness swept across the desert behind her, deep and impenetrable. Before her, blood smears on the glass did nothing to calm her fluttering heart.

Jessica wiped her sweating hand on her pyjamas; and then remembered the blood. She glanced down at the crimson streaks and her stomach turned. And then she remembered her friends and colleagues from Spiral_Q who had been murdered and loaded into trucks and helicopters, and her stomach did a triple flip. She swallowed her fear.

She was free.

She could make a difference . . .

She could flood the world with the schematics, with designs of how to construct and set up the QIII; she could reveal how WorldCode worked; she could reveal how it could predict the future using pure mathematics, formulae, code. She could blow the secret.

Spiral_Q would be stung, and stung bad.

Jessica needed to get to a powerful mainframe, and she realised the danger of her predicament. She was going to ruin their plans; they would want her dead . . . but then they wanted her dead anyway, right? Did they realise she had the QIII schematics? She doubted it – after all, they had been about to blow the building – and surely that had been the purpose of the bomb. To halt any possibility of pirating the cubic chip. But then, she could not rely on that, she could not rely on *anything* . . . she had to assume that they knew she had copies of the schematics.

But something confused Jessica. Why should Spiral – who she had always thought of as a brilliant organisation to work for – why would they kill a large group of their own employees? And why would they destroy their own building? Why would they blow up the QIII operation?

Something in the reasoning was flawed. Something was not quite right – like Feuchter planting the bombs, like the Nex assassins walking the Spiral_Q corridors.

She could not understand why Spiral would do such a thing.

Unless Spiral had been betrayed!

Jessica rubbed at her eyes and moved closer to the windscreen and the bullet hole that reminded her of how serious these people were – whoever they were. They knew that she was alive; they would have the airports covered for sure . . . so how could she get out of Rub al'Khali? She knew that Spiral_Q had the backing of the Saudi regime and that meant untold resources if they really *needed* to find her—

She racked her brains. What to do?

Prioritise, focus, she thought.

Get away from the Spiral_Q facility.

Dump the vehicle.

Find a disguise.

The engine stuttered, half-heard. Jessica felt a vibration on the accelerator pedal. Her eyes flickered to the dash and the orange light that indicated she was out of . . . fuel.

'What? You bitch,' she muttered. 'How is that possible?'

The engine stuttered again, and then stalled. She coasted to a halt on the dirt track, tyres crunching on small stones. She opened the door – and could immediately smell petrol.

'Shit. Shit!'

She looked around the inside of the car for anything that might be of use to her. There was nothing. She pulled the key from the ignition and, her feet jabbing painfully against stones, she moved to the back of the car and opened the boot. There was a canister. She unscrewed the top and sniffed: water.

'At least I won't die of dehydration,' Jessica muttered sourly, slamming the boot shut. Grabbing her small rucksack, and pausing for a moment to take several deep breaths and brush a few specks of fluff from her pyjamas, she bit the bullet of panic and set off down the road. Stones stabbed her toes again and she cursed herself for her disorganisation, her bad luck and, most of all, for choosing to work for fucking Spiral_Q Division in the first fucking place.

Carter returned from the outcropping of rocks, the Barrett in one hand, a canteen of water in the other. He yawned.

'How you feeling?'

Carter smiled, wincing at pain from a variety of locations. He glanced at Natasha; over the last few days she seemed to have aged incredibly. Lines and deep bruises of exhaustion circled her eyes. Her mouth had lost its customary upturned corners. Her body seemed . . . Carter searched for a word.

Deflated.

Pushed beyond the boundaries of normal human endurance.

'I feel like a camel danced on my head for an hour. What about you? You look wasted, girl.'

'I'm all right.' She smiled weakly at him. 'I need this break.'

'Me too. It's been a tough few days.'

'You could say that,' sighed Natasha.

After a brief break, and having made sure that they were not being pursued after the destruction of Spiral_Q, they climbed wearily back onto the BMW desert-bike and once again set off across the sand and stones. They travelled for an hour, until Natasha spotted something and tapped Carter on the arm, pointing.

'You see it?'

Carter glanced up. 'That's Feuchter's vehicle,' he said. 'The Land Rover I took out with the rifle . . .'

'Wonder who nicked it?' said Natasha. They exchanged glances, and both reached for their guns as the desert-bike crunched to a halt a few feet away from the stationary vehicle. They did not say the word *Nex* but the possibility was at the forefront of both their minds.

Carter climbed warily from the bike, eyes scanning the deserted horizon and the sand-blown vicinity. He moved around the Land Rover and saw the key in the boot. There was nothing inside on the seats and floor; he checked the boot. Also empty.

'Can you smell fuel?'

Natasha nodded. 'You think a Nex took it?' she said finally.

Carter glanced around. Natasha noted that now – in a possible conflict situation – he gave no sign that he was injured: all pain had been shunted aside, all agony wiped clear by adrenalin for the moment.

'Not sure,' muttered Carter, still scanning, the familiar heft of the Browning giving him little reassurance. 'But I don't like it out here – it's too open and we're still too far from Langan.'

'Come on, then.'

Carter jumped back onto the BMW and they crawled past the Land Rover, tyres growling on the dirt road. Carter kept the Browning in his hand and stayed vigilant as they set off down the desert track.

They drove with heightened awareness for the next

hour as the sun climbed steeply up the sky and smashed its rays down on them. They passed no traffic in that time, and saw no other living being. It was like being on the moon . . . albeit with a much warmer climate.

It was Carter who spotted her.

'Look. To the right, following a line parallel to the road.'

The woman hunkered down behind a small outcropping of rock when she spotted the BMW desert-bike. But by then it was too late – Carter's sharp piercing eyes had spotted *her*.

They halted and climbed from the bike.

Carter moved out onto the sand. 'Show yourself!' he called.

Nothing moved . . .

Carter pointed the gun at the rocks. 'If you piss me off by making me come in after you, I guarantee you a slow execution. You have three seconds. Three, two, one . . .'

The woman stood, slowly, arms above her head. She wore pyjamas and carried a small rucksack. Carter gestured with the Browning. 'Over there, where I can see you clearly.'

Carter moved closer, checking to see if she was alone.

The woman had long, curly brown hair and bright young eyes. She looked frightened, terrified even, and licked her lips nervously. 'Don't shoot me, please,' she said as Carter came closer.

He stopped, looking her up and down.

'How the hell did you get out here dressed like that?'

'It's a long story,' she said, smiling weakly. Slowly she lowered her arms, but Carter waved them up again. He stepped in close and checked her for weapons, sweat beading on his forehead under the sun's intense glare.

He stepped back. 'What's in the bag?'

'Nothing.'

'Show me.'

Jessica opened the rucksack; she showed him the inside which was indeed empty.

'What about the front pocket?'

Jessica unzipped the pocket. Slowly she withdrew a small silver disk and instantly Carter aimed the Browning 9mm at her face and her eyes went wide. Tears started to roll down her cheeks.

'Here, take it.'

'What the fuck *is it*?' barked Carter.

'So you're not from Spiral_Q?'

Carter smiled grimly. 'Well, we had a brief association with a man called Feuchter.'

Jessica jumped at the name. 'Where is he?'

'Dead. Are you going to answer my question?'

'It's the schematics for the QIII processor. So you're not here to kill me?'

'Don't even know who you are, love. Come on, walk over to the bike, you look like you're suffering from heat exhaustion.'

Jessica walked, with Carter a few paces behind her, a predator checking warily all around. When she reached the BMW Natasha smiled warmly, and Jessica was finally allowed to lower her hands.

'She's got the schematics for the QIII processor,' said Carter.

Natasha's eyes widened. 'You're fucking joking!'

'No.' Turning to Jessica, he said, 'I assume you worked there?'

Jessica nodded. 'Feuchter had a large section of the workforce murdered. I managed to escape . . . I took the processor schematics hostage. So you're really not from Spiral_Q?'

402

'If I was going to kill you,' said Carter softly, 'we wouldn't be talking. 'Come on, squeeze on the bike. I assume you need a ride out of here?'

Jessica nodded, and climbed up behind Carter, followed by Natasha, squeezing onto the tail-end of the bike, beside the stealth-exhaust pipes.

Carter fired up the engine.

'Where do you want dropping? Or alternatively, you can have this bike in about two hours . . .'

'Just get me out of Rub al'Khali,' Jessica said wearily.

'See what we can do,' said Natasha, smiling kindly.

They had paused for a break from the searing sun, shadowed by a low plateau of rounded rocks that had been smoothed by the blasting sand of the desert. Carter sat, head back, allowing a cool trickle of water to moisten his lips.

'We're running out.'

'Langan isn't far away,' said Natasha softly.

Carter nodded.

Jessica was seated some way off, staring out across the sand. Her pyjamas were stained, torn, and looked a sorrowful sight. Carter caught her attention and she moved over to him, accepting his canteen with a smile of thanks.

'How is it that you know about the QIII processor? It's a top top secret project,' she said, lips glistening with water.

Carter shrugged. 'Long story, love, and believe me, we don't really want to burden you with the information. Feuchter was the man with the answers and now he's cat meat. Fried cat meat.'

'So the building blew?'

'Oh yeah,' said Carter, smiling nastily. 'Tell me, does the QIII thing really work?'

'The QIII? Oh yes. It works all right. It is awesome in what it can do, what it can predict.'

Feuchter's words came back to Carter.

'The QIII. It is so powerful, so incredibly powerful – the WorldCode threw up a list of names that could compromise the very existence of the processor. It used probability equations, worked out which of the DemolSquads was the most dangerous and who we should take out. Your name was on the list.'

Carter started to get a crystal-clear picture: Feuchter and this other man Durell were acting as renegades against Spiral on information thrown up by a future-predicting processor in order to give itself longevity and them power and command. The Nex were sent in to kill him, and to kill other DemolSquad members who were considered a threat by Feuchter and Durell. They tried to take out Gol because he had the schematics for the QIII processor – and so could replicate this military device and fight them with a copy of their own weapon. And they had got to Gol; murdered him. Murdered lots of others in their quest for power . . .

But what next? Where would they go next?

What was their ultimate aim?

Fuckers, he thought sourly.

'I wonder if you could tell us something about the Nex,' muttered Carter, rubbing at his tired eyes.

'The Nex? You mean the people with the copper-coloured eyes?'

Carter licked his lips, focusing on Jessica. 'You know about them?'

She shook her head. 'They were the ones sent to kill the Spiral_Q staff.'

'Really . . .' Carter scratched at his heavy stubble; it was making him itch bad and he could smell his own stink. Gods, for a decent basic toilet! And a shower! And a cold beer! Or sweet Lagavulin . . .

'Holy shit,' hissed Natasha, scrambling at her pocket and leaping to her feet. She pulled free the ECube.

They all stared at it.

'It bite you or something?' snapped Carter. 'You made me fucking jump, woman. Spilled my water all down my shirt!'

'It's vibrating,' said Natasha.

'So what?'

'It's a receiver and it's receiving now.'

'Shit,' agreed Carter. He peered warily into the distance, and checked the skies. 'So whoever is sending knows exactly where we are?'

'Possibly.'

'I thought the Spiral mainframes had been destroyed?'

'They have, but someone must be routing through another ECube. They can work like that, independent of main servers in case the impossible happened and Spiral London HQ was destroyed – which it was.'

Carter ducked his head, looking warily around the nearby desert and scrub. He could see nothing very suspicious but that did not mean it wasn't there. 'Well then, you going to answer it?' he said as Natasha continued to stare at the little machine.

Natasha squeezed the ECube. It came to life with soft blue digits. Nats squinted at the tiny data stream. It read:

```
CLASSIFIED FUS100176510/ ENCRYPTED SIU
SEND: MOLYNEUX, G, SIU23446
REC: MOLYNEUX, N, SIU42880
```

'Oh my God,' said Natasha softly. 'It's from Gol.'

'That's impossible,' said Carter softly, wearily. 'We all saw what happened in Kenya.'

'Wait – think about it, Carter. If this was coming from the enemy, the Nex or whoever, then we would be dead now, yeah? We wouldn't be reading a fucking ECube transmission. We'd be fighting for our lives . . .' There was hope in her voice, and her eyes had become suddenly bright. The deflation he had witnessed earlier had gone, like dew burned off by the sun.

Carter looked suspiciously at the ECube, then at Natasha.

'I don't like it,' he said.

'And you think I do?'

Carter said nothing, merely gestured with the Browning for Natasha to read the message. She read:

```
I KNOW YOU THINK I AM DEAD: I AM NOT. I
SURVIVED, SAVED BY SPIRAL AT THE LAST
MOMENT; BUT THE DISK WITH THE QIII
SCHEMATICS WAS LOST TO ME.

I AM IN LOS ANGELES, CAN MEET YOU AT
FOLLOWING   CO-ORDS   034.626.555   -
CALIFORNIA IN 48 HOURS SPIRAL_F STILL
LIVES!

I KNOW YOU WILL THINK THIS A TRAP. IF
CARTER STILL LIVES TELL HIM ABOUT OUR
CONVERSATION, IN AFRICA, WHEN WE SHARED
CIGARETTES UNDER THE ORANGE TREES; TELL
HIM I SAID I FORGAVE HIM BECAUSE OF HIS
LOVE FOR MY DAUGHTER. IF YOU MAKE IT TO
THE MEET, ASK FOR A MESSAGE FOR CARTER
AT THE DESK// OUT //.
```

'He said he forgave you?'

Carter nodded. He walked up a nearby sand dune and stood in the BMW's tyre tracks, staring out across the barren hot wilderness. Cigarettes. He scratched his stubble. Damn, he thought, what I would give for a cigarette right now . . . trust a fucking ECube to remind me at the wrong fucking time.

Natasha moved up behind him. She took his arm.

'You OK?'

'Hmm. Maybe.'

'It's a trap, right? Gol is dead. We saw him jump.'

Carter nodded, looking down into Natasha's eyes; and he saw it, the desperation, the need for her father still to be alive. And yet . . . *could* Gol be alive? Could he have survived that terrible fall into the river? Could he have been rescued by Spiral at the last moment and even now be on the trail of the traitors to Spiral's cause?

Gol had been a *very* resourceful man. Maybe he had landed on a rocky outcropping; or used some sort of grappling device? And Natasha, Carter thought sombrely. If Feuchter was telling the truth; if you really do work for the enemies of Spiral – the 'traitors' – then you're a fucking good actress.

'We will go.'

Natasha squeezed his arm. 'Really?'

'Yeah, but don't get your hopes up – and we'll do it my way. You understand?'

'Carter, I know you think I—'

'Shh.' He placed a finger against her lips. 'Feuchter was lying, I know. But I've got a bad feeling about this – and yet, if Gol still does live, if the mad motherfucker survived that fall and managed to escape the Nex *and* reformed with other Spiral_F members . . . well, they're just about the only allies we've got. It's not as if Feuchter

407

was any great enlightenment . . . all we got from him was a name: Durell.'

Jessica had come up behind the two and Carter whirled, his gun in her face. He smiled weakly. 'Sorry, force of habit.'

Jessica waved his apology away. 'You said a name then, didn't you?'

'Yeah, Durell. He is – *was* – a Spiral top dog; originally based in Austria, near the German border, he was some kind of scientist researching genetics and medicines. His link with the QIII is probably on the semi-organic side – have you heard of him?'

Jessica nodded. 'Heard of him, met him, turned down an offer of sex with the slimy reptile. Thought I was going to get fired.' She laughed softly. 'Wish I had now.'

'What do you know about him?'

'Very little. He visited the Spiral_Q Division on numerous occasions. He was a taut little cockroach of a man. Tough, rough and hardy – but you should see his eyes.'

'Sounds like a nice guy,' said Carter, staring away over the sand again.

'You want to know the other amazing coincidence?'

Carter met Jessica's gaze. She smiled gently. 'Sorry, I've been eaves-dropping. But I think you'd like to know this . . . Durell, well, several times when he visited us, I overheard conversations with Feuchter – said he'd come straight from the US.'

'California, by any chance?' said Natasha, frowning.

'LA,' said Jessica.

'What a coincidence,' said Carter grimly.

'So what now?' asked Natasha; Carter could see it in her face. She knew the dangers, knew the odds, knew the possibility of the whole thing being a set-up, a trap, a plot to ensnare them. But she wanted – needed – to know if her father was still alive.

The bait was laid.

And the carrot was a juicy one.

They're either extremely clever and manipulative bastards, thought Carter. Or Gol is onto Durell . . . he's alive, and onto the leader of those dedicated to bringing down Spiral . . .

Decision time.

Decisions.

He scratched his stubble. He patted Natasha's arm. 'We'll go,' he said softly. And smiled. 'I have a lot of friends in LA.'

Night was falling as the BMW desert-bike reached the rendezvous. Langan was there and had lit the smallest of small fires, his almost trademark pan of coffee bubbling gently over the flames.

'Hey Carter, you break your nose again?'

'Long story,' said Carter with a glance at Natasha. 'Is there any of that coffee going? I think we could all do with a caffeine fix.' Langan nodded, and dished out three mugs.

He raised his gaze in Jessica's direction, and winked at Carter. 'You been a saucy devil, eh?'

'Hmm. Langan, can you fly us to America?'

'You want my gold fillings as well, Carter?'

'I can pay you. As much as you want, whatever it takes.'

'I work for Spiral; Gol wanted you helped, and so help you I will. I don't need your money, Carter.'

'You're in luck, then,' said Carter softly, his gaze meeting the pilot's. 'We've had a message from Gol. He's in LA. He wants to meet.' Carter watched Langan's face closely. The man looked a little shocked.

'Well, I'll be damned – that tough fucking insect.'

'Can you confirm this? Through your Spiral_F contacts?'

'I can try,' said Langan softly. 'But the whole Spiral_F network has been off-line, smashed along with the main Spiral grid. I think we can assume that security has been breached, yeah? The idea now is this: Spiral_F will contact me with updates and further missions when they think it safe, unless superseded by Spiral when they get their shit back on-line. Believe me, there's a lot of pissed-off people back in London . . . those that survived the explosion.

'So you're temporarily cut free from your duties?'

Langan sighed, scratching the back of his neck. 'It would appear that way, my friend. About LA: I can't take you to the city, it's a fucking nightmare there now – especially after the wars. It's so busy, there are LAPD choppers everywhere, military presence on the streets, you name it.'

'A little like London, then?' Carter smiled grimly.

'A little,' conceded Langan. 'Except amateur terrorists didn't accidentally detonate a fucking micro-nuke in London. Look, I could probably creep up over Mexico, shunt you over the border, let you find your way from there . . .'

'Great,' said Carter. He sipped the coffee, then held the mug out for more sugar.

'Carter?'

'Hmm?'

'Sounds like a trap to me,' said Langan.

'Yeah, yeah. I know. Just what I need, guidance from another bloody advice merchant.'

'Just trying to be helpful.'

'Just get us out of this furnace alive!'

'I'm going to need to refuel.'

'Any more good news for me, Langan?'

'It'll probably have to be in Egypt.'

Carter muttered something nasty into his coffee.

The Comanche was built to accommodate two people, in relative comfort, for prolonged periods of warfare; with Jessica added to the numbers the situation was a little insane.

Carter had decided that she could be of use; after all, Spiral was linked closely with the QIII, and she happened to have the processor schematics in her rucksack – something which Carter acknowledged could probably come in quite handy.

As the Comanche buzzed low over the northern plains of Rub al'Khali, Langan focused and working hard to keep them out of trouble, it also occurred to Carter that *maybe* Gol was alive and had been captured by the Nex. If he had been tortured, blackmailed, whatever, then maybe the QIII schematics could be used in an exchange situation.

'Jessica?'

'Yes, Carter?'

Her nose was four inches from his own, her bottom planted firmly on his knee. He could feel her supple limbs through the thin cloth of her pyjamas, smell the curls that bobbed in his face. He tried hard not to get an erection.

'You know the QIII?'

'I helped build it and program it; you could say I know it . . .'

'Don't be flippant or you can find your own way out of Rub al'Khali.'

'I concede – you are saving my life, even though it looked, from where I was standing, as though you were

411

saying that you should leave me behind and take the QIII schematics at gunpoint. I'm just saying that it looked a little to me like it was Natasha arguing my case and therefore Natasha's influential vote that has ended up with me hunched here on a pervert's knee.'

'Pervert?'

Jessica coughed. She wriggled a little.

Natasha laughed. It was not a laugh of support.

Carter flushed red.

'Like sitting on a fence post. I really wish you middle-aged men could control yourselves . . . I thought you lot needed Viagra or something, anyway? You know, to get it up?'

'Middle-aged?' Carter sounded aghast. 'Do you really think I look that old? Jesus, I knew we should have left you in the desert . . .'

'Carter, do you have a question for the poor girl or what?'

'Yeah. If we could get to this QIII – would it have information on Spiral? And people like Feuchter and Durell? Or even the Nex, for that matter?'

Jessica shook her head in a shower of curls. 'It's a processor, Carter, not a database. But get me the right equipment connected to the QIII and the little bitch will hack and crack anything . . .' Natasha's eyes lit up at that. Jessica continued: 'Point it at Spiral's mainframe and it'll worm its way through the code in under a second. There's not a computer system worldwide that the QIII will not crack; right down from world banks to the FBI, Wall Street, Parliament, Scotland Yard, the New IRA. That's why it's such a scary piece of hardware . . . nothing is untouchable; nothing is hidden from it.'

'What operating systems will it run with?'

Jessica shrugged. 'Anything, everything; fully compliant with OSs from UNIX-IX and WIN512, through Def76 and Stable05 – it will decode anything from BaseZ88 and 681270 to way beyond the current 256 and 512 Gigabit architectures. You see, it doesn't work like that, but if it did it would be comparable to a 256 million-bit processor . . . it is so incredibly fast, it's hard to describe . . .'

'I get the picture,' said Natasha.

'I don't,' grumbled Carter. 'Make it clear for me . . .'

'The QIII is that powerful it can decode and encode DNA in millionths of a second; it would take a conventional computer hundreds of hours. It is also loaded with what is called WorldCode – an incredible variety of statistics and equations that, supposedly, make the QIII able to predict the future . . .'

'Really? You mean it actually *works*?'

'It uses probability math; equations; it comes out with the most probable outcome of any given event or situation; we'd got it about 93% perfect, but it was getting better by the day when . . .' Jessica trailed off. She coughed, gazing out at the passing scrubland and marsh areas. 'We had practically finished our work at Spiral_Q, the processor was practically fully operational. It worked, it worked well – it was just being run through its testing stages.'

'So it was feasible to destroy Spiral_Q? Because you had finished?'

'Yeah,' nodded Jessica. 'But I don't understand *why*. There was never supposed to be just one processor, surely? What a massive waste of technology!'

'Unless you wanted the *only* one,' said Carter. 'Stop anybody else making one, and bingo, you're in a position for world domination if it tickles your fancy. A machine that can take over any other machine? A machine that can predict the future? A fucking machine that can control world finances, space exploration, nuclear weapons – armies, countries, the whole fucking lot. You could have the whole world at your fingertips—'

'A curse,' said Natasha softly.

'So the QIII could tell us what the Nex and Feuchter are up to?'

'Probably, if you could get your hands on it and feed it enough data.'

'*I* can guess if you feed me enough fucking data,' said Carter wearily.

'Yeah, but can you search all the world databases in a few minutes? Can you get into protected and encrypted archives in the blink of an eye or the time it takes to sneeze?'

'And this thing is capable of world domination?'

'You would need the right key codes . . . which means you would need to *understand* how the QIII worked, really *know* how to operate the processor to its fullest,' said Jessica.

'And, of course, Spiral would have the right key codes, and Feuchter and this man Durell also know how to operate the QIII seeing as they helped to fucking build it,' snapped Carter.

'Durell,' said Natasha softly.

Their gazes met; it sounded fantastic, but then, sometimes fantastic, improbable, *impossible* could happen. Take a man; a nobody; working on an incredibly ground-breaking new processor. He realises that he could be rich; control the world; cause the next world war; whatever. And he understands his own insignificance, his own mortality and decides to take a slice from the Fame Pie. To further his own ends. To play at being *God* . . .

'This is beginning to sound like a megalomaniac's wet dream,' said Natasha sourly. 'I don't think the world is ready for it.'

'You're probably right,' said Carter.

'Maybe that's why they pulled the plug on the Rub al'Khali HQ?' said Jessica.

'No. Destroying its own bases isn't Spiral's style; it would have dismantled it, not blown it to Kingdom Come,' said Carter. 'But I'm sure that when we come face to face with Gol once more – then he'll have some answers for us.'

The Comanche spun glittering across the mountains, twin LHTec engines humming with reined-in torque and power; it banked east, heading for the northern corner of Iran, then on into China, Mongolia, the northern tip of Japan and the Pacific Ocean beyond ... and then, of course, on to the West Coast of the United States of America ...

And the devastation of a city recently torn apart by a pocket nuclear device.

CHAPTER 21

LA

The Comanche flitted across the sky, a softly humming falcon, a predator – quiet, dangerous, deadly. It came in low across the Pacific and touched down briefly in a cloud of swirling, eddying sand. It was on the ground for precisely four minutes . . .

'I'll head south into Mexico – there are a couple of illegal refuelling dumps I can utilise.' Langan spat a mouthful of dust into the ground and rubbed at his tired eyes.

Carter nodded. 'If I need you, if it's a dire emergency I'll patch through on the ECube. The signal will probably be intercepted by the enemy but hell, if that's the case they'll probably be just around the corner anyway.'

Langan nodded wearily. 'Just make sure you give me enough time for a decent sleep before you need me to come swooping in from the heavens to rescue you – you hear?'

'I hear.'

'Carter,' grinned Langan, 'you are the definitive pain in the arse.'

'I try to be.' Carter patted Langan's HIDSS, and disappeared into the gloom.

Langan secured the cockpit; within ten seconds the rotors had spun up and the Comanche jumped into the sky, spun low in a semicircle overhead, and headed back out over the Pacific.

The night was hot and humid. Distant sounds of a party echoed across the bay, followed by several shotgun blasts and loud screams. A disco yacht filled with corpses bobbed on the edge of the Pacific Ocean and the searchlights of a naval vessel that had just riddled it with heavy-calibre machine-gun bullets probed the surrounding darkness.

The wide highways were quiet in the early hours of the morning. Phosphorescent gleams shone from the sand-blown concrete. A deep rumble penetrated the shadows thrown by the false sentinel lights as a V12 Corvette cruised along, tyres humming gently, the reined-in motor barely turning over at such low speeds. Light reflected dimly from the battered body panels, and in the once-plush interior Natasha leaned forward, gazing to her right over the lapping dark waters at the edge of the gently sloping beach.

'I always dreamed I would visit California.'

'We're not here for a holiday,' said Carter softly.

After the nuclear explosion, the city had been sprayed for weeks by aircraft pumping out radiation-dampening chemicals: a human crop-spray that had saved the city's basic habitability but could do nothing to save the thousands of buildings – shops, houses, civic buildings – all washed away in a sea of fire. LA was busy rebuilding, but the city was constantly on the verge of anarchy. The LAPD and the military could do little to serve and protect millions of people destined for a future of miserable hardship and radiation poisoning.

Dawn was breaking as Carter pulled the Corvette into a roadside motel. He paid for a room and came back with keys. The motel room was basic and clean, and Carter stared into the bathroom and sighed. 'A shower. A shave. And . . . a proper toilet. Heaven. Valhalla. Fucking *bliss*.'

Natasha squeezed past him. 'I'm first,' she said, slamming the door in his face.

Carter grinned back at Jessica. 'Something I said?'

'Hmm.' Jessica slumped back onto the wide bed, her hair fanning out behind her, her stained and tattered pyjamas doing nothing to diminish her natural beauty.

'I'm just popping out,' said Carter suddenly, moving towards the door.

'I thought you said you needed a shave and a shower?'

'Time for that later. I have errands to run; like I said, I have some friends in LA.'

'Carter?'

'Yes, Jessica?'

'Could you possibly get me something to wear? I left Rub al'Khali in a bit of a hurry.'

'See what I can do.' He closed the door, and a few seconds later the Corvette rumbled away in a huge cloud of nauseating fumes.

Jessica lay back, weariness overcoming her. She pulled the rucksack towards her, her gaze falling on her own hands, their shroud of filth, the dirt lodged under her nails. She smiled gently. Once, that would never have happened: dirt would have been an *impossibility*. But things had changed—

418

Jessica removed the QIII schematics from the rucksack and stared at the silver disk in her hands.

'I hope you're worth all the trouble,' she muttered, resting her head back against the pillows. They felt soft and luxurious – a complete antithesis to the last day . . .

God, had it only been that long?

Since Spiral_Q?

Since Feuchter and the Nex?

Since the murders—

She shuddered, then closed her eyes and was able – for the first time in days – to relax.

Her breathing deepened and she licked her dry lips. The bed was so comfortable that it made her want to cry with gratitude. Oh, to curl up and sleep for a million years; to curl up in a ball and *forget* . . .

Images flashed through her mind—

The Nex.

The Nex, with their menacing guns.

Feuchter, watching limp trailing bodies being loaded into the trucks.

The QIII speaking to her on her terminal; warning her.

Had it *really* been the QIII itself? Or some deviant hacker? Or had she been warned by somebody at Spiral_Q? Or was she going slowly and certifiably insane?

Jessica rubbed at her weary eyes as she toyed with the possibility . . .

They could have warned her. Spiral could have warned her – it *was* feasible . . . improbable but feasible . . . But then, why her? Why *just* her? Why not the others? Adams and Johansen? Skelter? Oliver? Ralph?

She closed her eyes again, picturing Feuchter and finding some gratification in the fact that he had perished in the explosion. By the time Natasha emerged from the bathroom wearing a towel and rubbing her fingers through her clean hair in well-earned ecstasy, Jessica was snoring softly in the embrace of a deep, deep, welcome sleep.

Carter returned just after lunch, as Jessica and Natasha were sitting down to cheeseburgers and fries. He carried several bags, and was wearing a tired but happy smile.

'Where've you been?'

'Shopping.'

'With what?'

Carter winked. 'Generous friends. Now, I have a few presents for you two *femme fatales* and I desperately need to use the toilet. Any objections? Thought not . . . and get on the phone, order me some of that food. Looks too good to miss.' The sarcasm in his voice was painful.

'You seem very upbeat,' said Natasha softly.

Carter winked. 'Got a few surprises up my sleeve.'

Carter stood in the shower, the hot water cleansing him of sweat, sand, blood and oil. He placed his hands against the tiles and allowed the water to run over the back of his head for a few long luxurious minutes, revelling in the feeling of cleanliness that was creeping over him and through him . . .

And to heighten the experience, his mind was clear.

Perfectly clear.

Not poisoned by the presence, the cancer, the tumour. The tumour of Kade . . .

He towelled himself dry, his gaze catching the ten small metal globes arranged neatly around the sink. Ten fully functioning, fully armed and extremely dangerous HPGs – high-pressure grenades that had no traditional explosive charge, working instead by a mixture of chemicals that created a huge build-up of pressure and an almost silent explosion. Now they were ready to use. And abuse.

As he left the bathroom, rubbing at his smooth and somewhat pinkly raw freshly shaved face, it was to see Natasha and Jessica modelling the new clothes he had brought them. Plain trousers and jumpers, and low-heeled boots.

'Very functional,' said Natasha.

'We won't be winning any fashion parades,' yawned Jessica.

'But then, we're not here to party,' said Carter. He grabbed a cheeseburger, and taking a bite, emptied another bag onto the bed. Ammunition magazines and bullets clattered free in a large pile.

'Fuck me,' said Natasha.

'Get busy, ladies, if you please.'

'Where'd you get all this?'

'You forget,' said Carter softly. 'I used to be a Spiral operative; I worked the DemolSquads for seven years; I know where many of the worldwide stashes are and I've got a few contacts in LA.'

'I don't think I can go through with this,' said Jessica, her face having paled at the sight of the bullets and the weapon mags. Her eyes lifted, met Carter's dark stare. 'I am not a soldier, I am a programmer. I'm not a fighter, I'm not a warrior. I'm in this shit way too deep . . .'

Carter smiled at the young woman, nodding and yawning himself. 'You are right – you have played your part,' he said. 'The best thing to do now is hand over the QIII schematics to me . . . I will make sure somebody gets a good slapping for what happened in Saudi Arabia.'

'Do you think Gol can really help you?'

'If the meet is genuine, then yes. If it is a set-up . . .' Carter shrugged. 'How about we rendezvous – I'll go in alone and meet Gol, then bring him out to meet you two if this thing isn't a trap? That way you're not in the firing line – you just play the waiting game.'

Natasha shook her head. 'I can't let you go in alone.'

'You have to,' said Carter. 'This thing screams of bad news; you can't expect me to put Jessica in such a dangerous situation – and as for yourself? Well, Nats, you know – and I fucking *mean* know – that I work better alone. If it really is your father, if he is alive, then so be it, we are on our way to recovering the QIII and stopping Feuchter and Durell's plans; if he has been captured, then I will do everything in my power to rescue him and I'll fucking get him out of there alive . . . and then we can move on to locating Durell . . .'

Natasha sighed. 'OK. You're right. When is the meet?'

'Two hours. I have just a few more things to take care of.'

'Where is it?'

Carter met Natasha's look and their gazes locked; he fell headlong into those beautiful, oval brown depths. He licked his lips slowly and could still taste salt. And the question at the front of his mind was . . .

Can I trust her?

Feuchter's words returned to him.

She's one of us . . .

But she had helped him get this far still alive. Without her he would be dead . . . And since Rub al'Khali Carter had been playing his cards much more closely to his chest – revealing nothing . . . the perfect poker player . . . the perfect gamesman.

Natasha smiled slowly.

'Don't tell me,' she said, sniffing, her eyes unreadable. 'I don't need to know the information and I understand that it could compromise you, yeah? Just tell me where you want to meet us afterwards.'

422

Carter nodded at Natasha and turned, gathering his equipment together. He glanced at Jessica. 'I'll leave the schematics disk here. I think it will be safer. If this whole gig is a trap, I wouldn't like to blunder into their lair with the very fucking item they obviously want from me. If Gol really is here in LA then the schematics could make a difference between his life and death . . . and I wouldn't like to piss that away.'

Jessica nodded.

Carter took the disk, a tiny silver platter, for a moment. He brought it up to his face and stared hard. 'Hope you're worth it, hope those fuckers need you more than they need me dead,' he muttered. Then he dropped the disk into Jessica's hand and headed for the door.

The Corvette rumbled to a halt in a deserted back alley. A recent fire had scarred most of the narrow passageway and blackened, cracked windows stared out at Carter. Papers blew across his path as the car door opened and Carter's boots touched the hot pavement under a bleached sun. He stood, stretched his back, and looked warily about: a predator, scanning his new territory, assimilating the piss-stink of markers, alert and ready for action. Carter reached back into the car, slipping various things into his trouser pockets and the pockets of his plain black waist-length jacket.

Carter buttoned up the jacket, checked his now clean-shaven features in the Corvette's cracked wing mirror, then smiled into the eyes of his own reflection. It was a strong smile. A convincing smile. It would have to be, to get him past the reception of the hotel where the meet was to take place: the Beverly Hills Hilton, recent survivor of atomic terrorism.

Carter walked, hands in his pockets, clearing his mind

423

for the meeting to come. He would have to be sharp; but then, if Gol wasn't there and it was nothing more than a set-up, Gol would be conspicuous by his absence and the bad gig would be pretty easy to spot – and pretty quick to go down.

Moving out onto the sidewalk, Carter walked swiftly. His gaze was alert, watching, gauging the few people he passed on foot, searching for weapons and bad intent. His eager scrutiny checked every car that purred down the scorched tree-lined sidewalk of South El Camino Drive, searching interiors, looking for anything suspicious, no matter how small. Reaching the corner of El Camino and Wilshire Boulevard, Carter halted again, looking around. He turned left and began to walk once more, again scanning the surroundings – the scarred fronts of buildings, the people, the battered cars, the burned trees. As he closed on the entrance to the Beverly Hills Hilton he slowed to an amble, searching for anything suspicious.

If they're here, he thought, if they're watching, then I won't see them. They will see me; but they will be ghosts.

Invisible.

He halted, leaning against a low wall and pulling free a packet of Camel cigarettes. He lit one and inhaled, enjoying the sensation and buzz of the nicotine. Shit, he thought, it's been too long, my little buddies. Far too long.

Ahh, the joys of civilisation.

The quiet cigarette allowed him time to examine his surroundings with a careful and practised eye. There were several spots on and in nearby buildings that would be fine for snipers; he could see no activity, but then, that didn't mean they weren't there.

Carter thought back to Africa.

Gol, running, the long jump out over the abyss . . .

The unheard scream, legs treading nothing but air . . .

The long dive towards the river far far far below . . .

Despite his own pain and exhaustion at the time, he still remembered the one word that had leaped unbidden to his mind . . . that came tumbling out of the bright red vaults of agony that had consumed him . . .

Dead.

There was no way that Gol could have survived that fall.

But then, Carter had also left him to die back in Prague; left him bleeding heavily on the road with the armed police only minutes away. Shot him to keep him *alive* . . . and Gol had survived that bad shit, escaped and survived like the tough cockroach bastard he was.

Carter breathed out a plume of smoke. Laughter echoed from further down the sidewalk and Carter's head snapped in that direction. He relaxed. Took another drag. Breathed deeply, calming his suddenly racing heart.

Analysis, he thought.

He closed his eyes for a moment; the frequent headaches he had been experiencing were thankfully absent; the stitches in his side were holding well and the pain there was nothing more than a dull throb thanks to an injection of pethidine. His nose which he had reset in the hotel room was throbbing with an annoying wave of soreness and the discomfort of his broken finger – freshly strapped – and cracked ribs were nothing more than dull aches that he had come to call his own. The pain was now integral to his existence, a part of him, unchallenged.

He finished the cigarette and flicked the butt into the bushes behind him.

Let's do it, he thought, checking his watch.

He walked up the long, winding drive, trying hard not to focus exclusively on the impressive but battered building, all the time scanning for anything suspicious as he neared the large turning circle in front of the glass-walled and steel-barred reception area. He glanced right, up at the six-storey building and the balconies that went round the exterior of each floor.

Carter's plan was simple. Ask for information at the Hilton reception desk, nicely at first . . . or with Mr 9mm as a bit of heavy reinforcement. He was sure events would unfold from there.

He nodded to the bellboy, climbed the low marble steps that ascended between lofty thick white pillars and entered the plush plant-littered foyer with catlike wariness. His gaze swivelled from left to right. Men reading newspapers, a few women apparently waiting for people, one talking animatedly on a mobile. Carter pressed the reassuring bulk of the Browning beneath his jacket and trod the plush carpets towards the reception desk and the beautiful beaming brunette with her shining eyes.

'Good evening, sir. How may I help?'

Carter smiled his winning smile as his eyes used the reflecting surfaces of glass, brass and polished marble to check events behind him. Then he said, 'Hi. I have a friend staying here by the name of Mr Gol. Said he would leave a message for me at reception about a meeting we have? My name is Carter.'

'Let me check, sir.'

The brunette turned to the pigeon-holes behind the desk. Carter leaned his elbows on the elegantly carved cherrywood surface, gaze scanning the people in the lobby. He watched a man with a full beard enter, carrying

426

a Nike holdall. Carter felt himself tense, and unbuttoned his jacket as the man with the holdall greeted a tall heavy-set man reading a newspaper. They left the lobby together.

'Yes, there is an envelope for a Mr Carter.'

Carter took the white A5 envelope. He tore open the flap with his thumb; there was a single slip of paper inside. It read:

ROOM 215. I'LL BE WAITING.

It was signed 'Gol'. The handwriting was Gol's and so was the signature. Carter glanced around once more, then put the slip into his pocket.

'Thank you,' he said. 'Can you direct me to room 215?'

'Take the elevator to the second floor. Straight ahead and to the right.'

'Thank you again.' He beamed at her and walked towards the elevator, his hand in his pocket curling around an HPG. The elevator door closed and Carter found himself staring at his own reflection in polished chrome. He blinked lazily, a predator, and ignored the urge to light another cigarette.

Alone, he thought.

The way I like it.

He pulled free the HPG and stared at the small reflective ball. He pulled the pin and held down the trigger, then cupped the globe in his hand thoughtfully, testing the weight. The HPG was hidden against his palm.

He carefully put the pin in his pocket and removed his battered Browning Hi-Power as the elevator doors slid open, revealing a bright corridor with plush carpeting and tasteful wood panelling and decor. Carter stepped out onto the thick carpet, his boots sinking into the pile.

'Very cosy,' he muttered. He checked left and right. Moved forward.

The hotel seemed quiet. Carter walked to room 215 and halted to one side of the door. He eyed the brass numbers suspiciously as something inside him screamed:

This is wrong, this is all wrong, Gol is dead, this is a trap . . .

Who wanted him dead?

Durell? The Nex?

There were easier ways to kill him than this. But then, now he had the QIII schematics with which to do a little bargaining . . .

He raised his fist. Glanced left and right.

Rapped on the door and took a step back.

'Come in,' came a clear, melodious, powerful voice.

Carter blinked. He licked his lips and realised that there was salt there. He realised too that his hand was slippery around the stocky bulk of the Browning. He holstered the Browning and wiped his hand on his trousers. He smiled nastily. Depressing the handle, Carter nudged the door open and drew the gun once more.

Gentle laughter came from inside the room. 'Come on in, Carter. There's no gun here waiting to blow your head off. No terrible plan of entrapment to ensnare you.'

Carter peered around the door frame. Gol was sitting in a chair by the window, a glass of brandy by one hand, a cigarette in his other. Carter checked the corridor, then stepped inside and closed the door behind him.

'Nice to see you again, Gol, but I thought you might be kinda dead.'

Gol turned then, and stood. He beamed warmly at Carter, and raised his glass, sipping at the brandy, his eyes on the Browning. 'Always a cautious man, eh, my friend? Although I *do* quite understand your concern . . . if our situations had been reversed, then I too would think it a trap.'

He moved, walking across the room to stare out of the window.

Carter moved forward suspiciously, all senses alert, Browning muzzle searching uneasily. When he was satisfied that they were alone in the room, he fixed his stare back on Gol, who had turned, his dark-eyed gaze settling on Carter.

Gol smiled warmly. He ran a hand through his greying hair.

'I know you will find it hard to believe, but I was rescued. By Spiral; they desperately wanted the schematics I was carrying but the irony was that in rescuing me, they forced me to drop that disk – and it became lost, leaving Feuchter with the only working processor in existence. Spiral were very precise – they had tracked me, were waiting when I took that leap of fucking faith. They plucked me from the sky like a fly being zapped.'

Carter looked him up and down. The man's beard was a touch shorter, neatly trimmed; everything else about Gol was exactly how Carter remembered him. Carter grinned wryly.

'You *do* look pretty good for a dead man.' He lowered the Browning. 'Natasha will be thrilled.'

'Ahh, my sweet little Natasha! I thought you might bring her along, but then – ah yes. A trap. You thought me dead, hah! Had you no faith in your old Spiral buddy – even though you left me for dead in Prague . . .' Gol's eyes twinkled as he took a step closer. 'But then, we won't go over that old ground again, eh?'

Carter smiled, holding Gol's dark gaze. 'How about a drink? You're there enjoying that brandy without offering me any? And after all the shit I've been taking from Natasha recently . . .'

'Yes, I heard about your exploits. Spiral_F has been following your progress with interest – although, it must be said, always a few steps behind you. Is that rogue Langan behaving himself?'

'He's doing fine.' Carter pocketed the Browning but kept the HPG hidden. He accepted the brandy and took a sip.

Gol's gaze lingered on the glass and Carter forced himself not to frown as the other man turned to stare out of the window once more. Something is wrong, screamed Carter's brain. He carefully spat the brandy back into the glass . . .

Gol turned again, a swift movement, a small black gun now in his large hand. 'I'm sorry, Carter,' he said. 'Really sorry.'

CHAPTER 22

THE DARK SIDE OF THE SOUL

Jam, Nicky, Slater and The Priest stood beside the two Chinook Ch-47s on the Kamus-5 landing yard, gazing inside the holds of the battered rainswept aircraft.

'They're ferrying crates,' said Jam quietly.

'Yes, but look at this,' said The Priest, leaping up into the back and kicking free a narrow crate panel. Nestling within straw were large shells, gleaming menacingly under the weak light.

'Big big bullets,' said Slater.

'Shells,' corrected Nicky.

'These,' said The Priest, 'are 12.5cm-calibre rounds.' He stared hard at the assembled DemolSquad. They looked from his fevered eyes to the shells, then back to his eyes.

Jam shrugged. 'You're going to have to enlighten us.'

'Warships use them,' said The Priest softly. 'In their large deck-mounted guns. They are devastating weapons.'

'So we're looking for a warship now?'

'They have abandoned this base,' said The Priest softly. 'What better position to operate from? If you have a large ship, filled with supplies – you are totally mobile. Now, in the briefing room here at Kamus I found maps and charts; most were of the Barents Sea and the Arctic Ocean.'

'That's a lot of fucking sea,' said Jam.

The Priest nodded. 'Yes, I agree, but did you notice the huge drums of oil in the storeroom? There were markings on the floor, suggesting that many have been recently removed. The drums were inscribed with a sales originator trademark: Kastevsky Co.'

'Russian?'

'Yes. The Kastevsky Co. operates out of Ostrov Vaygach covering the Barents Sea and Karskoye More. Spiral have always used them for oil when they've been operating in that region.'

'It gives us a starting point,' said Slater.

'I will send the remaining TacSquads to sweep the area; it is the strongest lead we have. We need to gather the remaining DemolSquads together ready for when the new threat is identified. Only then will we be in a position to do something about this Nex invasion.'

Jam nodded, enjoying his cigarette. 'I have an idea. If you are right and we are looking for a ship to link with these Spiral traitors, then we will need weaponry. Big weaponry. We can coordinate from here – Slater and Nicky can call the DemolSquads to the Kamus via the ECubes. This place has fuel, weapons – it is the perfect place from which to launch an offensive. You can locate the enemy and pinpoint their exact position; and I . . .'

'Yes? What skive have you dreamed up for yourself this time, Jam?'

432

Jam grinned.

'I have to see a man about a bomb.'

'I'm sorry, Carter,' said Gol. 'Really sorry.'

Carter grinned nastily, the brandy glass in his hand, the Browning in his pocket.

Stupid, he thought. Guard down . . .

Stupid.

'So, you alive, or dead, or what? The Nex get to you?'

Gol shook his head sadly. 'It's a lot more complicated than that, Mr Carter. A lot more complicated than you could ever believe. Now, I believe that you are carrying the QIII processor schematics. I would like them, please. They are ours. They belong to us and should have died in Rub al'Khali, just like you.'

Carter allowed himself to frown.

'You know when we worked together, out of Egypt. Do you remember the night in Luxor? When we were surrounded by Arabs with machine guns, just a veranda and the sea below us, the dark waves crashing against the shores at the height of the storm? You remember that?'

Gol nodded; but it was there. A flash across his face. A moment of . . .

Confusion.

'You mean . . . what we called the Fifth Night?'

Carter nodded. 'Gol, tell me what you said to me before we charged at those fuckers. Tell me the exact words you spoke to fill me with confidence on that dark night when we both thought that we would die.'

'I have no time for this, Carter. Give me the fucking schematics.'

'You are not Gol.'

Gol smiled then, a flash of white teeth through his grey beard. 'Shit, Carter, you have me there. So fucking what?

433

I *am* Gol – a part of Gol; but you cannot understand. I have been instructed not to kill you; there are a variety of people who would like a little . . . shall we say *chat*. But first you must give me the schematics you hold in your hands.'

Carter saw Gol's – or the *imitation* Gol's – finger tighten a little on the trigger. Taking up the slack, the taut; getting ready to reel in the line with the big flapping fish struggling on the end . . .

Carter smiled.

He uncurled his right hand to reveal the HPG.

'Surprise, fucker,' said Carter dryly.

Carter threw the HPG and saw Gol's eyes go suddenly wide, his mouth open in a silent 'Fuck!'

Reflexes took over; there was no thought. The large man reached up to catch the HPG—

His gun muzzle moved.

Carter's Browning was out and he was firing even as he dived for the bathroom. He rolled across the thick carpet as the Browning's bullets tore into the wall and then the window, which shattered with a crash of exploding glass . . .

Gol was running.

Carter aimed the Browning from the bathroom—

Just as the HPG detonated.

The room seemed to change suddenly from a normal hotel bedroom into the bizarre heart of a raging tornado. The furniture was picked up and tossed about and smashed up and out and down in a fury of chemical obliteration. The floor shook and trembled; glass shattered; there came the crunching of timbers and the scream of twisted steel. Carter cowered behind the bathroom wall, nose twitching at the heavy chemical stink as dust and debris spat through the doorway. He suddenly realised with horror that if the wall had been merely a plasterboard partition he would have been pulped and fucked up *bad*. There was a heavy *thump* as the wall buckled above him.

He glanced up, the tip of the Browning touching his nose, his eyes blinking in the sudden dust storm.

The shaking gradually subsided.

There was a rattle of plaster and wood hitting the ground.

Carter could hear the beat of his own heart. Hear his own breathing.

The soft *thumps* of his own *life* . . .

He glanced left. A chewed length of timber leaned against the bathroom doorway; dust was floating thick in the air and only then did Carter realise his ears were screaming at him—

Singing to him—

A song of pain.

The sprinklers suddenly burst into life, dampening down the dust.

Carter eased himself to his feet and peered around the doorway. The room was like a scene from a war movie. All the windows and their frames had blown out. The carpet had been torn up, twisted around the blasted furniture and the whole mess wrenched apart to litter the corners of the room. The walls were smashed and torn and scorched. The ceiling had partly fallen in, and there were several piles of unidentifiable rubble . . .

Gol had been running for the corridor . . .

'Gol?' screamed Carter. He wiped cool sprinkler water from his face and lips.

Somebody hammered on the main door, which had somehow survived the blast but twisted in its frame, wedging shut.

'Fuck you,' wept the imitation Gol.

Carter stepped out of the bathroom. He moved to the prostrate body of Gol, who was lying on his side clutching his twisted, smashed leg. The right limb had been almost ripped free and was only held on by tatters of muscle. A split second earlier and Gol would have made it to the sanctuary of the corridor and the protection of a genuine brick wall—

Carter grinned nastily. Put his Browning in Gol's face.

'Who the fuck are you?'

'I am not Gol.'

'Well, no fucking prizes for *that* answer. *Who the fuck are you?*' Carter jabbed the Browning against the side of Gol's head. 'Answer me – at least you're still fucking *alive* . . .'

Carter heard a zipping sound, and a buzz. Something warm raced across his cheek.

His hand lifted, bringing a vision of blood in front of his eyes—

'Fu-' he began as he dived for the ground and three more bullets skimmed overhead. Carter crawled away from the window, teeth gritted, shock registering in his system.

The sniper's bullet had taken a strip of skin from his cheek, and nicked his ear lobe.

Carter breathed deeply, calming his racing heart.

Close call . . .

Close call.

Millimetres . . . a single millimetre . . .

Fuck, he breathed—

'You got an answer, Gol?' he suddenly bellowed through the ringing in his own head.

The sniper's bullet took the imitation Gol in the face, punching his head back against the carpet. The man's

436

huge body seemed to sigh, to deflate, to settle back and finally lie still.

Carter's mouth became a grim line.

'Son of a bitch,' he hissed.

He crawled across the room, across the chaotic debris of the explosion. He could hear distant sirens. The fire service and LAPD. Could he trust either? He doubted it.

And then he heard a scream – from outside the room, in the wood-panelled corridor. Machine-gun fire shattered the door from its frame and Carter found himself back in the bathroom, ducking below the trajectory of the sniper's bullets and – thankfully – a little shielded by the frosted glass.

He heard boots, charging down the corridor—

Carter tossed another HPG; the globe bounced from the wall of the room and rattled across the torn floor—

He heard a single word.

'Shit—'

They ran for it.

The explosion rocked the room as Carter put a bullet through the bathroom window. The whole world seemed to have gone mad as Carter crawled to the ledge. The sniper's bullet had cut diagonally across his cheekbone and down to nick his ear lobe. That meant the sniper was above Carter's position and to the left—

He saw it: a nearby rooftop. Ideal—

Carter's sharp eyes spotted the tiny figure. Steadying his hand on the ragged glass-edged sill, Carter levelled the Browning and began to fire—

Five, six, seven, eight bullets.

He could see the distant stonework crumbling.

Twelve, thirteen. He switched mags, pulled a small device from his pocket, snapped it against the wall beneath the windowsill, took a step back, dropped an HPG in the middle of the bathroom and leaped out of the window—

Several things happened at once—

Five black-clad Nex slid around the corner, carrying sub-machine guns—

The sniper got to his feet, screaming in pain at the bullet in his shoulder, and painfully picked up his rifle. Shaking with anger, fatigue and the agony of hot metal piercing his flesh; he tried to level the weapon over the parapet and aim it at the opposite building—

The HPG detonated.

Carter bounced violently against the wall ten feet below the window on the end of the wire and the attached small black circular object – standard Spiral issue – that he held in his free fist—

The bathroom exploded.

Debris spat from the hole in the wall; even as the chaos erupted Carter swung himself around on the wire and, hanging suspended, unloaded another full magazine towards the sniper.

Then he flicked the release.

Buzzing filled his ears and he shot towards the ground; his boots touched down beside the Olympic-size swimming pool and a few onlookers who were standing, mouths agape, staring up at the room that he had suddenly and urgently vacated. Fire bellowed out, then was suddenly sucked back in. There was a splash as a scorched and flaming wall cabinet landed in the pool, where it hissed and steamed.

Carter glanced around, then sprinted for the nearest cover, switching magazines in the Browning as he ran. From the bushes he saw the police squad cars and two huge fire vehicles charging up the road, horns blaring.

Carter made it to the pavement, shoved his Browning back into his pocket and ran.

He was motoring on instinct now. All six cylinders.

He sprinted, boots thudding against the sidewalk. As he skidded onto El Camino Drive he saw the distant lights of cars and cursed. He dived over a low wall and watched the vehicles – three large black GMC trucks – go screaming past, engines howling. .

Bad, thought Carter.

Real bad.

He continued to run.

Two minutes later, pouring with sweat, he reached the Corvette. He jumped in, gunned the engine and floored the accelerator. The huge V12 roared and, leaving rubber tread smeared heedlessly against the concrete, he wheel-spun towards the end of the fire-scorched alley and out onto the road—

The GMC trucks were prowling, waiting, searching. Their engines howled as they raced down the highway after the Corvette as it appeared: wolves hunting down this running lamb.

All four vehicles screamed around a huge loop of tarmac, suspensions dipping as they veered round corners and ended back on Wilshire Boulevard. They slipped past the fire trucks and Carter, bent forward over the steering wheel, sweat dripping in his eyes, cursed his pursuers—

Carter pulled free his Browning and kissed the grip. 'You've saved me before, baby,' he muttered.

He fired through the Corvette's rear window. Glass exploded in a shower and the three GMC trucks veered, one mounting the pavement and sending a couple of pedestrians sprinting for cover, wheels churning an old man into the ground with quadruple impacts.

They regrouped on the road and, their lights dazzling Carter, accelerated towards him.

Where's fucking Kade when I need him? he thought. Closely followed by, I should have stolen a faster car—

The lead GMC truck smashed into the back of the Corvette. Carter was jolted in his seat, and almost lost his Browning. His foot slammed to the floor and suddenly he veered right, down a narrow slip road leading away from Beverly Hills—

The GMC trucks followed in tight formation.

They sped past a parked patrol car. Red lights flickered.

The police car pulled away from the kerb and gave chase.

Carter growled to himself. He fired another few bullets from the rear of the 'Vette and was gratified when he popped a headlamp. But that did little to take the GMCs out of action.

They're too high up, he realised. Their cabs are too fucking high up.

The lead GMC shunted him again.

Carter fired the remaining bullets; there was a high-pitched squeal and a rattle from the engine compartment and the truck veered off, hammering into a low wall. Carter caught a glimpse in his mirror of a dark body catapulted like a rag doll through the windscreen before the howl of police sirens made him drag the steering wheel to the left. The Corvette's wheels screeched at the abuse as the car power-slid around a corner through a crossroads, the back end hitting and bouncing from a set of lights.

More police cars joined the chase.

Who're they fucking chasing? he thought sombrely.

Me or them?

He pressed his foot to the floor. The engine growled.

Help, he thought.

The Corvette sped through an intersection; there was a multiple music-blare of horns as cars zipped insanely all around and Carter closed his eyes for a moment. Kade? Where are you, Kade? Come and get me out of this shit! Come and fucking *help me* . . .

He no longer checked his rear-view mirror. The view in it only seemed to get worse.

Engines howled close behind him, mechanical animals with their teeth bared, ready to tear and rend him with anger and hatred . . .

Once more he wrenched on the steering wheel, feeling the car lose traction as tyres slid around the corner, and once more he narrowly missed another vehicle – a fire truck, this time. The horn screamed at him and Carter involuntarily flinched, half ducking down in his seat . . .

Focus, he thought.

Meeting. With Natasha, and Jessica . . .

And Langan.

His gaze flickered up, checking the signs. He feinted a left turn, then dragged the Corvette over the grassy embankment and forced a U-turn through heavy traffic. Tyres squealed, horns blared; Carter caught a flashing, almost hallucinatory scene of angry faces and waving fists. The Corvette's rear bounced from the wing of a brand new Porsche . . .

'Motherfucker!' came the scream.

Carter checked his rear-view as he sped away. He had managed, by some twist of fate, by some fluke of gridlock, to cause a massive jam across the six lanes of highway; the GMCs had stuttered to a halt against a wall of metal. LAPD cops flooded the road, guns out – yelling—

Gunshots rattled.

He heard the wet *thump* of metal in flesh.

Carter ducked low and floored the Corvette's accelerator.

He drove for ten minutes as dusk began to fall, reducing his speed a little so as not to attract too much unwanted attention. As he sped down towards Inglewood and the meet, he checked his mirrors again.

There, in the distance, he could see a group of GMC trucks.

'No,' he muttered, frowning. 'Fucking impossible!'

He saw the trucks accelerating, still distant blobs, their grilles like teeth.

Smiling teeth.

Carter's jaw tightened. His foot hit the floor again and the Corvette jerked forward, spun right down a tight bend and into a McDonald's drive-through. He slammed on the brakes and the Corvette screeched to a halt beside a wooden bench under a group of flowering trees where Natasha and Jessica sat, empty Coke cartons in front of them.

Carter leaped out.

'We've got trouble.'

'Big trouble?' asked Natasha.

'Oh yes.'

Carter slotted a fresh mag into his Browning and as a car pulled free of the service window of the drive-through he pointed the gun and screamed, 'Get out of the fucking car!'

The Ferrari F355 Spider stopped abruptly. The engine rumbled, a deep-throated V8 purr.

'What are you doing?' hissed Natasha.

'You were right. We need something faster.'

'Hey man, you have *got* to be kidding!'

Carter met the man's outraged glare: he was young, wore a skull-and-crossbones bandanna, Oakleys and no shirt, revealing a heavily tattooed torso. When he spoke, his hands lifted from the steering wheel in emphasis.

'Get out.'

'You motherf—'

The Browning moved. There was a *blam*. A hole appeared in the passenger side of the windscreen – and in the fine leather upholstery beyond. The man stared at the hole in the windscreen, then at the seat. Then he leaped from the vehicle as if stung.

Carter, Natasha and Jessica jumped in.

'You know how much this car cost, man?'

Carter met the man's gaze again. 'Sue me,' he said as he slotted the tiptronic into first and floored the gas pedal; the Ferrari F355 roared, the bellowing of a 375-bhp lion, and shot off so fast that Carter was pinned back into the seat.

'You motherfuckers!' screamed the tattooed man, waving his fist and a strawberry milk shake in the air.

The Ferrari F355 became practically airborne from the speed bump as they took off past five black GMC trucks, the windows all blacked out, their engines rumbling and lights blazing in the gloom of the Californian dusk. He slotted the vehicle into sixth gear and felt the hairs on the back of his neck stand on end as the V8 3496cc motor roared with renewed vigour and the road became a blur of twisting concrete snake; it danced ahead of him like a scene from a bad trip.

Natasha leaned forward – both women had leaped into the cramped rear of the roofless sports car. 'Erm, Carter, how fast are you going?' There was an edge of fear to her voice.

'I don't know,' he said through gritted teeth. 'I'm watching . . . the . . . road.'

'Are we in that much trouble?'

443

'Yes,' said Carter softly.

'Did you see my father?'

Carter looked at Natasha from the corner of his eye. 'No, Natasha. I'm sorry.'

'Oh.'

She sat back, deflated. Carter wanted to say, *I told you so; you shouldn't have got your hopes up, love.* But he bit his tongue and concentrated on the road, a winding 180 m.p.h. roller coaster of orange and grey beneath the colourful bruise that was the sky.

'Who did you meet?'

'It was a set-up. I'm afraid I blew up the hotel room . . .'

'With what?'

'A couple of HPGs.'

'You lunatic! What did they – whoever *they* were – want?'

'It was the Nex,' said Carter sourly. 'And they wanted the QIII schematics. Hold on,' he snapped, slamming the Ferrari down a couple of gears and using the engine braking to get them sliding and squealing around a corner. Carter grinned like an excited child back at the two women.

They didn't look impressed.

Sirens screamed suddenly off to one side as a convoy of police cars burst from a junction, almost running the Ferrari off the road. Carter swerved violently, the motor roaring, and just made it around.

The squad cars took up the pursuit.

'Shit.'

Carter accelerated back up to 180 m.p.h., a wide grin on his face.

'Catch this baby, little piggies,' he muttered as they fell away behind him and he focused on the far distance.

'Natasha, get a message to Langan to come pick us up. There must be a thousand cops after us.'

'But the Nex will tag us . . .'

'So fucking what? They already know we're here.'

Natasha pulled free the ECube as Carter concentrated on driving; night fell over California as they sped south and left their pursuers far, far behind . . .

The motel was in the middle of nowhere; there were two pickups parked out front when the Ferrari F355 sped around a corner and came to a sudden halt. Carter lit a cigarette as Natasha and Jessica climbed out and stretched their tense, aching muscles.

'You're a lunatic,' said Jessica.

'I got us out.'

'What happened back there?' asked Natasha.

Carter shrugged. 'There were Nex waiting for me; they wanted the QIII schematics and we had a bit of a lovers' tiff. There was a bit of leg-slapping, hair-pulling and face-scratching and I had to make rather a sharp getaway . . .'

'You're hurt.' Natasha stepped in close, her finger brushing his cheek. Carter looked into her eyes then and smiled. He took her fingers, lifted them to his lips and kissed them.

'There was a sniper. Waiting for me.'

'Bad . . .'

'I think I hit him.'

The drone of the Comanche reached their ears and Carter gazed up into the darkness. Lights suddenly glared from the black as the chopper banked and, with a heavy wild *thrumming* of rotors, flashed overhead. It circled, then slowed and Carter, Jessica and Natasha backed away, shielding their eyes as the Comanche whined down,

445

its suspension bouncing as the machine landed lightly beside the Ferrari. There were several hisses and whines, plus the drone of incredibly powerful engines being gently but purposefully abused. The HIDSS-helmeted figure turned, looked out from the smoked cockpit and gave a thumbs-up.

Outside, the trees and bushes were tossed from side to side by the rotors' turbulence.

'Here's our ride,' said Carter, something unheard and unseen making him turn, his dark eyes peering out over the gloom and shadows of the nearby trees and dirty highway beyond the motel's parking lot. Something burned uneasily at the back of Carter's mind. His head turned as he glanced uneasily down the road, eyes searching for the dark GMC trucks that had so recently given chase . . . but there was nothing there.

Nothing out of place.

Nothing *wrong* . . .

Someth—

His gaze returned to the Comanche.

And he could hear it. A distant voice: like a scream, in passion, in anger, determined but pinned down, restricted, forced into silence against its furious force of will—

Something's wr—

Carter frowned. The whole world seemed to slow. The Comanche's blurred rotors whirled at a snail's pace, *thrum thrum thruuuuuum*. Carter reached for his Browning and it seemed that his hand took an age to reach the heavy weapon as his head was turning towards Natasha and his lips formed the words, 'Let's . . . go . . .'

There was a distant *crack*.

Carter's eyes caught the muzzle flash.

Something's wrong.

446

A hole appeared in the Comanche's cockpit canopy and Langan was punched backwards, flipping slowly across the inside of the helicopter, a huge splatter of blood mushrooming up against the smoked glass. Carter's Browning appeared instantly in his hand and he cursed the slowness and clumsiness of his own actions, cursed the sluggishness of the world around him and within him as his mouth opened to scream the words and both Jessica and Natasha turned, their movements painfully slow, to gaze in confusion up at the helicopter, the whirling rotors, the slumped figure in the darkened depths of the imprisoning and suddenly insect-like machine—

Carter dropped to one knee, shifting and dropping his stance, the Browning bucking in his hand: one bullet; two bullets; three bullets – and then he saw the shadowy figures detach themselves from the trees and come racing low with incredible speed across the grass and they were the Nex and a cold terror clamped Carter's heart as the world slammed back into focus and reality—

'What—'

'Oh, my.'

'Get in the fucking 'copter!' Carter screamed, firing the rest of the mag at the charging wall of Nex. They were dressed in identical dark grey body-hugging garments; they carried sub-machine guns but did not return fire; they were one of the most menacing, most terrifying things Carter had ever seen and his jaw clamped tightly shut—

Natasha was climbing, glancing back over her shoulder at the charging Nex. Then her gaze transferred down to Carter who grabbed Jessica and pushed her towards the Comanche, under the whining rush of the rotors that lashed the trees into frantic swaying with the power of those terrific reined-in engines . . .

Carter ejected the magazine. Slotted another into the weapon and sighted on a dark, masked face. The Browning barked in his hand and the figure pitched under the boots of another Nex. Carter's mouth was dry.

Fuck me, he thought.

There are *hundreds* of them . . .

Far, far more than in Africa . . .

They swarmed from all around now; like insects – dark-eyed and lethal. As if on some unspoken command their weapons lifted, muzzles swivelling towards the group—

'Fuck . . .'

Carter threw an HPG and watched Nex corpses thrown in different directions, limbs torn from carcasses, blood spewing from pulped flesh . . .

What the hell *are* they? screamed his brain. 'Get up there!' he yelled. He fired several more rounds, the Browning a dark comrade in his fist, an extension of his body.

The Nex, their sub-machine guns pointing, still did not fire. Carter's gaze darted up towards Natasha as—

Jessica reached up to the handholds. Carter turned, swiftly—

There came another distant *crack*.

Carter felt a hiss of heat beside his face and a blow against his back and turned to grab Jessica's arms – which suddenly draped loosely around his neck as she bounced from the DPM panels of the Comanche and fell against him. Her eyes were wide, confused and innocent as her gaze met Carter's stunned stare and her arms fell away from his shoulders. He grabbed her, his Browning forgotten, he held her waist and supported her sudden dead weight and gazed into those deep intelligent frightened eyes—

Eyes that held a million questions . . .

Why?

Why me?

Why now?

What is happening?

What is happening to me?

Jessica opened her mouth to speak, to ask him. A gush of red poured from her lips with a convulsion of her broken body, spilling down her dark jumper to stain Carter's battered jacket. She shivered, head flopping back now and shaking, curls soaked in blood. She tried to speak, but more blood flowed out from her mouth and across her cheek, a thick red river flowing into her eyes and down across her ears. She sighed, a bubbling of crimson spittle and exhaled air—

And then Jessica was dead.

'Come on!' screamed Natasha.

His gaze lifted and met the screaming panic-filled face of Natasha, her eyes wide, her tongue moistening fear-dry lips.

'Carter! They're—'

He whirled. The Nex were only feet away, arms outstretched, a swarm heaving to encompass and overthrow him. There was a heavy *boom* as the Browning kicked in his fist and then lifted, planting a second bullet in the closest Nex's face—

And then Carter was moving, leaping, the Browning kicking and blasting in his fist as the Nex went down with hot metal scything faces and throats and drilling eyes from their sockets. Gloved hands reached out for Carter as he grappled his way to the handholds leading to the Comanche's cockpit, but his boots lashed back and connected with heavy *cracks*. He gripped the bottom handhold and hauled himself up onto the helicopter.

449

Natasha was above him and confusion gripped him as she was suddenly punched from the Comanche's fuselage – a sudden violent lurching as blood splashed in a spray from her body and she spun above his head under the impact of bullets. Carter could not understand and the sounds of madness and attack washed over him and all noise was white noise and he reached up, fingers brushing Natasha's fingers as she fell but he was not fast enough and could not reach her and she toppled down into the mass of Nex and they closed over her body like a swarm and she disappeared from sight—

'No,' he said softly.

Carter's head snapped up from his red-stained hands. His gaze was filled with ice death, his lips a narrow line, his face a cold smash of silver against the darkness of the night.

And he realised.

Realised the horrible truth.

He was *alone*.

The Browning kicked in his blood-smeared hand; he swayed to one side on the handholds, movements mechanical, his body running on adrenalin and reflex. A line of bullets cut craters across the battle-scarred fuselage's alloy. The Browning kicked again and now it was Carter's only friend, only true friend, the only comrade he had left.

The bullet hit a Nex between the eyes.

Carter watched coolly as the light in them fled, as the Nex died.

More hands reached for him.

He kicked out, Browning pumping, his heart cold and emotionless. The dead man's click flicked on a switch in his brain. He reached up to the rim of the cockpit, slammed it upwards and leaped up dragging down the smoked glass. His hand slammed down on the controls; the rotors, still spinning, powered up with a roar of the twin LHTecs as Carter slammed down latches and watched the Nex swarm like dark grey bees around and over the Comanche—

And below him Natasha was lost.

He grabbed the control column. Flicked the power on and lifted the Comanche with a scream of engines, a shudder of the aircraft as the nose dipped and he shot up and out over the car park, MiniGun howling with a lethal stutter that punched down and merged Nex with the shredded grass and trees, pulped them into oblivion as Carter's cold detached stare watched their bodies and limbs and organs disintegrate under the awesome monstrosity of the war machine.

The Comanche banked, the concrete highway falling away below.

'Is Jessica dead?' hissed Natasha.

Carter blinked and looked over his shoulder.

But he was alone.

Natasha was gone.

Natasha was dead.

Carter, eyes focused on the night sky beyond, nodded to himself. He reached down, back, fumbling and shoving at the body of Langan lying prone and broken behind and beneath him. He grappled with the spare HIDSS helmet and settled it over his head. He activated the HIDSS, data flashing across his suddenly enhanced night vision—

'Whoa . . .' he said softly.

They were waiting for us, he realised.

Had they known about the meet, about the Comanche? Or had they just responded rapidly to the ECube patch?

How fucking far does this betrayal go?

'*All the way,*' whispered Kade. '*Hey, Carter, we've got company. Come on, buddy, let's taste some fucking blood . . .*'

Carter's gaze flicked to the scanners.

Three helicopters were coming up fast behind him as he headed out over the Pacific. His eyes narrowed and death sat with him like an old friend. His mouth was no longer dry. Fear was an ally; not fear itself but a love of the fear he would inflict.

Rotors roared as the helicopters approached at speed. The night had fallen, and moonlight glimmered from the rotors, dazzling through the holed cockpit canopy. Carter could see a single eye of silver where the bullet that had smashed Langan's life from his body had penetrated the aircraft.

And he thought about Jessica.

And he thought about Natasha.

He groaned.

'Natasha . . .' he whispered in pure agony.

Machine guns roared behind him; rounds clattered against the Comanche and Carter's mask of pain fell away to be replaced with something that even Kade could not replicate.

Hatred fuelled him now.

Hatred – and a need to kill.

Langan's words came back to Carter, hot words filled with a passion for his subject: the war machine. '*We are presently carrying 36 standard 70mm rockets, 18 Stinger air-to-air missiles and 6 Hellfire anti-tank missiles . . .*'

Carter's gaze swept the console. He reached forward, flicked switches, heard motors whirring within the Comanche; he glanced at the scanners, then looked quickly left and right. A squat black powerful helicopter had drawn alongside him to the right and he could see the copper eyes of a Nex. He slammed on the air brakes, dropping the Comanche with dipped nose through the skies, then with a roar of engines and a steeply banking turn that rammed his head back against the pilot's chair the Comanche veered, coming up behind the black helicopter. Carter engaged four Stinger air-to-air missiles – saw the glow from their tails as they detached and watched grimly as they hurtled into the black helicopter. It exploded with a roar and, glowing like the heart of a raging volcano, fell dead and spinning from the skies and smashed into the dark sea below.

Machine guns hammered, dragging Carter's hypnotised stare back to fresh dangers. Red lights flashed on the scanners and the Comanche fell from the skies, howling like an animal in pain to twist and skim close to the surface of the sea – so close that spray splattered against the cockpit and Carter could almost taste the salt.

He killed the lights.

Missiles plunged into the sea behind him.

'You want to fuck with me?' growled Carter. His finger reached out, tracing along the scanner, examining the target and analysis displays. He rammed the helicopter forward, the LHTecs screaming and vibrations pounding through the attack vehicle. The Comanche surged forward, and speed powered through Carter's brain; waves crashed just below the Comanche and there . . .

Against the black waves.

A tanker.

Carter swept low, the Comanche droning, followed by the two remaining helicopters and their Nex pilots. Carter banked the Comanche in low and tight, skimming the waves. The black helicopters followed. Machine guns fired. Bullets rattled against the huge oil tanker.

The Comanche lifted, skimming over the ship's elevated bridge and the black helicopters followed flying close to each other. The pilots were extremely skilled.

'Tune in,' said Carter softly.

He flicked several switches and engaged a digital readout. He smiled, a smile that conveyed only a longing for destruction and death.

'Turn on.'

He hit the air brakes. The LHTecs screamed in response. The two black helicopters veered, one to either side, in reflex response to his insane manoeuvre. Carter hurled the Comanche up into the air, climbing, lifting to ascend like a rocket, reaching for the stars. Carter gazed up into that black glittering expanse as the Comanche rumbled and screamed and vibrated around him and he prayed, prayed to a God he no longer believed in and tears rolled down his cheeks and his teeth ground in anger and hatred. As scanners blazed at him with low-oxygen read-outs he kicked the Comanche around in a tight arc and then dropped from the sky towards the distant tanker far below – his marker – twisting and spinning. The black helicopters were distant targets as Carter allowed the release of a single 70mm rocket . . . Exhaust plumed as the rocket ploughed into the spinning rotors of the second black helicopter, its cockpit and the Nex pilot and sent the machine crashing into the black sea, which swallowed it whole.

'Burn out, motherfucker.'

The Comanche spun, twisting, howling, and its rotors skimmed the sea, slicing through the waves as the aircraft cut an arc and spun and climbed once more with the final black helicopter following close behind with machine guns spitting fire and hatred and hatred and hatred . . .

They climbed towards the stars.

Wind howled through the hole in the cockpit.

Carter's tears chilled like crystals of diamond against his freezing skin.

And there, hundreds of metres above the sea, the Comanche levelled out and spun in a slow lazy arc. Carter slowed the speed, until the machine hung, hovering, stationary; his head drooped, eyes looking at nothing but the floor. And then his gaze lifted and he stared into the darkness ahead of him. His teeth clamped.

The last black helicopter came level, perhaps a hundred metres away.

Carter flicked the rocket restraints free.

His eyes narrowed.

'You want to fuck with me?' he whispered.

'Fuck him, Carter, make him taste blood,' whispered Kade like a bad injection of essence of ghost.

'I don't need your help,' snarled Carter.

Hatred was his master.

The black helicopter's engines howled; Carter could hear them even over the roar of the Comanche's LHTecs. Its nose dipped as it powered forward with its machine guns firing and Carter growled and hammered the Comanche on through the dark black bullet hail.

The two war machines hurtled towards one another. In the blink of an eye they had closed at speed, machine guns roaring, tracer bullets spinning lines of fire across the short distance. They veered, the Comanche twisting down and to one side, the black helicopter nearly over the top – but not quite ... A billion glittering crystal fragments shot out in a shimmering display as the Comanche's armoured rotors smashed the enemy's cockpit canopy into dust and sliced the Nex pilot cleanly in two.

The Comanche danced sideways, away from its dark and bloody deed.

Globules of blood spun up and out on ice-rimed rotors.

Within the black helicopter, the Nex looked down, mouth open in disbelief. Its body relaxed into two halves, the head and upper torso gesturing insanely in sudden panic as it slid into the footwell. The black helicopter tipped, Nex blood pooling in its interior, and screamed down into the sea. And was gone.

Searchlights from the crawling tanker strobed across the dark waves.

Carter breathed. Slowly.

'That was fucking nasty,' said Kade carefully.

'Fuck you.'

'Temper, temper.'

At a more sedate pace, the Comanche dropped lower, skimmed the dark waves and shot like a bullet across the watery desert desolation of the empty dark seas.

The Comanche flew on over the Pacific.

Carter glanced down at the corpse with which he was cramped into the cockpit, half seated upon: an unloving intimacy – the flesh was still warm, he could feel it through his own clothes. He tried not to think about the destroyed face and the pulp of blood and brains smeared over the inside of the cockpit. The smell made him want to be sick, though it had evaded his awareness in the turmoil of battle. Until now.

'You're better off alone, buddy. You know she was the enemy; you know she was bad.'

'Leave me be, Kade. I can do without your shit.'

'You need me, buddy.'

'I'm not your fucking buddy, *buddy.*'

'Ooooh, touchy.'

456

Carter licked at his lips and guided the Comanche low, no particular destination in mind, just needing to fly, to run, to flee, to get away from the Nex and the horror they represented, the *death* they represented . . .

What to do now? he thought. Carter sighed out loud. I'm tired, so tired. Tired of everything.

'And so we need to think; to plan. Contact Jam – he can help you, Carter; he can kick you out of this brain-fuck childish melancholy – hah, just because the bitch is dead. You need to become strong again, Carter. Jam will help you do that!'

Carter pulled free the ECube. In the insect-head-like HIDSS, a dark visor surveyed the soft blue digits. He scrolled and punched in Jam's descramble code and waited. The ECube rattled in his hand.

'Carter?'

'Jam – I'm in a world of shit!'

'Carter – you remember our motto?'

'Yeah?'

'Remember it.'

The ECube died.

Carter smiled grimly. *Remember the Kamus.*

Carter thought back.

Kamus-5.

And it sent a cold chill through his soul.

He chewed his lip for a moment.

'Fuck, I need a cigarette.'

Natasha.

He remembered her pretty face.

A little part of his soul said: No.

But he knew; deep down. They had her; there was no escaping. *No* fucking escaping.

'Now isn't the time to roll over and die,' snapped Kade.

'Why not?' said Carter gently.

'*Because you're stronger than that. Because we can get through this; all we need is time and a little brotherly solidarity — man, we can work together now that bitch is gone. We can be strong again.*'

'Kade, I despise you.'

'*No, you don't Carter. You are me; and you can't hate yourself.*'

'I always have . . . Listen, don't you ever get tired, Kade? Tired of the killing?'

'*It is why I exist,*' said Kade darkly.

Carter nodded, the HIDSS bobbing. He banked the Comanche, there was a drone from the engines and they spun out across the Pacific Ocean; beneath them the waves rolled and the sea seemed suddenly endless, a vast world of black merciless beauty stretching out for ever and beckoning for them to jump aboard and ride her into a sweet-tasting oblivion . . .

'Kamus-5,' said Carter softly, nodding to himself. The blood speckles and smears had dried on his hands, on his face, on his clothes. He looked demonic in the gloomy light. 'We made a pact; that the land of the Kamus was sort of holy; sort of *evil*.'

'*Are we going there, brother?*'

'Yes.' Carter nodded to himself.

'*You know, that motherfucker Langan stitched us up bad. Dumb fuck led them right to us . . . If I had known I would have shot the stupid bastard myself; drilled out his eyes and puked into his skull. I wish I had known. I wish . . .*'

Carter ignored Kade; Kade was an insignificant buzz of insect talk in his head. Carter felt sick. Carter felt cold. Carter felt alone.

Somebody is going to pay, he realised.

Somebody is going to pay bad.

458

CHAPTER 23

THE KAMUS

□ Ωclass relay □ qiii mainframe code logon
01001010
booting . . . sequences initiated . . .

Carter fell from infinite dark dreams out of one world of
pain and into another – a world of pain that was wakefulness. Pain: pure and white, it pounded his temples and
brainstem like a lump hammer. A diamond drill bit
pierced his eyelids and popped his eyes. A razor wire
sliced layers from his cerebellum. His mind was crushed
in an iron grip and held for all eternity.

He forced open his eyelids and looked up into a face he
knew only too well.

'How goes it, old buddy?' asked Jam, grinning. The
tall man was standing, leather coat wrapped around his
frame, hands in pockets, a smoking cigarette hanging
loosely from between his lips. His hair was still spiked,
his eyes dark-ringed and hooded but twinkling with an
inner humour laced with concern. 'Thought you'd fucking died on us out there. You touched down in that

battered war machine and bam, out you went like a fucking light!'

'Not good,' sighed Carter, wincing as he eased himself tenderly into a sitting position. He noted his Browning to his right, beside the bed where they must have dragged him. 'That to share, you stingy old bastard?'

Jam held the cigarette towards Carter. 'What's mine is yours, and yours is mine.' Carter's weary face brightened a little and he took the cigarette, took a long drag, passed the cigarette back and lifted the barrel of the Browning gently under Jam's chin. Jam blinked, hand outstretched to receive the weed. He coughed slowly.

'You seem a touch on edge,' he said at last, after a long meditative pause.

'Let's see both hands,' said Carter, and Jam could see there was no humour and no compassion and no give in the man he had once called a friend. Jam removed his other hand from the coat pocket and spread his fingers wide.

'What's going on, Carter?'

'Where's Slater and Nicky?'

'Out front.'

'Where?'

'On the landing yard.'

'Let's walk; you in front. And don't make me shoot you in the back, Jam, because it would be a fucking bad ending to a good long friendship. Unfortunately, events have conspired to fuck with my brain; I can no longer trust anybody. Not even you. The Nex are fucking everywhere.'

'We did Belfast together,' said Jam, his voice hoarse through gritted teeth.

'I know we did. And in a few minutes we'll either be sharing a drink or a new adventure in the Realms of the

460

Beyond. I shared a history with Gol, but a fucker who looked just like him still tried to kill me.'

They moved down the draught-filled stone tunnels, Jam's coat flapping in the gentle cool mountain gusts. Carter walked carefully behind the other man, aware of how fast he could move and how deadly he really was. He might have a glib tongue and a wicked way with the women, but he was a deadly killer. Very deadly.

They emerged into the darkness of pitch-black night.

Slater was sitting on his pack; Nicky had unpacked a small stove and was cooking food. They both turned as Jam and Carter entered—

'You OK, Jam?' growled Slater, rising quickly, hands straying towards his gun.

'No worries,' said Jam softly, waving for the large man to sit down.

Carter pocketed the Browning. Jam turned, gently patted the face of his old friend. 'You're a dumb mother-fucker, Carter, you know that?'

'Hey, sue me,' said Carter, moving over to the food. 'Smells good.'

'You pull a gun on him?' asked Nicky.

Carter nodded.

She shook her head. 'You mad bastard – he's here to help.'

'I'll be the judge of that.'

Jam jogged over and squatted beside the group. 'Right, then – to business, now that Carter has it solid in his mind that I am real. I presume you know what's going down with Spiral?'

Carter nodded. 'I know some of the Divisions have been wiped out, some of the DemolSquads have been murdered by assassins. There's some kind of splinter faction that has a processor that can take over the global

461

military and is intent on world domination. And it was being run by two men: Feuchter and Durell. Only I killed Feuchter back in Saudi Arabia, when Spiral_Q blew up.'

'Yeah, it really is that bad,' said Jam, grimacing. 'They've hit Spiral, and fucking hit them hard. Apparently they used this processor to hack Spiral mainframes, put us all in fucked-up situations where they could take us out.' He took a breath and his eyes were wild, flaring with adrenalin. He lit a cigarette, grabbed a fork and speared a sausage. 'Yeah, we found out much the same with the help of The Priest. Gol worked with Durell, way back, on something called the Nex Project – although no bastard seems to know what it was, or what it did. Gol pulled out, but Durell carried on with the work until Spiral withdrew the funding and moved him more on to medicines. Gol then moved to Prague – hey, and you know the history behind *that* little venture.'

'How did you find out about this Nex Project?' said Carter softly.

'Well, we've been talking to some of the remaining DemolSquads – Nicky and Slater have pulled a few in here to the Kamus. They're out now, helping The Priest with his *various projects*.'

'Thank fuck for that. So we weren't all wiped out?'

Jam grinned nastily. 'Take more than a few copper-eyed cunts to wipe this bunch of Squads from the face of the earth. Once we'd discovered the shit that was going down, we used ECubes to relay messages to the Squads who were still alive; created our own little network, piggy-backed on descramble codes. Then we started to work on finding out just where those fuckers have run to.'

'But?'

'Aye, there's always a but,' said Jam, blowing smoke into the night. He frowned as Slater shovelled food into

462

his maw without offering anybody a single sausage. Jam reached over and stole another one, peering at it in the gloom as smoke trailed from his nostrils.

'Demol16 was hot on your trail when you left England with Natasha. Apparently the TacSquads had a special interest in you – fucking secret police sniffing around your coat tails. Demol16 was sent to monitor you but always ended up being one step behind – they turned up to a fucking massacre in Africa; they nearly died there, Carter, fucking Nex crawling all over the place. Then they tracked you to Saudi Arabia, but lost you shortly after the explosion.'

'What did Demol16 find in Saudi?'

'A mess: the remains of Spiral_Q. But no Feuchter.'

'That's because I killed him,' said Carter through gritted teeth.

'There were no signs of his body. Even though he was involved in an explosion, they had top grade PFScanners and there were no genetic residues – no traces at all. *Somebody* must have come back for his corpse.'

'Why do that?' said Carter.

Jam shrugged. 'No fucking idea. What use is a fried chicken carcass? But anyway, we lost you after that until your ECube blast. Glad you remembered the descramble code, old buddy.' Jam bit into his sausage and chewed thoughtfully. Then he stood, walked towards the edge of the landing yard and the Apache, and stared out into the Austrian night. His long leather coat whipped around him in the wind.

Carter stepped up beside him.

Together, they stared out into the depths of blackness below. The wind howled around them, buffeting them on the cliff edge; here there were no parapets, no barriers – just a long steep fall into rocky chaos below. Far beneath the two men occasional lights twinkled: synthetic stars deep down towards the ground – bright yellow, white, and sometimes red.

'I love it here,' said Jam softly.

'Yeah. Love the insanity of the place.'

'They should never have closed it.'

'Well, your splinter faction *reopened it.*'

'Only as a temporary measure.'

The two men shared a moment of pleasure.

'What are your plans now?' said Carter.

'This splinter faction of Spiral has a mobile division based on a fucking warship, if you can believe that. Durell, the fucker, thinks he is going to dominate the world, or something shite like that. We've got to stop him.'

'We?'

Jam turned and grasped Carter's shoulders. 'You're part of our army now, Carter. You're a Demolitions expert; we need you.'

'I have my own war to fight.'

'And what war is that?'

'A war in my head,' said Carter softly.

'Well, I'll let The Priest convince you.'

Carter scowled. 'You've brought that mad fucker back here? He's a fucking liability.'

'Not just him,' said Jam. 'All of them.'

'All of who?'

'All the remaining DemolSquads,' said Jam, eyes gleaming in the glow of his cigarette. 'Durell and Feuchter – and those Nex fuckers – they have brought us a war. Now it's time for a little friendly retribution. There ain't enough time for the USA or China or Russia to get to Durell and his fucking warship . . . large parts of NATO's C&C – Command and Control – structure keeps crashing, spinning off-line and killing its own

464

data . . . It looks like Durell's plan is, well, going according to plan. I think we should fuck it up for him good and proper. Now, come over here. I suggest we sit down – drink the bottle of Lagavulin I packed especially for my old friend – and while we wait for the heavy mob, you can bring us up to speed on what exactly happened in LA.'

Carter smiled; the expression felt strange on his face. 'Lagavulin, you say?'

'Well matured.' Jam winked. He strolled over, booted Slater from his pack and drew out a bottle of whisky and some small glasses. 'Drink, anybody? A toast to Spiral's tough little boys winning against all odds?'

Carter laughed then; giggled like a schoolboy. 'Give me a glass,' he spat dryly. 'I need a fucking drink.'

Carter lay on the floor in the corner, snoring. Slater was curled up beside him, also snoring. Nicky had disappeared for a 'long soak in a bath'. And that left only—

Jam. He sat at the mouth of the tunnel, staring out into the night, mulling over thoughts of battleships and the Nex killers. He could not understand; could not understand why their eyes were so strange, could not understand why they were so good at killing. Because he knew that *he* was one of the best, and that he was totally outclassed by the Nex. In one-on-one combat with a Nex he would be dog meat.

'What the fuck did they do to you to make you like that?' he mused through a mouthful of smoke. 'What was the Nex Project? And why did Gol pull out in those early days?'

He watched the smoke as it was snatched by the wind and dispersed.

Like us, he realised. Dispersed. Broken up. Scattered . . .

465

And he remembered the pain on Carter's face; the pain from talk of Natasha's death.

Jam shook his head.

Shit always happens to good people, he realised. It's just the way of the world.

A low drone came from over the mountains.

And then, in a burst of anticlimax, a Piasecki Pathfinder-3 helicopter loomed from the darkness, hoving ponderously into view, and climbed slightly, then dropped, suddenly, unsteadily, rotors clattering, towards the landing yard. Engines screamed. The rotors whined in deceleration. There was a strange banging sound and a bad smell of old oil.

Jam shaded his eyes against the glare of the Pathfinder's landing lights, climbed to his feet and strode across the stone.

A grinning face met Jam's scowl, and a short squat man leaped down. He had powerful arms and shoulders plastered with tattoos from a life in the military; his head was shaved, bullet-shaped, and his round cheeks were a rosy red. 'How's it going, pussy?' he bellowed at Jam.

Jam blinked.

'Haggis – what – the fuck – is that?'

'It's a 'copter, ain't it?'

'I don't know,' said Jam slowly, walking alongside one rusted flank and staring in disbelief at the huge ragged hole that revealed nestling fuel pipes. 'Haggis, *where* did you get it?'

'Stole it. From an Italian. Is a long story.'

Jam sighed.

'You think we're going to wage a war using *that*?'

'Sorry, Jam.' Haggis gave a red-faced scowl. 'But we can't all nick fucking Apaches, right? They're not the sort

466

of thing that are ten a fucking penny! It's not like hot-wiring a fucking Escort!'

'OK, OK, calm down. Go and get yourself a brew. Are the others on their way?'

'Aye,' nodded Haggis. 'They're coming, all right.'

And come they did.

Shortly after the arrival of Haggis, the dark sky was filled with a clattering of rotors and howling engines. A squad of helicopters, two Lockheed AH-56A machines followed by a Sikorsky Black Hawk, made a majestic entrance and slowly touched down. Jam's face glowed as eight men and a woman disembarked. They exchanged greetings, Jam laughing at the custard spilled down Bob Bob's combats, and the weary group of DemolSquad operatives moved into the protective embrace of Kamus-5 in search of a brew and some chocolate biscuits.

Jam stood, hands on hips, staring at the six helicopters gathered in the yard; still the machines were dwarfed by the sheer rock walls, the huge expanse of barren stone, rocky and uneven, carved from the very mountain itself. His memories drifted back: he could still picture the base when it had been operational . . . but that had been twenty years ago when he had been a young bright-eyed man without the weight of years and the weight of murder burdening his shoulders.

Jam took his seat once more. Lit a cigarette.

'Hiya.'

He glanced up at Nicky.

'Hi, love.'

She handed him a tin mug filled with steaming tea. 'Lots of sugar, Jam, just how you like it.'

'Cheers.' He took a sip and stared back out over the darkness. Austria nestled below him.

'You OK?'

'Yeah,' he sighed, wrapping his leather coat around him. 'Just tired. Tired of it all.'

Nicky sat beside him, snuggling up close, and he looked at her, surprised. She rested her head against his chin and the smell of her hair filled his senses.

'Hello?'

'Mmmm?'

'You feeling horny or something?' He grinned his boyish flirtatious roguish grin; it was the sort of chat-up line that had got him beaten about the head on many drunken occasions.

Nicky met his gaze. His cheeky grin disappeared when he saw the seriousness there. 'You've always been an insolent fucker, Jam. But I have enjoyed working with you. I feel – I don't know – I have a very, very bad feeling about what we're going to do.'

Jam nodded. 'It's a war,' he said softly. 'Durell, and Feuchter – they brought us a war. They tried to wipe us out; now it's time to give them a bullet up the arse.'

'Yeah. But . . . not everybody is going to make it back.' She licked her lips. They gleamed in the light from Jam's cigarette. She reached up, suddenly, and kissed him. Their lips stayed pressed together, tongues darting, and Jam felt lust smash through his body with a ferocity that he had forgotten.

She pulled away.

Jam stared into her beautiful eyes.

'I need some company tonight,' she said, her voice husky.

Jam nodded. Speechless. And, standing, she led him inside by the hand.

As the tendrils of dawn light crept over the mountains, Jam rose bleary-eyed and happy from the pallet bed. The covers fell away to reveal Nicky's bronzed skin, a rounded breast peeking from above the covers. Jam rubbed at his eyes, then at his stubble, lit a cigarette and stumbled in his boxer shorts and socks down the draughty stone corridor.

Noise greeted him and, shielding his eyes, a cigarette limp between his lips, he stepped out into the dawn . . .

And into a hive of activity.

There were at least a hundred helicopters, filling the yard with their metal menace. Some had engines screaming, rotors hissing through the air as men and women stood by, staring into engine compartments or filling the machines with fuel. Others merely stood, waiting for the mission, glinting in the glorious dawn sunlight.

Jam's jaw dropped.

He could see Fegs, Bob Bob, Jones5 and Russian, all working on their helicopters, dark oil staining their arms and hands. Blitz and the sexy lithe Czech assassin named AnnaMarie were carrying jerrycans of fuel to their rusting steeds, while Carter sat nearby, his head in his hands, cigarette dangling from his lips as The Priest stood above him, quoting from his small leather Bible, a look of wild hatred in his eyes, spittle dripping from his impassioned lips. Jam's gaze roved across groups of men and women he had trained with and fought beside. Some he had trained himself. Hundreds of his DemolSquad operative friends had all been brought together here for the first time, the only time. The last time.

Pride filled him.

His chest swelled and he took a step forward. Several of those nearby glanced up, smiling, giving the occasional wave. A torrent of strength flooded through Jam and drowned his despair.

'Can I have your attention!' he bellowed.

Activity died down, and slowly all the DemolSquads turned towards this man in his underwear. His gaze met with that of The Priest, who gave him a quick thumbs-up sign.

Jam took a drag on his cigarette. 'I see you all standing in front of me,' he rumbled, his words coming out on a cloud of smoke, 'and it fills me with pride; it fills me with love; and it fills me with strength. There is a great enemy that we will face today, a fucker that we must smash to make the world a better place, a fucker we must kill. I talk about the terrorists who have sought to bring down Spiral from within; the people who have sought to murder us all over the last few months. The betrayers of the Spiral cause. The men who have betrayed not just Spiral but their *friends* as well.'

A few clapped.

Jam's wild-eyed gaze roved over the gathered group. He exchanged glances with Dublin, Sarah and Legs. 9mm gave him a small wave, her dark eyes flashing bright with love for him, and Jam beamed her a huge smile: they had been through good times together. His gaze took in Jupiter, Mongrel, Banks, Kavanagh and Ballard: all were ready, all had weapons primed, all were ready to go to war against the evil that was attempting to fuck the world and fuck it bad.

Jam smiled slowly.

'This processor, the QIII which the enemy possess – it is masking their presence, hiding their mobile operations, their *warship* from the world's military until they are ready to subvert all countries' own war systems – and that will be soon. Very soon. Once that happens, they will be unstoppable . . . Demol16 found them while sweeping the Arctic –' there came a small cheer '– and now *we* are the only ones who can make a difference. We are on our own . . . but we will win,' he said, his words soft as he tossed his spent cigarette down. 'We will break them. I will complete briefing of operations in thirty minutes; people, be ready to move in one hour. We have some madmen to kill.'

Carter walked slowly among the groups, between CH-47s, past a Bell UH-1N Iroquois – the famous Huey – and a 1967 Sikorsky HH-3 that looked severely the worse for wear. A hundred helicopters; many sported home-made artillery attachments and many had had heavy machine guns welded to their frames, feeds of ammunition dangling from makeshift containers made from plastic boxes. Inside many machines he could see bundles of explosives strapped together with masking tape, grenades, and anti-personnel mines that had been stripped and cobbled together as makeshift bombs. Pride swelled through Carter, and he understood just how Jam had felt; never before had he seen such a gathering of DemolSquad operatives. And these were the survivors; these were the toughest of the tough, the men and women who had fought off attacks by the Nex and had slain hundreds of them.

Every man and woman had a grudge.

Every man and woman had lost friends to the Nex – and to those who were behind the Nex.

Every man and woman wanted a slice of the payback cake.

Carter halted. The Priest had been following him around for the last hour, quoting from the Bible and reciting mantra-like phrases at him as if possessed. Carter turned and looked up into the big man's gold-flecked brown eyes. The Priest was large; one of the largest men Carter had ever seen.

'Can you *fucking* leave me alone,' said Carter.

'I see, my son, that you are aggrieved,' rumbled The Priest, closing his Bible slowly. The book was dwarfed in his huge hands. 'But I seek merely to make light of your pain, to fill your soul with joy in this most strenuous of times, to fill you with light before the coming battle with the evil God-mocking Satanic Hordes.'

'Well, don't – just don't. I need calm; I need to compose myself.'

'I see that you have suffered great loss at the hands of Durell and Feuchter. The Lord will pay back these evil men with flashes of lightning from Heaven; the Lord shall smite down our enemies, He shall fuck them up bad.' The Priest grinned then; he had lost many teeth, mainly in pub brawls while trying to convert Satan's unholy drinkers. 'Carter, my son, put your trust in the Lord and He will surely guide thee.'

'I'll put my trust in my Browning 9mm, Priest,' said Carter, smiling. 'It worked wonders on Feuchter, and it will work wonders today.'

The Priest frowned.

'Feuchter still has to be punished.'

Carter shook his head. 'Feuchter is dead, Priest; I killed him myself. Filled him full of holes, left him to suffer a bomb blast that would have ripped him limb from fucking limb.'

'You are wrong, my friend. For whatever reason, the Lord protected him; saved him for fiery retribution from the skies.'

'How do you know this? Demol16?'

'No – I saw him, when we intercepted an ECube transmission, a visual. He had sent a message to Durell; their arrogance is colossal, for they think we are as nothing. They think we are broken and ground as ashes into the dust. But Feuchter *was* alive, Carter. You can believe me on this.'

Carter's jaw clamped tight. 'That fucker just will not die.'

'There is more.'

'More?'

The Priest nodded. 'Natasha is there – on that warship, on that Spiral abomination. She was shot in LA, yes, but she did not die; she featured in Feuchter's message to Durell.'

'Natasha! Alive!' Hope died as soon as it had flared. 'Impossible,' growled Carter.

'Impossible that they would seek to save a bartering tool against you, their greatest proven enemy?'

'Me?'

'You scare them, Carter. They fear you. There is a dark demon in your soul, a seed there, and they can see it nestling within you.'

'They seek to draw me to them?'

'Like a lamb to the slaughter,' said The Priest softly.

Carter moved away from the hive of rag tag DemolSquad members into the cool confines of the Kamus mountain complex. He walked, for what seemed like hours, down darkened, long-disused corridors, his mind whirling, images of Natasha flittering like lost fragments through his brain, sadness overtaking him, then anger, then frustration, disbelief.

If she was alive, then he had to save her.

And Feuchter – alive, and using her as bait?

Carter smiled grimly.

'Our reunion will be a sweet one,' he said softly.

The briefing was over. The DemolSquads were making final preparations for their departure, including the incorporation of some highly sophisticated guns that could be mounted beneath their helicopters to help combat surface-to-air and air-to-air missiles.

From Austria, they were to fly to the north and east, across Europe and Russia, skirting the northerly Barents Sea and on towards Novaya Zemlya and the Arctic Ocean beyond where Jam and Demol16 and The Priest had tracked Spiral_mobile using The Priest's world network of spies, his illegal (even by Spiral standards) web of optical and digital communications, and good old-fashioned TacSquad scouts. There they would find a ship – a cruiser-class battleship similar in size and specifications to the Russian *Kirov* class. The ship was a dull matt black and had no name. Displacing 28,000 tonnes of water, it was a huge vessel that would no doubt hold many surprises for the attacking DemolSquads. But one thing was certain: all the men and women involved were willing to die to bring the enemies of Spiral to justice.

Carter stood watching the bustle, his Browning in his hand. Slater had checked over the Comanche and had refuelled her, ready for Carter's part in the battle. Carter did not care.

'Jam!'

Jam, now dressed, walked swiftly towards his friend. 'Yeah?'

'I need to ask a favour.'

'Anything.'

'I thought Natasha was dead but The Priest has informed me that I was wrong. Feuchter and Durell have her, they have her aboard the battleship. I need time, Jam; I need time to get in there and get her the fuck out before you blow it up.'

Jam stood, mouth open. 'What are you asking me, Carter? To hold up a fucking operation like *this*?'

474

'Yes. I need this, Jam; I need the chance to get her out.' Carter gritted his teeth. He stared into the eyes of his oldest friend. 'Come on, man, you can't let her die in there – I *know* what you've fucking got planned . . . come on, *please*,' he said.

Jam closed his mouth. He frowned, glancing over his shoulder. Then he met Carter's iron gaze.

'Just supposing I was to let you do this, how will we work it?'

'We fly in, and I use the cover of the battle to get inside the warship . . . and get Natasha out. It's all I've ever fucking asked you for, Jam; all I've ever, ever asked for.'

'You *do* know what I plan, don't you, Carter?' said Jam softly.

Carter nodded. 'Bomb in a bag?'

'Well, a nuke in a suitcase, to be more precise. A home-made neutron device. You need to be well the fuck away from there, Carter – this baby is going down *big style*.'

Carter's mouth was a grim line.

'I'll be out, Jam, with Natasha. If I'm not . . .' He left the sentence unfinished and Jam scowled, licking his lips.

'As long as you know the score, buddy. I can give you an extra few minutes . . . no more . . .'

Carter nodded; he knew the score, all right. He knew the dangers, the risks, the Hell that he would have to travel through before he could come out the other side and get his life back to normal. Normal? He laughed.

'Let's do it – and do it *now*,' said Jam.

□ Ωclass relay □ qiii mainframe code logon
01001010
booting . . .
booting . . . sequences initiated . . .

GetCommandLineAt □ GetVersion›
□ GetProcAddress & □ GetModuleHandleA }
ExitProcess ż
□ TerminateProcess ÷ GetCurrentProcess $ □
GetModuleFileNameA
□ GetEnvironmentVariableA u □ GetVersionExA □
□ HeapDestroy › □ HeapCreate ¿ □ VirtualFree Ÿ
□ HeapFree m
□ SetHandleCount
R6026
– not enough space for spiral initialisation
error
R6025
– pure virtual function call
R6024
accessing data scripts □
demolition squads// coordinates confirmed
attack procedures confirmed . . .

The sun had risen, glittering like a series of firework
explosions along the peaks of the ice-capped mountains,
filling the sky with a cool sapphire blue that surrounded
Carter and filled his soul with an easy gentle peace.

He breathed deeply inside the HIDSS.

Slater's repair on the hole in the cockpit was holding
up well, and Carter found it a pleasure to actually pilot
the vehicle without having to sit on the corpse of another
dead man . . . another dead *friend*.

As he flew, and the noise of the engines filled his
senses, he focused on controls and weapons, revising their
operation, revising the procedures. Kamus-5 and a slack-
handed Slater had provided full tanks of fuel. Carter
checked the navcomp.

Coordinates 000.002.006

South of the Arctic Ocean, of the North Pole.

A Continent of Ice . . .

When he was happy with the Comanche, happy with its motion and stability and his own confidence in operating the machine, Carter analysed himself: and he felt good.

No, he felt more than good. He felt fucking *alive*.

Behind the Comanche, a dark ragged line on the horizon, followed the remaining living DemolSquads in their massive range of aerial war machines. Carter took the lead not out of choice but because the Comanche housed the most advanced detection equipment of this group; this band; this new model *army*.

Walking point, he mused grimly.

And now he knew what he had to do. He had to get Natasha out. But more than that: this was about Jessica, and Langan, and Gol. This was about Spiral. This was about betrayal, and Feuchter and Durell. This was about life and death. This was about finishing what others had begun. This was about finding the truth. And this was about—

Revenge.

Not for himself, no. For the innocents, the people who had died merely because they were in the way. The people who didn't have a job where they were expected to take a bullet and be happy with the outcome.

Carter knew. Knew that he had to stop this thing and stop it fast.

What can one man do? mocked his subconscious.

One man can do enough, he replied calmly.

He dropped the Comanche's altitude, flying low over fields of snow in northern Russia and then down towards great sprawling forests. He flew fast over small villages of white-walled red-roofed houses; he even fancied he heard the ringing of church bells.

477

Sunday, then, he thought. Is it?

He checked the Comanche's computers.

Yeah, Sunday. The Day of Rest. The Day of Worship.

I'll give them something to worship, he thought grimly.

The Priest would not be a happy man, he chuckled to himself.

Carter checked himself: his body was sore, aching, suffering from a myriad of minor aches and pains and bruises and scratches. He flexed his bound finger; it was almost healed – or, at least, enough to allow him to use it sparingly. His ribs didn't click as much when he moved, although the soreness was a nuisance and his stomach still gave him twinges of pain. But he had taken some tablets and this irritant had faded . . . His smashed nose was his biggest problem. It was bent, broken. His nostrils were still clogged with blood. It had taken just too much shit to have healed and he knew deep down that it was his weak spot, his Achilles heel. To take another blow there? The pain would scream through his head and he would be blind . . .

Primary location for protection, then, he mused idly.

The Comanche hummed over a huge swathe of forest, closely followed by its lengthy growling wake of metal war machines, their shadows tumbling across the land and then over a cliff and down towards a huge inland lake. Carter checked to make sure that they were near no military or aviation bases.

They needed peace, not a chase.

And *he* wanted the serenity of the sea . . .

I wonder how Sam is? he thought suddenly, picturing the insane plump chocolate Labrador in his mind. He realised that he missed the dog; really missed it.

When Carter had kicked Sam out of his house on the approach of the assassin Nex, the Labrador would have made his way down the valley in search of food and the next cottage. Old Mrs Humphreys often fed the fat mutt and looked after him when Carter was away on missions.

She'd better be looking after you, you dumb fat mongrel, thought Carter.

Better be taking real good care of you.

With a shock he realised that he might never see the dog again. This annoyed him and he chewed his lip. The chances were that he would die; he would take the fight to them, fuck them up bad and sour their links with Spiral and then die . . .

And Natasha . . . well, Natasha could already be dead.

So be it, he mused bitterly.

He forced himself to relax as the Comanche at last flew low over the sea. Occasionally he passed fishing boats, and occasionally the fishermen would wave at him, forcing him to smile sadly.

What happy lives they lead, he thought.

What normal, happy lives.

Why couldn't I have been normal? he thought . . .

Because you kill – said a small voice in his head.

Because you kill and you are good at killing.

You might hate it.

You might loathe it.

But whether you like it or not, you are *good* at it.

A natural-born shooter.

A predator.

A tiger, rather than a lamb.

The world of ice waters opened up ahead of this ragtag army after they had traversed the Barents Sea: a harsh landscape of intense and frightening beauty, a terrible world of choppy freezing ocean with torn blocks of ice rising up, mingled and merged and tossed frozen together in rigid flow streams. The Comanche flew low, coming in off the unquiet cold waters as sunlight glimmered across the icy world.

He shivered. The Comanche shuddered.

Carter checked the coordinates and slowed his speed as he started to approach the estimated location of the battleship, the *Kirov*-class cruiser. The scanners still read zero: nothing. He flew. The Comanche, despite flying in temperatures well below what Carter thought would be its operating norm, was responding well and as long as no vicious storms came up over the bustling cloud-filled grey and sapphire horizon, Carter knew the 'copter would get him there in one piece . . .

A crazy thought slammed into his mind.

The Priest was wrong.

They were all wrong.

There was nothing; nothing but freezing sea, and cold cold ice flows.

Laughter welled up madly in his throat as he flipped free the HIDSS and with the power of ordinary human eyesight transgressed a billion dollars of technological development funding. Then he saw it. A black dot on the horizon: a matt black sentinel, squatting against the grey churning freezing waters.

Carter would have to be ready; he would have to be strong; he would have to be a machine without emotion . . . without fear . . .

The black dot started to grow; to materialise; to enlarge before Carter's very eyes.

The battleship was moving at a rapid speed for a ship so large; a churning wake of white foam followed it.

Carter grinned nastily within the insect-like HIDSS helmet.

All I want, he thought, are answers before I die.

All I want, he thought, is to kill those responsible – before I die.

He had resigned himself. Made his peace with God – or whatever other warped and wicked deity was waiting for him on the Other Side. Feuchter had asked him once if he was ready to die and now he understood, now he truly understood.

Carter knew.

Knew that he wasn't coming back.

□ Ωclass relay □ qiii mainframe code logon
01001010
booting . . .
□ GetStdHandle □□ GetFileType P □
GetStartupInfoA ² FreeEnvironmentStringsA
³ FreeEnvironmentStringsW Ò □
WideCharToMultiByte □□
GetEnvironmentStrings
□□ GetEnvironmentStringsW ß □ WriteFile □
HeapAlloc » □ VirtualAlloc
¢ □ HeapReAlloc ¿ GetCPInfo ¹ GetACP 1 □
GetOEMCP
Â □ LoadLibraryA ä □ MultiByteToWideChar S □
GetStringTypeA
V □ GetStringTypeW ¿ □ LCMapStringA À □
LCMapStringW / □ RtlUnwind
KERNEL32.dll ~ _AIL_lock@0 v
_AIL_get_preference@4 E □ _AIL_unlock@0
_AIL_lock_mutex@0 F □ _AIL_unlock_mutex@0 □
_AIL_set_error@4 Ê
»»»»»»»»»»»»
errors rectified
q111 01001010 100%on-line

```
operational procedures confirmed
HKLM,%KEY_OPTIONAL%,'sysmon',,'sysmon'
HKLM,%%\sysmon,INF,,'appletpp.inf'
SP1Q,%KEY_OPTIONAL%\sysmon,Installed,,'0'
SP1Q,%KEY_OPTIONAL%,'sysmeter',,'sysmeter'
SP1Q,%KEY_OPTIONAL%\sysmeter,Installed,,'0'
HKLM,%KEY_OPTIONAL%,'netwatch',,'netwatch'
SP1Q,%KEY_OPTIONAL%,'demolimminent',
'demolsquads=37'
HKLM,%KEY_OPTIONAL%\demol,INF,,
'squadthreat.inf'
script engaged script locking engaged
launch sequence initiated= threat=
demolsquad=37
co-ords 234.456.555.211 – eq%345.331
satellites= 248
satellites= qiii operational takeover complete
satellite request= granted
logged.
```

The warship, while not the largest cruiser ever built, was
certainly the most menacing. Its dull matt black flanks
crouched on the ocean crests and it growled through the
sea water, its heavy squat hull smashing the waves apart as
it powered towards its destination. Carter, like the other
members of the DemolSquads, had listened to Jam's
briefing, based on information gathered by a hundred different DemolSquad operatives, including The Priest.
Reconnaissance scouts had learned that the vessel was
armed with extensive weapons and guidance systems, far
superior to those a cruiser would normally carry. As well
as the standard surface missiles and guns, it had extensive
anti-submarine sensors and weapons, and a powerful Mk
IV phased-array radar giving 360° coverage able to track

up to 250 targets simultaneously. It carried fixed-wing aircraft and heavily armed and armoured support helicopters. And the ship was nuclear-powered. Unlike normal cruisers, this machine had a top speed of over 60 knots. And there had been no signs of a crew . . .

Carter hovered for a while at a distance, the Comanche humming softly to him, the HIDSS screaming proximity warnings at him. Below, the sea spun away in circular patterns, brushed aside by down draughts from the 'copter.

And yet—

And yet the cruiser was not on his displays.

The QIII processor, he thought.

It's fucking intercepting satellite, radar and scanner readings.

It's bouncing everything away from the ship!

No wonder it was never discovered . . . and now? Now that the QIII was quite obviously working?

Was he too late?

Behind, despite their agreed radio silence, Jam connected, using the ECube.

'You OK, Carter?'

'Yeah. You guys ready?'

'We're fucking ready. Me and Slater are heading off – we're gonna do our bit for the boys.'

'Be good, Jam. And if you can't be good?'

'I'm always fucking good,' snarled Jam.

Grinning, Carter eased the Comanche forward, leading this huge pack of metal wolves. They grouped closer now, machines coming up and around the Comanche to form a huge black swarm buzzing angrily against the Arctic heavens . . . Carter found himself suddenly tense, awaiting incoming fire, waiting for those huge 12.5cm calibre guns to spit their welcome . . .

The matt black cruiser groaned and growled through the crashing sea. Waves smashed against its prow. The odd seagull cawed, following the mighty vessel in the hope of some stray scrap of food. Sections of ice floated in the water, chunks that were brushed aside easily by the warship's ram.

Carter grimaced.

It began to rain, lightly at first, then a downpour of heavy droplets laced with ice from a tumultuous cold sky; clouds gathered and bunched, huge bruises against the skin of the heavens.

The rain and sleet fell with increased ferocity.

The dark sea churned, rain turning waves into dancing patterns among bobbing blocks of ice.

Against the sky sat an inky blot that expanded, multiplying, replicating; then what had been one blot against the backdrop of the sky became many smaller ones.

'Let's do it,' came the crackle of Carter's voice.

Insect-like, the DemolSquads advanced on the cruiser. They separated; aboard the helicopters, aboard the Lockheed AH-56As, the UH-1N Iroquois Hueys, the CH-47s, the MH-53Js, the MH-60G Pave Hawks, the Apaches and Black Hawks – aboard these metal monsters, these machines of war, stood men and women armed with machine guns and bombs, waiting to fight, waiting to suffer, and waiting to die.

In one machine stood The Priest. His eyes flashed with fire. He pointed down from the heavens; he pointed at the cruiser where a swarm of small black squat powerful helicopters lifted from the decks, rotors screaming through the rain, guns and missiles armed and ready . . .

'Here we go,' muttered Carter, arming the Comanche's weapons systems in a splash of coloured lights and flickering data within the HIDSS. Alarms screamed around him as, on the deck of the battleship, one of the gun turrets rotated on well-oiled rails. The 12.5cm-calibre twin barrels lifted in their angle of ascent; there was a massive concussive *boom* and the turret recoiled.

An advancing DemolSquad helicopter, a Pave Hawk, was plucked from the sky. Fire erupted, glittering bright orange and yellow against the grey sky, a ball of bright iridescence before it smashed down into the sea, rotors spinning screaming splashing into the churning waters where the blackened fire-filled carcass disappeared swiftly below the waves.

Swarms of small black helicopters came sweeping from the darkness and rain, their machine guns hammering.

The DemolSquads returned fire and the skies were suddenly lit by streamers of tracer.

Carter fired off two rockets and allowed the Comanche to spin, rotors scything, below heavy-calibre fire, closely missing a small black helicopter . . . he allowed the Comanche to drop – away and *down* from the battle, and towards the suddenly looming deck of the enemy ship: Spiral_mobile . . .

Above him, bullets crackled across the sky—

And the heavens were painted crimson.

Durell's twisted blackened fingers crept from beneath the soft folds of cloth and his hooded eyes stared into the void. His hand moved, slowly, a sliver of ice down the spine of the world . . . and he gently pressed RETURN.

Nothing . . .

And then a quiet hum filled the massive control deck. The computer monitors that lined the walls dimmed momentarily, as if bowing before some electronic deity, then brightened into life once more.

Words – QIII script – sped across the display. Then, from a laser encoder, a globe sprang into existence, a spinning white-laser representation of the Earth. It hung in front of Durell's face. His gnarled hands lifted and were bathed in white light that illuminated the deformed grotesque within Durell's heavy folded hood.

Durell laughed, a cold and ominous sound.

He reached out and pointed; the globe spun, located its target, and zoomed through layers of sparkling laser light to highlight Spiral_mobile, crashing through the waves. Durell pulled back from his own base and spun the globe; he located the nearest Russian air base and smiled softly.

'So you come to destroy me, my sweet young DemolSquads? Like virgins to the slaughter?'

He initiated the sequence.

The QIII hummed from the heart of the black terminal.

☐ Ωclass relay ☐ qiii mainframe code logon 01001010
booting . . .
HKLM,%KEY_OPTIONAL%,'Sp1on-line',,'sp1on-line'
HKLM,%KEY_OPTIONAL%\sp1on-line,INF,,'appletpp.inf'
HKLM,%%\sp1on-line,Section,,'sp1on-line'
HKLM,%KEY_OPTIONAL%\sp1on-line,Installed,,'0'
HKLM,%KEY_OPTIONAL%\CharMap556ar,Section,,
'CharMap'
SP1Q,%%,'ZipFldr',,'ZipFldr'
SP1Q,%KEY_OPTIONAL%\sysmon,Installed,,'0'
SP1Q,%KEY_OPTIONAL%,'sysmeter',,'sysmeter'
SP1Q,%KEY_OPTIONAL%\sysmeter,Installed,,'0'
HKLM,%KEY_OPTIONAL%,'netwatch',,'netwatch'
tracking . . . located Russian server
krostevskyTTQBGGH1#####
tracking . . . locked.

SP1Q,%KEY_OPTIONAL%,'demolimminent',,
'demolsquads=37'
HKLM,%KEY_OPTIONAL%\demol,INF,,
'squadthreat.inf'

script engaged script locking engaged
launch sequence initiated= threat= demolsquad=37
co-ords 234.456.555.211 – eq%345.331
launch MIG30 fighter config= 32armed
satellite request= granted
logged.

CHAPTER 24

THE SKEIN

The sea crashed and churned against the hull of the warship as it growled forward. Missiles and bombs detonated. There was a deafening roar of explosives from the ship's deck; steel shuddered; helicopters were smashed, burning insanely, from the sky to die, their flames extinguished in the waves. Guns roared, sparks spitting and kicking across metal and flesh.

Out of nowhere, a tiny black vessel was heli-dropped into the bounding waves. It sped at an incredible velocity and with absolutely no sound across the churning waters, crashing into troughs and riding them bravely before gliding up alongside the cruiser. There was a tinny *crack* and it secured itself.

Aboard, two figures gave one another the thumbs-up. Jam lifted his goggles for a second and stared into Slater's eyes. Both men grasped hands, and Jam said:

'This is it.'

'Good luck, brother.'

'If I don't come back . . . tell Nicky I love her.'

Slater guffawed. 'Such sentimentality from the King of Pornt?'

'A favour – for me.'

'Anything, brother,' said Slater, smiling kindly.

'Five minutes; then get the fuck out.'

'Five minutes,' said Slater. He replaced his goggles and hoisted the heavy machine gun, glancing up at the warfare raging above; at the flaming skies; at the turmoil of bullets and bombs and spinning rotors. Machine guns roared; so many guns that it seemed the whole world was at war – and on fire. Orange streaked across the grey of storm clouds.

'Good luck, brother.'

'Luck's got fuck all to do with it,' said Jam, grinning. Hoisting the wide black suitcase in his arms, he dropped backwards over the edge of the tiny boat and was instantly swallowed by the churning black abyss.

Slater sat for a few moments, staring down at the few bubbles that reached the rolling sea surface; then he concentrated on keeping the little boat stable in its umbilical link with the cruiser. He was so close that he could see rivets; he was so close that he could reach out and touch the cold black metal.

Slater nodded to himself.

Justice had to be served – like a plateful of napalm spaghetti, with nuclear dessert.

The Comanche banked low and hard, sweeping around past massive black gun turrets, so close that Carter could see the ship's railings and the windows of cabins. The Comanche banked, past more huge turrets that rocked with recoil and belched fire and shells. The cruiser flashed past in an insane blur, the Comanche screaming its own scream above the crash of the pounding Arctic sea. Carter dragged the machine, engines howling, around and brought it down to land on the deck with a swordlike *clash* of metal upon metal. The rotors howled as they wound down.

'It's a trap,' said Kade calmly.

'Like I give a fuck,' snapped Carter.

He lifted the cockpit canopy and wind and rain lashed in, stinging his skin. He stood, climbed up onto the rim, then lowered himself and dropped to the deck. His boots made dull thumps and he could feel ice, a slick layer beneath him. 'You've been a good girl,' he said, patting the Comanche's flank. The wind snatched his words in a shriek of laughter and twirled them away in a spiral of down draughts as helicopters banked and swept above him, machine guns roaring. A missile shot skywards and a helicopter was sent tumbling, a flaming ball of melting steel, into the freezing ocean.

Carter turned; focused; orientated himself. His stare roved the dark surroundings lit sporadically by fire from the sky and he could see nobody as he palmed his battered trusty old Browning – a small reassurance, but at least it gave him the ability to deal hot metal death to anybody who came near.

Natasha.

Where would she be?

With Feuchter.

'That fucker,' growled Carter. He moved quickly forward across the ice-slippery alloy deck, gaze lifting, scanning the bridges and gantries, the portholes and windows. This felt crazy, totally crazy and Carter felt the burden of his life lift from his shoulders because it did not matter any more, truly nothing mattered and if he was to die then—

So be it.

Carter sprinted towards the nearest doorway. But then everything happened at once – there was a concussive *boom* and a helicopter went hurtling past, low, rotors howling dangerously, and Carter whirled, crouching, bringing the Browning up to see—

'*Nothing,*' whispered Kade.

Behind him, Feuchter slid from the shadows, from the darkness, like a ghost or a demon emerging from another plane of existence. He held a small black gun and his expression was almost serene.

Carter turned and Feuchter nodded slowly. He smiled, showing tombstone teeth. 'Mr Carter, we are expecting you.' Carter fixed his glittering gaze on the muzzle of the gun that pointed straight at his heart . . .

He tried hard to disguise his shock at seeing Feuchter. 'I left you dead.'

'No. You left me *dying*. There is a subtle difference. Gods, the pain I have suffered at your hands, Mr Carter – it will be a pleasure to see you finally shuffle like a reptile from this mortal coil. Now, your gun, please?'

'What makes you think I'll give you it?'

An explosion rocked the ship. Feuchter did not waver, but nodded to something behind Carter. He turned. Behind him stood three Nex, copper eyes glowing, bodies black-clad, all bearing pistols and slung sub-machine guns. They had spread out in silence, and to his shame he had not heard them. These killers were subtly different to the other Nex he had met; they seemed larger, broader, more athletic.

'Previously, you met my scout caste, the 5Nex' said Feuchter. 'These Nex – they are different. These – well, they are the warrior caste.'

Carter licked his lips. He smiled broadly.

'Is Natasha here?'

'She is. She requests the pleasure of your company; she would weep and wail in your arms and seek one final kiss before you both die. Come this way, Mr Carter. Let me show you the Heaven we are building . . .'

'Heaven?'

'It will be a paradise of modern technology,' said Feuchter softly. He gestured with his gun, and Carter allowed the Browning to be taken from him. 'This way.'

'*You soft fucking bitch pussy,*' hissed Kade.

Carter stepped forward.

Towards the black door.

And the gaping maw of uncertainty beyond.

Feuchter led Carter through dim black corridors, metal floors and metal grilles beneath their boots. Light came from below and now that he was out of the wind and rain and ice, Carter could hear the deep distant drone of the cruiser's massive engines.

Feuchter walked ahead of him, his back a broad target. And yet, Carter could see something: a difference. The back of Feuchter's neck and head – it was scar tissue. Severe scar tissue, wrinkled and bright pink; his hair was re-growing but the new growth was not complete – and it was black and crinkled. *Different.* Abnormal . . .

Carter shivered. What the fuck is going on? he thought.

He glanced behind him; the Nex were there, guns trained on his back.

Carter followed Feuchter.

There was little else that he could do.

They descended; steep spiral metal staircases led down. The metal was cold beneath Carter's fingers and he felt his mind blurring; he could feel Kade squatting there, watching, observing, offering nothing.

Good, thought Carter at Kade.

492

Keep your fucking nose out of this.

This is my fight and I will do it alone.

They reached wider corridors and there was more bustle; Nex with gaunt haunted faces rushed about, and without their masks Carter could observe their strange asexual faces. Similar, and yet each one individual, each one different.

'Feuchter, what the fuck are the Nex?' he asked softly.

'Quiet.'

'Or what? You'll kill me?' Carter laughed, a bitter sharp bark. Carter looked Feuchter up, then down. His smile was sickly sweet. 'Come on, Feuchter, answer my question.'

Feuchter halted. He turned. His gaze was burning.

'They are human, Carter, just like you and me. But they are killers, incredibly efficient killers. I thought you were friends with Gol? And you mean to tell me that he never explained the phenomenon that is the Nex?' Feuchter sneered. 'We – Gol, Durell and myself – worked on them, or rather, took over work on the project named Nx5, nicknamed Necros – or Nex. They were pioneered in the 1950s by our predecessors when America and Russia were playing their Cold War games and developing nuclear weapons and intercontinental missiles to deliver their new, gleaming warheads. We then took up the research in the late 90s. Oh yes, we discovered many things back then; many things Spiral would have preferred us to keep hidden. They withdrew our funding for the Nex Project; our specimens were killed and we had to move on to other *more moral* areas.'

Feuchter turned and continued to walk. Carter followed.

'Durell and Gol – the horrors they created!' Feuchter chuckled, and the sound was cold; chilling; nightmare turned real.

493

Moving down busy metal corridors now, Carter felt the hairs crackling on the back of his neck. He kept glimpsing the faces of the Nex. There was something wrong with these people, these assassins who had hunted him for so long, these killers who had nearly wiped out the Spiral DemolSquads . . . but he could not put his finger on it.

Feuchter halted.

A door slid open and he ushered Carter through and onto a massive control deck. Computers lined the walls, their status lights glittering insanely. Display monitors were set up on benches, showing naval and air operations globally. And there, against the far wall, seated beside a small black terminal, was Natasha—

'Nats!'

'Carter!' She leaped to her feet, sprinted towards him and they fell into one another's arms. Carter kissed her passionately, then pulled away and stared down into her tear-filled eyes.

'They captured me,' she sobbed. 'I didn't betray you, Carter, I promise . . . they said I was their insurance policy, that you would do what they want as long as they could kill me . . .'

'Yes, yes,' snapped Feuchter. He strolled over to the small black terminal and placed the Browning on an alloy bench. He flicked a switch; there was a spiralling of metal plates, which spun out from the top of the terminal to reveal a small black cube. 'Behold,' said Feuchter. 'The QIII. Are you impressed, Mr Carter?'

'Is that it?'

'That's it. But what it lacks in aesthetics, believe me, it makes up for in ability. Thank your saviour, Mr Carter.'

'My . . . *saviour*?'

'Ask yourself this question – why did we take Natasha?

494

Why didn't I just shoot you up there on the deck? You think I give a fuck about answering your questions? You think I care about sparing your life for a few moments more? No . . . But the QIII's puzzled by you, Mr Carter. It can predict anything, *anything* – except your actions . . . and that worries the QIII, and it worries *us*. It thinks that there's something strange about you, Mr Carter, something dark *inside* you that makes you uniquely dangerous. And it's going to tear that secret from you – even if it fucks with your soul, even if it eventually kills you.'

Feuchter smiled, and it was not a nice smile. 'I, however, am sceptical; I want you dead. But *Durell* has other plans . . .'

Feuchter turned and ran a finger across the cold cubic processor.

It hummed softly.

'What's it afraid of?' said Carter softly. 'That I'll shoot you in the fucking face again?'

Feuchter turned; a fluid whirl. He smiled at Carter. 'Let me warn you, it is Durell who wishes you alive, and the QIII itself: not I. Do not antagonise me or you may push me beyond my boundaries. Now, this QIII is fully functional, as you witnessed when your sorry little group flew in to meet their makers – soon, you will see the full extent of our plans.'

'What, to take over the world?' sneered Carter.

Feuchter laughed then. 'You are so naive, Carter. So very, very simple. In your world everything is in black and white; not so in mine. Spiral had their power, had their fucking time. They abused it. Look at the way things are . . . it disgusts me. They have ultimate power and yet evil dominates, evil men walk the world with guns and bombs of HighJ fire. It is fucked up beyond belief, Carter.

Spiral: once I thought they were strong – but no, Spiral are weak, Carter – they grew fat and weak on the spoils of war. Now it is time for change . . . it is time for the strong to rule with an iron fist, and rule we will. We will turn the tables. We will annihilate evil. We will make the world a better place and make God proud of humanity.'

He stepped away from the QIII.

A white globe spun into the air; colours rippled across its surface, painting the simulated Earth with laser light. Around it spun satellites, and as the sphere expanded and rotated Carter could see activity within it: fleets of warships, squadrons of aircraft, battalions of tanks moving across this QIII globe of laser light.

The door opened. A huge, athletic Nex warrior entered, followed by a shuffling figure in heavy dark robes, its face hidden, its shoulders hunched as if in pain. The Nex nodded to Feuchter, who smiled once again. It was with unease that Carter noted the copper-eyed stare fixed on him.

'This is Krael,' said Feuchter softly. He turned and looked hard at Carter. 'You met his mate in Africa; I believe you destroyed her face with your bullets. Krael has asked me for a personal favour: he wishes to dance with you, Carter, he wishes to show you what pain is. The QIII wants you alive – I merely want you to suffer.'

Carter's gaze moved from the huge Nex to the shuffling figure; it had moved to the globe, and a cracked blackened hand came out, reached towards the digital hologram and was bathed, sparkling, by the ghostly witch-light.

The figure chuckled, a deep melodious sound.

'So we meet, Mr Carter.'

'You would be Durell.'

'I would.'

'You're the one in charge of this fucking yapping puppy called Feuchter.'

'Yes. Let me show you what we can do here,' came the voice of Durell from within the robes.

Suddenly, the globe spun with incredible speed. It showed the cruiser and the battle raging in the skies above it.

'You are privileged indeed, Mr Carter, to witness this moment . . .'

Durell's blackened twisted hand gestured, a complicated pattern of movements. Script flowed up and over the globe and the humming from the QIII increased in volume—

Natasha gasped. 'It's . . . doing it . . .'

Carter watched coldly as—

```
SP1Q,%KEY_OPTIONAL%\sysSATmeter,Installed,,'0'
HKLM,%KEY_OPTIONAL%,'netwatch',,'netwatch'
tracking . . . located Russian SAT 576 #####
tracking . . . locked.
script engaged script locking engaged
launch sequence initiated= threat= demolsquad
co-ords 234.456.557.212 – eq%345.331
config= armed and targeted
satellite lasers= granted
```

The fight was going badly. The DemolSquads were dying. And just when it seemed that things couldn't get worse, The Priest watched the darkened skies erupt with a burst of laser light . . . a column of white fire exploded from the heavens and blasted an Apache into glowing splinters of steel that rained sizzling down across the raging ocean.

The Priest swallowed hard. He blinked, and looked upwards.

And his faith was shaken.

The QIII showed it all.

It showed the destructive laser light smash down from the commandeered Russian PredatorSAT.

It showed, close up, the Apache with its struggling occupants.

There was a glow, incredibly bright.

Blood was vaporised.

Flesh torn from faces and hands and throats.

Screams – for an infinitesimal slice of time.

Death.

And an explosion of raining steel . . .

Carter's jaw tightened; he stepped smoothly away from Natasha, gaze scanning the room: the Nex, Krael, Feuchter and Durell.

'You are fucking insane,' he growled.

'On the contrary, Mr Carter,' said Durell, his hidden face turning towards Carter. 'We are quite sane. Only we seek to do what is *right* – by our own definitions of the term. You see the QIII now? The globe is spinning, a pretty light show . . . but thirty seconds ago it unlocked the World Banks – every single one. It now controls them. It has taken over every single satellite that circles the Earth. It controls the world's armies: their aircraft, their tanks, their infantry – their *nuclear weapons*. Shortly I will issue statements to all the governments of the World Powers – they will relinquish their countries to *me* in exchange for their lives. And then . . . *then* we will play this Spiral game my way.'

Durell's voice had risen in anger and, to Carter's ears, in madness.

That black crippled hand emerged and took hold of the QIII processor. Suddenly, the light was gone and Carter blinked . . .

Feuchter walked towards the door, following Durell.

He was almost nonchalant in his movements. His arrogance was total. His position of strength was clear. He halted and turned to Carter as Durell disappeared with the QIII . . .

'You asked me about the Nex, about what they are. I feel that it is my duty to give you answers. Show him, Krael. *Explain* your prowess. Oh, fuck it, Mr Carter, this little puppy thinks it is time for you to *learn*.'

The huge Nex took a step forward; he reached up, grasped his tight-fitting uniform, and ripped it up above his head revealing a heavily muscled torso. But at his sternum, trailing down, there was a light pattern of—

'Scales?' whispered Carter, frowning.

'Armour,' said Feuchter, his eyes bright. 'In the 1950s, when the Americans and Russians discovered the joys of nuclear weaponry, it was also discovered that many insects had, shall we say, natural in-built properties of which we, as humans, were envious. Spiral set up research centres to look at why insects were so tough, so hardy, so downright fucking lethal. Pull a leg from a spider, it doesn't die. It might *hurt*, but it's solid insular genetic structure makes it a force to be reckoned with. Take cockroaches: they are very resistant to radiation. Why? Why the fuck would that be? It was researched for years, answers were found – genetic coding is such a wonderful process – and then Durell and Gol took it one step further . . . developed the ultimate coding able to operate on today's nuclear, biological and chemical battlefields!'

'I thought they were all destroyed,' said Natasha. 'Back then, in Germany? Gol said they were wiped out.'

Feuchter glanced at her. 'Oh no, my sweetness. Durell and myself and your daddy were *very* busy. We call it Skein Blending: you take a human and an insect, or a series of insects and – you're going to fucking *love* this – you *spiral* genetic strands together. The host – insect genetics are quite parasitical in their nature – the host *receives* a whole new set of attributes: resistance to chemical, biological and radioactive weapons; an incredibly enhanced immune system; a massively increased pain threshold, quicker reactions, reflexes, thought processes. Their skin hardens, some grow external and internal armour to protect organs and bones – they become *incredibly lethal killing machines without remorse*. They become the perfect soldier. Their ability to repair themselves increases greatly, Mr Carter; and that is why I am not dead. That is why your bullets, and the explosion and the fire did not kill me . . . I am a Nex, Carter. It is well known within the scientific world that every true scientist should be willing to test his experiments on himself . . . I was the first Nex. I was the first *true* Nex.'

Carter stood with his mouth agape. He glanced at Natasha; she was pale.

'Tell him the rest,' she said.

Feuchter shrugged. 'What more is there to tell? The Nex are a blend of insect and human – nothing more. What Nature has denied us, Man has found a way to complement; to cure.'

'Tell them why Spiral cancelled the project and destroyed the specimens,' she hissed.

Feuchter merely shrugged again.

'It changes your mind state,' said Natasha softly. 'You lose all emotions; you lose all ability to care, to love, to nurture. Your mind becomes like that of an insect; you become the sort of man willing to betray everything he has ever known, ever *loved*.'

Carter dropped his gaze. Kade was screaming in his head and a wave of pain flooded over him. Distantly, there was a concussive *boom*. '*Kill him, and kill him now and we'll fucking go home . . .*' Kade was spitting in his mind . . .

Another figure stepped into the room; Feuchter spoke quietly, then smiled. 'It would seem that I am needed for a few moments – to take over the world,' he whispered. 'Krael, show him how far the Nex have *advanced . . . he wants his answers, give them to him . . .*'

Feuchter stepped through the door and was gone.

The three Nex with guns moved forward and grabbed at Natasha; she hissed a curse and everything happened at once. The huge muscled and armoured figure of Krael stepped forward with a narrow smile and a hiss, tossing his gun aside where it clattered against the wall, the dark armour on his abdomen glinting in the weak light, his asexual face under short dark hair – bristling black insect hair – serene and relaxed and ready to kill . . .

Yelling, Carter charged—

And Krael leaped to meet him . . .

They clashed in mid-air with a rapid exchange of blows so fast that the human eye could barely follow it. They parted, both landing and whirling on the dull black metal floor of the op centre . . .

Krael smiled. 'I will make you suffer like you have never suffered before.'

Carter glanced at where the three Nex had dragged Natasha to the door – but he was stuck, stuck with his own fucking problems . . .

'I will fuck your mind,' snapped Carter.

Krael charged, smashing a series of punches at Carter who blocked, dodged, blocked again and then hammered a right hook to Krael's jaw. Then he kicked out, boot lifting high to smash Krael in the chest, knocking him back with a grunt. Krael leaped again, high into the air, both elbows ramming down at Carter who twisted, whirling

501

with incredible speed as Krael met nothing. Krael landed; his boot smashed out, kicking Carter in the chest and sending him sprawling backwards, a look of pain flashing across his face. Carter hit the metal grilles of the floor with a *clang*, then rolled as Krael's boots landed where his face had been an instant earlier. They circled each other, snarling like caged tigers.

'You have slowed in your old age,' said Krael.

Carter laughed. 'I don't feel dead just yet.'

'You will,' said Krael, his eyes gleaming. 'Don't you understand? I am toying with you; I am fucking with you. You are *slow* compared to me, Carter; you are *weak*. I am going to make you suffer as you made Sharae suffer; I will send you to her and she will enslave your soul . . .'

'Stop talking and show me,' snapped Carter.

They closed—

Warily.

Carter threw a complicated series of punches, jabs, hooks and uppercuts – Krael blocked them all, then came back with a front kick. Carter sidestepped, catching Krael's leg and driving his elbow down at the joint – but Krael twisted, throwing himself up, the heel of his boot connecting suddenly with Carter's face, his nose, hammering Carter back sprawling onto the hard metal floor—

Carter screamed, blood pouring, hands moving to protect his face.

'No!' cried Natasha.

Krael landed in a crouch, then unfolded and stood. He walked forwards. He looked down. He dropped suddenly, one elbow hitting Carter in the chest with all his weight. There was a *crack* of breaking sternum. Carter screamed again – as his hands suddenly shot out, grasped Krael's head and dragged him forward onto the smash of a head-butt – once, twice, three times until Krael's fingers

502

prised Carter's hands free and he scrambled, coughing and blinded, backwards, spinning and dazed, away across the booming metal floor—

Carter, feeling sick, rolled to his knees, then to his feet, groaning. Pain lanced through his chest; he gasped, struggling to breathe, his fingers coming up to probe at his broken sternum. He glared across the op centre at Krael, who was shaking his head, a thin trickle of blood dripping from his broken nose.

The ship around them rocked and shuddered. Distant screams could be heard as scorched stressed metal ranted in fury. A low groaning rose as some distant explosion rumbled.

Krael smiled nastily.

And charged—

Carter braced himself; they punched, blocked, circled; Krael charged again, launching himself into a flying kick that Carter barely dodged. Again Krael came on and Carter backed away before blocking a flurry of blows and returning a combination of punches and kicks that forced Krael back for a moment—

They circled again, Carter panting, sweat dripping from his brow. Krael seemed untouched.

'I thought you would be faster,' said Carter.

'I am faster than *you*.'

'Show me, then, you fucking pussy.'

Krael howled and charged. The blows came thick and fast and Carter found himself retreating, panic-filled, under the insane barrage of punches and kicks. He barely managed to dodge and block – a blow caught him in the throat and he staggered backwards, suddenly trapped against a bank of computers.

Krael stood, panting, smiling grimly, watching the man in front of him as he scrabbled at his neck—

503

'Carter!' cried Natasha. She struggled with the three armed Nex, aware that even if – by some miracle – Carter managed to kill this warrior Nex, then he would have three more opponents with guns to deal with.

Carter clawed—

at his throat—

Clawed for air—

Carter clasped his neck, pain spearing him. Tears streamed from his eyes and he wiped them away with bloodstained hands. He looked up then, looked up into Krael's dark moody eyes and he knew: knew he was outclassed; knew he was beaten; knew he was *dead* . . .

'Is that the best you can do?' he wheezed through his damaged throat. 'I thought you were supposed to be a fucking warrior – your dead fucking mate put up a better fight . . .'

Krael's eyes widened and his smile disappeared. He screamed, charging again; Carter ducked a series of blows and launched himself across the metal grilles, a full-length dive, stretching for the wall and the bench and the stranded—

Gun.

His fingers curled around the Browning, carelessly tossed by Feuchter onto the alloy bench and left there in a fit of arrogance. Now his fingers curled around the heavy familiar weapon, around the heavy grip of his 9mm brother and he rolled onto his back, gun up and pointing at Krael who suddenly halted, dropping to a crouch—

Krael laughed.

Carter pulled the trigger.

The gun kicked as a bullet flew from its barrel. Krael flicked left and the bullet smashed into a bank of computers. Sparks flew. Carter rolled, the Browning coming around for a second shot with his broken sternum sending searing pain through his body—

He heard the metallic *clicks* – and despite the protest of his body he dived as the other three Nex in the room opened fire. Carter rolled into a metal panel with a *boom*, then scrambled behind a low bench and peered over the edge as guns blasted and sparks flew. The Browning was smashed from his hand, and a punch knocked him sideways.

Carter landed heavily, all breath knocked out of him. Acid pain ate him whole. He laughed through a mouthful of blood and saliva as the shadow of Krael loomed over him.

'*Let me,*' soothed Kade. '*I can take this fucker.*'

I can take him on my own, snapped Carter, slipping a long darkened blade from its hidden home in his boot. In a normal situation Carter never had to resort to knives . . . but this was a far from normal situation and he was fast losing faith and patience and *strength*. Krael loomed above him and Carter slammed the dagger up hard into the warrior Nex's groin, feeling the blade part flesh and muscle with consummate ease. Blood flushed warm and crimson over his fist and he dragged the knife to the side before pulling the blade out. Krael staggered, then slumped slowly to his knees. Carter rose, bathed in the Nex's blood, reached back and hurled the dagger across the ops room. It drove into the eye of one of the Nex holding Natasha – without a sound it toppled forward onto its face and twitched, a huge pool of blood gathering around its head. Bullets flew at Carter, and he ducked as sparks kicked up by his head. Natasha, screaming, was dragged from the room by the two retreating Nex and everything was suddenly silent—

Except for the moaning, writhing form of Krael.

Carter crawled to his feet and checked quickly around. He found the gun, slippery with blood, and moved to where Krael was squirming. The Nex's hands were coated in deep red gore. He looked up at Carter, his face a snarl, and licked at thin white lips.

And Carter felt—

Sorrow. Not anger, nor hatred. Just sorrow for this poor wretched creature at his feet.

He lifted the Browning. Wiped sweat, blood and saliva from his hand.

And placed a bullet in Krael's face, ending the Nex's pain.

CHAPTER 25

MORTAL COIL

Slater sat in the boat, frowning to himself. He checked his watch. Jam had been gone too long – far too long He peered down into the churning waters, but could see nothing. He heard a shout from far above. Glancing up the wall of black metal in front of him, Slater saw a pale round face; it disappeared.

'Great,' he muttered.

There was a *whiz* and a splash beside him.

Slater cursed. Glancing up, he saw the pale face again. Hoisting the heavy machine gun, he fired twenty rounds; some *zipped*, ricocheting, from the wall of black ship metal. Slater wasn't sure if he had hit the target. The pale face disappeared in any case.

'Gone for reinforcements,' Slater muttered. 'Shit. Shit shit fuck. Jam, you arse, *come on*!'

Carter limped warily across the operations centre where computers churned and groaned to themselves. One wall was glass, and looking down he could see a mass of activity; it had to be the ship's bridge. Carter could see

Feuchter and Durell, the white globe spinning between them as they directed their New World Order. Natasha was not there.

'You arrogant cunts,' he spat and hoisted his Browning in his blood-encrusted fist. He checked the magazine. Then he checked the other magazines stowed about his person.

He had bullets. Lots of them.

Carter smiled.

'Let's dance, Feuchter,' he said. And stepped warily from the room.

In the corridor, Carter could hear heavy-machine-gun fire. There were *booms* from the cruiser's big guns. Distantly, he could hear other explosions and the scream of engines.

'Doing your work well, eh, Jam?'

'He'll do a better job than you,' whispered Kade.

'Where is Natasha?'

'They've taken her to the bridge. To Feuchter. Everything is in a panic; somehow the DemolSquads have knocked out the navigation systems; the ship cannot steer except with the help of the QIII.' Kade sounded sulky; bitter.

Carter moved along the corridor, which sloped down. He came to steps and warily picked his way down their metal surfaces. He heard something behind him. Ducking into a hatchway, he watched a Nex rush past. The door to the bridge opened: Feuchter stood there, a look of anger and frustration on his face. Natasha was standing behind him, hands taped together, a warrior-caste Nex to either side of her. Behind, the QIII's representation of the world spun as the processor went about the final rounding-up of global electronic control . . .

Durell was dictating a message to the leaders of the

world; Carter caught phrases such as 'incredible destructive technology' and 'surrender all military currency'. He spat on the floor and gripped the Browning even tighter.

'Well?'

'The Demolition Squads are all but destroyed. They are retreating now, fleeing into the dark and the rain – but the thirty-two scrambled Russian Mig30s will be here within three minutes; they will finish off the last dregs. 'If only they knew who was issuing their orders now!'

'Good,' said Feuchter, smiling and glancing towards Durell. On the spinning globe of light he could see the distorted, angry, shocked, disbelieving faces of the world's leaders. Durell's cracked black hand was raised in a mocking salute, a gesture of *victory* . . .

Boots thudded along the corridor, and another Nex sprinted into view. He skidded to a halt in front of the smiling visage of Feuchter. But Feuchter could read something . . . something amiss within those bright copper insect eyes . . .

'What is it?'

'A bomb has been planted,' said the Nex calmly, eyes glittering.

'What kind of bomb is it?' snapped Feuchter. 'Come on, what kind of fucking device?'

'Our sensors read it as a micro-nuke neutron device of unspecified yield, magnetically attached to the underside of the ship.'

Feuchter's eyes widened. 'We need to get somebody down there. Now! You hear me?'

The Nex ignored him. 'We must vacate this vessel.'

'Won't our fucking armour protect us against this?'

'The formulation of the SPQ plating is incredibly strong. However, the blast will explode gas and air underneath the whole of the ship; it doesn't matter how strong

509

our armour is against bombs, there will be no water to support the cruiser's weight. The ship will break itself in half.'

Feuchter stared, dumbfounded.

A million thoughts whirled through his brain.

Out of the corner of his eye, he could hear Durell's triumphant ranting and see the black claw raised in the air in defiance of the world, in celebration at *conquering* the world . . .

And all this through a tiny processor.

Feuchter lifted his gun; a single shot through the eye ended the Nex's report. He turned to Natasha and smiled a thin cruel smile. 'It would seem your friends had an ace up their collective sleeve, Miss Molyneux. They're not running away from us, they're getting free of the fucking blast zone—' He gestured to the Nex holding her. 'Give her to me . . .' He grabbed her by the hair and dragged her roughly towards the door.

Feuchter hauled Natasha off the bridge.

Carter stepped out behind them.

'Let her go, Feuchter.'

Feuchter turned, Natasha held between him and Carter. He raised his gun and started firing, a mad smile creasing his lips, his brow furrowed in concentration. Carter dived sideways, back through the hatchway and into a wide metal chamber, sparks kicking up around him. A flattened bullet, ricocheting from the wall, spun like a circular razor across the top of his forearm – there was a moment when the wound was nothing but a narrow strip of red, then the muscle parted and blood gushed out. Carter clamped the wound with a curse and dragged himself to his knees. He heard running footsteps. He tore a strip from his shirt and bound it tightly about his forearm. Blood soaked through in an instant. Gripping the

Browning Hi-Power 9mm, he climbed unsteadily to his feet. His mind swam: loss of blood, constant pain, and a severe pounding at the hands and boots of Krael had left him weak.

'*It's also left you slow,*' sneered Kade.

Carter said nothing. Licking salty lips, he pushed himself forward and peered along the corridor; he could hear a bustle of insane activity from the bridge. His snarl went tight and muscles stood out like ridges of steel cord along his jaw.

He glanced after the fleeing form of Feuchter who was abducting the woman he loved.

And then towards the bridge—

And the processor that was intent on destroying the world.

'Fuck it.'

He strode onto the bustling bridge, past a huddle of Nex all intent at their terminals. He broke into a sprint as he heard Durell's voice triumphantly saying, '. . . And we will spare their lives . . .'

The Browning touched the back of the robes.

Carter could feel the body beneath the cloth.

Durell froze.

'But *I* will spare no fucking lives,' spat Carter as he pulled the trigger.

The bullet smashed into Durell's back. It ploughed its heavy way through his heart, exploding from his chest in an eruption of breast-shards, and left a spiralling trail of fine red spray up through the centre of the QIII-generated world display.

Durell collapsed.

Everything seemed to go silent on the bridge, as about forty Nex turned their attention towards Carter. He took a single step forward, glanced down at the QIII cubic

511

processor, levelled his Browning and sighted with one eye closed.

'It's been a long fight,' he muttered. 'Now it's game . . . fucking . . . over.'

He put ten bullets into the processor as a distant scream of 'No!' echoed from a Nex behind him. Bullets smashed the cold black QIII cube into a billion insignificant harmless fragments that blew violently outwards in a black mist.

The light-globe representation of the Earth shimmered and was gone.

'You've been hacked, fucker.'

Sub-machine guns and pistols blasted.

Carter sprinted, head low, as a Nex with a sub-machine gun cut ten of its fellow officers in half and stood, mute, wondering at its own stupidity. Bodies crumpled to the ground. Carter raced into the corridor with bullets kicking up sparks behind him and bounced from the wall, groaning long and low to himself as blood seemed to spurt from five or six wounds in his battered body. Then, gathering stored power from some reservoir of energy that he did not know he had, fuelled by the thought of Jam's micro-nuke and with Kade screaming obscenities in his mind, Carter sprinted as if his life depended on it.

Which it did.

Carter stumbled madly down the corridor in pursuit of Feuchter and Natasha.

'*You are slow and weak, Carter,*' mocked Kade. '*You cannot beat Feuchter now – but I, I can wipe him out for you. I can rip out his heart. I have strength you could never dream of – come on, Carter, you have had your fun, now let me out to play.*'

'I can do it alone,' snarled Carter.

He stumbled forward, rebounding from wall to wall. His sternum clicked with every jolt, making him want to cry out. He halted, fell to his knees, and vomited on the metal floor.

'*You are dying,*' mocked Kade. '*I don't like to say it, but I told you so. And that nuke is tick-tock ticking. Jam did his job well. You only have, ohhh, round about one minute and twenty seconds to get off this fucking ghost ship . . .*'

Carter spat out sour-vomit saliva.

Bullets kicked sparks from the floor behind him.

He heaved himself to his feet, swaying, and pushed on at a weary pace, stumbling, smelling his own stink. His boots thudded dully on metal walkways, up stairs, and to the door that had granted him entry. He heaved it open—

More bullets came at him, striking sparks from the door's metal rim; Carter dropped to one knee, Browning out and kicking in his hand. Feuchter was standing beside a waiting black helicopter and he dragged Natasha into the aircraft as rain pounded all around them.

Carter stepped out into the wind and lashing rain—

And looked around, dazed.

The skies were filled with distant fire and machine guns roared from all around. Most of the DemolSquad helicopters had retreated but a few had remained, buying time for their wounded fleeing comrades, sweeping in to drop bombs on the cruiser's booming gun turrets, keeping close so as to try and make the ship's weapons ineffectual. Nex in their small black helicopters fought short vicious gun battles against the raging sky. As Carter stood, mouth agape, a flaming Nex helicopter plummeted into the sea – closely followed by a wounded bullet-smashed Sikorsky, flaming, out of control, and heading straight towards—

Carter.

513

With a yelp he started to sprint for cover, all pain suddenly forgotten. The machine howled down from the sky, trailing fire, its guns blasting out of control. Bullets drilled a line of dents along the deck beside Carter, a parallel sprint as the machine crashed close behind him, a noise like thunder rocking Carter's world as an explosion and hot gases filled his senses and he did not look back, dared not look back—

There was a *whiz whiz whum* as Carter ducked, still running insanely with all pain and wounds and *everything fucking forgotten* now in this race for survival. A stray helicopter rotor flashed low over his head, so close that he felt the violent wind of its passing, a twelve-foot razor intent on his decapitation. The rotor clattered onto the deck up ahead and Carter turned to see the burning wreckage too close for comfort, thick black smoke pluming up into the sky, flames sizzling in the ice rain.

More bullets whizzed around him. Carter growled, glaring at the helicopter up ahead. It jumped into the sky and Carter could see Natasha struggling inside with Feuchter. He punched her in the side of the head, knocking her against the glass of the cockpit.

Carter, ducking low, sprinted for the Comanche.

Two Nex ran at him. The Browning's bullets smashed them from their feet, pulverising their faces. Carter did not even break stride. As he reached the helicopter, it was with despair that he saw the bullet-riddled fuselage.

'*It has been sitting in the middle of a battlefield*,' said Kade primly. '*You're lucky it's still in one fucking piece!*'

Carter clambered up and dropped into the cockpit. A lot of the instruments had been smashed, he noticed as he hit the engines. There was a grumble, and a whine. They did not fire.

'I don't fucking believe it!' Carter howled.

He punched the dash, then calmed himself. He tried again.

The twin 1380-shp LHTec turboshaft engines burst into life, and Carter lifted the screaming, groaning, wounded Comanche into the skies; it vibrated alarmingly, its engines howling. All around was a chaos of gunfire and flames and explosions; water dripped in through the holes in the cockpit.

As Carter gained altitude, he realised – with horrifying and undeniable finality – that the DemolSquads were being slaughtered. The cruiser's cannons had inflicted a massive toll and the Nex helicopters were dancing among the DemolSquads, picking them off—

Carter's mouth tightened in a grim sour line. His stare locked on the dot that was Feuchter's helicopter; it had headed out low over the waves and had then circled, describing a broad arc and returning to observe the outcome—

Carter powered the Comanche forward.

The killer 'copter dived howling towards Feuchter's small black machine. Carter flicked open the controls for the MiniGun and then realised, in horror, that he could indeed take the helicopter out easily. But that would mean slotting Natasha easily too . . .

Anger and frustration gripped his soul.

The Comanche, one of the greatest aerial war machines, could not help him perform this final task, this final act of revenge and justice and *need*. Feuchter had to die – but Carter did not have the weapons to do it . . . or, rather, his weapon was too *bad* . . .

Lights flickered across the console.

He had a fuel leak; he could see in the HIDSS display on his lap that avgas was pissing from the Comanche's fuselage. Carter forced the helicopter on in desperation.

Feuchter saw him coming and banked his own machine, on-board machine guns opening fire. Bullets whizzed past to left and right, and ate a line up one flank of the Comanche. Still Carter urged the aircraft forward and something, some inner sense made him eject the cockpit canopy in a hiss of hydraulics; it folded to one side to avoid the flashing rotors overhead and dropped away, shattered glass tumbling away into the sea. Rain and ice lashed down at Carter through the *thrumming* of the rotors, soothing him with their cooling numbness; then wind filled him with insane exhilaration as he veered right to avoid a head-on collision and banked the Comanche in a high wide sweep.

Guns clattered behind him.

Carter suddenly realised there were two small black helicopters on his tail; he realised they must have been flanking Feuchter, protecting this being who was their leader—

Guns hammered again.

The Comanche took more hits.

'*The fuel* . . .' hissed Kade in warning as the avgas spray streamed away behind the wounded helicopter . . .

The Comanche lifted rapidly, gaining on Feuchter's thumping black machine as it made its way back towards the cruiser. And then everything happened at once—

There was a low, deep sound, almost beyond hearing.

The world seemed to shake.

The cruiser *jolted*, as if stung, as the neutron micro-nuke planted by Jam detonated. There was a strange underwater roar, an aquatic scream; bubbles erupted and light and fire danced beneath the ocean, spreading out like the tentacles of some great luminous leviathan. The warship lifted and a rending, tearing, screaming sound of stressed steel ripped across the skies – huge cracks

516

appeared down the cruiser's flanks and it split, the midship dipping and the prow rearing into the sky on a gush of suddenly boiling water and steam, a massive split 'V' of steel revealing lights and compartments, tiny toylike items within the massive groaning structure—

Foam and flames burst into the sky, hot spray geysering upwards.

Bullets zipped past Carter, and he launched the Comanche down and *under* Feuchter's machine. He banked the helicopter so that it was flying on its side and fumbled at his belt, dragging free the wire that he had last used back at the Beverly Hills Hilton. He fired it up above him, attaching it to the underside of Feuchter's helicopter as more bullets flew towards him and a spark ignited the stream of aviation fuel trailing from the Comanche in a deadly umbilical to the devastating spark—

Carter felt himself tugged free.

The wind lashed at his dangling body.

The Comanche veered off, trailing a line of fire that quickly caught up with the war machine. Blazing bright, it careered out of control, and suddenly flipped and hammered into the waves, blossoming into a final bright bloom of fire and metal as Feuchter's 'copter flashed overhead.

Carter swung helplessly for a few moments. He was buffeted wildly, and swinging, turning, he saw that the other helicopters were still pursuing. Wind lashed at him, and ice rain. The pursuers opened fire.

Carter yelped as bullets roared around him, zipping past his unprotected flesh.

He reached up, grasping the enemy helicopter's landing rails. With a Herculean effort he dragged himself up, spun for a moment, and planted his boots on the rail, detaching his umbilical wire as he did so.

He appeared, suddenly, beside Feuchter.

Carter saw Feuchter mouth something. The helicopter veered left, banking sharply in panic. Carter smashed, helpless for a moment, against the door, his head hitting the glass and cracking its surface; he dragged the Browning up and placed the muzzle against the cockpit canopy. Even through the wind's noise he heard the tiny *clack* of metal against the window.

Feuchter heard it too.

He turned, staring hard at Carter.

His eyes glittered cold; his mouth was a grim sour line.

'Fuck,' screamed Carter through gritted teeth, the word snatched away instantly by the wind as his hair whipped wildly around his head, 'you.' He pulled the trigger. The bullet smashed through the canopy towards Feuchter's face. It drove through his top teeth and his palate and into the base of his skull. Feuchter slumped backwards, releasing the helicopter's controls as his brain erupted from the back of his head in a shower, splattering against the seat and covering Natasha in gore.

She gasped.

The helicopter lurched and flipped suddenly sideways.

For an instant she met Carter's shocked gaze. Then he was gone, lost in the darkness, lost in the ice rain, lost in the infinite blackness of the cold night storm.

Natasha grabbed the helicopter's controls, impeded by her tape-bound wrists. Feuchter flopped around beside her as she managed to steady the aircraft.

They were close to the fast-sinking cruiser. It was sliding beneath the bubbling super-heated waters, settling below the waves like some dying dinosaur.

Natasha suddenly became aware of her aerial entourage and banked the helicopter around in a wide

518

circle, her two *protective* escorts following suit. Then she suddenly spun the aircraft and opened fire with the on-board heavy machine guns.

The two Nex-piloted vehicles evaded the bullets ... and collided. In a sudden tangle of metal and twisting screeching engines, they plummeted towards the sea in a ball of fire.

Natasha smiled; she tried to calm her pounding heart but failed.

She steered the helicopter low over the sea, searching for Carter. Again and again she flew passes, her heart sinking, despair flooding through her. The helicopters that she had destroyed had sunk slowly beneath the cold waves.

Spinning the helicopter around once more, she watched as the battling DemolSquads, buoyed by the victory of seeing the cruiser – and its heavy guns – sunk, stormed through the skies, raining hot death on the remaining Nex.

The rain and ice continued to lash down.

Before very long, it was all over.

And a wounded group of heroes limped home.

CHAPTER 26

DEEP

Carter fell, and as he hit the icy waters all semblance of sanity was crushed from him in an instant as the freezing sea chilled him to the bone. Deep under he went, his Browning gone in an instant, bright white stars of pain forced into his numbed brain and body. He gasped, breathing in water. He spluttered, and realised that possibly, down in the depths of this polar black ice ocean—

'*You might drown.*'

'Leave me be.'

'*I should have warned you: you should have waited another three seconds so the positions of the rotors and stick didn't combine to flip the helicopter. Then you wouldn't be here . . . drowning.*'

'What do I have to do to be rid of you, fucker?'

'*You have to die,*' whispered Kade.

All force of will flooded from Carter. But then fire burned bright in his mind and he reached, slowing his descent into this awesome abyss, and struck out, fighting his way up, up, up, bubbles bursting from his tortured lungs. He broke through the surface, sucking in a huge

huge gulp of precious cold air. His breath streamed like dragon smoke. He realised that he was screaming.

Opening his eyes, Carter breathed deeply and saw the helicopter banking sharply. Machine guns roared and the other two Nex helicopters smashed and merged together, their rotors folding directly above him as Carter's grimace of madness dropped from his face—

'You're fucking *shitting* me . . .'

The twisted helicopters fell.

Carter dived, kicking with all his might, diving down and down, and the cold was forgotten in this sudden desperate race to get beneath the surface. Dimly he heard the impact – a dull *whoosh* – and his surroundings were illuminated by the burning helicopters descending above him through the cold waves, ignited fuel a torch lighting his way to a deep dark dominion named Death.

Kicking with all his might, Carter fought his way down; he risked a glance behind – above – and they were there, two glowing machines held in a metal mesh embrace.

He could see a Nex, struggling to fight free of the wreckage. But it was trapped.

The helicopters sank closer to Carter, who kicked to get out of their way.

Sorrow swamped him; he could faintly hear the Nex screaming.

The glow disappeared. Lungs burning, Carter kicked for the surface once more. The cold was numbing him to the point of death. He felt tingling all over his skin; he could not feel his hands and feet and face.

He burst free. Breathed deeply.

Debris littered the sea now. He glanced around.

Distantly, he saw the helicopter battle ending. More Nex were sent hurtling to their deaths and Carter felt sick deep down to his core. He watched idly as the cruiser finally succumbed to the cold dark waters.

Carter trod water.

And he knew that he had nowhere to go.

No way of saving himself.

Would they come looking for him? Or would the bastards think he was dead? Would they leave him to freeze slowly to death, alone with his memories for his last fleeting moments of life—?

There are worse ways to die, he decided sombrely.

But then, there are better ways.

He kept moving but he could not feel his arms or legs now; only the trunk of his body retained some heat. The pain had gone; all his pain had gone, numbed by the freezing waters.

How long will it take? he mused.

Minutes?

Seconds?

'What the *fuck* are you doing here?'

Carter turned around; there was a small black boat. A man peered down at him, goggles pushed up on his head, a cheeky smile on his broad face. Jam winked.

'We saw you take a dive. Thought you might need a ride,' rumbled Slater.

Carter grinned. 'Was that your firework display?'

'Nuke in a suitcase,' said Jam with a laugh. 'Low radiation yield – quite eco-friendly, when you think about it.'

The two men reached down and dragged Carter into their little boat, which bobbed alarmingly. 'You'll have to hug him, share your body heat,' said Jam, firing up the engine and heading out into the darkness.

'I'm not fucking hugging him. I'm not a poof!'

Jam rolled his eyes. 'Slater, look at the man! He'll die of hypothermia! Now, I'm not casting aspersions on your sexuality, but you really need to get him warm.' He stared hard at Carter who was shivering uncontrollably, eyes closed, pain his mistress. 'In fact, I think this is going to be a threesome if we don't want the fucker dead.'

They both gathered round Carter, and as the boat sped through the dark waves under the storm-filled heavens, they huddled close to him and waited for the dawn to come.

A cold late-autumn wind blew the brown and yellow leaves down the road, swirling them up into the air, decorating the tarmac with those symbols of summer's death and winter's impending onslaught. The gleaming black Mercedes sped through the wind-scattered leaves, turned left at the bottom of the street and headed out towards the deserted docks.

It was early. Five a.m. and not yet light.

The Mercedes stopped, engine ticking over, tendrils of smoke trailing from its exhaust; one of the rear doors opened and Carter – a bruised and battered Carter, missing a front tooth but cleaned and bandaged up and whole again – stepped onto the rough concrete and breathed deeply of the nectar that was the morning air. He limped slowly across the dockside, panting and wincing in pain as his broken sternum pierced his thoughts, and halted, staring down into the black, lapping water. He pulled free a packet of cigarettes, freed one from its paper cage with a heavily bandaged hand, and lit the weed.

Smoke plumed above the water and Carter sighed.

He turned at the sound of another car; the Range Rover cruised past the parked Mercedes and approached Carter where he stood beside the sea wall.

A cold wind blew as the Range Rover cut its engine.

Carter glanced in at the group of large men. One of the

doors opened and a figure stepped out; it was a man Carter had never met before, and yet Carter instinctively recognised him as Spiral; he was tall, and broad, and quite old. His grey hair was short, his eyes bright and pale. A neatly trimmed moustache and a long overcoat gave him something of the look of a gangster.

'Mr Carter.'

Carter shook the man's leather-gloved hand.

Carter nodded, drawing deep on his cigarette. 'Good morning, sir.'

'Yes, it is,' said the man. 'Come, walk with me.'

They walked along the edge of the docks, the wind blowing beneath their collars and making coat tails flap. An occasional seagull cried overhead as it swept low, searching for food.

'You know who I am?'

'No, sir.'

'That is probably for the best. But it has come to my attention that after your recent . . . exploits, shall we say, you have come to know rather a lot of things about Spiral that maybe you shouldn't. And yet we cannot forget your sterling service – albeit unknowingly – in leading us to the filth of the Nex, and in your destruction of the traitors known as Feuchter and Durell.'

'I appreciate that, sir.'

The man stopped and gazed deeply into Carter's eyes.

'Hmm,' he said. And then Carter saw it: the Browning 9mm. In the man's gloved hands.

Carter swallowed hard.

The man smiled.

'Here, this is yours. It was recovered when they dived for Durell's body. A miracle, don't you think?'

Carter took the gun. It was marked; scratched; old and worn. It had character.

'A miracle. Yeah.' He laughed then, staring out over the water. 'Did they find him?'

'No.'

'Oh.' Carter scratched thoughtfully at his brow. 'Look, sir, you can be assured of my loyalty concerning the things that I have discovered. I was maybe just a little pissed off at the beginning, because I thought that Spiral was trying to kill me at the start of these . . . shall we say, *adventures*. It would appear that I was mistaken.' Carter's voice had turned somewhat cool. His eyes glittered and his mouth tightened into a grim line.

The man nodded. 'Information is power, Carter. Look what too much information did for Feuchter and Durell. You cannot tell everybody everything; as DemolSquads you are only tiny cogs in the machine, only small players in the whole game. That happy pair of our enemies nearly brought Spiral down because of information: their knowledge; their complete understanding; the things that they *shouldn't* have known.'

Carter rubbed wearily at his eyes. 'Even if they had brought us down, others would have taken our place.'

'Yes.'

Carter nodded. He threw his cigarette butt into the sea. The black cold waves took the glowing tip and it disappeared from view. The wind howled softly; Carter shivered, remembering his thoughts of drowning in those distant ice-laden waters.

'I have some questions . . .' said Carter.

The man held up his gloved hand. He shook his head in the negative, just once.

'Maybe another time.'

Carter smiled sardonically. 'You mean another time as in never?'

'It is for your own protection,' said the man. He smiled

then, but it was an uncertain smile, a smile without a trace of humour – a smile on a face not used to the expression. 'I want you to remember, Carter, that our soldiers are never expendable.' He lit a cigarette. Held it delicately.

Carter met the tall man's gaze: grey eyes, hooded and masking a thousand emotions. Their stares locked for a long time. Carter held the man's cool look. Without another word, he turned and strolled leisurely down the dockside, admiring the dark expanse of churning sea. He climbed into the Range Rover which started its engine, turned, and was gone.

Carter turned back, staring out over the distant black waves. He shivered, pulling his coat tighter around his shoulders.

'Arse-kisser,' said Kade.

'What the fuck are you doing back?'

'I was lonely. I missed your company.'

'You're a fucking worm, Kade, and I am cursed with your presence.'

'You'd be lost without me,' said Kade softly.

'Why? What fucking possible help could you give me?'

'You're touchy today. Maybe you just need more time to think through our relationship.'

'What relationship is this? You driving me insane?'

'Lighten up, Carter: y'know, our relationship – me getting to kill people on your behalf when you need a little encouragement. That sort of brotherly deal thing? You scratch my back—'

'And you put a knife in mine?'

Kade laughed softly. *'Here, listen . . . I . . . I . . . I apologise. For sulking with you. There. I've said it.'*

'That was big of you.'

'You motherfu— No, no, you are right. I'll leave you. Let you gather your mental composure.'

526

'Better leave me for a *while*; say, a thousand years?'

Carter lit another cigarette. He heard the footsteps approaching and he did not turn. Natasha stood beside him, staring out at the sea and the distant buoys. Then she looked up at him. 'You all right?'

He nodded.

'They fire you?'

'No. Not yet. I think they'll probably want a few more psychological tests and medical reports. Then, if I'm real lucky, a desk job.'

Natasha took his hand; their fingers entwined and squeezed.

'You're a lucky man,' she said. 'Lucky to be alive.'

'Hey,' said Carter, grinning. 'Lucky is my middle fucking name.'

'Come on; the others are waiting. We have a party to go to.'

'Those other stinking curs? And at five o'clock *in the morning*?'

'Well, it's the tail end of a party. You know what Slater and Jam will be like. They'll still be pissed . . .'

Carter nodded. 'I'm game,' he yawned. 'Unless . . .'

'Yes?'

Their gazes met.

'I thought you were injured?' smiled Natasha.

'I'm not *that* injured. I still have, shall we say, various functioning parts.'

'I'm sure you have. Your place or mine?'

'Mine,' said Carter. 'I've got to pick up Sam.'

'He OK?'

'Great,' said Carter. 'Well fed on assassin, apparently. Made a right mess of the corpses in the woods; went back for a midnight feast when he was let out, the dirty dumb fat mutt.'

527

'That is one sick dog.'

'Hey – I suppose to his eyes it was fresh meat. Fair game. He was only thinking of his belly. Like the rest of us men. Listen, you go and wait in the car. I would like a moment alone.'

Natasha nodded. 'Sure.'

She moved away, and Carter stood staring out at the dark rolling sea. Waves crested with foam lined the horizon. The cold breeze reminded him of the coming winter.

From the pocket of his coat he removed a small object: a silver disk. It rested against Carter's cold skin and he stared at it for a while, wondering at the secrets it held. The riddle of how to rebuild the QIII. The code and data required to replicate events now done . . .

'You're better off dead,' he muttered.

Reaching back, he threw the silver disk as far out into the sea as he could. There was a tiny *splash*. The last copy of the QIII schematics sank without a trace in the dark waters.

Carter smiled softly.

'It is finally over,' he breathed. He walked back towards the Mercedes and climbed into the warmth of the plush heated interior. The gleaming vehicle turned with a crackle of tyres on concrete and headed smoothly for the network of UK motorways – leaving behind nothing but bitter exhaust fumes and the promise of an oncoming cold winter.

SIU Transcript 3

CLASSIFIED 000/000/artic SPECIAL INVESTIGATIONS UNIT
ECube transmission MEMO digMail sec:code:0056
Date: October 2XXX

```
Mission status: successful
```

Losses: 186 DemolSquad members dead resulting in the regrouping and collapsing of 38 squads. Training has been initiated and recruits searched for on worldwide basis.

Progress: the counter-attack by Spiral has culminated in the destruction of the mobile anti-Spiral warship and a loss of nearly 400 Necros. The rest have gone underground and SAD teams will be deployed on missions of extermination. The body of the traitor, Durell, has not been recovered.

Conclusion: a thorough clampdown on Spiral operatives and closer mental screening measures need to be implemented in the future. It was too easy for a small group to bring about some degree of internal collapse; power will be redistributed in future months.

Cartervb512: subject has been seriously wounded// condition presently under close scrutiny// severe mental monitoring required// return to DemolSquads doubtful at this stage.

\\###TRANSFER TERMINATED###

EPILOGUE

PARADISE

A turquoise sea lapped against a white sand beach. A gentle breeze dissipated the tropical heat, swaying the palm trees and heavy broad-leafed ferns that lined the wide white stone walls. Shells lay scattered among splashes of green seaweed, spatterings of pink and white, grey and blue, spirals leading trails from the lapping lagoons to the heavy foliage behind the bordering white wall.

The small boy ran barefoot across the sand, leaving footprints, his bronzed body gleaming with sweat as he sprinted towards the sea. Behind him, the shrill squeal of an angry mother followed with a promise of punishment, but for now the boy was safe . . . the harsh slaps would follow, but now he dropped to a crouch with his feet in the lapping waters and sucked at the fruit, juices running across his deeply tanned face, dripping from his chin into the blue waters.

The boy finished the stolen fruit and looked sharply to the right, his shock of black hair tumbling around his face. He stood quickly, and moved towards the shape lying half in and half out of the water. It was black, and at first sight resembled a thick tangle of old seaweed. But as the boy drew near he saw that it was vaguely human in shape, curled into a tight ball as if to ward off pain. Reaching down, he picked up a sun-bleached stick and crept close to the object. His nose wrinkled at the smell and, reaching forward, he prodded it gently.

When no movement was forthcoming, the boy shuffled closer, his interest piqued. The sea provided many treasures, but most of them the boy had long ago become tired of. This, however, was different.

He prodded again, then tentatively reached out and ran his fingers across the husk of black.

What is it? he thought in youthful wonder.

The object was rough beneath his fingers, like the old cracked leather his uncle cured from the hides of cows. He prodded it, harder this time, and felt the surface move over something within.

The boy stood, quickly bored, his wonder snatched away like a wind-stolen veil. He looked out over the sea. He shaded his eyes, searching for signs of the rich people's cruise ships that sometimes passed.

Something brushed his ankle.

He looked down to see a clawed black hand . . . that grabbed him in an iron grip, pulled him quickly to the sand and silenced his screams with a single heavy blow.

531

don't you **fuck with me**
don't you pull me down
don't shit in my face
don't you drag me around –

the day that **you die**
will be the day that I do
piss on your grave and on the rest of you

don't you **get it?**
don't you **forget it**

Get It [abridged]
Clawfinger

QUAKE

This book is dedicated to my brother Nick – for showing me how to clean spark plugs many years ago and instilling in me a love of all things mechanical, for his invaluable and humorous help when I destroyed my first car and for being the best brother a man could have.

CONTENTS

PART TWO
LITTLE FLAME

ACKNOWLEDGEMENTS

Thank you to Sonia and Joe, for giving me glittering diamonds of light through some very hard times.

Thanks must also go to my test readers, my agent Dorothy and especially to Tim Holman – for his faith.

And finally thanks to my mum, for endless Sunday morning bike breakfasts and her very special homemade soup.

PROLOGUE

INTERNAL COMBUSTION

The Tennagore Valley

Chile, South America

Carter's head snapped violently left, eyes narrowing as Kade's honey-treacle voice whispered a warning. There came a *zip* and something brushed Carter's ear. He flipped himself to the right, hitting the ground hard and smashing into a low concrete wall with a grunt. His hand came up, feeling warm slick blood smearing the lobe of his ear, and his teeth clenched tight in a sick parody of a grin – one that had little to do with humour.

'*It's a fucking sniper . . .*' It was the voice of Kade again. Carter frowned, closing his eyes for a moment, pain stabbing through his brain.

'Leave . . . me . . . alone!' he snarled.

A battle-scarred 9mm Browning HiPower appeared in Carter's fist and, his heart pounding, he checked its magazine. A sniper: that meant he had been spotted . . . At last a guard with more than a single brain cell! But no

3

alarms had sounded audibly . . . which meant he had almost been taken by surprise.

Almost: a razor-fine boundary between breathing the cold mountain air and lying sprawled in a blood-pooled hollow with no face and an empty skull, entry and exit wounds bone-ringed.

Carter slammed the mag back into the sturdy weapon and crawled to his knees, wind buffeting from the moon-lit cratered mountainside above. Shadows swirled in twisting black veils, plummeting and falling down from the high mountain passes and dancing delicately across the massive expanse of the dam.

Carter moved stealthily along the narrow concrete walkway and halted, shielded by a low, rough-rendered wall and glancing down at the shadowed KTM LC7 757cc motorbike, a special custom-built Spiral Stealth Edition packing 289 b.h.p. and a torque rating of 174 lb-ft. It squatted, camouflaged in the darkness and shadows, concealed behind huge steel drums and taunting Carter not just with its proximity but with the knowledge that to reach it he would have to pass once more in front of the cross-hairs of the infinitely patient sniper's scope.

He could see his escape route.

Compromised.

'*It's not going to be easy*,' Kade growled at the back of Carter's mind.

'You don't fucking say,' muttered Carter. His eyes scanned the layout before him, heart-rate increasing slightly at the prospect of the coming fight.

The dam sat high in the mountains, spanning the narrow rock-walled Tennagore Valley. Its highly advanced and masterfully engineered structure had been built at great expense by the Seckito Syndicate in collaboration with a corrupt section of the SNI – the Chilean secret

4

police – in order to irrigate plantations of coca plants, the basic source of cocaine. This refined product was in turn smuggled to the few countries that still prohibited hard drugs, where it commanded prices that were used to finance illegal heavy-duty military arms purchases by the Seckito Syndicate – who then handed the weapons out like candy to the eager grasping paws of the terrorist organisation JWKA and Spirits of Blood, located on opposite sides of the globe but ultimately having the same aim: civilian soft targets and high-profile media coverage.

Spiral had decided that it was time to smash the Seckito Syndicate with a blunt hammer. Seven operations were in progress. Carter's mission was to blow the dam, destroying the coca crop and pushing the Seckito Syndicate into an already-brewing private war against its untrustworthy arms suppliers. This would coincide with the assassination of several key figures, the destruction of three terrorist and corrupt SNI-protected drug factories and strikes by ZZ-guided long-range cruise missiles from HMS *Thunder*, moored over a hundred miles away in the Pacific Ocean.

Accuracy was essential.

The shit had to hit the fan – with perfect feculent timing.

Carter pulled free his ECube; the tiny black-alloy device vibrated softly in his hand and he thumbed a delicate sequence across its surface panel. Digits flickered at him, ghostly blue in the darkness. Three minutes, fourteen seconds until detonation . . . And Carter had initiated the Anti-Intrusion Filter on the bomb. Which basically meant that the explosion and subsequent destruction was unstoppable . . . the dam doomed within the next few minutes . . . the drug crop lost . . . the Seckito Syndicate smashed—

'But I'd rather get out alive,' he muttered.

Think!

Sniper: location?

Carter whirled, eyes scanning, calculating the angles and velocities involved; if he could climb down to the bike and fire the engine on remote using the ECube, then—

'Hey, *Mestizo*, what is this stinking bike doing here? It not look like one of ours . . .'

'I have no idea, *hombre*.'

The two guards were standing loose, one scratching his lank-ponytailed head, the other's face illuminated in a circle of orange from a home-rolled cigarette pluming lazy grey spirals of smoke into the cold mountain air.

The alarms sounded, shrill bitch screams, and both men sprung into immediate action, cocking Kalashnikov JK49s and glancing around with urgency and vigilance . . . ready for action and blood.

'There must be a *gringo* here . . .'

Carter heard more guards leap from their restful watches, fired into alertness by this sudden screech of intruder alarms.

'Shit.'

'*Do something*,' growled Kade.

Below Carter lay a spread-out collection of painted concrete buildings; and away from their scatter stretched the dam itself, its summit a metre-wide length of smooth gleaming concrete veering away in a slight curve for over half a kilometre. To the left, the choppy waters of the reservoir lapped, reflecting the shadowy peaks of the snow-capped mountains rearing above. To the right the dam fell away almost vertically, several wide channels gushing with white foam and dropping into the colossal open valley below.

Carter's eyes narrowed as he focused on the exit at the

far end of the dam's ridge. His stealth bike had cruised in unseen. And now there was only one – nastily compromised – way out . . .

He took a deep breath and leapt from the parapet, landing in front of the two startled guards whose eyes went wide, cigarettes tumbling from lips moist with fear spittle. Their JK49s twitched but Carter's Browning boomed in his fist once, twice, and both guards were kicked from their feet, brain slop and shards of bone splattering against the steel drums.

The bodies folded to the ground but Carter was already moving; a bullet zipped past his face, then another past his knee. He leapt, rolling and skidding to the opposite side of the steel drums and their unavoidably thin-walled protection—

'There! The fucking *gringo*!'

Machine guns opened fire and bullets howled around Carter. His Browning came up over the drums, thumping against his hand as he emptied a full magazine across the stretch of concrete and kicking another two guards from their feet in mushrooms of blood-mist. One fell into the reservoir with a splash, and was immediately lost.

Carter slammed his back against the drums and changed mags.

'*I told you so,*' said Kade smugly.

'What?'

'*I told you this was a bad idea. I personally would have used a series of automated rocket launchers. But no, you had to do your fucking James Bond bit and sneak in here like a throbbing gold-speckled peacock on heat . . .*'

'Kade,' growled Carter in the depths of his subconscious, 'we haven't fucking *got* automated rocket launchers – and this was supposed to be a low-key covert mission . . .'

7

'*Well, you've fucked* that *up then, haven't you? Every man and his bitch is out to shoot you now* . . .'

Carter turned, sharp eyes spotting the sniper's position high up in a shadowed bunker on the mountainside. Bastard, he mouthed. He hated snipers. Fucking hated them.

Carter suddenly stood, sighted along the top of the barrel of the Browning HiPower held uncannily steady in both hands, and fired a full thirteen rounds at the tiny firing slot barely visible in the face of the deep-set bunker. He saw spurts of stone-dust leap from the edges, and waited . . . No return fire came. He changed magazines again, then leapt across to the KTM LC7, firing the bike into life and scanning ahead. His ears picked out the sounds of guards approaching . . . He checked the ECube. Two minutes.

'*It's going to be tight*,' mused Kade darkly.

Tight? I'd love to get my hands tight around your throat . . .

Carter holstered the Browning, stamped the bike into first gear and flicked free the stealth exhaust mods; the bike could run silently, but silence leeched power. Now Carter needed the power more than he needed to remain undiscovered . . .

He screwed the throttle all the way round. The front wheel jerked into the air and the KTM screamed, LVA exhausts spewing from high-level pipes as the back wheel spun, leaving melted tread across the concrete. The bike shot like a needle bullet into the night from its suddenly hazardous hiding place.

Carter gritted his teeth, holding on tight and clamping himself to the broad tank as the front wheel touched down and the cold mountain air tried to smash him from the saddle. The KTM LC7 hammered through the night, a tiny black bullet skimming across the dam's metre-wide walkway; Carter could smell the fresh water to his left, could sense more than see the fearsome drop to his right.

Carter focused. On the narrow ridge of the dam.

On his road to freedom.

Water was gushing, roaring all around him. He accelerated, speedometer needle bouncing against the redline, the bike howling as it hit 220 m.p.h. The world flashed around Carter in a series of stuttering, splashing bright images.

'*Guards*,' hissed Kade in warning.

Carter palmed the Browning and blew the three guards from their feet before they even lifted their weapons. Two hit the ground, and one fell and toppled down the front of the dam, bouncing and flailing like a tumbling rag doll until he was smashed into a battered purple pulp-drenched carcass in the darkness far below.

Carter dipped the clutch and the KTM's front wheel kicked into the air again, the rear wheel ploughing through one of the corpses, losing traction for a moment in a supple compress of flesh and kicking the bike violently sideways. Carter felt, for a terrifying moment, his loss of control as the massive drop to the right tore his eyes from their target and fear rammed its fist down his throat. Then the KTM's front wheel touched down and the bike stabilised. Carter piled on the speed once more.

'*We've done it!*' crowed Kade. '*We're there . . .*'

Carter frowned. His eyes narrowed and he touched the brake, shaving speed out of instinct more than anything he could actually see or hear, his mouth opened, tongue darting against dry wind-chapped lips, and he realised that—

Hell, he thought.

It's a fucking *tank*.

9

The war machine squatted at the end of Carter's personal runway. Even as realisation hit, guards swarmed from behind the tank's protective armoured flanks and opened up with machine guns. 7.62mm rounds screamed like tiny tortured insects buzzing around Carter's face as he squeezed the brakes and left metres of tyre smeared against the dull white concrete. He kicked the bike around, wheel-spinning in a cloud of stinking burning rubber, then wheelied back the way he had come, ducking low over the tank as bullets howled past. Several slapped against the bike's exhaust pipes. It was a miracle no metal raped his flesh.

'*You've got one minute, Carter.*' Kade's voice was no longer filled with humour, or arrogance, or mockery. There was tension there. An edge of fear that chilled Carter to his very core.

'I – fucking – know . . .' hissed Carter through gritted teeth.

Up ahead, more guards had gathered.

Suddenly, he grabbed the brakes and twisted the KTM left; it shuddered to a halt, front wheel hanging over the terrible descent. Carter glanced down and Natasha's words came back to him.

You'll come back to me, won't you?

It's not that dangerous, he had lied.

I don't want to be left a widow.

But we're not married! he'd protested.

All right, then . . . I don't want you to leave your new child without a father . . .

But we haven't got a—

Actually – Natasha'd smiled weakly – I've got something to tell you . . .

Oh.

Their lovemaking had been gentle, teasing and soft – a

10

merging of flesh and sex – and in the warm afterglow, bathed in the iridescent flickering light of the candles, Nats had tickled her tongue down his neck and whispered in his ear, 'You make sure you come back to me, you reckless fucker . . . You make sure you come back to *us* . . .'

Now, Carter gazed at the vertical drop; 7.62mm rounds screamed around him and the world had descended into a blood-red insanity. His lips compressed in a grim line. Kade was screaming at him to turn back and he was counting, internally, the seconds left until the heavy HighJ detonation and subsequent shock waves cracked the dam, allowing the hugely titanic pressure of the reservoir to force its way violently and unstoppably to freedom—

He revved the KTM.

Revved it real hard, popped the clutch and allowed the bike to dip and fall over the edge—

Darkness and the world rushed towards him, gulleys of foaming white smashing to either side in an insanity of bubbling, roaring noise. The bullets were gone, fallen far behind . . . the bike was an insane bucking metallic bitch straining and heaving beneath him, trying its utmost to launch him from the saddle—

The tachometer's needle danced, bouncing against the redline, and Carter's teeth ground against each other as he grabbed the front brake and left a trail of rubber hissing down the concrete face of the dam . . . Then a string of detonations began to go off deep within the bowels of the dam . . . Carter felt them smashing through the wheels and suspension of the bike and he focused his eyes on the distant curve at the dam's base and the dense trees beyond – as the bike's speed peaked at just over 250 m.p.h.

Kade screamed in Carter's head, words of anger and words of insanity: pure hot curses of hatred—

—With a terrifying monstrous lurch the concrete dam moved . . .

—It heaved—

And, with a violent animal moan, exploded.

ADVERTISING FEATURE

The TV sparkled into life with a digital buzz of electro-hum, diamond-sharp images spinning and morphing into the jewelled-liquid logo of Leviathan Fuels.

Do you despair of the filth of low-grade fuel? Do you tear out your hair over the pollution, over the high cost, over the degradation of your children's futures and the destruction of the whole planet? YOU can stop this . . . YOU can change the world, YOU can make a whole big difference . . .

Scene pans: slowly, from belching thundering oil-slick diesel engines and black fumes suffocating the smog-heavy cancer-riddled twisted population of some tar-smeared contemporary dying city . . .

Scene morphs: into a crystalline metropolis, glittering skyscrapers, happy shining faces, definitive cleanliness . . . hospitals closed because there is no scum of dust and depravity and need . . . gleaming cars purring silently along free-flowing highways . . . healthy children of all cultures and religions and ethnic minorities playing together with an inflatable beach ball and laughing as they skip across dazzling white sand and crushed pink seashells . . .

Leviathan Fuels proudly present Premium Grade LVA, four hundred miles to the gallon, pollution-free with absolute guarantees. Go on, make the switch, because you know your children deserve a better future . . .

SCENE DISSOLVES TO BLACK

PART ONE

THE BOOK OF REVELATION

i see priests, politicians?
heroes in black plastic body-bags
under nations' flags

i see children pleading with outstretched
    hands
drenched in napalm, this is no Vietnam

i can't take any more, should we say
    goodbye?
how can you justify?

Blind Curve (Part v. Threshold)
Fish/Marillion

CHAPTER 1

GAME ON

Austria: 11:48 p.m. [GMT]

Durell's dark clawed hands clasped the small and ornately carved silver box tightly, almost reverently, to his chest: as if he carried the container which bore the ashes of God.

He moved, ghostlike and robed completely in black, down the long, damp stone corridors. He turned at intervals, picking passages through the labyrinth until he came to a small, ice-cold chamber. Despite its simplicity and bareness, there was something special about this place.

Something almost holy.

Durell's boots crunched on sparkling crystals. His breath plumed from the hidden folds of his hood.

Two men waited patiently. The first was tall and massively thickset, his hair greying and neatly cropped around a heavy skull. He was hulkingly muscled but his brown-eyed stare was serious and stern, fixed impassively on Durell; and he was as strong as steel.

In contrast, the second man was considerably slimmer, although he was wide across the shoulders in the

17

manner of an athlete; his eyes were blood red and set in a face that carried heavy, vicious-looking scars. The red eyes themselves were criss-crossed with angry, minute marble-veined lesions – a legacy of an old accident involving alkaline chemical agents and a gang of Colombian drug-purifiers. The man's vision had been saved by the miracle of nascent nanotechnology and the Avelach. His eyes were now fixed in a permanent and terrible expression of pain – and they throbbed with a burning hot-acid intensity in their sockets. He, too, exuded power but in a different, more subtle, even more terrifying way – and both men nodded as Durell entered, the small intricately fashioned silver box clutched within the cage of his fingers.

'Is it ready?'

The red-eyed man nodded curtly. Durell stepped forward, and there came a glitter of brightness from within the heavy folds of his clothing. He slid past the two men towards a narrow, tiny corridor. Stooping, he moved into its circular confines.

They journeyed along the winding passage. It led down.

And down . . .

After many minutes Durell finally stepped out onto a ledge, his breath catching in his throat with a sibilant hiss. It was terribly cold, at least minus fifty degrees centigrade, and he slipped slightly on the slick wide expanse of perfectly smooth rock. In front of his eyes opened a giant chamber, mammoth in its naturally carved proportions. Behind him his keen hearing detected the footfalls of the other two men.

The chamber spread out, dimly lit, the rocky walls frost-spattered and glinting, leading out into witch light and going on seemingly for ever. Within the chamber

18

stood men and women – suited in black and grey, masks covering their faces, gloved hands clasping ice-rimed automatic weapons. They stood immobile, insect-like in their poise, waiting.

Durell exhaled a plume of breath-smoke and smiled.

'Does it please?' asked the red-eyed man.

'Yes, they are perfect.'

'We have worked hard since you left us,' said the athletic soldier. His gaze surveyed the masked army and he smiled to himself, the smile playing gently across his iron-hard face. 'And our forces are still growing at an incredible rate.'

Durell passed the red-eyed man the small silver box. 'With the new nano-alterations to the Avelach machine, you should continue your work with more speed.'

Durell turned to the large bearded man. 'And you, my oldest comrade. Are you impressed with the scale of your invention? What it has achieved? What it can *do*?'

'*Our* invention, surely.'

'Yes,' purred Durell. '*Our* discovery. Our invention. From so many years ago, when the world seemed so much more – simple.' He let the word hang against the ice breeze, and then led the way down to the metal steps that spiralled down to the vast chamber itself. The two men followed, cursing as they left strips of skin against the freezing alloy of the staircase's guard rail.

Reaching the smooth rock floor, Durell walked among his soldiers, among the Nex, looking up into copper eyes and smiling with a deformed pride from within the hidden folds of the dark robes.

'Have you heard the news regarding our enemies?' came the voice of the older, grey-bearded man, his words rich and discordant in this place of cold inactivity.

'Yes,' soothed Durell. He gazed into the distance, past

19

hundreds of Nex. 'Spiral are fools. They think they have us crushed; they destroyed the QIII processor and thought that they had won the war . . . when in fact all they did was delay the battle. So naive of them to think that we had only the QIII to rely on – when in reality the processor was just a tiny slice of the cake. Their arrogance is a crime against all humanity.'

'And Carter? And Jam? And the other DemolSquads?'

Durell sighed. 'Thorns in my side,' he whispered. 'Carter has disappeared, but I have scouts searching for him. Jam has been targeted.'

'And the other squads? Spiral have been rebuilding their strength hard and fast since our . . . assassinations.'

Durell merely chuckled, breath-wraiths emanating eerily from within his dark hood.

'Do not underestimate Spiral,' muttered the bearded man in warning.

'Of course I will not underestimate them. But then, in a beautiful and ironic twist of fate, they have misjudged our strength and our aspirations – *they* are underestimating *us*. They have misread our intentions and they are arrogant enough to think that they have nearly destroyed the Nex with their pathetic search-and-destroy teams. The fools. Just look around you – look at our superiority!'

The two men glanced up, at the fifty thousand Nex who were grouped in battalions within the chamber. Their stares met – for the briefest of instants – and something unsaid passed between them. Hurriedly their gazes returned to the dark husk of Durell.

'We are stronger than we have ever been. Yes, they destroyed our mobile station and the QIII processor – but the development files still exist. The schematics still exist. It has merely cost us time . . . and in that time we have developed another weapon which should level the playing field somewhat.'

'May I ask you about the ScorpNex?'

'The ScorpNex,' said Durell softly, his voice low and menacing, 'was an accident. We have attempted to replicate the procedures that led to its creation and distortion, but each time the subject dies on the slab. If we could find the correct sequence and inhibitors we could build a superior Nex – but that is a problem for another day. Let me show you what the ScorpNex can achieve . . . Kattenheim?'

'Sir?'

'Our new companion needs a demonstration.'

They moved amongst the ranks of silent Nex – scouts, warriors and the elite assassin Nex5 – until they came to a small clearing among them. All around Durell and his two companions silent, immobile copper eyes watched without a flicker of emotion; the only indications of life were tiny trails of breath drifting from chilled lips.

Durell turned to Kattenheim and smiled. The lithe man with the scarred face and blood-red eyes nodded once and shouted in a language unknown to the older grey-bearded man.

Movement from the massive chamber made the large man look up, and he watched in horror as a huge figure lumbered into view. Its skin was jet black, chitinous and threaded with strands of raw pink; disjointed jaws drooled thick saliva from a face that was twisted in eternal pain.

'The ScorpNex,' said Kattenheim softly. 'Our new and . . . *accidental* breed.' He laughed softly. 'Let us say he is one of a kind.'

'Watch,' hissed Durell softly.

Kattenheim gave another call and into the circle came three Nex warriors, their movements perfect and smooth,

21

their copper-eyed stares fixed on the huge ScorpNex and then turning questioningly to Durell and Kattenheim. Kattenheim smiled at the Nex, and gestured towards the massive deformed figure of the ScorpNex.

'Kill it,' he said.

The Nex rolled, spreading out with perfect timing and unnatural fluidity.

The ScorpNex turned, folding its arms, talons slicing its own skin and allowing soft droplets of blood to fall sparkling through the icy air . . .

The Nex circled warily, then attacked as a single unit from three different directions, leaping forward with slim black knives extended. The ScorpNex swayed, smashed blows left and right, then backed away a step as a blade whistled past, a single millimetre from its face. Its taloned fist punched out, skewering a Nex and dragging free a squirming blood-gleaming spinal column. The Nex hit the ground screaming a shrill high-pitched scream as the ScorpNex tensed and attacked, blows raining thick and fast. Within five seconds all three Nex were dead, torn and shredded on the smooth rock floor, blood running into kill channels carved three thousands years ago into the ancient rock.

The ScorpNex folded its thick muscled arms and waited once more, covered in gore and gleaming under the soft light.

'Superb,' sighed Durell.

Blood was trickling, pooling into the stone channels.

'The ScorpNex is much improved,' said Kattenheim.

'Improved?' asked the grey-bearded man, kicking free a lump of meat from his boot in distaste. He stared at the huge figure as it twisted and hissed in front of him. 'This thing is *improved*?'

'It is fast, and it is deadly,' said Kattenheim. 'But the

coding is still far from perfect and needs an increase in conversion timings. And, of course, we need to master the sequence . . .'

'Another problem for another day,' said Durell. 'What matters now are the QEngines, the Foundation Stones . . . and the QHub – and their ultimate integration into the world as we know it.'

The large man with the grey beard frowned. 'QEngine? . . . I don't understand,' he said softly, bewildered by what he had just seen.

Durell's thin black clawed arm reached out and touched the man, almost tenderly. 'You have been asleep for a long time,' said Durell softly. 'You have much to catch up on, much to learn. And then I will show you the QHub and the things it can achieve . . . it will be like the old days, my friend: we will be masters and Spiral will be destroyed. The chaos of the Old God must reign fire from Heaven – before we can turn this world into the Eden we desire! Into the New World. Into Paradise!'

'Yes,' said Gol, nodding softly, rubbing at his greying beard. 'I have been gone for far too long; there is much still for me to learn.'

Northern Siberia: 05:10 a.m. [GMT]

One Week Later

The dawn wind howled and cavorted, kicking up flurries of snow and tearing across the harsh icy landscape, flowing and whirling towards the low darkened brow of the tree line that sported tangled webs of branches and glinting daggers of sculpted snow.

The derrick stood, ominous in its framing obsidian,

23

rigid and stonelike, a golem sentinel staring forlornly over the snow fields. This mighty behemoth guarded the precious drill string, the casings and collar, and the immensely strong titanium-carbide-VII drill bit.

Movement stirred within a lattice of timber, and a figure wrapped in thick furs moved slowly in heavy creaking oil-stained boots across the high wooden balcony built into the derrick. He lifted dDi binoculars to cold grey eyes that peered out above an ice-speckled bushy beard. A freezing wind blew, cutting through his clothing and biting at his skin with diamond teeth. He shivered, and longed for a large mug of hot coffee spiced with brandy.

A black Range Rover was moving, slicing the landscape in two with its distinctive 4X4 trail, exhausts pluming, engine a distant low growl as snow chains tore the ice. Lights glittered like jewels through the gloom. Gradually it drew closer, and the fur-clad guard reached out to hit a small digital buzzer that sounded muffled down below, off towards the trees where snow-encumbered huts and cabins lay under a smothering of snow.

The guard watched figures stirring, and his eyes flickered, darting from the cabins where the workforce was waking from sex-filled dreams and involuntary erections to the large and richly adorned HQ constructed from hardwood and flown to this prospective LVA site by Chinook. He reached down, picked up a Barrett IV sniper rifle with a digital sight, and settled into position against the rough timber railing. The Range Rover looked delectable in the digitally enhancing sights, a soft doe ready for violent slaughter. So easy, thought the guard in idleness. Bang! Dead. He smiled and unscrewed the cap on his vodka canteen.

Below, the door to the HQ opened and a broad-shouldered man stepped through, clad in a long black leather coat, stamping his boots against the snow and looking up towards the rapidly approaching vehicle. He wore his blond hair shaved to the scalp, a style which only emphasised his heavily scarred face and head.

Kattenheim's gaze was wide as he stamped his boots, shrugging off the ice-chill that tore at his skin, ignoring the ever-present pain in his eyes – as he always did and would always have to. He walked forward, his hands deep in his pockets, and stood, legs apart, his stance arrogant, eyes fixed.

The Range Rover came to a halt and the engine died. Plumes of exhaust smoke dwindled as doors opened, and five men with experience-lined brows and aged faces climbed down, slamming doors and approaching the man with the red eyes.

'You Kattenheim?'

The man in the leather coat nodded, slowly.

'We are the LVA Fuel Inspectors, TF Division, and we are currently responsible for Siberia and neighbouring states. I am sure that you have heard of us? Here are our papers . . .' A sheaf was presented, tattered and coffee-stained, curled at the corners. 'We have permission and directives from Director-General Oppenhauer, Commissioner for the Fuel Inspectorate of Eastern Europe, to inspect this facility and work out sequential plans for the eventuality of LVA discovery. My name is Petrinsky.'

Kattenheim reached out and took the papers, but he did not look at them, instead meeting Petrinsky's gaze. 'Oppenhauer exceeds himself with his timing, for only yesterday we were fortunate enough to hit a lode of LVA which would seem very promising. We are just determining its environmental boundaries, and currently await instructions from our science lab on the best methods for

25

extraction, and for the return of our exterior seismic trucks. Anyway, gentlemen, I am being somewhat rude. It is uncouth to speak like this in the snow. Please, follow me.'

Kattenheim's voice was curiously soft, a gentle low-level growl, and turning on the heel of one boot he led the group of Inspectors to the low steps of the raised hardwood cabin, up the steps and into the luxury of ice oasis within.

Out of the cold, Kattenheim removed his gloves and looked the men over, especially the one who had presented himself as Petrinsky. They were veterans, he could see that immediately, and probably as adept with machine guns as with diplomacy. They carried themselves well – ex-military of some sort drafted in to do what was an increasingly unpopular job – and Kattenheim searched the nuances of the leader's name and accent for hint of his origins; Russian, he finally confirmed, probably St Petersburg, but laced with a myriad of other inflections which suggested a lifetime of travel . . . either travel, or covert operations, around the globe. And now? Why employ ex-military men as Inspectors? Was the Fuel Inspectorate suspicious? Was the job *that* fucking dangerous?

'I will allow you a little time to compose yourselves, and then I will guide you around the complex myself. Please, make yourselves at home. There is vodka and brandy in the silver cabinet over there.'

'As you wish.'

Their gazes met, and Kattenheim smiled again, a slow feline smile without humour. 'Please excuse me.' He gave a brief bow and left the cabin, stepping once more back into the snow, his glance taking in the snipers at the tree line. He gave them a nod, and watched as they melted into the early-morning gloom.

*

Bright winter sunshine illuminated the scene, but was soon obscured behind threatening dark clouds. The LVA explorers had gone to work, and the titanium-carbide-VII drill was spinning slowly, searching the depths of the lode rock via its vanguard of diamond drill casings. The distant diesel engines rumbled, their power translated through the turntable at the base of the derrick, and large groups of engineers stood in and around the turntable near the blow-out preventer. The generators hummed through the gloom.

'What depth is this newly discovered LVA lode?'

'Eight kilometres.'

Petrinsky whistled softly, and turned to the other men; they scribbled on DigitalPads. Kattenheim's eyes narrowed, and he glanced left, past the huge spinning bulk of the titanium-VII drill to where the glistening black pumps waited for the removal of the derrick and their subsequent integration into the LVA extraction process.

The drill ceased; steam hissed from pipes as core samples were extracted and gas sensors were lowered down the carrier stem into the heart of this new breach in the Earth.

'We will have to carry out digital stability checks,' Kattenheim heard one of the men say over the noise. 'There must be some fucking pressure in that drill – I mean, look at the size of it! It must be ten times the size of a conventional oil drill . . . I suggest we close down the machines and reconvene in two weeks' time with the council, then decide upon . . .'

The other Inspectors were nodding.

Snow started to fall from the heavy broiling clouds.

Kattenheim sighed. As if in a dream, he lifted his left hand, gloved in the softest doeskin leather, and gave a small discreet signal.

27

The man who was speaking was struck suddenly and savagely between the eyes by a heavy-calibre round . . . a coin-sized circle of red appeared, there was a *smack* of suddenly struck flesh and his brains and skull erupted from the back of his head, showering his shocked comrades.

There was a moment of stunned silence, then Petrinsky screamed something incomprehensible as the Fuel Inspectors separated with military precision – Petrinsky whirled low, came back up with the accuracy of a boxer and hammered a right hook to Kattenheim's jaw. Kattenheim was rocked, but he rolled, absorbing the punch with a grunt before spitting out blood and a chip of tooth, his stare fixed on the fleeing men who were sprinting for the Range Rover.

Kattenheim lifted his clenched fist into the air; more shots rang out, and another two of the Inspectors fell. Petrinsky reached the Range Rover, yanked open the door and leapt in as bullets slammed steel slaps against the panels. The engine roared into life as the remaining Inspector reached the rear door of the Range Rover and was shot in the back. Strips of his lung tissue splattered against the black panels as his face thumped against the glass. And then he sprawled in the cold snow and his eyes stared fish-dead at the rear tyre.

Kattenheim looked down at the first man to be killed – his half-closed purple-lidded eyes, the V of blood down the bridge of his nose, his shattered head lying in the puddle of melted snow littered with tiny shards of bone.

The engine screamed, chains tore at the ice.

The Range Rover managed ten metres before the engine stuttered and died.

Kattenheim strolled towards the stranded vehicle, rubbing thoughtfully at his jaw. His gaze met Petrinsky's as he watched the Russian draw a large heavy seventeen-round-clip Smith & Wesson and point it as if in slow motion towards him.

Petrinsky, his face speckled with blood, his hair matted with gore and bone splinters, screamed harshly as he squeezed the trigger—

Kattenheim's weapon came up, smooth, precise, and there echoed a single shot that smashed Petrinsky's bullet from the air. Ricochets sang a brief song of metal. Kattenheim fired again, the bullet entering Petrinsky's shoulder, exiting from his back and drilling into the Range Rover's dashboard. The Fuel Inspector screamed in agony, and was forced to drop his heavy gun from fingers that no longer worked.

'Quite a right hook, Mr Petrinsky.'

Kattenheim held his Glock loosely, as if discussing the time of day. Petrinsky stared into those scarred red eyes, seeing the wide expression distorted by heavy scars, and realised that the emotion deep within that well of controlled pain was not surprise, hatred, loathing, or even a clinical determination to get the job done. The look merely held a sliver of deep insanity . . . trapped and fighting to be free.

And then he noticed something . . . something glittering behind the scars, behind the haemorrhage of finely woven tissue; it was a gleam, a bright gleam . . . the gleam of copper.

'Why, Kattenheim?' he asked. 'Why have you killed them?'

Kattenheim shrugged. 'I simply cannot allow the time deficit.'

Petrinsky frowned.

Kattenheim lifted the Glock and put a bullet into Petrinsky's face, smashing the man's teeth through the back of his head to bone-clatter from the glass of the Range Rover's windscreen. Petrinsky slumped back, a torn marionette. Kattenheim turned, and strolled off into the gently falling snow.

The bodies had been dragged to the edge of the mighty derrick; the titanium-carbide-VII drill was silent. The five corpses were perched on the edge of the Mud Pits, a huge crater of waste from the drilling process – dirt, rock, and any impurities that the drill had torn from the ground. Kattenheim watched the industrial Grade IV Element drop into the crater with a crash and sudden hiss; steam screamed from the pit as the frozen mud and rock and ice was loosened, and started to liquefy as the temperature rapidly rose above freezing.

And still the snow fell.

Kattenheim lifted a small black cube in front of his face and looked into the eyes of another man a thousand miles away.

'Are they dead?' asked Durell.

Kattenheim watched the corpses slither into the mud. The gaping cavity in Petrinsky's destroyed face – the now much larger hole where his mouth had been – filled with grey liquid shale and mud that then flooded his eye sockets until he disappeared from sight. Bubbles rose and died. The Range Rover was pushed to the edge of the giant pit and rolled into the rock swamp; steam rising around its metal flanks, it sank like a dying dinosaur. The industrial Grade IV Element was withdrawn; within minutes the Mud Pits would be frozen solid once more, a silent grey graveyard, a sinister hiding place for the murdered – the slain.

'Dead and buried,' said Kattenheim softly. 'Dead and fucking buried.'

Spiral Mainframe
Data log #12300

QIII

The QuanTech Edition 3 [QIII] Military Cubic Processor

The QIII was the first ever cellular processor – the prototype of a true electronic mind – semi-organic, silicon-based and with a mixture of synthetic substances at its core. Via design modes and mechs, the QIII processor was a totally independent piece of hardware.

Working around a digital model of WorldCode Data, the QuanTech Edition 3 was digitally capable of almost anything. A successor to the all-powerful QuanTech Edition 2 [QII] processor which runs at the heart of various Spiral mainframes across the globe, the QIII was capable and fully compliant with any and all global operating systems – from UNIX to Windows it could decode way beyond current 64- and 128-bit architectures. The QIII was so powerful that it could decode and re-encode DNA in millionths of a second when it would take a conventional computer many hours. The QIII was at least 50,000 times faster than any current processor in development. It was destined to have groundbreaking effects on all aspects of computing, from military applications to world economics.

The pinnacle of the QuanTech 3's development was the ability to use WorldCode Data combined with probability math – equations allowing it to successfully predict the future in the simulation of any given probable event. This feature was nearly 100% successful and required only occasional calibration.

The QIII was destroyed when a rogue Spiral operative named Durell abused the military processor (and its sub-systems) and attempted to use this all-powerful machine to take over global military systems, financial institutions and satellites, including the highly destructive Russian PredatorSAT modules.

The QIII was destroyed by Spiral operative Cartervb512. All schematics were lost/destroyed. Further development of this kind of mind were subsequently abandoned.

Keyword SEARCH>> QIII, NEX, SAD, SPIRAL_sadt, DURELL, FEUCHTER, Spiral_Q, Spiral_R, SVDENSKA, PAGAN

CHAPTER 2

BODY AND SOUL

Natasha leant on her elbow, staring out at the freshly falling snow. Mountains reared in front of her, grey and jagged rock scattered with ice and forests sprawling across the lower slopes, all viewed through a reality snow-globe that had been freshly shaken. She smiled, her pretty brow creasing slightly, gaze fixing on the dominant pyramidal peak of the Matterhorn and hand moving protectively to her slightly swollen belly where her baby nestled within.

'I wish you could see the snow and mountains, bubba.'

'Who are you talking to?'

A hand rested on her shoulder, and Nats turned, smiling up at Carter, who grinned. He was bearing a small silver tray on which were two squat glasses of Lagavulin.

'Baby.'

'Ahh,' nodded Carter with mock understanding cascading across his – some would say brutal – features. 'Of course – "baby". How is baby? Is he well?'

'He?'

'Just a wild stab in the dark.'

'Yeah, *she* is well.'

There came a long and comfortable pause. Natasha reached out daintily, took the proffered glass, sipped at the distilled warmth. 'I love this.'

'The whisky?'

'No, this place, the atmosphere. Snow falling gently outside with the Alps nestling in the background; the logs burning on the open fire and filling the room with real heat. The thick carpet between my toes, the glow of candle-light across the perfectly still surface of the whisky . . . and you, here by my side, the father of my growing child. Picturesque, eh, Carter?'

'Hm. How sweet. You've been reading that book by bloody Gillian Brewster again, haven't you? Tsch! Look, did I tell you about the new mod I've got for the Browning HiPower 9mm? It's brilliant, I got it from Simmo down in SP1 stores – a needle clip which slots on the top of the gun and . . . and . . .' He saw Natasha's dark frown.

'Carter.' Her voice was low and dangerous.

'What?'

Her eyes became more focused, her frown more intense.

'*What?*'

'My love, you are *so* romantic. Here we are, holidaying in Switzerland, our very own log cabin within the winter gardens of a five-star hotel overlooking the Zermatter Valley – a honeymoon of sorts for the unmarried . . . and you have to talk about your *large weapon*.'

'It's always worked for me before.' Carter grinned, knocking back the Lagavulin and allowing a look of ecstasy to pass across his battered boxer's features. Carter: ex-military, Spiral operative of the first order; his face had been used too many times to cushion the impact of large men's fists. But still, thought Natasha as she watched him through the crystal sparkling of Scotland's finest malt, he *was* handsome – ruggedly handsome . . . yes, battered and ruggedly handsome . . . yes, beat up, rugged, battered smashed and very definitely ruggedly handsome.

'Are you *flirting* with me, Mr Carter?'

Carter carefully placed the empty crystal glass down on the marble table top and gave her a fearsome scowl – the scowl that had impaled assassins, the scowl that had felled Nex warriors, the scowl that had detonated entire armies into piles of pulp . . . Natasha giggled as he swept her from the low couch with its fur throw-over and lifted her lithe supple form high in the air. He cradled her to him, to his chest, nuzzling her neck, inhaling her scent, prickling his stubble against her short spiked black hair. He could feel her agile limbs beneath the silk kimono, felt the robe writhe across her flesh in an incredibly erotic manner. This sensuous fabric standing between their coupling was far, far more erotic than simple nakedness. Carter's breathing deepened and he looked into Nat's mischievous sparkling eyes.

'You going to come snowboarding with me tomorrow, pixie?' he whispered, and kissed her full red lips. They were too good to abuse by leaving alone, and both of them enjoyed a languorous kiss that spun from long seconds to minutes . . .

Natasha finally pulled away with a pout. 'You *know* I can't do anything vigorous; not in my condition. The doctor ordered!'

Carter glanced down at her belly.

'Nothing vigorous? What a shame.' He sulked. 'I had so many fine games planned for you.' He trod carefully across the plush thick-pile carpet, towards the bedroom and the glow of candles within.

'Games?' Natasha seemed to consider this.

'You remember that DPM commando outfit I bought you?'

'You mean the peephole one?'

'Mm.'

There came a long pause.

'Well . . . if I must,' she murmured huskily as Carter's size ten military boot kicked the door closed and shut off the candles from the sight of anyone out there in the thickly falling snow.

The happy couple had failed to observe a broad-shouldered figure outside, arms folded across his black-clad chest, his balaclava-masked gaze fixed through the tumbling flakes on the window of the room where seconds earlier Natasha had reclined.

Snow fell.

And in the blink of an eye, the figure was gone.

Carter lay, dozing on the bed, Natasha's perfect long naked legs languishing beside his sleepy gaze. He moved close, nuzzling her sweet-smelling skin, and she murmured in sleep, rolling away from him and pitilessly stealing the heavy duvet. The room was dark, illuminated only by the glow of candles around the low bed. Carter rolled to his back, then sat up, stomach grumbling from a lifetime of whisky abuse. He popped a tablet, rubbed at his eyes, then picked up the small alloy ECube from the low carved pine table beside the bed.

An ECube was an electronic communications device issued by Spiral – the current model ran a V4.5 ICARUS operating system, sported a 24GHz RISC processor and 512 gigabytes of static RAM. The tiny alloy machine which doubled not only as a GPS but as a link to the massive Spiral CDb (Criminal Database) was completely solid-state, and had many tiny tricks up its little alloy sleeve. Communications, information, weapons system – the ECube was *the* invaluable asset for any Spiral field operative.

Carter grinned, tossing the ECube in his hand like a softball. He squeezed, and the surface came alive with soft blue digits. Reclining, Carter skimmed through recent reports – global activity, criminal, political, social. He yawned, and dropping the ECube beside the bed once more moved to the living quarters of the cabin, running himself a glass of water and standing, naked, staring out at the softly falling snow in the darkness.

It'll be dawn soon, he realised.

'*Exercise is what you really need,*' taunted Kade at the back of his mind. '*Burn off that puppy fat . . . show us you're the real man you pretend to be, fucker.*'

'Yeah, yeah – drop dead.'

'*You wish.*'

Carter poured himself a second glass of water, then moved to the low pine table and sat, staring at the small flexible GridMap entrusted to him by Jam. 'Keep that safe for me, fucker,' Jam had said, grinning over a pint of Guinness.

'What is it?'

'A map.'

'Of what?'

Jam had tapped his nose conspiratorially, giving his cheeky trade-mark grin. 'Trust me Carter, you do *not* fucking want to know. Just keep it safe. I'll be back for it soon.'

Carter stared at the GridMap now. On it were markings, coordinates, and tiny tags reading 'AnComm Post'. Carter had heard a rumour about AnComms, a back-up form of an analogue communication network Spiral were

37

– supposedly – in the process of installing in the event of ECube failure in the future. Of course, Spiral was admitting none of it. The official line was that the ECube was infallible. And if their digital wonder-toy was flawless, then why integrate a back-up system?

Still, Carter toyed with the tiny flexible digital GridMap. What was Jam up to?

Pushing the item to one side, he looked down at his paper notes – notes for his speech which he had been diligently working on. His discarded pencil accused him, and the sheets looked far too blank for his liking.

'Shit.'

He sipped the water and, taking the pencil, chewed the end thoughtfully as he remembered Natasha's words – *it's a huge responsibility, you mustn't fuck it up for Jam and Nicky . . . they have placed their utmost faith in you . . .*

'Yeah, right. I wish the bastard had asked Slater instead. I can do without entertaining a bunch of drunken friends and family . . . I would die for Jam, but perform his best-man speech?' Carter realised that he was grumbling to himself, and he forced his mouth to shut. He stared hard at the page, chewing splinters, but inspiration was denied him. He knew that this leisurely atmosphere, this heady relaxation in the mountains should be highly conducive to work and creativity: but the words just would not flow.

He read what he had already written in his untidy pencil scrawl:

The Marriage of Nicky and Jam: Alexander the Great, ruler of the Greek Empire between 336 BC and 323 BC and the only man to ever conquer the exotic continent of Persia, quantified his Royal

relationship with the Proletariat as
this:

*'It is better to rule by fear than to
rule by love. If you rule by love, the
people can give it - but they can take
it away. If you rule by fear, then you
can enforce the fear and nobody can take
that away from you.'*

Jam rules Nicky like Alexander ruled his
Empire!

Carter shook his head, dropped his pencil atop the
notes which slithered out in a fan, and cursed Jam for the
thousandth time. It was one thing performing a dual
parachute raid on a terrorist HighJ explosives den, but
quite another to stand in front of a group of people –
family people – and attempt to fucking entertain them.
Humour.
Carter snorted. He hated the word. Humour was
something that happened to other people.
He peeped in on Natasha, breathing deeply in sleep,
then on impulse moved to his bag and dug out his
Browning 9mm and a few spare clips. He toyed with the
familiar bulk of the battered old gun – it nestled in his
grip, an old friend.
'You expecting trouble?'
Carter ignored Kade, dressed, and grabbed his snowboard.
'I always expect trouble,' he muttered as he stepped
into a landscape of dawn pastel shades that were too good
to be true. A living breathing dreamland.

★

Carter stood on the edge of the mountain. Sunlight glittered revealing a virgin dawn, sparkling across the snow like blood wine across a fistful of sprinkled diamonds. He crouched, feeling the flexible solidity of the snowboard beneath him; he twisted his ankles slightly, checking the torque of the quick-release bindings, then kicked himself free.

Silence smashed him in the face. Exhilaration grasped his spine in its adrenalin fist and threw him head first down the mountain. He banked left, breath in a gasp, and a shower of snow hissed behind and to his right. Trees loomed. Carter ducked under branches and kicked gracefully around their grasping fingers. The board . . . sang. Carter grinned harshly behind the black neoprene face mask and ski goggles, breathed out slowly, and fixed his gaze on the vertical drop flashing past on either side in mad waves of liquid snow, white mercury . . .

Peace.

The wave descended across Carter like a white shroud. He was at one with himself; the horror of the past year was gone in a single rush of white injection. Gone, Feuchter and his twisted development of the military QIII processor; gone, the Nex assassins and their hunting and murdering; gone, the images of death and betrayal which had haunted Carter and forced Kade to the forefront of his violent mind . . . gone, the attempt by the rogue Spiral operatives to take over the world from a floating warship in the Arctic seas . . .

. . . And all were as inconsequential as a single snowflake.

Snow hissed by, and below him Carter could feel the board; it was a part of him – they had become one. Carter felt his speed increase and the wind howled past his goggles. He crouched lower, and as the ice trail descended through wind-swaying pines the world suddenly opened up to Carter's right. The mountains fell away into a vast open canyon where far, far below icy waters crashed through narrow rocky pools. Carter veered right, hit a low hump of snow and kicked himself into the air with the board raised in the vertical. Again, everything was silent, but this time with the whole world of ice and snow opening before him, there came a panoramic explosion of blinding white and blasting air . . .

The snowboard slid along the edge of the precipice and a devastating crevasse opened up in front of Carter's eyes. There came scraping sounds, rocks slicing the underside of the board at high speed and leaving deep grooves. But Carter was oblivious to this. Sunlight glinted from the ice and snow and distant peaks and he did not glance down at the far distant sharp serrated rocks or landlocked lakes. The board veered left, hissing away from the edge of the sheer drop in a shower of snow and Carter allowed himself to breathe once more.

The faster he went, the more peace settled over him.

Adrenalin brought him serenity.

But then— He felt something: a splinter in his soul, a hot needle drilling through his mind. The bulk of the Browning pressed against him reassuringly beneath his jacket but the other feeling, uncomfortable and real and nestling in his stomach like a cancer, made his head twitch as it came up, his eyes scanning his surroundings in a sudden panic born of experience and a life spent in deadly situations. It was almost a vibration, deep, subsonic, beyond normal hearing and it made him feel suddenly sick to his very core.

Carter licked at his dry lips behind the mask.

And then the feeling was gone . . . as quickly as it had come.

41

The board and its rider flashed beneath more conifers, adrenalin pumping Carter to even greater speed. Left and right he zigzagged down the insanely steep incline – more treacherous than any black run that a slope designer could dream up – until, finally, it levelled out and Carter's racing raging heart started to calm as the board straightened and he sped left, away from the cliffs and lethal terminal drops.

'*You're still a pussy,*' whispered Kade.

Carter smiled grimly, his face darkly demonic behind the mask.

'I must get it from you,' he muttered.

Reaching the outskirts of the hotel grounds, he snapped free of the snowboard and clipped a strap to the carrying D-ring; the hotel, the Coeur des Alpes, loomed ahead of him, an example of fine Swiss architecture constructed from smooth stone and beech, huge beams fronting finely sculpted gardens. Beyond, down snow-laden paths and cable-car tracks, sat the distant town of Zermatt, huddling under a winter shawl of cloud with curls of smoke reaching like grey fingers into the sky.

Carter walked slowly down the winding path, boots crunching fresh fallen snow, between decorative trees and a variety of winter flowers, splashes of colour from edelweiss, lilies and anemones. He stopped before he reached the entrance; a small group of people had arrived in a horse-drawn sleigh and were excitedly disembarking, carrying skis and sporting loud colourful jackets and louder voices. Zermatt was the 'village without cars' and Carter found some of the alternative modes of transport almost magical . . . another time, another world.

He slung his board over his shoulder and pulled free a cigarette, staring dolefully down at the crumpled weed.

'Last one?' He laughed, a gravelly bitter laugh battered

by a thousand battles and too many wars. Placing the cigarette between his lips, he grimaced as he lit the old friend and blew a plume of smoke into the soothing cool air.

Sitting, Carter watched the world go by, turning occasionally to stare up the slopes; he could make out the holiday slopes, just starting to bustle at this early hour of the morning. But he looked – no, he searched – beyond this façade, this mask, this replication of normality . . . searched for something – else.

'*You're imagining things,*' snapped Kade.

Carter snorted. 'Like your fucking voice, perhaps?' He turned and smiled up gently at a face blocked out by the dazzling sun.

'You OK?'

'Yeah,' sighed Carter. 'Just relaxing.'

'I was starting to get worried.'

Carter winked. 'Just, y'know, enjoying a secret cigarette. The wife thinks I've given up and I thought I'd try and sneak one in while she's back languishing at the cabin, doing all the cleaning and ironing. She's a bit of a dumb ass, thinks she can get her man – secure her victory like Alexander the Great – and then seek to change him by stopping his bad habits.'

Natasha sat down beside him, huddling close and linking arms. Sunlight bathed her beautiful, finely chiselled features, and her dark eyes surveyed Carter with casual violence as her hand curled around his steel bicep. 'So, this dumb-ass wife, what would she do if she caught you smoking out here?'

Carter shrugged, reached across, and gently pecked Natasha on the cheek. 'Probably beat me senseless,' he sighed, rolling his eyes.

'And you would let her abuse your body in this way?'

43

Carter grinned. 'Yeah, I've always loved the violent abuse of a woman.'

They kissed, lips moist and warm as a cool Swiss breeze blew from the mountains, and they drew closer until Natasha's bump pressed against him. Carter pulled away, met her gaze for a moment, then glanced down. 'You're definitely getting bigger. Turning into a right little porker.'

She ignored his jibe. 'I wonder, do you think he'll look like you? A mad little Carter running around, hair stuck up in all directions, cut-off combat shorts and podgy little face all screwed up as he searches for his plastic Browning 9mm?'

Carter's laugh burst free, a sudden explosion of sound. His hand moved over Natasha's belly, gently, protectively. 'I'm sure he'll be a little bastard, just like his father.'

'I can guarantee it,' snapped Natasha. 'Now, are you coming back to bed to warm the covers for me, or what?'

Carter scowled. 'What do I get in return?'

Natasha reached forward, dark eyes fixed on his, and flicked the end of his nose mischievously. 'We'll just have to see what I can come up with,' she crooned huskily.

Carter lay naked on the bed, still covered by a fine sheen of sweat from their sex, and listened to Natasha singing in the shower. He smiled, but the smile was laced with a distant agony and he remembered the bad times . . .

Sleep surprised him, and when his sticky eyes opened it was to see Natasha twirling in her new black dress in front of the mirror, her short dark hair spiked, deep brown eyes beneath well-groomed brows staring disapprovingly at him.

She tutted.

'What?' he croaked.

'Is the father of my child really such a dirty drunkard?'

''Twas only a nip, to keep the winter chill at bay.'

'You say that in the damn *summer*, Carter.'

He grinned, and scratched his belly. 'You finished in the bathroom, then?'

'I have . . . no, wait, let me get my make-up before you lock yourself in with a magazine.'

Carter sighed, and rolled grumpily out of bed.

The meal had been a particularly fine one, the following wine – and sex – almost too much for Carter to bear.

When he awoke, in the darkness, he was struck by momentary confusion. Sex-sweat had left him chilled, and he tried to work out how long he had been asleep. He frowned – why was he awake? He didn't need a piss, or a drink. That usually meant something bad and he rolled swiftly out of bed, palmed the silenced Browning 9mm and pulled on his trousers. If I'm going to fight, he thought, I ain't going to do it naked . . .

Carter hadn't lived as long as he had without being careful.

And clothed.

He moved towards the door, silent across the thick carpet, senses screaming at him that something was out of place; he could hear nothing, smell nothing but scented oil from Natasha's burners and candles, and yet something was wrong. He peered around the door and froze, waiting for his eyes to adjust. Like any hunter he knew that it was movement, mainly movement, that would give away a position – no matter how good the camouflage.

There was a large dark-clad figure, moving with extreme care.

Carter's eyes narrowed.

The man – or woman – was searching through the

45

cabin; Carter watched as hands rifled through drawers, then through Natasha's handbag. Carter stepped silently into the room – but, almost impossibly, he was heard. The figure's head, masked in a neat black balaclava, snapped around, eyes gleaming – then it whirled, dropping to a crouch and leaping with lightning speed at Carter who squeezed the trigger and the Browning spat, a bullet hissing free and smashing into the dark bulk of the figure before it crashed against Carter and sent them both flying back against the wall. Carter bounced to the floor, grunting.

The Browning was knocked free, a fist found Carter's jaw and he felt a tooth crack, blood flooding his mouth as stars danced in front of his eyes for a second. He lashed out with both fists, striking again and again at flesh beneath the mask and he carried on punching as he was picked from the floor and hurled across the room where he hit the wall again. A picture smashed this time, glass slicing strips of flesh from his back and he hit the floor once more, hard . . .

Boots stomped down but Carter rolled with lightning speed, coming up in a crouch and smashing an overhead straight punch into the attacker's groin – once, twice. Then, gaining his feet, he lashed out and gripped the attacker's windpipe. The large masked attacker pulled free Carter's hand with the ease of incredible strength and reached swiftly forward, fingers of both hands curling around Carter's throat before he could step beyond reach and lifting him from the ground with crushing force, dangling him breathless and kicking, eyes wide as the figure rose to his full height. Carter stared into dark slitted glittering eyes.

Carter choked, his hands gripping at the huge muscles in the arms which held him suspended. His eyes narrowed as he realised this huge fucker was much, much stronger than he, and he kicked out once, twice, three times but the grip would not release and Carter was choking, spinning white stars dancing patterns before his eyes and choking, choking and falling, he was shaken like a rag doll and he realised that he was suffocating . . .

Carter's hands dropped swiftly to the waist of his combats and with agony hammering through him and pain burning his brain with hot acid he slid free the thread of MercG that was sheathed there – hidden – as he heard the confused voice of Natasha calling from the bedroom. Carter sensed more than saw the attacker's change of stance, head turning to this new potential threat . . .

He had to act – and act fast.

His feet lashed out ineffectually against the attacker's groin and belly. Carter spun the mercury garrotte, a processor-controlled liquid metal thread activated by mind augmentations, so thin that it could be undetectably concealed and so astonishingly deadly that it could cut through steel, and with a flick of his wrist sliced through one of the attacker's arms. A burning hiss of slashed flesh and bone was barely audible.

The attacker screamed, a high shrill sound, releasing Carter who landed in a crouch beside the severed blood-pumping arm, limp-fingered and twitching and spilling gore across the carpet. The attacker spun, fleeing into the darkness without any further sound as Carter rubbed at his bruised windpipe and focused on regaining his breath and his vision. With his sight returned, he deactivated the MercG, located his Browning and crawled to the cabin door, peering out into the snow. But the attacker had vanished.

'What is that fucking smell?'

Natasha, bleary-eyed and naked, hair tousled, nose

wrinkled, stood in the doorway to the bedroom, looking confused.

'Yeah, thanks for your help,' croaked Carter, reaching up to flick on the light. An ambient cosy warm radiance contrasted with the stark images and thoughts that crashed through Carter's brain.

Natasha frowned, then stared down. 'Carter, there's a fucking *arm* on the carpet.'

'Really? You don't say. I wonder how that got there – could it have been something to do with the noise that roused you from your wine-induced slumber?'

'What was he after?' Natasha pulled a blanket around her shoulders and moved to him, crouching. 'Are you all right?'

Carter laughed, sliding the MercG back into its tiny hidden sheath at his waist and rising to lock the door of the cabin. 'Nice to see my health is third on your list of priorities.'

'Did he take anything?'

Carter prodded the severed arm with the toe of his boot. 'I don't know; I disturbed him before he found whatever he was looking for. Maybe he wanted Jam's GridMap.' Carter rubbed at his bruised throat again, noting Jam's map which had been covered by Carter's scattered wedding notes. The simplest hiding place was sometimes no hiding place at all!

'Can you get me a glass of water? The bastard nearly crushed my windpipe.'

'Hence the arm on the floor.'

'Yeah. And get onto Spiral, comm a genetic sample, see if the CDb can find us a match.' He coughed painfully as Natasha passed him some water. He checked first the door, then the carpet, then his Browning. 'The fucker took a bullet.'

'It didn't wake me.'

48

'That's because the gun was silenced and you were drunk. I never knew I'd curse the damn thing! I could have done with some help, even from somebody who was pissed.'

'You're bleeding . . . God, Carter, you've really been in the wars.'

'Yeah, you'll have fun picking the glass out of my flesh later.'

'Was this guy strong? A Nex?'

Carter stared with a frown at Natasha. 'Too strong,' he croaked, prodding at his windpipe. 'So much for the Utopia I dreamed about. Had to be a fucking Nex – and a big one at that. I was hoping the SAD teams had wiped them all out by now . . .'

'They'll never kill them all.' Natasha stroked Carter's cheek. 'And it looks like they still want you dead, my lover.'

'Yeah,' he grimaced, 'I'm a regular fucking hunted man.'

Music thundered, as if the Gates of Hell had been thrown wide open. Carter frowned, perched at the bottom of the stairs, smoke stinging his eyes, gazing out from this slight vantage point at the hundreds of people filling the hotel function room. After the previous night he was a touch on edge despite Spiral's reassurances that there was no Nex activity in the area. The results of the gene-coding sample had been returned negative: the attacker had not been a Nex. Just a real tough human son of a bitch.

Carter grinned nastily and searched the crowd for a large one-armed man. The Browning in his belt would sort things out if Carter happened across the intruder again . . . and the next time he wouldn't take just an arm as a trophy.

49

Natasha, behind him, gave him a little push.

'Come *on*, Carter, we're late.'

Carter grumbled and muttered something: something about it being too smoky, too crowded and too loud. And how he had recently been attacked and so should really be at home in bed with a hot whisky and lemon, three sugars.

'How old are you, you moaning old goat? Jesus, Carter, it's not like we go to *many* parties! Make a bloody effort or I'll break your spine.'

'Someone already tried that,' he grumbled, feeling the medical staples that Natasha had applied pull tight in the flesh of his back.

Carter watched Natasha's low-cut black dress disappear into the throng, and he followed, more sedately – like a dog on a leash, growling.

Carter blinked, then stared hard at the flamboyant and very well-presented breasts which had just bumped rudely into his chest. 'Excuse me,' came a voice slurred by High German and beer.

Carter's eyes flickered up from the impressive cleavage to a beautiful young face regarding him with positive appraisal. He shook his head, took a deep smoke-filled breath, and fought his way to the bar where he ordered a litre of Schwarz-Bier and sunk his face into its cold welcoming depths. The liquid nectar soothed his throat, soothed his brain and soothed his temper. Parties were not exactly Carter's scene; it wasn't the party *per se*, more the horde of bustling party people all with their own little agendas. Carter wasn't exactly the human race's greatest fan, and he had the word *cynicism* branded – hardwired – into his brain.

'There you are!'

Natasha twirled into view, giggling, a man on each arm.

Carter, with a Schwarz-Bier moustache, frowned at

her. His field-staples were hurting – he could feel the tiny pins piercing his skin and muscle – and the bruises on his throat were a testament to his recent attacker's formidable strength.

'Dancing! You coming dancing? This is Hans . . . and, and, and—'

'Mm!' grunted Carter, which translated through intonation to something considerably more rude.

Natasha took the hint, and disappeared, bump first.

Carter ordered another beer. He changed his mind, and ordered two. Then he thought: fuck it, and ordered a third, with a triple-whisky chaser. It's going to be a long night, he thought as the lights dimmed and more lasers kicked spirals of colour across the walls and beams – and the music's volume increased painfully.

'*You happy?*' came the taunting voice of Kade. Carter ignored him, ignored the tone of arrogance and deceit. '*Come on, Carter, talk to me! This is a fine place, full of fine woman flesh – look there! You see her hips? Fine child-bearing hips . . .*'

'Leave me alone,' said Carter softly.

'*But . . . Carter, I can't leave you alone, dickhead. We are brothers. And I feel I should warn you that things here are not as they seem.*'

'In what way?'

'*Ahh, that would be telling.*'

'Kade, you fuckwit, what's on your mind?'

Carter dismissed Kade with a mental surge of anger and, calming himself, leant back against the bar – good solid wood protecting his back – and watched the people around him, a tankard in his fist and a gun in his belt. Fuck Kade, he thought sourly. He was just a bad demon who'd got out of bed on the wrong side and fancied a little bit of shit-stirring as his starter.

51

Men and women gyrated in parodies of dance, as some Swiss musician massacred a song about the mountains and added GBH boot first to the tune with a happy accordion melody. Carter watched the people and the people ignored him – it was as if he wasn't there, an invisible player beyond the boundaries of these strangest of rules, this most esoteric of games. It always amused Carter: stay sober (or sober in comparison to those around you) and you could neatly sidestep the alcohol bubble; withdraw from the party sphere and allow yourself time to watch and study and fundamentally *learn* the mechanics of humankind.

The young German woman with the proud chest sidled along the bar towards him. Carter grabbed his Schwarz-Bier and was about to make a dash, but was too slow in his haste to salvage his drinks. Her talons curled around his bicep and she held him, trapped by manners, imprisoned by etiquette.

'Yes, love?'

'Ahh, English. You here to ski, yes?'

Carter looked into her eyes, saw the gleam of alcohol on her lips, eyed the painted decorative nails around his arm and swallowed hard. She was out for the kill.

'Yes, yes . . . well, snowboarding, actually.'

'Ah, the snowboarding man. Athletic! Can I buy you a drink?'

Carter eyed the three tankards and the huge glass of whisky – the kill-switch in his brain refused to trip. 'Yes, sure, don't mind if I do.' He mentally kicked himself, then caught Natasha staring at him from the dance floor and frowned at her. She gave him a broad wink and he stuck out his tongue.

Carter spent the next fifteen minutes stumbling through a broken conversation – broken because he refused to acknowledge his fluency in German, and thus allowed the poor girl to struggle with her distinctly bad English.

It was when her hand started brushing against his thigh that he made a lame excuse and, finishing his beer, headed across the dance floor and into No Man's Land.

'I'm getting a headache.'

Natasha tutted, boogying with Hans and twirling in a pirouette in front of Carter. 'Do you find me sexually pleasing to the eye, future husband and father of my child?'

'Yes, yes, but I've had enough of this. It's not my scene. I'm going out for a smoke.'

'Bad Carter.'

'Yeah, so shoot me. Every other fucker tries.'

Carter bounced from body to body and finally made the exit. Cold air hit him – crisp and fresh and exhilarating. The sky was partially clouded, but between the puffs of moonlit cotton twinkled stars brighter than crushed diamond. Carter breathed deeply, eyes closed for a moment of ultimate simple pleasure; then he pulled out a cigarette, lit the battered specimen and filled his lungs with a pleasant impurity.

He could hear the thump of the music and a cold wind blew across him, chilling his body after the sweating, heaving, dancing crowd. He enjoyed the cigarette, the beauty of the simple night air around him and the crisp stars above. Enjoyment, he decided, was something without action; without adrenalin; without the defying of death. But then – there was always an intense gratification after shooting a bad man in the face.

Slowly, teasingly, there arose a deep, distant, subsonic rumble.

Carter froze, smoke pluming around his slightly wind-chilled face, eyes narrowed.

The rumble came again, heavier, gravelly and deeply bass. Carter felt a tremor beneath his boots and his hand shot out to steady himself; and then he watched in horror as the hotel in front of him *moved*, shaking to the tune of suddenly screaming voices, and the whole world seemed to fill with a trembling roaring song as the structure thrashed backwards and forwards. The ground was shifting and flexing beneath him and Carter whirled, forgotten cigarette extinguished in the snow as he sprinted for the entrance to the party . . . which spat forth a machine-gun stream of screaming people, faces contorted in horror and fear. With a deep, climactic surge of noise the hotel buckled near its centre and part of the roof disappeared, slipping into darkness. Some of the lights went out in a domino swathe . . .

'Fuck . . .'

Carter fought his way violently through the throng of escaping, stampeding people, 'Nats!' he screamed as the rumbling continued, some Earth-giant coming awake beneath their very feet. The world was a confusion, a shaking, rumbling, heaving insanity and Carter plunged past flailing, screaming people who struggled against him, kicking and pushing, but he was fighting not to get out but to get *in* . . .

Natasha was dancing with Hans, slapping away his cheeky hands as the first tremor warned her through the soles of her boots. The smile fell from her face as somebody cried out. The ground suddenly roared beneath them, walls shaking, glass smashing from the bar and dropping from people's quake-slippery fingers. Beer washed across the floor amid broken glass and overturned furniture. As one,

54

the population of the party turned and ran, scrambling and pushing for the exit as—

Natasha blinked.

The floor opened and a jagged metre-wide scar tore towards her. With a yelp, she dragged free a concealed knife and leapt upwards, embedding the knife in a wide beech beam. It held her suspended as Hans hissed in surprise and disappeared into the gaping black cavity—

Warm air drifted up from the yawning crevasse.

Natasha blinked, licking her lips slowly, nervously.

Hans was gone.

Natasha watched, hands sweating in the sudden blast of heat, as a woman slipped, fingers clawing at the flagstone floor, and disappeared into a deep-seeming infinity of darkness. Warm air stinking of sulphur and other chemicals washed upwards over Natasha and she gagged, bile rising from her stomach, and still the rumbling moaned, then started to increase in tempo again as the crevasse – its movement halted briefly for a suspended moment in time – snaked across the ground once more in a bass-screeching zigzag of tearing stone, towards the terrified bar staff who froze like rabbis in the headlight beams of a fast-moving juggernaut . . .

'Run!' screamed Natasha, swinging her legs and leaping to the apparent safety of one crumbling uneven side of this sudden rift. The fracture crashed across the floor and the whole room seemed to tilt, to upend as the massive bar was torn, its woodwork screaming and spitting splinters like spears, whirled around in a vortex of unstoppable Earth energy and then dropped into the chasm, where it wedged tight at an angle.

The rumbling died.

People were still screaming, but this faded as the crowd fled from the chamber. The huge timber bar, stuck at an angle like a toothpick in a giant's maw, creaked in its undignified entrapment. Below it, in the darkness, Natasha could hear more screaming, one voice hysterical, another sobbing.

'Nats!'

'Carter, over here.'

Then Carter was there, his eyes wide at the jagged angular rift across the floor of the chamber, a tear in the fabric of the rock and leading – how deep? He frowned, glancing over the edge. His boots felt slippery against the loose stones.

'Nats, let's get the fuck out of here.'

More rumblings came from below the earth; the walls began to shake and the muffled sobbing increased in volume. Then the hysterical screaming suddenly cut short as the noise of impacting flesh bounced from walls of rock.

'No! Help them!' Her eyes were wide, pleading.

'Natasha! Get out of here . . .' But Carter knew that it was no use. She was too good a person to put her own safety first . . . her stubbornness was legendary and had led to a million fights. Carter grinned a bad grin: he knew a fucking lousy gig when he saw one, and the crevasse beneath him was definitely a gig to avoid . . .

Carter leapt to the edge of the precipice and kicked at the wide timber of the wedged bar; it was stuck, a ten-metre splinter length caught against a jagged fall of rock. Below, about fifteen feet into the chasm and caught on a narrow strip of rocky ledge, he could see two women clinging on for dear life, eyes streaming with tears, their revealing party dresses torn and ragged.

'Yeah, just like a fucking snowboard,' he growled, and to the cacophony of rising rumbles, the tearing of rock all around, the shaking walls and the vibrating of roof timbers Carter leapt onto the bar and slid down towards the two desperate women – descending into the darkness with its warm sulphur air currents and bad metal-rock stink.

The women's tears were flowing freely as he grabbed a hand, slippery with blood, sweat and saliva. His fingers closed around it in an iron grip and he hauled, lifted the woman in his arms and with all his strength threw her towards the top of the ragged vent . . . She was caught by Natasha's searching hands and pushed to freedom as another roar shook the room, more glasses smashed, and one of the huge ceiling beams split with a deafening crack, showering down jagged lengths of timber – and then collapsed with a tremendous scream, filling the chamber with clouds of debris and crushed stone, sending a shower of sharp rocks flying against Natasha and blocking out the light . . .

Dust engulfed Carter and he choked, balanced within the fissure of rock as everything shook around him, making him feel suddenly nauseous. With eyes streaming he steadied himself, traced the sobbing and choking noises and, reaching down, found the second woman's hand. He lifted her to him and she clung, limpet to rock, face buried in his neck, breasts heaving with panic against his chest. Holding her tight, Carter turned his face away from the dust and closed his ears to the rumbling roar of the world around him. He could feel the bar, perched treacherously and moving as if in rhythm with the shaking earth – he felt it sliding and with a sudden surge of adrenalin and an insane burst of speed and power he sprinted up the incline, boots pushing against the torn handles of beer pumps to propel himself upwards and onwards, somehow miraculously launching himself from the summit to roll, still clasping the woman,

57

to the stone- and -glass-scattered floor. The shards bit into his hands and arms and legs, slicing him open in a dozen places.

'It's fucking collapsing!' screamed Natasha.

Carter watched the bar slide into infinity. He wiped rock dust from his eyes and felt blood flow over his hands and arms. He looked up; the shaking had increased, the whole world was shifting and moving and bucking around them as if in the throes of inebriation, of sex, and he felt pure fear. 'Get the fuck out – now,' he said calmly.

They could die in this place.

Hauling himself to his feet, and dragging the hysterical woman along with them, they sprinted for the exit and the steps leading out into the fresh air. Another beam collapsed behind them, a mushroom of dust billowing around the two Spiral operatives and smashing them with stone buckshot from this natural shotgun. Up the steps they raced and burst out gasping into the cold crisp night air—

People were screaming, sobbing, searching for friends who were missing in the huge crowd. A couple of small groups had moved away from the hotel and were staring with wide eyes, dumbstruck at this incredible disaster. A few were trying to help others, less fortunate than themselves, who had been cut by broken glass or battered by heavy falling stones.

Carter could hear helicopters and distant sirens.

He prised the woman's fingers from their grip on his body, oblivious to her whimpers of thanks. His head turned to one side and he looked up. The screams were muffled by the continuing rumbles and vibrations. The whole hotel was tilted, partly collapsed, a deformed nightmare – and then Natasha was in front of him, her stare locked with his, her face almost unrecognisable through the dust and the grime.

'You can hear it as well.'

Carter gritted his teeth, stone dust grinding between them. 'I hear nothing.'

'You can hear her screaming . . . go and help her.'

Carter took hold of Natasha's face, looked deep into her beautiful eyes. 'No, Nats – I'm here for you. And our baby . . . I'm not part of International fucking Rescue.'

'She is fucking screaming in there . . . she will die. And it will haunt your conscience for ever.'

'Damn you, Natasha, I have our family to think about now . . .'

'Go,' pleaded Natasha, 'I will be OK here . . . go and help her.'

Cursing, and rubbing hard at his eyes, Carter looked up at the collapsing hotel. Then he was running, around the side of the swaying building, staring up at smashed windows and tilted sections of stonework, heading towards the buckled main doors. They were wedged in place by off-camber walls that showered pulped masonry from torn stone arteries. Carter's snow-crusted boot persuaded the doors to open.

The lights – and the hotel power – died.

The hotel was plunged into darkness.

The rumblings of the earthquake had died down a little, and Carter paused. He could still hear the screaming, but it sounded weary now, exhausted, a wail without hope. This fired him on and he ran into the reception area where fallen beams littered his path. He glanced up, could see a little moonlight far above and suddenly a snowflake hit him in the face. More fell through this smashed hole in the centre of the hotel and Carter headed for the stairs. They were twisted like a horribly deformed limb; Carter sprinted up them, boots slipping and outstretched hands groping his way forward. As he reached the landing, there was a terrible groan and the whole mammoth staircase toppled behind him, leaving nothing but a timber-spiked black expanse filled with rising clouds of dust and twisted fists of iron.

The noise subsided slowly.

'Fucking *wonderful*.'

'*Are we having fun yet?*' whispered Kade nastily at the back of his mind.

Carter grinned, a malicious lopsided grin, and wondered if he had made the right choice . . . hmm, a tough one. Standing in the safety of the snow, or rushing headlong into a collapsing hotel?

He glanced around; without the help of the hotel lights the whole place was a maze of shadows. Carter groped his way along one wall, using the fireman's trick of pressing the back of his hand against it instead of the palm – if he met a live cable, the shock would jerk his hand away; but if he searched with his palm open then the shock would cause his fingers to spasm and grip the cable, ensuring death by electrocution.

He paused, listening, the cuts on his hands and arms stinging with that glass-grated, flesh-peeled feeling he so detested. 'Hello?' he bellowed, and tracked the sobbing by sound.

The rumbling began once more.

Carter cursed vividly.

Gentle at first, the rumbling rose as Carter sprinted along a plush carpeted corridor and towards a door from behind which the sounds had come. The walls were shaking, and Carter's teeth rattled as he tried the handle – the door was locked. He raised his boot, but the whole hotel seemed to tilt suddenly and he was sent spinning backwards, smashing against the wall and hitting the floor hard, grunting as the staples in his back pulled tight and tore through living flesh. He felt a warm rush of blood flow down his spine as he heaved himself to his feet, blinking dust from his eyes and struggling to stand upright – and he knew . . .

Knew that he did not have long.

'*The floor isn't the right way up,*' advised Kade.

'I can fucking see that, moron.'

There came a distant, frightening, nauseating crackle. Carter's nostrils twitched as they detected smoke. The earthquake's rumbling continued to increase in intensity.

He kicked down the door and waded into the darkness. But then he stopped, confused by the sight that met his gaze. A man lay atop a woman in a broad bed; she was sobbing but he was gyrating in an act of wanton sex. Carter could see the gleam of his broad back and he took in the stockings on the man's legs and his PVC outfit. Carter's head tilted to one side as dust trickled down from the destroyed ceiling above. The woman was weeping and struggling ineffectually.

'*High-class whore,*' came Kade's unwanted intrusion.

'You think I'm fucking blind?' came Carter's vitriolic reply. Then, out loud, 'I think you two need to get out of here right now.' The woman still sobbed, but the man's hand clamped over her mouth and his wild drunken stare focused on Carter.

'Fuck off. I get what I pay for.'

Carter palmed his Browning and placed a bullet in the man's calf, merging pulped muscle and shattered shin with the bed sheets. The man screamed, rolling free and bouncing to the carpet, grabbing at the gush of blood. He stared up through drug-fuelled eyes, his hands stained with his own life. 'You shot me!'

Carter's boot hammered the man's face, and he picked up the limp, moaning woman from the bed. She was naked except for knee-high boots, and she cradled herself to him as the room shook. Carter moved to the window and stared down onto the decorative flagstones. Too high to jump. He moved back, into the corridor. The smell of fire was much stronger now, and without the staircase he would have to find another means of escape. Carter started to jog, near-naked woman in his arms, struggling to keep his footing on the sloping twisted floor. He could hear cries for help from the wounded man behind, bleeding in the room. 'Find your own fucking way out,' he thought simply. He reached the end of the corridor and stood staring through a huge bay window made up from lots of small panes but with only a few panels of actual glass remaining.

The rumbling ceased.

'Thank God,' Carter whispered in relief.

Rock tore and screamed, and from the window he watched the snaking crevasse appear, sucking snow from the slope directly before him and zigzagging crazily across the gardens towards the hotel. Time should have slowed but it did not, and Carter felt a sense of panic well up madly in his chest. He fought it down.

His mouth was still dry with sudden fear as the world cracked open in front of him, though.

The moaning woman shivered, cold in Carter's arms, as the mountain breeze stroked her skin. He looked down into her beautiful mascara- and tear-smeared face – her eyes opened slowly, confused, and she stared up at him, her full red lips parted slightly. Carter saw there a reflection of his own fear and a bewilderment about what was happening . . .

The sound of screaming, tearing rock filled his ears and the hotel began to sway, throwing Carter off balance. He kicked his way through the frame of the bay window, stomping its wood to match-tinder, and with a disbelieving prayer he leapt towards the snake of rapidly splitting ground.

The buzz of Air Zermatt rescue helicopters filled the air and the song of sirens rose from the valley below. They buzzed, muffled and distant, a dream.

Cold air howled past Carter, whipped at him as he fell helplessly towards the widening, speeding, zigzagging crevasse.

He closed his eyes against the horror . . .

Spiral Mainframe
Data log #12874

CLASSIFIED SADt/6778/SPECIAL INVESTIGATIONS UNIT
Data Request 324#12874

NEX

The Nex Project Nx5

Nicknamed 'Necros' or 'Nex', the Nx5 Project was pioneered in the 1950s as a response to the Cold War games of the USA and Russia.

The Design Brief was simple: create a creature that was a blend of insect and human, capable of withstanding chemical, biological and nuclear toxins. Using an ancient machine originally developed by the Nazis, Skein Blending allowed genetic strands to be spiralled together – woven into an artificial or enhanced creature. When the human element was kept dominant the resulting hybrid had many of the powerful characteristics of an insect. A much increased strength, agility and speed. An increased pain threshold. A resistance to chemical, biological and radioactive poisons with an incredibly enhanced immune system. Increased speed of thought processes. Some grew external and internal armour to protect organs and bones, and all became incredibly lethal killing machines without remorse. The perfect soldier, with an ability to repair themselves.

One downside was a change to the subject's mind-state. Many subjects lost all emotions, lost the ability to love, to nurture, to care. The mind became like that of an insect – sterile and completely focused on tasks.

Spiral withdrew funding following bad media coverage, several laboratory catastrophes and a growing concern over the moral standpoint.

Keyword SEARCH>> NEX, SAD, SPIRAL_sadt, DURELL, FEUCHTER, QIII, Spiral_NX

CHAPTER 3

SEARCH AND DESTROY

Jam and Mongrel stood outside the wide H2 military-green metal-studded door, their faces long, sulking like naughty schoolboys waiting outside the headmaster's office. They exchanged glances, and Jam wrapped his long leather coat more tightly around his shoulders as if this thick black skin was armour; a temporary protective exoskeleton.

'You ask him.'

Mongrel frowned, his naturally brooding Slavic features positively hangdog now. 'I ain't asking him.'

'It's your fucking turn.'

'But you *know* what that big dumb bastard said!'

'Yeah, he said he wouldn't give us any more ammo, and if we came back to ask for more he might just shove it up our arses. *That*'s what the bastard said. I just don't know if he was joking or not – you know, playing around in a friendly sort of fashion, or meaning it in an evil-bastardy sort of fashion. You know Simmo!' Jam scowled, seemingly unsure of himself.

'*Da*, I know him – and I know he fucking unpredictable.'

They both stared at the wide metal door. The plastic plaque screwed into the steel read: SGT SIMMO – STORES. Such a simple epithet, and yet one which had repercussions throughout the whole of Spiral_H, including the different H2, H3 and H4 divisions. In the same way that a secretary could run a school, the guard on a front gate could run a whole electronics corporation, or an air-traffic controller could coordinate an entire airport – so the nasty shaven-headed squaddie in charge of the stores could run the whole of Spiral.

Sort of.

Sgt Simmo was in charge of weapons, ammunition, gadgets, motorbikes, trucks, tanks and helicopters. If you needed something, you had to see Sgt Simmo. If you needed something in an emergency, you still had to see Sgt Simmo. And always, always, always . . . you had to sign for it in triplicate.

'Just follow my lead, pussy,' said Jam, and pushed the door open with a gentleness uncommon for the large killer.

Mongrel, muttering insults, followed Jam into the gloomy office which fronted the huge maze of warehouse stores containing a billion items of equipment. The office shouldn't have been gloomy – it was painted a bright military green, and had plenty of lighting. But something sinister nevertheless created an ominous murky half-light which one could only attribute to the personification of fear in the very air itself, lurking like the bad after-smell of a poisoned curry.

'He's not here,' said Jam, breathing a sigh of relief.

'Fucking horny old goat probably shagging Mrs Spud.'

Sgt Simmo rose from behind the counter, like a glacier sliding ominously into view. He was a mammoth hulk, a man-mountain with a shaved head, black goatee beard, fearsome bushy eyebrows, and the terrible narrowed eyes of a killer. He weighed in at around twenty-four stone and his barrel chest was just that. He insisted on wearing urban combats, even in desert or jungle combat situations. When asked why, he always replied, 'Wouldn't want to fucking blend in, would I?' even thought that, apparently, was the point. His arms, hands, neck and any other bare visible skin was heavily tattooed with lists and military script, and he grinned a nasty missing-toothed grin that told of a life of brawling in pubs.

Mongrel, who was a huge man himself, seemed dwarfed as Simmo reared up from behind that counter.

'What wrong with Mrs Spud?' rumbled Simmo.

'Nothing, nothing,' murmured Mongrel, reading the list of men that Simmo had killed that was tattooed on his throat with ticks against each name. Mongrel always read that list. It went: McGibbon, Dike, Hando, Pilchard, Begbie, Twat-57, Fat Bob Smith . . . and then trailed off into drunken tattoo smush which Simmo would never explain. Not that Mongrel asked, but he knew that if he *was* to ask then an explanation would be forthcoming – in a violent wide-fisted sort of way.

'Mrs Spud is fine lady friend of The Sergeant,' growled Simmo, frowning like an eyebrow avalanche, 'Mrs Spud, as well as cooking fine fish and chips in canteen and always giving The Sergeant his daily feed for free, also gives damn fine good blow job at no extra cost. There no feeling on this world that her false teeth not conjure, so don't you fucking be disrespecting Mrs Spud or The Sergeant be very angry man!' His voice had risen to a roar.

Mongrel was looking down, kicking his size thirteen polished boots against the bottom of the counter, guiltily. 'Sorry, Sarge,' he muttered. 'Really, really – sorry.'

Simmo deflated a little as Jam pushed Mongrel out of the way with a tut and slapped his hand on the counter. He beamed up at Sgt Simmo with the sort of insane wide-faced innocence that had deceived many enemies and sent them to their graves.

'Hi there, Simmo old buddy,' said Jam. 'Listen.' He leaned in close, much to the obvious distaste of Simmo. 'This – um – Mrs Spud . . .'

'Yes?'

'You and her – you a bit of an item then, or what?'

Simmo stared at Jam with eyes that had watched one thousand, four hundred and seventy-two men scream at the point of death.

'Yes,' he rumbled. 'That a problem for you?'

'No no no!' Jam beamed. 'Listen, hey man, it's your choice, she has a fine set of, um, cheeks, I'm sure, and those muscles in her square jaw surely must mean that she does what you said earlier, give a man a good BJ, and I'm sure that when she sits on your fucking face and pisses it gives you a happy warm glow inside – but hey, I need some fucking ammo and our Comanche leaves in five fucking minutes. So be a good lad, and open the fucking gate.'

Jam grinned up at Simmo.

Simmo's fists had clenched. Then he relaxed, deflating once more, and leered at Jam with teeth that had stripped the flesh from a dead comrade's thighs to keep a battle-weary Simmo from starving in the field. He laughed then, an explosion of rattling sound like bones in a tin can, which only confirmed in Jam's mind that The Sergeant was not used to laughing.

Simmo hit the buzzer, there was – predictably – a buzz and the huge iron gate behind him unlocked.

'Thank you,' said Jam, checking his watch.

'I know you only fuck with The Sergeant.' The huge soldier grinned and as Jam strode past a hand the size of a shovel slapped him on the back, nearly sending his face through the iron gate.

Jam coughed, and forced a laugh.

'Yeah, just fucking with you.'

Sgt Simmo frowned. 'You have three minutes. Get what you need and return here for the paperwork.'

'Will do.'

Mongrel followed Jam through the gate and into a wide strip-lit corridor that led on for as far as the eye could see. Doors and gates opened off this central corridor, feeding into hangars and testing stations, into firing ranges and mock terrorist positions; into stores filled with everything from 9mm clips to torpedoes and tank shells.

They headed for the ammunition warehouse, but on the way Jam suddenly stopped at an unmarked door. 'Hey, Mongrel, come take a look at this.' Jam pointed at the unmarked military-green door, which looked just like so many of the other military-green doors.

'I do not think we should,' said Mongrel uneasily.

'Come on, don't be a pussy!'

'Simmo might be watching,' whispered Mongrel.

'Fuck him!'

'Shh! He might hear!'

'Ahh, fuck him. Come on, you need to see this . . .' And Jam was already pushing open the green portal leading into a monumental underground chamber with a dirty stone floor and bare rocky walls stretching off into the distance. The lights were dim, and Mongrel squinted in the gloom as the door slammed shut behind him. A heavy boom echoed through the chamber, making Mongrel jump.

'What is it?'

'Over here,' said Jam, heading off across the dust. Mongrel followed, frowning. He could see nothing and such a huge chamber would not normally be wasted on empty space. Spiral never wasted space. He followed Jam's footprints in the dirt.

'I thought you only had five minutes?'

'Nah, Slater is still in bed and TT is getting our food supplies – funnily enough, from Mrs Spud. TT has a way with Spud. What about you – when do you leave?'

'About an hour.'

Jam nodded, chewing his lip thoughtfully. 'You off to Africa again?'

'Yeah. Nigeria.'

'We're paying a trip to Slovenia; we have a lead there. A hot lead, should see us shave a few more pounds from the Nex. Fry the fuckers and kill the pig, that's what I say. Always did have a thing for bacon.'

Jam halted in front of something covered with a huge green tarpaulin, grabbed a corner, and heaved. The tarpaulin rolled free, revealing the huge bulk of a tank, gleaming dully under a coat of fresh black paint and looking very big, very menacing, and very deadly.

'A tank,' said Mongrel, wholly unimpressed. 'Jam, I have lot of work to do before I head for Africa, I really think . . .'

'Look *closely*,' whispered Jam, placing a hand almost reverently against the flank of the mammoth metal beast. Jam was dwarfed beside the tracks, which rose to the height of his head.

Mongrel frowned, and was about to say something when he noticed the tracks. They looked somehow – wrong. That would never work, Mongrel thought. Then it clicked.

'An HTank?'

70

'Prototype,' breathed Jam, eyes gleaming. 'Beautiful, ain't she?'

The HTank was a tank so advanced that it made the most modern military models look no better than the French Char d'Assaut Schneider, the early prototype that had failed in the muddy battlefields of the First World War.

It was an HTank, a Hover Tank – with the ability to hover over obstacles, using the most advanced turbo-track matrix-fission engine and track displacements. If the HTank reached a near-vertical wall? The huge beast would tilt its nose to the sky and climb almost vertically with the aid of its colossally powerful engines. And it had a few other tricks up its sleeve . . .

Jam patted the machine, gazing up at it almost adoringly. 'You wondering why it's black?' He waggled his eyebrows in that cocky, cheeky way only Jam could manage, grinning at Mongrel's obvious frown.

'Go on, Jam, why it black?'

'It's not.'

'Da, it is. *Look*,' said Mongrel.

'No, it's not,' said Jam, grinning more widely.

'How that, then?'

'It's a CamCloak.' Jam paused, for effect more than anything, and Mongrel's frown deepened as he shifted from one boot to the other, obviously nervous at the prospect of getting caught by the humourless psycho who was Simmo.

'Jam, we not supposed to be in here!'

'Don't be a bean.'

'Jam!'

'Go on.'

'Go on what?'

'Ask me.'

71

'Ask you what?'

Jam tutted, running a hand through his short but growing black hair, which had been pampered and nurtured and had broken many a lady's heart. Often he would get grief from the other Spiral operatives – along the philosophical lines of 'Jam, you poof' and 'You look like a fucking girl, get a haircut.' But Jam always put forward the argument that his current locks got him laid, and for that fact alone they deserved respect.

'About the CamCloak, you dumb-spud monkey.'

'Go on, then, but make it quick. I got suspicion Sgt Simmo will be looking for us and waiting for us, and he will not be happy that we go snooping into classified military equipment . . .'

'Instead of just painting the tank, the CamCloak will replicate any environment at the press of a button; you want advanced blending, you got it. The HTank can operate in hostile terrain almost invisibly. And its weapons systems! Fuck, don't get me started on the weapons systems! They—'

'Jam, I going for ammo. Simmo will be really pissed off.'

'Aw, fuck 'im!'

Mongrel retreated, and with a final longing glance at the HTank prototype Jam followed Mongrel across the dusty floor, their boots leaving imprints. A hundred security cameras tracked their slow departure.

Laden with canvas sacks of ammunition in a variety of calibres, Jam and Mongrel made their way along the long straight corridor and paused at the iron gate. They waited, and then Jam peered through between the bars to where Sgt Simmo was seated at the high desk, a sheaf of papers in front of him, his finger poised delicately above something that had captured his attention.

Jam coughed.

There was no response.

Jam coughed again, this time louder.

Slowly, Sgt Simmo turned his huge bullet head on his thick bull neck, which spilled over the collar of his urban-combat jacket, and glared at the two men. Then, casually and without obvious hurry, he reached over and hit the release, which buzzed in an annoying fashion.

Jam and Mongrel stepped through this magic portal, their bags of bullets clanking as they paused in front of the desk and Simmo's raised bushy eyebrows. He grinned at them. It was a particularly nasty grin.

'We need to sign?' asked Jam softly.

'Oh yes,' crooned Simmo. 'In triplicate, on the correct military forms.' He pushed forward the thick pad and Jam stared with distaste at the stains. He took the pen on its industrial-grade chain and leaned forward.

'What the fuck is that?' snapped Jam, pointing.

'Chocolate.'

'You sure?'

'I very sure,' growled Simmo.

'And that? There! What the fuck is that?'

'That is blood,' said Simmo quietly, his rumble like the distant detonation of a nuclear device.

Jam met the large sergeant's eyes. 'How did you manage to get *blood* on your triplicate signing-out book?'

'Man refused to sign,' growled Simmo. 'Called me pedantic triplicate-signing paper-pushing motherfucker. So I stabbed him through hand with pen. Look, there is nick in wood where pen got stuck. It very messy. Got one of tendons wrapped around the nib.'

'Ahh, nice.'

Jam reached forward to sign. He signed.

'In triplicate,' said Simmo.

'Yeah, yeah.' Jam signed twice more.

'And him,' said Simmo, nodding at Mongrel.

Mongrel sighed. 'What you do if there was nuclear war and we had to urgently get whole battalion's ammunition in few short seconds because HQ about to be overrun?'

'You would have to sign in triplicate on the correct military forms. For every item.'

'But you have nuclear bombs blasting overhead, room shaking, lights flickering, nuclear fire screaming across landscape . . .'

Simmo stared hard at Mongrel. 'You would have to sign in triplicate on the correct military forms,' he said without any sign of emotion on his face, without any indication of humour, without any suggestion of anything other than consummate military professionalism.

'Come on.' Jam grinned, patting Mongrel on the back. 'You can see me off at the hangar.'

Mongrel nodded, and they trooped towards the door. Just as Jam reached for the handle, Simmo's low growl echoed across to the two men and made them freeze.

'Just one question, soldiers.'

Jam and Mongrel exchanged glances. 'Told you so!' hissed Mongrel, and turned with an unaccustomed beaming smile across his battered wide face. Jam turned, dropping the canvas sacks and placing his hands on his hips.

'Sarge?'

'You enjoy looking at my little toy?'

'You mean the HTank?' Jam nodded, and pulled out a cigarette, lighting it and inhaling deeply. Through a plume of smoke he said, 'Yeah, nice little piece of kit. Impressive CamCloak, and fucking thick armour, hey?'

'Nice machine,' rumbled Simmo, eyes gleaming.

'What you mean, "your" little toy?' said Mongrel.

'Is mine.'

'I . . . I thought it belong to Spiral.' Mongrel smiled carefully.

Simmo shook his bullet head. 'No. 'S mine.'

'You mean it's your HTank,' laughed Jam. 'As in, ownership documentation is stamped in *your* name, you have full financial possession, the HTank does in fact *belong* to you.'

'No. But it still mine.'

'OK, OK. Look, Sarge, it's a very nice tank. We were very impressed. Is it operational yet?'

'Only on The Sergeant's say-so,' rumbled Simmo.

'Whatever you say, buddy.' Jam grinned, placing the cigarette between his lips, squinting through the smoke, picking up his ammo and leading Mongrel to the door. As he was stepping through the portal, he turned. 'One last thing – if I ever need back-up, I'll be sure not to give you a fucking call.'

Simmo scowled, but Jam and Mongrel had gone.

Spiral Mainframe
Data log #12522

CLASSIFIED SADt/6345/SPECIAL INVESTIGATIONS UNIT

Data Request 324#12522

SAD

Search and Destroy Missions

When Durell and Feuchter's warship, currently tagged as Spiral_mobile, was destroyed, hundreds of genetically enhanced Nex soldiers were also destroyed. However,

even without the guidance of their masters –
the true enemies of Spiral – the Nex had a
network of systems in place across the globe
which enabled them to continue operations
and pose a minimal threat to Spiral agencies
worldwide.

SAD missions were instigated: teams of
DemolSquads whose mission objectives for the
past year had been to search out and
completely destroy Nex nests and relevant
minor military outposts.

The SAD missions have been extremely
successful in minimising current threat from
the Nex. Although all the Nex soldiers have
not been destroyed, intelligence shows that
they have almost been terminated. They are
currently running at a 4% strength when
compared to infestation numbers this time
last year.

Most recent find:
Brazil, 18km east of Humaita
Team:
Jam, Slater, TT [Demol12]
Nex destroyed:
40 genetically altered soldiers

Current SAD team leader: Jam [Demol_H]

Keyword SEARCH>> NEX, SAD, SPIRAL_sadt,
DURELL, FEUCHTER

The Hangar was huge, housing perhaps a hundred helicopters of different configurations and eight SX7 Harrier Jump Jets. Jam, Slater and TT stood, staring out at the rain beyond the corrugated walls and waiting for the Comanche pilot to arrive. They all carried huge canvas sacks – clothing, provisions for their operation in the former Yugoslavia, guns and, of course, ammunition. Slater had already overseen the loading of three KTM 800Vi motorcycles, which had been strapped unceremoniously beneath the Comanche in lieu of missiles, and all the group needed now was a pilot.

Jam smoked, watching the rain and listening to Slater and TT's idle banter. Slater was a huge man whom Jam had fought with on many occasions and who reminded him a little of Mongrel – both were tufty-haired and sported missing teeth from too many NAAFI brawls, and both took shit from no man. But whereas Mongrel was pure animal, very much in the mould of Sgt Simmo, Slater had more of a philosophical air, although it took a lot to get to know that side of him, and in truth it only rarely appeared after seventeen pints of lager.

TT, on the other hand, was a complete contrast. She was ex-Sniper squad and had moved sideways to the Demolition Teams, or DemolSquads as they were affectionately known. Tall, lithe and muscular, she was extremely reserved and aloof, rarely speaking unless it had to do with work. She had high cheekbones and short blood-red hair, pale blue eyes, and full lips hiding neat little teeth. She was oblivious to Jam's charms – much to his consternation – but had proved herself on many occasions with her skill with a rifle and telescopic sight.

'You OK, Jam?'

'Mmm,' he said, flicking his cigarette butt out into the rain and watching the heavy downpour destroy the filter.

77

Jam turned, gave Slater a small grin, then said, 'You check the SAD records? I have – just for my own personal amusement, you understand.'

Slater nodded. 'Current statistics show Nex strength running at just four per cent of this time last year when . . . well, when you blew their warship to Kingdom Come.'

'Ahh, the old bomb in the bag,' said Jam, his eyes hard. 'Makes you come over all warm and gooey inside. What the fuck does four per cent represent, anyway?'

'Statistics,' mumbled Slater. 'There are no current numbers . . .'

'Fucking suits and their fucking statistics,' snarled Jam. 'Real figures would had been more use – not four fucking per cent! What's four per cent of an unspecified amount? Jesus! Now, this is our chance to take out a few more unfortunates . . . drop it to two per cent of whatever, eh, mate?'

'Jam . . . better be careful we don't become complacent.'

Jam winked. 'Hah! We eat the fuckers for breakfast nowadays.'

Acting on tip-offs and local military intelligence, Jam, Slater and TT were due to investigate claims of a relatively small Nex 'nest' in Slovenia, close to a village named Trebija. The Brazil6 SAD mission had been the most recent large 'find', and SAD missions were becoming more and more infrequent and thus required fewer and fewer resources from Spiral. A large nest would entail complex military missions with interlocking paths from anything from three to twenty DemolSquads; but for a small gig like this? Jam was happy to do it on his own.

'Probably be nothing. Rice or something on their scanners,' growled Slater.

'You're so pessimistic,' said Jam, lighting another cigarette and cursing himself. He was trying – very unsuccessfully and at the request of Nicky, his wife-to-be – to quit. He inhaled the deep blue smoke and slapped Slater on the back, having to stand on tiptoe to do it despite his own six feet of height. 'Anyway, you haven't told me yet if you're coming to my wedding!'

'I have to check my diary,' said Slater.

'You still sulking because I asked Carter to be my best man?'

'No,' said Slater sulkily.

'Come on, buddy, you know I've been friends with Carter since fucking kindergarten. We've done some shit together, fought some fucking battles, been through some real hard times. And I know you and me are friends, but you have to accept my decision like a real man, not sulk like an arse . . .'

'It's just . . .'

'What?'

TT sidled closer, a smile across her full pouting lips.

'It's just . . .'

'Spit it out, man,' snapped Jam.

'He thinks if he's the best man it'll help him pull one of the bridesmaids, get him a bit of pussy for a drunken night of debauchery with fruit, or whatever it is that rubs Slater up the right way.'

'Thanks, TT,' spat Slater, reddening.

'Don't worry.' Jam winked, slapping the huge soldier on the back again. 'If it is a bit of pussy you're wanting, then Jam is the man to . . . to . . .' He stared hard at TT. 'What? What's that look?'

TT ran a hand through her cropped hair, then smoothed her eyebrows which were immaculately plucked. 'Do you realise that I went to prep school with

Nicky?' she said softly. 'We shared a dorm, were very good friends, in fact.'

Jam stared hard at her.

'We used to have midnight feasts, sneak out into the village and meet the boys, got up to all sorts of mischief – me and your soon-to-be wife.' She smiled sweetly at Jam.

'You're fucking with me, right?'

'Not at all.'

'Stop it, because you *are* fucking with me.'

'Why would I lie? You know I'm friends with Nicky, you've seen me talking to her enough times. We joined up together.'

'She never told me that.'

'Why would she? Do you know *everything* about your woman?' She gave a very dark smile. 'Because I doubt it very much, Mr Jam. But the things she has told me about you!'

The pilot chose that moment to arrive. He was a slim man, with bright eager eyes and the disposition of a puppy: always eager to please. He wore his hair long and generously curled like a middle-aged pop star or footballer, and it lapped around his shoulders, buoyed on a current of air, hairspray and expensive Italian conditioners. To Fenny, Hair Was Life. Which was why it had been with great irony that God had made this man bald at the crown – this Deity of Hair, this ultimately vain and narcissistic male of the species. And Jam secretly knew that if Fenny had decided to shun his flamboyant locks, to cast aside his self-love and hair-lacquer abuse, then God would have shown forgiveness and allowed him the mane of a lion.

God punishes those who punish themselves, he mused.

'Hiya, Fenny,' grinned Jam, slapping the pilot on the

back and watching with obvious amusement as his tresses bobbed – as if he were auditioning for a TV advert for the ultimate prodigal pelt.

Fenny carried his HIDSS helmet under one arm and surveyed the group with a convivial and easygoing gaze. This and other friendly characteristics had earned him many friends among Spiral, despite his love of getting drunk and pouring his pint into soldiers' laps.

'Your team going to Slovenia, Jam, you womanising old scoundrel?'

'Yeah,' drawled Jam.

'I think you'll find that there's lots of suspected Nex activity in the city of Ljubljana.'

'Possibly.' Jam grinned, his arm still draped around Fenny's shoulders. 'But I think you will find that it isn't enemy territory until we turn it into enemy fucking territory. Now, I have a question for you, my old friend.'

'Yeah?'

'Well, I don't want you to become tetchy, but every time I see you I always ask myself the question: why don't you shave off your curls? Get a good Number One, sorted.' Jam puffed at his cigarette.

Fenny looked a little confused.

'Why would I do that? Why would I want a . . . ugh . . . a *shaved* head?'

Jam spluttered. 'Well, mate, it's just your curls . . .'

'Yeah?'

'And, and . . . the curls bobbing, and the hairspray . . . it makes you . . . makes your curls . . . like . . . with their bobbing . . .'

'Yes?' Fenny was grinning broadly but with an iron twinkle in his eyes.

'If he had a pint, I'd choose this moment to take a step back,' rumbled Slater. He had walked home from the

81

NAAFI on too many evenings with a wet beer-stinking crotch and a strand of stray curl caught between his knuckles where Fenny had been too swift and elusive to suffer Slater's left hook.

'Well,' continued the politically inept Jam, 'I just thought you looked a bit, y'know, like a mad clown.'

'Leave him be,' said TT, sidling over. She pushed Jam aside and planted a large kiss on Fenny's lips, making the pilot grin even more broadly. 'I like the curls. Reminds me of—'

'A poodle?' suggested Jam.

'No, a real rock star,' crooned TT. And she slapped Fenny's behind. 'Now, are we mounting up and shipping out into the rain, or are we going to stand here all day and exchange pleasantries?'

'Always the spoilsport,' sighed Jam.

Fenny climbed into the cockpit and engaged the engines. Jam and Slater grinned at each other, as TT muttered, 'You guys are just so savage – you gang up on people and try to tear them apart . . .'

'Me?' squawked Slater.

'Ha,' said Jam. 'That's just fucking life.'

They followed Fenny and climbed into the Comanche's modified cockpit. As a war machine, the originally specced USA Comanche could only carry two pilots, whilst the Spiral Comanche VQ7s had a host of modifications to bring them in line with the requirements of anti-terrorism operations.

Once its occupants were settled, the Comanche leapt into the air, slicing up through the rain with the satisfying roar of twin LHTec engines, leaping into the darkened iron bruise of clouds and heading south, away from the nearby city of London and towards the dark churning mass of the English Channel. Fenny's curls bobbed from the exposed rim of the HIDSS helmet in time with the howling engines.

Southern Europe was still warm at this time of year, the sun beating down from a cloudless late-autumn sky. The Comanche landed in a remote mountain location, trees whipping and bowing under the onslaught of the war machine's rotors.

Jam, Slater and TT climbed free, stretching wearily after the insane strike across the English Channel, France, Germany and Italy. They walked through long grass, ducking beneath the idling rotors, dragging their kit and piling it beneath a large cherry tree. Slater moved off to release the KTM 800Vi motorcycles from beneath the Comanche as Jam lit a cigarette, checked the magazine on his SA1000 and walked out beyond their LZ, a hand shading his eyes. He propped his SA1000 against his thigh as he peered off into the hazy distance. He was sweating within seconds of landing under his heavy clothing, and his gaze took in the steep slopes leading to woodland and distant villages of white buildings with red-tiled roofs – a mountainous landscape of jagged grey peaks filled with a fluid beauty of deep green and the distant glimmers of a winding river.

Jam coughed on his cigarette smoke, his mind settling into a businesslike mode now that he was here on the ground, ready for work and ready for the killing to begin. His lips tightened as he thought of all the friends he had lost at the hands of the Nex; many good men and women, cut in half with machine-gun bullets, throats slit, limbs strewn around after massive terrible detonations. The war had become personal, and so Jam's hatred was personal – he would hunt the Nex to the ends of the earth and slaughter them in their sleep.

Slater approached. 'We're rocking.'

Turning, they watched the Comanche roar and leap into the air, huge rotors glinting in the sun, camouflaged flanks gleaming dully as the huge machine hovered for a moment, banked, and disappeared with a high-powered engine whine. The trees settled, the late-summer scents of the woods and the cherry trees drifting across to the small DemolSquad. The grass hissed in the breeze as Jam cocked his SA1000.

'Time for business,' he said.

Darkness was falling as Jam slowed the KTM on the winding unmetalled stone-littered road which sliced between woodland trails. Tyres crunched, skidding a little on the loose stone, and TT and Slater pulled up close behind him. The three bikes burbled quietly, their 800cc engines ticking over, stealth exhausts electronically steal-ing any sounds the machines might make and so rendering them, to all intents and purposes, silent.

'Everything OK?'

Jam said nothing. He sat, eyes surveying the incline ahead of him. Heavy woodland, conifers, beech and spruce sloped away to either side, their bases covered with the detritus of a hundred years of fallen branches and leaves. The Spiral operatives watched a deer, brown with soft white spots, wander aimlessly and pause, its head coming up to gaze at them with large oval brown eyes before it sprinted off between the trees, disappearing like a drifting ghost.

Jam gave the military hand signal for silence.

They waited, Jam watching the trail, eyes slowly scan-ning the tree line ahead and to either side where thick boles were scattered. Perfect ambush territory, his brain was telling him. Perfect . . .

84

With the unclenching of his fist they moved off, slower now, more warily. Something had spooked Jam, and Slater had known his friend long enough to trust the man's instincts. A drinking hedonistic womaniser he might be, but there were two things he was certainly good at: killing and, more importantly, keeping his men – and women – alive. It was an unspoken talent. A gift.

They cruised, moving higher into the mountain pass, the roads becoming more and more pronounced as Vs of worn stone shrapnel, the slopes steeper and more rugged, the trails more and more disused. As darkness fell Jam pulled to the side of the trail where a footpath or deer trail of some kind crossed the rough stone road. Jam pulled his bike onto the trail and, ducking branches which whipped against their faces and heavy canvas combat jackets, they rode through the woods until they came to a huge natural outcropping of massive boulders, some larger than a house and balanced precariously on one another to form a natural wall. Jam pulled his bike up underneath an overhang of rock, beneath a boulder so big that it would crush the three Spiral operatives like insects if it fell. Jam killed his engine, and Slater and TT followed suit. They dismounted, warily, and unslung their weapons, Jam his SA1000, Slater his trusty double-barrelled shotgun with machine-gun modifications, and TT her Barrett IV sniper rifle with digital sights.

They made a cold camp, seating themselves on a huge log which Slater dragged laboriously into the small clearing, and Jam spun his ECube into life. Dropping it in front of him it halted, spinning a few inches above the ground on a cold cushion of matrix. Tiny sections opened from the alloy chassis and a projection spread like liquid across the ground – a contoured map of their surroundings optically linked to the advanced AGPS signals that the ECube was intercepting.

Jam picked up a stick and poked at the green and blue image. 'We're here.' He lit a cigarette.

Slater, who had opened a huge tin of B&S and was shovelling the fodder into his maw cold, nodded in agreement and pointed with his fork. 'The white blobs signify intelligence sightings?'

'Aye. If we cross-section them it gives us quite a narrow field of operations – if you consider the contours of the terrain. If, for example, we give them the benefit of the doubt and assume that they are using bikes like us – then there are only limited paths open to them. Even less so if they are using larger, heavier vehicles.'

'You want to go in on foot?' asked TT.

Jam nodded. 'We'll take it more carefully from here on in.'

They moved with the precision and care of hunters. Slowly, deliberately, examining all the data available to them. Through the darkness the trio moved, in a wide triangular formation where they could provide one another with covering arcs of fire if necessary, but not so close that a single grenade or burst of machine-gun fire could take the whole team out.

They climbed the steep woodland incline, Jam at the apex of the triangle, leading the way forward, ECube set to max and scanning the environment for electronic trip mechanisms or mines or any of a hundred other devices that would give away their position.

Jam halted, dropping to one knee.

Somewhere in the distance, an animal rustled in the woods. Jam wiped a sheen of sweat from his forehead – his combats were heavy and the still woodland air was humid in comparison to the UK at this time of year. This, combined with the mountain inclines, was really making Jam and the rest of the DemolSquad work for their money.

The ECube flashed a warning – not with lights, for lights could be detected by the enemy, but with a high-frequency laser designed so that only Jam's eye could match the frequency and see anything there at all . . . Slater and TT, highly tuned to Jam's lead, dropped to one knee also and scanned their surroundings. Jam turned, giving the signal for optical tripwires – very advanced, and regular tactical favourites of the Nex. Slater and TT focused their own ECubes and they stepped silently over the traps.

Closing in, Jam thought grimly, and slipped free the safety on his SA1000.

They moved through the dark woods. More inclines passed beneath their boots, until finally the land began to level out before dipping away through sparse trees towards a small wooden hut built from rough-hewn logs and with an old moss-corroded red-tile roof The windows were blacked out and Jam could detect no sounds, even with the ECube's aural enhancers – but that did not mean that the hut was empty. Switching to thermal scanning, the ECube detected four bodies within the hut – and one seated just outside.

Jam squinted.

Motherfucker, he thought as he finally clocked the guard – a sniper – perched in a tiny hide of leaves and twigs, completely concealed from view. Jam, moving with extreme care, signalled to TT and she crawled forward on her belly and gently released the bipod, resting her silenced Barrett against the soft loamy ground.

Leaves and twigs sprang into view, and she zoomed in on the potential threat. She spotted him easily, for he was a Nex and had copper eyes. Always a give-away, she thought grimly. He was bearing a sniper rifle but did not have it trained on the surroundings.

'Lazy,' she muttered to herself as she squeezed the Barrett's trigger. There came the tiniest of hisses, then a rustle of dry leaves as the Nex guard was taken through the throat – and vocal cords – and sent rolling to one side, blood leaking to feed the tree roots, mouth working in a silent scream of pain, fingers scrabbling at the bullet wound. The second bullet smashed through the Nex's forehead, killing him instantly.

Jam gave the thumbs-up and they closed warily on the cabin. Jam's plan was simple – an MNK, or MindNuke, turned up on full and launched through the window. It would explode silently, and with no flash – and would scramble the brains of anybody within a twenty-five-metre radius. The MNK had different settings and could be used to take out harmless targets with what was affectionately called a 'fry-up'; the DemolSquads had found that on full power the MindNukes were particularly deadly against Nex, whose insect-blending made them almost impervious to bullet wounds unless an accurate head-shot was secured. As DemolSquad members had found the hard way, Nex were very, very tough in one-on-one combat; they felt little or no pain. MNKs evened the odds a little . . .

They halted, and Jam readied the weapon, twisting the two halves of the small silver globe. Having set it, he signalled to his companions and, his SA1000 gripped in one hand, crept through the meagre woodland towards the darkened cabin.

They're asleep, he thought.

Too easy?

Never look a gift horse in the mouth . . .

He reached the wall, his gloved hand resting lightly

against the rough bark of the timbers. He glanced back through the darkness and could just make out TT and Slater, scanning arcs, checking for enemies with ECubes primed and eyesight set to maximum overdrive. Jam eased himself up the wall and peered through the glass. He saw nothing but a small storeroom – but that was perfectly adequate for his needs. He placed the ECube against the glass and there was the tiniest of tinkling noises as a small rectangle of glass was sucked free. Then he pushed the MNK through the hole – and ran for it . . .

Skidding to a halt in the branches, he glanced back.

The DemolSquad sensed rather than heard the MNK detonate; a ripple seemed to pulse through the woods and they all shivered, aware of the damage that these silent and devastating weapons could cause. Then, standing and checking ECubes once more for enemy activity, they strode towards the cabin. Jam kicked the door down and moved forward with his SA1000 primed. The four Nex were dead in their beds, faces twisted in agony, dark copper eyes weeping blood onto their pillows. Jam poked one in the face with the SA1000's barrel and turned to Slater, his mouth opening to congratulate the large warrior on a job well done, a nest destroyed without casualty or even conflict—

A gunshot rang out.

TT was picked up and flung against Slater, her chest exploding to splatter strips of ragged flesh against the huge man, her eyes wide and her mouth spewing blood. Jam leapt forward as a second shot rang out, slapping into the back of TT's lolling head even as her weight carried Slater to the ground. He grunted as he hit the earth of the cabin floor, face to face with his companion, his friend, a woman who had saved his life on several occasions . . . Her eyes were wide, her gaze confused, blood pouring from her mouth to wash over Slater and sting his eyes and drench his hair and jacket.

Her hands were clawed, grasping Slater's combat jacket, but the fingers slowly went slack and Jam stepped over the two sprawled figures with a look of anger and hatred and disgust on his face. He opened up on full automatic, the SA1000's bullets strafing across the woodland in front of him, steel slivers screaming and howling between the trees, kicking sparks from the distance, splintering timber from boles and sending a dark figure suddenly sprinting for cover—

'Slater!' he bellowed.

'I'm with you,' grunted Slater, rolling TT to one side and grasping his shotgun in blood-slippery hands. He paused for a moment, looking down at her partially destroyed face and the pulp of mashed skull. He sighed, deep inside, and spat out her blood – which stained his teeth and run down his throat – onto the dusty floor.

Jam and Slater sprinted through the darkened woods, grim now, faces drawn with bitterness and need. A need to kill. They flicked their ECubes to *pursuit shell* – audible warnings would inform them of an attack from any direction, or other threats such as mortars, mines or approaching tanks.

And the two men put all their efforts into a hot pursuit through the woods . . .

The gunman was fast – incredibly fast.

Jam paused, Slater almost cannoning into his back, and they caught their breaths, their eyes scanning the steep decline ahead of them, leading down through a stand of trees to what appeared to be a narrow stream bed filled with leaves and old broken branches.

They heard the gunman crunch his way free, scrambling up the opposite bank.

Both men opened fire, bullets whining down the hill and embedding in the earth with dull impact sounds. Slater's shotgun barked out devastating shells that tore bark from trees, and the SA1000 hammered savagely. They paused, sweat rolling down their faces in the humid night.

A muffled engine growl sounded as a bike kicked into life. Jam cursed.

They set off, sprinting once more, down the steep slope and then up the other side; the engine noise was loud, but stuttering, an off-road bike of some kind. Jam reached the top of the slope first, launched himself forward on his belly across the branches and leaves and took aim. The bike was weaving between trees and bouncing off unseen obstacles in the gloom. Jam squeezed off a three-round burst. Then another. Then another—

The bike's engine suddenly screamed, its rubber tyres exploded and the whole machine flipped into the air, cannoning into a tree and depositing the gunman dazed on the ground with the smashed bike on top of him. The engine died and the wheels spun, clicking. Jam leapt up and with Slater close behind him sprinted towards the stricken rider who heaved the fallen bike and turned a sub-machine gun on his pursuers—

All hell broke loose as bullets ripped through the woodland. Jam and Slater slammed into trees, and Jam's SA1000 sent a stream of bullets into the darkness. The return fire ceased and the Nex – they had glimpsed his thin grey body-hugging suit and his balaclava that revealed only gleaming copper eyes – sprinted away, dodging athletically between the trees.

'The bastard just won't go down,' snapped Jam. The two large men set off at a sprint once more, arms and legs pumping, lungs heaving, too used to the good life, and they heaved themselves up another slope, boots ploughing through woodland debris until they reached the top—

The Nex was running hard, head down, powering along at an incredible rate. Jam lifted his gun and the Nex, ducking left and right, glanced over its shoulder as the SA1000 fired a single bullet. The Nex was picked up, sent spinning end over end and deposited in an untidy heap beside a small cairn of rocks. Beyond, Jam and Slater could see a drop of some kind, a rocky edge falling away into a dark, shadow-haunted valley.

Warily, the two men, their chests still heaving, moved forward down this uneven rocky slope. Closing on the Nex, both levelled weapons at the still body. Circling, eyes on the surrounding landscape, Jam pulled out a silenced Beretta XI pistol and placed three bullets in the Nex's head.

They stood, panting, covered in grime and TT's blood, faces grim as realisation and horror sank in. Their friend was dead – and the ECubes had given them no warning.

'I have a fucking bad feeling,' rumbled Slater slowly.

'It's like when the QIII processor hacked the ECubes. You get that same sinking feeling? Like you're naked? Vulnerable?'

Slater nodded in the gloom, staring down at the crumpled grey-clad figure. 'What's over there?'

'Well, he was sure running *somewhere* fast.'

'You think there are more Nex?'

'Maybe,' said Jam grimly.

They moved closer to the valley, dropping to their bellies as they neared the gash in the ground. 'I can't see anything,' muttered Jam, and they crawled up to the edge to peer down into the deep narrow V, scattered with dark trees and large piles of rocks, below them.

There was a distant log cabin, and Slater nudged Jam,

pointing with his gun. In the gloom Jam could just make out a narrow bridge of thick wooden sleepers connecting both sides of the valley. Large rocks were clustered around the opposite bank: a perfect defensive location.

Jam set his ECube to scan.

He turned to Slater, confusion in his eyes. 'The cabin and the bridge are not there,' he said softly. 'The ECube can't see anything. It's blind. What the fuck is going on?'

Slater muttered something evil, and Jam turned back, staring down at the valley where nothing moved.

'I'll go back, check the Nex,' said Slater.

'Yeah. You do that.'

Jam stared hard, trying to work out why the ECube couldn't scan these simplest of objects before him. Was there some kind of natural screening? Some source of strange radiation or IR that was interfering with the complex electronic mechanics of Spiral's premier agent device?

A noise interrupted his thoughts – a low, metallic sound – and Jam whirled, eyes squinting into the darkness. He came up onto his knees, his SA1000 presented for action.

'Slater?' he hissed.

Nothing. He could see nothing . . .

Climbing up to his feet, he crept forward towards the crumpled Nex. Then his adjusting eyes picked out the fallen figure of Slater and he dropped to a crouch, instantly freezing, scanning the surroundings. Fuck, screamed his brain as he checked his ECube.

The tiny alloy machine was completely dead.

Jam's face tightened into a grimace.

The SA1000 swung left, then right, as Jam's sharp eyes scanned for enemies. Was Slater alive? Dead? A sniper's silenced bullet? Jam dropped to his belly, and very slowly, using trees for cover, worked his way gradually towards his fallen friend.

As he reached Slater, he hissed, 'What the fuck are you doing?'

There was no response.

Jam crept closer, and to his horror he saw that Slater's throat had been cut. The big man's neck sported a gaping crimson mouth. Blood had pooled in the leaves beneath his head and Jam felt his own heart rate kick up a gear with bursts of injected adrenalin as his fingers reached out and took Slater's shotgun.

'Somebody is going to fucking die,' he growled, rising beside a wide tree for cover, his eyes glaring off into the gloom. He turned – and a huge black shape reared up in front of him, an incredibly sudden movement faster than a striking cobra—

Jam gasped as something huge and hard slammed into his face.

He remembered the rich scent of the soil, and the leaves.

And then nothing.

CHAPTER 4

SEVERANCE

The snow fell heavily. Carter could feel it whipping coldly against his face as his body curled, cradling the woman as they slammed into the flower beds. Carter rolled, bouncing roughly, the woman's scream suddenly halted as air was punched from her naked bruised frame . . .

Carter's eyes shot open as the crevasse loomed before him – a huge frightening maw smashing towards him. His boots kicked out violently against the narrow trunk of a pine tree and heaved them both away, rolling with grunts to the paved path . . . the crevasse roared past, rock grinding rock and spewing splinters, consuming the pine and disappearing beneath the swaying hotel – which buckled like a melted toy, folding around the dancing flames from the boiler room, debris exploding outwards as the earthquake's tremors eventually subsided.

Dust billowed, followed closely by fire. Sirens were still wailing, and helicopter searchlights swept the landscape.

Behind Carter another section of the hotel collapsed with an inferno roar. He could hear the stampeding of boots.

He looked down into the woman's eyes and released a pent-up breath. 'Thank you,' she said softly and reached up to kiss his cheek. Carter gazed once more into the darkness that had so very nearly claimed them.

'A close call,' he muttered—

And then felt it. A presence, behind him. Carter rolled free of the naked woman's embrace and stared up at Natasha's face. Her gaze was unreadable, skin glowing on one side from the hotel fires, eyes gleaming as a helicopter searchlight swept over them.

Natasha helped the woman to her feet and draped a blanket around her shoulders, talking softly to her as she shivered, fear deep in her eyes.

Carter shuffled away from the rip in the earth as stones trickled free at the edges and disappeared into deep blackness.

'This day just gets better and better,' he muttered, finger touching a tiny cut on his face and coming away stained with blood. 'Fuck me,' he hissed, gaze transferring from his finger to the abnormal crack in the world's mantle. A deep sigh escaped his lips and he calmed his raging mind.

They took the rescued woman to a red and white ambulance that had paramedics swarming round it, helped her into the back, then surveyed the full destruction caused by the earthquake. Rescue and emergency services were stretched to their physical capabilities by this sudden disaster.

Carter and Natasha watched sadly as brave Swiss firefighters battled the flames. They held one another tightly under the falling snow. A policeman tried to usher them into an ambulance, but Carter waved him away. 'I need a whisky, not the fucking hospital,' he drawled.

They moved away from the throng of emergency services

and the darkness started to close in around them away from the lights and the fire. Natasha lifted her ECube into her hand and her gaze met Carter's. 'It would seem we have a message.'

'What wonderful timing.'

Natasha activated the tiny screen, chewed on her lip and then smiled up at Carter. 'Some shit is going down; we are summoned to an urgent meeting in London, at the new Spiral_H buildings.'

'So, then,' he pondered. 'Our plan of action is that we find another hotel, get cleaned up, get some food . . . then flag ourselves down some transport and—'

'Now, Carter. They're coming for us *now* . . .'

'Bastards,' said Carter with feeling. 'They fucking *know* we're on holiday. I knew we should have left the ECube at home. Fucking work. Do they know about the earthquake? We're not in a fit state! We need some R&R!'

'It's important,' said Natasha softly.

'Not as important as my down time. Come on, we might be able to salvage something from the cabin – if the bastard is still standing.'

'The police are cordoning off the area – we'll be lucky to get in. They've set up a temporary shelter for the quake victims, further down the mountain pass.'

Natasha met Carter's gaze, looking at his steely eyes, the cuts on his face, his dust- and blood-stained clothes.

'Believe me, we'll get in,' he said, and taking her hand, led her towards the darkness of the hotel cabins and the yellow police tape.

As they walked through the snow, a roar echoed from the valley below. They stopped, turning, glancing past the flames and horror of the smashed hotel, and beyond to the glittering town of Zermatt . . . The roaring increased, rumbling from below and above, the sounds bouncing from the mountains and hillsides, reverberating and increasing until they became so loud as to drown out conversation—

'No,' whispered Natasha, eyes wide, lips gleaming.

The earthquake tore through the town with a single mammoth, clubbing sweep, smashing buildings into pulverised dust like toys stamped under a giant's boot, spitting chunks of shattered concrete, stone and timber up into the air in cascading arcs with shrieks of tearing and cracking; ripping the civilised world apart with appalling ease. Devastating trenches chewed through the rock, opening up to swallow whole buildings, bucking horses, spinning carriages, screaming pulverised people and in a final giant concussive boom like the ending of worlds the haze of lights that illuminated Zermatt was swept away beneath a tidal wave of evil and darkness . . .

In the aftermath, the only sounds were people moaning and the thumping of Air Zermatt's rescue helicopters fluttering uselessly above the terrible devastation.

**Leviathan Fuels: Premium Grade LVA
– go on, make the switch, because you know your children deserve a better future** . . .

The man wearing the fur coat and glossy yellow shoes stood on the runway staring up at the decommissioned Chinese MIG87 fighter and the small black DigiOpticDV4 camera attached to the nose cone just above the Chinese writing that read 'Death to All Non-Believers.'

'Is it attached?'

'Yes, sir.'

'Will it fucking *stay* attached?'

The technician reddened. His boss, the Big Man, Sir

Ronald Xavier IX and Corporate MD of Film & Film©
Incorporated, makers of Film and Supreme
Advertisements©, currently contracted to make one new
high-tech advert per week for Leviathan Fuels – their
biggest and biggest paying customer ever – was seriously
fucking pissed off.

More than pissed off. He was *losing money*. And to him
that was a crime worse than multiple sodomy.

'Yes, sir – I'm sure it's not going to fall off again.'

'It better fucking not,' hissed Sir Ronald Xavier IX
with passion. 'We've lost a day's filming, and that's cost
me US$38.7 million. I'd hate to deduct *that* from your
pitiful wages.'

The technician paled. He staggered back as if struck by
a pickaxe handle, wondering how long it would take him
to pay the money back if the unthinkable happened.

Xavier waved him away with contempt, and with a
'Fuckwit' thrown into the employee-abuse list for good
measure. He turned his attention to the pilot, who waved
in the sort of happy fashion associated with a knowledge
of one's own non-expendability. Xavier frowned.

'You know the run?' he shouted.

The pilot nodded, his features insect-like behind his
helmet. 'Like the back o' ma hand, man,' he drawled.

'Well, *go on*, then!'

The MIG87 taxied along a short length of runway and
then leapt into the air. A sonic boom followed soon after
as the jet reached altitude. For the pilot, the world
became a huge expanse of blue scattered with marshmal-
low wisps of cloud. The sun blazed from an infinite
heaven and he swung the MIG87, banking sharply left
with a scream of engines, then right, before settling into a
straight and even flight path.

'Have you patched me through yet?' came the annoyed

voice of Xavier, followed by a low 'Tut.' 'Well, fucking patch me through, you *moron*! What? He can hear me? Jesus Christ Superstar, you just can't get the fucking staff these days . . .'

The MIG87 howled around in a wide arc, plummeted back down in a steep dive and passed low over Xavier's head, making his strands of white hair, so carefully placed over his bald pate, wave wildly.

'Idiot!' screamed Xavier. There was a period of forced calm as he regulated his breathing – and his pacemaker, using external controls linked to his PDA. 'If you kill me, none of you get paid, you morons! Now, head for the first Zone.'

'Roger that.'

That MIG87 slowed, engines decelerating with a heavy whine, and headed for the first Zone. The desert opened up, a sea of undulating sand, towering dunes – a world of harsh and natural emptiness.

'Rolling Camera 3.'

'Roger.'

The MIG87 dropped low, skimming over the sand, huge clouds of it billowing up behind the fighter. The scream of jet engines sliced through the air as the warplane approached a massive rise of rocks – mountainous teeth of the desert, brown igneous rocks from an earlier age of the world, rising to reveal a valley dropping away into a sweeping expanse of sand and sparse spiked vegetation . . .

These mountain teeth were still distant to the camera.

The MIG87 hit its boosters, and the rocks suddenly appeared in the blink of an eye under massive acceleration – and then as suddenly jarred to a halt, rolling as the pilot slammed the machine into hover mode. Then he cruised easily down between two walls of jagged brown rock and on into the oasis within . . .

'Approaching Zone 2, over.'

'Keep it real slow for this bit,' said Xavier. 'Is Camera 5 still on standby? Good.'

From the desert reared a temple, a huge edifice of stone faced in the most wonderful brown- and golden-veined marble. Miraculously, it had not suffered the type of thefts that had robbed the Egyptian pyramids of the same era, and it remained a wonder of ancient architecture, protected by its natural environment, hidden by these towering walls of shrouding rock.

The MIG87 passed over with a throbbing drone. Behind the temple stood five mammoth derricks supporting gleaming black pumps, huge steel arms working to extract precious LVA from beneath the sand and rock. The jet banked, rising above the desert teeth, and then came around in a tight arc, dropping almost to ground level and zipping between the five huge pumps and the tiny specks of people working among the engines before climbing up once more towards the massive inverted ocean of blue sky . . .

'Wonderful!' came the crow of triumph from Xavier. 'A beautiful shot, truly spectacular. Now head for Zone 3 . . .'

Again, the MIG soared and banked, zooming across desert sand and then levelling out to take in the scene from far above: the mountains, their precious treasure of the temple within, and the squat pumps close behind, extracting LVA from below the desert dunes.

'I can see the text now,' said Xavier, voice heavy with treacly emotion. 'Leviathan Fuels – in harmony with our heritage, our ecology, our planet!' He chuckled to himself as the MIG87 soared, cameras still rolling, images still being frantically written to precious disk. The fighter plane passed over the huge slurry pits filled with rock and mud, the excrement of the earth dumped only 500 metres from this most precious landmark, scarring the beauty of the desert . . . it passed over the tiny scummy village that had sprung up close by to house the workers – labourers, engineers, drillers – and their servicing whores: the thick swathe of black bin-liners spilling jelly-shit refuse, the stinking open-air toilet facilities, the barking, snapping dogs . . . and finally past the rear of the temple where a group of humorous youths had scrawled fluorescent green garage-music graffiti over marble that had been hand-carved millennia ago . . .

'Shit. What's he doing? What are you fucking doing? Idiot! Jesus Christ Superstar . . . can we edit that out later? Right . . . is the audio off? Good. Fuck me . . . hey, yeah? Oh, hiya, hey, hi, Lindi, you're looking luscious for a sixteen-year-old, and I can't *believe* the size of your breasts! I was so impressed by the agency shots that I . . . What? Come and get a glass of brandy, love, you very shortly *will* have earned it . . . ooh, yes, that feels real good, yes, yes! Just ease it down and pull it out, yes, yes! Uh, keep doing that – a little bit faster now . . .'
Audio cut.

Due to the impact of the twin quakes, Natasha's ECube received an almost immediate update: new coordinates for a pick-up 160 klicks further east into the mountains, towards Strahlhorn and away from the scene of this colossal natural disaster and the subsequent heavy presence of the world's TV and press media.

Carter stood outside their cabin, yellow police tape wrapped in one fist like a boxer's bandages, a rucksack gripped in the other. They had skipped the cordons – the police had plenty of other priorities out in the darkness, and many screams could still be heard. Carter's gaze swept the grounds in the darkness and he sighed, a deep sad sigh. A heavy weariness and depression descended on two Spiral ops.

'What are those coordinates?'

Natasha repeated the list of numbers.

Carter cursed quietly and hoisted the rucksack. 'We'll need transport. I ain't fucking walking sixty klicks through snow-filled woodland and over mountain trails. I've hurt my back.'

'Could we steal one of the hotel's Snowcats? They're kept away from the main building, in the sheds over there.' She pointed through the gloom to where a rough-timber structure loomed through the falling flakes.

Carter shook his head, eyes hard after witnessing the devastation of Zermatt and listening to the distant echoing cries for help of hundreds of people.

'I was thinking of something a little *faster*,' he said.

Natasha, one hand on the rough-hewn timber of the shed doors, stared hard in the gloom lit only by Carter's Mag-Lite. 'Oh,' she said. 'I see what you mean. You've been snooping here before?'

'I snoop everywhere. It goes with the job . . . Come on.'

'We'll freeze!'

'Yeah, but it's fast. A Snowcat would take us hours! This is a Yamaha RX-16 Snowmobile, with an in-line 40-valve 2399cc Genesis-Extreme V engine, Pro-Action mountain suspension, titanium-fibre Deltabox chassis, Nail-skid resistance and a Camoplast Challenger track. This is the new promotional model – it has a 3D name badge and silver decals. Look, just above the tracks there. And it's been converted to run on the new Leviathan fuel, LVA, so we get real good mileage into the bargain.'

'Carter, you're a fucking geek.'

'But a geek who knows his vehicles. We'll be at the meet a damn sight faster on this than in a fucking Snowcat. Just get some warm clothing on and have a look for your ski goggles.'

Looking around to see if they'd been spotted, he straddled the machine and, using his ECube, within thirty seconds bypassed the digital immobiliser. The engine roared into life, and he flicked the switch for silencers, which slid into place. Carter revved the Yamaha snowmobile's engine and dipped the clutch, feeling the incredible torque just waiting to be unleashed as he watched Natasha pulling on two more jumpers, her Berghaus fleece jacket, ski goggles and thick Gore-Tex7 gloves.

'I hope you know what you're doing,' she muttered, climbing onto the machine behind Carter and pulling her rucksack onto her back – stuff that they had salvaged from the cabin which they considered valuable enough to drag to this emergency Spiral pick-up. Equipment and clothing designed to keep them alive.

Carter pulled his own goggles in place, blipped the throttle, then eased the clutch. The RX-16's 2399cc engine boomed quietly, straining at the leash to be free; the tracks dug in and the snowmobile eased to the shed doors, poked its nose out, then roared free in a shower of snow, banking left, its suspension dipping and tracks clawing the snow as Carter accelerated away from the hotel, away from the police, away from emergency services. And away from the quake zone.

They hammered up the mountain, the engine taking the huge ascent in its stride, snow spraying out behind them as the tracks dug deep and Carter eased the powerful machine between scatters of conifer. The broad sweep of the bright headlights cut slices from the chaotic darkness of the mountain night and tumbling snow, and Natasha looked behind her then, glancing back down the mountain, over the clumps of trees to the glow of the hotel embers and the steady sweep of police searchlights. Snow was still falling, blurring her view, and Zermatt and its horror was gone now. She turned back and hugged close to Carter, allowing him to buffer the wind-chill on this uphill flight to the Spiral rendezvous.

'Something is deeply wrong,' she muttered gently.

But Carter could not hear her.

They stopped for a breather, and Carter killed the RX-16's engine and lights. Darkness swept in like a huge velvet cloak. Snow fell all around, quickly covering their trail with a veil of white and stifling any sounds of movement. Natasha checked her ECube, then tossed it to Carter who scanned the blue digits and glanced up ahead.

There was no real trail to follow, just a newly improvised path – using the ECube to scope land contours, valleys and sudden crevasses. Carter lit a cigarette and the tip glowed in the darkness, illuminating his face through the falling snow.

'We're making good time,' he said.

'I thought you'd quit smoking. Or at least were trying to.'

'That was before the fucking Earth tried to eat me. Twice. And before that huge bastard broke into our cabin and tried to crush my windpipe.'

'That still makes me uneasy,' said Natasha, reaching for the proffered cigarette and enjoying a heavy drag. Blue smoke enveloped her face and she coughed a little.

'I thought *you* had quit,' smiled Carter gently, retrieving his weed.

'It's been a rough night,' she conceded, smiling, but Carter could read the exhaustion and horror in her eyes.

'Which bit makes you uneasy?'

'The intruder. Something doesn't quite fit – about him not being Nex.'

'I'm not the hardest man in the world,' said Carter softly. 'There are plenty out there who can take me in a fight; that's why I use Mr Browning.' He grinned nastily. 'But yeah, I know what you mean. A bullet and a fucking severed arm . . . I wonder what he was looking for? He certainly left empty-handed, if you'll excuse the pun.'

'Maybe he was a scout for the Nex?' mused Nats.

Carter shook his head. 'I don't think so. Those bastards are fairly thin on the ground now – the SAD teams have pretty much wiped that fucked-up genetic mess from the face of the planet.' He shivered, adding mentally that he was also glad that Feuchter, and Durell – his old and bitter enemies – were dead: dead and buried under the sea with the remains of their battleship and improvised war station.

Natasha nodded, and shivered. 'It's getting colder.' She glanced up. 'We could do with somewhere to stop.'

'I think the rendezvous is near a hut or cabin of some sort. We'll have plenty of time to rest when we get there . . .'

The Yamaha cruised through the falling snow, and soon the dawn arrived, its pink tendrils pushing between the snowflakes and turning the sky a cool grey. The falling snow eased until it was nothing more than a scattering of flakes, and the RX-16 found a narrow winding trail through the conifer forests. They cruised for a while, the snowmobile's engine buzzing quietly as it prowled along. Carter's gaze was focused and alert, sweeping the trail from left to right and back.

He halted.

The engine rumbled, spitting exhaust into the cold snow.

'What is it?'

Carter licked his lips, and lifted his goggles, rubbing at his eyes.

The land rumbled, and snow shook from the trees to either side of the trail. The rumbling continued for perhaps a minute, and then subsided. Silence filled the world once more.

'A gentle reminder,' said Carter bitterly.

'The sooner we get out of here the better,' said Natasha.

'I didn't realise that Switzerland was prone to earthquakes.'

'Neither did the Swiss.'

They cruised through the snow for another two hours, then left the trail and again headed cross-country through the forests. At one point the world fell away to the left, a massive vertical drop down into a huge canyon filled with snow and the occasional scattering of black, shining rocks. Carter stopped for another cigarette and Natasha stood, shielding her eyes with her gloved hands and gazing down in awe as the wind whipped at her. Snow began to fall again, scattering patterns down into the valley below, and both of them felt privileged to witness such a display of Nature's awesome power.

'We're so small,' said Natasha. 'So insignificant. It's like, one minute we're dancing at the party, the next the whole fucking hotel is swallowed by the Earth. We think we are so strong, so in control. And yet Nature – she could smash us in an instant.'

'Yeah, you hold on to that thought,' said Carter, flicking the butt of his cigarette away into the gulf of the vast valley. It spun, carried on eddies of snow and wind, and disappeared into the immeasurable expanse of bleak dawn wilderness.

It took them another hour to reach the cabin, located by the ECube's coordinate navigation. It was a small building set against a picturesque location and standing among huddled conifers. It had only a single room, and the outside log walls were piled high with snow. Still, the cabin seemed extremely inviting after the cold of the journey and the bleakness of the long stretches of mountain trail. The snow-heavy undergrowth surrounding the structure was dense and eerily quiet.

They killed the Yamaha's engine and Carter had to dig a path to the front door, which lolled open on broken leather hinges. Working together, they cleared the spill of snow and filled the fireplace with wood from a narrow protected log store out back. It took a good ten minutes to get a fire going because the firewood was damp, but as the small flames finally took hold warmth began to flood out. Wedging shut the door with a heavy, rough-hewn table, they pulled off their wet clothing and boots and set them steaming on the earth floor before the fire, and warmed their numbing hands and feet before the flames.

'The snow has got heavy again. Will the Comanche be able to fly through this?' asked Natasha.

'Our modified Comanches can fly through anything,' said Carter softly. 'They might not be able to land here, but they can winch us up; a real *chilling* experience.'

'How long to the rendezvous?'

'One hour.'

'I'll make us something warm to eat.'

Carter grinned. 'I thought you'd never offer. My stomach is like a Nazi's soul – empty.'

★

Carter stared at the bowl.

'I can't believe it.'

'What?'

'Of all the foodstuffs you could have brought with us from the cabin, all you brought was B&S.'

'What's wrong with B&S?' Natasha smiled encouragingly.

'Nothing, but . . . well, B&S is just standard military fodder. It's got a fair amount of roughage in it and . . . it's about as bland as bland can be, Nats. Couldn't you have brought something else?'

'Carter, we're only an hour from a pick-up. I wasn't going to go shopping for T-bone steaks!'

'Yeah, but . . .'

He stirred the red gruel. It seemed to be staring back at him.

As he ate, Natasha reclined and skipped through recent files on the ECube. 'You mentioned before that the snowmobile ran on LVA?'

'Mm.' Carter nodded.

'Seems like Leviathan Fuels are stirring up some interest. NATO's Fuel Commission are talking about investigations. The oil companies of the world are kicking up a right stink . . .'

'So they will.' Carter gesticulated with his spoon. 'Imagine, a new fuel springs seemingly from nowhere – best-kept energy secret ever: it's much cheaper than what's currently on offer, needs only a minor engine modification costing a few hundred dollars, and fuck me if it doesn't do eight times more miles to the gallon as well. The oil companies are fucking green with envy!'

'Apparently it's started a price war.'

'Yeah, and that'll get worse as the competition hots up. But hey, who am I to give a flying fuck about fat-cat billionaire oil industrialists with wads of banknotes falling out of their tax-free Swiss bank accounts? It's a free market . . . But let's be honest, if the petroleum moguls had clocked Leviathan Fuel researchers digging LVA out of the rock, then how long would those researchers' life expectancies have been? Nice man with a sniper rifle, anybody?'

'God, you're cynical,' said Natasha.

'I'm just the way the world made me.' Carter smiled sardonically. 'Anything else of interest on our little alloy friend?'

'Jam's still heading up the SAD teams; reports are favourable about the Nex extermination. I'd have thought they would have been wiped out by now, but every time Spiral think they've cracked it and the world goes a bit quiet, another bunch spring up.'

'Yeah, like a bad penny. I bet Jam's tearing his hair out. We're just lucky the Nex bastards haven't got Durell any more.'

'He was one insane motherfucker.'

'Tut tut, Nats, language like that from such a pretty face is most unbecoming in a lady.' He reached over and rapped her knuckles with his spoon.

'Carter! You'll get B&S juice all over me!'

'Don't be so soft. Look at me, fucking wrestling with a crevasse a few hours ago and you're bloody complaining about a little tomato on your dungarees!'

'Wrestling with . . . ? Ahhh, that was her name, was it? Nice pair of long legs Miss Crevasse had to her credit. And the way you saved her by mauling her naked breasts with your face was a true miracle to behold. Proper hero stuff, worthy of Hollywood.'

Carter grinned sheepishly. 'Hey, can I be blamed if the woman I rescue is naked except for a pair of knee-high

110

boots? Sometimes,' he muttered, a grim look on his face, 'you just have to take the rough with the smooth.'

Natasha moved towards him, on her knees, and grinned up into his face. 'You're a bad man, Mr Carter.'

'You'd better believe it.'

Thirty minutes later Carter and Natasha were packed and ready to move out. Nats had killed the fire, they had prepped both ECubes with SAR signals and now awaited their emergency holiday-destroying transport with some trepidation. Something big was going down, they could sense it; something big and bad and they were going to be a part of it. The tension within the two Spiral operatives was beginning to increase: emergency Spiral meetings on this scale were not called every day – nor even every year.

Snow was still falling, and Carter and Natasha stepped out to stand beside the Yamaha snowmobile; Carter checked his watch. 'They're one minute late.' He smiled, but even as the last syllable left his lips the sound of a helicopter echoed through the snow above the vast mountainside expanses of sweeping forest, the thump of armoured rotors reverberating through the falling snow.

Carter tutted. Natasha shook her head, staring at him.

'There's no excuse for sloppiness,' said Carter smugly.

'One minute!' laughed Natasha.

'One minute is one fucking minute. It can mean the difference between life and—'

Sudden fire illuminated the sky in smoking trails that converged from three directions. There was a scream of engines and a heavy bass boom; screeching rotor sounds destroyed the peace of the forest and a fireball blasted outwards suddenly in a flare of purple HighJ energy . . . The Comanche was plucked from the snow-filled heavens by three rockets that ignited it and sent it heaving skywards to hang for long timeless moments. Then it fell, trailing black smoke and spitting showers of superheated metal in all directions. It clattered through the trees, its rotors slicing branches and trunks and whining in screaming deceleration, and then crashed into the ground, crackling in the embrace of a sudden raging blue-white fire.

'—Death,' said Carter coldly.

'Three rockets,' snapped Natasha, her Glock in her hand and her gaze sweeping the trees. Carter pulled free his heavy battle-scarred Browning HiPower. His eyes were very cold. 'That should have been impossible,' he said.

'I know,' replied Natasha quietly, eyes scanning the forest with unease. 'The Comanche is supposedly one hundred per cent protected against SAMs. Whatever weapons they used, they were fucking advanced – and fucking invisible. Start the Yamaha.'

The two Spiral operatives backed towards the RX-16, automatically covering one another's arcs of fire as they searched for trouble. They were immediately a team, expecting an offensive; they immediately became as one.

Distant sounds of screaming echoed. The sounds of agony. The sounds of a man on fire . . .

'Fuck,' snapped Carter, firing up the Yamaha. He revved the vehicle and looked back at Natasha. 'You know we've got to check it out . . .'

'It's a trap,' said Natasha.

'*Damn fucking right it's a trap*,' hissed Kade in the dark recesses of Carter's brain. '*Go on, check it out, get a bullet in the brain and end up eating soil and you will be worm food, my brother . . . go on, do it, let's see what balls you really have, you dumb-arse fuck-brain . . .*'

Carter pushed Kade's comments from his raging mind. Anger threatened to consume him, but he controlled it. Out there in the snow one of his Spiral comrades was suffering, screaming and dying, and he could not leave him to cook, or to be shot by – who? The Nex?

Carter grinned a grin that had nothing to do with humour.

'You bastards,' he snarled as he opened the throttle. In a shower of cold snow-ice, he sped off between the trees.

Carter knelt warily beneath the tree line. The Comanche had gone down hard, rotors chewing wood and bark, body shell aflame, and now it lay buckled and twisted in a smoking, blazing mess. Carter's stare swept the opposite side of the small clearing and the trees that had been pulped by the plummeting war machine. Too nasty, he thought. And too fucking open . . .

Crouching, he crept forward.

And saw the body, smouldering in the snow. The pilot had managed to crawl a short distance from the Comanche's still-burning wreckage but his HIDSS helmet had been flame-fried to his face, melded to burning skin, blended with charbroiled flesh and muscle and hair. Carter wrinkled his nostrils, almost gagging as he moved closer. That man must be dead, came the unbidden thought. He must be dead . . . because to live—

It did not even bear thinking about.

Carter paused, gaze scanning the trees once more. Something was wrong, his senses screamed at him. Still he moved forward, and crouched beside the nightmarishly burnt pilot. He forced himself to look down at the scorched blackened face, and only then did the vomit truly force its way into his mouth as he saw eyes watching him from beneath a melted, caked brow and blackened crusted crispy skin . . .

A hand grasped his, a sudden movement that took him by surprise. Looking down, Carter saw that there was no real skin, only an oily, tarry mess of muscle and blood and crisped hide. The stench filled his nostrils and he vomited to one side and heaved until his stomach contracted and spasmed in a fist of horror. He met the pilot's gaze. The man was beyond screaming and his twitching eyes made only one entreaty and that was 'Please . . .'

Carter's Browning lifted and a single shot rang out across the small forest clearing.

Carter's eyes narrowed.

Three figures stepped out of the tree-haunted shadows. Nex.

Carter stumbled back towards Natasha as the Nex attacked.

Bullets spat from JK49s and Carter leapt swiftly into the forest, rolling behind a fallen conifer where Natasha crouched. The Nex sprinted towards the destroyed Comanche, kneeling beside the fallen pilot. Their grey-balaclava-clad heads turned as their stares fixed on Carter. They rose to their feet and began to run towards the Spiral agents.

Carter's Browning boomed in his fist. One of the Nex was sent slamming to the ground with its blended insect-human brain spreading in a bone-scattered pool of pink snow-mush.

'One down,' muttered Natasha, taking aim—

The other two continued their charge.

They moved fast – inhumanly fast . . .

But then, the Nex were not human.

Natasha fired, once, twice, three times. The Nex weaved left and right, keeping low, legs pumping, JK49s stitching a line of bullets in the log behind which the two Spiral operatives crouched, making Natasha yelp and duck. But Carter's Browning fired seven times, the gun heavy in his fist, and the second Nex was sent sprawling in

114

the snow with only a gruesome ring of smashed bone where once the masked face had been.

'*That's my boy!*' cheered Kade.

Carter snarled as the final Nex reached the log and leapt, its sub-machine gun tracking him as the Browning jerked up. Carter could still see the eyes of the dead Spiral pilot, surrounded by melted flesh: the HiPower jolted in his grip and five bullets sent the Nex lurching over him, legs kicking, blood spraying, to sprawl against a tree and fall twisted and dead among its roots.

Carter climbed slowly to his feet, panting, sweat stinging his eyes and the cuts on his face. Natasha leapt up beside him, licking fear-dry lips. 'You killed them,' she said, awed. 'You killed them all!'

Carter nodded emotionlessly. Pride was his enemy. And complacency meant death.

Natasha turned – and saw that ten more Nex had stepped into the clearing.

'Yeah, but here comes the main course,' muttered Carter as the killers opened fire with JK49s and the two Spiral agents fled, skidding on ice, sprinting as best they could for the sanctuary of the RX-16. Leaping aboard, Carter fired up the engine and with Natasha clinging on grimly he twisted the throttle hard round. Snow spat and streamed from the tracks as they raced off between the trees. Bullets hissed past them, gouging into tree trunks and whistling through branches. They weaved madly left and right, hunched low.

The firing finally stopped.

Carter pulled the Yamaha to a halt, spraying snow against a wall of black glistening rock where ice had formed long glittering stalactites. 'We lost them?' panted Nats through frozen lips.

'Listen.'

She concentrated as Carter killed the engine.

'What?'

'Shit.'

'*What?*'

And then she heard it. Engines. Screaming engines.

Carter fired the Yamaha into life once more and urged the machine on hard; snow shot up behind them as compact black snowmobiles with mounted SMGs appeared, weaving through the trees. The machine guns roared, fire flashing from their muzzles, and bullets slapped into trees and snow all around, ricochets striking sparks from the rock wall. Carter ducked and Nats hung on grimly as the snowmobile rocketed through the snow and trees . . .

Carter glanced behind. Through the haze of kicked-up snow he saw at least ten machines pursuing them.

'Fuck. I thought the fucking SAD teams had wiped out the Nex!' he screamed over the roar of the tortured engine.

'So did I,' shouted Natasha, clinging tightly to him.

Carter dragged the RX-16 around, heading up a steep slope, the engine pulling powerfully. The black snowmobiles started to fall behind as the Yamaha sped from the cover of the trees, swaying slightly through banks of snow and then skimming fast over a field of sloping ridged ice. Up they headed, towards another tree line and the sanctuary of the forest. Rocks glittered all around and with some skill Carter dodged through them, setting into a rhythm with the machine, feeling it as a part of him . . .

A few more bullets skimming past reminded him of their impending doom.

Carter powered the machine on, his stare fixed. Glancing back, he lifted his Browning in his right hand, sighted, fired off ten bullets but hit nothing. 'Moving too fast,' he muttered.

116

'*Or maybe you're just a shite aim,*' observed Kade.

Kade laughed at him, and that made Carter mad. He gritted his teeth, swerved the snowmobile into the line of trees and suddenly slammed on the brakes. They left a long straight line of grooved ice. Carter leapt free as Natasha screamed, 'What the hell are you *doing*?'

Carter was attaching something to his Browning.

'Remember I was telling you about the mod I got from Simmo? A NeedleClip?' There came a snapping sound, metal grinding metal. 'This is it.' He moved to the tree line where he could hear and now see the swathe of black snowmobiles speeding up the incline, their formation a tight V.

'NeedleClip?'

Carter glanced back, where Natasha crouched behind him.

'Fucking needle *bombs*.' He grinned savagely, holding the Browning two-handed and sighting down the bulky barrel. The NeedleClip had its own sight and squatted above the gun, a small black symbiotic metal cube, its sides laser-carved with a cryptic military designation.

He flicked a tiny switch with his thumb. There was a heavy deep hum which belied the weapon's size and Carter pulled the Browning's trigger. There was a soft click and instead of a bullet, a sliver of metal shot from the NeedleClip, glistening like a tiny, glittering dart as it flashed buzzing low over the snow and connected with the lead snowmobile . . .

There was a searing flash and then a massive boom as the snowmobile and the two that were closely following it were kicked up into the air, spinning, before blossoming into unfurling flaming petals. They soared briefly as the snowmobiles still on the ground skidded to a halt in clouds of powder snow. Then the mangled vehicles fell,

117

pluming black smoke and with their screaming Nex riders clawing at shrapnel-filled faces.

Heads looked up towards the tree line.

Carter fired again as eyes went wide and engines howled in hastily revved panic . . .

Another two snowmobiles were smashed skywards, Nex squirming as the exploding metal melted into their flesh. Black smoke blossomed and a crackling like fireworks going off reached Natasha's ears . . .

The other snowmobiles fled.

Carter turned to Natasha, but she was staring at the ECube. 'We have to get out of here, Carter.'

'What is it?'

Her gaze met his. 'There's more of them, up there through the trees. Hundreds of them.'

'Impossible!' he snapped. 'Why didn't the ECube pick it up before?'

'Remember the shields they used, back in Scotland?' A year ago an assassin had infiltrated Carter's house and had somehow managed to sidestep not only his own personal defence systems but the all-ranging scanners of the ECube. In essence, the effectiveness of the ECube – a Spiral operative's major defence mechanism – had been compromised.

'I thought we'd cracked their technology!'

'So did I.'

Carter cursed and glanced back at the black billowing smoke. 'We've just fucking advertised ourselves.'

'Better than getting bullets in the back.'

'Come on.'

They ran back to the RX-16, leapt aboard, and Carter started the engine, setting off in a straight line.

'Where you going?'

'Towards them.'

118

'Are you fucking crazy? The ECube's registering more than two hundred Nex. We need an airlift!'

'Yeah, and they'll have one.'

'Carter, they'll be sending search parties to check out the smoke! And the others have probably commed ahead and told them we're here.'

'Yes.' Carter smiled. 'Last fucking thing they'll expect us to do is head straight towards them. If the ECube is picking them up, I'm pretty damn sure they know about it. If they have ECube cloaks, then their technology is more advanced than we suspected . . . and there're more of them.'

Turning back, Carter opened the throttle wide and slid the exhaust silencers into place. Stealth came at the expense of power, but the machine was still functional as they cruised almost silently through the trees, weaving gently, Carter's vigilant stare on the lookout for the Nex search parties that he knew would come.

The engine clicked softly as it started to cool. Carter dragged some fallen branches roughly across the RX-16 in a crude version of camouflage, and Natasha and he set off through the snow on foot.

'I don't like leaving it behind,' said Natasha softly.

'Yeah, but we'll need to get close. The branches should hide it from air obs.'

Snow had started falling again, more heavily. The forest was quiet, almost silent, occasional falls of snow from over-laden branches crumping in the distance.

'What are the Nex doing all the way out here?'

'An interesting thought.'

'I bet Jam doesn't know about their existence.'

'I'm pretty sure *nobody* knows about their existence.'

They moved warily, guns out, the metal cold even

119

through their gloves. Natasha looked more closely at the NeedleClip, amazed that something so small could pack such a punch.

The cold was beginning to get to the two Spiral operatives as they weaved warily through the trees. They had to stand stock-still once as snowmobiles thundered off to one side, flashes of black between the distant tree trunks, and then they dropped to a crouch and waited.

Natasha kept a close eye on her ECube's scanners.

Several groups were moving, spreading out.

'They're searching for us,' she whispered.

Carter merely nodded.

They moved stealthily for nearly forty minutes, creeping from tree to tree, the falling snow their ally, the forest their protector. They halted while Carter carefully removed the NeedleClip and screwed the Browning's silencer back in place. As they moved off again through the thick snow Natasha watched the ECube, but was surprised when Carter's hand came up in a 'halt' signal. She met his gaze as he put a finger to his lips and gestured for her to wait and be perfectly still.

She watched him move carefully through the snow and then crouch beside a stunted conifer tree. He was moving with great care, placing each foot with an infinity of consideration. Then he levelled the Browning and aimed. She heard the hiss of a silenced shot and nearly jumped as a mound of snow seemed to collapse – to reveal a camouflaged Nex bearing a sniper's rifle. Carter signalled for Natasha to approach, and she checked the ECube again.

'He wasn't there, on the scanner.'

'I know.'

'How the fuck did you see him?'

Carter's breath steamed, and his eyes were twinkling. 'Let's just call it magic,' he whispered. He moved towards

120

the Nex and lifted the Heckler & Koch SN5 sniper rifle. 'Good weapon,' he said, hoisting it thoughtfully.

'He's dead?'

'*It* is dead,' Carter corrected gently. 'It was the perimeter guard – we must be getting close.'

'I don't understand: they cloak the guards but not the compound where the ECube is showing hundreds?'

'No point having a guard if he can be seen – even by a scanner. Nobody knows that this base – or whatever it is – is here. Why cloak it? What are the chances of somebody stumbling across it up here? Maybe it's arrogance, or maybe you can't cloak such a large group of Nex – we'll have to sneak in and ask them.'

'Very funny.'

'I'm serious.'

'That's what worries me.'

Moving on through the heavy snow they exercised even greater caution until once more Carter signalled for a halt. They had been climbing a steep incline, an embankment peppered with trees, that overlooked a compound of some sort up ahead. Trees ringed the compound on ridges of land and snow, and low buildings of grey concrete blended naturally with the ground, barely visible – especially in this climate of snow and mist and from the air.

'Probably left over from the Bright War,' whispered Carter, gazing down at the buildings. There seemed to be some activity going on in them but very little outside.

'They are all inside,' whispered Natasha.

'Well, they wouldn't be sunbathing.'

'The buildings look like barracks.'

'Maybe. Who fucking knows what they're doing? All I'm thinking about at the moment is one of those.' Carter pointed, his movements cautious, to where a high fence

121

surrounded a small square of cleared concrete on which sat four squat black helicopters.

'Airlift?'

'They look familiar,' growled Carter, remembering the great air battle that had taken place between the Demolition Squads and the Nex over the Arctic seas and the improvised WarCentre created by Durell and Feuchter after they had betrayed Spiral. 'Some bad shit is going down here.'

'A problem for another day,' said Natasha.

'I agree. Come on.'

They circled wide, Carter on the lookout for guards and snipers, his senses screaming at him and Kade making the occasional maddeningly sarcastic comment.

Carter halted, gesturing. A guard was stationed outside the compound, protecting the helicopters with a heavy machine gun. 'We need to get a bit closer.'

They moved carefully, coming in on the guard's blind side. Carter took him out with a single bullet to the back of the head.

The helicopter enclosure was protected by a digitally locked gate; Carter knelt beside the fence and stared at its metallic strands. 'Titanium IX, very advanced,' he said, impressed. He removed his own ECube and a tiny silver beam emerged from it, slicing through the Titanium IX strands, making tiny pings.

'How did you do that?' said Natasha, frowning.

'A new mod.'

'Why doesn't mine do that?'

Carter smiled, cutting the final strand and bending the glowing edges wide. 'Come on.'

They squeezed through the opening and moved warily towards the first black helicopter, which was cloaked with a veil of snow. 'This is too easy,' muttered Natasha.

'I agree, although I'm pretty sure they're not expecting us. You hot-wire this baby and I'll keep watch.'

'You think they know we're here?'

'Maybe. But maybe they're playing a game with us . . .'

Chilled by Carter's words, and with the hairs on the back of her neck standing up, Natasha gently opened the cockpit and climbed in. With ECube in gloved hand, she began the complex process of hot-wiring the helicopter's digital ignition, utilising her pre-Spiral hacking skills. She was illuminated by the curious witch-light of the snow-enclosed cockpit.

Outside, Carter's mouth was a grim line as his eyes scanned relentlessly around. The cold was seeping into his bones now. His head snapped to the right as a fall of snow toppled from the low branches of a wide pine. He realised that the Browning was already aimed and primed, and he lowered the weapon gently.

There was a distant, snow-muffled click and Carter dropped to a crouch, gun ready.

A figure stepped into the snow from one of the concrete buildings. He was athletic, broad-shouldered, and Carter could tell from his stance, the way he moved, that he was a warrior. He had shaved blond hair and a badly scarred head and face, and he was laughing unpleasantly. As he moved forward, a second figure strode out behind him. This individual was huge, towering a full head over the smaller man who was himself six feet tall. The giant wore a heavy black coat across his shoulders and his face was patched with black, as if he had suffered terrible burns that had scorched his skin. His eyes were small and round and copper, the face deformed and twisted to one side.

'I've done it,' whispered Natasha. 'What the fuck is *that*?'

123

At her hushed words, the deformed head swung round, stretching forward on a strange thick neck, the small eyes focusing on the helicopter, the crouched form of Carter, Natasha's peeping face . . .

'Well done,' snarled Carter.

'It's fucking looking at us!'

The blond-haired man turned and stared at them. Carter growled, 'Get that fucking chopper started – now!' He lifted his Browning as the huge figure shrugged free the black coat to reveal a heavily muscled body, bare from the waist up, skin merging with black panels scattered across his chest and belly, gleaming as snow settled against their chitinous surface.

'What is it?' wondered Carter.

'*Just shoot the fucking thing,*' hissed Kade.

Time seemed to slow as Carter lifted the Browning HiPower and took aim. The creature – or Nex, or whatever it was – lowered its head on bull-neck muscles and charged, heavy boots stamping through the snow, its speed incredible for something so big . . .

The door to the building, which still stood open, spat forth a stream of Nex carrying JK49s and aiming them at Carter and the helicopter. Kade was bellowing, '*Trap, it's a fucking trap,*' the words piercing Carter's mind as his trigger finger squeezed and the Browning kicked back hard against the heel of his hand—

The creature seemed to flinch to one side, and the bullet hissed past, taking a chunk out of the concrete of the building. Carter fired twice more, the third bullet ricocheting off one of the black armour plates but causing no damage . . .

Behind him the helicopter's engines started and the rotors began to turn, slowly at first and then rapidly picking up speed. The man with blond hair was smiling, stare

124

bright and arms folded, but there was something wrong with his eyes. Carter fired another two bullets as the giant creature reached the eighteen-feet-high fence and leapt, long claws extending from thick black fingers, and scrabbled upwards.

'Carter!' screamed Natasha.

Carter fired several more rounds as the huge creature, small copper eyes staring fixedly at him, clambered up the fence and reached the top. The Browning boomed again, bullets slicing through the air and screeching off the armour plates. The final shot punched the creature back off the fence to land in the snow. Carter watched in horror as it rolled easily and climbed to its booted feet. It snarled, drool pooling from crooked teeth as blood poured from two holes in its protected torso.

'*Give him to me*,' snarled Kade. '*I will fuck him bad . . .*'

More Nex were swarming from the low concrete building. Carter's gaze met the red-scarred stare of the man with the shaved blond hair who nodded, almost as if meeting a friend in the street. Carter bared his teeth in a grimace.

'Carter!'

The helicopter's engines screamed and howled under Natasha's rough ministrations. The creature clambered up to the fence once more, claws gouging a path upwards. Carter watched in horror and fascination, as if in a dream – a waking nightmare. It leapt cleanly up and over as Carter's sweat-slippery hands slotted the NeedleClip to the Browning with a precise click – the down draught from the chopper's rotors was beating against his back but his stare was fixed intently on the mammoth creature that landed in the snow in front of him. It was too close for him to use the weapon. To kill it would be to kill himself. It smiled with twisted fangs.

Carter sensed the helicopter lifting free of the snow. He felt the down draughts increase.

'*Let me,*' soothed Kade.

The creature flexed its claws, stained with its own blood, and Carter tightened his grip on the trigger.

To kill is to die, he thought . . .

'Carter, here!' screamed Natasha once more over the howling of the engines and rotors as he saw a massive group of Nex spread out beyond the fence with their weapons aimed and their faces covered by masks of grey and black. There were too many of them. Even if Carter killed this *thing* he would be cut to pieces in a machine-gun instant . . .

Carter bared his teeth in a tight-jawed grimace. 'You ready for me, you big fucker? You're one ugly piece of shit, that's for sure . . . Come on, let's see what you can do – let's fucking dance.'

Spiral Mainframe
Data log #11952

CLASSIFIED SADt/9083/SPECIAL INVESTIGATIONS UNIT

Data Request 324#11952

FEUCHTER

`Count Feuchter`

```
Count Feuchter; German professor, born in
Schwalenberg, educated in Munich, London and
Prague. Great-grandfather killed by the
Nazis during World War II after being
tortured somewhere on the German/Austrian
border. Mother and two sons fled to Italy,
```

then to England for protection after the war was over; Feuchter stemmed from this bloodline.

He was an expert in computing systems, specialising in processor function and artificial intelligence. He helped pioneer the QII and QIII military processors before turning traitor against Spiral with a group of other operatives.

Among other things, Feuchter was also heavily involved in the Nx5 Project and it is now believed that he continued this research illegally after Spiral withdrew funding and the project was killed. All the Nx5 subjects were apparently destroyed. It was unknown at the time that Feuchter had, in fact, experimented on himself and was willing to take his machinations much further.

He was responsible for many civilian deaths, and a Warrant12 was issued by Spiral in 2XXX after various Spiral DemolSquads were assassinated.

Count Feuchter was killed during the Spiral_mobile mission by operative Cartervb12. His body was never recovered.

Keyword SEARCH>>DURELL, QIII [lvlz], NEX [lvlz] SPIRAL_Q, SAD, SP1RAL_R

CHAPTER 5

BLACK PLANET

Jam swam in a world of darkness. Tiny fish-lights glittered and he watched them in fascination as they swam around and around as if in a bowl. But then a slice of red ripped across his vision and with it came a slashing glass shard of pain . . . deep heart-core pain that he could not push away.

His eyelids flickered open.

Darkness. Dry darkness.

And blows. Boots, suddenly crashing into his ribs and back and head. Dark silhouettes stood over him, amorphous shapes that wobbled and wavered, illuminated from behind by the yellow orange flickering of live flames. Jam curled into a tighter ball, his broken teeth gritting together and filling his mouth with blood and pieces of bone.

The blows continued, and a deep voice said, 'He's awake.'

The blows increased in intensity, smashing into Jam, pounding him against an anvil of agony. He felt a rib break with an audible crack but the pain flowed all through him and was everywhere, a dull throbbing interspersed with the thud of heavy steel-capped boots – connecting with his flesh. He felt blood pooling under his face on the dry dusty floor, on the cool stone and he watched it with interest, his vision shaking, vibrating, as the blows continued to rock him and the beating subsided. Gradually.

The dark shapes retreated. Faded like ghosts.

Jam coughed and tried to sit up. But he fell back to the stone floor once more. He closed his swollen eyes, his face pressed down against the warmth of his own blood and his eyes fluttered closed and eventually, after a long time, unconsciousness claimed him.

He dreamed of Slater.

Slater stood in the forest, talking through the gaping smile in his throat in a language that Jam found difficult to understand. 'What's the matter?' asked Slater, the flaps of sliced flesh puckering like lips. 'You don't fucking like what you see, eh? You did this to me, you bastard, you fucking did this to me . . . your fucking complacency led us all to our deaths . . .'

'But I'm not dead!'

Laughter, spraying droplets of blood.

Jam tried to say, 'I'm sorry,' and he tried, tried so hard to force the words from his mouth but it would not work, his tongue and lips would not cooperate and he could not breathe, awesome pain was smashing through his chest and ribs and he could not exhale the air with which to apologise to this man, one of his greatest friends.

Slater moved closer towards him, blood splattering from the wound with each footfall and raining down across the woodland floor. His eyes were filled with pain and sadness.

'You killed me, Jam,' he cried and tears of blood ran down his cheeks. 'You fucking let me die out there . . . and it hurts so much . . .'

And now Jam was spinning – then reality kicked him in the face with a blow of brightness. Flames, flickering orange and yellow and dancing like a demon of fire, washed across his face and he blinked rapidly, pupils dilating, mouth opening to allow a single silent sigh to escape.

'He's awake again.'

Shapes blocked out the flames once more, broad-shouldered figures that converged on Jam. A blow crashed against his shoulder, and he suddenly realised that they were using thick sticks like pickaxe handles. He tried to cry out 'Stop!' but the blows rained down and he tried to crawl away but his arm was broken and it gave way beneath him with a crunch as splintered bone poked and tore through his flesh and he screamed and that seemed to give his attackers a new lease of life as the blows rained heavier and harder and faster and the world was spinning spinning spinning and Jam fell into a deep well of Slater's slopping gore-filled blood and lay there staring at the stars and tasting bitter salt.

'When are you coming home?'

Jam stared at Nicky's face. It glowed with health and serenity. He took her chin in his cupped hand, smiled and, leaning forward, kissed her lips. She responded, and was warm and sweet and soft against him and he felt his love for this woman overwhelming his mind and their tongues danced and he felt at calm, at peace, at one with the world—

He pulled away.

Her mouth opened, and she said, 'You said you'd never

leave me, you'd said you were too good and they would never get you' – and a stream of black maggots spewed from her throat wriggling past her white teeth and they covered him, tiny jaws biting at his flesh and tearing at his eyes and he tried to cover his face but they pushed between his fingers sliding on their own slime and juice and Jam screamed and his eyes flew open—

The length of wood, the same diameter as the heavy end of a pool cue, connected with Jam's forehead with a dull slap. Stars spun across his vision and he rolled, trying to get away from the agony, but the blows rained down on his back and shoulders and neck. Suddenly he turned, snarling and rolling to his knees and lashing out blindly. There came a grunt of surprise as his broken fingers hit one of the attackers' groins and his fingers closed, his own bones crunching together as a heavy blow to the head smashed him down – so he grappled the nearest leg, pulling it close, and his blood-covered teeth closed on the struggling leg and he bit, he bit hard and he bit deep . . . he felt the cloth give way to flesh and the blows were thundering down across his back but he would not let go and the muscle was warm and wet and salted and sliming like an eel in his mouth. Jam bit and bit and he chewed and he ripped the sliming calf muscle from the bone, tore it like tender juicy steak to the accompaniment of a high-pitched shrilling sound – until darkness claimed him in its long dark flexing claws.

Jam came awake curled up in a ball, and for a long time there was no pain. Everything was gloomy, dry, and he stared at the black floor beneath him and the dust there, thick dust in which pools of his own saliva and blood had congealed. His tongue slowly worked around his dry mouth and he gently eased a piece of broken tooth to his desiccated lips, slowly pushed it out of his mouth and

131

watched it fall to the dust. Pain started to come then, in gentle throbbing waves and from every single molecule of his whole being. He realised that his eyes were filled with gunk, gritty and dry. And then he tried to move.

Pain lanced him.

It was as if a million knives stabbed at his flesh.

He suddenly realised that he was naked, but it did not matter. The pain was too great for him to worry about such trivial indignities.

Faces flickered through his mind, their lineaments forming photographs that were models of clarity. Nicky, her sweet smile, her loving eyes. Slater, his broad strong caring face. TT, her sardonic smile and mocking gaze. And Carter – broad and strong and battered, a face that could be trusted and that offered no compromise.

Gradually, the pain faded a little and Jam did not try to move again. Instead, he allowed his gaze to move around. At first he had thought this place was dark, but there was a reasonable light source – a dancing radiance from a flickering tallow torch. Flame-light caressed the walls, which were black and even and smooth, like obsidian or black marble although he could not make out any real details. He could see a bed, low down against the ground, a wide flat slab, again fashioned from obsidian or marble. And the floor, he realised, was not dust, but sand.

Jam coughed, and pain from his ribcage filled him with molten fire.

How many broken ribs?

He suddenly became aware of a figure standing behind him. He could tell by the shadows against the wall up ahead, and he tensed, waiting for the blows to rain down again. But they did not come, and Jam groaned from a dry throat as he rolled himself over and looked up at the slender dark shape in the gloom.

The figure was dressed completely in black, but instead of the trade-mark Nex balaclava, the face was bare and visible and gleaming in the flickering orange glow. It was deformed – only a little, but the evidence was still there. The Nex was not entirely human.

'You are the one known as Jam, Spiral operative on the TSAD Division?'

'Not me, pal,' said Jam slowly, his voice little more than a slurred croak. 'You've got the wrong guy.'

'Indeed, you have been responsible for the deaths of *many* of my colleagues.'

'Sorry, mate.' Jam forced a smile through cracked and bloodstained teeth. 'I was just out walking my fucking poodle when your thugs picked me up.'

'This is yours.'

The Nex produced Jam's ECube and held it up for him to see. Jam said nothing, and the Nex smiled, a gentle upturning at the corners of his slightly disfigured face. And then Jam realised what was wrong – the eyes were not quite right, slightly offset, and the nose a bit too low, and the teeth too . . . pointed.

'My name is Mace.'

'Pleased to meet you,' said Jam, huskily through his pain. 'I'd shake your hand but your men have broken my fingers, so I'll just have to wait until I can put a bullet in the back of your insect skull.'

'Tut, tut,' said the slender Nex. 'Such aggression is unnecessary.'

'Like the aggression your men have shown me?'

'An eye for an eye . . .' The Nex smiled softly. 'Do not think because we have been *altered* that we do not have feelings, do not have friends, do not have loved ones. Your people are responsible for the deaths of many Nex . . . there were a few retributions being sought.'

'Yeah, fucking great.' Jam went silent, his mind working. 'What do you want? Why haven't you killed me?'

'Bright, as well, for a non-Nex. As I was saying, my name is Mace and I will be your interrogator, your torturer, and ultimately your *friend*. We will spend many, many long hours together, you and I, Mr Jam. You will tell me everything that you know. *Everything*. And we will *learn* from one another – yes, you and I will learn one another's deepest and most intimate secrets.'

'Fuck you.'

'Now who is showing open aggression?'

'Fuck you.'

'Really, Mr Jam, you should learn more respect for those who dangle you from a thread, those who have the power to crush you like a –' he chuckled with dark humour, '– like an insect. Those who hold the power between your life and – ultimately – your death.'

'Fuck you.'

Mace moved closer, lowering himself to a crouch. Jam realised then that his hands were bound, with serrated titanium wire that dug through his flesh and ground jaggedly against the bones of his wrists.

'I won't tell you anything,' said Jam calmly, his stare fixed on the bright copper orbs of the Nex.

'On the contrary,' said Mace, his voice soft and hypnotic as he pulled free a leather pouch and removed a long, slender hypodermic. The syringe was filled with something silver – like the brightest of mercury.

The needle slid in.

The injection filled Jam's veins and *flowed* with every pulse of his heart.

His eyes went wide, and suddenly he screamed a scream so long and loud that he thought his lungs would bleed. Mace smiled, nodding understandingly as Jam writhed on the floor, knowing that the pain that the Spiral man had felt so far was as a tickle to a child, a brush of feather against skin, a mere inconsequence.

'On the contrary, Mr Jam, you will tell me *every*thing.'

```
Leviathan Fuels: Premium Grade LVA
- Go on, make the switch, because you
know your children deserve a better
future . . .
```

Charlotte smiled her sweetest smile, her all-winning smile, the smile that was guaranteed always to get her exactly what she wanted. She tossed back her dark curls and moved towards Freddy, one hand coming to rest lightly on his shoulder, her gaze meeting his, seeing the longing there, inherently understanding the bright lust lurking like a tiny flame within their amorphous depths. I have you, she thought. I have you eating from the palm of my hand. And you *will* do whatever I desire.

'I think we should make the switch,' she purred with alacrity.

'What?' Freddy's eyes went wide, not quite understand-ing, confused at Charlotte's sudden change of direction – from lust monster to base domestic conversation.

'The switch. To LVA. It's all the rage – every news report on the TV is bleating on about how wonderful this new fuel is. It's revolutionising the oil industry, you know.'

'Is it?' Freddy pulled away, dropping onto the settee with its floral pattern which he truly hated. The floral pattern was a concession he had made for a night's good hard sex, with a digitalVid showing Charlotte performing all manner of disgusting and perverse acts on his body – with her tongue stud – thrown into the bargain. He sighed at the thought, hating the fucking awful shifting couch, and was dragged back to the present. 'I don't think so,' he mouthed, slowly, uneasily, unable to meet her gaze.

'But LVA *is* all the rage! Everybody's doing it!'

'We're not.' Freddy smiled his false skull smile, transferring his gaze from Charlotte's supple form to the TV beyond. This was what he hated: the constant domestic chit-chat. It tortured his brain. Couldn't she see? All he wanted was peace and quiet! Couldn't she *see*? All he wanted was a few fucking minutes' peace every fucking day to compose his own fucking thoughts without domestic fucking haranguing.

His own space.

His own study! Now, that would work . . . a place he could call his own, a place he could be at one with himself. Shut – and lock – the door. Leave the world, and Charlotte's moaning and braying donkey laughs, behind.

'But everybody at work has switched to LVA.' Her lip came out then. A sulky one. 'Why do we have to be the odd ones out? We'll appear strange! Our friends will look down on us!'

'Keeping up with the Joneses, eh? It's got fuck all to do with your buddies at work, and everything to do with our depleted bank balance. How much was this fucking God-awful settee? Jesus, it's like an advertisement for vomit.'

'But you don't understand, Freddy!' she whined.

'The answer is no.'

Charlotte pouted again, moving towards the kitchen door where she leant against the frame and reached for the settee remote control. She spent a few minutes flicking through the designs and watching the floral patterns shimmer and morph across the surface of the settee while Freddy ground his teeth in total annoyance.

It gave him a headache.

A proper fucking *headache*.

How had she picked a settee with a hundred digital floral designs, with every single bastard one an absolute pile of shit? A pain to the eyeballs too. *And* a pain to the wallet . . . but no, she had to have one, had to have her way, had to maintain that pretence of social superiority and puerile domestication.

'But *everybody* is getting LVA! I know it sounds like a lot of money to get the transfer done, but we'll save in the long run, honest we will.'

'We've just spent six months of our fucking salaries on a world cruise! The damn holiday will take us the next two years to pay off! And now you want this? Now listen – which part of "no" don't you understand?'

'But *you* don't understand, Freddy!' Her voice suddenly changed, from an erotic purr to a schizophrenic snarl in the blink of an eye. Below him, floral patterns flickered and changed and he felt incredibly sick. His stomach *heaved* with the swirling remnants of a fried breakfast. But then, at least his decorative projectile vomit would be a far superior design pattern when compared with the swirling artistic smush squirming beneath his buttocks like dead frogs in a bucket of custard at this inopportune moment in time.

'No, Charlotte, you're fucking doing it again. We don't have a conversation any more! You get an idea in your head, and if I don't agree with it then you hit me with a tirade of "buts" until I wither and die like a rose under Bio-CHEM. I'm fucking sick of it, you hear?'

'Sick of it?' she raged. 'I'm offering you the chance to keep up with everybody else! I'm offering you LVA – it's always on the TV, always on the news, all our friends have got it . . .'

'But *we* haven't fucking got it,' snarled Freddy, rubbing at his moustache in annoyance. He climbed to his feet, grabbed his jacket and stared hard at Charlotte's face. 'You've changed since we met, you've really changed. I don't know you any more.'

He stormed from the house, slamming the front door.

'Please do not slam the front door,' called an automated voice with a comedy robot accent.

Charlotte chewed her lip for a moment. Her eyes flickered to the TV, where yet another ad for LVA ran for the full ten-minute slot. In any hour of TV, only twenty minutes was actually programme content – the rest was made up of ads, although her mother said that it had got worse over the years.

'Leviathan Fuels proudly present Premium Grade LVA,' burbled the ad as a smiling man filled his gleaming car with fuel, and then drove across a desert with his family on the rear seat playing happy family games. 'Four hundred miles to the gallon means you can drive across the Sahara on one tank! And it's pollution-free with absolute guarantees – go on, make the switch, because you know your children deserve a better future . . .'

Charlotte reached for the telephone.

When Freddy returned, it was dark, the wind howling outside like some diseased banshee. The house was quiet, except for a low burble of TV, and Charlotte was standing waiting for him. Freddy clutched a credit card receipt in his fist, and Charlotte's eyes dropped to the slip of paper.

'Ah,' she said.

'Yes, you might well say fucking "ah". I can't believe you went behind my back, Charlotte! I can't believe you've been bought by the marketing, the hype. You'll bankrupt us. We just *haven't got the money!*'

'But you *don't understand –*' Charlotte insisted with urgency.

138

'I understand perfectly,' said Freddy coldly, and reached for the largest gleaming kitchen knife.

'What are you doing?'

'Charlotte.' He took a deep breath, eyes gleaming in the gloom. 'I am making you see sense.'

As he murdered her, and she screamed and gurgled, the TV happily babbled the benefits of buying LVA fuel to a background symphony of slaughter.

Jam could feel movement. He came awake groggy, aware that he was being dragged across rough sandy stone by his ankles. Occasionally his head would bump against hard objects, such as steps, but thankfully most of the corridors were linked by ramps. Jam's groggy eyes came open and he could remember the pain following the injection – like pure burning molten metal had been flushed through his body, through every vein and artery and blood vessel. It had crucified him internally, seeped through every pore, wrought evil magic on every limb, every organ until pain had truly been his master. He had wept – but to weep was only to bring more pain on himself and it had gained him nothing.

And now he knew: every human had a breaking point. For some it was financial destitution. For some emotional rejection. For some, cancer. For some, torture. And they had found his limit, his threshold – for Jam had never felt anything like this internal rampant raging fire. And he knew that if they had asked him questions then, to his very great shame, his unbearable sorrow, he would indeed have told them everything.

But there had been no questions.

Just torture . . . and then they had left him until, after many hours, the pain gradually began to throb, to fade, to subside.

This worried Jam even more than a torturer's interrogation would have. As he was now dragged, bound with titanium wire, up and down sand-strewn ramps through narrow dark corridors and past sandstone walls created from mammoth rectangular blocks, his mind ticked over. If they had not asked him questions when he'd been ready to talk, then maybe they already knew the answers. And that thought chilled him more than anything had chilled him before.

What came next?

A welcome death?

Jam's head bumped against the ground and he grunted. The two Nex dragging him halted, looked back, smiled and kicked him several times. He took the kicks without a sound . . . after the injection, they were as nothing.

He was dragged along again, for what seemed an age; but in reality he had no real concept of time. Finally, they entered a chamber. It was large and cool: the floor was paved with white marble, and silver pedestals were set out in symmetrical patterns, each one capped with a shallow bowl containing a liquid which burned on the surface, providing light. At the centre were ten benches, ornately carved from marble and sandstone. As Jam was lifted and placed on one, he noticed curious grooves and channels – and his unease grew. It reminded him of a sacrificial altar.

'What's happening here?' he croaked through smashed lips. One of the Nex swiftly planted a wide fist in his face. Stars exploded in his vision and when he could see again he realised that he was alone.

For long hours he lay, shivering with the biting cold until a figure finally appeared.

It was the slender black-garbed figure of Mace.

'Hello again, Mr Jam.'

'What do you want of me?'

'Of you? Now we require . . . nothing.' He smiled and nodded, like a psychiatrist listening attentively to one of his patients.

'I thought you needed answers to questions. About Spiral.'

'We have cracked your ECube. As we suspected, you are Level One. You are a Prime. We have all the answers we could ever need. We know your identity, and we have your codes.'

'What the fuck is this?'

Mace simply smiled, and more figures moved from the shadows. These were cloaked and masked, and they carried metallic objects with slender silver pipes. Jam looked from one to the other, then Mace pulled out the hypodermic syringe filled with bright mercury and Jam started to struggle against the wires that bound him. They bit through his flesh, bit deep, and blood wept tears across his bruised skin.

'No!' he shouted. 'Get away from me . . .'

'I fear this will sting a little.'

As Mace came close, Jam stared into the twinkling copper depths of the Nex's eyes. 'I *will* fucking kill you for this, you cunt,' he snarled.

'Of course you will,' came the gentle reply. 'As you can see, my patients always do.'

He chuckled. The sound was ice.

The needle slipped into Jam's vein again. Fire screamed through his system and just as vision was failing and pain was consuming him in the flames of a billion infernos, he heard Mace's voice quietly say, 'Take his measurements . . . decide which advanced inhibitors will work . . .'

And then he was falling, falling into a well of desolation and he had always thought he was so strong, so powerful,

141

so in command and in control and these fuckers had reduced him to little more than nothing, a shell, a carcass of rotting flesh.

Jam awoke in his cell. This time he was lying in the sand, staring at the heavy stone door with heavy-set steel bars across a small opening that was an excuse for a window. It was through these slits that the flickering light came, and Jam slowly rolled into a sitting position, thankful at last to be alone.

He breathed deeply, but pain lashed at him from his broken ribs. He slowly rubbed broken fingers across his battered face – everything about him felt tender, loose, shattered. Bones in a tin can. He examined his hands – four fingers were snapped. His hands moved across his naked body: every inch of skin, it seemed, bore a bruise and was tender under his gently probing fingers. One ankle had a torn ligament, and there was some damage to one kneecap. His broken arm had been realigned and tightly strapped with some kind of bandage – blood-stained – but at least it meant they possibly had some further use for him. Besides these wounds, it was only his back that was giving him problems and he hoped to God they hadn't damaged his spine with their heavy blows.

Focus.

Jam settled his mind, using army meditation techniques taught by an old sergeant now dead. His breathing became more deep, more relaxed, and he inspected himself more thoroughly – internally and externally. Apart from the physical injuries, it was more the mental strain that worried him . . . and he felt it, nestling at the back of his mind like a dark maggot feasting on his brain.

Fear.

He acknowledged the word, the feeling, and realised

that it was something he was unused to. The fear was of the hypodermic and the silver fluid – and the incredible pain that would follow. Because he knew; Jam knew that they could do that to him, again and again and again until his will was broken. Until he was nothing more than a spastic shell.

Escape.

The word flared in his mind. Before, while being beaten by the Nex, the only feeling that had flared in his subconscious was a need for survival; but now that he had a moment to think and reflect he knew how great was the danger that he – and the rest of Spiral – were in. For a start, the Nex were far more numerous than he'd realised. Spiral were winding down the SAD anti-Nex teams when they should have been putting more man-power and more *fire*power into them.

These fuckers are far from fucking dead. And they're up to something bad . . .

But who commands them?

Who leads?

And just what are they doing?

He mused over this for a while, until the word sidled back into his tortured mind.

Escape.

The impossible.

How to achieve the impossible?

His stare scanned the walls; solid and slippery and very, very high. The room seemed almost to be carved as one unit, although he could in fact see very fine joins between the building materials. The floor was covered with a fine detritus of sand, which meant that they were probably somewhere hot – a desert region, or at least adjacent to one. Therefore he had been airlifted, carried some considerable distance from Slovenia.

The torturer – Mace – had claimed they did not need to question him due to their cracking of the ECube, but Jam doubted this very much. Yeah, just fucking with me prior to more torture, he thought grimly to himself. But then, if they *had* cracked the ECube, had wormed their way through its security features, then in theory they had access to all the Spiral networks and criminal databases . . . and maybe even staff files, mission specifications – everything was stored *somewhere*. They would know where the new major Spiral HQ was, in the heart of London . . . and the other secondary HQs . . .

He shivered, chilled to his very core.

Focus.

One step at a time.

Escape.

Jam dragged himself to his feet, using the low bed to lever himself into a standing position. Waves of pain throbbed through his injured body, but at least he could stand. He limped around the cell, and spotted a tray near the door with a bronze jug of water and a loaf of fresh bread. At least they didn't intend to starve him to death . . .

He ate the bread slowly, for it hurt some of his broken teeth to chew. The water stung his mouth but he forced himself to drink despite the curious stale taste. If they wanted to kill me, he thought, they wouldn't have to use poison – a single bullet would do the job more neatly.

When he had finished his spartan meal, Jam hobbled to the cell door and quietly peered through the bars. The corridor beyond was fashioned from the same huge sandstone blocks that he had seen when he'd been dragged to the large chamber for his second experience of torture under the needle. He could see two brands burning further down the corridor.

'Hello?' he called.

Nothing. No sound, no reply, no interest.

Returning to his bed, Jam sat and picked up the bronze jug. He drained the last few drops and went to work to see what weapon he could fashion from this primitive piece of metal.

The door opened. Three figures stood silhouetted against the flames of the torches.

Jam groaned, lying on the floor, and the figures moved to stand around him. Slowly, Jam rolled over and pulled himself into a seated position, shading his eyes – for with them his torturers had brought light.

As they halted, Jam noticed that one of the Nex had a limp. He lifted his eyes to connect with the burning copper gaze, and he smiled sweetly. 'Fine piece of meat.' He licked his lips. 'Put a bit of Savlon on that, did you, laddie? To take away the sting?'

The Nex growled.

Jam laughed. 'Come on, fucker, I'll eat your fucking heart.'

'Enough.'

The voice was rich, deep, commanding and Jam transferred his gaze to the speaker, who was shrouded and hooded but still dominated through sheer size. Then he glanced at the third figure, standing slightly back – again wrapped in a cloak but with a deformed face showing patches of black and a mouthful of crooked drooling teeth.

'My, but you're all butt-ugly. Like mescaline-popped whores on a crab-riddled Russian sailor.'

The dark figure made no sound, no movement. 'Let me introduce my companions,' came the rich deep voice. 'This is Yushalo.' He gestured to the Nex with the limp

145

whose gaze burned with hatred. Jam smiled, licking his blood-crusted lips. 'You owe him a great debt for his pain. And this is Xsala, apprentice to a Nex you know well – Mace. He would wish to test his newly found skills on your flesh.'

'Hey, you not brought Mace with you? We could, you know, sit down, maybe party a little. You brought any cider? It would be so much fucking fun.'

Xsala moved forward and looked down at Jam. He towered over the Spiral operative and growled something low and crude. His hands, black and twisted, came from beneath the cloak and long black claws slid free of sockets. 'Little man need know when not to speak with disrespect. We cause much pain.'

'Fuck me, bit of a drool problem you're having there, old fella.' Jam smiled, wiping the slime concerned from his skin. Xsala backed away, giving a heavy bass growl, and Jam transferred his gaze to the shrouded figure. 'You fucking want something, or have you just come to watch a weakened man suffer in pain, you perverse arse-fuck?'

'Perfect,' said the shrouded man softly, and turned with his colleagues, leaving the cell. The door closed and the light retreated as Jam frowned, face twisting with confusion.

'What the fuck does that mean?' he bellowed through the bars, but only a gentle hiss of cool breeze, sending a veil of sand swirling across the floor, replied.

Durell stood in the cold chamber, listening to the hum of the cooling fans. Ice rimed the smooth stone walls and made the polished marble floor treacherous to walk upon. The chamber was huge, the ceiling vaulting far above, the slightly concave walls stretching as far as the eye could see. Low slabs of stone were arranged in order, rough-hewn beds of natural rock, many bearing bodies covered with foil sheets.

Durell sighed, moving between the slabs, the cool air caressing him. He pulled his robes tighter around him, despite enjoying the cool air on his skin. He shivered.

It never used to be like this, he thought.

As he approached a slab, anonymous among all the others, Mace rushed towards him, a sorrowful look on his face which Durell knew had been placed there for his benefit. Nex felt few emotions, and a display was nearly always for effect – a throwback to the times when the Nex had been wholly human; a reminder of origins before the integration with insect kind; an almost unconscious physical echo.

'We can do no more.'

Durell reached out with a clawed, twisted hand and pulled back the foil. There lay a body – the body of a man called Feuchter. His head lay twisted to one side, most of the back of the skull missing and what was left glittering with ice. His body had been laid out: parts of the skin were scorched and while the face was perfect the contents of the brain behind it had been destroyed during the final battle he had fought so many months ago against Carter . . .

'He was like a brother.'

'The brain matrix is too far destroyed; we have tried and tried again to repatch and rebuild and model the organics, but there just isn't enough left. We could bring the body back to life, but not the mind. He would be in a deep vegetative state.'

Durell toyed for a while with the notion of bringing the body back, just so that he could look at his old friend animated again, just so that he could talk to him . . . But then, they would not be able to talk, they could not laugh

147

together, they could not *plot* together . . . Feuchter had been one of the few first Nex who had not been horribly deformed by the process of blending.

However, Durell himself had not been so lucky.

He reached out, one clawed hand resting against Feuchter's cold dead forehead. He closed his eyes deep within the folds of his hood, tears welling, burning his skin as they rolled from eyes that were no longer human. And he felt rage welling from some unknown source within him, burning him like a poisoned blade . . . and he knew that he did not have emotions, that he was cold and calculating but this finality and hatred came from somewhere deep inside him. He would destroy Spiral, he would destroy the DemolitionSquads – and he would kill Carter.

And that just as an aside. As a footnote.

Footsteps echoed across the cold stone, and Durell's head came up. Xsala was there, flanked by Nex guards with JK49 sub-machine guns. 'We have problem,' rumbled the huge warrior.

Durell nodded, tears still burning his skin, and covered Feuchter with the foil sheet one last time.

The door opened quietly and a Nex guard stepped in with a tray containing bread and water. His gun was slung across his shoulder negligently and he bent to retrieve the old tray – but it was gone.

'Surprise.' Jam grinned wildly, slamming the edge of the tray into the Nex's throat. Choking, the Nex dropped to one knee and Jam stepped in close, stabbing his new hand-folded bronze dagger through the Nex's eye. Blood poured out, staining Jam's hands, but he held the crude home-made dagger there tight in his fist as the Nex twitched and fought, kicking feebly. Jam drove the dagger in deeper, one hand cradling the back of the Nex's head until finally the legs ceased their kicking and he gently rolled the cooling corpse to the ground. He dragged the body into the cell and, after pulling his blood-smeared dagger free, he yanked off the Nex's trousers, thin cotton jumper and boots and squeezed into them, pulling them on with choked-back yelps and groans of agony over his broken limbs and his many cuts and bruises. The clothes smelt strange – metallic – but Jam was beyond caring. The boots were incredibly tight and they crushed his broken feet, but he did not care as he lifted the JK49, checked the full magazine, closed the door and stood in the corridor, nose lifted to the scent of a gentle breeze.

He felt empowered.

Jam grinned a crooked, blood-crusted grin.

'I'll show you, fuckers,' he muttered.

He reached down and activated his ThumbNail_Map. The ThumbNail_Map was a device, a tiny scanner which replaced an agent's actual nail; to any security equipment it scanned as organic – human tissue – and yet with the right mental augmentation it would illuminate and scan the surroundings, giving an operative an immediate indication of his or her whereabouts. The ThumbNail_Map was still a prototype, but Jam was thankful for it now as the tiny image spun across his nail and located him in the centre of wherever he was imprisoned – a maze of corridors stretching off all around him as he found true north.

Jam moved stealthily, eyes and ears alert.

It was night, although he'd had no way of knowing this while he'd been in his cell. He moved down a long corridor and came to an intersection. Following the ThumbNail_Map, and climbing up a long sloping ramp at a fast limp, Jam halted, blood drying on his fist and finger poised on the JK49's trigger. He listened carefully, listened past the pounding of the pain in his skull.

He moved swiftly, hiding in the shadows as boots trod the stone and four Nex glided past bearing JK49 submachine guns. They seemed alert – too alert, and Jam wondered if his escape had already been discovered. He had to assume that it had.

He limped on at speed, pain jolting through him, navigating, thoughts whirling through his now rapidly functioning brain. Priorities: escape, warn Spiral of possible security breach and apparent Nex hive – and Nex mission – kill a few Nex into the bargain and get the fuck away from whatever shit-hole they had dumped him in . . .

Which desert country? Africa? Iran? Australia?

The ramps flowed past. He could hear more activity, distant but coming closer. He forced himself on to greater efforts, pain pounding him from his broken bones and grinding ribcage. He came to steps and groaned inwardly, body jolting with each step, the agony making him want to howl and vomit at the same time.

'Where do you think you are going?'

Jam halted, JK49 trained on a dark figure up ahead, his broken fingers and constant pain making the gun's barrel waver a little. Light gleamed behind Mace, casting his frame in shadows that stretched down the ramp. Jam blinked, pain his master, and he could feel himself swaying and he wanted to scream, 'No! Not now, don't fucking let me down now!' but he was so weak and had lost too much blood and suffered so much pain that he thought, Fuck it! – and opened fire, bullets striking a spray of sparks from the stone by Mace's head—

Something smashed into Jam's back, forcing him down onto one knee. Bullets flashed across the space in spark

150

showers, and then the shooting stopped. Cordite filled the air and the silence was deafening, reverberating from metal-scarred stone. Again, a heavy blow crashed into the back of Jam's skull and his nose slammed against the stone ramp and broke with a terrible crack. He heard himself whimper in the voice of another man, a weaker man, a destroyed man. Got to reach freedom, he thought. Got to warn Spiral . . . he tried to lift the JK49, to whirl and take out the Nex that had crept up behind him in terrible silence – but his body would not work, his fingers would not obey his mental instructions. His vision was hazy and blood had flooded his eyes, filled his mouth and he gagged, drooling crimson to the stone floor. He tried to focus on Mace but a heavy boot stomped on his hand, and he heard his remaining working fingers snap.

Jam's vision swam.

And Mace was there. He held a hypodermic filled with bright silver.

'No!'

'What a shame you wish to leave behind our hospitality,' drawled Mace. 'I do, of course, humbly apologise in advance for the agony that is to come.'

'No . . . more . . .' said Jam through mangled lips, stare fixed on the hypodermic.

Mace bent and thrust in the needle. Jam arched his back, screaming . . .

A large dark-robed figure moved into view. Burnt hands came up and threw back the hood and Jam was transfixed by the horror within. The slitted copper eyes stared down at him with true malevolence.

'I did not introduce myself before,' came the voice. Shoulders moved with a crackling of twisted flesh and tendon.

Jam, panting, head spinning, tried to push himself

151

away from the monstrosity looming over him. With a curious movement, the heavy robed figure leapt at him and Jam writhed, trying to get away—

The unearthly eyes came close.

Their faces were mere inches apart.

'Who are you?'

'I am Durell,' hissed cold breath.

'But you're dead.'

The head shook, and with his evil eyes gleaming like metal Durell whispered, 'No. Carter shot me, the ship was destroyed . . . but I was never *killed* . . . oh Jam, our delicate nemesis – you have so much to learn.'

Jam's mind was reeling. The hot mercury screeched through his veins. He was crying tears of blood as his gaze passed from the Nex to Mace and finally back with a shudder to Durell.

'I will show you,' said Durell soothingly, 'I want you to know what it is to be a Nex. I want you to understand, my friend.'

Durell reached slowly, teasingly, towards the broken Spiral agent with the tentative care of a lover . . . reached towards the helpless body of Jam with long, curved, bloodstained claws.

And Jam closed his eyes.

CHAPTER 6

FOUNDATION STONES

The small copper eyes stared at Carter and the creature's twisted fangs drooled a little saliva. One claw dipped to touch its own body and it glanced down at its blood. Then it smiled nastily. 'I think you suffer much pain, little man.'

The wind from the black helicopter increased behind him and realisation suddenly struck Carter. Natasha had lifted the chopper into the air and she was dipping the nose, the rotors tilting to form a vertical wall of flashing blades. Carter dropped to the ground and rolled under the flashing tips of the armoured rotors as Nats guided the machine forward a touch. The blades hissed and skimmed the snow.

The creature tried to leap forward, but was beaten back by the violent wind and the promise of instant flashing titanium death. Carter stared from behind this thrumming wall of lethal blades. Natasha held the helicopter steady with a hum of cold matrix engines, wavering only a little, and Carter smiled at the entity as if from behind a shimmering screen of liquid metal.

'Next time, fucker,' he snarled.

'My name is Dake, and I'll be waiting for all eternity,' snapped the huge creature, blood pumping from the holes in its body – which it ignored.

'Carter, I can't fucking hold it!' came Natasha's panicked scream.

He moved fast, climbing into the chopper as the armoured creature turned and walked leisurely to one side. The Nex opened fire; JK49s thundered across the snow and Natasha urged the helicopter into the air, bullets leaving trails of tracer all around and striking a triple thump across one alloy flank.

'Quick thinking.'

'We're not out of this shit yet.'

They climbed steeply, engines howling and bullets screaming past them as the world of snow opened up like a huge white veil. The sky was a deep cool blue and Carter calmed his breathing, staring straight ahead, ignoring the whiz and hiss of bullets until the chopper finally sped out of range . . .

'*Well done,*' came the corpse-cold voice of Kade.

'Yeah, you want something?'

Carter could feel Kade smile – could sense the smirk as Kade mocked him. '*You should have killed it. I would have killed it. You are showing your weakness, Carter, showing your fucking age . . .*' Kade spat the word like a bullet. '*You're getting old, slow, weak, spineless, and it won't be long now, my friend, before some big Nex fucker cuts you in half and leaves your bleeding twin carcasses twitching on the pavement—*'

'I thought you were here to help,' whispered Carter.

'*Just trying to make you strong, brother. Just trying to warn you against the ravages of age, the natural slowing of the body, the terminal illness of the perpetually decaying mind . . .*'

'There's only one decaying mind here, and that's yours,' snapped Carter. He forced Kade away.

Carter realised that his eyes were closed, and he opened them, peering out across the spectacular snow-clad mountains of Switzerland and the villages and towns tucked neatly away in the Earth's folds.

He released a deep, pent-up breath.

'We lose them?'

'They're not taking up the chase.'

'We scared them away?' laughed Carter, an edge of disbelief to his voice.

Natasha looked at Carter and grinned. 'No, I think the dumb bastards shot up the other two helicopters! Jesus, give the Nex soldiers an IQ, somebody.'

'Better we don't make them too intelligent,' said Carter, rubbing at his eyes. Exhaustion hit him with a right hook. The recent quakes, the events at the hotel, witnessing the destruction of Zermatt, the chase through the snow, the destruction of the Comanche and the final escape from the massive deformed and twisted killer they had met in the snow – all combined to bleed him of energy. 'God, I'm fucking tired.'

'Get some sleep,' said Natasha. 'I'm OK with this thing.'

'You only got your pilot's licence recently . . .' He sounded a little worried.

'I'm fine, Carter. Get your head down, and then we'll switch in a couple of hours when we hit the bad weather.'

Carter's hand reached out and touched Natasha's thigh; then he dragged free his heavy quilted jacket and rolled it into a ball, resting it against the cockpit glass. The heavy thrumming of the rotors merged with his thoughts and the vibrations of the machine around him.

He dropped into sleep and fell through darkness. His dreams were like night.

The creature watched as the black helicopter soared high into the blue heavens, small copper eyes focused and intent. 'I know you,' it grated between horribly deformed jaws, and flexed its bloodstained talons. The sounds of gunfire echoed, chasing the fleeing Spiral agents and the being turned, looking at Kattenheim – who stood with arms folded, a slight smile across his brutally scarred face.

'You smile? They escape! You want we pursue?'

'No . . . Carter! He doesn't remember me,' said Kattenheim softly. 'Mr Carter does not remember me – which is a good thing, I think. But I surely remember him . . . although, in all fairness, I was less attractive then.' He laughed softly, fingers gently caressing his disfigured visage.

The ScorpNex chuckled too, a deep rumbling sound and a distorted mimicry of its master. It lifted a claw and made a reverberating cracking noise, like hollow bones snapping, like the cracking open of a human skull. The nearby Nex immediately ceased their machine-gun fire and turned to file back into the low concrete buildings, guns hot in smooth gloved hands, eyes emotionless and fixed on the next task ahead.

'You sure we not chase? We kill good, Kat.'

Kattenheim shook his head, and led the massive creature into one of the buildings. Inside, a soft orange light flowed around them, and there was incredible heat. They moved to a low-ceilinged chamber and seated themselves on the bare earth floor. The light bathed them both, glowing against skin and armour, gleaming from their glistening eyes.

'Kattenheim?' came a deep, rumbling voice.

'Durell. It is good to hear your voice.'

'You have an intruder?'

'A certain Mr Carter, I believe.'

'That fucker . . . an unhealthy coincidence that he found you, I hope – although I doubt it. Did you allow the ScorpNex to taste his blood?'

'Carter . . . escaped,' said Kattenheim, with a wry gentle smile. 'He is a very, very resourceful man. Once he was discovered he did not flee the area. He brought the fight to us.'

'It is extremely unfortunate that you did not secure his death,' said Durell coldly.

'The ScorpNex retained his scent. It got within inches of taking him out . . .'

'And yet, not close enough. Carter is too fucking resourceful.' Durell laughed, a cold, unlovely sound. 'It's almost as if he is one of us.'

'Yes.'

'Now, Carter is heading for London and that on its own may be enough for us to secure his demise. Have the Foundation Stones there been initiated? The QEngine testing complete?'

'The testing was perfect. We had one hundred per cent accuracy rates, and the engineering could not be faulted. The QHub is working smoothly and I will upload the processor links when we finish this dialogue.'

'Good.' Durell's voice was thoughtful. 'Kattenheim, my friend, it would seem that we are nearly ready for the assault. I know we were planning on building . . . but it would seem events are overtaking us . . . we are being pushed, as always, by the enemy that is Spiral.'

'They think themselves all-powerful,' said Kattenheim softly.

Durell laughed, a laugh of genuine humour this time. 'Spiral are fools and they will die like fools,' he said.

As Carter and Natasha flew further west, the weather worsened over Germany and Natasha had to activate the ECube to aid with navigation. Rain lashed down around the small black helicopter as they swept low over the sprawling Black Forest, dark and foreboding under heavy leaden skies. When Carter awoke from his slumber, he dictated a quick sitrep on their position and the ECube blipped an acknowledgement from the Spiral controllers. They already knew of the Comanche's destruction and had sent out automated scouts called PopBots – tiny semi-sentient globes of black alloy about the size of an apple that would analyse and report on the crash site.

The rain smashed against the cockpit and with much awkwardness Carter and Natasha exchanged controls, swapping seats and allowing the more experienced Carter to drop the helicopter even lower until they were flashing above the sweeping forests and banking past the occasional castle that stood on a jagged tier or cliff of rock.

The ECube rattled in Natasha's hands just as she was falling into sleep's welcoming embrace. Groaning softly, she squinted at the machine and read the data flashing across it.

'Shit.'

'What is it?' Carter glanced at her, one eye on the rolling sweep of darkened green below them, one eye on the shocked whiteness of Natasha's face. 'Bad news?'

'Very bad news. It's Jam's latest SAD mission; it has been reported as a failure.'

'A . . . failure?'

Carter stared long and hard at Natasha as the implication sunk into his weary brain. 'What are the CSRs?' The seconds seemed to last an age. He could not bring himself to acknowledge the very real possibility of Jam's death.

'The whole team are missing – Jam, Slater and TT. They were on a mission in Slovenia, up in the mountains researching a possible sighting by a local cattle farmer. PopBots were subsequently dispatched, but nothing has been discovered – no bodies, no vehicles, nothing. They have simply disappeared and all that remains is a coordinate from Jam's ECube's automated PanicBurst, nano-seconds before the ECube deactivated . . . or was forced to deactivate.'

'Not good.'

'They're not dead, Carter.'

'Have you heard yourself? ECubes don't fucking deactivate – they're nearly indestructible! And if his PB initiated, that meant vital signs gave his ECube a severe and violent kick up the arse. No, it's a bad situation . . . has anybody been assigned to an investigation?'

'Not yet,' said Natasha softly, her gaze fixed to her lover's stern jaw, the swathe of stubble across his face making him appear older and rougher. Whatever had happened, Natasha knew then – in that instant – that Carter would find out. Find out and kill like no other man on Earth could kill, if he thought it was necessary . . . and deserved.

'Once we have been briefed at this Spiral meet, then I will go and find them – if they're still alive.'

'But this looks important. Hundreds of Squads are being drafted in . . .'

Carter glanced at her, frowned and said, 'If there are hundreds of Squads being drafted in then they won't need me so much. I'll put in a showing and then I'm gone . . . find me the coordinates and put in an Investigation Request. Do it, Natasha, do it now.'

'You don't know yet what Spiral wants . . .'

'Spiral can fucking wait. This is Jam. This is my friend.'

They travelled in silence, rain thundering against the cockpit. The black helicopter lifted, rising into the deluge to skim over a series of high and densely forested hills, then dropped like a black bullet into a valley following the course of a wide river swollen by the storm. In the distance lightning flickered, illuminating the darkness for an instant in electric blue with a touch of blinding white.

Carter blasted headlong into the storm.

The gentler terrain of France provided an easier ride for Carter and Natasha as the rain slowly lessened, and there appeared several tentative glimpses of watery sunshine. But after the churning slate-grey waters of the English Channel the weather worsened once again.

Carter could not stop thinking about Jam . . .

Dead?

He could not be dead . . .

Carter's mouth was a thin grim line as they headed towards London and the Spiral meet at this most secret of HQs a couple of miles from the city centre. Disguised among a scattering of high-rise buildings, bland and nondescript, it was an architectural nonentity, bleached concrete with silvered windows. The Spiral HQ was a wholly unremarkable building above ground – but below was a warren of the most incredible high-tech activity, linked by mammoth networks of deep tunnels to other HQs, the SP1_Stores and several UK military bases.

It was also linked via the newly blossoming Spiral-GRID.

As the black helicopter swept across southern England darkness was falling. The 'copter whined low over rolling fields and damp autumn woodland, over drenched towns and bleak tarmac. Headlights cut swathes below, and Carter lifted the helicopter a little, avoiding urban areas where he could, and as the sprawl of the Home Counties stretched towards him and the population and housing density increased so he lifted the helicopter further and further into the storm until they were buffeted by wild winds.

'Not far now.'

'You'd make a wonderful navigator.' Carter smiled wearily. 'Your accuracy and grasp of details in navigational matters are astounding.'

'Yeah, Carter, and you'd make a superb comedian.'

'I try, I try. After all, life's a fucking joke.'

They were closing on the bleak concrete of the Spiral HQ as a sudden deep rumbling echoed across the world, reverberating and booming through the heavens, an almighty noise that drowned the sounds of the storm . . .

'Bad thunder,' said Natasha softly.

The chopper's rotors spun, glistening under the rain. Carter frowned.

The 'thunder' did not halt. It increased in tempo . . .

'That's not thunder,' said Carter slowly, eyes widening as the distant buildings far below seemed to vibrate, trembling and swaying, and he dropped the helicopter and suddenly, like a deck of cards toppling a whole section of streets collapsed, crushed by some invisible lump hammer. Carter's eyes lifted to the distant glow of London. He powered forward through the rain, the rumbling all around them, sometimes rising in pitch, sometimes dying off to nothing more than a distant grumbling.

The lights of London loomed close, and Carter closed on Spiral HQ's concrete tower. The wail of klaxons was springing up now from all parts of the city – fire engines, police cars, ambulances, their sirens howling through the storm – and Carter saw another building, a magnificent Victorian stone edifice, crumble and spew its contents across the street, whirling bodies tossed like pulp through the air to mash with the crashing stones—

'Fuck,' hissed Natasha.

Carter said nothing.

'What's happening, Carter? What the fuck is going on?'

They swept over the HQ; below swarmed a hundred Spiral operatives, some just recently arrived for the meet, all heavily armed and all glancing up from the wide expanse of roof as the helicopter dropped from the skies . . .

They brought the stolen Nex chopper down to land on the roof and immediately they were swarmed over by heavily armed guards. The earthquake took London in its fist and shook it and crushed it and fucked it hard . . . lightning flickered, illuminating a scene falling dropping *spinning* into Hell as streets compressed into piles of rubble and buildings were uprooted like concrete trees and spewed in a parody of dominoes . . . and below there was screaming, and the flashing of blue lights, the wails of sirens. Police and military helicopters took to the air as the networks were flooded by a million distress calls and all anybody could do was stand there and watch from the rain-soaked parapet as in a few short minutes the earthquake ripped the guts from London and left ugly rancid entrails showing from beneath the battered torn streets.

'I don't believe it,' hissed Natasha, rain soaking her hair and her pale shocked face, dripping from her eyelashes, lightning flashing in her eyes and tears mingling with the rain. 'I just don't fucking believe it.'

Carter stood, silent, eyes wide and absorbing the horror show before him.

The building shook.

'Get back in the chopper,' growled Carter, his hand touching Natasha's back, guiding her towards the vehicle. The rumbling beneath their feet intensified, vibrating through the soles of their boots to a distant backing track of screams. Spiral HQ suddenly lurched, and the men and women present were launched across the ground, some falling, others staggering. There came distant groans of stressed steel like a dinosaur screaming in pain. Carter was dragging Natasha now, towards the helicopter which – disappeared.

The building was torn in half, a huge gash ripping across the ground at their feet. Spiral operatives disappeared in the blink of an eye as the structure was separated, dragged into two halves by convulsions of the bucking ground beneath them. The helicopter fell, plunging through the gaping wound in the concrete, and the entire section of tower block drifted away from the severed other half and then halted, leaving a gap of perhaps three or four metres. The whole building was torn in two – a teetering parody of a skyscraper – and Carter could see offices, carved as if by a huge magic sword, sliced neatly in two. The helicopter crashed down further, smashing through the rooms and equipment and people, twisting and compressing until it became wedged a hundred metres below them.

A cold wind blew.

Carter's head turned swiftly left and right; people

163

were screaming, some hanging on to the edges of this sudden rift as their comrades rushed to help. The rumbling continued, a roar of concrete unrest. He licked his lips, realised that he was holding on to Natasha with a grip of iron and dragged her back as they moved away from the precipice.

Machine-gun fire rattled from the rubble-strewn streets below.

'We've got to get out of this fucking building,' Carter snarled.

Nats was pale, speechless.

Carter ran back to the parapet and watched the swarm of Nex sprint across the rubble, their sub-machine guns spouting fire. Several Nex were punched from their feet by return fire from the Spiral building. Below him, he felt the structure shudder – as if wondering whether or not to collapse . . .

'*You only have a few seconds*,' Kade whispered softly.

Being the Spiral HQ, this building which was nondescript to look at nevertheless had a host of innovative design features; one of these was safety chutes from roof to ground. As the people on the roof milled around in horror at the events unfolding beneath them, several activated the chutes which sprung into life, huge tubes jettisoning diagonally to the streets below. Carter tried to warn them but the noise was too loud. He watched helplessly as twenty or so jumped into the chutes and sped to the safety of the street below – and straight into a hail of JK49 fire at the hands of the crouching and merciless black-masked Nex.

Carter's Browning was out. He leaned over the parapet and started firing, a grim look of hatred on his face. Thirteen bullets found thirteen heads and blasted thirteen brains across the rubble. In a smooth movement

164

Carter released the empty mag from the gun and slotted a fresh one home. More bullets spat from the Browning. Others saw Carter's actions and followed his example – still more bullets rattled down on the Nex. The falling rain was joined by a hailstorm of metal and the Nex turned, retreated to a nearby building and took up defensive positions behind crumbling brick and stone, guns coughing and crackling whenever a member of Spiral tried to escape—

Natasha touched Carter's arm.

'We're fucked that way,' he snapped, whirling around. 'We're going to have to head for the tunnels under the HQ – head for the SpiralGRID . . .'

The earthquake chose that moment to smash and stomp its way across the helpless city of London.

Carter and Natasha and a hundred other Spiral people watched an invisible scythe sweep across buildings containing thousands of people, a wave of energy which crushed the buildings into the ground.

The collapsing edifices pumped dust and stone up into the rain-darkened sky and the screams were terrible to hear.

Natasha dragged Carter around and pointed.

'Look, there are children over there – on the other side of the gap.'

'What? *What?*' Carter's eyes narrowed. 'How fucking bad can it get?' he snarled. He sprinted to the edge of the precipice; the building had moved a little more, was still juddering and vibrating, responding to invisible signals at the heart of the quake. The wrecked helicopter had groaned and screeched its way down another few metres. He glanced hurriedly at Nats. 'What the fuck are children doing on the roof of the Spiral HQ?'

'There's a crèche, you moron.'

'For fuck's sake! A crèche *here*?'

There were five children, milling around the doorway to the roof, their small bodies framed by a rectangle of yellow. They moved slowly, in a daze, directly opposite to where Carter and Nats stood gazing over the chasm in front of them.

More machine-gun fire howled from the streets below as Spiral led an offensive against the Nex. Nex bodies were flipped spinning and spraying gore, until a large detachment of DemolSquads forced the Nex further back, away from the perimeter of the rumbling building, and set up a temporary front line of safety before the shaking Spiral HQ.

As Carter glanced up, Natasha turned, ran and leapt the four-metre-wide chasm between the two sections of the building.

'No!' he snapped – but it was too late.

She landed lightly, boots crunching stones, and glanced around, grinning back at Carter. She sprinted forwards and gathered the children to her, the girls crying into her shoulder, the boys with tear- and grime-smeared cheeks trying to look brave in the face of this nightmare.

She herded them towards the gaping rift, which groaned and grumbled.

The building – or its two separate halves – rocked dangerously, steel and concrete screeching in torture, showers of dust and tiny lumps of concrete raining down.

Carter whirled and grabbed at the nearest man's sleeve. 'We need help.' He met the huge man's stark grey-eyed stare. Carter pointed.

The man, bearded, clad in black and with an SA1000 slung over his shoulder, nodded and followed Carter to

166

the edge of the precipice. 'Hold my back.' Strong fingers grasped him, and Carter edged himself towards the crumbling torn edge.

The quake smashed more waves of destruction across London.

Again, Spiral HQ trembled as the earth beneath it was raped.

Natasha picked up the first child, a blond-haired boy with a red nose and snot covering his upper lip. Her stare met Carter's as she gave a smile of calm and control – and threw the child across the abyss. Carter caught a tight grip on Tigger dungarees, and he turned, depositing the child on the ground. 'Over there!' shouted Carter. 'Go to that woman over there!'

Seeing their plight, more Spiral operatives had come to help. As the earthquake roared around them and they faced certain death, they put aside their own fears and need for escape to offer help—

Natasha threw the second child. Carter caught it.

Stone crumbled from the edge where he stood and he glanced down involuntarily. The stolen Nex helicopter was a crumpled heap now, compressed and crushed between the heaving, buckling stone, brick and steel. Huge strands of reinforcing wire stuck from the concrete like severed rusting arteries. Far below, Carter could see fire and smell burning. Smoke trailed up towards him in lazy black spirals.

The third child flew across the gap, arms flapping, and smashed into Carter's chest. His own arms wrapped tight, securing the little girl, and he passed her back to the human chain that had leapt into existence to aid these stranded children . . .

The fourth child came, screaming, mouth wide. Carter grasped at her as she bounced and slipped, but his strong powerful fingers grabbed her clothing and passed her gently to the ground.

'Mummy!' she whimpered.

The huge man with the beard smiled, and patted her head. 'She'll be on the ground now, luvvie. Go on over to the chutes – it'll be fun and then you'll see her again.'

'Thank you.'

The big man smiled again, then grasped Carter's jacket more tightly.

'One more.'

'One more,' agreed Carter, breathing deeply.

Black smoke billowed up from the unnatural crevasse. His gaze met Natasha's through the smoke and heat as more tremors roared around them. Carter could feel the building moving beneath his boots and he suddenly felt sick to the core of his soul.

What the *fuck* is going on?

Natasha lifted the last child in her dirt-smeared fingers. A little boy, short hair, chubby tear-stained face, but with a look of defiance on it: he dangled precariously from her grasp. She took a step back and Carter could read the exultation of rescue in her face, in her glowing deep brown eyes as she launched the boy across the chasm and through the smoke and Carter's hands grappled blindly, slipping from the boy as the Spiral man behind him reached forward, plucking the child from Carter's fumbling grip and hauling the boy to safety . . .

There came a deafening, screaming roar that went on and on and on and Carter wanted to cover his ears and his eyes were streaming and then he was engulfed by a wave of dust from below which cut into his eyes and mouth and he yelled, saliva drooling from grey lips. The section of the building on which Natasha stood began to sway crazily and she lost her footing and fell to one knee.

Her stare was fixed on Carter through the dust as the building moved, shifted and started to crumble . . .

'*No!*' snapped Kade.

'I can save her,' growled Carter.

He leapt across the chasm, into the dust.

The TV sparkled into life with a digital buzz of electro-hum, diamond-sharp images spinning and morphing into the jewelled liquid logo of Leviathan Fuels.

You may be wondering who Leviathan Fuels are? After all, we have only been on the scene for a few months, but with this . . . Over-cheerful Japanese scientist holds up a small metal object with a complex series of tubes and dials . . . *you can convert your road vehicle, be it diesel, petrol or gas, to run on LVA for only a few hundred dollars – LVA, a new fuel for the future, the fuel of choice for over two million happily satisfied customers. . .*

Scene dissolves: two cars driving through spotless mountain passes high in the Alps. One car runs out of fuel and an angry man stands by the kerbside, kicking the tyre and pulling his Mr Bad Mr Angry face, whilst the second car . . .
Scene cross-fades: drives on, and on, children [1 × black, 1 × white, 1 × oriental] singing happily on the back seat and playing extremely violent hack-and-slash-'em-ups on their 3D HoloStation . . .

400 hundred miles to the gallon! Go on, make the smart choice . . . choose Leviathan fuels. Your children deserve a better future . . .

Scene/text scroll R→L [Arial black] acr. vid: *And now, we have over 11,000 fuel outlets across the civilised world!!! Be smart! Become a Leviathan! Leviathan Fuels will change your life.*

SCENE DISSOLVES TO RED

CHAPTER 7

BREED

When you're a kid, summer lasts for ever. School finally shuts in a tumult of chaos and high spirits, and the weeks stretch away for an infinity, long days spent running through tall grass, down the park, the Church Fields, through Witch Woods and towards Jacob's Ladder and the Old Nazi Bunker where they imagined a previous litany of war crimes had taken place.

Summer lasts for ever . . .

'*Until you die*,' sneered Kade.

The pain whirled inside Carter's brain: the agony of memories; the poisoned narcotic needle of childhood; the atomic blast of innocence and naivety and the high bright insane fucked-up whirling loss of these delicate treasures . . .

'It could never be the same again,' he muttered.

As the black quake dust filled his mouth.

'*Oh, to be a child again*,' mocked Kade. '*To languish in the mire of mockery, to paddle in the piss-stream of puerile poetry, to reel in the eternal uncertainty of pain and confusion and*

*hate . . . it is like a dream to me, a bad dream, a dark
dream . . . the best of dreams, my dark and twisted brother.'*

'Remember it?' whispered Kade.
   'Remember it, my friend?
   'Surely you hadn't forgotten?
   *'Surely you hadn't forgotten about . . . Crowley? How
poetic. How romantic. So beautiful I could be fucking sick . . .'*

It was summer. The days were long. The summer holi-
days had come and school was like a distant mad, bad
dream. The days flowed into one another as the boys
played on Church Fields: one day they were soldiers
engaged in some terrible war against terrorism – just like
their dads – another they were space heroes spat out into
the universe on a terrible mission. On yet another they
were aircraft pilots, killing all the evil and terrible drug
barons in Colombia. They ran through the grass, into the
woods, down to the river. They played in the park, in the
concrete tubes, on the swings and the slide. They paddled
in the shallow fast-flowing river, imagining incredible
depths sporting terrifying monsters. Morris brought his
BMX-i with Alloy-Kick2 to enable high stunt-jumping
and they built a ramp off the top of the steps leading
down the edges of the Church Fields; they dared one other
to jump the two-metre drop and Carter was the first,
flying through the air with a shout of triumph, the BMX-i
landing with a violent wobble and a clang as the back
wheel bottomed out through under-inflated tyres.
   The days were long and good.
   Childhood, it seemed, would never end.

*'But you're not thinking, Carter, not thinking straight. Have
you forgotten Crowley? Have you forgotten that bastard? What*

he and his friends did? Don't tell me you pushed that out of your mind as well, you spineless worthless cheap whore bastard . . .'

'Get him!' came the roar.

'Run!' hissed Carter.

'Why?' asked Jimmy in innocent fear.

'Run!' Carter cried.

They ran, Carter holding Jimmy's hand, guiding his blind brother down the narrow woodland trail; they stomped through mud, kicked nettles and plants from their path, could hear the distant roar of the river. They suddenly changed direction, trying to lose their pursuers. We can hide by the river, thought Carter, Jimmy's hand sweating with fear in his own. He tugged Jimmy along, guiding the younger lad, his brotherly need to protect intense . . .

'And the rest,' mocked Kade, *'Don't blank it out, Carter; remember it. Remember it all.'*

'We're going to kill you!' came Crowley's hoarse thundering yell.

Evil laughter drifted down through the woods; a comedy accompaniment.

Carter could hear the river growing closer. He increased his speed, dragging Jimmy along behind him. The two boys hurtled down a narrow trail, weeds and nettles whipping at their bare legs.

'I can't run any more,' wept Jimmy.

'Come on, push yourself . . .'

'I can't!' wailed the younger boy.

'Come *on*!' Carter hissed, slapping his brother around the back of the head. 'You'll get us both caught and

Crowley will mess us up bad. You remember what he did to Morris? You *remember*? He's still in the hospital!'

With Jimmy wailing they pushed on, the sound of the river coming closer and closer and closer; and then it exploded into view in a burst of colour and noise and movement and Carter dragged Jimmy to a halt. There was a steep drop directly ahead of them, sheer rock falling into the fast wide flow that cascaded violently over pebbles and large water-polished boulders.

'Where are we?' came Jimmy's panicked voice.

Carter's twelve-year-old gaze swept along the river bank. And then he saw it: a huge wide pipe crossing the river. A makeshift bridge whose interior was used to carry sewage. It was bright green and had two high iron-railing fences at each end to protect its precious cargo from the abuse of vandals.

'This way.'

They ran along the top of the river cliff towards the pipe.

The boots of Crowley and his band of followers – Glass, Trigger and Johnny Jones, and a couple of nameless giggling girls in the chase for fun and the cheap thrill of bullying – thundered after the two boys. Rain started to fall from a suddenly dark sky.

The narrow ledge rapidly became muddy, slippery and treacherous. Jimmy clung with one hand to Carter, and with his other to clumps of grass, his mouth gasping at the sudden violent downpour, his lips twitching with fear and surprise at this sudden change in their fortunes . . .

'You're making me wet!' screamed Crowley from behind them, his logic twisted, his hatred a physical entity living like a demon within his big fists.

Carter stopped and turned, his hair plastered to his head. Crowley was grinning at him from the beginnings of the narrow ledge; behind him his worms jostled, vying to see what was happening. Carter heard the giggles of the girls, Mandy and Trish, the stink of their cheap child-whore perfume drifting through the rain.

'Don't come any closer,' said Carter, his voice low and suddenly dangerous.

'Or what?' said Crowley. 'I'll do to you what I fucking did to Morris. And he's still in the fucking hospital.'

'Why don't you just leave us alone?'

Crowley said nothing, just grinned a real nasty grin. His shaved head gleamed under the rain as the smirk fell from his face, leaving a mocking evil in its wake.

'We know you're strong,' said Carter wearily, wiping rain from his own face. 'What have you got to prove?'

'Nothing,' snapped Crowley. 'Nothing at all. I just like hurting people.'

Jimmy shook Carter's arm, his grip tight.

'What, little brother?'

'I'm frightened.'

'Come on, we'll go across the pipe. The girls won't be able to follow – because they're girls. I can see them get-ting fed up already – they didn't expect to get wet.'

'I don't think I can get across the pipe – we tried before, remember?'

'But you're bigger now,' said Carter soothingly, despair creeping into the edges of his soul. He tugged at Jimmy's hand; obediently, the younger boy followed.

Why wouldn't Crowley give up?

Why didn't he clear off and torture somebody else?

They crept along the muddy ledge over the suddenly raging river. The drop below the two boys was terrifying, at least thirty feet down to rocks and the raging waters beneath. They edged along and, glancing up, Carter grit-ted his teeth. Crowley, Glass, Johnny Jones and Trigger were following. They had left the whining mud-splattered girls behind.

It became a race.

A slippery, treacherous race.

Sliding in mud, grabbing on to the wet grass for support, they edged along towards the distant green sewerage pipe; the fans of iron at each end – designed to stop people using the wide pipe as a bridge as well as to protect it from vandals – grew slowly closer, gleaming slick in the rain.

'Are they getting any nearer?' gasped Jimmy. He was splashed with mud, his face red with exertion, his hands bleeding from the sharp blades of grass and occasional thorns.

'No,' said Carter.

They raced on. Once Jimmy slipped and Carter grabbed his collar, hauling the younger boy back onto the ledge. After a few minutes the pipe loomed close, gleaming under the rain, a wet, gradually sloping green tube connecting the two banks over the raging torrent—

They reached one end of the pipe, panting for breath, and Carter leapt lightly onto the slick surface and helped Jimmy up. 'You remember? Remember last time how you climbed?'

'I . . . I think so,' said Jimmy.

'You little bastards!' shouted Crowley, still wrestling his way through the mud. He was splashed and coated with it and now his face displayed true fury and a controlled hatred. His black Guinness T-shirt was plastered to his rotund and stocky barrel frame.

Carter hoisted Jimmy up, and the boy grasped the iron rungs; his feet found purchase on the horizontal cross bars and he began to climb. Carter jumped up behind his brother and hand over hand they climbed to the top.

Jimmy tentatively reached across and eased himself over the crooked lip, with Carter close behind, giving him support—

They climbed down and landed lightly on the other side.

Crowley reached the foot of the iron fan. He grasped the vertical bars, pressed his face against them and glared at Carter and Jimmy – only a foot away from him but protected by this barrier.

'Better get used to that look,' said Carter.

'I'm going to kill you, then make you watch as I smash and kick your little shit of a blind brother to fucking death,' said Crowley, illogical as always. He spat through the bars at Carter who backed away, turning to follow his brother tentatively across the slippery pipe—

Crowley, Trigger, Johnny Jones and Glass were all climbing, Crowley in the lead as was his right by physical strength. His boots made short work of the climb. He launched his body over the top and landed in a crouch. His gaze lifted and fastened on the retreating backs of Carter and Jimmy.

'Stop!' he shouted.

Carter and Jimmy turned at the sound.

'You've got nowhere to run,' growled Crowley, his voice husky and filled with the heady emotion of the hunt and its climax: the kill.

The rain pounded; in the distance thunder rumbled, the snarling of the storm. Black cumulonimbus towered over the boys – insignificant insects far below against the tiny glossy green pipe. Beneath the pipe the river raged, its torrent crashing across the stones in a fury of savage, natural power.

Carter moved protectively in front of Jimmy. Jimmy's hand came to rest on Carter's shoulder.

'What's happening?' whispered the younger boy.

Crowley moved closer. Grunting, the other boys landed on the pipe behind him and moved to back Crowley up, slipping and sliding on the wet surface, their faces split into grins.

They had played his game before.

And the outcome was always the same . . .

Pain.

'You want to fight me here?' sneered Carter, peering nervously over the edge of the pipe.

'Why not?' growled Crowley.

And then—

'Remember it, Carter? Remember the details, the gory details? Don't push it away like a pussy—'

There came a sudden wail.

An abrupt and shocked cry, filled with desperation . . .

Jimmy slid from the pipe, hands trying feverishly to grasp the slick wet metal. He slid from view, his scream echoing forlornly through the rain—

The slap of the impact sent a shiver through Carter.

But he did not look down.

He stared; stared hard, icily at Johnny Jones, at Trigger, at Glass; and then stared with an infinity of hatred at Crowley. The stances of the boys had changed; they were leaning, peering over the edge, rain pouring down around them.

Crowley was the first to look up, his face ashen, transfixed by Carter's dark stare.

'Shit,' he whispered. 'You see? You see his fucking head?'

'All his brains came out . . .' whispered Trigger.

The boys' faces were locked in masks of shock; their eyes wide, their mouths forming silent Os.

Carter did not look down. He stared, arms hanging

180

limply by his sides, dark eyes drilling into Crowley – and the others . . .

Crowley took a step back.

'Don't fucking stare at me, Carter – it's all *your* fucking fault! You brought him here!'

Carter said nothing.

The storm pounded him with its darkness.

Trigger and Johnny Jones turned, ran down the pipe towards the metal fan; they were closely followed by Glass and the three boys climbed the iron grillework and thudded heavily into the mud on the opposite side, leaving—

Crowley, facing Carter.

They stared at one another. Crowley's face was ashen, sweat- and rain-streaked, his tongue darting out to lick at his lips. Carter's head dipped a little, his eyes hooded, before peering back up at Crowley, his mouth a solid straight line without expression. His was no longer the face of a child and echoes of something dark squirmed across his features.

Carter moved first.

Slowly, he knelt on the pipe. Only then did he glance over at the river below. The torrent had already washed away the brains and the blood, but Jimmy lay twisted on a bank of large oval rocks, water gushing and white foam bubbling over and around him, one hand flopping loosely in the flow.

His head had been cracked open like a macheted coconut.

And he was quite obviously dead.

Carter stood in one fluid movement.

Crowley licked his lips and began to back way, rubber boot soles squealing on the pipe.

'Fight me now,' said Carter softly, his words almost lost under the downpour of rain.

'N – no.'

'Fight me *now*, you fucker.'

Crowley turned, boots slipping and sliding on the pipe; he sprinted, then leapt at the iron fan and scrambled up and over. He jumped from the top, sprawling face down in the mud; he did not stop then, but scrambled to his feet, his dirty face twisted in pain, and limped off into the woods.

The rain lessened.

The storm's pounding finally stopped.

Shafts of sunlight broke through the heavy black clouds, beams slicing vertically from the heavens. They picked out many things: rain-glistening rocks, wet leaves on trees and plants, a boy standing on a pipe with his arms hanging limp by his sides . . . and they gave a sunlight halo to a twisted dead boy amidst a tumult of churning white foam.

There came a steady, slow, rhythmical dripping sound.

Drip, *splash*.

Drip, *splash*.

The drips connected with a square tile, white and gleaming in its hospital sterility – a frame for the small puddle of blood forming on it. Slowly, very slowly, the pool of blood grew – widened – a Rorschach image evoking gore and torture and hell and death.

Carter sat on the blue plastic chair, his head clasped in his hands, staring at the white tiles of the hospital corridor. Occasionally a bustle of trolley and tubes and nurses would rush past him, accompanied by a distant cacophony of sirens and engines and shouting. Carter's hair was matted with dirt and oil and smoke and blood. His face was a blank canvas peppered with cuts and bruises and streaks of grime. His broken nose leaked blood to the tiles. His eyes were vacant pools leading deep into the void.

'Mr Carter?' A soft voice; the voice of somebody used to delivering bad news.

Carter did not respond.

'Mr Carter?' A little louder.

'Yes?' His voice was gravel. His voice was the scraping of tombstones.

'We have stabilised her.'

'You have?'

'Yes . . . but I don't want to give you false hope. It's bad. It's really, really bad.'

'And . . . the child?'

'It's hard to tell at this stage – we need to run more tests . . .'

There was a whirl of violent movement and the doctor blinked, the cold metal of the Browning pushed under his chin tilting his eyes towards the tiles of the suspended ceiling and the bright strip lights. The man swallowed hard and did not move. Did not blink.

'Well, run more fucking tests, then,' snarled Carter.

Slowly, the doctor backed away and Carter could read many signs in his face: panic, fear, anger, hurt. Carter felt bad. He knew that the doctor was doing his best. Doing his best in the insanity that had become every London hospital still standing . . .

Slowly, Carter slouched back to the blue chair.

Tears ran down his cheeks, tracing lines through the concrete dust there. He rubbed them savagely away with the back of his hand, and placed the Browning on the blue plastic beside him.

'*Don't worry about him,*' said Kade. '*All fucking doctors are vermin. They deserve to die horrible deaths, deserve torture and carnage in their souls.*'

'Fuck off.'

'*Don't be like that, Carter . . . I saved you out there, in that fucking chaos.*'

'Fuck off.'

'*Carter—*'

'I said fuck off!' screamed Carter, lurching to his feet. Blood from his nose sprayed out, splattering across a sterile white wall. Three nurses stood stock-still, staring at him with undisguised horror.

Carter slumped down once more, glancing at his own appearance. His clothing was grey and torn. His hands too were grey with dust, scratched and cut and battered and bruised. He could feel dust grinding in his eyes and it filled his mouth and throat and lungs, making him cough and choke.

He knew that he looked bad.

And outside, hundreds of others looked far, far worse . . .

The nurses scuttled away. Carter laughed suddenly, then started to cry again with his head in his hands, his blood dripping to the white tiles on the floor.

Natasha, he thought.

Natasha.

After the jump from the building he remembered little. The sensations of falling, heavy lumps of concrete and masonry smashing into his body from all directions . . . and then dust, filling his vision and his rasping lungs.

He awoke choking, coughing, choking again. Everything was grey and, strangely, there was no pain. And suddenly the noise smashed through his world, an insanity of sound – crashing and smashing, rumbling, screaming, hundreds of people screaming, shouts and wailing sirens, the bark of orders, the distant muffled roar of engines and a throbbing of helicopter rotors . . .

Hands pulled at him, rolling him from the mountain of collapsed rubble. He sat on a buckled pavement surrounded by lumps of rock and stone, staring up at firemen, police, JT8s with sub-machine guns slung over their shoulders. People were carried past on stretchers. A fireman stooped to touch his shoulder with surprising tenderness.

'You OK, mate?'

'Yeah,' he coughed, and spat a ball of grey phlegm onto the cracked pavement.

'Were you in the fucking collapse?'

'Yeah.' Carter nodded, dumbly, and could read the look in the fireman's eyes. A look of awe.

His head was spinning. He could still see the look of fear on Crowley's face from his dream and he rubbed at his eyes, stinging with dust and dirt. Screams invaded his consciousness and Carter pulled himself to his feet, pain pulsing through him in waves. Everything felt weak – battered by concrete, pulverised by the toppling building.

Natasha.

He lurched forward, limping, looking frantically through the people lying on stretchers and waiting for the next wave of emergency vehicles. He moved towards the helpers wading through the rubble and pulling bodies free, some living, some motionless and battered and dead.

People were crying, standing beside the collapsed building and crying.

All around him, London was a living chaos.

Carter started to dig, pulling free a huge section of concrete and rolling it down to the pavement. He worked with other grim-faced men heaving rubble, digging with

185

his hands, pulling at beams and twisted metal. With five other men he heaved free a huge section, which rolled with a thud to the pavement.

They waited for a crane, which did not arrive.

More distant sirens wailed.

The sounds filled the world.

For hours Carter worked.

Until his fingernails snapped.

Until the bloodied skin was worn from his fingers.

Until he sank into a crumpled heap on the pavement and slept, crouching under the black dust.

'Carter?'

He wasn't sure if the tears were tears of gratitude or fear. He took her trembling hands in his.

'I love you, Carter, you hear?' She coughed, her face twisted in pain.

'How is she?'

'We need to get her to the hospital. You can ride with us if you want.'

'Yes. Thank you.'

They had found her crushed under a heavy section of twisted concrete, semi-conscious, mumbling for help. It had taken hydraulic lifting equipment to free her and Carter, acting on impulse, maybe through some twisted sixth sense, had homed in on her as she was carried to the ambulance. He had stumbled forward through the rubble and dust and screaming confused people to drop to his knees by her side.

The ride in the ambulance had been a long, tense experience—

And now?

Now they would play the waiting game.

★

'Mr Carter?'

Carter's head jerked up. The doctor he had threatened with the Browning stood with three other doctors huddled close by. They all stared at him suspiciously.

'How is she?'

'The news is not good.'

His face grim, Carter climbed to his feet, hands hanging limply. He walked slowly forward, and said simply, 'Tell me.'

'Natasha has severe internal injuries. She has a ruptured spleen, heavy internal bleeding – we've managed to stem most of the blood loss but there are still problems, and we may have to remove one of her kidneys. After operating, she failed to regain consciousness and is currently in what we call a state of obtundation, or coma.'

'And the baby?'

'The baby is still alive.'

'Thank God,' whispered Carter.

He seemed to slump then, his whole frame collapsing against itself. He seemed somehow smaller, less menacing, almost . . . weak.

'*Every man has a breaking point,*' whispered Kade. '*Don't let this be yours.*'

'Fuck you.'

Carter moved backwards and sat down tiredly in the seat. The doctors looked at each other, then seemed to shuffle forward a little, gaining confidence in numbers.

'Ahh . . . Mr Carter, this isn't the waiting room. You really should move back through those doors where all the other relatives and friends are waiting—'

Carter's head lifted.

The doctors stared hard at him.

One muttered, 'Well, maybe . . . maybe on this occasion . . .'

'When can I see her?'

'You may come through for a short while now, if you wish . . .'

Carter nodded, pocketed his Browning and followed the doctors. They left him at the door with the words, 'Five minutes only,' and then they dispersed into the corridors and wards of a hospital pushed way beyond its limits.

Carter stepped through the portal.

The lighting was subdued, the background filled with the hum of machines. Natasha was linked to myriad matt-black monitors that glittered with small coloured lights. Tubes snaked from her nose and side, and she was attached to an umbilical cord of IV fluids and drugs.

Carter looked down at her face. Her eyes were closed, her face scratched and heavily bruised. Carter reached out and touched her cheek gently but there was no response. He could feel the warmth of her flesh beneath his battered fingers.

'Don't you die on me, girl,' he whispered.

His hand moved, coming to rest gently on her abdomen. He imagined that he could feel the precious cargo within her womb: beating with life, struggling to grow and survive and to be free.

Carter bit his lip and gritted his teeth so that cords of muscle stood out along his jaw. His gaze returned to Natasha's face and he crouched low, his mouth to her ear. 'Come on, baby, come back to me. Don't leave me on my own. Not now.'

He bowed his head and cried.

The nurse gently prised him away from Natasha, smiled understandingly and helped him from the room to the white-tiled corridor. There was a shout and Carter's red-rimmed eyes failed to focus through the aftermath of tears. He blinked them away, to see Mongrel and Nicky striding towards him.

'Carter, we just heard,' growled Mongrel. 'How is she?'

'Bad, Mongrel, she's in a real bad fucking way.'

'Oh, Carter.' Nicky embraced him, held him, and he buried his head against her neck, smelling musk and sweat and woman; they sank to the seats and Carter suddenly looked up into her eyes.

'Any news of Jam? And Slater and TT?'

'No, nothing . . .'

Carter nodded. He could read her pain. And desperation.

Mongrel spat onto the white tiles. 'Spiral have regrouped, and retreated between HQs 2, 5 and 7.'

After the original bombing of the Spiral headquarters in London a year earlier by the traitors Durell and Feuchter, Spiral had rebuilt itself – but had realigned its structure using the same premise on which the Internet was based. No single hub in complete control – but a myriad of powerful cells, units that could act independently of one another, each containing a core of the whole and strands of the Spiral mainframes . . . so that in times of crisis, no single devastation could make Spiral weak again.

Mongrel continued, 'They work hard to find out just what happened in London yesterday. London not the only city hit – Moscow, Paris, Hong Kong. We need you to come back with us to HQ2 – we need your help, Carter . . .'

Carter glanced up at Mongrel then, frowning suddenly. 'Sorry, mate, I'm staying here.'

'There's nothing you can do, Carter. Natasha is in coma – and they'll let you know when she awakes. We desperately need your help . . .'

Carter stared hard at Mongrel. 'How the fuck do you know that Nats is in a coma? You said you had just heard. What's fucking going on here? What are you not telling me?'

'Tell him,' whispered Nicky as her eyes filled with tears.

Mongrel sighed, glancing around. 'This place not secure.'

'Just fucking tell him,' she snapped, and Carter held her tight, feeling her trembling.

'We have intel on Jam,' said Mongrel. 'He not dead – despite the PB from his ECube. We think he being held hostage, possibly in Slovenia, more details to follow . . . I need your help to get in there and get him out.'

Carter stared hard at Mongrel, who held Carter's gaze without flinching, without weakness, without backing down.

'I love Jam,' growled Carter slowly, carefully, his voice controlled. 'But as you can see, I have my own fucking problems. Or hadn't you noticed?'

'I need you, Carter,' said Mongrel. 'I can't do this alone.'

Carter got to his feet, turned and stared at his two friends. A battle raged within him. 'Look – a few short hours ago you know, you fucking *know* I would have jumped at the chance . . . I would never let Jam suffer and I would give my life for him. But now . . . have you any idea what you're asking me? I am needed here, Natasha needs me . . .'

Mongrel took a deep breath . . .

And Carter caught the connection, the quick glance between Mongrel and Nicky.

'What?' he snarled. 'What the fuck is it?'

'Let us say that doctors have not quite been candid

190

with you, my friend,' said Mongrel softly. He moved closer, placed a hand on Carter's shoulder.

'What do you mean?'

'Natasha is dying. Slowly, but she *is* dying.'

Carter stared hard.

'And when Natasha dies, your baby will die with her.'

'Fuck you,' whispered Carter.

'It's true,' said Nicky softly.

Carter shook his head. 'No, it's not true . . . it can't be true . . .'

The Browning pressed against Mongrel's chin. The metal was cold and hard and Carter's face was a twisted nightmare of insanity and hatred.

'Be calm,' whispered Nicky.

'I will fucking burn you,' hissed Carter, staring into Mongrel's eyes. 'How can you feed me this shit? How can you fuck with my mind like this?'

'I need your help,' repeated Mongrel, voice strong, gaze unwavering despite the pressure of the Browning. 'Put your gun away, Carter. You won't shoot me. Not here, not like this.'

'Want to take a fucking bet?' he snarled.

'There's more,' said Nicky softly.

'Much more,' said Mongrel. 'Tell him about the Avelach.'

'The SAD teams have been killing the Nex; hunting them down and slaughtering them. But Jam was onto something – a machine, a machine they call the Avelach that is used by Durell and Feuchter to *create* the Nex. The Avelach is old, really old. The Nazis discovered it during World War Two – but for decades it remained unused.'

'So what?'

'This machine that's used to create the Nex – well, its

191

primary function is to heal. It could bring people back from the brink of death, save those who were mortally wounded . . . only Durell and Feuchter found a way to subvert the mechanics of the machine, to twist it and force it to create abominations . . . Blending, they called it.'

'Jam knows where machine is,' said Mongrel softly. 'If we find Jam, we can get machine and we can heal Natasha.'

Carter took a step back, his gaze incredulous. 'I don't believe it,' he hissed. 'You would use Natasha and my unborn child to force me into helping you to bring Jam out alive? In the hope that some fictional fucking machine will save her?'

'It's far from fucking fictional,' rumbled Mongrel.

Carter met his gaze.

'You cunt,' he whispered, his head shaking.

'I never claimed to be anything else,' said Mongrel, his heavy-browed face filled with thunder and power, his iron-strong voice steady, unwavering.

Carter sat down. Slumped. Pocketed his gun. Put his head in his hands.

Mongrel and Nicky exchanged glances. Nicky gave a tiny shake of her head.

They waited . . .

Finally, Carter looked up. His eyes were filled with tears. He licked his battered lips. 'I want proof,' he said softly. 'I want proof that Natasha and the baby are dying . . . and I want proof of the fucking machine's existence.'

'We can show you,' said Nicky gently.

Carter frowned then. 'If you're fucking with me, I guarantee you one thing.'

Mongrel nodded in understanding.

'A single bullet in the fucking brain.'

'Let's go – we're wasting time,' said Mongrel, and strode off down the hospital corridor.

Carter sat in the doctor's plush office, toying with his Browning. The main doctor delivering the report, Pat Callaghan, a tall dark dashing stud of a man, was looking nervously from Carter to Mongrel – and then back again.

Carter stared at the medical notes.

'So – she is dying.'

'Yes. Very slowly. It might take a single week, maybe two. But the damage is too great; we could try nano-implants, but in terms of replacing kidneys and liver, they are unproven and we have been getting high failure rates . . . and in the current situation they are not the easiest mod to come across. The biggest problems lie in Natasha's internal structural damage – her body is reject-ing her own organs, and we cannot work out why.'

'And the baby?'

'If you look at Scan 5, you can see it is currently healthy and alive. Kicking, shall we say.'

'Can you not deliver the baby? By Caesarean?' Carter's voice was cold, almost uninterested . . . but Mongrel and Nicky knew that he was forcing himself into a state of detachment – working out the best way to get the job done . . . the job being the saving of Natasha and their unborn child.

'We *could* deliver, but the trauma would certainly kill Natasha immediately. Due to the crushing injuries she has sustained, several organs and arteries have been moved – they are in the way. There is no clear path to the child without immediately putting Natasha in, shall we say, a terminal situation. And the other angle is that it's almost as if Natasha's body has caged her baby. The shock of such a long-drawn-out operation could also kill the child. In fact, I would say there was an extremely high probability. It might work . . . but then, we wouldn't do it until there was absolutely no alternative.'

Carter tapped his Browning against the desk.

'Doctor Callaghan, can you leave us for a few minutes?'

'What? But – it's my office . . .'

Carter stared at the man, his battered grime streaked visage a picture of menace. Without a further sound the doctor slipped from the room. Carter stared hard at Mongrel and Nicky.

'Our motives are not completely selfish,' said Nicky softly. She placed a hand on Carter's shoulder. 'We want Natasha back as well – we love her, you know? But Jam needs our help, and he holds a key to a machine that can save Natasha and the child. With no compromise . . .'

'*If* the machine exists, and *if* the machine works like you say it does.'

'Jam was onto it; had been for a long time. Yes, he was heading up the SAD teams, but down in Egypt we stumbled across metal sheets with diagrams, instructions – took them from the dead fist of a Nex scout. The diagrams were on metal sheets carbon-dated to 6800 BC – some of the oldest "documents" ever discovered by man.'

'Who has this machine?' asked Carter tenderly.

'We're not sure. Jam had coordinates that he was going to check out after his mission in Slovenia. But then the shit hit the fan and the team went AWOL. He carried the coordinates in his head.'

'What makes you think Jam is still alive?' asked Carter. 'For his ECube to initiate a PB he must have been on the verge of death. That's the way it works, yeah?'

194

'Yes, he was assumed dead initially. But the Spiral mainframes, piloted by the QII processor, were sending out random signature scans – they picked up a signal from Jam's ThumbNail _Map. It only activated for about three nanoseconds, a distorted burst that the mainframes couldn't pin; but it meant he was using the implanted device. Which meant he had to be alive.'

Carter sighed.

'You can stay here, Carter, while Natasha slowly deteriorates. Watch her die,' said Mongrel, his face grave but showing no weakness. 'Or you can come with me, help me track Jam and find this Avelach machine.'

'The machine used for creating the Nex,' said Carter softly. 'Oh, how ironic. I would use it to save Natasha's life! The machine responsible for so much *taking* of life.'

'They have abused it,' said Nicky.

'Yeah, somebody always does.'

'A gun is just a metal box containing bullets – unless there's a finger to pull the trigger,' she whispered.

Mongrel nodded. 'Nicky will coordinate between HQ2 and here, checking on Natasha; she will study metal sheaves we have, work out how to operate this machine for when we find it and steal it. That way, we signal her to rendezvous – and all we have to do is pull machine out and get here. Before that, all we need to find this Avelach device is Jam and coordinates in his head.'

'I don't like this,' said Carter.

'We've been granted clearance. Grade AA. Straight from top. With full-support WarCover and WarClearance – if we need any help.'

'Our starting point?'

'Where Jam was taken out,' said Mongrel softly. 'We'll pick up his trail. He must have stumbled upon something.'

195

'I thought it had been scanned by PopBots?'

'It has,' said Mongrel, 'but I believe human eye see more than dumb-ass electronics.'

Carter climbed to his feet, face sombre.

'You need time to get cleaned up? Have a MedScan?' Mongrel was looking him up and down.

'No. I just want five minutes alone with Natasha.'

'We'll wait by hospital entrance.'

Carter nodded and left Mongrel and Nicky behind. He could read their uncertainty, their fear, their *need*. He walked back down corridors, some filled with screaming wailing patients, overflowing from waiting rooms with relatives and friends, and finally reached Natasha's side room. The ward Sister made eye contact with Carter in the corridor and smiled wearily; he let himself in.

The monitors were chattering and bleeping with the subtlety of harmonics.

Carter gazed down at Natasha.

Tears filled his eyes but he pushed them angrily away.

He took Natasha's hand. It trailed tubes.

'I will save you – save you both,' he said, smiling gently.

'*Another of your empty promises,*' snapped Kade, emerging from the depths of Carter's mind. His arrival was a black blossom opening its petals to welcome the radioactive death-light of a black planet.

'Empty promises? No,' said Carter softly, shaking his head. 'I will save her. I *have* to save her.'

'*There are other fucking women.*' Kade chuckled smugly. '*You don't need this one. Ultimately, she's just another dead bitch. Come on, Carter, let's fuck off, find you some fresh slick meat from the nightclub pork-market.*'

'I have to save her,' repeated Carter. 'Because, if Natasha and the baby die . . .' His voice went quiet, its volume dropping to that of an unsettling lullaby. 'If they die, then I will bathe the world in blood. I will seek out and butcher God – and all his children. This I swear.'

Kade did not – for once, could not – reply.

Carter's emotions *burned* him. And, silently, Carter's dark twin departed.

CHAPTER 8

SCORPNEX

In the dream Jam walked down a long dark corridor. There were a thousand black obsidian doors all leading from this central aisle and Jam strode, gaze flicking from one to another, his long black coat flapping around him, heavy leather boots stomping through the cold frost and leaving heavy tread imprints. And then he stopped. He could feel the malevolence beyond.

Slowly he reached out, turned the handle and was flooded with a wash of violet light. Shielding his eyes for a moment he heard the growls creeping from within, and he stepped tentatively forward – could suddenly see the horribly deformed Nex emerging from the violet mist – and he said, 'What is wrong with you?'

'Everything went black,' whispered the deformed ScorpNex through twisted fangs. 'They changed me, they made me into . . . this.' It looked down in horror at the merging of carapace and muscle which still bled between strands of twisted spaghetti flesh.

It moved forward, a bloodstained claw coming up towards Jam.

'Help me,' it said, drooling thick yellow saliva laced with skeins of blood.

'Please God, help me . . .'

Jam's eyes flickered open. He was cold, terribly cold, and his breath flooded out in smoke. He could see a massive vaulted ceiling above him and it was rough-hewn stone, hung with glittering ice stalactites. He groaned long and low, agony throbbing through him like a distant scalpel carving his flesh. He turned his head to the left and saw hundreds of stone-slab tables spreading off into the frosty, gloom-laden half-light. Each supported a body: some were perfectly still, some twitched, some were bent into arched shapes and frozen in a rictus of torment – a stop-motion dance of suffering.

And then Jam saw the wide straps holding the victims in tortured bondage against the thick stone slabs.

He tried to move, then realised that he too was strapped down.

He hissed in pain and frustration.

'Don't move. It won't be long now.'

Jam's head jerked to the right – and there, fore-grounded against a backdrop of human suffering, stood Mace. His face was pale, gaunt, just a little deformed, and smiling softly.

'Where am I?'

'This is where we create the Nex,' said Mace. He removed a small leather case from which he took the syringe. The needle glinted brightly against the gloom. The silver liquid glistened within, holding Jam's gaze in anticipated horror.

Jam licked his lips nervously.

'No, not again, you fucker,' he croaked.

'You will like it this time,' said Mace softly, placing his

199

hand delicately against Jam's forehead. 'The inhibitor has worked . . . you will feel no pain.'

'No . . .'

The needle slid into his flesh and Jam tensed, tensed so hard that he thought he would burst. There came a burning sensation . . . and then nothing. He floated, gently rolling through a mental landscape of silver blossoms.

Another voice. Drifting lazily in the dream.

'Do it.'

Jam opened his blurry eyes and could see the black robes of Durell, the hint of slitted copper eyes within the hood. He smiled, filled with warmth – and then cold tore through him and he gasped. Mace was holding something that wriggled and Jam blinked, slowly, eyes stuck with honey – three times he blinked, and then focused on the—

Scorpion.

'What . . .'

He was going to ask 'What are you going to do with that?' but his mouth would not work properly. The coldness had flooded him, turned his blood to ice, his saliva to frost, his eyes to glittering insect jewels.

Mace came closer.

The scorpion was struggling, its shell a dark and glistening terrible black – as if oiled and carved from stone. Mace held up a clenched fist and Jam tried to struggle as the need for survival kicked in. Durell produced a small silver box and opened it with a tiny click—

Mace lowered the scorpion into Jam's mouth. He wanted to scream but could not, wanted to struggle but the ice injection had hijacked his limbs and his will. He could feel the scorpion move inside his mouth, its legs pressing against his tongue and gums. He gagged, nearly vomiting, but the cold injection held him in thrall. The arachnid's claws brushed his teeth, the sting lashed out – once, twice, three times – but there was no pain even though Jam could sense the poison entering his system like bad blood. Mace's fist opened and he held a horde of squirming scuttling cockroaches, their stench stinging Jam's nostrils. He poured them into Jam's mouth alongside the scorpion and all Jam could feel was a hive of activity in his mouth and then down his throat. All he could think was, *This is a dream, a nightmare, I will wake up soon*, but whenever he opened his eyes he was still in the stone chamber and Mace was still staring down at him like a scientist conducting an experiment.

Another injection. This time in the throat.

Jam tried to scream, but the insects blocked his mouth and in panic he realised that he could not even breathe.

Durell handed a black disc to Mace, who stepped forward and smiled down at Jam.

'Soon it will all be over,' he said, copper eyes shining with—

Kindness?

Fuck you! screamed Jam's brain, but he was too busy trying to thrash his head from side to side to disgorge the crawling insects. Mace placed the disc over Jam's mouth and stepped back—

'You must welcome the Avelach,' he crooned, almost singing the words.

The disc was terribly cold and then it felt like liquid yet simultaneously solid metal. Jam felt it move and spread and change and *expand* as the thick black catabolic substance spread out from his mouth to his throat and neck and head. Then it sped across his naked torso and over his arms and legs until he could feel the tight cold metal cage clamping his flesh. It covered his skin completely, this dark liquid metal, spreading across all of him.

201

The Avelach coated him.

It entered him.

It *raped* him.

And for a moment it soothed his pain. The cold spread over his naked skin like a chilled layer of smoothest silks – and then flowed into his eyes, and into his mouth to scorch his lips and tongue and gullet. It burned, and it burned bad.

Jam tried to scream and the cold oil-metal flowed and filled his lungs and merged with the insects in his mouth and throat. He breathed sulphur and insect blood. He drowned in white phosphor. He imbibed napalm.

The pain was eternal.

The agony burned him for a billion years.

And then it was over, and a dry and dusty harmattan blew across his soul. His soft tears ran like silver droplets of molten ice across his scorched skin.

The imago had begun.

Durell sat back against the black leather high-backed chair, the cold all around him, soothing. His hands rested against the freezing leather. His head drooped, his slitted copper eyes gazing down at the stone floor.

As Mace entered, Durell glanced up, hood thrown back, his horrendous disfigurements producing no more than a flicker of momentary interest across Mace's face.

'It is done,' said Mace.

'Has it been successful?'

'As you know, we have changed the coding of the sequence and the make-up of the inhibitors – and we've used a slightly different breed of cockroach. Only time will tell if this will yield another ScorpNex.'

Durell laughed softly. 'The problems of trying to

replicate a mistake! How many specimens have died so far? I have lost count.'

'There have been sixty-eight attempts,' said Mace, his copper-eyed stare fixed on Durell.

'And this is the sixty-ninth? With luck Jam will prove his toughness and his will to survive. That was what made him *Spiral*.' Durell spat the name like a ball of sulphur phlegm.

'Yes. He has thus far shown great resilience – and we have done our utmost to keep the Blending pure.'

'How long?'

'The next few hours will enlighten us.'

'Good. Keep me informed.'

Mace moved forward through the gloom. At this time of the night everything was silent; the Nex attendants were in their nests and Mace was completely alone . . . except for the hundreds on the stone slabs in this cold underground world.

He stopped in front of Jam . . . the Avelach had long since retracted to its former shape and the black metallic disc, the *machine*, had been removed from Jam's face and mouth and placed back in the sanctuary of the silver box that had been fashioned to protect and recharge it.

Mace moved forward. Jam's head was tilted back, his eyes closed, his face a deathly white. His lips were tightly closed and, reaching out, Mace prised open Jam's mouth and clenched teeth. Reaching inside, he pulled out the shell of the scorpion – which was so brittle that it crumbled to dust under his fingers. Carefully, Mace scooped out the remains of the cockroach carapaces and allowed them to fall to the stone floor, across which they drifted softly in response to the cool breeze. Then, slowly, he undid the straps that fastened Jam to the bench and ran

his hand down Jam's naked and treacherously cold flesh.
It felt glassy, cold, hard – and slightly tainted with oil.

Mace smiled.

'Good,' he said, nodding to himself.

Jam could feel them inside him. He tried to force them
away but they would not and could not leave him.

we are together

merged

as one

they have made us one

Pain blended them in fire and flowed like acid through
his veins. A metallic copper stink like the stench of old
bad blood pervaded his nostrils and tattooed his tongue
and it was him, a part of him, injected into his flesh and
blood and brain.

Jam fell into a dark pit of despair.

Then awoke.

He lay for a long time on the stone, not really thinking,
just mentally searching his body for signs of injury.
Everything was cold. Stone was beneath him. The air was
crisp and biting against his lips and tongue. He was
breathing, his chest rising and falling, and he could feel
air entering his lungs and then smoothly leaving again.

Slowly, he opened his sticky eyes.

There was no pain.

That was the first real thought that struck him.

No pain.

He had spent the last few days suffering physical and
mental torment so severe that he thought he would
break – both mentally and physically. But now the pain
had gone and all that remained was the cool and soothing
embrace of frost.

He moved his hand, lifted it to his face. His flesh was white, chalk white and he examined his hand, its structure, the tapering of his fingers, the roundness of his nails. He turned his head to one side, realised he was in a cell . . . but not the dry dusty cells of his initial beatings, rather somewhere cold and sterile. There was a single light source, tiny against the damp stone wall; nothing more than an insect glow.

Jam sat up, looking down at his chalk-white nakedness. A bad metal taste was in his mouth and he spat again and again. But it would not leave him.

'Was it just a dream?'

His voice rattled hollowly in the stone cage of his skull.

On a low table there stood a clay pitcher of water and a cup. Slowly, testing himself, Jam stood, bare feet shuffling on stone, and moved to pour himself a cup of water.

Something did not feel right.

Within himself . . .

His body felt . . . somehow *wrong* . . .

He drank the water to quench his terrible raging thirst, and staring down at himself he was deeply confused. He remembered with a shudder the insects in his mouth, but then he also remembered long dreams of corridors and fires and Slater shooting ice bullets into his face.

He rinsed his mouth with water, but still the metal taste would not leave him.

And then a wave of nausea convulsed his body and he dropped to one knee, vomiting the recently imbibed water onto the stone floor. His athletic frame heaved, and heaved again . . . his stomach disgorged bile until there was nothing left. But still the nausea swamped him and he continued to heave until his muscles screamed at him and he thought that his stomach would tear itself physically apart . . .

Then it was over.

On his knees, panting, drooling saliva, sweat beading on his forehead, soaking his hair, Jam stared down at his shrivelled penis and flat stomach bathed in a sheen of sweat. He was trembling violently, and cursed his lack of clothing . . .

Is this just another form of fucking torture? raged his mind.

An insane anger filled him.

A true need to *kill* . . .

He stumbled towards the door, raised his hand to knock and sensed rather than heard or saw figures outside – looking in on him, anonymous. He smashed his fist against the door, then recoiled in horror as he felt the bones of his fingers crack and splinter within the padded flesh of his fist. A gasp escaped his cold blue-tinged lips, more shock than the sudden pain that flared from the six broken bones and he whirled . . . but felt his ankle snap and dislocate and compress. He stumbled, fell, felt his left leg shatter within his flesh and lifted his gaze to the ceiling, screaming as he collapsed onto the stone.

Outside, Durell said, 'The pain has begun.'

Mace nodded, deep in thought. 'It will not be long before the imago is complete.'

The room had thick plush carpets and a roaring fire in the hearth. Gol stood in front of the weaving flames, warming himself and staring at the painting above the immense stone fireplace – *The Education of the Virgin* by the Austrian artist Franz Anton Maulbertsch. Gol traced the fine strokes of oil on canvas, his gaze absorbing the flying angels and almost demonic use of blacks and reds above this seemingly pure act of instruction. The fire crackled, an aural background to Gol's calm, and he turned to warm his back as he swirled the brandy in the glass thoughtfully.

He took a gentle sip of the 1794 Hennessy, and the spirit burned his mouth and warmed its way to his belly like liquid fire. Gol sucked in air and surveyed the room.

Small single-pane leaded windows looked out over a heavy rain-filled valley under deep veils of darkness. The walls were panelled ceiling to floor in oak, and lined with many bookshelves sporting dusty old tomes. Furniture was period, in keeping with the fine theme of the room – and of either Austrian or Swiss lineage.

Rain rattled against the windows and a savage night wind howled outside, driving down with animal fury from the mountains.

Gol sipped the brandy again, its mellowness soothing him. He looked up as a huge heavy oak door swung silently inwards and Durell moved forward at a slow pace. He stared at the fire for a while, then turned towards Gol.

'Is everything all right?' Gol asked.

'Yes,' said Durell softly. 'It is too warm in here.'

Gol nodded. 'Thought I'd light a fire . . . is that OK?'

'I do not like the warmth; it makes me itch.'

'I can have it put out . . .'

'No, no.' Durell held up a hand. The cloth fell away to reveal something black, crusted and glistening. Gol swallowed hard, staring into the depths of the hood that hid the slitted and almost feline copper eyes.

'Is it working? With Jam?'

'We think so. But due to such high previous failure rates we are keeping a very close eye on him. He just has the nominal pain and metamorphosis to complete and then –' Durell smiled '– then he will be one of us. No other specimen has reached this far.'

Durell moved to a large table and it seemed to ignite,

207

to glow, as the surface became digitally alive. Durell and Gol stared down at the glowing map and Durell pointed.

Gol nodded. 'Have the Foundation Stones for Core3 been initiated?'

'Shortly,' said Durell.

'Then we are close?' asked Gol, sipping once more at his brandy.

'Yes. We are close.'

Jam dreamed a hard bad dream. He was falling, through a long dark tunnel that seemed to lead downwards for ever. Wind ruffled his hair and the world was filled with a complete silence. Jam shifted in the slipstream, fear a distant echo, pain a distant dream . . . The walls around him were fashioned from glistening black rock, speckled with frost, glimmering with ice, and suddenly a ledge loomed out of nowhere – a jagged, rocky extrusion with which Jam collided, grunting in pain, spinning off with stars fluttering in his mind to career from the opposite wall of this vertical tunnel—

Down.

He could taste blood – and something else.

And then he saw it. Just as he thought that the fall would be eternal and he could drift lazily in the cold air currents for a blissful eternity, he saw the water spread wide and the tunnel disappeared above him, sucked away into blackness. Jam could make out distant glittering waves. The sea was an oil, a dark obsidian mercury, and he sped down towards its cooling enveloping embrace . . .

He saw it *shift*.

Move.

Squirm . . .

And he realised that it was alive. Crawling and alive.

He flowed towards the sea of insects and fear suddenly

208

struck him with a cold left hook. He could feel it, panic bubbling in his throat, and then he realised that the feeling was the skittering of tiny legs on his body and tongue and teeth. His mouth was filled with cockroaches frantically squirming to break free of this teeth-barred organic cell.

He could feel their panic.

Their will to survive.

He bit down, crushing some of their bodies, and felt their blood run down his throat, a flood filled with torn legs and tiny pieces of carapace. And then the scorpion moved up his throat and Jam felt vomit heaving within him. The sea rushed towards him, and engulfed him and darkness flooded his world. He smashed through the crust of crawling insects and into an oil which burned his flesh and stung him. He realised with horror that it was a toxin, a thick and swirling poison and he was finally able to scream out a verbal ejaculation of spewing wriggling insects—

Jam sat up, sweat pouring from his brow. He screamed, fingers scrabbling at his mouth, and he looked down in the gloom. He could see something that had crawled up from his ankles and shins, covering his lower legs with a sheen of glistening black, and had then halted around his knees, merging with his pink flesh, twisting between strands of shredded skin and muscle . . .

This cannot be happening to me, he thought.

This cannot be real.

Nicky . . . Nicky . . .

He pictured her sweet face, hair tied back, eyes twinkling—

He pictured her moving towards him, mouth parting slightly, sweet breath tickling his lips, his eyes closing as her kiss taunted him and lust surged through his body like a drug—

He pictured her dying, screaming with insects in her hair like tiny black blossoms, squirming.

'No . . .'

He sat up, hands moving down to the hard skin of his lower legs. What is it? Just what the fuck is it?

Pain welled inside him, and he suddenly noticed a swelling in his groin, to either side of his testicles. The skin there was inflamed, puckered with tiny spikes of black. Jam arched his back as he felt the spikes prick his skin under his questing fingers and he screamed, screamed and screamed and screamed until there was no more breath and no more light. And no more hope.

Jam awoke on his side, curled into a ball. He felt strange. There was no pain.

He rolled onto his hands and knees, and looked down curiously at the backs of his forearms. Merged with his brown skin was a series of thick black marks with tiny spikes poking free. He rocked back onto his heels with a clack of chitinous armour and flexed his forearms. Spikes sprang free, rippling up his arms and glinting eerily in the gloom.

Jam breathed deeply.

His mind settled.

He blinked lazily.

There came a sound at the door and his head jerked left, spikes erecting along his forearms, eyes compressing to narrow copper slits. The door opened, flooding the chamber with light, and Jam recoiled with a hiss, armoured feet clacking across the stone—

Durell stepped in.

'Welcome,' he crooned, throwing back his hood.

Jam rose to his full height, spine crackling softly, and he could feel saliva pool from his twisted jaws. His head swung left, then right, and he could smell the scent of fear.

'Follow me.'

Durell left the cell and Jam stooped, armour scraping the stonework as he followed Durell down a series of long stone corridors. They came to some steps and Jam leapt lithely down them, landing heavily and cracking a stone flag. They travelled on down stone ramps under the dim glow of electric bulbs into the depths of the castle.

Not once during the journey did Durell turn round.

And Jam found himself surveying the dark expanse of Durell's back. His head swayed from one side to the other, eyes fixed on that broad back and strange metallic thoughts flickering through his brain

Kill

Kill

Rip flesh burn and turn and flee

Master

Control . . .

Master

Durell led Jam into a huge stone chamber decorated with tapestries and burning brands in iron brackets. Set in the floor, scooped from the rock was a large sunken pit lined with huge blocks of rectangular stone, measuring maybe ten metres by ten. There were intricate old weathered carvings set roughly in some of the blocks lining the pit; the floor was criss-crossed with grooves and gutters leading to wider channels feeding off around the edges.

Gol stepped into the chamber and Jam's copper eyes locked onto the large grey-bearded man. Jam saw Gol swallow, hard, and walk tentatively around him to reach Durell's side.

'Is he safe?'

'Yes.'

'I fucking hope so . . .'

'I will show you.'

Across the chamber, through a narrow stone arch, came Kattenheim. He held a man by the arm, a man who seemed deflated, beaten, withdrawn. As they walked his head came up and his stare widened in horror as he saw Jam—

'Fuck, no,' he gasped.

Kattenheim heaved the man into the pit, where he landed heavily before scrambling to his feet, pushing his back against the stone of the wall. His gaze roved wildly searching for an avenue of escape. Kattenheim lifted a huge-bladed axe and tossed it into the pit where it clattered with a shower of sparks against the stone. The man scrambled forward, lifting the weapon. He understood the game.

'This is Scarlet, a former captain of the Australian SAS and latterly of Spiral, DemolSquad 142. We captured him and a few others of his ilk in Tibet on a mission that went badly wrong.' Durell reached out, patted Gol's shoulder, smiled a hidden smile. 'Don't worry. Watch.'

'Come on, you fuckers,' Scarlet was screaming, anger firing him into action, brandishing the large-headed axe in both hands and readying himself for battle.

'Kill him,' said Durell softly.

Jam's triangular head tilted, dark copper eyes fixing on Durell. Then, with a hiss, he leapt into the pit and strode towards the man swinging the axe. The axe whirled, then smashed down.

Jam spun, ducking low under the sweep of the heavy blade, and powered a right hook straight against Scarlet's jaw that sent the man spinning to the ground to lie

212

stunned. The axe clattered uselessly against stone. Silence suddenly reigned.

Jam paced up and down, seemingly unsure. Then he leapt into the air, both armoured feet coming down with a heavy crunch on Scarlet's head. The Spiral man's skull cracked open, spilling liquid pulped brains into the kill channels. Jam's face lifted questioningly to Durell.

'Athletic,' said Kattenheim softly, red eyes watching the proceedings with interest. 'Much faster than the other Scorp.'

'Summon the Nex.'

Three Nex warriors were called and they arrived, wearing their tight black suits and thin boots, and carrying Armalite X sub-machine guns. They stood silently, waiting, copper-eyed stares fixed on Durell. Gol forced himself not to take a step back. He set his face in the cold stone mask of the stoic.

'You are unsure?' asked Durell.

'Let us see,' said Gol softly.

'Kill it,' snapped Durell, pointing at Jam.

The three Nex moved swiftly apart, Armalite X guns lifting and opening fire. Dozens of 5.62mm rounds screamed across the chamber, striking sparks from stone. Jam leapt high into the air, bullets spinning and whining beneath him. He twisted in mid-flight, kicked off from one bare stone wall and landed suddenly among the Nex—

The Armalites ceased firing.

Jam punched left, then right – he flexed his arms and spikes rippled upright. He slashed them across the first Nex – ripping its face clean off. It fell, screaming, to one knee, blood pumping between its fingers. More bullets spat from muzzles. Jam whirled low, kicking the legs from under a retreating Nex and then slamming his fist through

213

its back to explode in a slurry of purple from its chest. His free hand plucked the Armalite X from its twitching fingers, and with his fist still embedded in its ribcage and with bullets skimming past his head Jam fired off the magazine's contents into the third Nex's face. He watched emotionlessly as it collapsed into a smoking heap.

Cordite smoke drifted lazily.

Jam withdrew his fist with a slurping noise from the still-twitching Nex and it collapsed, spewing blood that ran down the walls into the kill trough and along the channels designed to carry away the detritus of slaughter.

Jam calmly found a fresh mag from the Nex's ammo belt and moved towards the Nex without a face. It was making a low keening sound and rocking on its knees. Jam filled its head full of scything metal and then allowed the Armalite X to clatter to the stone floor, his eyes lifting to stare at Durell and a snarl flickering across lips that had once been human.

'Well done, my child,' said Durell softly.

'I thought they were supposed to fight *inside* the kill trough?' said Gol, having felt the passing of bullets and looking at the blood on his boots and lower trousers.

'Jam improvised,' said Durell. 'What think you, Kattenheim?'

The German ex-para nodded in appreciation. 'Strength, speed, agility, improvisation, lack of mercy. Ideal. A beautiful weapon to turn against Spiral . . .'

'And the DemolSquads,' said Gol softly.

'One final test.'

'Is that necessary?'

'Oh yes,' said Durell.

Kattenheim disappeared, then returned with a small group of Nex soldiers. Between them they dragged a woman and three children – and without breaking stride they tossed them into the kill trough. Durell watched with amusement as two of the children became hysterical upon seeing streams of blood down the wall and the split-skulled corpse of Scarlet. The woman cradled them to her, covering their faces. She glared up at the small gathering with hatred across her face.

'An innocent family, how sweet. A positive example of what the human race can achieve – pinnacles of organic evolution,' said Durell softly, smiling sardonically. 'Jam – kill them.'

'But . . .' hissed Gol, his head turning—

Jam leapt forward into the pit and, arms glistening with human and Nex blood and gore and brains, moved towards the cowering family. His dark eyes surveyed them, head swaying a little, and tiny spikes sprang up along one heavily muscled and armoured forearm.

'Is this necessary, Durell?'

Durell's slitted eyes gleamed. 'Death is always necessary,' he said, his words forming sombre lyrics to the music of anguished screams and gurgles that followed.

Gol sat in the room which he used for meditation. The castle in which Durell now based his operations was huge. Built of grey stone many hundreds of years previously, and modified by Durell to certain very specific details, it held an ancient feel; the walls were thick and designed to repel invaders, and much of the décor – oil paintings, tapestries, Swiss and Austrian furniture, thick German rugs scattered throughout the many stone corridors and rooms – was original. Huge black iron brackets lined the walls. Windows were edged with lead and rattled in high winds.

Gol was seated on the large bed, naked, legs crossed, eyes closed. Rain howled against the windows, but he was switched off from the current reality; in his meditation he relived his past—

Running, running . . . pursued by the Nex. He could hear the sweep of the Comanche's rotors overhead, hear the whine of its LHTec engines, feel the presence of the Nex and their submachine guns close behind his sprinting form – with his arms pumping, fist holding the precious silver disk with the schematics for the QIII processor. He had done the honourable thing, done the only thing he could to protect the information and give Spiral a chance of winning the war—

Sacrifice . . .

He leapt from the clifftop. Into the narrow chasm with the glittering river far below.

A Nex ran over the cliff behind him, not because of any programmed response but through a lack of ability to kill its speed.

Gol fell, wind tearing through his beard and hair—

Tears flowed across his cheeks and were snatched away by the wind of his fall—

Something hit him in the back of the head, and twisting mid-fall Gol saw the Nex trying to lift its sub-machine gun, copper-eyed stare fixed impassively on his face and its single focused intent obvious—

It would not let him live.

It wanted to place a bullet in his face – as extra security in case the impact following the fall didn't kill him.

Free-falling, the glittering river speeding close, Gol lifted back his mighty fist and delivered a thundering left hook. Blood spurted from the Nex's mouth, along with a tooth, and Gol hit it again – and again. Bullets suddenly howled as the Nex pulled the trigger. Gol reached out, grabbing the hot barrel. It scorched his flesh and bullets flashed off over his left shoulder, cutting

216

lines in the stone walls of the flashing, speeding canyon—

They grappled, spinning.

Gol pulled the Nex close, slamming his head into its face once, twice, three times, four times – until it went limp and they were spinning, spinning and falling and the river loomed up suddenly close and frighteningly real and—

They plunged below the waters, the Nex first, Gol wrapped closely in the creature's loose embrace. The force of the impact seemed to knock all life from Gol. Blackness swamped him, and he felt the second impact against the river bottom with a blow of pain pounding through every limb. He felt the Nex's body come apart beneath him, and felt his own frame smashed against the river bed like a corpse flung by the sea at an unforgiving wall of rock—

Blackness poured like dark honey into his mind.

And then . . . nothing.

Gol had awoken on the river bank, both cliffs towering far above. Ten Nex stood around him, their copper eyes staring into his face.

'Is it dead?'

'Not yet.'

Cold laughter rippled.

'Drag it to the truck. Durell might want to question it.'

Gol caught a glimpse of the silver disk, the disk he had given his life to protect, shoved beneath dark grey clothing. He was dragged along the ground and heaved into the back of a truck where pain screamed at him from every part of his battered body. Unconsciousness claimed him.

★

Darkness, as violent jolts hammered through the truck's suspension. Gol kept his eyes tight shut and did an internal diagnostic. He could feel both legs and one arm broken, and something was wrong with his spine. He also thought his jaw was broken. The jolts from the truck did not help. They fed the pain a diet of need and Gol welcomed the darkness when it finally – eventually – came once again.

When he awoke, bright lights were shining into his face.

'This will hurt a little,' said Mace, smiling down as the needle slid into Gol's throat. The burning came over him as a rush and he screamed as Durell approached, copper eyes staring down with a hint of . . . compassion . . .

'Welcome back, my oldest friend.'

'Fuck you, Durell, you are a traitor . . .'

'Ahh . . . we will speak again in a little while. Mace, take the sample for the clone.'

'Yes, sir.'

The pain had consumed Gol as the liquid burned through his veins and the insects filled up his mouth. Then he was eaten and swallowed and raped by the Avelach.

Gol opened his eyes in the present – and breathed calmly. Rain clattered against the windows and the night had fallen as Gol had relived his transformation from human to Nex.

He smiled.

Strange, he mused, how betrayal is all about perspective.

But now he was Nex, now he was part of Durell's army – and now he could see everything clearly.

And still . . .

218

Something was wrong: a splinter in his brain, a tumour in his soul. He knew now that he was fighting for the right side and that becoming a Nex had saved his life and transformed him into a superior life form – even if they had used different experimental inhibitors so that his Nex status was slightly – how would they describe it? – different. They would destroy the evil named Spiral. They would turn it, as Durell had said, into a New Eden. They would rule, and they would be like gods looking down from Olympus . . .

Gol smiled.

His body relaxed.

He felt the slow pulse of blood through his Nex veins.

Gol uncurled from his meditative crouch and leapt to the floor. He padded over and poured himself a brandy, allowing the liquid fire to scorch his throat and warm his belly.

Something disturbed him.

Gol wasn't like the other Nex.

He didn't crave the cold, like the other Nex.

And although his emotions were subdued, he still felt empathy to a greater extent than the cold copper-eyed killers . . .

And his eyes—

Something had happened – or, more importantly, had *not* happened to his eyes. Most Nex had copper orbs, a side-product of the inhibitors used and the Blending process . . . but for some reason, this physical transformation had not affected Gol—

And it set him apart.

He was different.

A mongrel among pure-breed Nex.

Gol moved to the window, staring out at the rain. He sipped his brandy and the face of Natasha popped into his head, surprising him. My long-lost love, he thought with a wry smile. My child, I wonder where you are now? I wonder what you are doing?

Still fighting for Spiral?

These thoughts were idle because he knew that deep down in his soul the emotional link between himself and his daughter was severed. And despite his intelligence telling him that this was a part of being Nex, still something burned deep within him, a tiny candle flame which didn't so much feed his emotions as make him remember what it used to feel like.

'It's better to be alive, yes?'

'Kattenheim, you made me jump.'

Kattenheim padded across the rugs and poured himself a brandy. Then he turned, red eyes surveying Gol with interest – with a sparkle of scarred intelligence that made Gol wary.

'Am I right?'

'Yes, but that's a strange question for you to be asking.' Gol moved and pulled on a thick jumper and a pair of heavy combat trousers. Dressed, he turned to stare out at the rain once more.

'I've seen you . . . and Durell has seen you. We understand – that you are different from the other Nex. This is not a problem.'

'But?' Gol turned, laughing softly in his deep melodic voice. 'There is always a but . . .'

'Durell trusts you implicitly.'

Gol's deep brown-eyed stare met the blood-scarred gaze of Kattenheim and he saw nothing but strength and single-mindedness there. A focus of purpose. The intent of the insane. Gol breathed deeply, then sighed, moved to the window and looked out over the rain-swept forests, hazy in the distance. 'You, however, do not trust me. You

220

see me as a threat. You think Durell is mistaken in his trust because of our old bonds, our old ties. You think he is misguided.'

'Yes.' Kattenheim moved closer and Gol could feel the threat. His body tensed involuntarily, awaiting the first blow as the Nex part of him fired into immediate readiness . . .

Gol turned his back on Kattenheim.

'You couldn't have killed the women and children,' said Kattenheim softly.

'No.'

'Why not?'

'I cannot explain it.'

'I can. You are not fully Nex . . . the Avelach Skein Blending was interrupted; the machine did its work healing you, and the process of merging you with your insect companions had begun . . . but it happened when the war was at its height. Mace was called away during the process – it was left incomplete. You are not fully Nex. You never were.'

Gol shrugged. 'It's of little consequence.'

'No,' said Kattenheim. 'It is of *great* consequence . . . You are a half-breed, Gol, and I think you are the weakest link in the chain to our future. I am watching you – and the Nex are watching you. It was my suggestion that we either finish the process – but apparently this is an impossibility – or . . . kill you.'

Gol turned with a snarl. 'Fuck you, Kattenheim. I believe in what we are fighting for – if you want to fuck with me then we can take it down to the kill trough. Now, if you've nothing constructive to add then I suggest you fuck off and complete your duties – we have a lot of work to do, the QHub can still be refined and I need my sleep.'

Kattenheim turned and left. Gol smiled, releasing a deep breath.

Still got the fucking fire, he thought.

I can still kick some fucking ass—

But Kattenheim?

Gol had seen him fight, and knew deep down that he could not beat the man . . . the *Nex*, he corrected himself. Kattenheim was just too fast. Too deadly. But then, it didn't matter because they were on the same side. Right?

The same side?

Gol stared out at the rain, which fell in vast vertical sheets, driving across the landscape, across the trees and slopes beyond the castle, running in cold rivulets and streams along the crushed-stone road that led from the heavy steel gates down through the dark forests and into the valley below.

I'm not sure which side that is any more.

SIU Transcript

CLASSIFIED SR12/7252/SPECIAL INVESTIGATIONS UNIT
Hacked ECube interception
Date: September 2XXX

California CT15: Sector XH

Seismic Reactor Research Facilities **[SRRF]**

Dr Brian,

In short, we are deeply confused. The recent devastating quakes measuring between 7.2 and 9.6 on the Richter Magnitude scale which have hit Beijing, Salvador, Moscow, London, Zermatt, Bangkok, Berlin, Stockholm, Paris, Budapest, Tokyo, Baghdad and New York do not

222

relate directly to previously understood contours of seismic activity. Quakes have always followed patterns - the contours of geological plates and known fault lines in the world crust. This new breed of quake, however, does not seem confined to such known parameters and areas of historical and recent seismic disturbance.

Here at the SRRF we find this extremely disturbing, and combined with the sudden flurry of seismic activity apparently on a worldwide scale, would go so far as to suggest a moderate state of global emergency. Something seems to be happening to the world which we cannot understand nor link to any physical activity - earthbound or solar. In short, we are stumped. Suggested courses of action are:

- Intercontinental surveys of known faults and suspected recently discovered fault lines

- Satellite-instigated land and sea surveys to be carried out within the next 36 hours

- Undersea exploration subs to digitally scan recently discovered fault lines or expected fault lines

Please advise ASAP.

Dr Jeremiah Sulokov

CHAPTER 9

THE HUNT

The small black helicopter howled through the storm, rain pounding from its insect-like shell as rotors sliced through the downpour and low-lying storm clouds. Below, dark fields rolled into one and occasionally the chopper skirted a town or village, its lights glowing distantly under the storm's onslaught. Mongrel peered down, trying to work out their location.

'You know where we are?'

Carter, cigarette held in one fist, ignored Mongrel's question as smoke curled up past his face and gathered in the tiny cabin of the chopper. Mongrel scowled, and leant forward to Fenny.

'Where we are?'

'Near Merthyr Tydfil.'

'Is that close to the Sp1_plot?'

'Another couple of minutes. Better get the ropes ready.'

'Roger that.' Mongrel smiled his toothless smile.

'You OK, Carter?'

Carter flashed him a weak smile, then allowed it to drop from his battered face. He dropped his cigarette, crushing its glowing tip under his heavy boot. 'Fuck it, come on.'

They moved into position and each readied their coils of rope, one on each side of the fast attack chopper. Suddenly, Fenny slewed the vehicle around and both Carter and Mongrel stared down into black nothingness. The rotors thumped and the wind howled.

'Out, guys.' Fenny grinned, curls bobbing, and flicked the release.

The doors swung open and Carter and Mongrel dropped their ropes into the darkness. Carter tightened his gloves, and watched Mongrel disappear into the rain and the black.

'You're a good lad, Fenny.'

Fenny nodded, still smiling. 'Send me a postcard, eh, Carter?'

'Where I'm going, you wouldn't want to see the sights.'

Then Carter was gone, dropping down the rope which hissed under his leather gloves. Rain and cold struck through him immediately, making him gasp, and he pulled tight just above the ground, bobbing for a second, then jumping free and landing in a crouch. Trees reared around the two Spiral agents and they found themselves buried in the depths of a storm-darkened forest.

The black chopper leapt into the sky, trailing the fast-ropes and reeling them in as it climbed. Within seconds only the sounds of the storm could be heard, howling and grumbling.

'Which way?'

Mongrel pointed, then stowed away the gentle glow of his ECube.

They set off at a steady but fast run up a steep incline and deeper into the woods. The going was tough under the heavy downpour, the woodland floor slippery and treacherous with mud, branches and a layer of leaf detritus. Dressed all in black, the two Spiral agents dropped to a crouch. Both carried M24 carbines that fired 5.46mm bullets and had MicroX2 mags, which could hold sixty 'compressed' bullets each.

'How far?'

'Three klicks.'

They ran, pushing on through the rain. Darkness swallowed them and occasionally they would halt and check their ECubes, scanning for possible enemy activity. After the quake in London and the sudden re-emergence of Nex soldiers cutting Spiral agents in half as they fled the building, Spiral found itself in a high state of emergency.

The enemy, it would seem, were far from dead.

Carter pointed his carbine into the darkness. Below his clothing nestled his trusty old Browning and within his head squatted thoughts of death and revenge.

They moved at an easier pace now, closing on the SP1_plot in an old abandoned farmhouse. Its walls were overgrown with vines and ferns, the roof long ago fallen in, leaving rubble cascading in terracotta waterfalls across blankets of moss. Mongrel's ECube showed no sign of enemy activity.

Mongrel rose to march ahead, a smile on his face, his head turning – but Carter grabbed him, dragged him back down to the ground and placed his finger against his lips. Mongrel nodded, and slowly Carter eased himself forward on his belly, rolling down his balaclava and allowing himself to blend with the darkened trees and the soft floor of the water-soaked forest.

Inch by inch he moved forward, his eyes and ears alert. After every inch he would halt – check around himself in all directions, listen, make sure of his next small step.

For long minutes he lay in the rain, then edged forward. Wait, move. Wait, move. Wait . . . move . . .

And his sharp eyes saw them.

Nex.

Motionless: waiting, watching. One was perched on a low wall against the farmhouse itself, merging chameleon-like against the tangle of ferns in the gloom. The second crouched just inside the farmhouse doorway, and the third – the hardest to spot – was squatting under a bush beside a tall oak tree which spread out its branches to touch the leaning outer wall of the derelict building.

Fuckers, thought Carter.

'*And even more serious,*' whispered Kade, '*is the fact that the Spiral plot has been compromised. Bubbled. They know the location . . . I wonder if they know you're on your way?*'

Slowly, with murderous care, Carter retreated.

Inch by painful inch—

'What is it?'

'Nex,' said Carter.

'Let's take them . . .'

'Wait. Don't go fucking rushing in there – check the ECube again.' They both watched the tiny face of the electronic cube. Carter tutted when it scanned, again and again, showing no sign of Nex intruders – or of any life whatsoever – in the vicinity.

'Come on, Carter,' growled Mongrel. 'We used to fucking eat these bastards on the SAD missions . . . pile in, blow them to fucking Kingdom Come. No problems . . .'

'This is different,' said Carter.

'How?'

'I can't explain it. Something has changed.'

'You're fucking imagining it – come on!' Mongrel moved forward. Cursing, Carter moved off to one side to provide him with cover. The carbine was slippery in his gloved hands and he checked the safety, nudging the mag to make sure that it was firmly in place.

Mongrel moved forward through the trees.

Carter circled off to the right, putting distance between himself and his comrade, positioning them for an attack on two fronts. He crouched, rubbed rain from his face and eyes, and fought to control his breathing.

He eased himself forward and caught sight of the Nex on the wall. He halted, pacing himself, then heard the blast of Mongrel's carbine sound from the woods as it punched bullets through the door frame.

Carter lifted his own M24. The Nex on the ground jerked its head left, copper eyes staring straight at Carter. It seemed somehow different from the Nex on the SAD missions and those he had met out in Switzerland. It moved with such incredible speed that Carter was still rolling as the bullets from its weapon tore a line of smashed twigs and shredded leaves into the air and cut a vertical stripe up a tree. Carter rolled, his carbine bucking in his gloved hands but the Nex was gone between the trees—

A vanished ghost.

Carter could hear Mongrel's gun. And return fire. Bullets zipped through leaves, slammed into tree trunks.

Carter scrambled right, then sprinted down a small slope and around towards the back of the house, trying to catch sight of the Nex. Then he saw it. Their eyes met and those copper orbs drilled him and he smiled a bitter smile and both their guns roared at once, and Carter felt the breeze of bullets ripping past his face as the carbine barked in his hands and the bullets picked the Nex up, flipping it over to crash into a tree, drilled and bleeding and—

It crawled to its knees and tried to change mags.

Carter sprinted forward, his boot smashing against its face and sending the Nex rolling against the tree's roots. Carter placed his boot on its chest and its head lifted to look at him coolly.

'Luck,' it hissed, its voice soft and asexual, copper eyes glowing.

Carter grinned. 'There's no such fucking thing,' he said, and drilled the Nex's face full of metal.

'Carter!'

Mongrel's voice was tinged with panic. Carter sprinted up the incline and dropped to his belly. He caught the muzzle flash of guns firing from the edge of the house, and crawled forward until he was beside an old, crumbling outbuilding.

The sounds of automatic fire halted.

Carter calmed his breathing, and wiped a speck of blood from the back of his glove.

'Carter!' came the call again. More sub-machine-gun fire – and Carter realised that both Nex had pinned Mongrel down. He sprinted forward, using trees and ferns for cover, past the farmhouse. Mongrel had to be in the shit—

To call Carter's name?

Out loud?

Carter veered right, ducking under tree branches. His carbine juddered in his grip, cutting one Nex in half. The other whirled, and as Mongrel's bullets tore into its chest with metallic blows Carter lifted his M24 and put ten bullets in its head, hammering it to the soft ground where it lay still, blood weeping from its wounds.

Silence fell.

Cordite smoke was smothered by the rain, which fell softly.

Mongrel sprinted to Carter, a look of deep shock on his face.

Carter checked his weapon, then sighted off among the trees, checking for further signs of enemy movement.

'Thanks,' panted Mongrel, fishing for a new magazine in his belt. 'They nearly fucking nailed me.'

Carter said nothing, merely looking off through the rain.

'They much faster than I remember,' muttered Mongrel sombrely. 'I not fucking hit them! Fired whole magazine at them but nothing, not hit one fucking thing . . .'

'Something's definitely wrong,' said Carter softly. 'I can feel it in my bones. We have become complacent . . . but these Nex, they were not some soft target.'

'I'll listen to your advice next time,' said Mongrel.

'Just don't be so fucking eager to jump in boots first, mate. This ain't a fucking game.'

They moved across to the farmhouse, scouting left and right. Standing in the doorway, Mongrel initiated his ECube. This Sp1_plot was a large armoury – as distinct from some of the more moderate stashes that were located in other parts of the world. This was an Sp1_plot specifically used for AA clearance – WarClearance.

There came a distant mechanical noise, a soft whirring sound and the interior of the farmhouse folded free to reveal a wide metal ramp leading down. Mongrel walked down the ramp, boots echoing hollowly on the rain-slick alloy, and Carter followed, carbine ready for action in case of nasty surprises within.

'I've not been here before,' said Mongrel.

'I have . . . before the TankerRuns; me and Jam had a mission – a big Demolition.' He smiled grimly as he was swallowed by the earth and the clever intersections of alloy ramp folded above him to leave the interior of the ruined farmhouse exactly as the two men had found it.

Tooled up with weapons and supplies, Carter moved through the huge alloy bunker and said, 'Mongrel, grab that end of the sheet.' Mongrel obliged, and they hauled the heavy tarpaulin from the Comanche. They stood lost in wonder for a moment as they stared at the machine's matt-dark roughly camouflaged flanks. Missiles were already in place, and Mongrel wheeled a KTM LC7 stealth bike free of its stand and checked the machine for fuel. 'We taking one or two?'

'Two,' said Carter, lighting a cigarette. 'You never know when we might have to split. Double the firepower. And we can still carry plenty of missiles.'

'You really out for fight this time, aren't you?'

'Stakes are fucking high,' said Carter coldly.

They spent a few more minutes checking out the KTM motorcycles, fired them into life a few times and checked the on-board guns and fuel. Then Mongrel hitched the two machines beneath the Comanche as Carter rolled four missiles across the stone floor with a clattering of steel against stone and stood them in the corner, red nose cones menacing in the gloom of the bunker's emergency lighting.

'Weapons of death,' rumbled Mongrel, staring at the missiles with a strange look on his face – a mixture of distaste and pleasure. Carter merely nodded, cigarette held limply between his lips, squinting as the smoke stung his eyes.

Within minutes they were ready. They had checked their carbine magazines and tooled up with extra-*special* weapons, advanced first-aid kits and many other supplies that they thought they might need. Some they

231

stuffed into packs, other equipment they packed into the Comanche.

Climbing on board, they settled into their positions. Carter flicked a few switches and watched the glow of instruments light up in a glittering array. He pulled free his rolled-up balaclava and settled the insect-like HIDSS over his head.

– Battle data initiated, came a soft smooth female voice in his skull.

– All weapon systems primed.

– Targeting sequences aligned.

– Your Comanche is ready for battle.

'Ready for action?' Carter said.

'Always ready,' rumbled Mongrel.

Carter punched a button and above them the interior of the derelict farmhouse folded into a tunnel of alloy panels that cleared them a vertical path. With engines whining, then increasing in pitch to a dull roar, Carter focused on his displays and eased the Comanche up from the ground, nose lifting slightly higher than the tail. Alloy panels passed his vision, followed by the damp moss-covered bricks of the old farmhouse. Then they were up into the dark and the rain.

Behind, the alloy panels fell neatly and precisely back into place.

'Phew . . .' breathed Mongrel, rubbing at his eyes. 'I hate vertical take-off.'

'That's nothing. Look down there.'

Mongrel glanced down – just as distant automatic fire punched through the darkness and bright tracer-round streaks sped towards them.

'Nex?'

'Hmm,' said Carter, arming the mini-gun. Its mechanism whined as it spun into action. Carter lifted the

Comanche up into the broiling dark clouds, where it hovered for a moment. Then it dived, engines howling, towards the dark mass of woodland below and Carter pulled the trigger. Hundreds of heavy-calibre bullets cut and punched through leaves, branches and Nex – bodies were mashed and pulped into the Welsh soil as the Comanche's nose lifted. The dark war machine banked with a howl and sped off into the night, mini-gun smoking and glittering rain-slick rotors thumping with the rhythmical thrumming of precision engineering.

'How many you hit?'

Carter shrugged. 'Not enough. But it'll give the fuckers something to consider as they plan their next move.'

They sped on in silence, the Comanche vibrating with restrained power. Carter guided it south, and within minutes they hit the Bristol Channel, glass-black under the canopy of night. The Comanche dipped low along the coast, coming up over Exmoor and hugging the ground as it sped on at insane speeds. Carter lifted the chopper high through clouds and rain as they passed over the M5, a solid snake of gridlocked traffic, lights stretching off in skeins of immobile metal.

'What's going on down there?'

'Probably a knock-on effect from the quakes . . . is there any sitrep on them?'

Mongrel pulled free his ECube and scanned for a few moments, battered face lit by a ghostly blue. 'London was the most heavily hit – some coincidence, no? A series of quakes smashed across south coast, from Kent to Devon, and also in Manchester and Glasgow . . . fuck, looks to me like most of United Kingdom has been hit . . .'

'What about the rest of Europe?'

Mongrel nodded. 'Lot of seismic activity – Europe

233

affected, Africa, Middle East, Russia, China . . . something very fucking wrong here, Carter.'

'Tell me about it,' Carter said bitterly, picturing Natasha's face.

The Comanche powered on low over the English Channel, across France, Germany, and then to Switzerland. Carter found himself gazing down and remembering events from only a couple of days before when life had seemed so good and he had been complaining about his party lifestyle.

'*You fucking fool,*' mocked Kade.

'Yeah, like I need you to remind me.'

'*And look at the big hero now, rushing off to save Jam . . . you'll end up getting us both killed, Carter, you big pussy. This gig is an arse-fuck and you fucking well know it—*'

'Leave me be.'

'*Don't come crying to me when you're dead in a shell hole with your brain full of Nex metal, just like—*'

Carter frowned at the sudden silence. 'What's wrong? What are you not telling me?'

Kade remained silent, brooding, and then Carter felt him depart. It was like a weight lifted from the inside of his brain.

'You all right?'

Carter glanced round at Mongrel, who was staring at him strangely, concern in his dark eyes. Carter nodded, taking a deep breath and calming his battering heart.

'Yeah, never felt better. We'll be passing near the Kamus soon . . .'

'A wonderful sightseeing opportunity,' snapped Mongrel. 'Just great for the kiddies.'

Carter laughed then, a short sharp bark, and took another deep breath. Tiredness was creeping up on him but he pushed it away. Mongrel was no pilot – and so Carter had to keep going on reserves of adrenalin and energy that he had forgotten he had.

'We need to refuel?'

Carter gazed out, down at the distant mountain that lay below, glittering with ice. 'No. We'll get to Slovenia without a problem – and if we're desperate for fuel there are stocks at the Kamus. Spiral keep an S1_plot there now.'

'So I heard. Not happy about that.'

Carter turned again, helmet tilting sideways. 'You there when the troubles kicked off?'

'*Da.*' Mongrel nodded. 'Me and Slater, and a few others – we found some of the bodies.'

'Was it ever explained?'

'Was it fuck,' snorted Mongrel. 'And even if they'd found out what sent them people crazy, blowing each other's fucking heads off with shotguns, do you think they'd tell us humble squaddies about it? Hah. I spit on the Kamus. It bad place. Carter, there some things in this world we don't understand – we claw our way into space but there still a million secrets here on the planet . . . things we will never understand and never explain. And that mountain, where they build the Kamus complex – it bad place, Carter, real bad place.'

They flew on in silence through glittering clear skies.

Carter landed the Comanche under cover of night, thirty kilometres away from Jam's last recorded ECube coordinate. The rotors spun down, making the surrounding trees thrash wildly, and the air was warm and humid with the promise of a brewing storm.

Engines hissed and clicked, the Spiral agents dumped their kit on the ground and jumped free, and Mongrel unlocked one of the KTMs and wheeled the bike across the grass, kicking its stand into place and placing his hands on his hips. He took several deep breaths and smiled a warm smile.

'I love Europe. I love this place! Smells like home!'

Carter frowned. 'Where exactly *is* home for you, Mongrel?'

'Ahh!' He tapped his nose, dark eyes hooded.

'No, really, where do you come from?'

'Eastern part of Europe.'

'Which country? Europe is a big place.'

'I big guy! Ha! I come from lots of places. Well travelled, you might say. Son of a Thousand States.'

Carter lit a cigarette and rubbed at his tired eyes, drawing deeply on the weed and coughing heavily. 'Like that, is it? Right, I'll get a brew on, then get my head down for an hour . . . I can't remember the last time I slept rather than being simply unconscious. You up for stag?'

'*Da*, Carter, you get some shut-eye. I'll guard.'

Mongrel patted the weapon and glared off into the surrounding trees.

They sat, each with a half-pint mug of sweet tea, a small pan of water bubbling between them on a tiny frame heated by a hexi-block. The Comanche squatted behind them, a terrible dark machine, engines still hot. Around them long grass waved in the wind, and the last dying scents of autumn invaded their nostrils, soothing their souls and transporting their minds – at least temporarily – away from the horrors of the recent earthquakes.

'I need you to tell me about the machine,' said Carter softly, after finishing his fourth cigarette and most of his tea. He dropped in another teabag and five spoons of sugar, and gently poured water from the bubbling pan.

Mongrel, who was still staring off into the trees, his

236

M24 carbine ready for action, gave a small sideways glance at Carter.

'What you need to know?'

'Everything.'

'I already tell you.'

'No,' said Carter, cold eyes fixing on Mongrel's face. '*Fucking* everything.'

Mongrel gave a little laugh, and scratched his cheek with dirt-crusted fingernails. 'Ahh, *fucking* everything. That's different, then.' His face became a little more sombre and he stared off, steaming brew in one hand, other nursing his sub-machine gun. 'We were on SAD mission in Nicaragua – one of world's most active earthquake zones. Odd, that, no? We in northern mountains east of town called Ocotal. We were scoping out a silver mine, where several Nex apparently seen trying to break in one night. It was hot, humid, I was relaxing while Jam was on stag . . . next thing I know I fucking staring straight up at Nex. He look surprised to see us, that for sure, in our little bivvy. Jam took bastard out with single bullet between the eyes. Dropped fucker there on spot while I was still having horny dreams about air hostess on the flight over Caribbean.'

Mongrel sipped at his tea, then reached over and added another two sugars, stirring the brew with a plastic spoon. He grinned at Carter, showing his missing teeth, and said, 'I do like a sweet drop.'

'I can fucking see that. Go on, what happened with the Nex?'

'He was carrying metal sheaves – encoded. We tried to descramble codes on spot, but they were too complex; we took them back to Spiral HQ after mission and Jam got some top guys on job. Took them fucking *month*, and we got call when we were on other job in

New Zealand. When we got back, Jam went into meeting with these guys and afterwards gave us restricted briefing. He said it had gone straight to top within Spiral, and sheaves had been very important find. They had detailed a machine, named the Avelach, which was very, very old.'

'How old?'

'About 10,000 years.'

'That's before all modern civilisation.'

Mongrel nodded. 'I know that. That what confuse us all, because machine very, very complex. Too complex to come from such primitive age – unless there been another civilisation hidden from us, or dating techniques not accurate on substances found.'

Carter sipped his brew, staring off into the warm night darkness.

'Go on.'

Mongrel shrugged. 'All I know, Jam did some missions alone, and on his final one he said he thought he'd found out location of machine. I asked where it was, he gave me cheeky Jam grin and then headed out here for what appears to be his last Search and Destroy mission with TT and Slater . . .'

Carter frowned. 'He *thought* he'd found it? So he hadn't *actually* discovered the location?'

Mongrel shook his head, gaze meeting Carter's. 'It's our best shot, old buddy, our best chance. If anybody know where this machine is, it is Jam.'

'It must be at an old Nex base. After I killed Durell and Feuchter, the Nex had no command structure left; it could be fucking anywhere. Would the normal Nex even understand what the machine was if they had it?'

Mongrel shrugged again.

Carter lay back and closed his eyes, mind working.

238

They sat in silence for a while. Finally, Mongrel said, 'You very down, Carter. Let Mongrel cheer you up.'

'No, no . . . you're OK.'

'No, really, Carter. I have story make you piss pants.'

Carter's eyes fluttered open. Mongrel had yet another half-pint of tea clasped in his mitt and Carter grinned. 'If you drink any more tea then *you*'ll be the one pissing his pants.'

'A man needs tea when he on stag,' said Mongrel seriously. 'Help keep guard awake!'

Carter sighed, and propped himself up on one elbow. He stared at Mongrel, and could feel the malevolence within the huge man: the tension, the violence, the hatred. Mongrel was a psychopath born and bred, a poison-brained fucker of the lowest order, a face-smashing bone-pulping kneecap-breaking spine-tearing dirty low-down son of a bitch. Carter loved him, but also hated him.

'You OK, Carter? You look at me funny.'

'I'll live.' Carter smiled, rubbing at his eyes. Despite his weariness, sleep eluded him.

'That wasn't fucking question,' Mongrel said. 'Listen, I tell you of my wonderful sexual exploits . . .'

'Well, if you really, really, really must,' said Carter uncertainly.

'Har har,' said Mongrel, beaming. He settled back, resting his huge hands on his knees, his eyes dark and yet filled with an inner humour that Carter had rarely seen in this large killer. Carter smiled softly to himself, realising Mongrel's ploy. The psychopath was trying to bring him back down to earth, to cheer him up; to take his mind off the violence to come and the horrors that awaited them . . .

And to sidetrack him from thoughts of Natasha.

'I was stationed in Burma, at Pyinmana. We had great NAAFI, run by some of hottest chicks ever to wear sweaty shorts.'

Carter nodded, hooded eyes half-closed, the weariness of the past days creeping up on him. 'And this is your story of how you bedded all these hot chicks with quirky chat-up lines?' Carter yawned.

'Nah,' chuckled Mongrel heartily. 'It story of how I end up with worst chick in universe. Imagine this, I'm in for quiet drink with Tequila, tall broad-shouldered red-shaved son of bitch, and me and Tequila minding our business, like we always do, not looking for no trouble or nothing like that . . . except for time we threw that man through plate-glass window, yeah, and time Tequila set that woman on fire, but yeah, we minding our own business and Tequila at bar, talking to this fucking hag. I mean, she was *fucking* hag. Bitch-bag of the lowest echelon, har. Tequila comparing tattoos with this bird . . . now, I don't like to labour point, but she was fucking dog, Carter. A fuck-een dog. She was tall, long black hair like rat-diseased barbed wire, big arse like two badly parked Land Rovers. Kara she was called. Hmm . . .' There came a long pause.

Carter rolled his head, easing the tension in his neck. His hand came to rest on his Browning. It was cool and reassuring, battered and yet – perfect. His friend. His comrade in death. His metal lover.

'Yeah, Kara Red,' said Mongrel at last.

Carter propped himself up on one elbow again, momentarily intrigued. 'Red? Strange name?'

'Nickname,' grunted Mongrel, pulling out a packet of cigarettes and offering one to Carter. Carter, with a look of pain, waved the weed away and Mongrel laughed a hearty cruel laugh. He lit up, inhaled deeply and winced as smoke stung his eyes. Gravely, he croaked, 'Kara Red – she'll take you to bed, and fucking bleed on you.'

Carter cringed. 'I wish I'd never asked.'

'That's nothing to what you'll soon fucking wish, mate. Right, so Tequila at the bar, pissed out of his shell, comparing his fucking tattoos with this bitch whose face, Carter – fuck me, it was that bad, putting your fist in it would be doing her favour. It was like she was sucking heifer's arse soaked in vinegar. Like she was being seriously bum-fucked by steroid-pumped Australian donkey. Tequila comparing tattoos—'

'Is this a long story, Mongrel? I'm pretty tired . . .'

'You'll like it. I promise you.'

Carter sighed. 'Go on, then.' He eyed Mongrel's cigarette hungrily.

'I got eighty spare, mate.'

'I've given up. As from now.'

'Only in body, but not in soul.'

'Just tell your fucking story before I change my fucking mind and shoot you.'

'Temper, temper. Tequila comparing tattoos with this death-bitch, they talking about fade and quality of lines and other drunken arsery. I wander over, staggering, sloshing beer down my front like real man should – just as this bitch announce in high-pitched donkey-cackle that she's got tattoo on her big toe.

'"Let's see it," I say, playing with one of my few remaining broken teeth. This Kara goes through this lengthy rigmarole, kicks off her shoes, peels off her blue and black striped tights – class bird, this – and then peels off her sweat-soaked sock to reveal red rose laid delicately across the skin of her large toe, toenail missing, presumed dead. Me and Tequila, we exchange glances, and it a fucking miracle we didn't puke our beer back into our glasses and I peers at her through the old beer goggles and says, "Does it *smell* like rose?"

'This Kara stares back at me, without a hint of humour. "Nah!" she squawks. "It smells like *Stilton*." We reeled at disgust of situation, and as you imagine, outcome was as you expect.'

Carter chuckled. 'You shagged her?'

'*Da.*' Mongrel nodded. 'Nothing wrong with that – when class cheese-bitch offers roll with her Stilton feet, you take it on chin like man and accept it like drunken arse with possibility of no future.'

Carter stared long and hard at Mongrel as the huge ugly ex-squaddie finished his cigarette and immediately lit another, coughing on the blue smoke.

'We live in different worlds, Mongrel.'

'It get worse.'

'How can it fucking possibly get worse?'

Mongrel grinned. Most of his teeth were missing. Carter often wondered how he chewed, but every foodstuff imaginable simply slid into Mongrel's gaping maw and disappeared without any apparent need for mandibles. Steak never caused him a single problem. Bacon was shredded with ease.

'Well, I'm shagging this Kara, right, and she really going for it – sweaty arse high in air, me on my back, her tits wobbling like jellies in dark above my face. She pumping me like fucking milking machine and moaning and screeching like mangling of badly meshed tank gears. I thinking I proper king, despite her smell, but then – and this gross even me out, mate – she farts: proper evil-stinking cloud of poisonous mustard gas that engulf fucking room like fucking nuclear winter.'

'Mongrel, that is *bad.*'

'It get worse,' Mongrel threatened for the second time.

'How . . . no, no, just finish the story and then I can get my head down.'

'Har. Well, this Kara Red, she shit all over me.'

A silence followed.

Carter stared hard at Mongrel.

'*Really?*'

'*Da.*'

'She, like, shit. All over you?'

'*Da.*' Mongrel beamed, and smoked his cigarette.

'Did this bother you?'

'*Kanyechno*. I threw her down stairs.'

'Is that the end of the story?'

'Pretty much.'

'Mongrel, you're a fucking animal – but I concede, Kara Red was, shall we say, a thousand times worse.'

'She change her name to Kara *Brown* after that. After she got casts taken off her legs. But then, at least it gave her opportunity to air her fucking Edam feet.'

'Stilton.'

'Whatever.'

Carter finally managed to catch an hour's sleep. He awoke groggily, Mongrel passed him another cup of tea, and he resigned himself to a smoke.

'You see anything?'

'It's as dead as a croaked beetle out there.'

They packed up their gear and, several hours before dawn, set out on the KTM LC7 bikes with stealth mode engaged. Carter rode one machine, Mongrel the other. The bikes left the fields and woods leading down from the deserted hilltop and joined up with narrow tarmac tributaries, each side dusted with gravel and loose stone and spreading off into moonlit fields. A river flowed to their left and they cruised along in silence without lights,

Mongrel with his M24 gun across his lap and holding onto the KTM with one hand, eyes focused and looking for trouble.

They travelled the dark roads for an hour, only passing a couple of cars – a Mercedes and a Skoda – which they skimmed past in silent dark blurs. Finally, leaving the roads behind, they headed up dirt trails until they finally pulled the bikes off the tracks and rode, standing on foot pegs, over rough ground until they halted the machines on hissing Brembos and killed the hot engines.

They cammed up the KTM stealth machines with ferns and branches. Then Mongrel checked his ECube and they moved off through the gently rustling trees, packs shouldered and M24 sub-machine guns at the ready, proceeding patiently – and with care. As if their lives depended on it.

Which they did.

'There.'

Carter squinted at the distant cabin and allowed his breathing to ease. He pulled out his Browning and checked the mag for the hundredth time, then flicked free the safety on the carbine.

'You sure?'

'Yeah.'

'You cover me . . .'

Carter moved forward, and Mongrel rocked back on his heels, squinting around in the pre-dawn glow. Carter approached the rough-walled cabin warily, weapon ready for action, mind screaming abuse and firing him into a full adrenalin state . . . he reached the doorway and dropped to a crouch, glancing back at Mongrel who was covering arcs of fire.

'*You need at least three men for this,*' chastised Kade.

'You offering your services?'

'*Well, you know what they say: if the going gets tough—*'

'Then Kade gets going?'

'*Fuck you, Carter.*'

'Temper, temper, little man.'

Carter moved warily into the cabin. It was deserted and he moved cautiously through the rooms, but his sharp eyes could see nothing. He was just turning to leave when he saw it – a tiny square of glass missing from the window. An ideal size and position for a—

'*Mindnuke,*' said Kade.

'Hmm.'

Carter touched the edges of the hole; they were perfectly smooth and had obviously been sucked by an ECube ready for MNK insertion. And an MNK meant . . .

Nex.

Carter returned to Mongrel. 'He was here.'

'Fucker, I fucking knew it. They should burn those PopBot scouts. They're a waste of fucking time!'

'The question is, what happened next?'

'No other signs?'

Carter scanned the surrounding countryside, and shook his head. 'No, nothing obvious. Come on, I'm going to have to do some tracking the old-fashioned way . . .'

It took Carter an hour to pick up the trail. The sun was rising steadily in the sky, making both men feel uneasy.

Carter pointed. 'You see it?'

'See what?'

'Look closely.'

'What at?'

Carter sighed. 'Boot imprint – Spiral issue. They were

245

fucking here all right, and running in that direction.'
Carter pointed with the muzzle of his carbine.

'Come on.'

'Wait . . . slowly, Mongrel. These things take time. And let's not forget the DemolSquad's recent fucking disappearance.'

They moved cautiously through the woodland, from tree to tree. Stopping, checking distances, checking other trees and foliage for signs of passing. Occasionally they risked a scan with the ECube, but knew now not to trust the device at all . . . it seemed that the Nex were playing their covert games once again and had access to digital superiority.

Carter crouched beside a tree with strange markings in the bark. 'Something big, heavy and metal hit this.'

'Like what?'

Carter shrugged, 'A bike, something like that. I tell you, Mongrel, some bastard has tried hard to cover this up – there should be fucking tracks everywhere. And look – even metal particles have been removed from the trunk.'

'Could it have been Jam's bike?'

'I'm not sure. But it looks like we're going in the right direction.'

They squatted in a clump of thick bushes where the valley dropped off to one side. They watched for several hours as the sun toiled across the sky. A cooler wind blew from the south but it did little to relieve them of the sweat drenching their thick clothing.

Carter had pointed out the bridge leading over the valley, with rocks clustered at either end. They had spent a good hour watching the small log cabin down in the valley bottom, but had seen no activity at either location.

246

'I think we at dead end,' said Mongrel eventually.

Sweating beneath the bushes, prickled and poked and uncomfortable, Carter pulled free his ECube and activated the tiny black alloy device. Lights flashed in his eyes and audio signals blipped.

'That's . . . strange.'

'What?' Mongrel shuffled closer, smelling of fallen leaves.

'Neither the bridge nor the cabin appear on the ECube. They're invisible to the scanners . . .' Carter shook the alloy device.

'Yeah, that always work for me – four billion dollars' worth of development technology fail to function so give the little fucker shake. Kicks it up its arse good.'

'I don't understand,' muttered Carter. Then he killed the tiny device and glanced out from their shelter.

'You want go look?' asked Mongrel cautiously, staring into the valley, his eyes straining to detect movement.

Carter nodded.

'I think we wait for nightfall,' growled Mongrel. 'I think good idea we sit back, wait, then get closer look without sun bouncing off our guns to give away our position, eh, Carter? *Carter?*'

Mongrel turned.

Carter had gone.

'Fucker!'

Mongrel crawled from beneath the prickling bushes to see Carter gliding towards the rocks shielding the bridge; he dropped down and disappeared. Mongrel eased his own bulk forward, keeping trees and bushes to his right – until he finally stopped in a good spot and glanced all around, nervous now, licking sweat from his lips.

He glanced around for Carter, but could not see the man.

'Mad fucker,' he grumbled. 'Why we not wait for night? You get us both shot!'

And then he saw Carter – underneath the bridge, fastened as if by magnets and moving beneath the thick wooden boards which stretched out between the two horizontal iron H-section supports.

'What he doing?'

And then Mongrel saw the dull glint of a machine-gun nest – just a hint. It lay concealed among the rocks and he caught a fleeting glimpse of black – a barrel sleeve with drilled holes for cooling during firing. It could be nothing else . . . and it was positioned in a brilliant natural defensive location overlooking the only way to cross the valley:

The bridge.

'What you doing, Carter? You get yourself fucking drilled!'

But Carter was committed and, eyeing the bridge, Mongrel knew that he himself had neither the skill to negotiate the structure in the way that Carter was doing nor the strength to sustain his own body weight for such a lengthy climb.

I need to lose bit of weight. If I survive that long, he added to himself.

Sweat rolled into Carter's eyes like acid and he blinked as it stung him. He licked his dry lips and found a fresh handhold, moving over another few inches beneath the thick ancient timbers of the bridge.

The temperature beneath the bridge was high, the air humid, stagnant. And he couldn't reach his water canteen. *Bitch.*

Slowly, Carter advanced, his mind switching between images of Natasha lying supine in the hospital bed with tubes emerging from different parts of her body, pictures

248

of the baby on the scan imager – a tiny white blob against a background of glossy black, barely distinguishable as head, torso, arms and legs but miraculous nevertheless – and then to Jam's smiling, cocky, mischievous face, stubbled, a dangling loose cigarette, and holding the coordinates for the machine that could save both Carter's woman and their child.

The wood above him was bleached by the Slovenian sun; it creaked occasionally and tried continually to spit dust into Carter's upturned face.

He moved on in this inverted crawl, inch by painful inch, boots tucking into crevices, fingers finding holes and gaps, muscles screaming at him.

Don't blow your position, warned his brain.

But another part of him, the shell inhabited by Kade, wanted to rush in with guns blazing and kill everybody, slaughter them like sheep. But then, what did *he* want? He wasn't even sure what he was looking for any more . . . surely anybody who had covered their tracks so well out in the woods wouldn't leave Jam's body or his KTM motorcycle lying casually around?

And then he heard it.

A low engine rumble.

No, he cursed. It can't fucking be!

But it was: a truck, a big eight-tonne vehicle with heavy off-road tyres and a canvas roof. It approached with a steady growl and a meshing – a thrashing – of gears and Carter worked harder, moved faster, but realised—

He could not beat the truck.

'Son of a bitch.'

He heard the vehicle drop two gears, its engine pitch increasing on the slight incline before the bridge – and then twin heavy thumps as the front tyres mounted the span. They clattered across the thick wooden beams, and

Carter was almost knocked from his perch by the initial crashing impact. He gritted his teeth, tightened his muscles, and prayed . . .

The truck's six rear wheels slammed onto the bridge.

The whole structure started to vibrate.

Badly.

Carter felt a shout welling in his throat as the truck's wheels bludgeoned the wood and vibrations pulsated through his arms and legs. Dust and dirt poured down into his face, causing him to cough and choke. Spitting, Carter glanced down at the terrible drop beneath him—

The shaking and battering seemed to last for ever.

It pounded him like a piece of metal between a hammer and an anvil.

It felt like a train rolling over his head.

And then it was gone.

Carter choked back a sneeze and cursed, his eyes slits of anger, and then continued his horizontal climb with fingers and arms burning, his Browning digging into his ribs. He finally reached the side and swung himself onto the tiny narrow ledge underneath the bridge, panting. Then, climbing around the iron struts, he pulled himself up a little, peered around, hoisted himself up onto the rocks and leapt into the tiny protected circle of the machine-gun nest.

It was small and circular, sand scattered on the floor. The large T80 Heckler & Koch heavy machine gun sat on a tripod pointing out across the open expanse of bridge and was manned by a—

A merc?

Human.

Carter grinned at the sudden surprised and horrified look on the man's bearded face. He slammed his fist into the soldier's nose – twice, three times, splattering blood across the sand and pounding the man into unconsciousness. Carter peered out from the back of the machine-gun nest, grinning fiercely as he saw Nex dismounting neatly from the back of the truck that had tried to dislodge him and send him tumbling into the valley. Grunting, he dragged the tripod across the sand, checked the belt of ammunition, and levelled the T80 out of the back of the machine-gun nest. The Nex had assembled in ranks of eight – twenty-four in all – and they stood to attention with weapons by their sides, their copper eyes focused.

Carter waited, his own eyes bright, picturing Natasha . . .

And he remembered the Nex outside the Spiral HQ as the quake pulverised London – murdering the innocent, fleeing Spiral operatives, men and women, without remorse or even a flicker of emotion. To Carter, the situation had looked suspiciously like a trap.

The Nex outside the truck were joined by more of their kind, mixed with a few mercenary soldiers. 'Sorry, boys,' muttered Carter, feeling himself go cold and dead inside. 'You're fighting on the wrong fucking side . . . hope the money tasted good and you spent it well.'

He opened fire.

The T80 roared and bucked beneath his hands as a hail of bullets flew across the narrow stretch of land, mowing down the Nex in a swathe of bloodied flesh.

Some reached for weapons.

Some turned to sprint—

Some leapt.

All were pulped by the onslaught of the heavy machine gun.

Scythed down.

Slaughtered.

Bullets slammed into the rear of the truck, puncturing

all six rear tyres in tiny deflating explosions. The vehicle settled slowly down.

Carter released the trigger and his pent-up breath and surveyed the destruction with a cold eye. He heard a moan from the mercenary at his feet, looked down, saw the man struggling with his own SA1000 and palmed his Browning, placing a single shot in the contract soldier's brains. The merc crumpled back, eyes glassy and staring. Carter sighed and shook his head.

He suddenly felt sick of death. Sick of killing. Sick of slaughter.

'*Don't be a pussy,*' said Kade.

'I'm just tired.'

'*Don't be so soft – people trying to slot each other in a fun-filled military scenario is what makes a human* human; *it's what sets us apart from animals . . . it's what makes life so fucking worth living.*'

'Not for me.'

'*Want to bet?*'

Warily, gripping his M24 carbine, Carter stepped away from the machine-gun nest. He could hear the truck's engine, still idling with a low grumble and spitting exhaust fumes. Boots pounded the bridge behind him and he whirled low – to see Mongrel's face looming into view. Carter returned to cover the compound in front of him with his weapon.

'I hear heavy gunfire – what fuck happened?' Mongrel stumbled to a halt. '*Bozhey moy!*' he whispered, surveying the carnage.

Carter lit a cigarette.

'You kill them all?'

'Let's find out.'

Covering opposing arcs of fire, Carter and Mongrel moved warily forward, halting and staring at the

252

compound across which they had stumbled while on Jam's trail. The buildings were all fashioned from wood, some painted in brown, a couple in dull blue. They were raised on low piles and beneath each hut was a dark and gloomy patch of dead ground. There were ten huts, set out in a semicircle in a natural hollow. Rough vegetation grew between the decrepit old buildings, and many walls had been badly patched with crooked joinery.

'A good place to defend,' said Mongrel, his gun pointing from building to building.

Carter nodded, drawing heavily on his cigarette. 'This is an old Second World War barracks or camp,' he said. 'I've seen pictures of this place before . . .'

'Used by?'

'The Nazis.' Carter smiled bitterly. 'How fucking fitting.'

They moved through the camp, clearing the buildings one at a time but each knowing instinctively that they were alone. The Nex were not the sort of enemy to set up camp and hide – in battle they were fearless and would not squat in a building waiting to be discovered. They would attack . . .

Happy that they were finally alone, Carter moved to the truck while Mongrel moved over and nudged one of the Nex corpses with his boot. 'By fuck, they stink . . .'

'You think *they* smell bad? You should have tried the TankerRuns,' said Carter, reaching into the idling truck's cab and killing the engine. Silence settled across the camp and Carter shivered. 'A million rotting diseased bodies . . . now *that* was a fucking smell. Christ, this place is awful – you can feel it in your bones. It has a *bad* history.'

'Yeah. Come on, we need to find out where they took Jam . . .'

'If he's still alive.'

'Yeah, if he's still alive.'

Most of the wooden huts were empty, or had nothing but simple camp beds and the most basic of equipment. One stood out as the obvious HQ and had many locked cabinets and high-tech computer equipment – which appeared out of place against the ancient and rotting surroundings.

They searched the HQ and used Mongrel's ECube as a SecScanner, flicking free digital locks and hijacking the computer systems to allow access to hidden files. After thirty minutes of snooping, Mongrel slumped back in a chair and wiped a fine sheen of sweat from his forehead.

'It's all fucking financial data,' he said at last, confused.

'Yeah, food supplies, stone and cement prices, exchanges of stock for things like diesel and LVA fuel.'

'Have you scanned these?'

Carter shook his head. On the desk were several thin metal sheets, with encoded data pitted in their surfaces. Mongrel idly ran the ECube over them and projected a digital beam onto the nearest wall.

Figures flooded the surface in eerie blue as the ECube decoded: columns and rows of numbers and data.

'More buying and selling,' said Mongrel.

'Wait.'

'What?'

Carter peered through the figures, the beams of the projected blue light cutting neatly through his cigarette smoke. 'Look, the third column details the transfer of titanium-carbide drill bits. And the fifth is cooling oil, used in drilling.'

'So?'

'This looks like equipment for mining – oil or . . . LVA?'

'This irrelevant to us, Carter.'

'No, look at the digital stamp and the signature. Director General Oppenhauer, Commissioner for the Fuel Inspectorate of Eastern Europe. He's the guy who inspects all the new LVA drilling operations that have been opening in Eastern Europe – why would he be authorising sales, purchases and transfers of this equipment? And what the fuck have the Nex got to do with LVA?'

Mongrel shook his head. 'Maybe after Feuchter and Durell were killed the Nex signed on as mercenaries. Maybe they protect places like this and you just machine-gunned a load of innocent merc soldiers.'

'It's still illegal to employ a Nex, ever since Spiral shut down the original operation decades ago. An abomination against God, one politician called it, although in my humble opinion all fucking politicians are fucking abominations against God themselves. Just by their very natures.' He grinned sourly.

'What connection then?'

Carter scratched at his stubble. 'Not sure, Mongrel, not sure . . . what could the Nex possibly want with LVA? It's just a fucking fuel – sure, they could make money out of it but . . . you make money out of lots of things.'

'Maybe they funding another war . . .'

Carter met Mongrel's stare. 'Doesn't even bear thinking about,' he said softly. 'Come on, I don't think we're going to find anything here to do with Jam – we're at a dead end. We should go down and check out that second log cabin – maybe he spotted another nest of Nex there.'

'Yeah, and those dead Nex you kill, they stink.'

'Lead the way.'

'After you, Mr Carter,' said Mongrel, a glint in his dark eyes. 'This looks like your gig now.'

★

It was late evening and Carter halted beside the truck. Mongrel nearly stumbled into the back of him.

'Don't fucking move, and don't make a fucking sound,' said Carter.

'What is it?'

Carter rolled his eyes. 'There's a sniper up on the hill . . .' He eased free his Browning whilst his visible hand dangled free, holding the M24 carbine. His left hand disguised by Mongrel's bulk, he turned his body slightly, an easygoing smile on his face as his head turned and—

The Browning flashed up.

And Carter began firing . . .

The cliffside was steep, rocky, scattered with bushes and a few tiny clinging trees. Bullets whined, spitting dust from rock and thudding into vegetation. A scream echoed, followed by, 'Stop! Stop!'

Carter, dropping his M24 to the hard-packed ground, ejected the Browning's mag and slotted another in its place. Mongrel lifted his carbine and covered the hillside. Carter took the Browning in both hands and sighted down the short barrel.

'Throw out your weapon,' he bellowed.

There came a short pause, and a rifle with a telescopic sight attached sailed through the air and landed on the hard ground with a clatter. Then a woman stood up, waving weakly, one hand to her shoulder where blood was visible, seeping between her fingers.

'You hit her,' said Mongrel.

'Good.'

'But it's a woman . . .'

'Good.'

'But she . . .'

'Yeah? She could still have put a round in the back of

256

your fucking dumb-skull head. Mongrel, you've always been a dickhead when it came to women – go on, help her down and I'll cover you.'

Mongrel moved forward, warily, as the woman scrambled down the steep cliffside and slipped, rolling and sliding the last twenty feet to hit the ground hard. She sat up, covered in dust, coughing. She had a sweet oval face, perfectly unblemished skin, and thin blonde hair tied back into a ponytail. She wore rugged outdoor clothing with natural colours designed to blend with her surroundings. And blood was pouring from her shoulder.

Casting around, eyes and ears alert, scanning the rest of the hillside, Carter followed even more carefully and watched Mongrel help her to her feet.

'Who are you?'

'Please don't kill me.' Her English was good, but laced with a heavy accent.

'That depends on your answers.'

The woman's gaze moved to the truck, and the pile of Nex. 'Oh,' she said, eyes riveted on the carnage, the strewn limbs, the gaping maws, the strings of flesh.

She peered into Carter's face. 'You kill them all?'

'Yes. Now answer the fucking question or you'll be next on the fucking pile . . .'

'Carter!' snapped Mongrel, frowning.

'My name is Mila. I work for a small unit called the SVLA who seek to kill those . . .' she gestured. 'They have invaded us, our country, they have camps all over the world . . . and they killed my brother . . .'

'So you were going to pick them all off with your little pea-shooter?'

'No, I was just observing, watching them come and go. You have done a job for us all . . . I cannot believe you spotted me.'

257

Carter ignored her, turned, and moved to the rifle. It was old, polished, well cared for. More like a family heirloom than a working weapon. Carter threw it to Mongrel, who caught it in one huge hand and looked at the scratched stock.

'She survive?'

'I need few minutes to clean wound,' said Mongrel. 'Luckily, your round tore through muscle and not shatter bone. Lucky your fucking aim was out.'

'There was a bush in the way.' Carter grinned. 'Now, come on, we need to move out . . . we need to get away from this place. You can sort her out in the woods.'

'Why are you here?' asked Mila, her features screwed in pain but her teeth clenching as if trying to put on a brave face.

'We're looking for somebody.'

'Mongrel, you dick!'

'What fucking harm, Carter? She might have seen something! She say herself she been sat watching the Nex . . . maybe she see our friends? Yes?' He glanced towards Mila, who was nodding.

'A man? Short dark hair, short beard, travelling with a real big man and a woman?'

Mila looked nervously from Carter to Mongrel, and then back again.

'Yeah.' Carter nodded, eyes suddenly wide. 'You saw them? Here?'

'Here,' said Mila softly, blood running between her fingers.

Carter ignored her obvious pain. 'Had they been captured?'

'The first man had, yes. They beat him – kicked him when he was on the ground. But the others . . .'

'Yes?'

258

'They loaded their bodies into the back of a truck. Like that one. With dark grey motorcycles.'

'Gotta be them,' breathed Mongrel. 'Fuck . . . that means Slater and TT dead. Fuck. What did they do with man who still alive? One they beat?'

'They took him to the Kataja Quarry. I could show you . . .'

'How do you know this?'

'I followed. I was gathering information, remember? Watching them. But I couldn't go too close, these people – with the copper eyes – they are crawling all over the place. It is far too risky for me to approach the quarry itself.'

'How far is it?'

'About fifty kilometres from here.'

'Come on, let's get back to the bikes – we can sort out her wound and plan our route.' Carter turned and allowed Mongrel to help the woman along the dirt road behind him.

They passed the pile of Nex corpses and Carter did not look down.

They were nothing more than dead meat.

Reaching the bridge they stepped out onto the wide thick timbers. Carter turned, gesturing to Mongrel to check his weapon, when he saw something, a glint – a change – in Mongrel's eyes. His head snapped round to see, at the entrance to the bridge, a *creature* . . . it was a good head over six feet tall, with a huge neck and a face from a nightmare. It had twisted, drooling fangs and small copper eyes – and torched black skin, as if this *thing* had been burnt. The body was heavily muscled and bare from the waist up – but from the lower abdomen black armour merged with flesh and scattered in irregular glinting panels down its groin and legs. Long claws extended

259

from thick black fingers and Carter stared in horror as the figure sighted him—

And seemed to smile.

Like a bad drug-induced dream his words came back to haunt him. 'Next time, fucker,' he had snarled . . . and suddenly his show of bravado didn't seem like such a good idea.

'*My name is Dake, and I'll be waiting for all eternity.*'

Unfortunately, this particular eternity hadn't actually lasted that long.

It had come around much quicker.

Carter swallowed hard.

'What is it?' yelled Mongrel, his carbine lifting—

And then they realised that the creature carried a weapon.

It opened fire, heavy boots pounding swiftly across the bridge towards them, saliva pooling from the twisted deformed mouth and bullets hammering from the sub-machine gun it carried—

They turned and dived for the protection of the machine-gun nest, rolling into temporary safety. But before they could do anything there came a crunch of boots on rock and the creature was staring down at them, twisted jaws working silently—

'Carter,' it hissed.

Carter's M24 opened fire and the Nex was punched backwards from the rocks under a hail of bullets. The gun yammered in Carter's hands until he released the trigger; the explosions echoed around the valley, fading rapidly, and in the silence that then fell Carter glanced at Mongrel.

'It fucking *knows* you?' Mongrel scowled.

'Long story.'

'I hope you just killed it.'

'Don't fucking bank on it.'

Carter poked his head warily from the confines of the machine-gun nest. Then, followed closely by Mongrel and Mila, he stepped onto the packed earth of the road—

A roar erupted from the opposite side of the rocks.

Carter calmed his breathing.

'Go on, then,' said Mongrel.

Carter glanced back at him and smiled grimly. 'Cheers, mate,' he said. 'Why don't *you* go first?'

'I ain't going first,' mumbled Mongrel. I got fucking wounded woman to look after . . .'

Carter moved forward – and the ScorpNex attacked, slapping Carter's sub-machine gun out of the way with a heavy claw. The gun skittered along the dry road. Carter ducked a heavy blow and whirled low, skipping backwards . . .

'You remember me, little man?'

'I could never forget a face like that,' snapped Carter dryly.

Again it leapt at Carter with awesome speed, and he dodged a blow, swaying to one side and then skipping out of the huge ScorpNex's way. Suddenly it whirled on Mongrel, and with a mighty blow sent him flying backwards to land on his back, blood flooding from his nose. Carter charged as Dake whirled—

He slammed his fist three times into the creature's nightmarish face, heavy smashing right hooks, then ducked low under a double whirling slash of the creature's massive claws. He dodged left and hammered a side-kick to the ScorpNex's chest – but the impact had little effect and the creature grabbed Carter's leg. It launched him through the air to land heavily on the ground where he bounced and rolled to a halt. Carter uncurled, stood smoothly and drew his Browning, snarling.

He started shooting.

The ScorpNex took five bullets – flinching with each impact – by the time it reached Carter, but had managed to sidestep five more. It struck the gun from Carter's grip and blood splashed his face and arms as it grabbed him by the head in both heavy claws and lifted him from the ground. Carter gasped, the pressure pounding through his brain, but he lifted both boots smoothly and with his heels he hammered the ScorpNex's face once, twice, three, four, five, six, seven times until he felt its fangs and then its jaw crack—

It dropped Carter—

Who sprinted towards the bridge. In a second the ScorpNex was after him, bounding along almost on all fours, heavy arms and claws lowered to help drag its twisted frame along the ground. Carter sped out onto the bridge and the ScorpNex was right behind him. He knew then that he could not outrun the creature. It was faster and stronger and infinitely more powerful than a mere human . . .

'*Let me have him* . . .'

'*I will burn him* . . .'

'*I will fuck him* hard . . .'

Carter fumbled in his webbing, pulled free an HPG – a chemical grenade – and dropped it onto the bridge, where it rolled for a moment, awaiting the initiation burst. Dake leapt at Carter who dodged a heavy blow, smashing a fist into Dake's battered face where Carter's boots had already wrought serious damage. Carter evaded another blow, then a third and he was backing away across the bridge's beams as he counted—

And initiated the HPG sequence with a mental impulse from an implanted augmentation.

262

The HPG exploded and Carter caught the edge of the blast. It picked him up and threw him down the bridge, where he landed tumbling, limbs flailing, and rolled to a confused halt. The ScorpNex was flung, twisting and thrashing, against the heavy iron struts of the bridge, crushing bones and snapping one thick iron beam which sagged, its supporting bolts severed.

A ragged hole appeared in the timbers of the bridge, four metres in diameter, its edges splintered with thick daggers of wood. The valley lay below the hole – a distant expanse of greenery.

Silence seemed to reign for a moment—

'Carter!'

Mongrel was sprinting as Carter rolled to his knees and coughed, spitting and heaving onto the beams beneath him. He took a deep breath, calming himself from the sudden explosion of violence, blood streaming from his nose and ears. Then he climbed shakily to his feet and started to jog back towards the jagged hole and the prostrate figure of the ScorpNex.

Is it dead? he thought.

It just took a fucking HPG blast . . .

It *must* be dead . . .

There came a crackling of chitinous armour.

Slowly, the ScorpNex uncurled and climbed to its feet.

The blast had sliced a layer from the side of its face, arm and torso, and one eye was mangled, hanging against its black armoured cheek. Its claw moved to its side and there was blood and gore there too – from the incredible impact with the bridge's iron strut. But it pulled itself to its full height and a deep-throated chuckle rolled out across the bridge.

Carter faltered but his face set in a grim line. He knew he had to finish this thing and finish it now. He accelerated towards the ScorpNex, blood coating his face in a violent demon mask. The creature suddenly dropped to a crouch and leapt forward powerfully to meet Carter head on.

CHAPTER 10

WORLDSCALE

Jam dreamed.

'You killed them.'

He stared at Nicky's face. Tears flowed down her red-puffed cheeks and he hung his head in shame, staring at his scuffed boots, then rubbed at his face and looked up again.

The accusation in her eyes felled him more easily than any bullet.

'It wasn't me,' he said softly, his own tears flowing.

'You even killed the fucking children,' she snarled. She stepped forward and hit him then, a heavy right uppercut that made him rock. He absorbed the punch, eyes staring down, and tried to explain but everything swirled in his brain and his thoughts were clouded, sluggish, confused.

'You ripped them apart.'

'It wasn't me!'

'You tore off the children's faces, you fucking bastard, I saw it, saw it all . . . and you will rot in hell for what you have done . . .'

Jam's head jerked up. His eyes suddenly narrowed, and

he lashed out, claw slicing through Nicky's neck and ripping her from collarbone to breastbone with a sickening wet crunch of torn flesh and crackles of snapping tendon and gristle. Her body peeled apart in two segments that hit the ground dead, without making a sound. Her blood pooled out and her eyes grew glazed, staring blankly at the wall. Jam's head tilted to one side, staring at her in contemplation and he reached out to nudge her separate halves with his foot.

Jam awoke in the dark. He was crying. The chamber was cool and that pleased him, the chill on his flesh soothing his raging mind. He shifted, awkwardly, joints stiff as he rolled to his feet with clacks of armour. His head tilted and he could feel saliva pooling in his mouth, between jaws that would not close properly—

But then—

That was him, wasn't it? He had always been this way.

He moved to a wide bowl of water and stared down through the gloom at his gently swaying reflection. His small copper eyes took in the patches of black – almost as if it was scorched – armour on his face, twisting and merging with raw pink flesh. His jaws worked continuously, tiny movements almost as if he was chewing, and he could feel his back teeth grinding together.

Remember?

And he remembered the woman from his dream.

She had been crying.

Why? he thought.

The children he'd killed – they'd been nothing more than fresh meat, the meat of the enemy. They would have grown into soldiers and come looking for the Nex with guns and death – it had been a simple extermination process. In the same way that you would step on an insect . . .

Jam frowned, his mind spinning.

He could still see the look of pain in the dream-woman's eyes, and it confused him. She knew him; but he could not remember her name and that was strange. It burned him . . .

Her pain.

Jam curled up and sleep claimed him quickly in a black embrace.

Durell stared down at the map, its glow softly illuminating his disfigured face. Colours glittered across this synthetic microcosmic world and Durell nodded to himself, small tongue darting out to lick his dry lips.

He felt . . . nervous.

Things were coming together.

Plans were merging.

And he could feel the shifting of power.

Spiral, he thought.

He felt Gol enter the room behind him and he tensed a little. He laughed softly to himself, revelling in the knowledge that Gol was Nex, a slice of Nex, but not quite a pure-breed.

Not so Jam.

No. Durell smiled. Jam had turned out a thousand times more pure than he could ever have dreamed possible. Jam had proved himself to be beyond reproach . . . a true Nex . . . true *ScorpNex*—

'It failed,' said Gol.

Durell turned, unable to read the emotion in Gol's expression.

'So be it. We were lucky with Jam; the ScorpNex protocol is extremely difficult to replicate and it will take time. However, with Jam's conversion I am pleased that we have yet another general willing to die for our cause.'

'Yes.'

'Gol, I believe you had a little chat with Kattenheim?'

'Yes. He—' Gol smiled. 'He does not quite believe that I am with you. He doubts my loyalty, I think.'

'Ignore him. Kat always did overreact. But he is strong and powerful and fast – don't antagonise him unduly because I need you both with me.'

Gol gave a single nod.

'What are your thoughts on Natasha?'

'It is a very sad day,' said Gol carefully. 'She is my daughter and I love her. But she has chosen her own road in life. She has chosen Spiral and she has chosen to die for Spiral . . . I cannot protect her for ever. She is her own person now.'

'Very philosophical. Now.' Durell's hand came out, resting on Gol's shoulder. Gol looked deep into those slitted copper eyes and sensed that Durell was waiting for a reaction: a glimmer of horror or disgust or revulsion—

Gol forced his face to remain calm, unmoving.

'I have a job for you. A delivery.'

'The Foundation Stones?'

'Yes, four of them. I want you to go with Kattenheim and Jam, make the delivery and check their installations. Then we can work on links to the QHub and initiate the QEngine with its final settings.'

'Is the army mobilised?'

'Nex soldiers are on the move,' said Durell softly. 'The pieces of the jigsaw are slotting neatly into place.'

Gol nodded again. He understood.

The small black chopper piloted by Kattenheim came in low over the desert, swirling a dust storm in its wake, the thudding of its rotors echoing over the vast flat plain. Rocks loomed from the shifting sand dunes and Kat brought the chopper down with swift precise movements. The blades spun down whining as Gol leapt out onto the flat rocks, closely followed by Jam who shielded his eyes with an armoured black forearm.

Grabbing a pack, Kat followed and the three of them stood on the desert sand. They gazed at the twenty Nex who had spilled from low wooden barracks to meet them, sub-machine guns at the ready. One of them came forward and saluted.

Kat returned the salute. 'Are events progressing?'

'They are,' came the sibilant, asexual voice. 'We have been expecting you.'

They walked across the sand-blown rocks under the beating sun. Gol could see a massive pen where perhaps a hundred huge trucks were parked. As they moved past the rocks the true scale of this particular encampment opened up in front of him – there were a thousand hastily constructed wooden barracks containing perhaps thirty thousand Nex in all. The desert camp during this hour of the day was quiet, with only a few Nex scouts running errands – it was at night, during the cooler hours, when it truly came alive.

Entering a wooden cabin, where fans cooled the dry desert air, Kat moved immediately to a table filled with maps. Gol stood, waiting, and looked occasionally at Jam.

This new ScorpNex – a Skein Blending of a man he had once known – had shown no recognition. Years earlier Gol had scripted several missions with Jam – in their younger and wilder days – but this transformation, this blending seemed to have eyes and mind for one thing and one thing only: combat – combat leading to death and destruction.

'What do you think?'

Jam turned, small copper eyes staring at Gol, and Gol resisted the urge to take a step back. Jam's huge shoulders rolled as he moved and turned and stared out over the desert.

'Too hot,' he rumbled.

'No, the scale of the Nex.'

'There are many,' Jam said, drooling long strings to the wooden boards. 'They put up good fight when the time comes – they put up good kill.'

'And that time may be sooner than you think,' said Kat, rejoining them and smiling grimly. 'We got some nosy fucking Americans in an armoured column advancing a few kilometres to the west – I think we need to go and give them a taste of our power.'

'I thought we were under orders to avoid conflict until the time had come?'

'The time is here and now,' said Kattenheim softly, his red eyes alive. 'Durell has given the order. From this point forward we are Active.'

Kat led the way, and Gol and Jam followed, climbing back into the small black helicopter. Within a few seconds the rotors spun into life and the chopper jumped into the air.

'There,' said Kat.

Fifty tanks, engines revving, moved out from a giant compound with thick timber walls and a massive sagging tarpaulin roof; in desert colours they blended in well. Around fifty black helicopters leapt into the air behind Kat and flew past in air support of the heavy section of armoured ground vehicles . . .

'This should be good kill,' said Jam.

'This is just a taster,' replied Kat, and powered forward in the wake of the small army.

The American armoured column had halted, engines rumbling, awaiting the return of their scouts. Infantry and desert-modified Humvees backed up the thirty M1 Abrams tanks in full desert regalia. The units had been detoured due to intelligence provided from an anonymous source. There were perhaps a hundred men in the column, and they were not expecting a fight.

Sergeant Thorpe stood on the tank's turret, digital binoculars held to her eyes and tongue licking at desert-scorched lips. She watched the scout's Humvee bumping back towards them at high speed, a trail of sand whirling in its wake. She tutted in annoyance.

'The dumb bastard will make us stand out for miles!'

She scanned the horizon but could see nothing else of interest. She cursed the desert for making her feel so hot and dry. She watched the Humvee slew to a halt, tyres half-buried in the soft sand, and knew, her heart sinking, that they might be digging the huge bastard out in a few short minutes—

The driver, a squat reliable soldier named Hamill who sported a crew-cut, a good tan and expensive Croc-III shades, leapt out as if on fire and screamed, 'They're coming!'

'Who are coming?'

'The enemy!'

Thorpe frowned from her position on the tank. She felt a shiver course through her despite the heat. 'What fucking enemy?' she growled, her voice husky with a sudden taint of fear.

'Tanks!' screamed Hamill, heading for a truck, boots ploughing sand. 'Lots of fucking tanks!'

Thorpe scanned the horizon once more. All she could see was the slowly settling wake of Hamill's Humvee.

'Cleo, scanners?' she shouted.

'Nothing, sarge.'

'You sure?'

"I'm fucking *sure*, sarge.' Cleo sounded mightily pissed off. 'Hamill must have been on the fucking vodka again, the drunken bastard. I tell you, he puts all our lives at risk . . . what is it?'

'Cleo,' came Thorpe's calm, calculating voice. 'Are you *sure* those scanners show jack-shit?'

'One hundred per cent positive, sarge.'

'Contact!' screamed Thorpe, bringing around her machine gun as the Nex tanks filled the horizon and the black swarm of helicopters leapt into view. Their sounds smashed across the desert and Thorpe watched in horror as sudden explosions echoed across the undulating plain . . .

Everything became a sudden madness. There came a whistling, then a *crump*. Thorpe saw one of the M1s picked up and tossed across the desert, fire blazing around its hull, gun twisted as it described an arc and connected with the ground, ploughing a trough and being ripped apart. Another tank was picked up, then another – and then the helicopters came in as Thorpe hit the dirt hard, rolling, her SA1000 rattling in her hands as the choppers swept overhead—

Bullets flew all around.

Trucks exploded.

Thorpe heard screams.

Something happened, and with her head spinning Sergeant Thorpe was thrown through the air. Something hit her hard in the back of her head, and she remembered staring at the sand and hearing roars and concussive booms all around her, and she wanted to roll over, to fight this sudden unprovoked enemy that had come from nowhere.

'I can't believe it,' she moaned.

She seemed to lie for an eternity where she'd fallen.

She could feel blood running across her hips and belly.

Her throat was dry, parched.

Water, she thought. Just . . . water . . .

Hands rolled her over. Three dark figures stood over her, blocking out the sun, and in her confusion she could have sworn that their eyes glowed like copper, like tiny molten suns.

'Water?' she whispered.

'Be quiet, bitch.'

The sub-machine gun touched her face and blasted her pretty features in a spray of gore across the desert sand.

The BBC London helicopter swept over the Thames, camera panning from the destroyed Houses of Parliament to the leaning, mortally wounded tower of Big Ben.

'The whole of London mourns today for all those killed and maimed in a great tragedy,' came the sombre voice of Mr McSouthern. 'Here we witness the aftermath of the most terrible earthquake ever to hit the United Kingdom.'

Again, the camera swept across the carnage.

It zoomed in on collapsed buildings, cars crushed by massive slabs of concrete, exposed steel wire and sections of fallen brick. Emergency personnel and civilian volunteers picked their way through the devastation and tanks and bulldozers were being used by the military to clear a passage through some of the blocked roads.

The vid_scene switched to the London Underground, where collapsed tunnels spewed crushed Tube trains, full of twisted limbs and bodies, to fill the screen. Blood pools lay still under flickering strip-lights as water gushed from smashed pipes above the subways and silent, stationary escalators, washing dirt, blood and mucus from the rictus

273

death-grins of a thousand crushed commuters caught underground when the quake struck . . .

BBC London's camera viewpoint switched then. It moved to the south coast of England, where a collapsing coastline had swallowed individual houses and whole small villages in a mammoth cave-in, taking them tumbling and sliding into the English Channel.

No part of the country was unaffected; there were sweeping vid_scenes from Inverness, Glasgow, down through Manchester, Birmingham, Nottingham, Oxford, London and onwards to Portsmouth . . . fallen buildings, loss of power on a massive scale, overcrowded hospitals – a nation pushed to the limits of its emergency services in the sudden aftermath of an insane devastation.

'The roads are severely gridlocked up and down the country,' came the voice of Mr McSouthern, 'and are causing endless difficulties for military personnel and vehicles who have been drafted in to help with the country-wide disaster zone . . .'

Within the hot, dry Libyan drilling station, the titanium-carbide VII drill bit rotated at high speed within its protective Plas-7 sheath, the rock and stone detritus sucked up and away by thick alloy-rubber hoses. Ivers stared from behind a mask of mud and rock flecks, eyes searching for defects or any hint that the drill bit was faltering – variations in speed or angle of descent, excess vibration, changes in the extracted rock slurry.

The platform was a huge hardwood structure, set some four kilometres below the earth's surface. It nestled, together with the Sub-3KM control quarters of the drilling rig, in a small hollow of rock. Ivers and his team of LVA-ENG Level-2 engineers worked in shifts and analysed data deep below the earth's surface to make sure that the drilling process went smoothly. As their superiors always stressed: a drill that doesn't drill is a drill that loses money.

'Slow her to twenty-five,' shouted Ivers, back over his shoulder, then returned his gaze to the spinning drill bit. He felt tense, nervous. He hated this job. It had the allure of being extremely highly paid, but it was even more dangerous. If a titanium-carbide VII drill bit snapped at anything over 32 speed, then its operators would all be pulped to blood and liquid flesh.

Ivers chewed his lip, craving a cigarette. Instead, he reached into his overalls and popped a stick of chewing gum into his mouth. He didn't like gum but at least it gave him something to do with his jaws.

Of medium height, with sandy-coloured hair, Ivers was quite stocky, with the trade-mark powerful arms and shoulders of the LVA engineer class: as the saying went, 'To work a rig, a man has to be stronger than a fucking pig'.

A red light flashed, reflecting from the Plas-7 sheath. Ivers turned, frowning, and Kesstelavich gestured that somebody was coming. Ivers cursed, stepped forward to the TBD console and checked the readings. All were OK, tiny needles flickering in the amber. They were on target. The drilling was going according to plan, despite them pushing the machinery hard.

Ivers turned, waiting for whoever it was to arrive and wiping sweat from his brow. Probably another fucking fuel inspector, he thought. I fucking hate inspectors. If a child, teenager or adult shows any inclination of wanting to become educated in the inspectorate, they should be taken behind the bike sheds and fucking shot in the back of the head, he growled to himself through his tough and tangy strawberry chewing gum.

That's how much he hated them: always fucking whining. Always finding some little tweak that supposedly had to be made, some fucking little justification for their hugely disproportionate salaries, and forever covering their own arses with a plethora of pointless paperwork.

Wankers.

Ivers frowned as the two figures came into view. The first was heavily robed, face hidden within the folds of a black cloak and, with a sudden, sinking feeling of dread he realised it had to be—

The top man.

The money behind the LVA phenomenon.

The Big Boss.

Ivers knew of this almost mythical figure through reputation and gossip. He had never met the fellow before, but had spoken to the friends of friends who had been inspected by this dark-robed money man, this suit without a suit. They said that he wore the robes because he had contracted some horrible disease that had eaten his flesh. Ivers shivered, feeling a little sick as he imagined strips of flesh hanging from a green pus-filled face.

And Ivers knew: this man was *strict* – far worse than any snivelling waddling bureaucratic turd of an inspector with a comedy clipboard.

Behind the dark-robed figure stood a large man with greying hair and beard. He had huge hands and a violent look about him, as if he should be wearing desert camouflage gear instead of the dark trousers and loose jacket that he now wore.

Ivers put a false smile on his face as the figures ignored Kesstelavich – who Ivers saw sigh with relief – and headed straight towards him and the TBD console.

'Ivers,' came the cool, intelligent voice from within the folds of the robe.

276

'Yes, sir. It is a great honour for you to pay us a visit . . . ahh.' He glanced up, but could see nothing but darkness within the folds of the hood, abetted by the natural gloom of the working LVA extraction platform. When nothing else was forthcoming, he blurted, 'I – have not got another inspection scheduled for at least three days. I thought that our work was satisfactory and, and, and—'

'It is,' came the smooth voice. 'Do not panic, Ivers. I am not here to inspect; in fact, your team has provided sterling service while in our employ.' A hand – a *claw* – emerged from the robe and Ivers found himself taking the metal sheaves and staring at the place where the twisted darkened hand had briefly been. Suddenly, realising his rudeness, he glanced up into the darkness of the hood and felt sweat roll down his entire body, sticking overalls to his flesh in a clammy, uncomfortable embrace.

'Release orders. You and your team are relieved of duty for exactly one hour.'

'I . . . but . . .'

'Scan the documents. They are all the authorisation you need.'

Ivers turned, clumsily juggling with the metal sheaves. He scanned them on the console and then turned back, a look of confusion on his face. 'I . . .'

'Drop the speed to five.'

'Five? But it—'

'Do not question me, Ivers. Drop the speed to five – then take your unexpected one-hour break and be thankful that you do not need to hear answers to questions you really should not be asking.'

'Yes, sir.'

Ivers gathered his documents and together with Kesstelavich, Rothwell, Oldroyd and Kenny headed for the pressure lifts. He glanced back once as the figure watched him depart, and saw the large grey-haired man produce a small pack and stare at the engineers until they disappeared into the gloom of the vertical ascent . . .

Durell threw back his hood as Gol passed him the QEngine – the 'Foundation Stone'.

Durell smiled, the smile looking strange against his deformed face.

'Let us show the world what we can do,' he said softly.

The Priest wore a grey robe, wooden rosary beads swung against his massive barrel chest and a small battered leather Bible nestled in his huge palms. He stroked the cover, his gold-flecked brown eyes closed for the moment, mouth silently incanting passages from his Holy Book – the words of his God. Outside the cockpit windows of the Comanche the desert rolled by, and eventually The Priest opened his eyes. His keen gaze focused on the featureless expanse beneath him.

'We shall be there soon,' said Heneghan, her voice soft. Her head was encased within the HIDSS and hid her shoulder-length hair and smiling oval face.

'We will be there when God allows, sister,' came the soothing voice of The Priest as he folded his hands humbly in his lap, at peace with the world.

The Comanche flashed through the clear blue skies, its engines humming.

The sun beat tattoos of light across its dull desert camouflage.

And below, the world rolled by uncaringly.

An hour passed, and The Priest came awake with a start. Getting old, he chided himself sombrely, and yawned, stretching his considerable frame in the confines of the Comanche's cockpit. Getting too old for *this*.

'ETA four minutes.'

'Thank you, Heneghan. May God bless your children.'

'I'm sure he already has,' she said.

'No, no,' said The Priest shaking his head in all seriousness. 'I would know about that sort of thing.'

The HIDSS helmet turned, the blacked-out insect-eye panels staring hard at The Priest. He smiled gently at the pilot and gazed out of the window at the distant mountains past Al Hijaz. Saudi Arabia – the Arabian Peninsula.

Rub al'Khali – the Great Sandy Desert.

Rub al'Khali – three hundred thousand square miles of mostly unexplored desert. Three hundred thousand square miles of sand and rock, a plateau baked under the scorching sun for millennia, a land without any obvious attractions . . . And once the home of Spiral_Q: a high-tech base where the major development of the military QIII Cubic Processor had taken place under the watchful gaze of a man named Count Feuchter.

The Priest watched calmly as the Comanche banked, sunlight gleaming from its fuselage, and soared in a huge arc around the blast zone that marked the erstwhile site of Spiral_Q. A huge crater squatted against the desert – and although the preceding year had allowed much of the area to be reclaimed by the desert sands, the enclosed vertical shaft beneath the surface still remained – along with much half-buried detritus of twisted alloy, steel and shattered glass.

'Take us down,' said The Priest softly.

The Comanche settled gently, its rotors whipping up huge sand eddies. Heneghan slowly shut down the engines but left them primed – in case they needed to lift off in an emergency.

Heneghan had been on missions with The Priest before.

And they were never simple . . .

Opening the cockpit, The Priest stuck his nose out into the heat and looked around. He climbed down and jumped, sandals sinking a little and the hot desert sand burning his toes. He breathed deeply, enjoying the fragrance of purity within the Empty Quarter; enjoying the sudden rise in temperature. It reminded him of thick black coffee, lapping blue sea water on luxurious sandy beaches, and snorting camels with thick strings of saliva between their evil teeth.

Smiling softly and ignoring his new-found discomforts, and still holding his Bible, The Priest moved across the sand towards the site of what had once been Spiral_Q.

'It's been a long time, Lord,' he muttered, glancing up into the vast blue vault above him. The sun burned down and the Priest felt a single trickle of sweat roll down his body beneath his grey robes. He smiled, nodding in understanding. 'These things are sent to test us.'

Heneghan had set the Comanche down a good distance from the Spiral_Q blast site; the Comanche's scanners had reported that the ground was extremely unstable – especially for heavy vehicles – and so The Priest toiled across the desert under the sun, occasionally reaching up to touch the string of wooden beads around his throat and muttering words into the sky.

He halted as he came to the first signs of the bomb blast and High-J explosion.

A twisted length of alloy, perhaps eight metres long, lay half buried by sand. Parts of the metal were fused with glass. The Priest found himself shivering involuntarily.

It must have been a huge and devastating explosion, he realised.

A true vision of Hell.

He waded on through the soft wind-blown sand, past more twisted melted struts and a huge ball of fused glass, twisted and deformed and blackened. The Priest gradually worked his way towards the epicentre of the explosion site, reaching the edges where a rim of sand had been superheated into black glass, now sand-blown and weathered in rugged sections. He halted and gripped his Bible tightly as if seeking some strength from above.

'The infidels wreaked much havoc on our world!' he boomed, his voice echoing around the pit in the sand. His eyes went suddenly wide in his broad strong face, and his hair whipped wildly in the desert wind. He grinned then, and sidled towards the edge of the huge crater.

The Priest moved closer, pocketing his Bible in a hidden pouch inside the long grey robe. He dropped to his belly and edged even nearer to the edge. He felt the ground shifting beneath him, gently, in warning, and gritted his teeth as sand blew into his eyes. A warm wind drifted up from the pit.

Pulling free a tiny alloy device, The Priest looked behind him and attached it to a large block of melted metal. Tiny motors whirred and the device – a 'Parasite' Skimmer – ate into the metal and secured itself. The Priest pulled on a pair of gloves and, gripping a length of thin, almost silken thread, turned to lower himself over the edge of the abyss . . .

The world seemed to go suddenly quiet. And dark. Sand drifted down after him, getting into his nose and mouth and making him splutter a little. His sandals scrabbled against the wall and then he swung out, drifting through nothingness. He dropped like a lead weight, rotating slowly into the gloom, which slowly enveloped him.

As he descended, tiny motors droning almost silently above, his eyes began to adjust so that he could scan the walls and the remains of the twisted beams. For a moment he touched down, on an old section of buckled alloy floor. His descent halted, The Priest pulled free his Spiral-issue ECube and set it to scan. Blue digits flickered, illuminating his face with an eldritch glow.

```
> ECube v5.0 ICARUS
> Initiating GTf Scan
> Scanning
> Codecs secured; Δ### ...
> 01001101 01010101 01011111 512enc
> Results ... ... ... 00000
```

The Priest cursed, and spat heavily into the gloom. More sand drifted down from above, spiral eddies which made the huge barrel-chested man want to sneeze.

Sandals slipped treacherously on the old smashed floor. He allowed himself to step free once more into the vastness of this blasted subterranean cavern and, dangling like a fish on a hook, he lowered himself deeper into the enveloping darkness.

He seemed to drift downwards for an age . . .

The Spiral_Q building had been excavated *deep* . . .

His sharp eyes scanned continuously, and three more times he halted to initiate his ECube. Three more times it gave him negative results.

'Why hast thou forsaken me, Lord?'

The Priest rolled his eyes heavenwards – the heavens being a small square hole of light high above him – and then lowered himself deeper into the pit.

He saw more and more detritus that had survived the insane chemical stomping of the original High-J blast. Buckled panels littered with sand, huge sections of mingled glass and alloy twisted into bizarre alien formations and shot like bullets to embed themselves into the walls.

Molten metal had run down the walls and cooled to hang in glittering globular stalactites from girders and battered steel H-sections.

Finally, he reached the bottom.

The Priest's sandals touched down on a surface of merged metal and glass. Most of this hard base was covered with sand, which rose in great piles at either end of the huge blasted site and lay scattered in humps and drifts.

The Priest looked around in the ghostly light.

He shivered.

This is not a place for man, he realised.

Not even a place for God.

Warily, he pulled free his ECube and stopped, his hair ruffled by some cool breeze. Listening, he was now on the alert for intruders as he pulled a Glock 9mm from inside his robes, the gun small in his huge hands. He flicked free the safety catch with his thumb. His tongue licked against the dryness of his mouth.

Are they here?

Nex.

The Priest scanned again, then set his ECube to search for interlopers. His eyes narrowed as the tiny alloy device confirmed that they were alone. But he did not trust it. He was the sort of man who put his faith in his eyes, his ears and The Almighty – not in billions of dollars' worth of computing technology.

The Priest made a short tour of what had been the structural basement of Spiral_Q. Below his sandals, through a four-foot slab of fused glass and metal, lay the original floor of the building – the base's original *base*.

```
> ECube v5.0 ICARUS
> Initiating GTf Scan
> Scanning
```

```
> Codecs secured; Δ### ...
> 01001101 01010101 01011111 512enc
> Results ... ... ... 11110
```

The Priest moved a few feet in one direction, eyes focused now, the Glock forgotten in his hand. He dropped to one knee and placed the ECube against the once-molten floor.

```
> Scanning
> Results ... ... ... 11111
```

'Bingo!' he called piously.

The Priest climbed back to his feet and shook a little sand from his sandals. Again, something seemed to haunt him and his nostrils twitched. There was a faint metallic scent. He whirled around in a low crouch, Glock in his grip and stare searching—

'Nothing.'

He laughed a hollow laugh and glanced up at the sunlight far above. He felt as though he was at the bottom of a huge coffin, or a deep tomb leading straight down into . . .

Hell.

He traced patterns against the ECube and blue digits glowed for a moment. Then a narrow white beam sliced from the tiny alloy machine and swiftly cut a neat slender shaft of metal and glass from the recently formed false floor. Tiny claws gripped the top of this column and, grunting, the Priest pulled it free and laid it to one side.

The Priest knelt once more and peered down into the space thus exposed. He could make out a small alloy panel at the bottom, dusted with black from the original fires that had raged in the insane inferno . . .

'Ah,' he said.

In the gloom behind The Priest, something uncurled.

'Found you, you bugger.' His gold-flecked eyes shone and a smile spread across his broad face. With the ECube buzzing, and his Glock forgotten on the floor to one side, The Priest shuffled and leaned forward, his gaze fixed, his hand stretching out and his brain spinning at the implications of what he had discovered . . .

A cold breeze blew—

Behind The Priest, talons slid free of their armoured casings, touching softly against the fused glass floor of Spiral_Q as slitted copper eyes opened – and blinked lazily in the gloom.

Spiral Mainframe
Data log #12327

CLASSIFIED SADt/5345/SPECIAL INVESTIGATIONS UNIT
Data Request 324#12327

DURELL

All existing files relating to Durell were destroyed (by the man himself) prior to his betrayal of Spiral.

It is known that he was heavily involved in the Nx5 Project early on in his career. He worked with Gol and Count Feuchter. It is known that he carried on with this work illegally after Spiral withdrew funding and closed down the operations.

It is believed Durell was the instigator in creating the Spiral_mobile, an anti-Spiral warship designed to overthrow world powers and take control of the world's military and financial institutions via the all-powerful QuanTech Edition 3 processor.

Cartervb12 filed a report in December 2XXX relating to the death of Durell at his own hand. No body was ever recovered and there is suspicion that Durell is still at large.

Durell is the most dangerous individual ever encountered by Spiral. His knowledge and lust for power are insatiable. He is considered extremely dangerous and ranks No. 1 on Spiral's terrorist hit list.

Substantial rewards are offered for information leading to his capture and/or extermination.

Keyword SEARCH>> NEX, SAD, SPIRAL_sadt, DURELL, FEUCHTER, SPIRAL_mobile

PART TWO

LITTLE FLAME

and i hate your country
and i hate your world
i hate your god's people
who breed on earth

over to the other side
i'm caught stepping out
i'm gonna recreate a religious experience
to tear my fucking heart out

Chord of Souls
McCoy/Fields of the Nephilim

ADVERTISING FEATURE

The TV sparkled into life with a digital buzz of electro-hum, diamond-sharp images spinning and morphing into the jewelled liquid logo of Leviathan Fuels.

Leviathan Fuels are proud to announce their recent acquisition of important contracts . . . not only are most global emergency services signed up to have vehicles converted to LVA, but 78% of military contracts have been acquired worldwide – this gives LF a dominant share of the world fuel market and they thank you all!

Smiling American soldier puts armoured arm around dishevelled refugee figure and gives him a hug, ignoring the JK49 swinging against the feeble refugee's legs – **Scene dissolves into**→ A disco full of Korean and Norwegian soldiers, drinking together, laughing, soon joined by mechanics with greasy arms and oil-stained fingers who proclaim loudly the benefits of LVA mod upgrades→

Scene folds into cube/spins around a digital representation of the Earth and then fades into→ An entourage of fire engine, police squad car and emergency ambulance, all cruising the tarmac in an unspecified country and sweeping majestically around curves – *be smart, the whole world is converting to LVA and you don't want to get left behind in the dirt . . .*

Scene dissolves into→ Children running along a dirt road under the pounding rain. Behind them stands a small unkempt boy in the road, hair dishevelled, face grubby, eyes red from crying. He is squawking as his ex-friends run away and leave him whining in the road . . .

– Four hundred miles to the gallon! Go on, make the smart choice . . . choose Leviathan Fuels, your children deserve a better future . . .

Car sweeps past, stops, picks up the little boy – the sun comes out, the world burgeons with greenery and sparkles with flowers, the boy giggles and everything is all right. Car disappears, sporting bumper sticker saying: **LVA, make the RIGHT CHOICE**

Scene/text scroll R→L [Arial black] acr. vid:
(*Be a part of the club, join the fastest-growing user group in the world – check out **www.leviathanfuels.com** for more information on your nearest dealer, stockist and fuel emporium.*)

SCENE DISSOLVES TO BLUE

SIU Transcript

CLASSIFIED SR19/1178/SPECIAL INVESTIGATIONS UNIT
Hacked ECube interception
Date: September 2XXX

Our breaking headline for this evening is the assassination of the President of Leviathan Fuels, Chanya Verisimilov, who was gunned down today at 3pm on the marble steps leading to the Central Leviathan HQ in Prague, Eastern Europe.

Four men wearing balaclavas and bearing

assault JK53s opened fire without warning from a truck, killing Verisimilov and three bodyguards instantly and severely wounding many reporters and paparazzi who were standing nearby taking statements and photographs.

Special Forces were immediately deployed and cut off the truck's escape route. Despite some eyewitness accounts of the men surrendering and holding their hands in the air, all the assassins were accidentally shot in the forehead at point-blank range and have therefore been unable to comment.

Leviathan Fuels have currently been storming the globe with massively expanding fuel sales, an economic alternative to petrol- and gas-powered vehicles that requires nothing more than a simple engine modification. They recently acquired emergency-service and military contracts on an almost global scale, and it is rumoured that they are in the running to supply a new type of LVA which NASA and other space agencies can use to power contemporary developments in space-going propulsion systems. They are also rumoured to be developing a new type of shuttle engine with NASA, the RFFSA and the CPLSA.

Verisimilov's family were unavailable for comment on the brutal, vicious and bloody execution of a beloved husband, father and grandfather - despite constant and repeated questioning from a variety of media.

CHAPTER 11

INFILTRATION

The pain from the HPG blast and the fight fuelled Carter. His teeth gritted as the ScorpNex leapt towards him on the bridge across the valley – but even as the huge creature leapt, the Browning flew from Mongrel's sweating bloodstained fist. Carter caught the weapon, skidded to a halt, lifted the gun and fired—

The first bullet missed.

The next two crashed into Dake's already battered chest . . .

The fourth glanced from an armoured plate on the ScorpNex's face, and its leap faltered. It fell, landing clumsily, a claw coming up to its side in a reflex gesture. A low growl spat from its twisted mashed fangs and Carter sprinted forwards, booted feet connecting with Dake's already smashed face. The ScorpNex teetered – then stepped backwards and toppled through the ragged, splintered hole left by the HPG blast.

It vanished . . .

And everything suddenly fell silent.

Carter and Mongrel met on opposite sides of the hole

and looked down where the ScorpNex tumbled towards the ground far below. There came a deep, echoing crunch.

'What fucking ugly son of bitch,' said Mongrel.

'You looked in the mirror recently?'

'What was it, Carter?'

'Some kind of Nex.'

'You did well them, *compadre*.'

'Thanks for the Browning.'

'A pleasure. Cup of tea?'

Carter grinned wearily through the caked blood on his face. 'I'd fucking love one, mate.'

Darkness was creeping softly over the horizon and insects chirruped in the long grass, calls echoing back and forth from their hidden sanctuaries. Trees wavered gently in a breeze that mercifully dispersed the humidity of the early-autumn evening. Carter dropped to the ground, winced at the pain in his body and limbs, then fished out a cigarette and lit the weed with shaking fingers.

'I thought you were quitting.'

'Yeah, yeah, fuck off and see to your new girlfriend.'

Mongrel reached down and placed a hand against Carter's shoulder, making him wince a little in pain. Carter glanced up into eyes filled with concern. 'You OK, mate? You did well back there – really, really well . . .'

'I'll live.'

'Which is more than I can say for that ugly fucker,' snorted Mongrel. He patted Carter's shoulder and moved to the KTM's packs and the medical kits within.

Carter sat for a while, savouring the cigarette smoke and allowing his body to calm itself after the violent adrenlin rush of the previous few hours. He looked at his hand, which was still shaking, and smiled to himself. A long time since I got the shakes, he mused.

'*Yeah, which just shows that you're returning to your mental roots.*'

'Meaning?'

'*That you're growing soft again. Where's the tough-fuck Carter I know and love? The one that blew the faces from three terrorists in Egypt with a High-J shrapnel bomb and kept their face skins as souvenir masks? Where's the cold-hearted bastard who shot that South African woman in the back of the head, even after she had surrendered? And where's the fucker who murdered them all – the men, the women and the fucking children – on that hot sunny day in Belfast?*'

Carter's cigarette smoke plumed blue into the sky. He watched idly as Mongrel helped Mila remove her holed and bloodstained jacket.

'In Egypt, I kept the face of *one* terrorist because that was all that was left of him, and Spiral wanted DNA samples to link him to bombings across four different continents. The South African woman had killed six DemolSquad members with a sniper rifle, one of them a very old friend and I knew she would fucking get off on some international diplomacy clause and continue her reign of slaughter . . . and Belfast?' Carter's voice went terribly cold. 'Why, Kade, Belfast was all *your* doing.'

Mila was lying back, her head resting on Mongrel's jacket. He was laughing and joking with her.

Kade faded, gently, slowly, leaving Carter with a throbbing head. He killed the cigarette and ground the butt into the soil with his boot.

Kade was wrong, he knew.

Kade was wrong about him . . .

Once, a young and newly recruited Spiral operative on Demol18 had said to him, 'Wow, you're Carter . . . the

Butcher . . . the man without fear.' The young man's eyes had glowed with awe and apprehension – and a need to be like Carter.

It had disgusted him.

Made him feel unclean to his very core.

There are no more heroes, he thought.

No more heroes.

They just didn't get it. Killing wasn't something that was good, that was fun, something you could just do and go home, have your tea and put your feet up and watch TV, secure in the knowledge that a good shower would wash away the blood. Killing was just something that Carter had to do because he had to do it. He was good at it, he acknowledged . . . brilliant, even. And he was intelligent enough to understand that the people he killed, the people he murdered, were bad men and women, killers themselves, terrorists with soft civilian targets in mind. He was protecting the innocent. Cleansing the scum from the earth.

And yet he knew that his hands would never, ever be clean . . .

And it burned his soul with darkness; with bad blood.

'Carter!'

He glanced up, lit another cigarette, and was glad to see that his mild case of the shakes had subsided. He stood, groaning at the pain. The HPG had kicked the living fuck from his body and he started to wonder if retirement wouldn't be such a bad idea after all. Yeah, retirement – again.

'Aye?'

'You need to hear this.'

Carter moved closer, looking down at Mila who glanced up at him, a nervous smile on her lips. She looked to Mongrel for reassurance, and he beamed a winning, encouraging smile – the same smile that had bedded him many a drunken lady. Carter shook his head in weary disbelief.

He forced a smile to his face, despite the pain.

'Yes?' he sighed, catching the canteen that Mongrel threw. Standing slightly behind Mila, Mongrel cupped his hands to his chest and winked. Carter shook his head again and took a long drink of warm water.

'Tell him about the quarry.'

Mila smiled again, seeming to relax a little. Mongrel had dressed the wound well and her painkillers were kicking in.

'There are many of these, how you say, Nex there. They always wear masks, they always have those bright copper eyes and they are so fast . . . so fast . . .'

'You say they killed your brother?'

'Yes. He was only thirteen, out with four of his friends. They were children, Mr Carter, they were only little boys. They tried to get away, ran through the woods. One had lagged behind, saw them all shot in the back by these Nex and then dragged off through the trees. They were given no warnings, no mercy.'

Mila was crying now, tears flowing freely down her cheeks, her face looking down at the ground and her mud-crusted boots. Carter felt his chest tighten, his heart going out to this beautiful young woman . . .

'*Careful . . .*' hissed Kade.

Carter ignored him and, reaching out, took her hand. It was lightly tanned with long fingers and rough nails. But it was a pretty hand and Carter looked up to realise that she was looking at him, looking at him strangely.

'You say there are many Nex at this quarry. How many?'

'I have seen maybe one or two hundred.'

'*What?*'

'There are barracks. And there are human workers there as well, men, engineers who work on the machines.'

'What machines?'

'The pumps.'

'Pumping LVA?' asked Carter softly.

'Yes, the new fuel, I think. It is taken in tankers – I have seen all this.'

Carter smiled, squeezing her hand, and said, 'We need to see this place. Are you ready to move?'

'Carter, she's just been fucking shot . . .' said Mongrel.

'Are you ready to move?' he repeated.

'I will show you. Are you going to kill them?'

Carter pulled free his Browning HiPower and checked the thirteen-round magazine before hammering it back with a solid *click*.

'Yeah, we're going to kill them all,' he said coldly.

'*There's my boy,*' sneered Kade. '*Just like the old days . . . Welcome back, Butcher.*'

Darkness flowed over the woods. It flowed over the mountains. It gradually extinguished the light in the sky like a thumb and forefinger snuffing out the glow of a candle flame.

A gentle wind stirred the tall grasses in the valley, and blew the warm scents of a dying summer over the rocks where something moved. Slowly, a dark shape gradually uncurled and turned small copper eyes towards the moon.

The ScorpNex growled softly, claws moving across its body and dipping into the wounds it carried, wounds that went deep into its frame and caused it a burning agony it would never forget.

Pain pulsed.

But, more than this, a need pulsed within its mind.

A need to kill.

Revenge.

A need to kill Carter . . .

The ScorpNex rolled onto its side and lay drooling for a while, and then it heaved its bulk onto its knees and vomited on the ground. A low keening sound came from its broken jaw and it managed to pull free a tiny grey ECube – a copy of the Spiral-issue device. The grey plates spun free and a voice spoke.

'You failed.'

'Yes.'

'How could you fail?'

'Carter . . . he is . . . hard to kill.'

'Can you walk?'

'I . . . think so.' Claws clamped tight shut in pain. Copper eyes glittered.

'Can you hunt?'

'I need help.'

A sigh. 'Stay where you are. We have your location – we'll send in a chopper, bring you out.'

The signal died, the grey ECube copy whirring to itself.

The ScorpNex rolled onto its back and made soft sounds of pain. But in its eyes burned a singularity of purpose and a need for revenge.

The two KTM motorcycles cruised down the dirt trail as darkness finally fell. Much to Mongrel's disappointment Mila had chosen to ride with Carter. As they cruised, tyres crunching, Carter was painfully aware of her delicate hands on his hips, the slim and beautiful woman pressed close behind him, her face against his broad, heavily muscled back.

Focus, he thought.

Flicking on their headlights, they slowed their speed as falling darkness impeded their progress. Mila pointed out the mountain trails they were to traverse.

They travelled through the night, passing down a long winding trail that descended alarmingly along the side of a mountain through dense woodland, switchback bend after unlit switchback bend, hairpins chasing hairpins until it briefly levelled and then began to climb steeply, straightening as they ascended another mountain trail through night scenery of moonlit splendour.

At one point Carter rolled to a halt and Mongrel pulled up beside him.

'What is it?'

Carter pointed. There, ensnared in his headlight beam, was a brown deer, eyes wide, nostrils flared. It suddenly started, galloping off into the darkness. Carter grinned.

'I love this place,' he said.

'Such a shame we have dirty job to do.'

'Yeah, a real shame.'

They travelled warily for perhaps a couple of hours along dangerous roads and trails. Eventually Mila patted Carter's thigh and he pulled over to the side of the road.

'It is best we leave bikes here,' she said, her lips close to his ear. 'You want me climb off?'

'Yeah.'

The two Spiral agents quickly cammed up the bikes and then, allowing Mila to take the lead, they set off through thick forest, once more climbing a huge rugged mountain and fighting their way through the trees.

Occasionally the moon fell behind clouds. Then complete darkness dropped like an obsidian cloak. Mila stayed close to Carter who refused to return her rifle, allowing a disgruntled Mongrel to strap it to his pack instead and hump the excess weight like a pack mule, muttering a string of expletives.

Both men carried their M24 carbines with reloaded magazines. Both felt twitchy, watchful after their realisation that Jam had not been on such a simple SAD mission – but a much more dangerous operation.

Poor Jam, thought Carter sadly.

When had he realised?

Thought he was taking out a few rogue remainders – a few specimens left over from the war of a year ago. When in fact he was stumbling headlong and blind into a whole fucking battalion!

And they had captured him.

Beat him. And . . .

Murdered him?

Carter could think of no other fate that might await his friend. But then, Nicky said that the Spiral mainframes had picked up signals from Jam's ThumbNail_Map – many hours after his disappearance and apparent ECube PB. Which meant that they had not killed him – at least, not straight away – and he had managed somehow to escape . . . for a little while at least. Or maybe he was free now and they were chasing ghosts?

What now?

Carter's mouth was a grim line in the darkness.

If the enemy had him, then Jam's future did not look rosy.

As they walked, Carter's eyes scanning left and right for signs of danger, ears alert for any slight change that could signal the presence of an enemy, he found a part of his mind drifting, wandering. He was focused on his journey, but a part of him fell back to remembering the old days—

Reading in the sun, wearing shorts and T-shirt, and

301

Natasha running outside with a bucket of water to drench him to the bone . . . Carter chasing her, screaming and threatening, with Samson barking around their feet, almost tripping them in the long grass, Carter lifting her in his arms and then dropping her into the dirty green water of the dog's paddling pool amidst the shed dog hairs as she squealed with indignation and disgust . . .

Wandering hand in hand on a distant foreign beach, toes curling in the sand, laying out a rug and unpacking their impromptu and hastily purchased lunch. They had eaten, drunk beer, lain in the sun until the tide had crept in and the waves had splashed their dozing bodies . . .

'Here.'

Carter halted and they dropped to their bellies, peering up the incline to the ridge above them that was scattered with conifers and sycamores. 'You sure there are no look-outs?'

'No.' Mila's face looked bleached in the moonlight. 'This is the place I have always come to watch – and learn. I have been here maybe ten times. I have never been seen.'

'You two wait there,' Carter ordered her and Mongrel.

He dropped his pack to the ground and eased himself forward cautiously up the slope, inch by inch, careful and precise in his movements. At the top the ground levelled off between the trees and Carter waited patiently, allowing his eyes to adjust to the moonlight falling between the branches and leaves. Then he eased forward, M24 carbine held loosely and Browning secure at his hip.

He saw the ghost night-glow of perimeter halogen lamps.

And then the world opened up in front of him . . .

The Kataja Quarry was huge, a mammoth circular depression between high steep red rock walls tumbled with vegetation and rock scree. The rock walls fell away to a massive flat basin, again littered with rocks and scrub bushes, with the odd pine standing forlorn and isolated. To one side squatted six large barracks, each capable of housing perhaps a hundred men – or Nex – and built from rough-sawn timber. They looked relatively new. All the windows were blacked out, but Carter could just about distinguish a few chinks of light round the edges of the blackout curtains. Beside the barracks stood a smaller building, obviously some sort of operational HQ. On the corrugated roof were sophisticated satellite scanners and transmitters. This Op HQ too looked newly built.

Away from the barracks stood a set of buildings, made from corrugated galvanised steel, which were obviously older. These buildings hunkered beside the huge black gleaming LVA pump which even now was quietly thudding and churning, pumping the new fuel into five gigantic container tanks – each at least forty metres in diameter and painted a dull matt black. Near the barracks stood a couple of grey tracked tanks, their engines off, and perhaps fifteen large six-wheeled trucks like those Carter had seen back at the old camp. They were obviously used for troop transport.

Carter scanned the quarry.

'Quite an operation you've got here, fellas,' he muttered, and shuffled himself around to get a better look.

The Kataja Quarry was fed by a single wide road. Four more tanks served as heavy protection, and two tall timber guard towers stood bleak against the night with two snipers posed in each of them. Two more towers were positioned towards the back of the quarry, each tower again sporting two snipers. And then Carter saw them – almost perfectly camouflaged beside the four rough-timber sniper-towers:

SM-7 surface-to-air missiles.

Deployed from Mini-SM7.8 Blocks in III/IV and IVa configurations, the SM-7s were much more compact and discreet SAM weapons than had been used in earlier wars. They employed electronic countermeasures in the form of mono-pulse send/receivers for semi-active III-TR radar terminal guidance and inertial midcourse guidance. Launched from the SM7.8VLS Vertical Launching Systems the SM-7s were perfect for both low- and high-altitude threat interceptions and had almost total success rates even if target aircraft employed electronic counter-measures such as the ECM-6, Lockheed 52s and Sikorsky 2212 ASAMs.

'Shit. There goes a fucking air strike.'

Carter waited patiently, watching, counting, observing.

The ground area was policed by Nex, heavily armed with sub-machine guns and pistols. They patrolled in teams of four, and there were at least eight teams operational – which meant a minimum of thirty-two Nex on the ground, eight operational snipers, and six T76 tanks which Carter had to assume were armed and ready for action. And all that backed up by serious SAM support and God only knew how many Nex in the barracks.

'*A lot of firepower,*' said Kade.

'The game's getting bigger.'

'*You think Jam is in there?*'

'He could be. This is where they took him, and the bodies of Slater and TT. If we don't go in this is where our trail stops. This would be our dead end . . . and the death of Natasha and my child.'

Kade did not reply.

Slowly, Carter eased back and rejoined Mongrel and Mila.

'Big?' Mongrel asked.

'Fucking huge,' said Carter softly. 'Four-man Nex patrols, snipers in watchtowers, and tanks.'

'I hate tanks,' rumbled Mongrel.

'What I don't understand is why so many Nex are there. They suddenly protecting the LVA? Mila, have there always been this many soldiers based here?'

'No. Originally it was quite small camp, when they first start mining. Only in last few weeks have they brought in so many more men . . . these Nex. Now whole area is deserted; they frighten everybody away, and even police keep away.'

'Greasy backhanders,' said Mongrel.

'Maybe.'

'What's your plan?'

Carter smiled, meeting Mongrel's fearsome gaze. 'Quite simple. You and Mila wait here, I go in alone. I'll find out if Jam is being held there.'

'No.'

'What the fuck do you mean, "no"?'

'I brought you in on this, Carter. I go in to see if Jam is there. He's part of my team, I am responsible for him getting caught . . . I should have been there.'

'What?' sneered Carter. 'You think if you'd been present it would have made a difference? Use your brain, man – all it would mean is that I'd be here alone looking for four dead bodies instead of three.'

'Or not here at all,' growled Mongrel.

'Listen, I know how you feel, Mongrel – but look at the facts. You're a demolitions expert – that I'll grant you. If this place needed blowing up, I'd be happy to let you waltz in with your High_J and get the job done. But I'm good at covert; in fact, I am the fucking best. And you know it.'

Their gazes locked.

'You know it, Mongrel. I'll be in and out in one hour.'

'Let me come with you, Carter. It too dangerous.'

Carter shook his head. 'No, no, my friend. You have your new companion to babysit. After all, you can't say we really know her. What if this is a set-up? A trap.' The word tasted bad on his tongue.

'She not one of them, Carter.'

'Prove it.'

'I know it. In here.' The huge man put his fist to his heart.

'You know fuck all, Mongrel. The only way you come with me is if we put a bullet in her skull. Are you willing to do that? Then stop your fucking whining . . . you came to me in the hospital when Natasha was dying because you needed fucking help – and yeah, I've got my own motivations but you came to me for a reason: because I get the fucking job done. Now leave me to do it.'

'What you want me do?'

'Looking at the fucking defences, I'd say an air attack is out of the question. Bastards have learned from past mistakes, eh, Mongrel? Our only option would be heavy tank back-up to take out this Nex *army* – and the other main problem is the single road in and out. It channels an attack . . . but then, that will only be a problem if I bubble it.'

'I think Spiral need to know about this place now. They can form their own conclusions.'

'OK. You send out a WB as I head in. Call in some choppers and tanks in case the game goes a little pear-shaped. I'm going in now while we still have the cover of darkness . . .'

'Why not wait for back-up?'

'I've got a bad feeling about this place . . . and there's no time like the present. Time is running out. I need that

306

machine . . . *Natasha* needs that machine. Or –' Carter's eyes went hard 'I – won't be held responsible for my actions . . .'

Mongrel watched Carter disappear into the night, fading like a ghost in a bad dream. He wore his balaclava once more, and had armed himself with some serious weaponry.

Mongrel sat with his back against a tree, M24 across his lap as he hurriedly composed his digital report for Spiral and sent it on in the form of a WarBurst. Highest priority. Straight to the top.

Mongrel smiled grimly to himself.

'Will he be all right?' said Mila softly, blonde hair blowing in the gentle breeze.

'Yeah, Carter is the best,' said Mongrel.

'Shall we keep watch?'

'We will have to be careful.'

'I've been watching these people for months and I've never been caught. I am careful, and I am invisible.'

'Carter spotted you – up on that slope.'

'Yes.' She nodded. 'He is good. How you say, a killer? A psychopath?'

'I wouldn't go that far,' said Mongrel.

'I would,' said Mila. 'I see it in his eyes. He is a little insane, I think.'

'In this world, *Iyubimya*, I think we all are.'

Carter crouched in the darkness at the edge of the quarry, senses alert and ready for anything. He clipped free his Sp_drag – nicknamed a Skimmer or Parasite Skimmer – and connected it to a rock. Tiny drills ate into the stone and secured the device. Taking a deep breath of humid night air, Carter stepped off the rim and into the Kataja Quarry.

Below, halogen lights glowed.

Trucks were coming and going, engines revving in the floodlit rock arena. The LVA pump worked effortlessly, ceaselessly, and he could imagine the thick pumping of the rich fluid into the huge containers – ready for refinement and distribution around the world . . .

Focus.

Jam . . . location?

The obvious. Op HQ.

Carter's boots trod the almost vertical wall with infinite care; a single loose rock, a single trickle of stone and he could be highlighted, sighted by a sniper – and pop. Dog meat. Carter took his time. He had another three hours of darkness . . . there was no immediate rush.

Squatting on a large protrusion of rock, Carter waited, wire coiled behind him and giving him a life-umbilical to the rocky mother wall. He watched the Nex patrols again, his sharp eyes noting their movements, their efficiency and yet their – complacency? Or was it arrogance?

Carter grinned. He'd given a few arrogant Nex presents that they would never forget.

Moving off once more, he eased his way down the wall and imprinted on his brain a map of the layout of the military installations and buildings and the Nexes' patterns of patrol. As he reached ground level, touching down softly, he flicked a tiny switch and the Sp_drag released from its hold on the rock and wound itself slowly together, allowing Carter to stow the device away in his belt.

He crouched, calming his breathing.

He palmed his Browning and secured the M24 carbine tight across his back. He screwed the Browning's silencer into place and remembered the last time he had used the mod – back in Switzerland when it had almost got him killed. Now he needed its stealth . . .

Carter eased his way through the bushes and rocks and halted, watching the patrolling Nex. They worked well – tight units with heavy firepower.

Carter focused on the Op HQ. The door opened and three men stepped out, moving across the flat hard-packed ground to the group of corrugated rusting buildings beside the LVA pump. He chewed his lip, listening to their conversation . . . but got no clues about whether Jam was present, a prisoner, dead or had been shipped away to some distant location.

Could he risk an ECube scan?

No. The enemy might pick up the electronic tracking pulses. And then he would be fucked.

Carter rested back on his heels, calming his thoughts, forcing images of Natasha and their unborn child from his mind. He could not afford to think of them now.

Carter waited . . . a good half-hour passed and activity seemed to lessen. Five trucks roared off in support of six large LVA tankers; their lights cut through the night and their engines howled, heavy wheels whirling up the dry dust and then leaving a deathly stillness in their wake.

The patrols seemed to lessen.

Carter checked his watch.

3.20 a.m.

Time to move.

Taking a deep breath, and timing himself between Nex patrols, Carter set out from the rocks around the edge of the quarry so that he could zigzag across to the rear of the Op HQ through as many shadows and trees as possible . . .

And hope that the snipers didn't spot him.

Mongrel checked his watch.

3.17 a.m.

'Come on, Carter, what the fuck you doing?'

Mongrel and Mila had watched the quarry for some time, noting the loading of Nex troops into trucks, the filling of LVA tankers, the continuous drone of the LVA pump. Then, when he could see no sign of Carter, he eventually decided that it was too risky to keep popping their heads over the ridge line . . . it could get them shot.

So they retreated down the slope a little and listened, waiting for any sounds of infiltration or discovery – sirens, gunshots, anything.

'You OK?'

Mila nodded. She was tired, pale, and looked very weak. She was trying hard to put on a brave face but Mongrel could sense her weariness.

'I am fine.'

'How old are you?'

'Twenty.'

'That's young.'

She shrugged. 'I am still full woman,' she said, smiling.

'You need to sleep?'

'No!'

'Come here, girl.' Mila moved over to Mongrel and he took her in his arms. She rested her head against his huge chest. Her eyes closed, and Mongrel looked down at the top of her head, the fine silken web of hair. He inhaled her perfume. Lust was not far from his thoughts.

Mongrel's eyes scanned from left to right, then he shifted a little. Mila sighed against him.

He hefted the M24 thoughtfully, wondering idly how Carter planned to get Jam out in the event that the Spiral agent was unable to move under his own steam.

Carter would think of something. He would probably secure Jam in that event and await heavy back-up . . . And soon – with luck – the tanks would arrive.

310

Mongrel nodded to himself, his tongue chasing a crumb around the cavernous toothless interior of his mouth. Damn crumbs, he thought. Closely followed by, Fucking teeth.

Metal pressed against the back of his head.

It was quite obviously the barrel of a gun.

'Drop the carbine, fucker.'

Mongrel froze – the hairs on the back of his neck prickled.

They emerged from the darkness, drifting like ghosts with sub-machine guns levelled at his face and the sleeping form of Mila. They were Nex. And there were twelve of them . . .

Slowly, Mongrel dropped his M24 and shook Mila awake.

'Oh!' she said, her gaze alighting on the Nex. 'Oh.'

'Well done. You led them straight to us.'

'I . . . I did?'

'We've been watching you for weeks,' said a Nex softly, copper eyes burning into Mila's face. It stepped forward and smashed the butt of the gun against her head, sending her sprawling across the ground to lie still, blood flowing freely from her wound.

'And you . . .'

Mongrel launched himself at the Nex, who neatly sidestepped, its fist lashing out to slam against Mongrel's jaw. He rolled, countered with an uppercut but the Nex dodged and rammed the sub-machine gun into Mongrel's face.

The large Spiral operative hit the ground.

Five heavy kicks sent him spinning into unconsciousness.

They bound the two captives with wire, and dragged them down the slope towards the truck which idled, exhaust fumes spitting grey into the dark humid night.

'Just one more.'

'How perfect.'

The truck disappeared quietly into the night.

Carter dropped to a crouch, a low hiss escaping his lips, the Browning tight in his fist. He rolled into the shadows under a wide pine tree, felt needles prickling through his clothing and waited until the stealthy footfalls of the patrol had passed.

Releasing his breath slowly, he crawled to the edge of the wooden walls of the Op HQ and moved to the nearest window. It had been blacked out but, standing, Carter could see through a chink in the curtain.

The Op HQ was empty . . .

He watched for a while, just to make sure.

Carter, hand touching the wall, slid along the side of the building and glanced up again towards the sniper towers. He could see two Nex, motionless, copper eyes scanning like those of automatons. With a swift movement Carter reached the door and slid inside, closing the heavy wooden slab behind him.

The Op HQ was a large room, perhaps twenty metres square. On one side of the chamber was living accommodation – low single beds, four sets of bunk beds, a wide, rough-hewn oak table with a scattering of chairs – and in the corner a kitchen assembly with cooker, sink, kettle and a disarray of pans and cups. To the right the whole twenty-metre wall was taken up by oak benching littered with all manner of computing equipment, scanners, a satellite-control deck, and other complicated machinery that Carter suspected had something to do with the SAM defences. Lights glittered on small grey alloy consoles – blipping orange and green, then a cascade of purple which seemed to shower across the displays. Beside the high-tech computer equipment were several large wall boards containing maps and documents, and a fixed digital map; it was towards these that Carter gravitated.

'*It's too quiet.*'

'I know.'

'*It could be a trap . . .*'

'But I need to find Jam. It's no use sitting in the woods all night.'

Carter stared up at the maps. They ranged across several continents and seemed to display LVA sites operational and potential – and several that were under investigation by the Fuel Inspectorate. Countries included Egypt, Afghanistan, China, Peru, Russia, Norway and Australia. Carter lifted his ECube and it captured the information with a digital whine.

Moving to the console, he activated it and the digital map buzzed into life. Passwords were requested and Carter rested his ECube against the computer terminal – it clicked softly, and letters and numbers flickered at incredible speed across the display as the ECube hacked the terminal and the digital map spun into focus . . .

Again, LVA sites were displayed . . .

And other markings scattered across the map, highlighted in a bright orange that glittered softly.

Carter's eyes were drawn towards London as—

Glass smashed from all around the room as five windows imploded and Nex rolled to their feet with sub-machine guns levelled. Carter whirled low and the silenced Browning was spitting in his fist as he dived for the benching. Two Nex took bullets in their faces, blood spraying in bright arcs and were flipped into untidy dead heaps against the wooden floor.

Carter reached for another magazine—

As a gun barrel touched his head.

'Getting slow,' said the Nex, voice soft, asexual, a gentle croon. It had come in through one of the windows behind Carter as he fought.

Carter grinned. 'Yeah, I'm too fucking old for this game.'

The other three Nex approached, forced Carter to stand, and took his Browning and M24 carbine. They bound his hands tightly behind his back with wire and one of the Nex – seemingly the leader, although they wore no insignia or marks of rank – turned and stared at the two Nex dead on the floor.

He spun back, copper eyes burning, and moved close to Carter.

'You have been a thorn in our side for a long time.'

'Good.'

Carter's own Browning smashed against his head and blackness whirled in patterns against a sea of red, floating with bright brittle stars. He was dragged to his knees and blinked, working his jaw, and spat a little blood onto the boards.

'Can we kill him?'

'Not yet. They're bringing the others.'

Carter cursed inwardly and, licking his lips, scanned the room. He tried to loosen his bonds and caught another blow from his own weapon that sent him crashing to the wooden boards with a heavy thump. He lay stunned for a few moments, pain pounding him. The Nex dragged him to his knees again and he started to laugh, a long low evil sound.

'What's so funny?'

'The detonation.'

'What detonation?'

'Better get looking, little worms. Not long now before

314

this whole fucking LVA plant blows sky-high . . . after all, you dumb motherfuckers, I *am* in a Demolition Squad . . .'

The Nex exchanged glances, and two whirled, leaving the Op HQ at speed.

'*Down to two*,' whispered Kade.

Carter did not look, but was aware of his ECube nestling against the digital map's terminal. He calmed his breathing, head throbbing with pain, and turned a little to reposition his body, relaxing his muscles, waiting . . .

The door swung open.

First came Mongrel, badly beaten and bleeding from mouth, nose and forehead; he was bound tightly and he was – understandably – scowling fiercely. Two Nex held him. Then came Mila, also bound, staggering weakly and moaning in Slovene; again, two Nex followed and Carter cursed as they piled into the room . . .

'*This should be more fun*,' said Kade.

'What the fuck does that mean?'

'*More bodies for me to burn*,' he said darkly.

And then—

Then came Durell and another figure: a tall man, with a grey-flecked beard and neatly trimmed greying hair. He was large, a powerful man, and his gaze fixed directly on Carter as he entered the room. The pair halted, leaving the door wide and a cool breeze flowing in from the night.

Silence fell. Then—

'Mr Carter,' said Durell softly, throwing back his hood to reveal the monstrosity that was his face. His narrow slitted copper-eyed stare burned into Carter. 'How nice to see you again. This is such a pleasant surprise.'

'I thought you fucking killed him!' murmured Mongrel.

Carter nodded. 'I'll make sure I shoot him in the

315

damned face next time, mate – although since he looks so fucking hideous I think somebody already tried.'

Durell chuckled, drool pooling from his twisted jaws.

'I commend you for your tenacity, Mr Carter. It has been a long time since we had an enemy so worthy of us.'

'Too bad he has to die,' said Gol, eyes still fixed on Carter.

'So you the real Gol, or what?' snapped Carter, turning his attention from Durell to his old friend and ally. 'I saw you fall from a mountain, and then I gave you an HPG to eat – both times I saw you fucking die. It would appear that you have a little bit of immortality flowing in your blood.'

'The first time I did not die,' rumbled Gol. 'The first time I was saved . . . by Durell. And the second time you met a—' He smiled softly. 'Shall we say a changer . . . a form of Nex we worked on a long time ago.'

'And now you show your true colours?'

'True colours?' Gol frowned. 'This is no betrayal, Carter. Spiral has had its day. Spiral is weak. It has had its time and now it needs – shall we say – a little gentle persuasion to move over.'

Carter said nothing.

His gaze moved to Mongrel and the two Spiral agents exchanged a silent communication.

'This LVA all your idea, Durell?' growled Mongrel.

'Who is this puppy who yaps at my feet?' snarled Durell – and whirled, a true blur of movement, an incredible display of speed as claws emerged from the depths of his dark robes and hammered into Mongrel's head. The big man was picked up and tossed across the Op HQ to clatter against the wall, falling heavily to the ground, blood spilling from his mouth. He groaned, looked up, then slumped back down and lay still.

'What do you want with us?' said Carter coldly, amazed at this show of speed from the twisted husk.

'No,' said Durell, slitted eyes burning with anger. 'What is it that *you* want with *us*? Are you here to destroy the pumps? Or to look for . . . enemies?'

Carter stared into Durell's eyes, breathing deeply and calming himself. 'We have come to find Jam. We tracked him here; this whole discovery of your LVA set-up is incidental and, to be honest, I do not give a fuck about your aspirations for world fucking domination – I just want to find Jam.'

'*Strange.*'

Durell paced up and down as the cool breeze brought in night scents. He moved towards Mila and one claw cupped her chin, lifting her face so that she had to stare at his deformities. Her eyes were wide in terror, her mouth agape.

'Tell me, Carter – your needs would seem unbalanced.'

'My woman, Natasha, is dying. Jam can help her. Is he here? Or is he dead?'

'Ahh, the sweet Natasha. I remember her well. She had a hand in the fall of Spiral_mobile . . . well, Carter, my oldest and bravest adversary—' Durell seemed to smile. Releasing his grip on Mila's chin he turned and moved, making crackling sounds, to stand in front of Carter where he lowered his head until his broad twisted face was only a few inches from Carter's own. 'It would seem that you are in my control once more. So, unfortunately, things will not be going to plan for you and your little band. Yes, in answer to your first question, Jam is here. And no, he is far, far from dead . . .'

Durell backed away.

Carter could smell the strange Nex stink that had haunted his darkest nightmares. He shuddered. Blood rolled down his wrists as the wire continued to cut into his flesh.

Something moved in the doorway, and a massive shape filled the frame, stooping to enter. It unfurled, its triangular head coming up with tiny copper eyes fixed directly on—

Carter.

It moved forward, its heavy armoured feet booming on the wooden floor, and halted, swaying a little, its eyes blinking in the bright light.

'It is too warm here,' said Jam.

'I agree,' replied Durell softly. He glanced at Carter. 'Welcome our new ScorpNex. It has taken a long time to achieve such a fine specimen, but shall we say that this time we had a rewarding subject on which to build; from which to *blend*.'

Carter frowned.

He stared at the huge ScorpNex in front of him – and then the lines of the deformed face clicked into place. Carter blinked, and felt his knees go weak. He staggered against the two Nex who held him tightly and shook his head wildly in disbelief . . .

'It . . . it can't be . . .'

Jam, the ScorpNex, smiled. Drool pooled from his twisted jaws, stretching to the floor in viscous strands.

'No, it fucking *cannot be*!'

'Hello, Carter,' said Jam, his voice soft and deformed – but still recognisable. Just.

Carter found tears on his cheeks.

'Jam! What have they fucking done to you . . .'

'Carter –' the ScorpNex spread its arms wide, making tiny crackling sounds as its chitinous armour shifted '— this is good, this is progress, this is *evolution*.'

'*Jam?*'

Jam's head moved, dipped, turned to stare at Mongrel who had crawled to his knees in the corner, blood coating his face, eyes wide in horror.

'Welcome to my home, Mongrel,' Jam growled softly.

Durell chuckled. 'Such a beautiful moment. Oh, my heart bleeds . . . but now, now to business. Jam?' Jam turned his gaze on Durell.

'Yes?'

Already the Nex were backing away, dragging Mila towards the door. The two Nex holding Carter suddenly dropped his arms and stepped away, leaving Carter and Jam in the centre of the room and Mongrel on his knees in the corner.

They left the building with Gol. Durell remained . . . watching from the doorway. 'They wanted you, Jam. Now they've found you. Kill them both.'

Jam's huge head wavered, shifted, and his stare fixed on Carter who stood, head down, eyes dark and brooding, his hands bound behind his back.

Jam seemed to grin, light reflecting from the tips of his long twisted teeth.

And in a blur of movement, he attacked . . .

CHAPTER 12

WARHOST

The Priest's eyes narrowed.

Something clicked against the hard floor.

Then there was a long, low and terrible hiss . . .

He whirled in the gloom that was speckled with light from far above, as a huge bulk rushed towards him. He reached for his Glock but too late – he was thrown across the chamber, grunting with pain, hammering into the wall and crumpling into a heap. Wheezing, The Priest struggled to his feet and peered through the darkness, his sandals scrabbling against the loose sand scattered over the fused glass floor of Spiral_Q.

It moved slowly towards him.

The Priest's eyes went wide.

'What in God's name are you?'

It moved on all fours, like a huge cat; its head was triangular, armoured and tufted with thick strands of fur, and its eyes were a deep and iridescent copper.

Its head dropped low, almost touching the ground, eyes looking up at The Priest with a kind of primal curiosity. Then its lips curled back to reveal long fangs and it snarled and claws clacked against the floor and thick heavy corded muscles bunched—

'I know you,' said The Priest, placing his hand against the Bible within his robes. 'You are a Sleeper and I remember you.' He smiled gently, nodding, his face lit with a serene light as he was listening to some distant voice.

The creature snarled and The Priest saw it ready for the kill: each fraction of a second filled with a rippling of muscle, a vibration of sinews, a focus of intent . . .

He sighed, hand moving from his Bible, brushing past his wooden beads as his sandals fought for purchase on the uneven sandy floor and dipping beneath his robes to reveal—

A big, broad-bladed, serrated knife.

'You are an abomination under God's Law,' he said, his voice now strong, booming almost, and eyes glittering in the gloom. 'And as such you must – die . . .'

The Sleeper attacked, bounding across the chamber towards The Priest who leapt forward to meet it, his huge frame silhouetted against the gloom as they smashed together. The huge jagged knife slashed up, and then out, slicing fur and bone and sending a dark spray of blood up over The Priest's face, splashing against the wall and floor.

He gasped in shock at the icy coldness of the blood as the Sleeper hissed in pain, rolling to one side. It skidded across the ground and The Priest ducked, whirling in a circle. Then it uncurled and stared first at the deep bubbling wound in its armoured flank, then back at the Priest.

He smiled, arms spreading wide, blood dripping from the tip of the glinting blade.

'Come, my friend. God has a very important lesson that he would wish me to teach you.'

The Sleeper rolled to its feet and edged forward, with infinitely more care this time, clawed pads clattering against the ground in a slow, hypnotic rhythm. The Priest moved away from the wall, face settling into a calm mask of understanding. The knife weaved in front of him, the steel blade his only defence . . .

The Sleeper charged.

The Priest rolled with awesome speed as a claw flashed past his face and the bulk of the creature smashed against him. The knife struck out, but the creature had spun to one side and whirled, huge heavy head swinging from side to side like a pendulum, to return and glare at The Priest – who ran at it, sandals flapping against the sandy glass floor as the Sleeper leapt again at the huge man. There came a sudden flurry of blows, and The Priest's powerful arms encircled the blood-dripping Sleeper. The large-bladed knife clattered across the floor and they hit the ground hard, rolling to a halt against the wall in a tangle of violence—

The Sleeper snarled.

The Priest head-butted its lower jaws, three, four, five times—

The Sleeper suddenly scrabbled against the huge man like a cat trapped in a cage, claws shredding his robes and the flesh beneath in a spraying shower of crimson. The Priest's face compressed in a titanic strain of effort, going through shades of red and purple as muscles writhed like eels along his arms and chest and his eyes searched desperately for the fallen blade—

A claw shot up, slicing through the already tattered grey robes. The Priest felt a warm sluicing of blood as the claw continued, and there came the wooden clatter of rosary beads against the glass floor.

The Priest's eyes went wide.

'My beads!' he hissed.

He slammed his right fist into the Sleeper's triangular head again and again and then kicked himself backwards, scooping up the blade and leaping at the stunned creature. The knife slashed down five times, and blood splashed across the floor and over his grey robes in pumping arcs. The Sleeper seemed to deflate and lay still, wheezing in the throes of death. Its huge head turned and the copper eyes bored into the blood-soaked Priest, hands slippery with gore and beard spattered with tiny pieces of armoured shell, which had been pulverised by the pounding blows of the broad serrated blade.

The Priest was panting, his eyes wild.

Staring down, he said in a deep and solemn voice, '*My brethren, be strong in the Lord and in the power of his might. Put on the whole armour of God, that ye may be able to stand against the wiles of the devil. For we wrestle not against flesh and blood, but against the darkness of the world!*'

He took a menacing step forward.

The Sleeper snarled, its blood forming huge pools on the ground. It struggled to rise, claws raking the glass, but sank back again as The Priest stooped towards it. Their stares became locked, joined to one another by dark threads of understanding . . .

'. . . *Wherefore take unto you the whole armour of God that ye may be able to withstand the evil day* . . .' The blade rose high above The Sleeper's head, and the beast's copper eyes lifted to follow the eerie glint of steel. '*And having done all, to Stand!*'

The blade plunged down, striking just above one eye.

There came a heavy crunch.

And the Sleeper died.

Panting, The Priest backed away and looked around the chamber, searching for more enemies. He then got down slowly onto his knees to retrieve his rosary beads.

He returned swiftly to his task. He cut through the alloy panel and reached inside, hand curling around a sheaf of metal documents. He stowed them beneath his robes, found his Glock, and with sandals leaving bloody imprints in puddles of death he moved to his Skimmer so that he could ascend from this pit.

Heneghan stared down from behind the facial shield of HIDSS as The Priest toiled across the sand. As he climbed into the Comanche's cockpit she half-turned, glancing at his shredded and bloodstained robes; the dark splatters on his hands and face; the look of thunder in his features.

'You been fighting again, holy man?'

'The bugger tore my beads!'

'I can see how that would be your greatest worry during a bout of violent combat,' the pilot said softly, eyeing the vicious serrated blade, which dripped blood onto the floor of the Comanche's cockpit.

The Priest's gaze met Heneghan's.

He was serious. Deadly serious.

'It was an act of blasphemy!' he growled.

'Was it?'

'The beads were my mum's! Now – take me to Greece.'

Jam's claw lashed out towards Carter's face and the Spiral agent rolled swiftly to one side, rising smoothing to his feet and launching himself into the air. Both his boots connected with Jam's triangular head, knocking the ScorpNex back a step. He gave a grunt and a deep hiss of surprise—

Carter landed and sprinted, arms still wired behind

324

his body. Mongrel had produced a hidden knife from his boot and cut his own bonds . . . now he cut Carter's as Jam charged.

'Don't do this, Jam!'

Claws lashed out and Carter ducked, landing a savage right hook on Jam's armoured head. He punched again and again, then dodged a blow by the ScorpNex and skipped to the left, boot lashing out in a powerful side-kick to connect with Jam's chest. Jam caught Carter's leg and tried to force him down but Carter flipped himself into a roll, boot hammering twice against Jam's face as he kicked himself away and rolled fluidly back upright, despite his previous injuries . . .

'Jam, stop!' he bellowed.

Jam halted, his copper eyes staring at Carter. Mongrel, who was watching almost paralysed, started to sidle towards Carter's Browning and the sub-machine gun on the side benches—

'You the enemy now.'

'We were friends!' snarled Carter. 'Don't fucking do this! I can help you.'

'How?'

'I don't know . . . but I don't want to fight you, I don't want to—'

'Kill me?' Jam chuckled with genuine humour. 'Show me Carter, show me how you will kill me . . .'

Jam leapt and Carter dodged again. Jam came down and spun in a blur, arm lashing out to smash Carter from his feet. Carter hit the ground hard, rolling to a stop and grunting, coughing and holding his chest where pain hammered through him with an intensity he had rarely felt before.

Carter rolled again and Jam's armoured feet landed where his head had been, cracking the thick wooden floorboards which splintered and spat shards of wood into the air.

Carter got to his feet and attacked – launching himself at Jam who plucked him from the air and threw him across the room. He landed heavily, crashing into one of the bunk beds and sending it tipping over – and with sudden panic Carter realised that he was tangled in its strewn wooden slats—

Mongrel grabbed the sub-machine gun.

Growling, Jam charged as Mongrel opened fire. Bullets spat across the Op HQ as Jam swerved to one side, the fusillade tracking him—

And then the whole world seemed to shake with the boom of a devastating explosion. Shrapnel scythed the building and the ground shuddered. Mongrel ceased firing, smoke curling from the gun's barrel—

'Jam!'

Durell was gone from the doorway.

Jam rose smoothly to his armoured feet as Carter clambered from the wreckage of the bed. Their stares met as Mongrel trained the gun on their old friend, snarling.

'Wait,' commanded Carter.

Jam glanced over at Mongrel, then back towards Carter. Another shell howled overhead and the world shook again. The remaining windows in the Op building rattled, and they could hear the roar of distant engines and the sudden clattering of heavy machine-fun fire.

'Tanks!' said Mongrel, eyes gleaming.

Jam stared at Carter. 'Until the next time,' he said, his face twisting into a strange smile.

'No, Jam . . . stay here . . .' Carter was clutching his chest and wheezing from the impact of the recent heavy blow. 'We . . . we need your help. Natasha is dying, Nicky is with her—'

Jam's expression changed – from a twisted smile to a snarl. 'Stop, Carter, stop . . .'

'We need the machine, the Avelach . . . you know where it is . . . it was used on you – to *change* you. Listen to me, man, if I don't get the machine then Natasha will *die*—'

Jam whirled, and was gone into the night.

Carter and Mongrel staggered to the doorway to see two of the LVA storage tanks billowing fifty-metre columns of fire into the sky with deafening roars, lighting up the quarry with false daylight. To one side the two armoured tanks sprang into life, engines roaring, tracks rumbling as at the distant head of the valley a group of Spiral SP57 tanks appeared, in desert camouflage – their tracks tearing at the hard-packed ground as they mowed down the perimeter fence and ploughed through barbed wire—

Nex spilled from the barracks.

There came a *whump* and one of the barrack buildings exploded in a titanic ball of fire sending a hundred screaming burning Nex flailing up into the sky where they disintegrated into flurries of charred flesh. The Spiral tanks advanced, churning the earth. The Nex tanks' guns fired and an SP57 was blown into the air and sent crashing into another tank. The two war machines exploded in a massive blossoming purple fireball . . .

'What can we do?' hissed Mongrel, eyes wide.

He turned. But Carter had gone . . .

The quarry was a battlefield.

Nex with sub-machine guns had taken up defensive positions and their JK59s roared. Another barracks was sent flashing into the sky at the same time as a Nex tank. It spun lazily on a rising blanket of fire, its gun blasting a shell up towards the heavens even as it rose and was slowly consumed by purple HighJ fire before arcing gently and toppling back to earth as a burned and blackened steel carcass . . .

Carter sprinted across the quarry, head down, Browning in one hand, face grim . . .

Four small black attack helicopters leapt into the air. The SM7.8VLS Vertical Launching Systems whirled on heavy-duty motors, arming the SM-7 missiles . . . but they did not engage.

They recognised their own.

Carter forgot stealth as bullets and shells screamed all around him. His face was illuminated by the light from the burning LVA tanker stores. Machine-gun fire stitched a line of dust spurts in front of his boots and his Browning smashed a Nex from its feet. He halted, dropping to a crouch beside the Nex warrior which scrabbled at the hot metal in its throat . . .

'Where is Durell?'

But the Nex died before it could say anything.

Behind the tanks came the roar of machine guns as DemolSquads on foot came to their aid. Using the heavy tanks as shields, they advanced across the tracer-lit quarry, an SP57 pushing a burning Nex truck chassis out of the way. Then the tank climbed over it and crushed it under its heavy tracks.

Carter saw the distant small black helicopters. Jam was climbing into one of them. He looked left, towards the nearest sniper tower. His eyes narrowed as he watched its two snipers firing, reloading, firing again and he ran towards the tower, grabbed the slippery alloy ladder and started to climb.

Bullets whistled past him, making him flinch and curse. Carter palmed the Browning and took out three

Nex with three head shots. They hit the ground, rolling, rag-dolls whose brains merged with the hard-packed ground in streamers of gore.

Carter continued to climb.

Below him the quarry spread out, a battlefield populated by a couple of hundred Nex and Spiral DemolSquads. The tanks had centre stage and, off in the distance, Carter saw more Nex tanks rumbling from some distant reserve post—

'The fuckers.'

To his right, the helicopters containing Durell and Jam started to climb into the night air, engines howling, mounted machine guns raining bullets down into the battle raging below. Carter increased his efforts, sweat rolling down his face and body, breath coming in gasps, stare switching between the battlefield and the ascending choppers—

Carter reached the top of the ladder.

The two snipers were busy – busy dealing out precision death.

As Carter's boots touched down on the rough-sawn planks, the Nex whirled round, suddenly looking confused. Carter shot the first one in the face at point-blank range and saw the pale white features disintegrate in an instant as blood sprayed across a wooden beam. The second Nex threw a punch but Carter ducked, came up on its left and powered his right elbow into its face. It took a step back, and Carter smashed a right kick into its chest – it hit the barrier, and was flipped over to topple to the ground far below.

Carter grabbed at his belt, produced a tiny matt-black disc the size of a small coin – a TrackingDisc – and as the helicopters lifted past the tower he pulled back his arm and threw it with all his might. It spun across the void and connected with a click to the tail section of Durell's helicopter – which disappeared up into the blackness.

Panting and shaking, Carter glanced down at the raging battle.

Machine-gun bullets slammed into the beam behind him, spitting splinters of scorched wood into the air.

'Cheers, guys,' he muttered, taking hold of a Nex sniper rifle. He hefted the Barrett SilverScope III thoughtfully, then leant it against the wooden parapet and sighted on the nearest sniper tower directly opposite.

The two snipers there leapt into view as the sight clicked and buzzed. The Nex were busy with their shooting, rifles kicking smoothly and emotionlessly in black-gloved hands.

Carter sighted his weapon and sent a bullet across the gap.

It hit a Nex in the side of the head, the high-calibre round smashing it from the platform with only half of its skull left. The second Nex looked momentarily stunned, then whirled as the bullet hit it high in the chest and it, too, was punched backwards from the tower to flip and fall, legs kicking as it spun towards the ground.

Carter turned his attention to the third tower.

And, smiling coldly, killed the snipers there too.

'*I fucking hate snipers as well,*' snapped Kade. '*Go on . . . give them a taste of their fucking medicine . . . do you know, in the Fourth Gulf War if we caught a sniper we used to—*'

'Kade?'

'*Hmm?*'

'Shut up.'

Carter sighted on the final operational sniper tower. They were raining hot death down on the DemolSquads supporting the SP57 tanks below and Carter sighted on the first Nex – could see the copper eyes leap into view

330

through his scope, could read the focus of intent, and licked his lips, allowing breath to flow easily from his lungs as—

The whole tower top exploded in a sudden bright inflorescence and disintegrated in a bloom of purple.

The Nex snipers were vaporised.

Carter frowned, and followed the line of trajectory. And there, on the top of the cliff, squatting like an angry insect against the hard ground with its matrix-engine hissing was the HTank – the Spiral Edition HoverTank – driven by Simmo.

Carter grinned.

Then saw the gun start to track round—

Towards him.

'You've got to be fucking—' But he was moving, climbing onto the ladder and praying like a lunatic. He clamped his boots to the outside of the ladder and loosened his grip . . .

The ladder thrummed under his gloves.

The ground rushed towards his boots – as his eyes saw the kick of fire from the HTank's massive barrel and the tower above him exploded in a shattering blast. The shock waves sent him crashing from the ladder, chunks of hot wood raining down on him, to land in a bush.

All the air was kicked from his lungs.

Carter lay there, dazed. He watched the HTank engage and with a cold matrix-engine hiss flip over the lip of the canyon and speed to the wide floor of the quarry down the rugged near-vertical slope – and behind the positions of the fighting Nex.

Three shells sent bodies sailing, burning, through the air.

Another shell destroyed the final Nex tank.

Carter looked up, looked around.

Mongrel was grinning. 'Carter, what the fuck are you doing in that bush?'

Carter realised that he was on fire, and hurriedly patted at his flaming clothing. 'Trying not to get shelled,' he muttered, as Mongrel helped him from the spiky branches with small curses and yelps.

'They got away,' said Mongrel, as Simmo's HTank roared up behind the Spiral agent and Mongrel looked calmly over his shoulder. The hatch opened with a clang and Simmo's huge shaved head appeared, throat-tattoos glistening under a layer of sweat.

'The Sarge think that fine sport!' he yelled.

'Not done yet,' said Carter, pointing.

One final small black attack helicopter was trying to take off. It rose into the air, then fell back again, its engines screaming. Then it leapt once more—

'Simmo take care of this.' He disappeared.

Carter and Mongrel exchanged glances.

The HTank, so close that Carter could have reached out and touched it, elevated its bulk on a cold-cushion of hissing vapour and the gun fired a shell that caught the helicopter's tail section, ripping it free and sending the machine into a spinning nosedive. It crunched against the concrete landing pad and fire erupted along one flank from severed fuel pipes . . .

Simmo leapt down from the HTank and strode towards the chopper.

'What you doing?' yelled Mongrel over the sounds of distant gunshots.

Simmo just shrugged, reached the burning copter, and pulled free a lithe but muscular man with a heavily scarred face and red eyes. He was unconscious from the impact, bleeding, and Simmo calmly dragged him away as the black chopper flared bright and exploded, sending a thick plume of black smoke up into the moonlit night.

'There are more tanks coming,' said Carter. 'From down the valley. I saw them from the tower.'

Simmo nodded, dumping Kattenheim to the ground. Mongrel rolled him onto his belly and bound his wrists and feet with wire. Simmo spoke quietly into his ECube and a group of waiting SP57 tanks turned, tracks grinding against the hard earth and turrets rotating smoothly to face this new threat.

'We get call,' said Simmo proudly. 'We come! Heli-lift tanks in from local depot in Italy and many of TankSquad men fast-jet here from London . . . including me! Well done, Mongrel! Your message tie in with The Priest's and suddenly it make sense!'

Carter lit a cigarette.

'And I see you brought the HTank there, Sarge.'

'My HTank. Italian prototype. Ducati engines.'

Carter frowned, smiling softly. 'You mean *Spiral*'s HTank, surely?'

'Is mine.'

Carter breathed deeply, then nudged Mongrel as Simmo climbed back into the HTank and revved the cold matrix-engine. 'Me go kill more Nex!' he shouted down. 'The Sarge not seen battle for too long! The Sarge soon run out of tattoo space!' He steered the thundering HTank across the quarry, scattering DemolSquad teams who were clearing the area of any remaining Nex . . . and disappeared from view.

'We need to get the bikes and get back to the Comanche.'

'You got a plan?'

'I tagged Durell's helicopter.'

'So we know where they're going? Smart move.'

Carter took Mongrel's ECube and punched in a code.

333

It hummed as it tracked trajectories and gave a list of possible destinations. 'Yeah, looks like we're going to . . .' He groaned.

'Where?'

'Of all the fucking places!'

'Where is it, Carter?'

Carter grimaced. 'Looks like we could be going to Egypt.'

'I thought you were a wanted man in Egypt?'

'I am. Everybody wants me *very* dead.'

'Why?'

'It's a long story, my friend.'

Mongrel kicked the trussed-up body of Kattenheim. 'What we going to do with this piece of shit? You think he might have some answers?'

'I'm pretty sure he does. If we ask the right questions.'

'I bet,' said Mongrel, sharing Carter's cigarette as machine guns blasted to one side and five DemolSquad operatives found the last remaining Nex and drilled it full of holes. 'I bet he's one of those tough bastards who just doesn't want to talk.'

'Simple solution,' said Carter, eyes glittering.

'What's that?'

'We'll let Sergeant Simmo question him.'

Mongrel nodded, enjoying the smoke and gazing around at the fire, the bodies, the devastation. He laughed out loud then, and shook his head, eyes haunted.

'You thinking of Jam?'

'Yes,' muttered Mongrel. 'Come on. I want to get out of this place.'

'Let's tool up and move out,' said Carter. 'Simmo can give us information while we're on the move.'

'Can I come with you?'

Carter turned, and saw Mila. She was watching him

334

with a strange look on her face. Blood had dried on her skin and he smiled kindly, wearily.

'No.'

'We might need a sniper,' said Mongrel.

'No.'

'Listen, you can't leave me *here*,' Mila said, gazing round in horror at the battlefield and the corpses. 'This is my fight as well – these Nex, they are my enemies. I have helped you get this far – without me you would not be on the trail of that . . . *creature* you need to hunt.'

Carter glanced – murderously – at Mongrel. What else have you blabbed? he thought.

'It will be dangerous,' said Carter softly. He placed a hand against her shoulder, gently, feeling a little guilty for having placed a bullet in her flesh.

'I can look after myself,' Mila said.

'So be it,' nodded Carter.

'*Pussy*,' whispered Kade, a dark sneer in his tone.

CHAPTER 13

RENDEZVOUS

The lights were dim inside the barracks.

Simmo stood at the centre of the room, wearing nothing but combats and boots. His chest, heavily scarred and heavily tattooed, rippled with muscle. The huge soldier carried not one ounce of excess fat.

Around the outskirts of the room designed to house a hundred Nex warriors stood several grim-faced DemolSquad troopers. Haggis and Mo stood side by side, huge squat bullet-headed men, one British and one Pakistani: both awesome fighters. Lurking in the shadows, weapons held loosely in their hands, cigarettes trailing smoke to the ceiling stood the TankSquads – Fegs, Kavanagh, Oz, Remic, Root Beer, Rogowski, Falconer, Sagar, Graham and Holtzhausen. Kinnane and Samasuwo both held brews in their big scarred fists, and Bob Bob was looking forlorn, still with custard – his favourite food – staining his combats. All of them watched with barely suppressed hatred as Simmo reached down, dragged Kattenheim onto the chair at the centre of the room, and slowly tied him tightly to the thick wooden frame.

Simmo stooped a little, looking into the red eyes.

'I know you're a tough lad,' he rumbled, 'and The Sarge be honest – he not really like doing this sort of thing. Well, not much. Well, not unless he in bad mood. But you know answers to our questions and we want answers.'

'Fuck you,' said Kattenheim softly, and stared straight ahead.

Simmo shrugged, flexed his shoulders, and delivered a crashing left hook. They all heard the crack of bone before the chair hit the ground and Kattenheim lay, stunned and bleeding and staring at the wooden boards.

'Simmo?' said Fegs, holding a cigarette casually between his tattooed fingers.

'Yeah?'

'Aren't you supposed to ask him a question?'

'Hm. Yes.' The Sarge nodded, then dragged Kattenheim upright once more.

'Nothing like a fair trial,' said Kattenheim smoothly; his face was swollen around his cheek and his gaze lifted to meet Simmo's. 'Once, when I was on para-ops in Colombia, I was captured by the enemy. The drug-puri-fiers tortured me for five days with alkaline chemical agents – and you see the results of their handiwork. And do you know something, Sergeant Simmo? I spoke not one word. Not one fucking word until my team mates found me and burned the enemy – alive – in large pits. I have a pact with pain, Mr Simmo. Me and pain, well, we just agree to disagree.'

Simmo nodded, then delivered a right that smashed Kattenheim's nose and sent the chair crashing backwards, thumping against the boards. A splash of blood stained the timber. Simmo moved forward and stood over Kattenheim, staring down, his face twisting as he felt his

337

massive temper rising. Simmo felt the other TankSquad men retreating further into the shadows. When Simmo exploded, nobody wanted to be close.

'The Sergeant very sorry you suffer at the hands of your enema.' He chuckled nastily. 'But I have watched one thousand, five hundred and sixty-three men – and, ah, Nex – die. One could say Sarge is professional. One could say Sarge have no soul. One could say Sarge have pact with the Devil. Whatever, you need answer questions or your pain will be incredible.'

'Pain is something I can live with,' said Kattenheim softly as the chair was righted and somebody handed Simmo a long, heavy, rusting iron bar. Simmo weighed it thoughtfully.

'You have made your peace. That good, Sarge thinks. Now, I need know links between Durell and the LVA fuel. I need know why Nex are guarding LVA pumping rig. And I need know where Durell has gone with little cronies.'

Kattenheim stared straight ahead, mouth a grim line.

Most of the TankSquads looked away as Simmo swung the heavy bar.

And they knew that the night was going to be a long one.

The Comanche's twin LHTec engines were humming softly as they cleared the south-west coast of Slovenia and headed out over the Adriatic Sea. The sun was rising in the east, casting tendrils of soft orange light over the silver waves, and the huge expanse of water stretched out ahead of them.

Carter, still weary and exhausted, checked the blip from the TrackingDisc and smiled to himself. He thought of Natasha lying in the hospital bed and the smile changed immediately to a grim scowl.

His mind spun with confusion.

And hatred.

And . . . exhaustion.

How much longer can I go on? he asked himself.

How much longer can I fight? Kill?

'*For ever and ever. Amen,*' said Kade.

'Who dragged you kicking and screaming back into this universe?

'*I was just thinking.*'

'About?'

'*About Jam. I know his weakness.*'

'Which is?'

'*Ahh, now that would be telling. Let's just say that when we meet the fucker again, let me have a stab at him. We'll see who's the fucking daddy then.*'

'The only stab you'll ever get is a nine-inch blade in the back.'

'*Your humour is what keeps me alive, O Master,*' chuckled Kade.

The Comanche flashed low over the sea, heading south-east a couple of miles off the coast of Croatia and then Albania. As they headed over the Ionian Sea to the west of the Greek mainland Carter's ECube buzzed softly.

'Yeah?'

'Carter, this is The Priest.'

'Long time no see, you religious maniac. What do you want?'

'We need to meet.'

'I'm a little busy.'

'Make time.'

'You're not listening, Priest. I'm a little fucking busy to be arranging social events with Bible-wielding lunatics – even if they are in charge of the Spiral secret police.'

'Carter, this is important. It involves Spiral, it involves Jam, and it involves Natasha.'

Carter was silent behind the insect-visor of the HIDSS helmet.

'What do you suggest?' he said, finally, quietly.

'You are heading for Egypt. The Spiral mainframes have you plotted. Touch down in Crete, coordinates 224.361.762. I will meet you as soon as I am able.'

'How long?'

'I cannot say. We have just discovered Durell's game. I will bring you up to speed when we meet.'

'This better be important, Priest.'

'It's important, Carter. Trust me and trust God.'

'God? I'm pretty sure that fucker has abandoned me.'

The ECube cut out and Carter was left staring at the silver sea below his humming war machine. He thought back to everything that they had been through; thought back to Feuchter and Durell and the QIII processor and The Priest's involvement in the events that had almost toppled the world.

'*You think he could be a traitor as well?*' asked Kade.

'No . . . I don't know. I find it hard to trust people in, shall we say, the current world climate.'

'*Let me kill the fucker,*' said Kade.

'Jesus, don't you have another fucking tune to play?'

'*The day that I die will be the day I stop killing,*' said Kade. '*And you are the same, my boy, my brother. You are the same. We are as one; peas in the same pod.*'

In silence they cruised towards the distant shimmering island of Crete.

Freddy killed the engine and sat in silence, in the absence of the Honda's 8600cc rumble. He nodded to himself.

340

Hmm, he thought, this LVA seems to be running a treat! Maybe Charlotte had been right after all?

He climbed from the cabin and stood in the darkness, hands on hips, and then lit a cigarette. He noticed that his hand was shaking – just a little bit. As the weed touched his lips he could just distinguish badly scrubbed blood-stains on his fingers.

The ground trembled beneath his boots.

A gentle caressing.

A tender warning . . .

The quake singing a soothing grinding lullaby.

Freddy stood on the moors, filling his lungs with nico-tine. He moved around to the boot of the Honda and popped the catch. It slid smoothly upwards to reveal a dark interior.

And there lay the bin-bag-confined body parts of Charlotte.

Freddy sighed.

Why couldn't you have been normal? he thought.

He reached in and pulled out a long parcel. It was wrapped very neatly and Freddy prided himself on the tight binding of the silver duct-tape around the seams that made sure that no blood could possibly escape.

He chuckled to himself as he stepped onto the heather and headed away from the Honda. The heather was wet, springy, sinking a little beneath his footsteps. He carried Charlotte's leg under one arm and a spade in his free hand.

It wouldn't have to be a deep hole.

Just a shallow grave.

He found a suitable spot.

Rain started to drizzle down. As he dropped the par-celled leg on the heather, it made a wet thump. He slammed the spade into the earth, cutting neatly through heather with the sharp edge of the blade. The blade struck four times, creating a square of sliced vegetation and soil – and then Freddy levered the mound free and threw it to one side.

Slowly, Freddy began to excavate.

After twenty minutes he was panting hard and his breath was steaming in the light rain. The hole was quite big – almost big enough for the body of his ex-lover, at any rate.

Freddy felt a twinge of guilt then.

He acknowledged that Charlotte probably hadn't deserved what she had got. He acknowledged that death and dismemberment were gifts that one shouldn't really bestow upon one's girlfriend. And he acknowledged that burial on the moors was perhaps rather savage a punishment for perpetual moaning, whining, bickering and emotional blackmail.

Freddy smiled.

His eyes glinted – a little insanely.

But then . . . but but but fucking *but*!

He shovelled another spade of earth onto the pile of waterlogged soil. It smelled creamy, rich, musty – like a proper grave on the moors should.

Something glinted through the rain, distantly, across the heather.

Voices drifted; the sounds of ghosts.

'Pedal, fat man, pedal!'

'Is this insanity – or fitness training?'

'It must be insanity. We never see any other fucker out in the rain, ice and snow!'

'Fucking warm-weather riders. Bunch of pussies to a man.'

'Yeah, bit of frost and they fanny out! The little girls.'

Freddy's head whipped left. His eyes narrowed. Water dripped from the tip of his nose.

Lights glittered dazzlingly through the rain.

'What the hell is *that*?' he muttered.

Two sets of twin halogen lamps sparkled. Freddy could hear puffing and panting – laughter. Through the increasing downpour came two mountain bikers, their silver titanium full-suss machines sloshing easily through the mud, lamps glittering. The riders were wearing full army combats, wet-proofs, and floppy desert army hats. They splashed to a stop a few feet away, halogens cutting a bright slice from the night and illuminating Freddy, his spade, his hole, and a bin-bag-wrapped leg.

The two bearded men stared hard at Freddy.

Then they looked at one another.

'What the fuck is *he* doing, Ravioli?'

'Fucked if I know, Worzel.'

They both stared back at Freddy, eyes narrowing to glares as they stepped from the saddles of their mountain bikes and allowed the machines to fall in the mud. They took a step closer, then another. Freddy took a step back.

'What you doing?' said Ravioli, goatee beard making his tapered face look quite evil in the gloom.

Freddy shrugged a little, spade loose in one hand.

'Is that a fucking *grave*?' spat Worzel, round face, bushy eyebrows and thick black beard glistening in the murk.

'I've got a bad feeling about this – worse than the time you swallowed that mescal worm and I had to take you to the hospital when the alcohol-infused grub burnt away part of your lip! Hey, and what's that parcel wrapped up there?'

They moved forward, curious.

Again, Freddy backed away – and in a fit of sudden panic, dropped his spade and ran for it. He sprinted across the moors, stumbling across the heather in the darkness, heavy rain obscuring his vision, blind panic filling his soul with a need to get away. He ran and ran, pushing himself to levels of exertion that he had never realised he could reach. Then, suddenly, he splashed to a halt, panting, eyes scanning nervously as he spun around – twice – in circles.

Where am I?

Shit.

Where's the car?

Bitch!

He calmed his breathing, and listened to see if the two men were pursuing him. He whirled in the gloom, twitchy, nervous, mind filled with leaping shadows.

And he could sense—

Sense something there.

Freddy stared as hard as he could into the darkness. He knew that the night could play tricks on you, and places like the moors were renowned for being spooky in the dark. He had been in the habit of coming up here with Charlotte a few years earlier, before they had their own place – the moors had been a good place for covert sex. But many times, even during their soaring passion and Charlotte's moans for a new toaster, vacuum cleaner or tropical holiday, the light could move in such a way, or the wind moan through the oppressive darkness and you could believe that a knife-wielding maniac was only a few feet away.

How fucking ironic, he mused bitterly . . . as something large and black and moving faster than thought slammed into him. He caught a glimpse of bright gleaming copper and then the pain screamed through him. He gagged and choked on his own blood as a fist like a sword tore open his chest. The dark heather was so cool on his

344

face – it smelled fresh, like that summer's day when he had first brought Charlotte up to this romantic desolate haven . . .

Worzel knelt by the package and prodded it gingerly. He glanced up at Ravioli who was staring – a bit aghast, mouth open and nose wrinkled in distaste.

'Open it,' growled Ravioli.

Worzel scowled. 'I ain't fucking opening it. It might be a body or something.'

'What, the body of a midge?'

'You mean midget.'

'Whatever. Go on, it won't bite you. If it *is* a body then it's obviously dead. But it'll just be a porn stash or something.

'There's nothing wrong with porn!'

'I never said there was.'

There was a pause for thought. 'So why *bury* it?'

'I don't fucking know. Are you going to open it or what? Or are you just going to start crying about being the most unpopular man at the party again – just because you have to drink a half-pint of tequila? Like a big pussy?'

'At least I haven't got a ginger fucking afro!'

'Hey, I had that shaved off a long time ago, so—'

Something clicked.

From the gloom, past the dazzling halogen headlights shining across the rainswept moorland and tufts of heather nestling at ground level, came the sound of padding armoured claws.

A bulky shape stopped in the gloom, tantalisingly hidden by the edges of shadows cast by the bright bike lights.

Ravioli and Worzel ceased their petty argument.

A large dark rain-slick triangular head swept towards

them. There came a gleam of copper eyes. The ground trembled softly underfoot, and Ravioli and Worzel took a step away from the hole, the spade, and the severed leg. They licked dry lips and swallowed, their throats coarse. They glanced nervously at each other – as if to confirm that this was not a bad moorland night-mirage.

'Nice doggy,' said Worzel.

'That ain't a doggy.'

'You think I don't know that? You think I think it's a fucking donkey or something?'

'I think we should run.'

'Run or fight?'

'Or . . . the third option?'

Ravioli produced a Mars bar. He took off the wrapper and broke off a chunk of chocolate, stretching strings of soft toffee. Worzel stared hard at his friend.

'What the *fuck* are you doing?'

'I was going to entice it away with chocolate.' Ravioli looked suddenly a little uncertain.

The creature . . . growled.

Ravioli and Worzel turned to run – and felt something crash into them with the force of a train smashing into a wall. Claws rent flesh in the darkness, slashing left and right with economical movements. A spray of gore and blood filled the temporary shallow grave. Two bodies rolled away in several separate pieces, skin, bone, intestines and muscle flapping loosely – and blank dead eyes stared up at the heavy downpour.

The Sleeper turned, its own eyes glowing for an instant like miniature twin suns caught in the beams of the halogen bike-lamps – and from behind the bikes came more shapes, moving through the rain: two, three, five, ten . . . twenty . . . dark bodies glistening with chitinous exoskeletons. They moved on armoured claws, warily, heavy muscles bunched as the world trembled in the fist of the impending and building quake. Their eyes turned towards the distant lights of the city and the scent of the humans beyond.

They sprinted into the night.

And were gone.

Ivers stared with incredible boredom at the titanium-carbide VII drill bit rotating at high speed within its protective Plas-7 sheath. The platform was solid beneath his feet, his lust for Michelle even stronger as the minutes until their next amorous meeting ticked by . . . but something else had wormed its way into his brain—

A needle.

A needle of . . . curiosity.

'Hey, Oldroyd?'

'Yeah?'

Oldroyd was in his late thirties, and although only small in stature he made up for his lack of height with his character. He was chirpy, cheerful – bouncing, some would say. He always had a clever quip, a witty put-down, a humorous piece of pornographic verse: many underestimated Oldroyd, but always to their own cost. With a smile he could destroy a room full of cocktail party guests. With a quip he could decimate a legion of underrated comedians. With a baring of his arse on live TV, he could offend a nation. Which he had done on four occasions in life, thus far.

'You know when that inspectorate team came here, with the guy in the robes?'

'Durell.'

Ivers met Oldroyd's look but for once the small man's humour had evaporated. Ivers waited for the punch line – none came. I suppose there are some things in life which are just not funny, he mused.

347

'I think they went down the tubes under the Sub-3KM control quarters.'

'Why do you think that?' Oldroyd's normally cheeky expression was deadly serious.

'I don't know . . . the equipment looked like it might have been moved.' Ivers shrugged. 'Forget it, forget I said anything about it. I'm just fucking imagining things.'

Oldroyd tutted. 'Aye lad, you should get yourself a girlfriend.' He smiled roguishly. 'That usually cures supernatural imaginings for me.'

Ivers chuckled, and went back to checking the titanium-carbide VII drill bit. Fantasies played through his head – fantasies of small cars with large engines, his ambition to rebuild and customise a Helix Coupe 6.0 litre, replacing the motor with a 1250 bhp 24-cylinder monster . . . and his inherent need to lavish love, care and attention on his most favourite of favourite hobbies: bike racing – preferably on 1296cc Ducatis.

Kenny's voice came from the ComChamber, whining a little. 'Something's going on. Upstairs.' 'Upstairs' was their nickname for above ground. Away from the drilling sites.

Ivers frowned. 'Like what?'

'The order's come down to shut down the drill bit.'

'What, slow it down?'

'No, *shut* it down.'

Ivers shook his head, but Kenny was already punching in the digits. The huge bit slowed to a crawl and, hissing loudly, rolled to a halt. A strange silence seemed to pervade the underground site.

Ivers glanced upwards, almost nervously.

He could feel the weight of the world – and it weighed heavy.

'Come on.' The others were ascending the pressure lifts and Ivers followed, watching his fellow LVA-ENG team members disappear up the tubes. He stumbled just before the tube engaged, fell to one knee on the hardwood deck – and then glanced up.

Buzzers were sounding across the console.

Ivers turned and moved swiftly to the hatchway leading to the tube which in turn led under their control deck; it was intended for service personnel and led down towards the bottom of the shafts to allow deeper servicing of the titanium-carbide VII. He popped the hatch and stared down into the gloom.

He licked his lips.

Going down there is a sackable offence, mused his inner voice.

But he knew. Knew that something was *wrong*.

Taking a deep breath, Ivers climbed into the tube and hit the SEND button; he felt his whole body *compress* and then he stepped out in the tiny alloy work bay.

It was very dark. But something was glowing – displaying soft blue digits.

Frowning, Ivers moved forward and stooped, finally dropping to his knees to get a closer look. There was a long thin grey box, with a small alloy cube attached. Digits flickered across the cube, and it was these that glowed.

'What is it?' he muttered.

And then he heard a noise – a scuff behind him.

He whirled – to see the barrel of a gun pointing straight at his face. He blinked, swallowed, and tried to step back. But the alloy wall was there – and he had nowhere to go. No escape. No path to freedom and life.

The figure was slim, athletic, wearing a body-hugging grey jumpsuit and a balaclava. The eyes glowed like

349

molten copper and burned into Ivers with their fearsome fixed intensity.

Ivers lifted his hands in front of his face, as if they could halt the bullet.

'No . . .' he whispered.

The Nex moved forward, gun nudging past Ivers's defensive fingers until the barrel touched against his forehead, sliding a little against the sudden sweat there. Ivers closed his eyes. He prayed, images flickering like movie scenes through his scattered thoughts . . .

Tears rolled down his cheeks.

The Nex's finger tightened imperceptibly on the trigger.

'*No . . .*' whispered Ivers.

And then – the unimaginable. The pressure of the gun was released, and Ivers opened his tear-filled eyes. The Nex had tilted its head, its copper-eyed stare still fixed unblinkingly on his face.

It gestured with the gun.

'Huh?'

'It's your lucky day. Go on. Fuck off.'

'Th— tha—'

'Just go. But first, a word of advice.' Ivers halted, reluctant to turn his back on the entity with the gun. Those copper eyes made him want to pee his pants – but stinking of urine was not something that filled him with enthusiasm so he contained himself. 'There are some things that you are destined never to see in life,' the Nex said softly, its voice asexual. 'This is one of them. I suggest that you keep your mouth shut. Or I will have to shut it for you.'

Ivers scuttled away.

Calmly, the Nex folded its arms and retreated into the shadows.

★

The Comanche spun low over the Mediterranean Sea, rotor blades flashing in the sunlight as the LHTec engines whined.

The war machine came in wide across the lapping silver waters, crossing the coastline of Crete midway between Keratókambos and Ierapetra on the large island's southern shores. Carter touched down on a section of rough ground that Spiral used for such covert operations – miles from civilisation – and he and Mongrel quickly unloaded the KTM LC7 motorbikes and cammed up the chopper using netting woven with fake foliage.

They fired the bikes into life and Mila scrambled on behind Carter. They headed a short distance cross-country until they reached the narrow winding coastal road. Here Carter halted the KTM and, its engine rumbling between his legs, he peered out over the sparkling waters as the autumn sun rose above, high into the sky.

He breathed deeply, feeling simultaneously free and enslaved – jerked back on his leash by The Priest and his request for a meeting. Carter knew it would be important – and The Priest had specifically mentioned Natasha.

'Ah, fuck it.'

He twisted the throttle hard and the rear tyre spun, kicking out sand across the wind-scarred dusty tarmac. Then he virtually fired the bike down the road on an insanely accelerating surge of power.

Mila clung tightly to the back, her hair whipping in the mad breeze – and wondered at their wisdom in wearing no helmets—

Carter, eyes streaming, relaxed into the bike's rhythm and allowed his mind to merge with the machine. He could feel the thump of the tyres over the rough terrain, the violent vibrations from the broken ground through

351

the handlebars – and he grinned without humour into the wind as a sharp corner reared ahead. He leaned deep into the bend, feeling Mila squirming behind him – fighting the kick of physics – as tyres slid and barely managed to keep their grip on the dusty trail.

Behind them sand clouds bloomed.

Mongrel coughed in the dust-trail and cursed Carter with all his might.

Ten miles saw them reaching the outskirts of Ierapetra on a high coastal cliff which looked down over the distant narrow streets of Kato Mera, the old town of Ierapetra and the Kales medieval fortress which had once housed Saracen pirates.

Carter stopped the bike again and they stared down at the traditional white-walled buildings. Mongrel finally caught up, coughing on dust and glaring at Carter.

'You fucking maniac on that thing!'

'I try my best,' Carter drawled through gritted teeth. 'We going up to the Serakina?'

'That's where the co-ords specified.'

Carter wheelied the bike up the beginning of the rise, feeling Mila's hands digging like claws into his hips, and as the front wheel touched down they hit the *really* rough trail, bouncing and bumping their way along.

The Serakina was a small white building, a single-storey hotel and bar overlooking the Mediterranean. The road to it led between two mounded hills, effectively giving a single entrance into and out of the compound. Tables and chairs had been set out on a wide lawn that ended with a fence and a steep drop down a cliff onto rocks and crashing waves far below. A couple of cars were parked next to the building, beside a large 5.0-litre BMW X550 off-road vehicle with tinted windows and heavy knobbled tyres.

'I see George is home,' muttered Mongrel as they kicked the bikes on to their stands in the shade beside the white wall of the Serakina, and stretched their aching backs. Shouldering their kit, they moved to the front door which was open, allowing access to the cool interior within.

'George?' bellowed Mongrel.

A large black man appeared, his biceps thicker than a normal man's thigh, his face stern and scarred. But the scowl broke into a beaming smile when he caught sight of Mongrel. The two embraced like old friends, laughing.

'The Dog is back.'

'Nothing but a half-breed,' agreed Mongrel. 'You remember Carter?'

'I remember Carter,' said the heavily muscled man, transferring his focused round-eyed gaze and fixing Carter with a dangerous glare. 'You not bring trouble to my house this time.'

'That's a promise I cannot keep,' said Carter softly.

George stared for a while, then transferred his gaze to Mila. 'My, what a pretty creature. What is your name?'

'I am Mila.'

'She's travelling with us,' added Mongrel helpfully.

George nodded. 'Why don't you go sit in the sunshine – I bring you out drinks. You look worn out.'

'Is there somewhere I can have a bath?' asked Mila.

'I will see to you in a moment, my sweetness,' crooned George and Mongrel flashed him a wicked smile.

'She could do with some fresh clothes. And chuck her a sterile pad while you're at it. I know you're a dab hand at dressing injuries and you not turn down the opportunity to maul her flesh.'

Carter and Mongrel walked across the grass towards the cliff edge and the timber tables. At that time of year

353

the tourist trade had quietened – trailing off after the heat of high summer – and with the recent earthquakes and their unpredictable effects and locations many people worldwide had chosen not to fly. The tourist trade had been seriously damaged by the quakes, but this suited the Spiral agents.

Mongrel slapped Carter on the back. 'How you feeling?'

Carter sighed, glancing at Mongrel 'Sore. I thought that fall from the sniper tower was going to break every fucking bone in my body. And it didn't help with Jam trying to cave in my head . . .'

'*Da*, you've been through the wars, mate.'

'I've felt worse.'

Carter went quiet suddenly and glanced out over the sparkling sea. They could just hear the crash of the waves on the rocks down below. In the distance the town of Ierapetra glittered like some ancient story of Arabian deserts and miracles.

The sound of an engine reached them, a large engine working hard up the incline towards the cliffs. Carter automatically found his hand on the Browning. Both he and Mongrel stared at the single entrance leading to the land in front of the Serakina.

A black Toyota Land Cruiser 70 4X4 rumbled into view and parked. The door opened and a lithe athletic woman stepped down. She glanced across at the two men, almost nonchalantly . . . and then froze. Her gaze met Carter's.

'Isn't that . . .' stuttered Mongrel.

Carter nodded, swallowing hard.

She was tall and slim, pale-skinned and dressed in black trousers and a short-sleeved black blouse. Her face was oval and had a light sprinkling of freckles below piercing green eyes. Her hair was long, straight and dark

354

brown, fanning behind her shoulders. And she wore a red hat, a striking contrast against the black of her clothing.

'Didn't you two . . .'

Carter nodded again, slowly, watching as the woman tilted her head – almost in confusion, almost acknowledgement – and then turned and disappeared into the cool interior of the building.

'*What's that bitch doing here?*' snapped Kade.

Carter did not reply.

Carter couldn't reply.

It had been a long time since he had seen Roxi.

A long time since he had tried to *murder* Roxi.

And the feeling tasted bad in his soul.

George arrived, bearing a tray with four bottles of beer and a plate of food. Mongrel stared at it suspiciously.

George grinned. 'Don't look like that, bad dog. That is *vrasti gida*, and that is *kolokithocorfades*. You will enjoy, this George promise you!'

'It looks minging,' growled Mongrel.

'Minging?' George frowned and boomed laughter. 'Now, you eat your breakfast and drink your beer. The sun is shining and there is lovely lady who need bath and expert medical help from ol' George.'

'You be good to her.'

'I always am.'

'Different cultures, different customs,' said Carter softly. 'Don't be such an English egg-and-chip heathen!'

George ambled across the grass in his flip-flops, his huge size making him look out of place. His shoulders squeezed together to allow him to fit through the doorway. Mongrel grasped his beer and took a long, refreshing pull. He slapped his mouth and patted his lips in appreciation. 'I fucking needed that. Didn't think I was ever

355

going drink beer again, not when that Nex put gun to my head and beat me and threw me in the truck. Carter, we up against some bad enemies this time.'

'The fuckers just won't lie down and die,' agreed Carter, taking the beer and staring at the brown bottle. He placed the chilled glass against his lips and heard a sharp intake of breath in his mind – Kade's hiss . . .

Carter paused, then closed his eyes and took a long cool drink.

It tasted good.

'What the problem between you and George?' asked Mongrel, poking suspiciously at the *kolokithocorfades*. He could have sworn the dish was staring back at him.

Carter shrugged. 'I shot some of his customers once.'

'Bad men?'

'I always shoot bad men,' said Carter sombrely. Standing suddenly, he said, 'You wait here. I'm going to call Nicky.'

Mongrel's battered face paled. 'Are you . . . you . . . ?'

'Am I going to tell her about Jam? You've got to be fucking joking! What would you say? Oh yeah, we found Jam but he's not dead, and the enemy seem to have deformed him into some kind of super-breed of Nex and he's grown body armour and tried to kill me. Should go down real well.'

'Somebody has to tell her.'

Carter rubbed at his weary eyes. 'I – just can't do it. I'm running out of energy, Mongrel. Yeah? I'm running out of the fucking will to live. This world has just got so fucking crazy.'

Mongrel nodded, and watched Carter move towards the cliff edge. He watched Carter lean over the low fence and for a moment – a split second, a fleeting slice of infinity – he thought that Carter was going to jump. Carter fished out his ECube and punched digits into the tiny alloy device.

I'm running out of the fucking will to live.

Mongrel shivered.

If someone like Carter is nearly ready to give up, then what hope is there for the rest of us? he thought viciously.

'Nicky?'

'Carter. Any news?'

'We're on the trail.'

'Have you . . . seen him?'

'No.' The lie felt bad. 'But he's – not dead.'

'Thank God!'

Carter felt a spear of ice pierce his heart. He could picture Nicky's face. Read her eyes. Understand her tears . . .

'*Tell her,*' said Kade softly at the back of his mind.

'No.'

'*Fucking tell her. She's a big girl, she can cope with it. Go on, make her fucking* century.'

Carter gritted his teeth. 'How is Natasha?'

'Stable. After you left she went into decline, but the doctors worked hard; they saved her life, Carter. But you will have to hurry – they can't say how long she can hold on.'

Carter gazed down at the cliffs and the crashing sea. The gentle blue rolled away for eternity, and the sea breeze filled him with a sense of vastness and life. He took a deep, deep breath. The air felt good in his lungs.

'Don't let her die on me,' said Carter softly.

'I'm doing my fucking best,' said Nicky. Carter could hear the strain in her voice. And he did not know why he said the next sentence; could not explain to himself the lie . . .

357

'I will find Jam. I will bring him back.'

They cut the connection and Carter stayed leaning over the fence, allowing the sea breeze to ruffle his hair and soothe the bruises on his battered face.

'Fuck.'

The frustration tasted bad.

Suddenly, Mongrel was there. His hand rested on Carter's shoulder and for once Carter was glad of the contact, glad of the company. He turned red-rimmed eyes on Mongrel and felt his anger melt away like heated butter.

'I'm scared, Mongrel.'

'Don't be.'

'I'm scared she's going to fucking die on me.'

Mongrel clumsily embraced Carter, hugging him hard. 'You fucking listen to me, Carter – I never seen you like this before, but you just remember I here by your side and I give my life for you, I give my life for Natasha. We find this machine, and if we have to kill Jam in process then he is casualty of war. We not make these fucking rules – and we not have to play by them. Now, you come and sit down and damn well drink this beer, or Mongrel drip-feed it to you and make sure you be drunk when The Priest arrive!'

'The Priest.' Carter laughed, rubbing at his eyes. 'Mongrel – cheers, mate. Thanks. You might be a dog and a cunt – and I know I toyed with the notion of shooting you in the face back at the hospital . . . but – just thanks.'

'You not mention it, bruv.'

The sky was heavy with purple contusions of cloud. Huge swirling banks filled the night sky, blocking out the moonlight. Occasionally, a beam of white would delicately find

358

its way free and creep tentatively across the sea, across the black oil of churning waters. Tendrils would dance across the waves, taste the crests of foam, caress the rough cliff face leading up to a low rough fence, against which a figure leant, dressed completely in black. The figure stood nonchalantly, at ease, a sea breeze ruffling his short hair. From between thin, tight lips hung a home-rolled cigarette, staining the darkness with a silver plume of smoke. The figure coughed on the harsh Greek tobacco, gazed up at the shafts of moonlight shining down from the dark broiling heavens – then lifted a bottle to his lips.

He took a drink.

A long drink.

'Fuck it,' he said. 'I can't wait any longer.'

'*You have to,*' whispered Kade.

'Why do I have to?' The snarl was filled with whisky-fuelled violence. 'What the fuck do *you* know about it?'

'*The Priest is coming. He has information. But he may betray us – and I will kill him. I will savour the death.*'

'Kade . . . I truly am fucking sick of you. I'm sick of the metallic stink in my brain. I'm sick of your bad fucking advice . . . What are you? What do you want with me? Why won't you just *leave*?'

Silence.

Carter lifted the bottle of cheap Greek whisky. He took another long pull. A little spilled down his black jacket and whisky spittle gleamed wetly on his lips, which he licked, leaving a nasty gleam.

'*You know she is going to die.*'

'Fuck you.'

'*Don't hide from the truth, Carter. Don't hide behind your stupidity!*'

'Like you give a shit.'

'*I . . . I would like to help you.*'

359

'The only person you help is yourself.'

'*Not true, Carter. Not true at all – what about in Egypt, all those Arabs with machine guns? Or in Poland? That fucker with the garrotte? And then in Belfast . . . don't get me started on Belfast . . . You should leave this place, Carter. Leave now. Get back to the Comanche, fuck Mongrel and that sniper bitch into the night and it will be like old times, just the two of us . . .*'

'I will wait for The Priest.'

'*You won't like what he has to say.*'

'And what would that be?'

'*Trust me,*' said Kade smugly.

'Get out of my head.'

'*The Priest will be here in a few hours – at dawn. You need to make your decision and make it now . . . if you meet with him you won't like what he has to say. It will be a threat to Natasha's life . . . and fuck only knows you've moaned about that dying bitch for long enough . . .*'

Carter frowned. He drank the cheap whisky, which burned his throat and his belly with its unrefined harshness. 'How could you possibly know that? How could you know such things?'

'*Trust me. I know.*'

Kade's sinister voice faded, and Carter listened to the sea crashing against the rocks in the moonlight. He frowned to himself, remembering random events from his life all leading to the insane moment where Natasha had gone down with the building under the crashing fury of the quake . . .

He remembered leaping, and being engulfed by concrete.

He remembered their last kiss. A long and lingering sweet-tainted caressing of lips.

And he remembered Kade . . . haunting whisky dreams with his vitriol . . .

Kade.

Kade . . .

Something pressed against Carter's back – a hand, its outline and the familiar pressure. It was Roxi, behind him, looking out over the dark sea. For a long time he said nothing, just allowed his mind to calm. Then, finally, he turned and looked into her emerald green eyes. Her hand slipped down and rested on his hip like an intruder.

Carter shivered.

'You like a whisky?'

'I thought you'd stopped drinking that.'

Carter grinned wryly. 'You never did like my Lagavulin addiction, did you?'

Roxi smiled then, and her oval face beamed like the birth of a new sun. Carter took a drink from the bottle and then reached out, touching her cheek.

'I just want to say—'

'Shh.' Her finger touched his lips and she shook her head. 'You don't need to say it. I understand.'

'You *understand*?'

'Yes.'

'About him?'

She nodded, then stepped to his side and leaned on the fence. The breeze from the sea whipped her straight brown hair out behind her and she closed her eyes, revelling in the coolness.

Carter blinked.

And remembered:

The bedroom. Her high pert breasts, the sheen of fear on her brow, the trembling of her fingers, the enticing pulse beating rapidly in her throat.

'*You're fucking insane!*' she had shouted, eyes on the gun in his fist and her tongue darting out, moistening her fear. And Kade had been like a worm in the back of his

361

mind, whispering, hissing, filling his brain with confusion . . .

'Kill her. She will betray you – betray us. And we shall be nothing. We shall be ashes and dust. Do it . . . or, if you're such a fucking coward, let me do it . . .'

Carter had walked past her, thrown the gun into the lake and Roxi had left him, hurriedly pulling on her clothes, their manic animal sex of the previous night forgotten in her need to get away from him . . . From the shores of the lake he had watched her leave.

Returned, lain on the bed where he could still smell her sex and the lingering bright dregs of her perfume . . .

And cried . . .

'I believe you have a problem.'

Carter snapped back to reality. He glanced sideways at her. He found it strange – almost surreal – to be talking to somebody he had assumed he would never see again. It had been years – four or five at least, he could no longer remember, since she had walked out of that cabin room. She had not reported him – his threats, his apparent insanity. He had contacted her ten, maybe twenty times but she had ignored his calls and he could not blame her.

Their missions for Spiral had never crossed from that moment forward. They had never met.

Not until now.

'We all have problems,' said Carter coolly.

'With Natasha? The ECubes are alive with news of the quakes ripping across the world and the resurgence of the Nex soldiers. I saw Natasha's name mentioned . . . she was injured . . . *is* injured. I'm sorry.'

Carter nodded, watching the sea.

'You here on Spiral business?' he said, finally.

'Yes.' Roxi produced a cigarette, lit it, then passed it to Carter and lit another for herself. He could taste her subtle lipstick on the weed and long distant memories came flooding back—

Her naked, arching back—

Her soft skin, the welcoming velvet between her legs . . .

'No,' he hissed to himself, exhaling smoke. He met her strong gaze and she smiled, hand reaching out, stroking his stubbled cheek, thumb rubbing at a mark on the end of his chin with obvious affection.

'I've missed you.' Her words crashed like sweet thunder in his brain.

'I missed you,' he found himself saying.

She reached forward to kiss him, but he halted her, smoke stinging his eyes and carried away on the breeze. 'No, Roxi. Not now, not like this. I loved you once . . . still love you. But my mind is fucked up – I haven't the time for complications.'

'All life is a complication,' she said, moving closer, her voice husky. He looked deep into those green eyes and her beauty was astonishing to him. He could feel her body pressed against his and he was waiting for Kade to jump in, but the dark side of his soul had apparently vanished . . .

Carter pulled away, and took a long drink of the whisky.

'I cannot. *Will* not.'

Roxi smiled. 'I hated you. For a long time.'

'I understand.'

'Do you? You kept me in the dark. *He* forced us apart, wanted me dead. But what hurt me the most was that you did not tell me. You couldn't trust me, and that hurt more than a bullet in the face.'

'I was . . . scared. Scared I would lose you.'

'Like you're scared you're going to lose Natasha?'

'No, that's different.' Carter sighed, and took another long drink. He turned his back on Roxi and it took all his strength, all his will-power not to look round.

'Maybe in another life,' he said softly.

She came up behind him. Kissed his ear. 'I still love you. I always will . . .' She laughed. 'Maybe in another life-time, as you say, my love.' And then she was gone, gliding into the darkness.

Carter shivered, retaining her scent.

He remembered it well.

It reminded him of . . . sex. And more.

It reminded him of love . . .

Carter retired bitterly to his room to finish the bottle.

Carter was spinning, spinning down into dark dreams and the sand was hot under his bare feet, ragged trousers flapping around his ankles as the Arabs marched him out into the desert and the sun scorched his back.

Shit. Cairo7.

The Battle for the City.

Occasionally, the whip would crack against the bare raw pink skin of Carter's sunburned shoulders and through sweat and blood he glanced left at Slater – who grinned a savage grin through his own individual pain – and Carter ground his teeth as the leather bit deep. The Arab screamed at him and he whirled in the sand with eyes narrowing and lips mouthing motherfucker—

'*Let me,*' Kade had whispered.

Like silk.

Smothering his fevered brain in an ice-cool shroud.

'No.'

They heard the scream of the fighters. They thundered overhead, long and dark and gleaming, engines glowing and their noise a sonic boom that filled the heavens. Cairo stood, a massive swathe of buildings and here, from the distant desert, the pyramids squatted in front of the group – the glowing scene a vast expanse of beauty, almost a perfect postcard, with the city ranged behind the pyramids. Then the bombs began to fall—

The pyramids were shattered. Smashed into rubble. Cairo was crushed by HighJ and spinning silver steel.

Carter and the other captured Spiral agents watched with mingled horror, fascination, fear and awe as buildings were swept away in a tide of fire and billowing bright gas. An armoured Egyptian column caught beside the pyramids was lifted on a wall of flame and sent spinning and howling up into the fire-filled sky.

Machine guns rattled.

Men screamed . . .

Carter watched solemnly as the distant soldiers fought. More fighters howled. More buildings were destroyed and, slowly, the Cairo skyline began to change, to warp, to disintegrate . . .

'That way!'

The whip cracked and sub-machine guns poked into backs.

Carter and the ten others were herded further into the desert, away from the savage destruction behind them. They stumbled on through the sand.

On they ploughed.

'Where are you taking us?' snarled Slater – and caught the butt of a sub-machine gun in the jaw for his persistence.

The Arabs, all brutal and battle-hardened soldiers, herded the prisoners through the fast-falling darkness. The men stumbled clumsily across the sand, hands bound tight and bodies covered with the marks of heavy beating.

The group halted, and were all given sips of water.

Carter felt himself growing weary, and for once he welcomed the return of Kade.

'*They're taking you to be executed.*'

'No, we are political prisoners. There will be an exchange. Maybe a ransom.'

'*No. They know you are Spiral. They will execute you in cold blood.*'

'Why don't they kill us here, then? Why not now?'

'*They need fucking permission from their leader, a man called A'shiek Elmora. You should keep more up to date with your fucking reading, Carter.*'

One of the captors, a short squat powerful man dressed in a grey shawl and wearing sandals, slowly approached. He offered Carter water, but as Carter reached for the cup he poured it at Carter's feet. His eyes glistened with challenge.

'You the Spiral men!' he snarled, dark eyes filled with hatred. 'You have killed many of our people . . .'

'No,' said Carter, shaking his head.

The man pulled free a long curved knife, the blade black and heavily chipped from battle use. Carter stared up at the Arab, could see the twenty other shamag-cowled men surrounding him. Camels were grunting wearily in the heat and the drone of a distant Land Rover sounded in the desert air.

'*Let me,*' crooned Kade.

'*Let me fuck them . . .*

'*Let me eat their souls.*'

Carter had smiled at the man then, staring at the scars across his cheeks with hate-filled eyes and said out loud, dry voice a croaking command to slaughter:

'Fuck them, Kade.'

And slitted feline eyes opened on a desert scene carved in black and white.

*

Kade calmed his breathing. The scene was bleached – shades of desert grey that suited Kade just fine as he tested the strength of his bound wrists and glanced down. Rope? '*Fucking amateurs,*' he snarled and—

Kade leapt towards the Egyptian, and the knife came up in a clumsy movement so sudden was Kade's attack. He twisted, and the blade sliced neatly through the rope, freeing Kade's hands. His boot came up, connecting with the Arab's chest as he whirled and took the curved blade from the man who grunted in pain and surprise, stumbling back under the force of the heavy blow to teeter and fall –

Everything seemed to move so slowly.

Kade grinned.

Kade leapt again, the blade hacking into the Arab even as the surprised man fell – and as he hit the sand the man's blood gushed out in a pulsing arc. Kade stabbed him in the face and left him gurgling as the rest of the twenty men turned their attention towards this *blur* of an escaped prisoner—

Shouts split the cool desert night – tinged with panic. Sub-machine guns were cocked in twitching hands.

Kade surged forward with a savage snarl. The blade slashed left, then right, leaving scarlet globules hanging suspended for microseconds as throats gaped wide and blood flooded from the wounds . . . Kade spun low and rammed the curved knife into another Arab's groin, wrenching it to the side as the man screamed, hands clutching at the warm flow of blood. Kade smoothly took his sub-machine gun . . . instantly bullets blasted from the muzzle – heads and chests caved in under the heavy impact of flying metal as Kade strode forward, deep into the group, with the gun hammering away in his powerful death-dealing hands—

Bodies flipped to the sand, torn wide open. Heads popped. Jaws were smashed from faces. Bullets chewed flesh and Kade swept his dark gaze without emotion across the men who died screaming and scrabbling at his feet . . .

The noise slowly died down.

Camels were barking with nostrils flared at the scent of blood and at the noise of the guns. They stamped on the sand, tethered and nervous.

Two men were groaning, lying prostrate on the desert floor.

Not a single Arab had fired a shot.

'Carter!'

Kade's head snapped left. The other Spiral men were bound, and Kade grinned at them savagely and said, 'Just give me a moment to provide an encore, gentlemen.'

Kade picked up another sub-machine gun and moved to the two groaning men. He knelt beside the first, looked into the dark cruel eyes, then smashed the butt of the gun against his forehead several times, cracking open the skull.

'Carter, man, what the fuck are you doing?'

Kade lifted the gun and pointed it at the group of captured Spiral agents.

'You got a fucking problem?' he screamed, insanity dancing in his eyes, across his twisted face. 'I'll fucking kill you all, I'll fucking smear your blood on my face and—'

He glanced down.

Shot the last Egyptian in the face. Emptied the magazine until there was nothing left of the man's head, just a dark purple pulp with shards of bone splintered obscenely on top of a bullet-torn neck stump strung with skeins of twitching muscle and ligament.

The body jerked spasmodically, a last pulsing of its blood staining the sand.

Kade climbed to his feet, staring around at the twenty dead bodies. He realised that he was breathing hard and he dropped the gun to the ground and started to laugh. 'Welcome to Egypt,' he screamed as the other Spiral operatives looked on in horror. 'Yeah, welcome to fucking Cairo as well!'

And instead of this being the end of the horror, it was, in fact, just the beginning.

Carter awoke, shivering. The whisky bottle was by his side, drained, and his head was pounding. Weak light crept from behind the shutters. A diseased rat had crawled into his mouth and died.

Cairo7.

He shivered again, horrified at the dream – at the reliving of Kade's first bout of true insanity, on show for others to appreciate.

Before Cairo7 Carter had always retained some semblance of control. But in the desert that night, Kade had pushed Carter into a deep mental recess and locked the door. Kade had mocked him. Kade had punished him. Kade had fucked him very severely.

Carter still remembered, as they made a cross-desert dash for friendly lines, the fear emanating from his own men, the other Spiral agents whom Kade had reluctantly released. They sat near him only so not to antagonise him further. They shared their water only so that he would not shoot them in the face.

Not Slater.

Slater had watched him with a dark intelligence.

Slater had shown no fear.

It was as if Slater had understood.

369

Carter heard their comments as they made camp without fire in wadis, hunkering under outcroppings of rock or in shallow caves. They had whispered among themselves.

'*Did you see him move?*'

'*He was so fucking fast . . .*'

'*Like a fucking demon . . .*'

'*He killed twenty armed men single-handed—*'

'*They couldn't even fucking touch him!*'

'*And what about when he unloaded a full clip into that poor bastard's face?*'

'*He was fucking insane . . . did you see it? In his eyes? He was* possessed *. . .*'

Carter rolled from the bed and stood, naked, scratching his belly. He moved to the sink and poured himself a glass of water, downing it in one. His door burst open and Mongrel stood there, fully kitted and ready to move.

'Carter?'

'Hmm?'

'The Priest is a couple of miles away. The ECube comm says he'll be fifteen minutes. Get your shit together.'

Carter smiled at Mongrel. 'I told you not to let me drink the whole fucking bottle.'

'Hey.' Mongrel spread his hands, gaze fixed on Carter's face. 'You looked like you needed it, mate. I'll meet you out front in five.' He stared, frowning, at Carter's dangling penis, his nakedness, realising Carter would need time to dress. 'Better make that ten. And don't forget to put your fucking pants on!'

Then he was gone, leaving the door wide open and a cool breeze invading Carter's privacy.

'You're an animal,' muttered Carter, searching, eyes bloodshot, for his clothes.

★

Carter and Mongrel sat in the dawn sunshine, looking down over the steep winding trail and waiting for The Priest.

Carter sipped at his steaming coffee.

'You feeling bad?' muttered Mongrel with a smirk.

'I've felt better.'

'Did you speak with Roxi last night?'

'Yes.'

'Did you fuck her?'

'Mongrel! Natasha is dying and my only thought is of saving her life . . . do you really rank me so low in the scheme of things? Lower than a fucking reptile?'

'*I* would have.'

'She's pretty,' acknowledged Carter, 'but I think my energies are best put to other uses. And my bastard ribs are cracked, I swear it. That bastard Jam didn't half give me a kicking . . .'

'Have you thought any more about him? And that ex-Spiral fucker Gol?'

Carter downed his coffee and refilled his mug from the jug, tipping in plenty of sugar and milk. He sighed, shaking his head. 'Hey, Mongrel, as far as I'm concerned the whole world has gone mad. We've got earthquakes ripping up various countries, Jam transformed into God only knows what sort of experimental entity by Durell, Gol back from the dead, and now I've got Roxi drifting into my life from a past I had practically forgotten – a past where I tried to murder her. I can't really say that anything else could possibly surprise me.'

'Well, let's see what The Priest has to say.'

'It better be pretty fucking damn important,' growled Carter, 'because he's wasting my time right now.'

'You soon ask him,' rumbled Mongrel, gesturing at the trail.

371

The Priest laboured up the path.

His grey robes flapped around his titanic frame, his bushy beard swayed in out-of-synch rhythm with his rosary beads, and his sandals trod the rocky sand trail with an awkward step. He carried his Bible in both out-stretched hands, like a magic talisman, a totem of power.

Carter and Mongrel watched the barrel-chested man's long haul up the mountain.

It gave them some small pleasure to see him sweat like a pig.

The Priest finally arrived on the plateau and smiled down from his great height, sweat streaming from his forehead and great patches of it staining the cloth under his arms. 'Behold, my children!'

'At last, the prodigal returns,' said Carter through a veil of smoke. 'Coffee?'

'Yes. Six sugars.'

'*Six?*'

'A growing lad like me needs to keep up his strength. Now, down to business.' From within his robes he brought out two ECubes and passed one to Carter, one to Mongrel.

'Updated?' asked Carter.

'More than an update, my son,' said The Priest. 'These are new revisions, running V5.0 ICARUS op systems, now up to 18GHz dual-RISC processors and 1024 gig of Optical-RAM. The whole network has been revised after many recent breaches by the Nex – the whole encryption stage has been revamped, and if you key in your DSquad code then you can see the schematics and check out all the new functions. There are a few new little tricks. The Lord would be proud of such innovation.'

Carter and Mongrel handed over their old units. The Priest took his coffee and sat cross-legged on the grass.

The sea crashed distantly, and a cool breeze ruffled his beard and cooled the sweat on his brow.

'I have answers,' he said, simply.

'What is going on?'

'Since we sunk the Spiral_mobile battleship just over a year ago, we have become complacent. We thought the Nex were on the decline. The SAD teams were doing their job, exterminating what Nex filth they could ferret out in small pitched battles. But we have all been wrong. The Nex soldiers that the SAD teams were taking out were *rejects* – the weak and the lame. Apparently, when a Nex is created there can be many problems with the DNA coding and restructuring – the blending, as Durell would call it. For the past year we have been fed these mewling weaklings as decoys while Durell built an army.'

'An army?' rumbled Mongrel. 'You mean . . .'

'We estimate that Durell has a quarter of a million Nex soldiers, although he could have more. He has also enlisted many thousands of mercenaries to do his bidding. It would seem that his company – Leviathan Fuels – has provided him with the funding he needs.'

'LVA?' said Carter. 'So Durell owns the fuel company?'

'More than that,' said Durell softly. 'I have encoded documents – the code took us many hours to crack and I risked my own life and limb to retrieve the items concerned. They show a machine – a machine, built to a very specific and strange design, that can control *earthquakes*. Now, there seem to be strategic points around the globe where Durell drops a shaft, mainly under the pretence of mining LVA, when really the LVA is a *catalyst*. In every shaft he plants a machine – which he calls a QuakeEngine, or Foundation Stone – and when networked through a "QuakeHub", a central unit devised to focus all this power and allow networked command globally, our enemies can force earthquakes at quite specific locations.'

'Why would he want to do this?' rumbled Mongrel.

Carter sighed. 'Durell believes that Spiral has grown weak and fat on the spoils of war. He believes that he and his happy band of Nex can do a fucking superior job. But first he has to persuade everybody that he's the boss. If he can target cities, even whole countries with earthquakes – fuck, combined with quarter of million Nex soldiers in support he can hold the world to ransom. What he failed to bring about with the QIII processor, it would seem he now seeks to achieve with brute force.'

'His Achilles heel is that the network is not fully functional,' said The Priest. 'For whatever reason, events are accelerating beyond his control and his QuakeHub network is not quite fully operational. Governments have received encrypted messages outlining how the quakes that recently ripped through London, LA, Moscow, Paris . . . they are just warning shots. Jabs to the nose. Tasters. But when the network is complete then he can truly play God. His sacrilege will be complete and he will be ready to administer a smiting from Heaven.

'You did an excellent job in Slovenia. Spiral have instructed Simmo and the TankSquads to hunt out the LVA pumps and destroy them – if we move quickly then Durell will not be able to get his QuakeHub network fully functional, and even though he can control the quakes it will be as nothing to the power he could unleash if all the sites are linked and uploaded. Spiral is working with world governments even as we speak, and if we move with enough speed we can destroy his sites quicker than he can build them . . . we can halt Durell and his army before they begin to march. All it needs is the cooperation of the international powers.'

'You could have told us all this via ECube,' growled Mongrel. 'Why you drag us from our mission? Why waste our time sitting here on dumb arses getting fat and frustrated?'

'The whole network is compromised,' said The Priest sombrely. 'Hence the new ECube machines . . .' He glanced then at Carter, and the Spiral operative felt suddenly, deeply uneasy.

Cold.

Kade's words came back to haunt him.

'The Priest will be here in a few hours – at dawn. You need to make your decision and make it now . . . if you meet with him you won't like what he has to say. It will be a threat to Natasha's life . . . and fuck only knows you've moaned about that dying bitch for long enough . . .'

Carter fixed his stare on The Priest. Smoothly, under the table and out of view from the cross-legged Spiral man, he eased free his Browning and it rested bulky in his palm like an old friend. Something was not right, Carter realised. This whole meeting was *wrong*.

'What is on your mind?' said Carter softly.

The Priest bowed his head for a moment. One hand touched his rosary beads, as if for reassurance. Then he met Carter's glare with his piercing gold-flecked eyes and there was strength there, an inhuman strength that could only belong to the head of the Spiral secret police.

'You must abandon your mission,' said The Priest.

'What mission?' said Carter easily. He flicked free the safety catch.

'You seek the machine that creates the Nex. You seek to use the machine for its original purposes – that of healing. You wish to bring Natasha and your unborn child back from the brink of death. All these things I know to be true. All these things I understand.' The Priest was

375

calm, and perfectly collected. He did not blink. 'But you must still abandon this mission.'

'Why?'

'The answer to this question is a complicated one.'

'Fucking try me,' snapped Carter. Mongrel placed his hand on Carter's arm, and Carter could sense his friend's sudden fear. 'You ask me to abandon my fucking woman. You ask me to let her fucking die and you will not give me an answer? Fuck you.'

'I do not ask,' said The Priest softly. 'I tell.'

'Tell?'

Carter laughed harshly and The Priest found himself staring down the Browning's dark muzzle. 'I think you need to give me some fucking answers, Holy Man – before I send you to meet the God that you claim created you.'

'So be it,' said The Priest softly, his eyes glittering. He sipped at his coffee, his huge frame relaxed in his seated position on the grass. Then he smiled, as if amused by some internal dialogue.

'Carter, put the gun away.'

Carter ignored Mongrel.

'Durell has machines that were built before our civilisation arose. One is the machine used to create the Nex, the Avelach. Another is the QuakeEngine – which is based on the design of the original machine found by the Nazis in 1940 and unlocked decades later by Spiral research teams led by Feuchter, Gol and Durell. These machines are thousands and thousands of years old and use archaic electronics similar to those of the machines we currently field, but they operate using different materials and superior processes. In truth, they are much more advanced than our own technological developments.'

'Get to the fucking point.'

The Priest sipped at his sweet coffee once more, unperturbed by the Browning and the thirteen rounds in its magazine. 'You seek the machine that will heal Natasha. Durell holds this machine – as he holds the QuakeHub. And yet he is in delicate negotiations with major world governments right now . . . If you stumble in, firing off a thousand rounds of ammunition, and take this machine from Durell – or piss him off in some other unexpected way – you could accelerate proceedings. You could destroy the bridges that the politicians have worked so hard to build.'

'You think I would start a war?' said Carter incredulously.

'Maybe unwillingly. We cannot antagonise Durell directly. You must put off this mission – at least for a couple of days. When the politicians – the governments of the world unite against this gigantic threat, and when the TankSquads start hitting the LVA mines, then events will escalate at a catastrophic rate . . . But we cannot move until we are ready . . . We are buying time, Carter, buying military muscle, and the last thing Spiral needs are loose cannons. I fear Durell has become too powerful even as we speak. We *need* this time . . .'

'In a few days Natasha may be dead.'

'Then Natasha will be dead. She will be a casualty of war. Her fate is in the hands of God.'

'Not my fucking God,' said Carter brusquely. 'There is something you're not telling me, Priest. You're holding out on me . . . come on, who are the other players in this game?' He waved the Browning towards The Priest's face.

'There are some factors of which I cannot speak. I can only repeat the direct order – which has come right from the top. Spiral is ordering you to abandon this mission – to *postpone* it, if you will – until you have the all-clear. If

377

you choose to ignore this direct order then I have instructions to kill you.' He glanced at Mongrel coolly. 'And any who stand with you.'

Carter lifted his coffee and drained it.

'I think that you should leave.'

The Priest climbed ponderously to his feet and stared at Carter. Hard. 'I know it is a bitter pill to swallow, but trust me, Carter. There are things at work here that you could never understand. The doctors give favourable reports about Natasha's progress – you may yet have the time to save her. But the world does not. It is a sacrifice that we must all make – it is what she would expect. What we would *all* expect. The sacrifice of one to save many . . . Natasha is not divine, Carter. She cannot live for ever.'

'You have no idea what you ask,' whispered Carter.

'I do,' said The Priest gently, his gaze softening. 'Don't make me come looking for you, Carter. Don't make me hunt you down – it would be a waste of a good man. One of the best we have.'

The Priest turned and lumbered towards the trail. There he met Roxi, and they exchanged quiet words. The Priest disappeared behind the house and they heard an engine fire up.

Roxi approached.

'Will you do as he says?'

Carter frowned. 'You are working with The Priest?'

'Yes. This was our meeting point.' She reached out to stroke Carter's cheek but he pulled away. 'Until the next time, lover.'

'There will never be a next time.'

Roxi smiled, a dazzling smile, bright green eyes glinting. 'Oh, but there will.'

'*Do you want me to burn her?*'

Roxi moved away and climbed into the Toyota Land

Cruiser. Wheels spun and the big vehicle disappeared in a roar of black fumes. Carter sat down again, toying with his Browning idly, his face an unreadable mask.

'More coffee?'

'No, we're moving out.'

Mongrel frowned at Carter. 'Where to?'

'After the machine. Fuck The Priest, this isn't his woman dying on a doctor's slab. I don't trust him – I think he is spinning us a whole crock of shit. If we find Durell, then we find the machine to heal Natasha *and* the QuakeHub – we can take out his control of the earthquakes. And a bullet in his brain will end his thoughts of world domination once and for all.'

'They will have people on that,' said Mongrel softly. 'Specialists.'

Carter laughed hollowly. 'And what the fuck are we? No, there is some other game being played here and I will not follow their rules. I refuse.'

'You heard The Priest. He said this was an order. Straight from the top.'

'I don't care,' said Carter. He glanced at Mongrel. 'It's up to you, Mongrel. You can either come with me, or you can stay here. Either way I am going after Jam, I'm going after Durell – and I will find that fucking machine or die in the process.'

'I don't know . . .'

'Make your mind up. But do it fast.'

Suddenly, George came pounding out of the house carrying three Heckler & Koch MP5 A3 9mm sub-machine guns. He tossed one to Carter and one to Mongrel. Mila appeared in the doorway, face ashen, the sniper rifle gripped in her shaking hands.

'What is it?' growled Mongrel.

'I've just had a call. There's been trouble. Down in the

town, a shoot-out with local police. Eighteen dead local policemen – murdered by masked killers. They are in three trucks and are heading this way.'

'You sure?' snapped Carter.

George nodded, heavy brows creased.

'Nex,' said Mongrel.

'Has to be. Quick, get your shit together . . .'

George pointed. 'Too late, my friends.' He cocked the weapon in his huge hands and Mila sprinted over to the small group. Coming up the distant trail, engines screaming and dust pluming around their wheels, came three squat black trucks, sunlight glinting menacingly from their darkened windows.

'Fuck. Mongrel, go grab the packs. We'll cover the road.' Carter's eyes scanned the trail, which led up through sparse woodland and mounds of rough grass and coarse sand, then checked the two natural hills – low humps of grass-covered rock that formed a natural funnelling point ideal for defence, before the road opened out once more onto the plateau on which the Serakina was built overlooking the sea. 'Mila, you get up there with your sniper rifle. Start shooting as soon as you can. George, you get on the other side.'

'And where are you going?' rumbled the huge black man.

Carter grinned wolfishly. 'I have a fucking surprise for our little masked gatecrashers.'

The three black trucks lurched up the rough trail, tyres bouncing in ruts and suspension smashing into over-stressed chassis. Carter calmly checked the magazine of his Browning, holstered the weapon and weighed the Heckler and Koch MP5 thoughtfully in his grip. The trucks were coming closer quickly and he could spy the distant glinting Mercedes logos splashed proudly across matt black grilles. With howls of metal agony, the trucks were being hammered by their Nex drivers . . .

Mila started to fire . . .

Heavy-calibre sniper rounds flew through the early-morning sunlight. The lead Merc's windscreen took two hits, then the front tyre exploded in a shower of mashed rubber and the truck veered to one side, listing danger-ously before rolling onto its side and sliding across the rough ground towards the edge of the cliff . . .

'Keep shooting!' yelled Carter, sprinting up the incline behind Mila to gaze down at the stricken truck. Carter pulled free the tiny black alloy cube and slotted it neatly onto the Browning. There came a deep hum as Carter aimed at the vehicle with the NeedleClip-modded Browning. There was a click and the tiny missile flashed from the gun's barrel. The doors of the Mercedes were opening as the projectile hit the underside of the chassis. Metal exploded and the van was picked up and tossed over the cliff in a fist of curled flames. Trailing thick black smoke, it disappeared into the sea far below—

Mongrel appeared as Carter sprinted back down the incline. George opened fire on the two remaining trucks from the opposite hill; bullets slapped along their flanks as Mila continued to fire shots from her sniper's weapon. Mongrel tossed Carter his carbine, and with their sub-machine guns they opened fire from the centre of the trail . . .

Bullets ate the grilles of one truck and Carter and Mongrel split, sprinting in opposite directions as the vehi-cles broke through onto the plateau and skidded in wide arcs. One Mercedes crashed through the wooden tables and scythed in a circle, tail end smashing through the fence overlooking the sea—

Doors slammed open and bullets tore the turf at Carter's feet. He dropped to one knee, and his return fire picked up a masked Nex and spun the rag-doll figure over the fence and down towards the crashing waves. One truck's rear doors opened and everything became an insanity of bullets and crackling gunfire. Mongrel crouched by the edge of the Serakina's white building and drilled the trucks with bullets. Hot metal tore a line of holes up the wall by his face and he retreated, changing mags, concrete dust stinging in his eyes.

Three Nex charged at Carter.

He shot two of them in the face as their bullets zipped past his shoulder and throat. Then a heavy-calibre round cracked from behind him, exploding the third Nex's face in a bloom of blood. The body fell into the grass, tumbling up to Carter in a tangle of limbs, and Carter whirled low, hearing another exchange—

'Carter!' shouted Mongrel. 'The back of the trucks are empty!'

Carter cursed. Of course – the rest of the Nex would be coming in on foot from different directions. The trucks were a decoy . . . He glanced up to George – who was shooting at figures unseen. *Something* chilled Carter's soul.

He sprinted across the ground, yelling, 'Mongrel, start your fucking bike! And take Mila with you!' George was changing mags as Carter reached his side, and Carter gazed down on the rough hillside to the east of the track. Across the rough ground raced thirty Nex from different positions, firing as they came, using the trees for cover. Carter ducked back, but George took three rounds high in the chest. His blood splashed sickeningly across Carter's face and he was tossed limply down the slope and rolled to a halt at the base, his huge limbs quivering.

Carter scrambled down to George's side as Mongrel's bike started. With an abused-engine howl, the KTM rocketed up the hill and Mila climbed onto the back. The bike churned rough ground, skidding in an arc towards Carter who pointed down the road.

'Get the fuck out of here!'

Mongrel's anger-filled gaze surveyed George's blood-speckled face.

Then, without a word, he screwed the throttle hard around, the back wheel spat sand and grass, gripped and then propelled them down the road and away from the Serakina. Carter heard Mongrel's sub-machine gun fire from the road . . .

He stared at George.

The large black man smiled, blood staining his teeth.

'I thought you said you not bring trouble to my house?'

'I'm sorry, my friend.'

George grasped Carter's hand with an iron grip. 'Shoot a few in the fucking face for me, Carter? You manage that?'

Carter nodded. 'I'll see what I can do . . .'

But George was already dead.

Carter dropped the MP5. Swinging his M24 carbine across his back, he sprinted to the KTM LC7. He fired the engine, locked the front brake, spun the bike around in a circular skid then released the brake. The front wheel lifted and Carter dipped his head low, chest touching the tank as he howled the bike towards the road leading from the plateau mountain top.

The bike raced from between the small hills, through the natural gateway and onto the dusty trail. The Nex were closer now, coming in from different areas of cover. Bullets whined past him as Carter palmed his Browning and glanced left. He launched ten NeedleRounds into the charging ranks of the Nex.

The explosions stuttered like fireworks, fire leaping into the air with charred bodies spinning in its midst. Nex were slammed into one another, into the air, into the ground, into the trees and rocks with their flesh pulped, their weapons mangled. The explosions blasted, and flames curled and ate flesh.

The Nex were consumed . . .

The KTM powered down the track.

Bullets chased Carter, and he held the throttle full open as the first bend – and temporary safety from bullets – loomed ahead.

Something slammed into his back.

The KTM faltered . . .

Carter leaned into the corner, pain pulsing through him, and increased the speed of the bike. He hammered along a dusty road, the dirt trails dropping away under his wheels from the immediate danger behind.

Carter coughed, his tongue thick in his mouth.

The road seemed to shimmer ahead of him.

Suddenly, agony took Carter in its fist and crushed him. The bike's front wheel slammed against a rock with a crunch of steel and Carter, weight pitched forward from the blow against his back, felt the front suspension sag on heavy oil. The handlebars slammed to the left with a snap of metal against metal. Nausea flooded him with horror as he was flung from the KTM at eighty miles an hour and the world rushed around him in a confused blur as he tried to curl into a ball and behind him the bike screamed a high-pitched metal scream grating along the trail pissing its death sparks across the gravel . . .

The ground slammed up to meet Carter.

He hit hard, all air kicked from his body, and slid along the rough trail for what felt like a lifetime. The bike spun off to one side, twisting and groaning in metal defiance.

Still sliding, gravel biting through his clothing, Carter wanted to scream, to reach out and halt himself, to tell himself this was just a bad dream. But a bend in the trail loomed and Carter struck a low ridge of rough sand and grass. He was catapulted up, flung tumbling into a sparse copse and rolled to a final crunching halt on dead wood, old leaves and discarded pine needles.

Carter lay stunned, just trying to breathe.

For a lifetime.

Pain hammered through him.

In the gloom under the canopy of trees the world had suddenly gone very dark. Carter, finally managing to breathe in heavy gasping gulps, saw that most of the skin had been scraped from his right arm. He groaned and tried to sit up but rocked back as pain punched him down.

And then he was suddenly looking into copper eyes.

The Nex stood, sub-machine gun loose in its gloved hands.

Part of its mask was scorched and torn, the skin on half of its face beneath the eye a mess of molten flesh. It was watching Carter as it breathed smoothly, apparently undisturbed by its half-melted visage.

With hands that – Carter noticed – did not shake, it ejected a spent magazine, which tumbled lazily to the ground. Slowly, it retrieved a fresh one and slotted it home. There was a click that seemed to last for ever.

Carter tried to reach his Browning.

Then realised the weapon had gone.

'Mr Carter.'

He glanced at the Nex. 'Yeah, fucker?'

'It's been a pleasure.'

The Nex lifted its gun and pulled the trigger.

CHAPTER 14

BRAWL

The WIC – or World Investigation Committee – had a central headquarters in Washington DC. The building was massive, an incredible modern structure of glass, steel, alloy and stone glinting menacingly in the strong sunlight. It sat in grounds patrolled by soldiers armed with seriously heavy weaponry. Sniper towers and advanced air defences squatted at every corner. At any one time the WIC HQ was manned by elite soldiers from no less than fifteen different countries.

At the HQ's heart lay the Central Chambers, attended either in person or by digital personifications of world leaders. One such meeting was in progress, chaired by General Tetalyahevsky of Russia, Patron San Lee of China and Lady Emma C. Dickinson from the United Kingdom. Nearly five hundred officials from around the globe were present, and a general murmur was echoing softly around the huge vaulted stone ceilings of the Chambers. The noise died to a hush as the images of earthquakes and global chaos faded from the huge fifty-foot optical-plasma screen against one wall to be replaced by a dark, hooded figure who lifted one finger and held it up as if waiting for something of importance . . .

The murmurs increased in volume and Durell looked out from the digital screen at this gathering of the world's most important and influential people, who had their fingers on the red buttons of nuclear doom.

Durell smiled within the folds of his hood.

And when he spoke, everybody present was totally focused on his soft, gentle voice.

He had gained their attention. 'You have seen before you the power of the quake. And you have been shown the proof that I have complete control, and can command the earth's plates to move at will.'

There came a hiss of alarmed voices.

'Now, ladies and gentlemen, I have a most serious proposal for you.'

The sky was a massive expanse of blue, a huge vault soaring over the gentle curve of the world. It was scattered with trailing wisps of bedraggled cotton-wool cloud and brightness glinted off a small black alloy object that spun – and hammered past at an incredible velocity.

A rolling sonic boom followed it and the tiny single-seat aircraft, nicknamed a *Mànta*, banked gently, sunlight glittering along its pulled-back black alloy wings. The twin tail jets glowed white with cold matrix fire as the machine hit 1,900 k.p.h.

'PDSK57 calling in, over.'

'We have you, PDSK57. Over.'

'I've found a Charlie. Sending coordinates now.'

'Thank you for that, PDSK57. Out.'

Haggis looked over at Mo and gave a thumbs-up. Mo nodded, and slowly – inching forward – the two men moved through the rainforest on their stomachs, crawling through the thick dense foliage and evergreen *Chinchona*, noses twitching at the heavy fragrance of the flowers.

Twenty miles behind them sat ten TankSquads, awaiting their report and an update from the Spiral mainframes. They knew there was an LVA site there – south of San José del Guaviare, Colombia – but had been put on hold just as they thought they were about to see action. A wave of disappointment had swept through the ranks and Haggis and Mo had scouted ahead to gather any possible further intel.

The two men slowly emerged on a clifftop, a jagged ridge tumbling away to a basin of dense jungle foliage. The sun beat down and the men – both of them large – were sweating heavily, their clothing sporting huge stinking stains.

Mo ran a hand across his shaved bullet head, wiping off a sheen of sweat, and turned his obsidian-eyed gaze on his partner, who passed him a canteen.

Haggis, who chain-smoked a hundred and forty a day, was quivering from nicotine withdrawal. He nodded down into the basin to where a huge section of hardwoods – mahogany, oak and lignum vitae – had been cleared and bundled with wrist-thick strands of heavily woven rope. The mammoth logs formed an outer perimeter wall. The LVA pump was working hard, and the drone of distant engines could be heard over the rich and exuberant sounds of the jungle.

'I fucking hate jungle missions, said Mo, dribbling water down his triangular black beard. 'It's just so bloody hot! I was not built for this kind of climate . . .'

'Yeah, you're a bit of a fat walrus, mate.' Haggis grinned. 'I've relayed the coordinates. Better get back or that lunatic Simmo will go bananas! Come on.'

The two men turned, and eased themselves back into the jungle.

From the cloaking darkness of the thick vegetation, Nex soldiers watched them leave, their copper eyes bright and emotionless.

The wastelands of the Arctic spread out in front of Jader as he dropped the jet's speed and heard the decelerating whine of the engines. He spun the *Manta* low over the broad undulating plains of ice and could see an awesome, colossal arc of white. Ice crackled from the *Manta*'s wings and Jader dropped the SK even lower, skimming the snowy expanse. Below him he could glimpse the mad rush of wind-sculpted ice-towers, the diamond sparkle of stalactite-crusted chasms and a territory that was wild, vast and untameable.

Jader grinned.

He loved the magic of the Arctic.

Lifting the *Manta* he soared up into the cloudless freezing skies. Engines howled with cold matrix pulses and he levelled the Spiral jet, which seemed to float for a while. His scanners scrolled fat green readings of data over the jet's monitors. Jader watched them with one eye, again slowing the *Manta*'s speed and peering out.

'There,' he muttered.

Hidden among a small range of ice hills, and surrounded by walls of banked white ice sat an LVA pump. It had been painted, obviously to camouflage it against this Arctic landscape, but Jader's sharp eyes had picked it out.

He blipped the coordinates.

'Well done, Jader. Over.'

'How many we got, Control? Over.'

'That's eighty-six Charlies. You coming home? Over.'

'Be home soon, Mother. You make sure my tea is ready.' Jader grinned within his HIDSS. 'Out.'

As he killed the ECube-linked comm, red warnings suddenly scrolled and flashed over his monitor. 'Shite.' Jader jinked the controls and the engines screamed as the jet leapt forward. Something glinted beneath it, a sudden snapping flash of silver. The jet banked and Jader's eyes went wide as a sliver of alloy spun in a wide glittering arc ahead of him and then—

Hung. Suspended.

Jader smashed the *Manta* down towards the ground and the glinting missile dived, following closely, locked on. Jader banked right and severe-turn and proximity warnings lit up on the console as he felt his guts wrenching within his suddenly fragile human shell. The missile powered past over one wing and Jader steadied the jet – then spun it in a tight curve and began to climb.

The missile followed.

Heading away from the LVA site, Jader licked his suddenly parched lips and the HIDSS flickered through different types of offensive weaponry, attempting a match. It could not target the missile, could not recognise the weapon – and so could not suggest the best evasive action.

Jader urged the jet until it was clipping 2,100 k.p.h., a tiny black blur flashing low over the landscape. The missile paced it, just behind and slightly to one side. Jader felt himself go cold and dead inside. This was like no missile he had ever before encountered – or seen – even in the high-tech development cells below several Spiral HQs.

'PDSK57 to Mother, I have been compromised, I repeat, I have been compromised. Sending images now . . .' The HIDSS whirred around him and relayed data on the missile. Jader dropped the jet towards the ground, eyes frantically searching—

The ice blow him rose and fell.

And then he spotted it, a wide crevasse glittering blue and as inviting as death . . . He spun the *Manta* in a tight circle and then down into the crevasse, reducing his speed slightly as the walls leapt up above him and he was suddenly plunged into a world of cold ice and shimmering frozen slick walls.

The jet flew through the deep blue silent gloom.

Engines whined, noises reverberating from the ice walls.

Still, neither the HIDSS nor the on-board computers linked to the Spiral mainframes showed an enemy: no missile in hot pursuit, nothing. The *Manta* jet flittered through and beneath the ice, which flashed past at a terrifying rate to either side. Data crackled across Jader's scanners. And then—

The crevasse plunged under snow. An ice ceiling appeared above the jet and Jader felt himself slowing it even more, his eyes searching for the missile. Rear scanners displayed nothing – it was no longer tracking him but something told him not to believe that he had evaded his pursuer.

It had been too—

Too . . .

He groped for a word. And settled for 'sentient'.

Now, encased in ice, Jader spun through the Spiral mainframes' inventories.

'Jader? Over.'

'Yeah, Mother. You find anything?'

'Sorry, Jader. Unidentifiable. You're on your own, buddy. I'll keep you online, see if anything materialises while you—'

'Fuck!'

The jet was smashed down, wings flashing into the

vertical as a fall of ice and rock invaded the space within the crevasse. Then the world opened up above. Sunlight glinted through snow and ice and Jader tentatively brought the jet to ground level and shot like a bullet from an ice gun up into the waiting infinite sky—

The missile was hovering.

Patient.

It accelerated at an awesome rate and ploughed into the underbelly of the *Manta* like a needle piercing flesh. There was a sudden, silent microsecond of impact – of suspension—

And then a purple explosion. Gases bloomed and curled, like flames around the edges of paper. They sucked in on themselves until they glowed, an intense inferno of melting alloy and steel merging with dripping white-hot flesh and liquid bone.

Jader and the *Manta* became, for a nightmarish instant, as one.

And then scattered in glowing arcs across the ice in a scree of twisted detritus.

The explosion echoed across the snowy wilderness.

Simmo sat on the HTank, elbow on his knee and chin on his fist. His expression was thunderous. His eyebrows were dark-bushed storm-clouds. His lips were razors of ruby lightning. His eyes were pools of comet-fallen mercury. And his clenched fists were the threatening knots of tropical hardwoods battered by the eternal elements.

'Are you . . . OK?'

'Of course I'm not fucking OK!' screamed the Sergeant, gazing down at Oz and Rogowski. The two men took a step back at Simmo's wrath, Oz spilling his tea from his plastic pint mug, huge crooked nose wavering a little. 'We're here, in the fucking Colombian jungle, fucking sweating like fucking pussies, we've found the enemy and what do Spiral HQ fucking say? The fucking politicians are fucking working on a fucking solution and so we can't bomb the fuck out of the bastards.

'Of *course* I'm not fucking OK! In fact, I'm ready to . . . *kill*.'

His dark gaze swivelled around to where Kattenheim was seated on a felled hardwood tree – his face and upper torso a mass of battered, bruised and *sliced* flesh.

Kattenheim was staring at Simmo. And then he smiled.

Simmo felt his temper exploding, but calmed himself.

'You want a cigarette?' said Oz uncertainly.

'The Sarge not smoke cigarettes.'

'A drop of whisky?' suggested Rogowski.

'You boys should know by now! Sarge not drink on ops.'

'Yeah, I know, but I just thought . . .'

'Yes?'

For such a simple word, it carried a wealth of threat. Like a barbed wire maggot in an apple. Rogowski, a soldier who had been shot in the head once and in the body fourteen times, was oblivious to such verbal niceties.

'. . . I just thought you might savour a nip, you know, after Kattenheim there wouldn't speak despite your best efforts with the iron bar – God, I thought you were going to kill him! And then we get lifted all the way out here, spend ten hours piloting fucking tanks through jungle lanes just to find . . . to find . . . that we . . . we are . . . we are not allowed . . .'

He finally faltered.

Simmo's scowl could not get any blacker. He glanced again at Kattenheim, seated calmly on the log with his hands tied tightly behind his back with wire. His ankles and knees were also bound tight. Spiral were taking no chances with the Nex warrior.

Simmo drank from his canteen, then hopped off the HTank and moved forward past the stationary bulks of other tanks to where Kattenheim sat. Simmo glanced down at him and the Nex looked up, scarred red eyes defiant, gleaming.

'You want a drink, fucker?'

'That would be pleasant.' Kattenheim's words were a little distorted by his broken jaw and cheekbone. Simmo stood, drinking, water dribbling down his chin.

'Well, fuck you. Talk to us and I might allow you to drink. And eat. And maybe even sleep a little.'

Kattenheim merely smiled, a smile that disheartened Simmo. Deep down he wanted to kill the Nex – but Spiral had instructed him to bring him back alive for trial.

He moved back to the HTank, frustration gnawing him.

There came a call from the jungle, and some of the TankSquad men lowered their weapons as Mo and Haggis moved into view, M24 carbines held pointing towards the ground in case of NDs.

Mo made his report to Simmo, who nodded, face blank. Then they sent the report to Spiral and awaited further orders. Simmo sent some more scouts out, securing a wider perimeter around the tanks. As night started to fall the men began slinging hammocks between the tanks and some surrounding mahogany trunks. Simmo had only once – obstinately – slept on the floor in the jungle. He'd suffered 239 ant bites, huge swellings that had left him in blood-red throbbing agony and in no fit state to piss, never mind fight in a covert jungle operation. Simmo was a big man, who hated hammocks – but in this contest with the vicious and uncompromising rainforest

394

he had backed down after the first jab, never mind waiting for the end of the first round.

Darkness was falling quickly.

They kept a cold camp, no fires, and the jungle seemed to creep in on the TankSquads. The huge black outlines of the silent weapons of war became shadow-haunted structures around which the enemy could creep and hide. Trees reared all around, sometimes erupting with bursts of monkey chatter or the hiss and click of large invisible insects. Other jungle night sounds warbled around the sixty or so men, some of whom stood guard, eyes alert, and some of whom relaxed within the barricade of heavy steel and mammoth metal tracks.

Simmo squatted next to Rogowski, Mo and Holtzhausen. They were boiling a pan of water for tea over two chemical kem-blocks, which glowed softly in a tiny ring of stones.

'You want some tea?' drawled Holtzhausen in his German burr.

Simmo nodded, dropping a bag and spooning sugar into his mug. He held out the plastic vessel and Holtzhausen poured the boiling water in. Simmo inhaled the steam hungrily. Simmo was the sort of man whose appetite was eternal. And if you fell asleep, he wouldn't just eat the last slice of pizza, he'd steal the entire contents of your fridge.

'You like your sugar,' said Mo, grinning. He too held a large plastic mug, larger than everybody else's – from which he drank a whole litre of tea. His mug looked more like a paint pot.

Simmo nodded. 'The Sarge surprised you not piss all night, drinking so much tea.'

'Hey, Sarge, what did you do with that fuck Kattenheim?' Holtzhausen spat on the ground and continued to sharpen a sliver of wood with his broad-bladed combat knife.

Simmo frowned. 'What you mean? He over there.' Simmo turned, peering through the darkness. Their little camp was lit by nothing more than kem-blocks, the occasional dull luminescence of a NightCube, and the glowing tips of a few cigarettes. Simmo squinted.

'*Where?*' asked Mo. 'I can't see him.'

Simmo cursed, spilling his tea over his combats as he lurched to his feet and sprinted forward, tea sloshing over his huge fist. A sound alerted him even as he reached for his holstered SigP7 9mm pistol strapped to the small of his back and he turned – into a heavy uppercut punch that rocked him back on his heels and sent stars spinning through his head . . .

Simmo staggered, dropping his tea.

To see Kattenheim, fists raised, grinning at him with a mouth full of broken teeth. The huge German ex-para came forward slowly and there was a chorus of clicks as several of the TankSquad men cocked their weapons.

Simmo grinned nastily, holding up his hand. 'No, lads. The Sarge handle this.' His fingers were covered with blood from his split lip. 'You do well slipping the wire, Nex.'

'Lots of practice,' said Kattenheim, rolling his shoulders and then settling into a boxer's stance. 'You gonna fight me fairly this time, you ugly hunk of army meat?' Sweat was rolling down his heavily scarred head and in the weak red light of the NightCubes he looked totally demonic. His red burned eyes seemed to glow – and within their depths shone the copper heart of the Nex warrior.

Simmo cracked his knuckles by clenching his fists, then strode forward.

'Lads – if he kills me, then you can fucking shoot him. But as long as I still live you will be disobeying direct order and The Sarge have you up on a charge!' He squared up and looked down at the smaller man. Nex, he thought. It is not a man, it is a concoction. Either way, I pulp fucking face.

Kattenheim attacked, a fast fluid combination of punches – straight right, right hook, left hook, left upper-cut, right straight. Simmo found himself backing away under the flurry of heavy precise blows which he managed – just – to block with his forearms. Simmo returned with a thundering right straight but Kattenheim rolled smoothly to Simmo's left under the punch and came up, hammering a right hook that caught Simmo on the side of his head and staggered him with the colossal impact. Another right straight shook Simmo's head again, and then a front kick to the face sent the huge man stumbling down on his knees.

Kattenheim stepped back, folded his arms, and waited.

Slowly, Simmo climbed to his feet.

He is too fast, realised the huge soldier. Just too fucking fast.

Simmo approached warily, and Kattenheim still had his arms folded across his chest, a look of arrogance on his face. Simmo spat on the ground and around him he could feel the pressure of the TankSquad soldiers, of the Spiral agents who were watching and understanding and he knew that he had to kill this fucker with his bare hands – and rip out its spleen.

The Sarge was a legend.

To lose a fist fight?

With a fucking *Nex*?

'Better off dead! Sarge not let that happen!' he said, unintentionally out loud, and then threw himself at

397

Kattenheim. They exchanged a series of heavy blows at great speed, and Kattenheim tried another kick, but Simmo punched down on his opponent's kneecap. The onlookers all heard the splintering of bone.

The two fighters drew apart.

'You move well, for such a big man,' said Kattenheim. He displayed no obvious pain but had altered his stance, favouring his left leg instead of the right and moving so that the damaged limb was partially shielded by the one that was still sound.

'And Sarge *kill* well for such big man – as you find out.'

Simmo charged again, teeth glinting in the red light.

They exchanged punches, and Kattenheim landed another right hook that shook Simmo. Growling, The Sarge launched himself on top of the smaller Nex warrior and gripped him in a tight bear-hug, lifting him from the ground and exerting a massive pressure on the Nex's spine. Kattenheim growled, and slammed his head into Simmo's face – but after the second blow Simmo twisted and shook the Nex like a rag doll . . .

Kattenheim continued to head-butt Simmo – in the neck, in the face – as tendons popped along his spine. Somehow he managed to free an arm and started raining down blow after heavy cracking blow until Simmo was forced to drop him. Kattenheim leapt high into the air and came down with the butt of his elbow on the crown of Simmo's head. Simmo hit the jungle ground hard, stunned. Blood seeped in pulses from the wound and Kattenheim stood over Simmo, who was rocking and groaning, down and temporarily blinded and out of the fucking game . . .

Kattenheim glanced around, to see what stood between himself and freedom.

And only then, in the dull jungle glow, did the TankSquad Spiral operatives suddenly realise that the Nex held Simmo's matt black SigP7 gun.

The pistol lifted and, as shots that sent bright muzzle-flashes piercing the gloom rang out, the men split up. They leapt for safety, their own weapons coming up but unable to fire because immediately in front of Kattenheim was Sergeant Simmo . . .

Simmo felt as if his skull had been cracked open. Pain pounded through the centre of his brain and pulsed like hammer beats as blood soaked his shaved scalp. A rage like nothing he had felt for years arose – a red tide engulfing him. He could not speak, scream, shout nor curse because this intense, and insane tidal wave of hatred consumed him and carried him to—

Consciousness.

His eyes flickered open.

Kattenheim was firing *his* pistol at *his* men.

'Cheeky motherfucker,' Simmo snarled. He lifted back his boot and from his position on the ground kicked as heavily as he could at Kattenheim's injured knee. This time a real crack echoed through the jungle as the knee folded in on itself and the leg collapsed, pitching the man to the ground as he howled through blood-speckled lips and clenched teeth. Simmo grabbed the wrist holding the gun and they both lay, locked for a moment, staring into one another's eyes.

Simmo slammed his head into Kattenheim's nose. Then he released the hand that wasn't gripping the gun and, reaching down, punched at the twisted broken knee – five times, six, seven, eight. Then he took the gun like a man taking an ice cream from a child, and climbed ponderously to his feet.

Simmo levelled the SigP7 at Kattenheim's face.

'Say your prayers.'

Kattenheim said nothing, merely glaring at Simmo with hatred.

As something leapt from the darkness of the jungle, something huge, armoured and with a triangular head.

Simmo's gun came up as he spun round. A bullet smashed in the ScorpNex, which scooped Kattenheim from the ground and disappeared into the blackness. Submachine gun rounds ripped after the Nex, slicing through leaves, tree trunks and ferns and spitting soil from the ground. Ricochets whined all around as bullets bounced off hardwoods.

'Cease fire!' screamed Simmo.

The gunfire stopped.

The TankSquad men turned towards Simmo. Both Mo and Haggis had taken rounds from Kattenheim's crazy erratic firing and Haggis was seated, nursing his stomach. Simmo glared around angrily. This wasn't supposed to be how the game went.

'Fuck. Get your shit together – we as compromised as a man fucking his brother's wife in his brother's bed as his brother walks in. In other words, we fucked from both sides – by exposure of our location and by Spiral.'

'We going in, Sarge?'

'Yeah, we're fucking going in.'

'I thought the order was to wait.'

'They're the enemy, aren't they?' snarled Simmo. 'Hundreds of them tried to take us out back in Slovenia – tried to turn us into mincemeat. And now we supposed to sit by as fat-arsed politicians argue over who gets the rights to the LVA fields when all this over? Fuck 'em. We do this Simmo way! That LVA installation guarded by Nex. Nex are outlawed. We have licence to kill.'

The Sergeant's eyes gleamed.

All eyes were on his blood-encrusted shaved head, which was still pumping thick crimson that glistened in the red gloom.

'So let's kill,' he growled huskily.

Jam sat in the dark frost-filled cold, breathing slowly. He watched the clouds of vapour exhaling from his twisted jaws and something pricked his memory; something was different. And then he realised, with a growing sense of horror, that his eyes had physically shifted. They were in a different place; his head had broadened, flattened, and his eyes had moved further apart, thus expanding his field of view – his *predator*'s vision.

He considered Carter – and their exchange.

He knew that he could kill Carter.

Ultimately, he knew that he *would* kill the man . . .

But Carter's words had disturbed him – somewhere deep down in his twisted soul. Jam had sensed the reluctance to fight. Carter had some long perverse connection with the past, some distant impulse of honour and friendship that Jam could understand in a cool and detached way. And Jam had been happy to slice the fucker in two, smash his bones into splinters and then piss on his grave. But the words . . . the distant words from a warm and welcome deathbed . . .

'*No, Jam . . . stay here . . . we need your help. Natasha is dying. Nicky is with her. We need the machine. The Avelach . . . you know where it is . . . it was used on you, Natasha will die—*'

Jam pictured Natasha's face; her short dark spiked hair, her deep brown eyes and slim, athletic figure. Jam's head tilted softly. He could see – see Carter and Natasha together, laughing, holding hands as they walked along the pier, kissing in the rain—

The images flickered.

And Nicky was there, her sweet oval face, piercing bright eyes filled with tears. Was she unhappy? he wondered. And if so, for what reason?

Words drifted to him—

Words from a million years ago—

'It's a war – Durell, and Feuchter – they brought us a war. They tried to wipe us out; now it's time to give them a bullet up the arse.'

And Nicky; smiling weakly, standing there on the . . . on the Kamus, the disused Spiral base in the Austrian alps. 'Yeah. But . . . not everybody is going to make it back.' Reaching up, suddenly, she kissed him – and their lips lingered, tongues darting.

Jam stared into her beautiful eyes.

'I need some company tonight,' she said, voice husky, and she led him by the hand inside the cold confines of the dark and dank mountain base . . .

Jam lowered his huge triangular armoured head.

He stared at the floor, remembering their lovemaking.

Something is wrong with me, he realised.

I loved this woman. Loved her.

And yet – yet now I feel . . . *nothing*?

He spat, and lifted his head once more, breathing deeply, making strange rasping sounds. But a connection – from the man he wanted, *needed* to kill, this Carter and the two women who touched him in some strange way in his dreams, in his memories – something hard to grasp, something esoteric twisted inside his head. He could hear the whisper of deep voices he could not understand.

And Durell?

And *Feuchter*?

Jam lowered his head again, and the deep coldness

402

seeped into his limbs and into his brain. It soothed him. The cold calmed him, relaxed his mind. His worries bled away and his anxieties melted away and he rocked, on armoured heels that bit deep grooves in the stone cell floor.

With tiny clicks his eyes closed.

The World Investigation Committee central headquarters in Washington DC was in a turmoil. Voices rang around the huge vaulted ceiling of the chambers in a myriad different babbling languages. Human and electronic interpreters babbled, adding to the confusion; and Runners sped between benches and tables, in and out of doorways.

Voices could be heard above the hubbub, rising shrill, borne on currents of anger, disbelief, outrage, frustration, incredulity—

'I think he's fucking insane . . .'

'But he's got us by the balls . . .'

'Who is this man? I think it is one huge bluff!'

'But haven't you seen what he can do? The reports are flooding in from a thousand different media agencies – this is no insane dictator whom we can ignore . . .'

'The countries of the world should stand together, unite. We can mobilise millions of men and this Durell could not stand against such a tide of world strength—'

'But who would lead the armies?'

'Why, the USA, of course . . .'

'Why not the UN?'

'I think China is the obvious choice . . .'

'We can crush this worm before he moves—'

'Assassination would be more direct – a fucking sniper bullet in the back of the skull.'

'Yeah, when we find him – but if he *is* controlling the

earthquakes, then he can hit any central government, any capital city, any military installation in the world.'

'It is a preposterous claim, impossible!'

'Who is backing this lunatic? Which fucking countries? There must be some here who know of him. This is an outrage! It would spark a—'

'World war.'

The words hung like a storm cloud on a static-charged summer evening: heavy, ominous – and threatening.

The wide oak doors at the head of the chamber slammed open, smashing against the walls with twin crashes. Slowly, the noise subsided as faces turned to peer at the man who stood in front of them, the man who – with his stern silence and bushy-eyed frown – commanded their attention.

He was a huge barrel-chested man.

He wore v-neck grey robes, with dangling rosary beads which bounced against his curly-haired chest as he walked.

His sandals slapped against the floor as he moved to stand on the Central Podium. All attention focused on him. Many of the world leaders knew the face but could not name its owner.

The Priest seemed to be angry.

Furious.

His face was red, lips curled back, beard damp with sweat. His intense gaze swept the gathered men and women in front of him, and he pointed, eyes bright and holding a glimmer of insanity. Then he pointed again, his mouth working spasmodically, and again and again and again until total silence descended on the chamber—

'You *argue!*' boomed The Priest at last. 'You stand here, with the power of the world at your fingertips, and you – you bloody *squabble* like monkeys over a dead maggot. You whine at one another like spotty children in a playground arguing over a lollipop. You must *decide* . . .'

People began to shuffle their feet.

Nobody spoke.

The Priest began to rant, spittle flying from his lips and drenching his beard, '*Woe unto you, scribes and Pharisees, hypocrites! For ye are like unto whited sepulchres, which indeed appear beautiful outward, but are within full of dead men's bones, and all manner of uncleanness* . . .'

His stare roved.

'I say,' began one of the English delegates, 'that seems a tad harsh, old chap . . .'

'Shut up!' screamed The Priest with the fury of God flashing like lightning in his eyes.

All eyes were on him now.

And he felt—

Filled. With the Power. With the Glory. With Divine Insight.

'*And almost all things are by the law purged with blood; and without shedding of blood there is no remission!*'

Faces were turned towards The Priest; no one spoke. Despite their power, despite their learning and wisdom, in this moment of greatest confusion the leaders of the world truly did not know what to do . . .

'*And I saw as it were a sea of glass mingled with fire: and them that had gotten the victory over the beast, and over his image, and over his mark, and over the number of his name, stand on the sea of glass, having the harps of God* . . .'

'We should fight.'

'No, he could destroy us. He has the power of the earthquakes at his fingertips . . .'

'How many infantry can you field? 80,000? 100,000?'

'Yes, but mobilisation takes time, and if he sees the armies of the world mobilising then he may attack first . . .'

'May attack, will attack,' boomed The Priest. 'You have heard his demands, and you must here – and now – decide among yourselves whether this Durell is a threat to world peace. If you bow to his demands then decide here and now – with a single voice before God! But if you choose to fight – and a hard fight it will be – then decide it *now*. You do not have the luxury of time. *We* do not have the luxury of time. Things move apace, my brothers and sisters, and I beg you, before the Holy Father—'

Voices rose.

Squabbles broke out.

And The Priest looked down in despair at these, the most powerful people in the world, unable to decide upon the best course of action for the future of the whole planet.

Politicians, he thought sourly.

And slumped to the ground, listening to a hundred languages and a thousand dialects washing over him. People swarmed about him now, but The Priest ignored them. They shouted questions at him but he merely shook his head, clutching his Bible.

And by the end of the day they had made a decision.

The world leaders had finally made a decision.

They had *finally* decided to meet again in three days' time after lengthy discussions – to make the ultimate and *final* decision.

Some countries wanted to fight.

Some pressed for peace.

Some would mobilise armies.

Some would prepare talks.

The unanimous agreement was disagreement.

The undisputed choice was a non-choice.

The definite decision was no true decision at all.

'Chaos is finally here,' muttered The Priest.

SIU Transcript

Section WORLD SCALE MOBILISATION INFORMATION/
Spiral Information Transcript

Selection: Units 12-18, from total info
units 2844

US Army Pacific:

Hawaii - 35,300 troops mobilised from 2nd, 4th,
6th and 9th Battalions and comprising 20th to
43rd Infantry Regiments; 400 soldiers from 30th
through to 78th Aviation Battalions with UH-78
Black Hawk support; Paratroopers from 1-501st
Parachute Infantry Regiment deployed; 3rd, 8th
and 10th Battalion Field Artillery Regiments
deployed. 16,000 troops from the 9th Theatre
Support Command scrambled and put on High
Alert, including USARJ at Camp Zama.

German Federal Armed Forces:

16,000 Mechanisierte Division troops
mobilised, made up from Femmelde and
Aufklarungs Batallions, Mechanisierte
Brigades; also 3800 men from the Division
Spezielle Operationen, Division Luftbewegliche
Operationen and Heerestruppen-kommando units

407

made up of Artillerie-brigade, Pionier-brigade, Heeresflugab-wehrbrigade, ABC-Abwehr-brigade and Logistik-brigade.

2400 jets have been scrambled across Europe and are currently on a state of High Alert, both Luftwaffenführungskommando and Luftwaffenamt.

600 naval units have altered their patrol courses, both Flottenkommando - Flotille der Marineflieger and Zerstörerflotille, and Marineamt Kommando Marine-Führungssysteme, Schulen der Marine and Marinestützpunkte.

Australian Army

A total of 52,000 personnel deployed from:

1 Armd Regiment; 1 Fd Regiment; 1 JSU; 1/19 RNSWR; 10/27 RSAR; 12/16 HRL; 12/40 RTR; 13 Fd Sqn 13 CER; 11 CSR (141 Sig Sqn); 16 RWAR; 2 Cav Regiment; 2 HSB; 2 RAR; 2/14 LHR (QMI); 2/17 RNSWR; 51 FNQR; 6 RAR; 7 Fd Bty 3 Fd Regiment; 7 Fd Regiment; 8 CSSB; 8 CER; 9 CSSB

The Chinese People's Liberation Army Navy have mobilised over 2200 naval units including:

Destroyers
Type 956 Sovremenny
Type 054 Luhai
Type 07 Anshan

Guided Missile Boats
Type 520T Houjian
Type 343M Houxin
Type 021 Huangfeng

Amphibious Warfare
Type 074 Yuting
Type 072 Yukan
Type 073 Yudao

Frigates
Type 059 Jiangwei III
Type 057 Jiangwei II
Type 053K Jiangdong
Type 065 Jiangnan

Submarines
Type 094 NEWCON SSBN
Type 092 Xia SSBN
Type 093 NEWCON SSN
Type 091 Han SSN
Type 039 Song

The Chinese reserve militia currently numbers sixteen million personnel and mobilisation (of unknown scales) is in progress.

** We are on the brink of war.
** The verge of chaos.
** The edge of destruction.

more intel to follow>>>>>>>>>>

CHAPTER 15

EGYPT

Carter stared up at the Nex – watched the bright light in its copper eyes and thought:

What are you?

What do you want?

What does Durell *really* want?

'*We'll never fucking know . . .*' came the bitter, acid response from Kade as—

The Nex pulled the trigger.

There came a click – not the dead-man's click of an empty magazine, but the heart-pounding click of a stoppage. A bullet that the hammer had failed to kick into life and out of the barrel because the previous bullet casing had not been smoothly ejected . . .

The Nex glanced down and shook the sub-machine gun—

As Carter growled and his boot lashed out and up, slamming into the Nex's groin as the Spiral man rolled, whirled low and came up with his battered and bruised body screaming at him from a thousand different places. Carter felt a warm flush down his back and realised . . . he had been shot. Staggering back, the Nex dropped its gun and charged at Carter, who sidestepped and rammed a right hook against the masked face, knocking the Nex to the ground. The Nex rolled and came up smoothly, its stare fixed on Carter. They circled like caged tigers, awaiting the opportunity to pounce.

Carter's arm was throbbing; he could feel the skin hanging loose and weeping crimson tears. His lower spine was aching, as was his right shoulder and neck from the impact when he'd fallen from the KTM LC7 motorcycle. And the bullet wound . . . blood was pooling down and soaking into the waistband of his trousers, and he could feel something pressing hard against the back of his ribs, grating against the clicking bone within . . .

Carter spat.

Mainly to see if there was blood mixed in with his sputum and so find out whether the bullet had damaged his lungs. He was relieved to see no traces of blood but the pain was still excruciating and the waves of agony rolled over him and he felt himself sway—

Darkness started to spiral in front of his eyes, like the thick black corpse-smoke from piles of burning bodies just before the GreyDeath TankerRuns – before the governments finally realised that burning the disease-riddled human corpses merely spread the terrible designer disease and did not exterminate it . . .

'*My turn*,' said Kade.

'Kill it . . .' said Carter despondently as he felt pain overwhelming him. The trees swayed nauseatingly around him, whirling in some sickly sweet hallucinogenic vision of crystal insanity . . .

Kade opened his eyes.

He saw the copse in black and white, gloomy and filled

with hollows and shades of grey. Kade savagely pushed the pain aside and quickly analysed his wounds as the Nex circled in apparent slow motion. Kade smiled fiendishly and launched Carter's tortured body forward at an incredible speed—

Kade delivered ten blows in rapid succession and the Nex blocked them all, responding with a low sweep over which Kade leapt. Kade's boot came up, a high kick that caught the Nex under the jaw and lifted it from its feet to summersault backwards, landing lightly and smiling back at Kade.

'You are too slow.'

'Come and taste my pain,' snarled Kade, blood staining his teeth.

They danced through the black and white shadows of the trees. The Nex punched Kade, connecting twice, but he rolled easily and grabbed the Nex by the throat, dragging it to the ground and pounding his fist repeatedly against the mask. Something rammed between Kade's legs, and the Nex's fingers found the bullet wound in Kade's back, dug gloved fingers in with all its strength and wrenched sideways—

Kade's scream was filled with a dying animal's urgency.

He rolled through the leaves, mind overcome for a moment.

Red flashed over the scene in grey—

And for the first time Kade knew colour.

He growled, pushed himself to his knees in the tangle of vegetation and looked up—

Into the barrel of the Nex's gun.

'Let's fucking try again,' snarled the Nex. Its composure had gone and Kade realised, grinning savagely through his pain, that he had hurt it. He lifted his middle finger, face in a broad smile . . .

'Any time, cunt.'

The Nex's trigger finger tightened—

And its head exploded as a heavy-calibre round struck the side of its skull. There was a moment of compression as the cranium caved inwards, its shape becoming deformed . . . and then a rapidly expanding cone of flesh and bone and brain was forced inwards, creating a funnelled intensity of pressure that smashed free from the opposite side of the Nex's skull in a bright red, white and grey spray that pattered down onto the ground. Kade met the copper stare. The Nex looked momentarily stunned. Its gun tilted, barrel down, and fell from twitching gloved fingers. Then its knees buckled and it toppled sideways, rolling slightly downhill with leaves and twigs sticking to its gore-encrusted clothing.

Kade rose to his knees. Glanced right—

To where Mongrel and Mila were making their way cautiously forward through the trees. Kade spat on the ground, pain ripping him. He slumped into a seated position and tracked his two companions as they approached. Mila held the sniper rifle, Mongrel his M24 carbine.

'We wondered what was keeping you.' Mongrel grinned.

'You took your fucking time,' snapped Kade.

Mongrel frowned. 'But she a good shot, yes? She prove herself to you?'

Kade nodded, chewing his lip in thought. 'You brought your pack? I've got a fucking bullet in my back and you're just standing there like a dumb fuck, letting me bleed to death.'

'I see your manners have not improved,' said Mongrel coldly, and dropped to his knees, opening the pack. 'I'll have to work quickly – there are fucking Nex everywhere. This might hurt a little.'

413

'Just do it,' said Kade, turning away from Mongrel. His face contorted and he forced himself into a kind of calm. Kade hated Mongrel. In fact, Kade just hated people in general. *All people. . .*

Mongrel cut away Carter's jumper with a broad-bladed knife and inspected the wound. Bits of cloth had been dragged into the wound and, unwrapping a sterile pack, Mongrel slid a hypodermic needle into the crust-circled edge of the bullet hole and injected antibiotics and a chemical agent devised by Spiral for emergency field surgery. Kade gasped a little at the coldness of the injection . . .

'*Let me back*,' hissed Carter.

'I want some fun,' said Kade.

'*Fucking let me back!*'

'Wait . . . there's something wrong . . . trust me Carter, just for a dumb-fuck moment in your life, *trust me* . . .' Kade surveyed the scene again, in black and white, his stare examining the forest scene. He knew, he could *feel* that something wasn't right.

Mongrel placed an SSG – Spiral StapleGun – against Kade's back, which was also Carter's hot flesh, and there was a *kerchunk*. Kade ground his teeth as white-hot agony flooded his body. Mongrel pressed a second time, then a third before removing the device and reaching for another hypodermic needle.

'Last one.'

Kade threw himself backwards with all his might and sent both himself and Mongrel toppling over to roll a few feet down the slope – as a shot hammered the silence and a heavy-calibre sniper round tore into the soft earth. Kade reached out, picked up the syringe, spun and hurled it with every ounce of strength that he possessed—

Mila, standing with her rifle aimed, took the

414

hypodermic in her left eye. The needle struck deep, splitting her eyeball and sending blood pumping down her face. She did not scream, so sudden was the movement and the blow . . . she merely gasped, dropping to one knee as Kade climbed to his feet and Mongrel looked around, stunned.

'She would have shot me!'

'Us,' corrected Kade, retrieving Carter's Browning and checking the magazine with care. He turned to confront Mila. 'You fucking led us, didn't you? To that quarry? The Nex knew we were coming. You fucking set us up, you little bitch.'

Mila said nothing. She had tried to take hold of the needle but had just screamed: it was too painful to touch. Blood was flowing freely and she glanced up at Kade, her other eye wide. Her blood-splattered hand reached out to him pleading, her sobs echoing through the copse.

'Please,' she said.

Kade lifted the Browning.

The muzzle stared, small and round and black and unwavering.

'You betrayed us,' said Kade softly.

He fired.

The bullet took Mila in the throat, pitching her backwards. Kade walked over, staring down at her pretty face. 'I fucking hate pretty little blonde bitches . . .' he snarled and lifted the gun as rage swamped his brain. He wanted to destroy that face.

Carter at last wrenched Kade from his body and dropped to his knees, the Browning hanging in his limp grip. He breathed deeply, pain rocking him, and stared down at Mila's face – still pretty but undeniably dead.

'Why?' said Carter softly, almost despondently. 'Why did you do that?'

415

Mongrel placed his hand on Carter's shoulder. 'You did what you had to do. She would have killed us both – tried to on several occasions, in fact. I was a fucking blind man.'

'We were both blind,' said Carter softly, looking up at his friend. Carter stood, swaying, resting against Mongrel's broad powerful shoulder. 'God, I fucking hate killing women.'

'If it left to me, we would now be dead,' said Mongrel softly.

'Yeah, me too,' whispered Carter, reliving the scene – the mad scene with the syringe thrown like a knife and then the fatal bullet to the woman's throat.

They left the small copse behind, left behind the heavy scent of pine and the last warm dregs of the Greek autumn, left behind the body of a Nex and the bloody corpse of a woman whom they had trusted and who had betrayed them.

Just two more deaths.

Just two more corpses . . .

'Sometimes I think this madness will never end,' said Carter as wretchedness filled him.

'You OK?'

The Priest glanced sideways at Roxi and shook his head, lips pursed tightly, eyes glancing back down at the ground. 'We are ruled by morons,' he whispered. Frustration ate him from the inside out. It made him want to weep – to stand there and weep huge tears and beat his hands against the Comanche's war-spattered fuselage.

He sent the message to Spiral.

Kicked it through a thousand miles of space.

His ECube rattled, and he squeezed it softly, expecting a reply from the WIC to his update. Instead, the blue letters glowed and The Priest read them with a further sinking in his heart. He climbed up and belted himself in behind Heneghan, the pilot. Roxi leapt in and took her position beside The Priest in a supple, easy movement; she was all glistening leather and bristling guns.

'Now you look even worse,' she said, large oval eyes watching him with concern.

The Priest sighed, hands in his lap, folded protectively over his Bible. Without looking at Roxi, he said softly, 'These fools cannot decide whether to run, stand or fight. They cannot make a single decision and with each passing moment Durell grows stronger. He needs to be stopped – for his power has become great, so great that I fear he could overthrow many, if not all, of the world's governments. And that would give him a firm handhold on the face of the earth – and from thence he would move forward in great strides, for he is ruthless indeed. By far the greater and more noble decision is to fight. But we must stagnate for three days, awaiting the decision of the men in power. Who knows what might happen during that time to give Durell the opportunity to deliver the first blow?'

'What did the ECube say?'

The Priest sighed again, meeting Roxi's beautiful gaze. 'It is Carter. He has not heeded my warnings – nor Spiral's orders. He is disobeying direct instructions from the very top. He is going to Egypt. Our intelligence shows that Durell is currently in Egypt. Carter could jeopardise everything.'

'And?'

'I have been ordered to intercept him. To stop him. At any cost.'

'To *kill* him?'

The Priest nodded, his eyes hard. 'Yes, to kill Carter. If that is what it takes.'

'That *is* what it will take,' said Roxi, squeezing The Priest's hand.

'I know. The Lord will guide me,' he whispered, and closed his eyes.

The Sikorsky Comanche cruised into Egypt from the north-west, coming in over the Mediterranean Sea just west of Alexandria on the coast. Carter fancied he could almost feel the heat shimmering up from the long-baked sands as he slowed the chopper and its twin LHTecs whined down to spit their fumes into the arid Egyptian night.

As the darkened coastline gave way to a mixture of ancient and modern hotels scything along the coast in a glittering string of false emerald and ruby lights, Carter banked the Comanche over the half-lit suburbs around the heavily built-up centre of this, the second largest of Egypt's cities. The machine cruised calmly through near-total darkness.

'How are you feeling?'

Carter glanced back at Mongrel, thoughts racing through his mind. He shrugged, turning to gaze out over the poorly lit shanty towns, suburban sprawls where *fellaheen* subsistence workers lived in densely overpopulated crushes of seething humanity. The buildings were crazily crowded masses of mud-brick, breeze-block and red-brick dwellings, built in and around and often on top of other buildings. Between houses stood pens, some with corrugated roofs erected for animals. Some of the narrow streets sported small iron braziers that glowed like tiny fireflies as Carter eased the Comanche in stealth mode over their owners' unsuspecting heads.

'About what, in particular?'

'I don't know,' rumbled the large man, rubbing at his

eyes. The Spiral agent looked suddenly tired in the weak cockpit glow, huge rings circling his eyes and his face taking on a slightly haunted look. 'It worry me, that thing what happen with Mila.'

'You mean killing her?'

'Yes, and her betrayal of us. It sit bad with me.' He shook his head, sadly. 'I know you had to do it, I know you in pain about – Jesus, Carter, a syringe in the eye?'

'It was the nearest weapon,' said Carter slowly, carefully. He could remember the pure adrenlin-high ecstasy of Kade's exultant glee, his joy at seeing the woman fall with blood pouring from her eyeball – and he shivered.

Passing over the last straggling streets they headed south above dark undulating sands, pacing themselves and flying parallel with the Nile. Carter checked his ECube constantly as well as the tag – the TrackingDisc – that Carter had risked his life to attach to Durell's helicopter as the leader of the Nex made his escape.

The darkness flowed over and around them. For a while Carter remembered his good times in Egypt – the *best* times – and then, making him shudder, Kade's memories came back to haunt him and he remembered the *bad* times: the killing of his Arab captors in the desert, which was just the beginning of Kade's all-powerful consuming insanity—

And then the horrors that had come later.

The murders . . .

The events that had made Carter a hated, wanted and *feared* man across the whole of Egypt. A man wanted dead not just by the military, but by the civilian population as well . . .

And I can't say I blame them, he thought.

If I was them, *I'*d want me dead.

I'd want me crucified on a cross of crumbling bones.

419

'What happened down there?' asked Mongrel suddenly, intuitively, his face lit by an eerie soft blue glow, his eyes focused as if reading Carter's mind.

'I'm sure you read the reports.'

Mongrel nodded. 'Yeah, I read them. I know about the murders in the desert, the killing of twenty Arab captors and how you single-handedly rescue all the Spiral men – but that only tip of iceberg, I thinking.'

'What do you mean?' Carter felt a craving for a cigarette. He wanted to feel the nicotine buzz in his veins to help ease the pain from his bandaged arm, his battered bruised body, the stapled bullet wound. He was still carrying the flattened slice of metal in his back and he could feel it pressing against the slope of his ribs. The powerful painkillers seemed to be ignoring his agony.

'I run several missions in Egypt, in Cairo, Alexandria, Beni Suef, Sohag, Luxor, even over in Port Said at the Suez Canal and as far west as Al-Tor at foot of Mount Sinai. I speak good Arabic, make good Spiral agent in these parts and look damn fine in *galabiyyas* robes and, hell, even enjoy smog that pass for air in Cairo. I can dance with *tahtib*, even do a bit of Sufi dancing and only thing I not like here is damn food, just not never as good as egg and chips back in Yorkshire, bloody funny bits of meat in rolls with God only know what stinking fiddly herbs all black and shrivelled. I know rules of Islam so not make fool of self, and can blend in on streets and can pass as construction worker or *bawwab* without problem. In all this time, for the years I work here and after you finish your run of three missions, they put up wanted posters – *everywhere*. And not just outside police stations, but lining roads, up on big mad billboards usually used to advertise movies. They wanted you dead, Carter. Very dead.'

'I don't want to talk about it.'

'Well, I reckon it must be bad.'

'It *was* bad,' said Carter softly, remembering Kade with the long blackened knife and the soft flesh that had parted with such ease . . .

'Well, I know they had your face plastered on billboards for what seem fucking *years*. And you look no different – just little bit older and more careworn. I think lot of people remember you. We definitely have to stay covert when we go down there on streets and in desert.'

'Yes.'

Mongrel stared over Carter's shoulder, at the ECube. 'Where it taking us?'

'We'll cut across Cairo, then head south and east down over the Eastern Desert. Looks to me like we're heading just west of Hurghada, near the Red Sea Mountains.'

'Hmm. I've not been there.'

'Well, you can add it to your list of interesting places visited in the name of demolition, can't you?'

'I thinking Carter not in good mood.'

'Well, you be fucking right. I've been shot, come off my bike at eighty per and played "Grate my fucking skin with a gravel road" – a wonderfully fun little game. I've been pounded to fuck by God only knows how many Nex and by Jam, my oldest and best friend who just so happens to have become a mutated monstrosity. And then I had to shoot a woman in the throat, which isn't exactly something that makes me sleep easily at night. You could say I'm a bit fucking *tetchy*.'

'Mongrel take your point.'

Engines humming, they reached the outskirts of Cairo and within minutes had passed the shanty towns and city buildings – indicated by a proliferation of lights. The Nile snaked through the centre of downtown Cairo; they passed the glittering mosaic that was Tahrir Square and the bright pointing finger of Cairo Tower and flew on past the lights of the Arab League Building, the Cairo Opera House and Gazira Island where Cairo's money people resided. The Nile was split by lights cutting over the Sixth of October Bridge, and Carter reined in the Comanche. They hovered near Tahrir Square, gazing out over the visual confusion of advertisements for Coca-Cola, Sushi Burgers and AOL that adorned most buildings higher than a single storey and sent a million wavering colours cascading across the night-ebony waters of the Nile.

'Bad memories?'

Carter nodded. 'It was being bombed last time I was here. They have rebuilt well.'

'The Egyptians are a resilient people.'

'You have to be these days. Jesus, I could do with a cigarette.'

'Let's go there and get this done, then,' growled Mongrel, and Carter eased the Comanche forward. They spun darkly over the bustle of lights and the bumper-to-bumper traffic that filled the roads, pumping out yet more black pollution into the already toxic air. Even from their height they could hear shouts and the general rumble of the traffic, the sounds of a city crammed with people to the point of meltdown.

Carter gradually increased their speed, and the Comanche lifted gently, banked and left Cairo behind. They followed the winding course of the Nile for a while and then cut out over the desert towards Gebel al-Galala al-Qibliya.

'Long time since I been on the plateau,' Mongrel muttered.

Carter said nothing; his eyes were dark, haunted with memories . . .

Memories of Kade.

The Eastern Desert was far from being a flat and feature-less plain. As dawn broke, its pale tendrils spearing the horizon with a gentle glow and a promise of intense baking oven-heat to come, Mongrel yawned, rubbing at his eyes.

The desert world was a nightmare of sand-baked val-leys, hills, mountains, troughs and massive boulders. Huge sheer scree slopes battled with high walls of moun-tainous rock and gentle undulations of rock and sand.

'Beautiful,' said Mongrel.

'Not when you're being marched out to be shot.'

'It's better to die in beautiful surroundings,' chided Mongrel, smiling. 'Better than dying in a sewer in Soho with all the other fucking rats.'

'Better not to die at all.'

Carter kept the Comanche low and as the sun crept up the sky they cruised across the gradually rising plateau, which sloped upwards from the Nile towards the distant jagged volcanic mountains lining the Red Sea. As they approached, Carter spun the Comanche around and they settled easily into a small basin lying deep with windswept sand. The rock bowl lay scattered with massive oval boulders, each larger than a house and seemingly tossed casually across the basin floor. A few sprinkled date palms, acacias and jacarandas sat half within the shade of several boulders, indicating a water source of some kind.

Carter brought the Comanche down beside a sprawl-ing jacaranda that was not yet in flower, its branches spider-webbing out to the green baked leaves at their tips. The rotors buffeted the tree, and as Carter shut down the

423

engines, so the swirls of rotor-swept sand slowly died with them, settling. Carter leapt out under the baking sun and looked up at the clear deep blue of the sky.

'Fuck, it's hot,' breathed Mongrel, jumping down beside him. 'How far we got to walk?'

'Two or three klicks. Maybe a little more, depending on the terrain. I didn't want to get too close – we don't know what sort of air support they have. Back in Slovenia they had some serious weaponry but it was all linked close to the quarry. It seems they could have a similar set-up here.'

Mongrel leant his back against the trunk of the tree, and took a long swig from his canteen. 'You think Jam will still be here? After all, we've had to detour and delay thanks to The Priest, that moaning bastard . . .'

'The TrackingDisc led us here, and the bugged helicopter hasn't moved. There's always the possibility they've travelled onwards, using a different vehicle –' Carter smiled grimly '– and if that's the case, then we're probably fucked.'

'Let's get moving then,' grunted the large squaddie, pushing himself away from the tree. 'Longer we stand talking, more chance they have of escape.'

The two men quickly sorted their equipment, travelling with light rucksacks, black shamags wound around their heads to protect them against the relentless sun.

Walking across the basin floor, they climbed the gentle rocky slope leading up and out to the rising plateau of rock and sand, and then started the short trek in silence, eyes alert and M24 carbines slung across their backs.

It was only when he started walking that Carter realised how weary he was; exhausted, in fact. And now they were heading into the lion's den – heading towards the enemy with no back-up and no prospect of calling any. Spiral had forbidden Carter to travel to Egypt but though it hurt him deeply to do it, if this was what it took to save Natasha's life the insubordination came easily.

I wonder if this was how Durell felt?

How Feuchter felt?

To bite the hand that feeds . . .

The sun pushed slowly on up the sky.

Carter and Mongrel moved steadily on, using the new ECubes to navigate and hoping that this new model was as secure against Nex digital infiltration as The Priest had promised. Wading through hot sand that came up to their ankles, they climbed ever upwards, tabbing between walls and gulleys of red rock, sometimes dropping into a narrow wadi and negotiating their way forward towards—

The rock basin, and the town that lay within.

Carter and Mongrel knelt beside a large jagged outcropping of rock, which overhung the steep drop ahead of them.

The basin spread out and was filled wall to wall with a town built from stone and mud bricks. Carter rested back on his haunches and Mongrel dropped to his belly as they sweated heavily under the burning sun, gazing down on the activity below.

The basin was perhaps a kilometre and a half square, three sides bordered with steep jagged volcanic walls rising to a high peak over to the north-east. At the head of the basin there was a temple of some kind, a large imposing building built from the red rock of the mountains and faced with marble, the upper layers of which had been stripped off. Ancient carvings, wind-worn and smooth, sat along a balcony above thick circular pillars, and sand swirled around the steps that led down to a main street, which in turn sliced through the heart of the town.

'Looks like the town built up around the temple,' said

Carter, soothing his parched throat with a gulp of water.

'Yeah. And look.' Mongrel pointed. Beside the temple, in a narrow fenced-in and sand-swept yard sat five black helicopters, squat and gleaming and shaded by the high rock walls.

'Nex,' said Carter softly, indicating with his canteen.

They moved in patrols through the main street and the narrow side-streets of the town. They moved in twos and threes, dressed in black, heads shrouded in black shamags and carrying machine rifles of various types. They moved easily among the populace of the town who seemed to ignore the Nex, almost accepting them as their own.

'What is this place?' asked Mongrel.

'Durell's secret hideaway? Who fucking knows? But our tagged helicopter is in that compound and I would bet that Jam and Durell are inside that temple: with the machine.'

'What's your plan?'

Carter rubbed at his stubble. 'I'll be honest, Mongrel – I'm tired of fighting, and I'm in no fit state to be taking on people like Jam. All I want to do is get the fucking machine and get back to Natasha . . .'

'What about if we disable Jam? Knock him unconscious and take him with us?'

Carter looked into Mongrel's eyes and saw the pain there. He wanted to say, *Don't be insane – Jam has been changed into a Nex, he's fucking dead . . . he's the enemy . . . he will try his utmost to kill us, to burn us.*

But he could not bring himself to speak the words.

'What we need to do,' said Carter carefully, 'is move in – covert infiltration: steal the Avelach and then get the fuck out, using one of their helicopters. If an opportunity arises then we can take Jam with us.'

Mongrel shook his head. 'No, that not good enough. And we also have problem with Durell and the earthquakes. He ripping the world apart, Carter. We got to stop him.'

Carter pursed his lips.

'*You shot that fucker once, through the heart,*' said Kade softly. His voice whispered through Carter and he felt himself shiver despite the heat of the desert.

'I thought you'd disappeared – gone off somewhere to shoot more women in the face, you fucking coward.'

'*Tut tut, Carter. You can't use me to do your dirty work and then criticise me when it's over. That just isn't* sportsmanlike. *She would have shot Mongrel in the back of the head – you know it, he knows it, and I fucking know it. And anyway, Carter – shooting pretty blonde bitches is as easy as shooting fish in a barrel.*'

'What do you want now?'

'*I want nothing more than to offer good advice.*'

'Such as?'

'*Kill Durell. Then kill Jam. Then kill all the Nex in the whole town.*'

'Wonderful,' muttered Carter sourly. Then he realised that Mongrel was looking at him, head tilted to one side, face a frown within the folds of the black shamag.

'You OK, Carter?'

'Yeah, yeah. What do you have in mind?'

'Well, when we find Avelach I'm thinking we find Durell. Let's take fucker out, *then* steal machine and drag Jam out to helicopter. I'm sure two men like us can pull quite simple suicide mission.'

Carter shook his head. 'We do this one step at a time. Carefully. No fucking mad dashes, nothing without us agreeing. Yeah? Or we'll both end up as minced dog meat.'

Mongrel stared down at the town. Watched the patrols of Nex, amidst the barking of the occasionally excited dogs that ran through the streets. He knew from experience that dogs made covert travel at night quite impossible.

'I think first we got to get to temple.'

Carter grinned. 'I've got an idea about that.'

With sunset came a respite from the heat. Carter and Mongrel watched the glowing orb sinking slowly over the shimmering horizon, over the distant desert plateau which dropped off in kilometre-long strides towards the far distant Nile.

Carter focused his actions to stop himself fidgeting with frustration. All he could think about was more waiting, more hanging around while Natasha lay dying on a cold hospital slab. He cleaned and oiled both his Browning HiPower and his M24 carbine, checking and reloading their magazines, oiling the moving parts of the weapons. Back in Crete when the Nex killer had been about to shoot him in the face and its gun had suffered a stoppage, he had been made aware once again just how vulnerable life could be – hanging by a thread, awaiting a cruel twist of fate that would swing the pendulum of favour from one combatant to another. The Nex was dead, slowly decomposing next to the body of Mila the sniper. And why? Because his submachine gun had been dirty, or lacked oil, or the bullet had been poorly manufactured.

Mongrel, after quenching his thirst and chewing on dried beef to satisfy his huge deep-bellied hunger, finally followed Carter's lead and oiled his own weapons. As the sun set and the blue faded from the sky, allowing darkness to cast a veil over the town, the two men found that they were finally ready.

Carter watched a small sand-coloured scorpion scuttle in front of him and pause, seeming to turn and look at him. He aimed his Browning casually – and watched the scorpion scuttle away, its sting held high and proud.

'You little fucker. No compassion in your insect brain, is there?'

Dogs barked in the distance, and Carter and Mongrel shouldered their packs. Clutching their guns in their hands, they moved off slowly against the now dark sky-line.

Their boots trod softly against the rock and sand, along the ridge that dropped towards the main gap leading to the village. Halting some distance away, they saw several Nex standing idly by the roadside. The two Spiral men crept down through the steep rocks until they reached, panting and with sweat-stinging eyes, a narrow back street. It was unlit and had an unpleasant aroma of some-thing rotting.

'What now?'

Carter gestured, and they moved forward. For six hours he had been watching the Nex patrols and planning a way across the town towards the temple. He had the route imprinted on his cortex.

They halted, carbines at the ready.

As they waited, three Nex drifted past, boots silent on the sand-scattered street, heads scanning left and right. Deep in the shadows Carter and Mongrel held their breath – and once the Nex had passed they moved from one backstreet to the next, hugging the shadows and treading carefully, their eyes alert.

A dog barked, the noise echoing across the town. Another mutt took up the call, and for a few minutes about twenty of the beasts decided to make a nuisance of themselves, their echoing barks reverberating through the town and out into the desert.

'I understand why they fucking eat 'em now,' muttered Mongrel, who had made no pretence of liking Egyptian food, and referred to most foreign dishes placed in front of him as a mishmash of either shredded dog, donkey or camel.

They crept along through the shadows, halting often, listening to the local denizens chattering in Arabic. Small groups of men wearing *galabiyyas* robes in varying colours and styles sat outside some of the houses at small wooden tables, sometimes smoking strong Egyptian tobacco through bubbling hookahs and drinking tiny cups of thick black treacle-like coffee. They kept their voices low. There seemed to be an undercurrent of fear pervading the air.

Finally, Carter called a halt and dropped his pack to the ground. He handed his M24 carbine to Mongrel and rolled his neck as if readying for action.

'What are you doing?'

'Wait here.'

'You said no single-handed heroics! We need know what both up to!'

'I'm buying us our passage into the temple – unseen.'

Mongrel frowned, then watched Carter draw a long black steel blade from a boot-sheath. Mongrel licked his lips, tasting dried sweat-salt caught in the stubble around his mouth, and watched Carter move towards the end of the narrow darkened backstreet.

Carter crouched between an overflowing bin stinking of old vegetables and a square cardboard box reeking of rancid, pungent dog piss. He waited, eyes almost closed, counting . . . and then sensed rather than heard the footsteps of the two Nex guards . . .

He uncoiled from his hiding place like a striking cobra,

leaping forward without a sound to plunge the long dagger through the eye and into the brain of the lead Nex. Blood gushed, drenching his fist, as his left boot kicked up and out, cannoning into the second Nex's throat. Carter whirled, pulling out the knife in the same movement and, spinning low, brought the blade up, ramming it into the second Nex's heart. It fell forward against him, and Carter withdrew the blade, supporting the Nex as blood poured out onto the sand and their stares met for a long horrible moment. Carter waited impatiently until it died in his arms.

Dragging the body back down the alley, Carter dumped it behind the bin, then sheathing his dagger he ran and dragged the first Nex corpse back, depositing it next to its companion.

'Strip them.'

'You want us to look like the Nex?'

'Can you think of any better way of sneaking in?'

'I bloody hope Simmo not arrive.'

'Yeah.' Carter grimaced, remembering the incident on the sniper tower. 'So do I.'

They stripped the Nex bodies of their clothing and pulled themselves into the outfits, finally rolling the thin balaclavas over their faces and turning to check one another.

'It stinks,' complained Mongrel.

'Don't you ever stop moaning?'

'And we haven't got copper eyes! They spot us for sure!'

'Jesus, Mongrel, we're not supposed to satisfy intense scrutiny in this Nex gear, just casual glances. We're going over the fucking roofs until we reach the street – it's just for the last few feet.'

Moving back out into the alley, Carter swept sand over

the blood as best he could. They took the Nex's weapons, slinging their own carbines over their backs. Then Carter led the way down several more alleys until they came to a low building and Carter leapt up onto a bin, then jumped, hauling himself to the low roof. Mongrel followed, muttering morosely to himself as he heaved his bulk up and scratched his dragging belly against the roof's rough edges. Then they crouched for a few moments in the darkness, getting their bearings.

Moving along behind the parapet, they climbed to the next building, finding easy handholds in the badly constructed mud-brick breeze-block wall, and then looked out over the main thoroughfare.

Fires flickered, casting long golden shadows.

Occasionally Nex patrols would pass. Carter focused his gaze on the opening to the temple – six steep steps, blown with sand, leading to a dark interior with a ramp. Were there any guards inside?

He took his ECube and stared at the tiny alloy device for a few moments. Digits glittered. Carter bit his lip, frustrated and mistrustful. Could he risk it? Was the new version of the ECube truly undetectable?

Could he trust it?

Carter stowed the tiny device away once more and calmed his breathing, peering into the temple. He took a SniperScope from his pack and lifted it to his eye, flicking it to night-vision mode. The world sprang to life in green and purple. Carter zoomed in on the temple but could see only the ramp rising out of view. He watched for a while but saw no movement.

They moved from roof to roof, slowly, carefully, making sure that they made no noise. They could not afford the hiss of cloth scraping against stone, or the negligent kick of a pebble that would rattle against mud brick.

Any such mistake could not only cost them their lives, but the lives of others who relied on them . . .

Finally, after further climbing and more of Mongrel's silent curses – which he threw with mental vitriol at Carter's back – and sweating like pigs, they reached the edge of the street overlooking the temple.

It reared ahead of them, supported at the base by heavy carved rounded pillars and rising to a single sculpted spire about a metre in diameter whose top rose just above the high cliff wall behind. Carter glanced down at the small black helicopters, and then up and down the street.

They waited, watching the occasional Nex patrol.

'They seem quite relaxed,' said Mongrel.

'Good.'

'Maybe it a bluff?'

'Maybe.'

'What happen then?'

'Then we're dead.'

'Oh.'

A pause. Silence. The stone around them, after baking all day in the sun, was now releasing the naturally stored heat. Both men were sweating heavily, and the Nex-scented balaclavas did nothing to relieve their sombre mood.

'You see anything?'

'No,' said Carter softly.

'When we going in?'

'When you learn to shut the fuck up.'

'I need to be moving. I'm overheating.'

'Your body or your brain?'

Mongrel frowned. 'You not take piss when I on bad mission with you. You listen hard, Carter boy, I not take this sort of—'

433

'Shh.'

Mongrel lapsed into silence.

'Come on.'

They climbed onto the parapet, jumped onto a low ledge, then lowered themselves to the ground. Nothing stirred, no breeze to cool the air, no wind to blow the sand on the street around. Carter and Mongrel strode towards the entrance to the temple with heads held high, weapons in hands and hearts in mouths . . . waiting for the shout to halt . . . waiting for the blast of bullets that would eat the backs of their skulls . . . Their breath coming in short gasps, they jogged up the sand-blown steps and disappeared into the temple's gaping black maw.

The room had a red sandstone floor, gently grooved from a thousand years of use. The lower sections of the walls were lined with panels of marble and obsidian. Light came from globes in the high vaulted stone roof, and benches on which rested the most advanced computing equipment in the world stood against the walls.

Durell stood by a rectangular black screen. The surface of the screen seemed to ripple as he touched it. Then it sprang into liquid fire and lights glittered around his twisted black clawed hand.

He smiled within the folds of his dark hood.

And his copper slitted eyes glittered.

'Are we ready?' came Gol's voice from close behind in a hushed whisper.

'Yes,' said Durell, and touched the screen. 'We are finally ready.'

Carter and Mongrel crouched in the gloom, weapons primed. They were allowing their eyes to adjust to the

434

weak light cast from well-spaced flickering torches whose amber flames danced in iron brackets along the smooth red walls.

From where they waited, senses alert, one long wide corridor stretched off, filled with nothing but shadows.

'It's like being back in the annals of history,' said Mongrel, shivering.

'Yeah, I always had a thing for Ancient Egypt.' Carter smiled and slowly unfolded from his defensive stance. He glanced around, moved forward cautiously a couple of steps, then halted once more. His head cocked and Mongrel came up beside him, sub-machine gun gripped in unsteady fingers.

'I do not like this,' said Mongrel softly.

'Where are the guards?' asked Carter.

'They would not leave this unguarded,' said Mongrel. 'Something very wrong.'

Carter nodded. He activated his ECube and scanned on different frequencies. 'Over there – a wall of blue k-laser. Invisible to the naked eye.'

'A fucking digital tripwire that cut you in half with delayed action!' muttered Mongrel. 'Very nasty. You any idea how we get past?'

'Yeah.' Carter stared at Mongrel hard. 'And so should you. Where were you during the seminars?'

Mongrel shrugged awkwardly. 'I had this bird, down in the town. She had great pair of breasts that wobble all over place . . .' He petered off when he saw the look on Carter's battered face. 'I sorry,' he finished. 'I really am. But you should see tits! They mark a step in man's way forward through life . . .' Mongrel trailed off feebly.

Carter moved carefully on while Mongrel covered their backs. Stopping within the stone-floored corridor, Carter lifted the ECube and digits flickered, tracing patterns across its alloy face. Nothing seemed to happen – visually – but physically they had become surrounded by an invisible globe of blue k-laser.

'Come on.'

They walked slowly forwards, with Carter's gaze never leaving the flickering read-outs on the ECube. As they moved through the invisible wall – the digital tripwire capable of cutting the two men into cubes of flesh – the ECube absorbed the sentry laser into its own field and allowed the signals to flow uninterrupted by the physical intrusion of the two men. They slid silently free on the other side and stood, Mongrel panting softly, looking around in the flickering light of the corridor.

'We through?'

'Yeah.' Carter checked the mag on his sub-machine gun. 'I kind of expected spikes, or something.'

'This not Indiana Jones!'

Crouched in the shadows once more, the two men waited patiently. Carter allowed the ECube to perform a full scan – realising that it could save them many hours. Anyway, if the new version of the ECube had been breached by the Nex then they had already been discovered.

A drift of fine sand blew across the floor, and a cold breeze wafted from the temple's depths.

'What you doing?'

'Shh.' Carter held up a finger, then turned the ECube to Mongrel. Mongrel nodded, eyes wide. 'This is some fucking huge temple. Look, it goes back into the mountain rock for nearly two kilometres.'

'We never find Jam in here,' said Mongrel.

'I have an idea.'

Carter played with the ECube for a few minutes.

436

Whilst not an expert on the machine like Natasha or The Priest, he could navigate his way successfully through the myriad coded terminals and keys and rhythms. Finally he smiled. 'Yes, it's here.'

'What you doing? This place giving me the willies.'

'The *willies*?'

'I been watching some *old* vid recently.'

'The fucking *willies*?' Carter laughed then, a brittle sound in the cool dry interior.

Mongrel touched his arm. 'It good to hear you laugh. I know you not got much to laugh about. It good to see you keeping it together.'

'Hey, insanity is my middle name. Now, when the Spiral mainframes picked up a stray signal from Jam's ThumbNail_Map it held a pattern. A grid of the location that Jam was trying to traverse . . . If I can match that grid to a pattern of corridors here, then we have a link, yes?'

Mongrel looked sideways at Carter. 'You crafty fucker.'

'So you agree? That's a possibility?'

'Aye,' nodded Mongrel. 'Sound feasible to ol' Mongrel.'

Carter played with the ECube for a few more moments. Then he smiled. 'Game on,' he said.

They moved through the shadows of the stone corridor, most of it just bare sandstone-block walls, scuffing through the fine sheen of sand that scattered beneath their boots. Three times Carter had pulled them into smaller corridors that led off as teams of Nex moved slowly past, JK49s held with barrels pointing at the ground.

Three times they waited, risking discovery and a sudden blazing firefight that would end their quest . . .

Three times the Nex moved on silently, their black boots leaving nothing but imprints on the sandy floor.

From the wide central corridor at the entrance to the temple, they moved steadily downhill towards a hub – from which radiated another ten stone walkways, some leading up, some down, and some spanning away on the same level. All these corridors were extremely narrow and had no distinctive features to differentiate one from the other.

Using the ECube, Carter navigated them through the *labyrinth*.

For the next twenty minutes they moved slowly, gently pressing their hands against worn stone-block walls. Mostly, ceilings were high and obscured by distance and darkness. At irregular intervals iron brackets held flaming brands, some guttering low and leaving the two men practically without light. They had the back-up of NVGs but night-vision aids gave off a subtle whine that was easy for the Nex's superior senses to pick up.

'What is this place? I never heard of it before?'

'I don't think it appears on any tourist maps,' said Carter, leading them down a steeply sloping stone ramp. He halted at the bottom, holding his hand up. Mongrel glanced nervously behind, the muzzle of his gun wavering.

'What?'

'Listen.'

They could hear a noise, like a gentle rasping. Leather against glass. Or—

'What the fuck is that?'

They crept forward and suddenly the walls ended and the ceiling soared high above them, disappearing into blackness. The floor fell away into a dark wide pit with gently sloping sides. The flat expanse of floor was spanned by an ornately carved stone bridge which arced gently over the depression, which in turn was filled with—

'What the fuck are *they*?'

Carter and Mongrel stared. In the darkness, apparently sleeping, were a hundred or so *creatures*. They each had four limbs ending in savage black claws, and their bodies were tightly and hugely muscled, armoured with contoured interleaving plates. They were big – bigger than any wild feline – and their heads were triangular and tufted with thick strands of fur.

The large group were all breathing softly, intertwined in sleep.

'You get the feeling we truly fucked if they wake up?'

Carter scowled at Mongrel, and prodded him in the chest. Then he moved forward, slowly, placing each footfall with care. He checked with the ECube and found another blue k-laser digital tripwire near the centre of the bridge.

'*A beautiful trap, don't you think?*' said Kade.

'Shut up.'

'*Lure you to the centre of the bridge and – bam! – a hundred fucking Sleepers descend on you and rip out your belly with their teeth. Fucking primeval!*'

'What did you call them? Sleepers? How do you know that?'

Kade remained silent, watching, dark and brooding at the back of Carter's mind.

Carter stepped onto the bridge.

He began to walk forwards. Below him, the creatures continued to breathe deeply, their eyes closed and Carter felt the tension rising in his chest. He licked at dry lips.

Out of the darkness rose columns, six-sided and carved from red and yellow stone. On the summit of each squatted a finely carved and crafted figure like nothing Carter had ever seen. These carvings were strange, alien almost.

Halting, Carter activated the ECube and the two men

439

slipped neatly through the digital trap, then padded down the other side of the bridge and into the relative safety of another narrow stone corridor. Mongrel wiped sweat from his brow and then rolled his Nex balaclava back into place.

'You OK?' said Carter.

'I've felt better,' muttered Mongrel harshly.

They disappeared like ghosts into the dimly lit corridor. Behind, in the pit, there came a glimmer of movement as one of the Sleepers opened its eyes.

Copper slits glinted.

And slowly, gracefully, it began to uncoil . . .

The tunnel led down.

It was horribly claustrophobic, with a low rough ceiling which made both Carter and Mongrel stoop to avoid banging their heads. The narrow walls of the tunnel were mostly rough-faced, with some crumbling edges worn by time, but they would sometimes blaze with panels of ancient Egyptian hieroglyphs. The walkway was rough, and grooved down either side. Carter pointed, frowning, and Mongrel merely shook his head.

They moved even more slowly now, even more warily. Ahead, a strange noise sounded: a high-pitched keening wail, not altogether human. It rose in pitch, then faded away until it was nothing more than a distant dream of aural melancholy. Then it would wind up once more, into a terrible thrumming whine that hurt the men's ears. Carter scanned with the ECube – but there was nothing.

'I got bad feeling about this.'

'Yeah, me too,' said Carter. He checked his Browning and continued forward. He pulled off his Nex balaclava with a cursed, 'Fuck it,' and rubbed at his face. 'I don't think we'll need these disguises now.'

'But what if—'

'Then we shoot the fuckers in the face.'

The corridor continued to lead down. Sand swept around their feet, pushed by a cool breeze that moaned softly. Carter's nostrils wrinkled as a coppery and unpleasant odour drifted past them.

They passed the holding cell which they assumed was where Jam had been imprisoned. It was empty, with a few shards of twisted copper on the ground accompanied by a few dried bloodstains. With no other option, they continued to follow the passageway . . .

Which led further down.

'I do not like this. It feel like the Kamus.'

'And that place was haunted,' said Carter softly.

The whining sound lifted and fell, a ululating call of stressed metal. Occasionally there came the sound of a heavy impact like stone crushing stone. Both men felt their hackles rising as the tunnel came to an abrupt end. They crouched by the edge, looking out into a mammoth cavern.

It was almost circular. A million strange patterns were carved across the floor, walls and high distant ceiling, and the floor was littered with huge engraved blocks of stone, marble and granite. The floor was divided down the centre by a crevasse of black – which not only cut across the floor but up the walls as well, almost giving the impression that the huge hall *floated*. It was very dark, and a bad smell was carried by the cold – by a now chilling – breeze.

Carter gazed at the crevasse, the sheer drop that they would have to cross. It measured perhaps ten metres and was too wide to leap over. His gaze scanned from side to side, following the gap upwards and noting that it also crossed the ceiling. He also saw a bank of carved rock on the floor, a bridge across the actual ceiling that spanned the black crevasse, and a strangely angled doorway at the distant opposite side of the hall.

The wail returned, moaning softly from the depths of the gash in the rock.

'Shall I check it out?'

'Wait,' said Carter softly.

They waited, watching, sweat beading on their brows despite the chill. This is some puzzle, decided Carter.

He scanned with the ECube, but it revealed nothing.

His stare raked the ceiling, the walls, searching for spikes, or holes, or tips of barbed spears.

'*An active imagination you have,*' sneered Kade.

'What do you want?'

'*To help, of course.*'

'Yeah, to help yourself.'

'*Let me have control and I will get you past the traps.*'

'Fuck off. What do you know of this place?'

'*I have my contacts.*'

'Yeah, and I have mine.' Carter pointed and lifted his M24 carbine as a tall, broad figure stepped out from the crooked stone doorway opposite. The man held his large hands wide in an act of supplication, and his face was at peace, filled with serenity. His grey-flecked beard was just how Carter remembered it and the brown eyes were the brown eyes of the killer, the Spiral killer – the Spiral *traitor* . . .

Carter stepped down—

And almost fell.

The rocky floor seemed to sway, to shimmer. He felt it move like ball bearings beneath his boots and his M24 slammed up. His eyes narrowed and fixed on Gol as he strode across the subtly moving stone floor towards the segment of falling space.

The stench grew worse.

'Welcome to our laboratory,' came the deeply melodic voice of Gol. The man had halted beside a group of red stone cubes stacked beside the crevasse.

Carter moved closer, warily, glancing all around. He could sense Mongrel behind him, frantically searching for a source of danger. Carter glanced at the ten-metre-wide drop that separated the two men.

'How are you, Gol?'

'In truth,' said the huge man, letting his hands fall to his sides, 'I have felt better. I find it sad when those who show themselves to be enemies by their actions but not by their morals must die.'

'Meaning?'

'Meaning that I no longer have a choice.'

'You always have a choice,' said Carter softly. His senses were screaming at him, and Kade – the blood-scream demon in his brain – was howling like a pig stuck on a spear.

'You have come for the Avelach? To save Natasha?'

'Yes,' said Carter, staring hard into Gol's unreadable eyes. The big killer had always unnerved Carter. Natasha had once claimed that he and Gol were the same – men, yes, but murderers too, fashioned from the same mould. Carter had reluctantly acknowledged then that she was correct. But now, staring into Gol's eyes, he was not so sure. 'How the fuck did you survive?'

'They turned me into a Nex,' said Gol softly. 'They saved me, using the machine that you seek. The Avelach. But they deviated from the normal formula.'

'You do not have copper eyes?'

'What makes you think all Nex appear the same? It is down to the different chemicals in the inhibitors.' Gol's voice was deeply melancholy, an actor's voice, a voice belonging on the stage, not in an ancient temple.

443

'You have a question for me?' said Carter.

Gol smiled then, seeming to relax a little. But Carter did not; the M24 remained trained on Gol and he felt the Browning creep into his left hand. He could almost hear the frantic searching of Mongrel behind and he allowed himself to flow with the situation, to calm his heart and brain and notice everything . . .

The floor rolled gently – nauseatingly – beneath him.

The distant wailing and stench poured from the crevasse. Moving towards the edge and glancing down, Carter saw it disappear into an apparent infinity.

Beneath his boots, the carved stone shuddered softly, then started to move. There came a deep and thudding crunch of rock against rock and, glancing up, he saw the ornately carved bridge creep across the circular ceiling and towards the side of the circular cavern. Spanning the ten-metre gap that separated the two men, it would soon provide a means of linking them . . .

Carter smiled, suddenly understanding.

'How do you know that I have a question?' asked Gol.

Carter tilted his head, eyes fixed. 'We are talking, not fighting.'

'The fighting will come later. You remember the QIII? The cubic processor developed by Quantell . . . Spiral_Q? By Feuchter and Durell? You remember it? The processor that you blasted into oblivion with your bullets and hatred?'

'How could I ever forget?'

'It could not see you,' said Gol. 'How was that so?'

'I do not know. Where is the Avelach, Gol? Where is Jam?'

'We both want something,' said Gol, spreading his hands again. 'We need to know why the processor could not see you. Could not predict you.'

444

'I do not know.'

'Who is Kade?'

Carter froze, his stare fixed on Gol. His mouth was suddenly dry. His eyes drilled like diamond bits into Gol's face.

'I don't know what you mean.'

'Kade, the demon in your soul. Who is he, Carter?'

'I think – think you are mistaken.'

Gol smiled then, and Carter's attention shifted back to the distant doorway. Durell stood there, and now Jam heaved his bulk forward, swaying softly as his claws struck tiny sparks from the stone. Jam started to move forward, swaying as the uneven floor rolled beneath him. Carter's gaze returned to Gol who now held a pistol, a heavy Sig P5, black and evil in his huge hand.

The floor continued to move, pushing Carter off balance. Kade was screaming in his head but still he did not open fire; there was something strange about Gol. The big man's mouth opened and Carter shifted his aim to where Jam strode purposefully forward, heavy triangular head swaying gently from side to side—

'Kill him,' Jam snarled.

Gol's stare met Carter's.

'You seek to save Natasha,' Gol said softly. 'When you find the Avelach, the codes and the secret to its control are inscribed on the silver box that protects it. They must never be separated.'

Gol smiled, then turned and opened fire on Jam with a sudden booming burst of bullets. Jam moved with incredible speed, taking one round in the torso as he bounded forward. He gave a deep gurgling growl and flipped suddenly to one side . . . Gol was moving, sprinting forward, still firing as he leapt to meet the larger Nex—

The gun was smashed from Gol's fist as a huge

445

whirling blow sent the big man spinning from his feet. Jam reached down *into* himself, his claws coming up with dark blood. He glanced over at Carter, then reached towards Gol who kicked out, hatred in his eyes . . .

Jam grasped Gol, lifting the grey-bearded man by his groin and throat. Gol's boots lashed into Jam's head, powerful blows that rocked the Nex, but Jam pulled Gol into a bear-hug. Their stares met, their faces almost touched and it was as if Carter was witnessing some bizarre act of love. Jam's claws came around and slammed into Gol's back. There was a tearing of cloth and flesh, followed swiftly by a heavy pattering of blood droplets.

Gol's body kicked. Spasmed. Went limp . . .

Then spewed blood across Jam's armoured torso.

And Jam allowed the dead rag-doll body to fall, to lie limp and broken and torn apart on the stone in a crumpled heap. Jam's head came up, glistening, and he stared across at Carter—

Who opened fire, M24 bullets shrieking across the crevasse as the bridge rolled around the walls towards the two combatants. Jam leapt back behind the bank of red stones; more noises of stone on stone were heard, and the bridge slid into itself until there was nothing but an incredible fall into the black pit keeping the two enemies apart.

Carter ceased firing, smoke rising to sting his nostrils.

Jam turned and sprinted for the opening in the following wall. Carter sent more bullets blasting after the fleeing Nex – but failed to hit him.

'Carter, we're trapped.'

Carter glanced around at Mongrel. 'What do you mean, trapped?'

'I leap out to give supporting fire, and this stone door slab thing come down behind me. It block us in.'

'Shit.'

Carter moved forward and stared down into the crevasse. The floor was still moving beneath him and he could see Gol's mangled corpse on the opposite side of the hall.

What's fucking going on here?' he thought.

He glanced up to where the ceiling was revolving and he suddenly realised that it was getting harder to stand. Glancing back, he saw the far end of the chamber slowly lifting, so that he stood on a slope leading down towards the spinning abyss—

'Carter, you stop this thing . . .'

'The whole fucking chamber is suspended, it's going to tip us into the pit . . .'

The angle of elevation gradually increased.

Gol's corpse started to slide away, rasping against the stone, back towards the far distant end of the chamber, leaving a long smear of blood in its wake.

'There no way out, Carter!' Mongrel's voice was filled with panic.

Carter's boots started to scrabble against the rock as it tipped him towards the crevasse. The whining of distant machinery increased, and again crashes of stone on stone reverberated around the huge cavern.

'Bloody Egyptians!' howled Mongrel.

Carter felt himself slipping.

Ahead of him the looming chasm seemed to spin crazily closer, and he felt suddenly sick, filled with an insane nausea and vertigo.

How ironic!

How sweetly fucking ironic.

Not for Carter hot scything steel in his brain, nor a snapped and twisted spine from a crazed motorcycle crash, nor machine-gunned in half on some distant future battlefield. No, this was death by stone—

447

The old-fashioned way.
The abyss loomed closer—
Death grinned with a mask of dark, aged bone.
And Carter could do nothing to stop them falling . . .

CHAPTER 16

SYSTEM SHOCK

The stone chamber spun, elevated on the scream of ancient gears and tried to spit Carter and Mongrel to their deaths. Boots scrabbling, guns clashing against the stone floor that lifted in front of him, out of the corner of one eye Carter saw something incredible—

Gol was moving. His head came up, beard stained with blood, and his stare fixed on Carter. He heaved himself along the floor, grunting with pain, hauling his torn and shattered body across the incline towards the precipice that threatened to swallow both Carter and Mongrel . . .

Carter fought to stay on his feet. He felt himself slipping towards the revolving crevasse and glanced over at Gol, who was leaving a trail of blood against the intricately carved floor.

Gol had halted, ten feet from the cubes of red stone.

He was panting. Blood was dribbling thickly down his chin.

'What that fucker doing?'

Carter smiled crazily, the whining noise filling his head

and making his ears want to bleed. 'I think he's trying to save us.'

'Why he do that?'

'Mongrel, *stop asking fucking questions*!'

Both Carter and Mongrel could not help themselves; they slid closer and closer towards the edge of the abyss. Gol fought his way upwards until he disappeared behind the red stones – and suddenly the noise died. A terrible eerie silence now filled the massive, tilted, disjointed chamber.

The world halted.

Carter glanced at Mongrel.

'I think he stop it,' said Mongrel.

'I hope so.'

'I hope so too. Not good way to die.'

'What isn't?'

'Falling into a stinking pit. It remind old Mongrel of a story . . .'

'Not . . . fucking . . . *now*.'

Sounds of machinery wailed up from the crevasse once more and for a terrible heart-wrenching moment it seemed that the two men were going to be pitched to their deaths after all. Instead, the whole chamber started to right itself. Carter and Mongrel slumped backwards to the ground, and sat staring at the stones that hid the mangled body of Gol.

Finally, levelling out, the bridge slid out into an arc of interleaving stone panels over the ten-metre gap. Carter climbed to his feet, pulled a grumbling Mongrel up behind him and together they padded over and placed their booted feet warily on the bridge.

'This not another trap?' asked Mongrel.

'Only one way to find out.'

Carter marched across the bridge and stared down at

Gol. He lay on his back, staring up at Carter. His eyes were wide and bright.

'Why are you still here?' growled Gol, spitting through blood and froth. 'They've gone to Austria. Every second you stand here you are letting them get away!'

'Why did you do this for us?' asked Carter softly, kneeling and taking Gol's huge hand in his.

Gol met Carter's gaze. 'Maybe I'm just going fucking soft,' he spat through blood-froth.

'I thought you were the enemy?'

'I have been blind, blinded by that fucking machine. But Carter, the Nex . . . they are not just life unworthy of life . . . they feel, they have emotions . . . they can be *changed*.'

'I think you are different to the others,' said Carter.

'Find the Avelach. Use it to heal Natasha. Then you will see, then you will understand . . . but first, up ahead, you will find Durell's control centre for this place, his laboratory . . . there are digital maps, explanations of the Foundation Stones and how LVA is used to control the earthquakes – but you must move quickly . . .'

Carter stood. He exchanged glances with Mongrel as Gol started to cough, his whole body convulsing, blood pouring out of his mouth and nose. Carter lifted his Browning, and sighted it on Gol's forehead. He met the man's gaze.

'Do it,' gurgled Gol.

Carter . . . froze.

'Don't fucking leave me for the *Nex*.'

Carter closed his eyes, and a single echoing shot rang out across the carved stone chamber – ending Gol's life.

The black helicopter lifted from the ground, rotors swirling wide arcs of sand and blasting the other choppers, the wire-mesh fence and the temple walls. Engines howling, the small aircraft lifted off vertically – high into the black Egyptian night – spun in a tight circle and headed off into the darkness towards Cairo.

Lights glittered in Durell's eyes.

'Do you think they are dead?'

Durell glanced at Jam, at the twisted jaws that had straightened a little since he had last examined his subject, allowing Jam's speech more of a human quality. 'Nobody has ever survived that chamber.'

The helicopter spun through the darkness, following the plateau as it fell away from the Red Sea Mountains. Away from the town the pilot dropped them closer towards the rock and sand, and without lights they spun like a black bullet through the night.

'When will we begin the Domination?' asked Jam quietly. The Nex's huge triangular head tilted to look at Durell and Durell found himself shivering at the look in the slitted eyes of the creature he had . . . created.

'Mace tells me that all Foundation Stones are in place. He tells me that the World Investigation Committee is playing games with us, stalling for time and I believe they will never give in . . . I believe they will not relinquish control. I thought some of the weaker states might have folded without a real fight – but I feel our demonstrations are still being viewed as natural events. I will give them something more to play with. I will smash their armies, I will crush their navies and air forces. I will bring down every fucking government building in every fucking city of the world. And only then will I seek to negotiate. Only then will I seek to talk about peace. Once again I find myself surrounded by weakness and indecision, the very factors that will topple Spiral and world governments from their heights of abused power!'

452

'And we will orchestrate this from Austria?' asked Jam softly.

'It can be the only place.' Durell smiled from the darkness of his robes.

The Priest climbed up into the helicopter, and Heneghan turned, meeting his gaze from behind the HIDSS.

'Code Black?' she whispered, her eyes haunted by the touch of fear.

'Code Black,' rumbled The Priest with a great melancholy in his voice.

The Comanche's twin LHTecs howled as Heneghan hurled the machine into the night sky, cutting through the rain and sleet that pounded against the fuselage of the war machine.

The Priest settled back, lips pursed together, gold-flecked brown eyes narrowing as he considered the mission to come.

It was very simple.

To the point:

Hunt down Carter and stop him. By any means necessary.

'Why did you do this to me, you foolish old bugger?' rumbled The Priest to himself. 'Why did you force me into this path of unrighteousness? I do not want this . . . I do not want to see you die.'

Because he knew.

Knew in his heart and in his soul.

Carter would not cease with his mission to save Natasha . . .

He would never stop.

And he would condemn them all—

The only way to 'stop' Carter would be to kill him.

'Damn you,' muttered The Priest darkly, hand on his

small Bible, which was of little true comfort now as they howled through the dark night's rain and sleet.

Mongrel followed Carter into the chamber, stooping a little beneath the rough red sandstone archway. The lower section of the walls were lined with panels of dark marble containing veins of some mineral that glittered softly. All around the room were benches on which sophisticated computing equipment lay. Carter's head swung back and forth, his eyes narrowed, his M24 clasped tight.

'This place is *old*,' said Mongrel. 'I do not like it here.'

'Is there anywhere you *do* like?'

Mongrel thought deeply, nodding to himself. 'Brothels,' he announced after a few moments.

Carter moved forward, to a large rectangular black screen. The surface of the screen seemed to ripple as Carter reached out and touched it. Lights danced gently around his fingertips and it made a soft lulling sound.

'Kebab shops.'

Carter moved his hand, and with a shock realised that the screen obeyed the same movements as an ECube. Of course – Durell was ex-Spiral. The betrayer. His technology was based on Spiral technology. His computing equipment was a bastardised deviant version of all that Spiral used . . . only warped, twisted and perverted.

'Porn museums.'

'Mongrel, *shut up.*'

Carter traced patterns with his hand and the screen sprang into life. He scrolled through intricate interwoven data, strands coiled with DNA. His eyes searched and he became lost in the digital world. *The chamber no longer existed, this temple in Egypt no longer existed . . . Mongrel pacing the room, keeping a lookout – none of it seemed real as he sunk into the data and felt himself* absorbed . . .

After a few moments, Carter disengaged.

'You find anything?'

'Oh,' said Carter softly.

Mongrel stared at Carter's face. It was ashen.

'Now I understand,' he whispered.

'Is it bad?'

Carter nodded. 'It's fucking bad, all right. We have to tell Spiral. We have to stop Durell.'

'Is it the earthquakes?'

'It is worse than earthquakes,' whispered Carter, turning away and grasping his machine carbine tightly. 'If Durell makes a wrong move in this game he's playing, he could destroy the world.'

'You mean take over the world, right?' growled Mongrel.

'No.' Carter shook his head. 'If Durell fucks up, he'll take us all out with him. Every single living creature on the planet. Have you got that ECube booted up yet?'

'It's flickering between states of stupidity and unreliability. I think the Nex may have compromised the network.'

'Give it to me. We have to tell Spiral – and tell them *now*.'

Simmo halted the HTank and breathed deeply, staring down at the tiny DigitalMap on the tank's ECube-linked scanners. Crushed under the wide heavy tracks, trees and other jungle vegetation creaked softly and Simmo could feel sweat running down his head, stinging the cuts to both the crown of his skull and lesser wounds on his face from the pounding he'd had from Kattenheim. Beneath him cold matrix engines hissed.

They know, said a small voice in his head.

They know you are coming.

Kattenheim has warned them . . .

The LVA depot deep in the Colombian jungle was a large one; it was perhaps five times the size of the one back in Slovenia and one of the largest finds reported by Spiral men across the globe. Hence, logically to Simmo, it had to be the one he personally came to investigate – and destroy. Twenty-four huge tankers containing fuel squatted in the darkness and Simmo's scouts had reported back that there were at least fifty enemy tanks, grey-tracked Nex TK79s supported by another twenty or so six-wheeled Can-trucks.

Simmo's TankSquad itself sported only thirty Spiral SP57s armed with twin 135mm M512 smoothbore cannons, firing HEAT-X2 combat rounds, and triple heavy-calibre machine guns. They would need the element of surprise to win this one . . . and in Simmo's mind they had been guaranteed that simple necessity before Kattenheim's escape.

Now they would have to make the best of a shit situation.

'I should have let the guys shoot him,' Simmo muttered.

'You OK, boss?' rumbled Oz, his mission co-op.

'Hmm. I is thinking the plateau is nice and wide, hard to protect at front – this why they have so many tanks and trucks. We need to hit them – fast and *now*.'

'Frontal assault?'

'Poor tactic but we have little option. I will take HTank in from behind, down the gulleys and through perimeter fence when you engage. Send message to Rogowski – synchronise for five minutes.'

'Will do,' growled Oz.

Simmo lifted the hatch and poked his head up into the night. A deep dense blackness surrounded him and he felt

456

sweat dribbling under his shirt and down inside the legs of his urban combats.

Parrots shrieked somewhere in the jungle, followed by the chatter of squabbling monkeys. Insects buzzed. Simmo squinted, staring off into the darkness. On the scanners below, he could see the SP57 tanks moving smoothing into position, their twin cannons looking ominous in the gloom.

'You think they know we're here?'

'Maybe,' said Simmo. 'They not move on scanners. ECube reports no engines starting, no activity whatsoever.'

'If this attack is not a surprise, we're fucked, Sarge.'

'You think Sarge not know that?'

'Sorry, Sarge.'

'Is all right, lad.'

The valley was a wide scoop from the Colombian jungle, with steep walls climbing from the basin's base in an insane flurry of tangled trees, flailing creepers, nature-ravaged trunks, ferns and climbers, all competing for life and light. Trees tumbled across trees in great cataracts of spewing vegetation. Ferns mated with creepers, snaking over and around and through huge hardwood mahoganies and oaks. The whole basin was an insanity of jungle through which a wide road had been scythed, leading to the Colombian LVA depot at its heart, and bordered by a natural rough-sawn mahogany barricade at the rear – a huge impassable arc of titanic trunks.

Rain started to fall from heavy clouds swirling in dark skies. It increased quickly to a tropical downpour and Simmo lifted his face, revelling in the large warm droplets which filled him with a sudden vigour – a feeling of youth and indestructibility.

He glanced down at the scanners and watched his

TankSquads moving into place through the rain and wet vegetation. Once a time had been agreed the men kept radio comm and ECube silence.

'Still nothing,' came the voice of Oz. 'Looks like you were wrong about Kattenheim.'

'Don't be too sure.'

Simmo clambered back down and took the controls; he liked being at the controls, he liked to be *in* control. He revved the HTank quietly, engines hissing and cold matrix fumes blowing from exhaust ports in the darkness, then activated the CamCloak. There was a tiny hum. He grinned through his own personal pain.

Easing the HTank forward, he drove it carefully through the thick jungle. Tracks crushed trees and vegetation – and with each sound Simmo winced, hoping to God that his intel was correct and there were no scouts or enemy lookouts nearby.

The huge HTank slowed as it reached the precipice of the valley wall in front of him. Trees scattered off into a treacherously steep black abyss – and distantly he could see bright halogen-II lights through the torrential downpour, illuminating the hive of activity that was the massive LVA depot. He peered at the vid. The tangle of fallen, twisted trees were like dark black emaciated limbs and the strings of creepers were like shrivelled muscles stretched across black pitted bone.

Simmo shivered.

The tracks crunched to a halt, matrix engines hissing.

'Here we go, then,' he whispered.

In an inverted V formation, the SP57 tanks crept forward, two at the point of the advance, then a considerable distance break with most of the remaining tanks following. Tracks crunched and crushed their way noisily through the foliage. The two lead SP57s halted, engines rumbling, and their turrets began a smooth traverse as the tanks readied for a sudden high-speed assault—

From nowhere, the darkness to either side of the lead Spiral tanks suddenly became alive with unexpected explosions and flashes of tank cannon fire. Twin combat rounds flew from the darkness and struck with precision timing, crushing the two lead Spiral tanks from either side and lifting them, suddenly blazing with HighJ purple fire, spinning high into the air where metal disintegrated and dripped flowing in a liquid stream to the forest floor far below.

Rogowski, in the second row of tanks behind this sudden onslaught, froze for a moment as realisation struck him like a brick. There were TK79s camouflaged in the jungle to either side of the trail . . . the Spiral TankSquad had rumbled into an ambush.

Simmo had been right . . .

They had been compromised.

And, thankfully, they had sent the two lead tanks in on REMOTE – as bait, for the enemy to make the first strike and expose their positions. This would give Simmo justification for attacking without specific orders.

It would have been a trap—

Without Simmo's simple but effective battle strategy.

Suddenly, the night lit up like day as tanks camouflaged with jungle vegetation surged forward and pounded shells into the formation of Spiral tanks, which returned heavy-metal fire as the battle exploded in an onslaught of violence. Engines screamed and tracks ploughed towards the centre of the LVA camp as the Spiral heavy armour roared ahead in a sudden planned attack—

Spiral tank turrets whirled.

Shells spat at savagely close quarters.

Tanks, both Spiral and Nex, caught fire and burned with hellish flames.

Noise ruled.

Noise and fire and destruction . . .

A TK79 was hit, skidding along under the impact, tilting and then collapsing onto one side as it slid through the mud, bulky chassis and heavy tracks crushing five workers to the accompaniment of screams and the snaps of broken bodies. It struck a huge spherical storage tank of LVA fuel. A million gallons of LVA washed out over the trail—

From his vantage point, Simmo stared down in grim silence, watching the raging battle.

The timing has to be right, he thought.

Growling, he dropped the HTank into the darkness . . .

Shells were booming through the halogen-illuminated rain, which swept down in great dark sheets. Fire belched from huge gun barrels as they thudded back in recoil. More tanks were pulverised, sent hurtling skywards in unfolding veils of purple and violet. Exploding gases and billowing bursts of fire seemed to envelop the whole world . . .

'There.'

The HTank fired. The shell hit the TK79 target, spun it round and sent it tumbling through the LVA camp. Machine-gun fire rattled, ricocheting by chance from the HTank's camouflaged armour.

The TK79s were converging now, pursuing the Spiral tanks to the centre of the site. There were more Nex tanks than the Spiral men had at first thought, perhaps seventy or eighty, and they seemed to be unstoppable.

Simmo's HTank squatted at the base of the steep rocky tree-clad slope. He watched as the outgunned and outnumbered Spiral SP57s turned, engines screaming,

460

and started a hasty retreat through the mud and crushed trees.

The TK79s pursued them.

Simmo watched impassively from the safety of his camouflage as he realigned the HTank's superior gun and waited for the right moment . . .

Another LVA tank had been smashed by a well-placed shell. LVA soaked into the glistening mud. The SP57s retreated, crushing a barracks as they apparently fled the enemy in a sudden panic – and the Nex tanks formed into a fighting unit with their guns facing forward. They slowed to manoeuvre through the bottleneck leading from the LVA depot—

Simmo smiled, sighted, and hit the launch key.

Six programmed K-TF8 guided missiles were loosed from the HTank's camouflaged and electronically invisible hull. Rockets trailing blue jets of fire sped out, seeking the massive containers of LVA premium-grade fuel . . .

Simmo and Oz hunkered down inside the HTank and prayed.

Engines howling, the SP57s fled from the LVA-depot basin, the site of their supposed ambush . . .

Missile warheads detonated.

LVA ignited.

And the night was suddenly lit with an unfurling of gas and fire which seemed at first to creep into the sky, consuming vegetation as it went, tracers spinning around the ever-expanding cloud of destruction—

Then came a roar of infinite devastation.

Followed by the sounds of nearly a hundred TK79s being smashed together, superheated and fused into a single solid lump of steel and alloy. Melted Nex briefly ran like candle-wax fat and were then vaporised in the sudden apocalypse. Barracks were kicked into oblivion, the LVA containers disintegrated into shards of twisted steel which then melted and rained fiery droplets from the now-contracting fireball—

A deep rumbling followed.

The very earth shook.

Simmo, panting, waited for the noise to subside. He checked his scanners – and learned that the SP57s had followed their orders precisely, forming a huge wall in their apparently chaotic but well-timed 'flight' and flinging up combined protective shields against the fury they knew was about to engulf the camp.

Simmo flung open the hatch, which clanged against the HTank's hull as he climbed up into the rain. All was darkness and shadows, lit by a million scattered small fires at the edges of the blast zone – the perimeter of the titanic combined missile and LVA explosion. Simmo could smell gas and the stench of burning vegetation. The whole LVA depot had been disintegrated, vaporised – destroyed.

Simmo jumped down onto the hard-baked mud. He strode forward with his Sig in his fist towards the twisted, fused block of steel and iron, its shape almost organic in its sculpted curves and waves.

Oz joined him.

Rain poured down on them.

'Good plan, Sarge,' Oz said. 'We sure nuked the fuck out of those bastards. Good job the lead tanks had no crew, eh? Did *we* lose many in the rest of the battle?'

'We always lose too many,' growled Sergeant Simmo. 'But no – we lose only four men this time. Four good men. But at major loss to enemy! Go get me a sitrep from the rest of the TankSquad. And get some scouts out, do some ECube scans, see if there are any other fuckers waiting for us . . . and get the fucking shields recharged.'

462

'Aye aye, cap'n' said Oz, grinning.

'And Oz?'

'Hm?'

'You *ever* speak to me like a Trekkie again, and I will shoot you in throat without trial.'

Oz gulped. 'OK, Sarge.'

Simmo sat on the HTank's hull, watching the fires that still lit the jungle through the rain. ECube scans had revealed no organic traces of Kattenheim in the massive tank wreckage, nor organic slivers in the rubble of the barracks and the surrounding destroyed LVA storage tanks. What remained of the derrick and pump were nothing more than tiny blackened stumps, broken fingers poking forlornly into the tropical downpour.

Rogowski approached with Mo, who was carrying his usual huge mug of tea. Simmo watched the curls of steam from the Pakistani's massive container of sweet brew for a moment, then transferred his gaze to the two men's worried faces.

'Anything?'

Rogowski made his report. 'Another squad of Nex tanks has been alerted. They're at some sort of refinery twenty klicks down the river. We reckon about sixty machines in all, TK79s again with a few TK82s thrown in for good measure and bang-per-buck firepower. There's still no sign of Kattenheim, although that doesn't mean he escaped.'

'You sure are a mean motherfucker, Sarge,' said Mo, dark brown eyes gleaming. He sipped from his huge mug of tea, grimacing as he burnt his tongue. 'That was a very clever manoeuvre, getting them to chase us and line up with the LVA tankers . . . *nasty*. I wouldn't like to be on the opposite side to *you* in a war.'

Simmo scratched at the weeping red line on his skull,

463

where his head had been stapled back together again after Kattenheim's heavy blow. He smiled a dangerous smile as he surveyed the fused work of art. 'Better fucking believe it,' he growled, and lit a cigar. Puffing out huge grey clouds of tobacco smoke, he muttered, 'A refinery, you say? It not appear on our Spiral scout maps?'

'They must have missed it. Or it was too well camouflaged to be spotted from the air,' said Mo, glancing around nervously at the flickering shadows. Raindrops sent concentric ripples across his lake of tea and the huge Pakistani soldier tried to shelter his precious brew.

'You gonna send an ECube blip? Let Spiral know what went down here?'

'Yes.' Simmo nodded. 'But only after we pay this LVA refinery a visit. Don't want to spoil our fun, do we?'

'So we're a private army now, are we?' said Oz softly, meeting Simmo's gaze.

'No – we just carrying out orders *before* they been issued. You trust The Sarge on this. The Sarge never been wrong in battle. *Never.* We just taken on and destroyed a force more than double our own . . . and you still here sipping your tea. Now we go visit refinery and see how this new Nex tank threat measure up. You with me, lads?'

'We're with you, all right,' said Oz, eyes glinting in the light of the fires of the burning LVA site.

'Sure, we'd follow you to Hell and back,' said Rogowski.

'Not wise offer to make,' said Simmo, drawing heavily on his cigar and still constantly scanning the periphery of the destroyed LVA refinery. 'Because before this thing over, Sarge think you may have to do just that.'

Carter paused on the steps, his body screaming in raw agony, and glanced further down the stone spiral to where

464

Mongrel stood, legs braced, chest heaving and a look of pain and nausea on his broad face.

'Come *on*!'

'I'm shagged. You go on without me!'

'I'll put a fucking bullet in your head if you don't shift your arse.'

'Suddenly, Carter's Browning lifted and there was a deafening series of shots as five bullets spat from the barrel, skimmed Mongrel's shoulder and took a pursuing Nex in the face. Its body flipped backwards and toppled down the narrow stairwell.

'Looks like the rest have realised that we're here.'

Mongrel grunted something incomprehensible, and started to sprint up the steep stairs after Carter. The two men ran, their bodies throbbing with pain, sweat coursing down their faces.

A cold breeze blew from above and they suddenly emerged—

Into the Egyptian night. A short walkway led around the side of the temple from the small hole – Durell's escape tunnel – where the two Spiral operatives had appeared; it was paved with black marble and led to the—

'Helicopters.'

'They're on the move,' muttered Carter. 'Come on.'

'Should we not go back for Comanche?'

'*Why?*'

'It ours. It Spiral's. It fucking expensive. I don't want *that* deducted from monthly salary payment, that for sure. I want to retire as fat old man, happy with pension, not paying for damn stupid mistake in desert with billion-dollar combat helicopter.'

'God,' said Carter, 'it's like being on a fucking mission with my wife. Stop fucking nagging.'

They crept around the outskirts of the temple and

could see further squads of Nex in the street outside. But none inside the compound. Quickly but cautiously they edged towards the four remaining black helicopters—

As machine-gun hell broke loose from behind them . . .

Bullets, some of them tracer, flew all around. Carter sprinted for the nearest chopper as Mongrel shoved his shoulder against the temple wall and opened fire. Carter dropped to one knee beside the machine and opened fire, allowing Mongrel time to retreat to his side and change mags. Then Carter leapt into the cockpit as a line of bullets slammed into the alloy beside his head. He flicked the controls, set the rotors spinning and palmed his Browning, holding it double-handed and taking careful aim—

Tracer lit the sky.

Carter shot the Nex in the face.

Silence reigned for a few moments. Then engines whined, the rotors started to spin and Mongrel clambered up beside Carter.

No alarm sounded, and there were no shouts of distress or warning. But suddenly a huge swarm of Nex came out of the darkness. Carter hurled the small black helicopter up into the night with Mongrel shooting furiously from the doorway, his face lit by muzzle flash, his few remaining teeth clenched in concentration and grim determination.

The temple and small town fell away. A few rounds of tracer spun past them up into the darkness and were lost as Carter armed the chopper's machine guns.

'What you doing?'

'Hold on.'

The helicopter, engines screaming, suddenly levelled and then dropped nose first from the heavens, plummeting towards the temple, the valley and the three remaining helicopters. Bullets blasted from the on-board heavy machine guns, cutting lines of sparks across the three remaining choppers.

There was an explosion and Carter lifted the helicopter higher on a cloud of flames that reached out with a yellow fist to smash the Nex into oblivion. Fire raged across the helicopter landing yard, scorching the ancient walls of the temple, followed by the clatter of falling metal panels, twisted and blackened.

Carter and Mongrel cruised through the darkness.

The blue glow from the ECube lit their faces.

'Where they going?' Mongrel was breathless, sweat staining his brow.

Carter frowned. 'It looks like Cairo.'

'I thought Gol said they go to Austria?'

'Who fucking knows? But they have the Avelach and the QuakeHub, and we must stop them.'

'I just think it strange they off course.'

'Maybe they're avoiding SAM sites we know nothing about.'

Mongrel shrugged.

Carter pushed the helicopter hard, crossing the desert over Gebel al-Galala al-Qibliya, heading towards Cairo. Engines howling, it took them a little over two hours and as the dawn light started to creep over the horizon so the scatter of buildings below began to increase in number as they approached the Nile.

'We're gaining on it,' said Mongrel.

'Good,' snapped Carter, eyes weary, hands gripped tight on the helicopter's controls.

'No – wait.'

'What?'

'It's stopped.'

'*What?*'

'No . . . no, I've lost it.'

Carter glanced at Mongrel. 'How can you fucking *lose* it? The ECube is never wrong.'

'I fucking tell you Carter, I lost damn thing! It not on ECube scanners, and it . . . oh.'

'What now?'

Mongrel shook the ECube, and Carter met his gaze, scowling. Digits flickered, then died. Mongrel's expression grew puzzled and he placed his finger against his lips.

'I'm thinking . . .'

'Don't just fucking think,' snapped Carter, peering through the helicopter's cockpit at the dawn-bathed city below them. 'Sort it!' He cruised closer, reducing his speed as the towers, apartment blocks, statues and minarets came gradually into view. They passed the Nile, and the Tahrir Bridge. Even at this early dawn hour the city of Cairo was heaving, a bustling hive of activity. Faces turned up towards them as they buzzed overhead.

Machine-gun fire erupted and Carter slammed the controls to the right. The helicopter flipped to one side, diving towards the city below with a wail of engines as Durell's machine closed on them at high speed, gun barrels blazing fire and rounds slamming into the hijacked chopper.

Carter spun the machine, flipping it down almost to street level and then slamming along, people cowering beneath him as he wrestled with the controls. Durell's machine followed closely, machine guns blazing as bullets chewed up the street and sent civilians to their deaths in showers of fine blood mist. Carter dragged the chopper back up into the sky, narrowly missing a shabby tower block.

Mongrel glanced out of the cockpit.

'They close, Carter.'

Carter growled something obscene and the helicopter dipped again, thrumming low towards street level and the closely packed structures. Durell's machine followed as Carter tried to shake them, weaving between buildings, spinning through the narrow streets, thousands of faces staring skywards in wonder and fear as machine guns fired once more and a bullet ricocheted from the stolen 'copter's rotors—

'Carter!' yelled Mongrel.

Carter slammed the helicopter to the right, whirling tightly around a minaret and heading for a densely packed group of crumbling suburban apartment blocks sporting neon roof signs for Coke and SmashVID. Dipping lower, the helicopter raced through the streets, buildings tightly packed to either side, Durell's howling machine close behind.

More machine-gun fire followed.

'This is getting tiresome,' growled Carter, spinning the helicopter in a tight bank down a side street. Engines screamed, the whole helicopter vibrated and the landing struts scraped a shower of concrete dust from an already tottering wall.

Durell's machine pursued.

Carter slammed the helicopter left, then right. They powered away from the cluster of apartment blocks as the following heavy machine-gun fire chased them relentlessly.

The sun was rising higher in the sky.

Light bathed Carter's face, blinding him for a split second.

Guns blasted.

Machine-gun fire over Egypt,' sighed Kade. '*Now that* is *a beautiful sight. A Wonder of the World, no less.*'

469

Carter found his way back into the maze of three- and four-storey apartments. Activity seemed almost to have ceased on the ground below as people abandoned their cars and took shelter wherever they could.

More bullets slammed into the back of the stolen helicopter and Carter cursed, Kade screaming inside his head, unable to shake the pilot of Durell's helicopter. Panic washed over him in a wave but he forced his body to relax and grow calm – and tried to think.

He slammed the machine to the left, dipping low, landing struts almost clipping the roofs of the cars lining the street bumper to bumper. Men and women ran for cover, hands raised futilely for protection. Some cowered in doorways as the screaming engines smashed over their heads.

Bullets chewed a wall to Carter's right.

He started to lift the helicopter, but realised that something was wrong as Mongrel shouted, 'We've got a fucking fire.'

'Jump!' Carter yelled.

The helicopter started to wobble furiously in its trajectory and Carter realised with horror that he could no longer control the wounded beast. Below, people were running, screaming and sprinting for cover. Mongrel's stare met Carter's and Mongrel stepped to the doorway as a building loomed close. Powered by instinct and without a second to think, he leapt.

Mongrel fell through the air, arms flailing wildly, and hit a concrete roof hard. It slammed into his face and body and he rolled madly for what seemed an age, his gun cutting into his ribs, until he slammed to a halt against a yellow-painted parapet, crushing a plant pot between himself and the wall. Shards of pottery speared his flesh like terracotta knives.

Mongrel tried to breathe—

But could not.

He levered himself up and saw the helicopter connect with an apartment block. It seemed to fold in upon itself, rotors bending at right angles as the machine compacted with a shriek of tortured metal and then—

Then it exploded.

A huge wave of fire erupted upwards and outwards, and Mongrel blinked at the sudden gaping hole in the apartment block. Black smoke rolled up. The flaming helicopter carcass shifted and then dropped from the hole that it had smashed for itself in the concrete wall and hit the ground, crushing eight people.

Hearing their screams as they burned, Mongrel staggered to his feet and scanned the sudden chaos below. People were swarming everywhere. Car horns were honking, men were shouting, women crying, and Mongrel searched in vain for Carter as pain stabbed him from a thousand sources and he tried hard just to breathe . . .

Where are you, Carter?

But he could not see his friend.

'Fuck.'

Suddenly, horrified at his vulnerability, Mongrel ducked and glanced up at the sky. But Durell's helicopter had gone. He glanced back down at the chaos and saw a few snarling men pointing his way.

Mongrel frowned.

Bullets ate a line along the parapet.

'What?' he wailed down at the gun-wielding Egyptians. 'It was a fucking accident!'

More bullets nearly took his head off.

'You fuckers.' He returned fire, then ran for it, head low, towards an adjoining roof. He leapt, missed the parapet, and fell a single storey, landing heavily on a folding table stacked with bottles of beer. Glass smashed all around him.

People started shouting, their voices harsh.

Bullets crackled from various handguns.

Stinking of cheap Egyptian beer, Mongrel put his tufted head down and ran for his life.

CHAPTER 17

QUAKE

Carter was being attacked from all sides. Sandstone blocks came out of the darkness and hammered him against the desert. People were screaming – and he realised that it wasn't people but an engine, howling through the centre of his brain. He felt himself falling, wind rushing through his hair as a blood-red insanity screamed through him. He gasped and the heat rushed up. Pain smashed through his body and he lay, panting, listening to the sounds of his own ragged breathing. He felt the horrifying warmth of blood running slowly over his flesh. And then screams, and chanting, words recited over and over again in an Arab dialect that he thought he understood, in words that he should have known. But his understanding fled him. The chanting reverberated around his skull. And then he felt boots and sandals kicking him and he curled into a ball in the sand. Single gunshots rang out, then the rattle of automatic gunfire – and the physical blows suddenly stopped.

Carter opened his eyes warily.

He could see a sandstone wall, smeared with beautiful

curving red swirls of Arabic graffiti. And he could see sand and feel the heat. And smell the camels.

More voices shouted.

In the distance, there came the roar of an explosion. People screamed. Carter could smell burning flesh. He sank into a state of unconsciousness and he thankfully allowed the blackness to take him. He remembered no more.

We need to tell Spiral. About the Foundation Stones – and about the LVA and how it all links in with Durell and his fucking QuakeHub . . .

Well – you're no fucking good like this.

What has happened? Where am I?

Open your fucking eyes and you'll find out.

I don't want to open my eyes. I am afraid of what I might see.

Your worst fucking nightmare, my friend. You remember them kicking you? The mob kicking you? They remember you, Carter, remember your face . . . from before. They know who you are, they know the things you did, the children you slaughtered . . .

Children? Where am I Kade?

You are in Egypt, Carter. And you are a prisoner.

Oh my God . . .

Yes, Carter, your worst nightmare . . . you remember? Me and Egypt – well, I will teach that fucker a lesson it shall never, ever forget . . .

Oh no, Kade, I remember the last time I let you loose in Egypt—

So do I, gloated Kade.

Carter fought.

He fought for a long time. But too much had happened – he

474

*had lost a lot of blood, taken too many beatings at the hands of
men and Nex intent on his murder. His fears and frustrations
over Natasha had put him in a prison of his own horror and
weakness.*

Carter folded.

Folded like damp newspaper.

And Kade took control.

Kade opened his eyes.

The scene, as ever, glistened in glorious black and
white. Kade tilted his head, felt the smash of pain
hammer through his body and with a silent snarl of contempt hurled it away. The bruises and bumps, the cuts
and grazes, the cracked ribs, the fractured knuckle, the
stapled gunshot wound in his back, the loss of skin and
the impacts from the KTM crash, the battering from the
helicopter crash – were as nothing, merely ant stings to an
elephant. Kade surveyed his grey-spectrum surroundings.

He was in a cell made of light grey sandstone. Bars ran
from floor to ceiling, and without moving his head Kade
could see a broad rough-timber desk on which a fan
whirred softly, stirring a sheaf of papers held down at one
corner by a makeshift paperweight. A gun.

Kade's stare fastened on the weapon.

It was Carter's Browning. And he could see that the
magazine was still in place, the safety catch off. Kade
smiled, a flickering of his lips – a dark expression, something that should never be seen on the face of a mortal.

Kade watched a man moving around what he assumed
was an office. He shifted his head slightly, took in the row
of perhaps fifteen cells, some occupied, most empty. The
other cell occupants – separated from Kade by floor-to-
ceiling barriers of bars – looked bedraggled, worn, poor
and ill. Kade wrinkled his nose in distaste.

Fucking criminal scum, he thought.

Kade watched the policeman shuffling papers, then turning in response to a call and shouting a reply in Arabic. Kade shifted gear in his brain and tuned in.

Shut up, or you'll get another beating, the Egyptian policeman had said.

Kade pushed himself up on one elbow, hearing a broken rib click. Despite his stealth, the policeman heard him and turned, smiling humourlessly. He had very black hair, quite shaggy, and bushy eyebrows. He also had a moustache that drooped over his top lip and down to the line of his jaw. His eyes were dark and Kade noted how lithely he moved. Like an athlete. A *warrior*.

'Ah, the bad man awakes.'

Kade said nothing.

'Oh, it was such joy when you were delivered to us. God punished you, my friend. He brought you back to us for repayment.'

The Egyptian moved closer to the bars and Kade stood smoothly, stretching with an almost feline grace, arching his back. Kade leant his head left, then right.

The Egyptian placed his hands on his hips and grinned at Kade. It was a savage grin. 'Do you remember? Do you remember the things you did here, English man?'

'You have the wrong guy,' said Kade smoothly. 'I am a citizen of the United Kingdom and I demand to see a representative of my country immediately.'

'Well, I am Abdul Hassaq, and I *know* you, I *know* the things you did here. I was a member of one of the many teams who helped to clear away the bodies. I was involved in the search for you after the burned children were scraped from the streets. I do not forget. I am not stupid. And you will *die*. Now, I suggest that you sit down and make your peace with God, if that is possible. He will

476

judge you for your crimes, and deny you your rights – by all that is holy.'

'No, no, my good man, you really have made a most grievous mistake. A case of mistaken identity, in fact. I am a journalist here to investigate the recent earthquakes and seismic activity in different parts of the globe. Jonathan Swift is my name, a graduate of Oxford, ha ha . . .'

Kade clasped the bars. His knuckles were white. He smiled and his eyes held pure dark evil. His gaze danced from the Egyptian policeman's face to his clothing to his belt, and then to the gleaming smooth leather holster that held his *gun*.

Kade slipped free the MercG from his pocket and spun the mercury garrotte to activate it. The liquid metal thread flashed in two powerful horizontal swipes and Kade stepped back, watching as four thick metal bars tumbled and clanged to the stone floor. The Egyptian's expression turned from righteous contemplation to sudden and acute horror.

The policeman froze for an instant, and Kade leapt through the neatly sliced hole in the bars as the man grabbed at the holstered pistol at his hip and aimed it. Kade lashed the MercG like a whip – which sliced vertically down the weapon's barrel, continuing on to cut the policeman's hand in two as far as the wrist. There was a clatter as the two parts of the weapon hit the ground in a shower of bubbling crimson. The Egyptian was staring in disbelief at his pumping appendage even as Kade whirled and, in a continuation of the same movement, placed the MercG through the Egyptian's neck with the precision of a Samurai swordsman.

Kade lifted himself from his crouch and deactivated the MercG, coiling the thin wire into the pocket of his badly torn and bloodstained trousers. He tilted his head, considering coolly the shocked gaze of the Egyptian policeman – and the narrow line of red across his throat. Then one of his knees buckled, blood flooded down his chin, turning the tips of his moustache into a dark glossy beard, and his head slid free and slopped onto the floor. Kade saw the yellow glimmer of severed spine within fat-pulp and flesh.

He gave a mock shiver.

'Ooh, I am *dangerous*,' he crooned softly and lifted the Browning from the table, settling the stocky grip in his battered hand.

One of the other prisoners, the nearest one, started to get a bit twitchy. He was peering through the bars of his cell and could make out the severed head of the police-man lying limp and bloody on its side, spilling a little yellow neck-fat to the stone floor. He opened his mouth and started to shout something . . .

Kade hissed, in Arabic, 'Shut the fuck up or I'll cut off your balls.' The man took one look at the levelled Browning and retired to the corner of his cell, curling into a ball and closing his eyes to blank out the demon gaze of Kade's insanity.

Kade took a large bunch of keys, including digital PlasSticks, from the policeman's pockets, and found a small bag of chewy sweets. Popping one into his mouth, he started to hum as he moved to the barred windows and stared out into the street. Across it, on the other corner, a group of people had gathered – and Kade could see by the looks in their eyes that they were a lynch mob. Obviously they did not believe that the police would conduct a fair trial with him, and believed that their own meat cleavers could deliver a finer slice of retribution to the evil man in the cell.

'Dum de dum de dum.' Kade chewed his sweet and

strolled – almost happily, certainly calmly – to the front door of the police station, locking it and sliding three thick bars into place. Then he heard a voice shouting from the station's interior and he moved smoothly to the doorway, standing discreetly to one side.

Another policeman appeared, carrying a yellow folder. He stopped. His gaze dropped and he gasped. Kade blew his head open. Still chewing, Kade stooped and pulled the policeman's gun free, checking the magazine.

'Yum yum, cherry flavour,' said Kade, helping himself to another sweet. More shouting erupted from the interior of the police station and Kade sighed, almost resignedly, hoisting both weapons in his blood-slick grasp.

He tilted his head, smiling at a cowering prisoner and shaking his head almost in sadness.

'Time to go to work,' he sighed.

It had been a hard climb, but at least the two pilots on the roof of the *Egyptian Times* news building had not been armed. Two punches and two broken cheekbones later, Mongrel had dragged them away from the civilian helicopter and stared in horror at the white flanks of the RT10 with their bright red and yellow stripes. Mongrel glanced around, realised he had been caught on some form of CCTV, and decided that standing next to two unconscious men while armed with a sub-machine gun was not going to endear him to the journalistic staff of the building below – nor to the inevitable security and police forces who would follow.

Mongrel stared at the name etched on the machine's flanks.

An RT10 Dandelion.

'An RT10 fucking *Dandelion*,' he muttered.

Mongrel fired up the helicopter, and listened in agony

479

as the rotors began their snail-speed acceleration. There came a curious metallic squeaking sound that made Mongrel shudder.

From a nearby building Mongrel had watched Carter being beaten up by a mob, and had been just about to open fire with his M24 when five policemen had waded in, driving back the crowd who were armed with sticks, bottles and rifles, and dragging a bloodied Carter into their battered old Land Rover. Thinking that he and Carter needed transport fast, Mongrel had decided to secure the helicopter from the nearest logical source – the news building. But, just after punching the two pilots into oblivion, he had heard the familiar distant report of Carter's Browning from the police station below – and decided that his best option was to take to the air and monitor events from there . . .

Carter was obviously looking after himself.

The 'copter spun into action and Mongrel climbed on board. He hated flying – and admitted to everybody including himself that he was, basically, an awful pilot.

The RT10 Dandelion helicopter waggled into the air, a dangerous combination of underpowered civilian engines, a worn rudder and a lack of engine oil. Mongrel's lack of experience and confidence didn't help. Mongrel watched as men ran onto the roof of the *Egyptian Times* news building, waving their arms at him. He swooped high over their heads with the metallic noise singing a discordant song in his ears, and headed off to the west in what he considered to be a decoy manoeuvre in case these men wanted to chase him.

Mongrel came around in a wide arc, noting that crowds seemed to be gathering in the streets below. Many seemed to be armed, and were waving and chanting.

'Not look good,' mused Mongrel.

And something else gnawed at him. He tried to place his finger on it. It was something to do with the guards on the rooftop.

What had it been?

The helicopter thrummed around again and Mongrel was searching now. Where would Carter emerge from? It would not be the front door – there was a crowd there already, hammering against the old worn wood. The roof, then? It had to be his only way of escape.

Mongrel prayed that Carter had seen him . . .

He swooped, the engines whining in a strange way that he had never heard before inside a chopper. And then he saw it: on the roof of the police station a door flew open and Carter came into view, firing a gun in each hand. Blood pooled across the floor at his feet and he slammed shut the door, reaching and grasping a bar and sliding it into place through rope hooks.

Mongrel dropped the helicopter.

It still nagged at him: what had been wrong with the men on the roof of the newspaper building?

The helicopter touched down on the police station roof.

Carter leapt in, and his dark-eyed stare moved over Mongrel arrogantly. Carter was soaked in blood, and for a moment Mongrel thought he was wounded . . .

'You OK?'

'You took your fucking time,' snapped Kade. 'I'm fucking covered in blood, had to kill sixteen fucking policemen in there – not that that's a bad thing.' He flashed a shark smile. 'All fucking police deserve to die, whatever their nationality.'

'Carter?'

'Hmm?'

'You're not hurt?'

481

'Nah, never felt better.'

A figure appeared on a neighbouring rooftop and opened fire with a sub-machine gun. Bullets kicked up tiny showers of dust and Kade stepped calmly away from the civilian chopper as the rounds ate their way towards his legs. He aimed the Browning and the gun bucked in his fist, firing three bullets that smacked into the Egyptian soldier's head and dropped him in an instant.

'Now the military is involved. What a bummer! I was enjoying shooting the pigs,' he chuckled darkly.

Mongrel lifted the chopper into the sky. He was frowning . . . and knew that something was badly wrong with Carter. It did nothing to relieve his misgivings about their situation.

And now the Egyptian military as well?

Shit . . .

Kade popped another sweet into his mouth. He held out the bag to Mongrel as the chopper wobbled over Cairo, rotors whining above them as crowds of civilians, police and military swarmed through the streets below in an attempt at pursuit.

'You want a sweet?'

'A fucking *sweet*?' bellowed Mongrel. 'We've got the fucking Egyptian army fucking after us now, and you ask if I want a fucking *sweet*? There'll be fucking military 'copters here in a few minutes, with fucking heavy machine guns.'

'Yeah? So? It's only a fucking sweet!' snapped Kade, frowning. 'And anyway, what's wrong with this pile of shit? Couldn't you find something a little more –' he searched for a word, licking at his cherry-tinted lips – '*exciting*?'

The rotors whined again, and now there was a grinding note in the sound.

And then Mongrel realised what had been wrong with

the guards on the rooftop. They had been waving their arms to him – and yet they'd carried sub-machine guns slung over their shoulders. Their intention hadn't been to stop him . . . but to *warn* him.

Why?

Another grinding sound came.

'I think you've picked a dud fucking chopper, my fat friend.' Kade fired a few bullets into the swarming crowd below, laughing as bodies rolled in the dust.

'What are you doing?' hissed Mongrel.

Kade ignored him – then suddenly whirled, pointing down. 'Over there. Towards the south. There's a military airfield. Take us there *now*!'

Mongrel flew in silence, jaws clamped tightly closed, his mind whirling. He glanced across at Carter – and saw an expression on the man's face that he had never seen before. Mongrel looked at Carter: the battered and torn clothing, the cuts and bruises, the drying blood, the pieces of brain tissue and fragments of bone in his hair. He was a demon figure, a nightmare horror-show walking the earth, dealing out hot gunfire from his bruised and sliced hands . . .

He feels no pain, Mongrel realised.

And no remorse . . .

The chopper banked, leaving the surging crowds in the streets behind. It swept down low over buildings, mostly built from sandstone and a few from breeze-block and rusting corrugated metal sheeting. Dogs barked, and women shouted.

The rotors continued to scream above the two men—

And then the control-panel dials started to flicker madly as certain pressures dropped.

Kade caught Mongrel's stare. 'You fucking looking at something?'

'Yeah, something bad,' snapped Mongrel.

'There.' Kade pointed. 'The El Kashem airfield. I don't think this bag of shit is going to get us anywhere. You see that grey plane over there?'

'You mean the MiG?'

'Aye.' Kade nodded, smiling slyly, and popped another sweet into his mouth. 'Land next to it.'

'And what about those guards with those big fucking dogs?'

Kade slammed a fresh magazine into his Browning. 'You leave them to me,' he growled, sucking hard.

Carter tumbled through darkness, falling for ever. He spun, curled in a ball, round and round and round, wind lashing through his hair. His eyes were clenched shut and he contained the *pain*. It was an animal raging within him and he cursed Kade; Kade had trapped him, ensnared him within a cage of agony and in fury Carter punched out at the dark invisible veil all around him—

He heard the gunshots. The yelps of the dogs.

Carter's jaw tightened grimly.

The pain beat in huge tidal waves against the shore of his brain.

Pulsed, like an evil cancer.

Smashed him with the eternity of death . . .

Light flooded in, as if somebody had torn a hole in the canvas of darkness surrounding him. Carter pushed away the pain, felt it slide between him and Kade as Kade fought him with claws of steel. He dropped to his knees, spittle drooling from his mouth and the desert sun scorching his eyes, lancing directly into his tortured cerebellum . . .

Carter coughed.

The Browning felt solid in his throbbing fist.

484

He glanced up – at the airfield, at the sand under him, at the corpses of Egyptian soldiers – and four dead Alsatian dogs, their heads twisted back, long canine tongues protruding and their blood staining the desert.

Carter breathed deeply, cursing, as Kade's laughter drifted into a haunting nothingness. He glanced back at Mongrel, who was staring at him with disgust.

Carter climbed to his feet.

'I'm back,' he said softly.

'What's that fucking supposed to mean?' snarled Mongrel.

Carter approached the large man, weariness suddenly hitting him with an incredible intensity, sucking away his will to go on. He reached out and placed his blood-caked hand against Mongrel's tattered Nex clothing.

'I am sorry, Mongrel. That was not me.'

Mongrel's eyes glittered. 'What you mean, Carter? I don't like what I fucking see here.'

Sirens wailed from the distance. Carter stared down at the eight dead Egyptian soldiers, their faces and bodies blown apart by the wrath of the Browning. He felt something go cold inside and he made a promise to himself – when this was all over he would find a way to kill Kade. He would burn that fucker in the furnace of his mind.

'Those men did not deserve this,' said Carter softly.

'What?' snapped Mongrel. 'I seen bad things in my time, and you one of them, Carter.' And Carter caught it, the big man was afraid.

And Carter felt shame.

A deep shame that burned him.

The sirens were getting louder. Across the airfield jeeps sped into view, displaying the red flashing lights of military police. Carter stooped under the grey belly of the big Russian MiG 8-40 MFI – *Mnogofunktsionalny Frontovoi*

Istrebitel – and kicked out the wooden block from behind the front wheel. He moved under the wings, kicking out the rear blocks as Mongrel heaved himself up the narrow ladder to the cockpit and climbed into the co-pilot's seat.

Carter followed him up. He stopped for a moment, glancing over at Cairo. The sights and scents of the city had filled him with an awe that he would never forget. But he knew that he was cursed in this place, hated and reviled, condemned to die. He could never again witness its wonders without risking a bullet in the back.

Carter breathed deeply, dropped into the cockpit and pushed the ladder into its housing. He stared at the controls in front of him, reached out, and flicked on the power. Powering-up whines came from the aircraft's batteries and Carter touched the control screen, which sprang to life with a display of Russian and subtitled Arabic.

'Hmm.'

'You know how to fly this, Carter?'

'Aye.'

The sirens were getting uncomfortably close. Carter started the engines, which roared into life with the awesome, deafening thunder of quad Saturn/Lyulka A184-F turbofans and the reined-in energies of 200,000 pounds of thrust. Grasping the controls, Carter eased the MiG 8-40 around in a circle to face the long expanse of sand-blown tarmac. The runway stretched into the distance, meeting the horizon through a shimmer of desert heat.

Excitement welled in Carter's breast – excitement at such awesome and mind-blowing power, mixed with his fear of flying and falling and heights. He also had the terrible certainty that if he fucked up then he would be dog meat, pulped in a battered can, within about thirty seconds flat . . .

Machine guns rattled from the jeeps.

Bullets zipped over the wings . . .

Carter hit the burners. The MiG 8-40 MFI's engine note rose to a scream and the fighter juddered around the two men. It screeched down the runway, leaving trails of rubber on the dusty tarmac, lifted its nose towards the sky and the orange sun – and soared smoothly up into the heavens . . .

Sunlight gleamed along the fighter's grey flanks.

The wheels lifted neatly into the machine's underbelly with tiny and precise clicks.

And the MiG 8-40 banked, wings gleaming, and headed towards the south and west.

'We're going in the wrong direction.'

'No, we're going to pick up the Comanche.'

'Why?'

'All our equipment is there. And our explosives. Everything we could need.'

Mongrel frowned. 'How long will it take?'

'In this?' said Carter, gazing out over the rapidly undulating desert. 'Well, we're currently cruising at 2,000 kilometres an hour – so a little over ten minutes. Now *that*'s pretty fucking fast.'

The MiG 8-40 MFI was a multi-functional front-line fighter. It was built primarily for air-to-air combat but it also carried payloads both in its belly and on pylons beneath its wings for tactical air-to-air surface strikes. Built by MiG – the Mikoyan & Gurevich aviation, scientific and production complex of the MAPO military-industrial corporation of the Northern Russian Confederacy – the war machine had quad Saturn/Lyulka A184-F engines with turbofans and Needle_injectors capable of upwards of 200,000 pounds of thrust when using afterburners. It had

System5 thrust vectoring channels to allow the fighter to make extremely sharp turns. The jet could supercruise at an awesome 2,600 km/h, had a top thrust speed of 3,245 km/h and a flight ceiling of a little over 27,500 metres. The plane was a cranked delta-wing, with triple tail fins, and it had intakes under the nose. It measured twenty-two metres in length and had a wingspan of sixteen metres. It sported Phazotron Plasma TW-35 phased-array fire-control radar, rearward-facing N-018 radar and Global PK18 TSAM control radar. It also carried the latest generation of plasma-cloud stealth systems – known as PCSS-5s – for the simple beauty of undetected infiltration.

After scanning the machine's systems and struggling through the Russian and Arabic instructions, Carter could see that this machine packed quad 30mm canons, and carried eight R-80 AA-e Aphid air-to-air missiles, and twelve KH-68 AS-13 Kilter tactical air-to-surface missiles, each 4.98 metres long.

Carter grinned to himself sombrely.

Fucker must be worth a few million, he mused.

One could say that airfield security had been lax.

And somebody was going to lose his job, and then his balls.

There was silence for a while, interrupted only by the noise of the engines as they cruised at low altitude. Carter knew that he wasn't a fighter pilot and despite arming the PCSS-5s he still felt nervous. He didn't want to engage in air-to-air combat with pilots sporting thousands of hours of training.

'Mongrel, we need to talk.'

'So talk.'

'That wasn't me back there.'

'Who was it, the fucking Queen? I didn't realise she was so fond of shooting dogs with a Browning.'

'Mongrel, listen to me. There is a demon inside my head. Sometimes I go a little – *insane*. I try to control it, really I do. But sometimes, when I am weak, or I've been beaten up or shot – sometimes the demon takes control.'

Mongrel was silent. The engines hissed behind the two men. Below, the desert flowed like golden mercury. Rocks flowed past and the distant landscape lay cratered like the moon.

'I find that hard to accept.'

Carter took a deep breath. 'You have heard Natasha – and I – mention the name of Kade? I know you have. It is the name of the demon in my soul, the dark brother I have to carry like a seed. And yes, he is evil, and yes, I wish him dead. But I cannot banish him, Mongrel, I cannot get rid of him without terminating my own fucking existence. And I want to, believe me, I want him to die . . . but he lives, inside me, in my brain, and sometimes he breaks free . . .'

For decades Carter had carried this secret.

And he realised that he was talking as much to himself as to Mongrel. And now he was exorcising his secret, the words flowed with ease, like fine sand in an hourglass.

Carter realised that there were tears staining his cheeks.

'Sometimes I do really bad things,' he whispered. 'But it is not always me in control. Sometimes I have no say in my actions. Sometimes Kade holds me in his fist – trapped behind the bars of his strength – and there is nothing I can do.'

Mongrel leaned forward and tapped Carter on the shoulder. Carter turned, savagely wiping away his tears. Mongrel smiled at him, his dark eyes glistening.

'I accept this for now, but later we must talk. When this – this *Kade* is out, he have real attitude problem. I considered putting bullet in him with M24. He real fuck-wit.'

'Yeah.' Carter laughed. 'Fucking tell me about it. I have to listen to his voice 24/7. It drives a man a little mad.'

'So what the plan now?'

'I'll drop you by the Comanche . . . shit, you *can* fly it, can't you?'

'Ha, I'll fly anything! Not very well, but I fly it.'

'Then we'll rendezvous in Austria. I'll scout ahead. The fucking speed of this thing, I'll probably get there before Durell and Jam!'

'I doubt that. We spend too much time fucking about here.'

'I knew coming to Egypt was a bad idea. Have you checked the ECube?'

Mongrel fished out the machine. It glowed blue.

'It's working. But I fear Nex still have control of systems, despite this new revision of our magical little alloy friend – real piece of shit The Priest gave us here, I am thinking.'

'Send an ECube blip on the WarChannel. When the shit hits the fan, my disobedience will be as nothing – and the world is at stake here, our whole civilisation at risk. We need Spiral back-up; I doubt we'll come out of this alive without *some* aid . . .'

'But you are disobeying Spiral's orders!'

Carter nodded. 'I will save Natasha – and I will destroy Durell. But I cannot fight a war alone. Let Spiral do what they will do – if they cannot see I fight for the greater good, then fuck them to the darkest reaches of Hell. But I won't turn down a bit of heavy artillery help, that's for sure . . .'

Mongrel nodded, and started to spin the ECube in his

fingers. 'If Durell *does* have control of channels, when I send this he might know we're still alive. He might know we're coming . . .'

'Fuck him,' said Carter. 'Send him one as well. And tell him I look forward to our next joyful meeting, because there will be only one fucker leaving the room – and it won't be him.'

The MiG cruised on, sunlight glimmering along its dull grey hull. The Russian tri-colour was the only bit of colour on its otherwise blank alloy fuselage. Soon the machine dropped, howling from the deep blue skies, and skimmed low across the desert rocks of Gebel al-Galala al-Qibliya – and then on towards the Red Sea Mountains, searching for a place to land . . .

■
■■
■■
>>>>>
>
■quakehubQIV initiated
waiting
waiting
waiting
  proc zgrade
matter (q) clocks initiated
zones (q-z): checking . . .
■
```
OPEN 6364786398-QIV{
   isort(A, 0); check(A, 0)
   genid(A, 1); isort(A, 1); check(A, 1)
   genrand(A, n); isort(A, n); check(A, n)
   gensort(A, n); isort(A, n); check(A, n)
   genrev(A, n); isort(A, n); check(A, n)
```

```
identical integers //q12
  genid(A, n); isort(A, n); check(A, n)
qq)

function isort(A, n,     i,j,t) {
  for (i = 2; i < = n; i++)
  for (j = i; j > 1 && A[j-1] > A[j];
j--) {
  # swap A[j-1] = A[j]
  t = A[j-1]; A[j-1] = A[j]; A[j] = t \\\}

zones cleared;
  call fzone sort; 7y879ehwi
  x897xx89x897x90
  x5x675x45x5657b
  x876x79-x076x9x7
  x6xx454x76x765x
  call 76538973454784
  call 43876438973492
  call 23765723862348
■
quakehub systems online
quakehub foundations linked
quakehub systems operational
01010111ok
10101010ok
11101010ok
10010101ok
10000010ok
00000000ok.
```

492

```
qengines complete
please specify targets ...

OPEN tactical :GUI

done.
████
```

New York, the United States of America

Darkness flowed majestically over the sleeping city. Lights glittered from a billion different coordinates, a swathe of electronic eyes focusing and keeping the world alive. Cars moved in tracer streamers along the twisting concrete highways, headlights slicing the dark and adding to the great sweep of phosphorescence flowing up and out towards heaven.

The night was peaceful.

Sleeping.

The rumble seemed to shake the whole world. Buildings started to tremble, softly at first, jiggling against their foundations as windows clattered in frames. Several shattered, glass shards and slivers tumbling in long glittering falls to the sidewalks far below. From Queens to Staten Island, from Brooklyn to Manhattan, the Big Apple felt the clenched and threatened fury of the quake's titanic fist-fuck.

Cars started to rattle against road surfaces, bouncing on protesting suspensions.

Shop windows cascaded onto sidewalks in huge sheets of diced glass.

Alarms started to squeal from a million different tenement blocks and wounded vehicles.

The George Washington Bridge began to shudder, swaying violently.

On the subway, trains ground to a halt as rails were distorted, twisted, wrenched from concrete blocks, their tortured bolts torn.

And then the quake seemed to grow, to expand, to rise swiftly into a sudden fury – as it washed across the whole city in a titanic crush and devastating smash of unleashed energy worse than any single warhead that had ever been directed at the United States . . .

Buildings toppled.

Houses disintegrated.

Cars were crushed.

And all to the accompaniment of a constant wail, a high-pitched eternal cacophony, a moaning writhing bleeding symphony-scream of apocalyptic human suffering.

Shanghai, China

In Shanghai Harbour at the head of the Yangtze River, the water trembled gently. Small boats started to bob, the rhythm gentle at first but growing more violent until they jiggled as though they were on wires. Moored ferries started to rock, crunching against wharfs and one another, and on the mainland the streets started to move, some actually erupting as tarmac buckled and thrust upwards in grey-black showers. The new T12 HyperTubeway ground to a halt, and screams echoed as the waters from the Yangtze poured in, picking up trams and spinning them violently down the wide bright underground tunnels, washing people like sticks of debris from the platforms, drowning those who were already trapped and struggling.

The Huxinting tea house, built in 1784 and nestling like a proud jewel, a national symbol of heritage at the centre of Nanshi's ornamental lake, shifted as dust drifted down from its ancient supports, peppering the still lake waters with tiny flakes of debris. There was a beautifully constructed zigzag bridge, linking to Yu Yuan, that was said to keep evil spirits away . . . As it tumbled into the still waters a roar so loud, so devastating that it could dwarf the sound of a nuclear explosion, scythed across Shanghai. The whole area moved and tipped and a devastation, an abomination like nothing the city had ever seen smashed down without mercy through the darkness . . .

To leave a mass of pulped flesh in its wake.

Delhi, India

The Red Fort of Delhi, quarried and built in 1648 from the local deep red sandstone and once serving as the imperial palace of the Mughal Emperors, started to shake. The Lahore Gate and the Delhi Gate started to rattle against their ancient iron hinges, and stonework began to crumble around sand-blasted fixings. The two-and-a-half-kilometre defensive wall began to buckle, writhing like a huge red snake in its death throes, and all around people stared up in wonder – and horror – as the ground trembled beneath their feet.

The huge and beautiful Great Mosque – the *Jama Masjid* – was shuddering as if some great hand had taken the tapering minarets and rounded bulbous domes and was shaking them. Several minarets toppled to the ground far below, scattering debris like a child's abused building blocks under the fists of a tantrum-screaming toddler . . .

The River Yamuna shook as if in the grip of a fit; it sloshed up its banks, smashing boats and overturning several small ferries. A huge wave washed up, over, dragging people and barking dogs from the banks and away in a sudden deep swell of flood waters . . . In the suburbs surrounding the city people came outside to stand in the street, staring up into the sky or over towards the crumbling Red Fort, which dominated the skyline and seemed to *shimmer*.

And twelve million people watched in muted terror as the quake made its presence felt, smashing, stomping and branding its presence into the brain of every screaming human who endured its buckling stampeding smashing *torturing* onslaught . . .

'Is it done?' asked Jam through twisted jaws.

Durell shook his head. 'No, my boy, it is not yet done.' His eyes stared down at the screen, at the swirl of colours, at the scattered flickering images of destruction being relayed back to him via thousands of satellite eyes around and above the globe.

He reached down beside the screen where a small black box sat, its lights flickering softly. He glanced down, a curious smile etching his face within the folds of the dark hood. Frost coated the box – the QuakeHub – and with blackened claws Durell flicked open the lid to reveal a dark cube squatting at the heart of this terrible weapon that was wreaking such havoc across the world.

Jam peered closer.

'What exactly is it?'

'The heart of the QuakeHub. It is a processor, Jam. The most advanced military processor ever designed. It is controlling the earthquakes, and it is controlling the world . . . watch closely, for no more will we offer ultimatums, no more will we bow under the onslaught of world powers and world armies and the slime that is Spiral . . . we will control *everything* because, my friend, as you can quite clearly see, the QIV processor, the QIV military-organic-cubic processor is now fully operational and permanently on-line.'

The Nex poured out in their thousands from hidden bunkers – cold-storage facilities, secret subterranean chambers – across the globe.

As satellites became blind and governments and army leaders panicked, appalled at their sudden terrifying loss of control, the Nex attacked targets that had no idea of what was coming.

In Germany, armies clashed in the streets as civilians fled, screaming, to be machine-gunned in the back. In Sweden, the Nex landed in swarms of black helicopters, storming airfields and army and naval bases, taking them in minutes. With stumbling leaders blind, oblivious to the fact that they were even under attack, nuclear power stations were overrun and complete control was taken of poorly defended nuclear missile silos – from Russia to America to China.

The Nex – thanks to the QIV military processor – had control of digital locks, satellite navigation, world finances. In certain high-tech army barracks hundreds of thousands of men were simply locked in. No need for bloody warfare in such cases, no need for hand-to-hand combat in the streets – the Nex could prevail with far inferior numbers due to technological and digital superiority.

The power base across the surface of the globe began to shift.

Durell stood over the QIV processor, revelling in his supremacy, revelling in his power, his apotheosis – and he turned, throwing back his hood as his glittering eyes surveyed Jam. He placed a claw on Jam's shoulder and smiled. There was a taste on his lips like . . . *revenge*.

'Carter is coming,' said Jam softly.

'I care not.'

'And Spiral, with their TankSquads.'

'I care not.'

'We should leave this place.'

'No, Jam. This Carter, he must die. By coming to us he simply makes this game easier . . . he cannot stand against you, and he cannot stand against *us*. It is too late, the game is in play, the world is toppling even as we speak, we blink, we breathe. The time for running is over.'

'Is the QIV processor blind to Carter? Like the QIII before it?'

'It is.'

'Why?' asked Jam. 'Why can it not see him?'

'Carter is an anomaly in the system. A bug in the software. A virus in the code. He needs to be ironed out; he needs to be quarantined; he needs to be *eliminated*.'

'I will do this,' said Jam softly.

'Good,' whispered Durell, nodding with satisfaction, and he turned back to the screen which rippled like mercury. His hands moved deftly over the controls as thousands of images flickered across it, showing scenes of battle and death.

And all the while they could hear the deep and distant rumbling of the quake.

The huge hospital car park on the outskirts of London was dark and rainswept, filled with shadows. Sections of it were packed with cars gleaming glossy under the downpour; several spaces provided nothing more than raindrops dancing on tarmac. A soft noise echoed through the darkness at the perimeter fence – where a single Sleeper Nex stood, water gleaming on its shell. It turned copper eyes within its triangular head, left, then right, and dropped to all fours like a huge cat. Muscles bunched and its whole body quivered. It seemed to scent the air – then, eyes glinting eerily, it turned its nose towards the Accident & Emergency neon sign and the bright glare of strip lights inside. An ambulance had just pulled up, blue lights flickering.

The entity sniffed again and, head dropping, its claws raked the tarmac as it headed towards the bright entrance and the heavy stifling stink of the people within.

Earthquakes had ravaged London. Most wounded had been airlifted away because the capital was said to be still unstable, at best – with the threat of more quakes to come. People were leaving the capital in their thousands – or, rather, sitting on motorways, crawling along bumper to bumper.

It had been suggested by the hospital authorities that Natasha should be removed along with other patients, airlifted to a quieter hospital by military Chinook, to a city that had not been savaged by the fury of the earthquake, such as nearby Oxford or Coventry. Nicky had made it plain to the doctors that Natasha would be going nowhere and had sat at her friend's bedside for long hours, holding the cool flesh of Natasha's hand.

Nicky came awake with a start.

The steady beep-beep-beep of the monitors soothed her suddenly racing heart and adrenlin kicked her system into wakefulness. She glanced at Natasha.

What woke me? she thought.

She tilted her head, listening.

Something felt wrong. Out of place.

She tied back her hair, pulled tight the laces of her boots and lifted free her Smith & Wesson 11mm pistol, checking the 24-round 'compact-shell' magazine and flicking free the safety.

Tiny hairs prickled across the nape of her neck.

A distant shout echoed from the depths of the hospital. Nicky glanced at Natasha's recumbent form, and moved quietly to the door.

Somewhere, distantly, a woman gave a muffled scream.

There came a crack.

What's going on? she thought, blood nightmares raging in her skull.

Nex?

Mercs, even?

The return of the quake?

She tugged free her ECube and paused for a moment – Spiral were already stretched to full capacity . . . and beyond. The last thing they needed was some jumpy bitch sending in an Urgent Request for Heavy Back-up – just because a locally anaesthetised patient on a cold operating slab was being sliced open by a careless doctor.

She toyed with the tiny black alloy cube for a moment.

Then pocketed it.

Pull yourself together, girl, she thought with a long blink and a deep breath.

Clutching the S&W pistol tightly, she moved down the corridor and then stopped, listening, head tilted slightly, eyes narrowed in concentration.

Nothing.

'See? Panic for nothing . . .' she muttered to the stagnant air.

She moved towards the double swing door, boots

squeaking a little on the sterile tiles of the hospital corridor. A man screamed – a long low animal sound, full of pain and horror and ending with a savage nasty gurgle.

Nicky paused then—

A real pause.

As a fist of fear punched her in the brain.

She started to reach for her ECube, thinking *Fuck it, they can send me some of the boys* – when something rounded the corner at the end of the corridor, about twenty metres directly ahead of her. Something big and black, heavily armoured and moving stealthily like a large cat. Thick armoured legs supported a wide stocky chest and a triangular head, with tiny copper eyes. Claws raked the ground and the head snapped up, around, a blur of movement. She saw blood dripping from twisted jaws.

Twin copper eyes focused on Nicky.

There was recognition there, in that bright copper-eyed gaze. It *knew* her. Dropping its head it started to pound towards her, leaving trails of blood from its claws against the white tiles . . . she could see strips of flesh flapping from its twisted maw . . .

And she realised—

For whatever reason, it had come for Natasha . . .

Come to murder Natasha . . .

And any one else from Spiral who got in its way.

Gritting her teeth, Nicky fired off five deafening shots, then heeled back through the double doors and began to sprint towards Natasha's room. In her pocket, she stabbed a PB on the ECube and let out a little gasp of fear, glancing over her shoulder as the huge black gleaming monstrosity hammered through the doors, wrenching them from their hinges.

Nicky slammed through into Natasha's private room, kicked shut the door and slid the bolts into place – gun up and pressing against her cheek as the pounding claws suddenly halted and silence flooded the corridor.

Nicky backed away from the door.

Fear beat a tattoo within her chest.

And she watched in horror as the triangular head, twisted jaws drooling and trailing strings of human meat, lifted – slowly, purposefully – and those tiny copper eyes tilted and stared in at her through the rectangular frame of wire-mesh glass.

Nicky lifted her gun and took slow and careful aim.

CHAPTER 18

AUSTRIA

After a hurried desert landing to allow Mongrel to hop from the MiG 8-40, Carter gave a small salute with blood-encrusted fingers and urged the jet over the hard-packed desert rock, aviation-shocks pissing oil from their abused suspension. Leaving a huge dust trail in its wake, the tortured war machine climbed from the ground and powered hungrily into the vast blue bowl of the sky.

Carter flew the fighter north – skirting Cairo in a wide arc and heading out over the Mediterranean Sea.

The sun was high, and climbing to an altitude of 23,000 feet Carter breathed the crisp oxygen-recyc of the cabin and stared out over a cloud-carpeted world. Below, Durell had somehow managed to gain control of the Earth, and the savage fury of its earthquakes. Both Carter's and Mongrel's ECubes had been screaming – reports, intelligence, damage information, casualty figures, panic calls, mission briefings – the tiny alloy devices had never been so much in need.

Carter hit the wide expanse of the shimmering sea and found himself focusing, calming his heart and mind.

Kade squatted, silent and dark and sullen in the back of his brain, refusing to speak and refusing to share his pain. This suited Carter just fine.

The MiG banked as he headed north and west. Behind him, quad engines thundered and Carter took the time to familiarise himself with the weapons systems. He watched in horror as Russian script flowed across the control monitor. Carter used his limited knowledge of languages to translate some of the instructions from Russian, some from Arabic and fill in the rest through context. Still, he wasn't happy.

After a half-hour, alarms sprang to life.

'What now?' he muttered.

'*You have company,*' said Kade.

'And how the fuck would you know?'

'*I just do. I read Arabic better than you, I think. The MiG has identified the aircraft – Lockheed choppers and five British-made Sea Harriers. They have Sea Cat missiles, and they're piloted by Nex.*'

'You sure?'

25mm cannons roared, and shells screamed past the fighter, several thumping home as Carter banked the fighter sharply, cursing. Engines howled, the System5 thrust vectoring channels kicking in, and Carter lifted the machine, nose up, peering intently at his scanners as the sky spun.

'They're not on the scanners – nor the ECube,' he cursed.

'*Durell must have some way of shielding them.*'

He banked the machine once more, dropping in a tight arc, and saw the enemy: five Harriers SK15s – hovering and turning – with perhaps fifteen choppers accompanying them. Carter's jaw set grimly and he wondered if they had been on their way to intercept him. In Cairo? Maybe at the Red Sea Mountains? But they had been too slow to the call, and he armed the MiG's weapons systems almost without thinking, Russian flowing through his mind as he settled into the mindset of combat and sped below the Harriers – which accelerated after him in deadly pursuit.

Engines howling, Carter saw the Harriers spread out behind him, losing the entourage of helicopters which were far too slow for this kind of aerial battle. Carter raced across the skies, climbing, and sensed rather than saw the AAMs detach and accelerate away from his pursuers. Carter banked again, more tightly this time, and the Sea Harriers couldn't match his manoeuvre. The MiG flashed up through cloud as the six missiles forged ahead and he wheeled, rolling, and then dropped from the skies and powered with only inches to spare between the clustered group of searching black helicopters—

Six missiles met six targets.

Thunder rolled across the sky as the choppers exploded in gaseous balls of flame. Another two choppers caught fire from being too close to the explosions and were sent spinning, rotors screaming, into the Mediterranean where they plummeted beneath the waves, leaving wide circles of churning foam.

'*Neat*,' said Kade. He sounded a little sulky.

Carter lifted the machine, vibrating under his battered hands, and armed his own missiles. His Global PK18 TSAM control radars started to buzz but he couldn't understand the flashing Russian commands. Carter looped, coming up behind the Sea Harriers, which had temporarily lost sight of him – and sighted, smiling savagely as he accelerated towards the five glinting machines—

Wing pylons retracted. Four of his eight R-80 AA-e Aphids released as he was almost upon the Harriers and he flashed overhead, climbing steeply. The missiles ate into the Sea Harriers like hot knives into soft fresh butter. There came the sounds of four impacts, like rapid detonation charges exploding in quick succession. Flames roared into the sky, purple and orange globes of fire spinning off hints of green and blue from superheated burning slivers of steel and alloy. Nex pilots melted into their seats, faces ridged in screams, and were then vaporised, spat up and out and finally down into the all-encompassing waves.

There seemed to be a moment of silence.

A long, long silence . . .

'*One left,*' said Kade smugly—

As Carter dropped the MiG and opened fire with the quad 30mm cannons. Huge heavy-calibre rounds roared across the bright blue sky, slamming into the Harrier and taking out its fuel tanks. There came a blossom of purple fire and the jet nosedived into the sea where it sank in an upsurge of foaming bubbles. Huge white rings spread out from the point of impact, and Carter watched for a moment as they dispersed.

'*You remind me more of me every day,*' said Kade.

'Fuck off.'

'*Tch. Tetchy again, Carter. Hey, where you going? You've left some choppers behind . . . hey, Carter, you're leaving some of them alive! You fucking pussy! Where are you going?*'

'I've seen enough of death to last me a million lifetimes. They'll never catch us.'

'*Carter! Breaking your own fucking rules, my man. Never leave an enemy behind, that's what you always told me. Come on, brother, let's see some more of those diseased fuckers burn . . .*'

Carter ignored Kade, and with his tight-lipped mouth a grim line as he wiped sweat from his hands, he thundered through the skies towards the coast of Greece, Albania, Yugoslavia and then onwards and up into Austria . . .

'*You butcher*,' muttered Kade, before disappearing from Carter's sombre thoughts.

The engines were whining softly.

'You make sure you come back to me, you reckless fucker . . . You make sure you come back to *us* . . .'

Natasha's face came into his mind, her twinkling eyes, her short spiked hair. He sighed, wondering if he would ever see her again.

He remembered those words, just before the dam detonation at the Tennagore Valley in Chile, South America – where everything had gone horribly wrong and he'd gone speeding down the face, screeching motorcycle bucking out of control beneath him, the near-vertical concrete surface flexing beneath him like the wildest of roller-coaster rides . . . and as the dam exploded and the waters picked him and the bike up, threw them down the valley on the surging crest of foam he had truly believed that he would die . . .

'*You make sure you come back to me, you reckless fucker . . . You make sure you come back to* us . . .'

Much later, Natasha's tears had awoken him. Spiral had picked him up, unconscious, half-drowned, in a Chinook chopper. Her tears had dripped into his face and Carter had hugged her, wincing from the pain in his broken bones.

'I love you, Nats. You knew I was coming back.'

'You nearly died out there, you fucker. And you *promised* . . .'

And now? The sweet irony! A reversal . . . a need not to kill, but to *save* and every bastard who got in his way was paying the ultimate *ultimate* price – but Carter felt like he was on a wild pillion ride straight into the heart of Hell, and the only way he could surface to heaven and reality was to cling on and ride the throbbing screeching insanity engine all the way – down the deep dips and through a world of madness and death, hopefully re-surfacing on the other side clutching the Avelach and with the ability to bring Natasha back from the brink of death . . .

'*No fucking chance,*' mocked Kade.

'Shut your face.'

'*You know my philosophy Carter, there are more fresh bitches in the sea. All you have to do is prime your maggot and do a little fishing. It's really not that fucking* hard *to understand.*'

'Shut up!' he screamed, slamming one fist against the inside of the MiG's cockpit. He coughed then, and a pain smashed into his head and it reminded him, back when he had been in Africa with Natasha and the pain had crippled him, dropped him like a bullet and the pain washed over him in great pulsing waves and he was almost blind, crippled, flooded with an intense pulsating vision and for a long time he drifted on the verge of consciousness and allowed the auto-pilot to correct the navigation of the MiG fighter's journey—

Engines hissed.

Sunlight sparkled, then dropped behind towering clouds which rolled billowing shadows over the sea far below. And Carter fell into a world of wonder and better times, when Natasha had been well and their lives had seemed so simple, so pure, so *complete*.

Before his world and sanity had seemed to finally end.

Simmo's HTank roared towards the unsuspecting Nex tanks guarding the refinery. Shells screamed overhead and this time they *did* catch the enemy by surprise. Guns thundered, smoke billowed in clouds and the Nex hardly knew what hit them. Tracks ground heavily across damp ground and when the battle was over Simmo leapt free, sinking up to his ankles in mud and gazing around, a beam on his broad flat face. He lit another cigar, and coughed a little on the blue smoke before letting it drift lazily from his nostrils.

'We do well, lads!' he roared, and the TankSquads cheered, standing on the hulls of the battle-scarred SP57s and throwing their helmets and water canteens into the air. Several Nex had been herded together and bound with wire, and Mo, Haggis and Rogowski were scoping out the smoking remains of the actual refinery, which, by some miracle, still stood amidst the twisted tank carnage and smoking devastation.

The TankComm rattled. Simmo picked it up, eyeing the TankSquad squaddies who fidgeted nearby. Simmo's face fell from elation to horror as he realised that he was speaking with Field Marshal Jacobs, Acting Commander of the Spiral TankSquads.

'Yes – Simmo, isn't it?'

'Yes, sir.'

'OK, lad, clearance has come through for you to take out that Nex-held LVA position in Columbia. Do you foresee any problems?'

'Um, no, sir.'

'Good, good.'

'Um, sir?'

'Yes, what is it, Simmo?'

'We also spot a refinery a few klicks away and it not on Spiral scout map. You want us investigate and take out if necessary?' Simmo eyed the smoking ruins in front of him, his shoulders hunched, teeth bared in a grimace.

509

'Yes, you go and investigate. If there are hostiles, by all means destroy them.'

'Yes, sir.'

'And Simmo?'

'Sir?'

'We have a Code Black across all bands. You will shortly be forwarded scrambling points. It would seem there is a madman on the loose with the ability to control earthquakes.'

'Ah. OK, sir. Thank you. Out.'

Simmo stared at the TankComm with obvious relief. Then he grinned. 'It turning into a good day,' he muttered.

Mo and Rogowski appeared, shaking their heads.

'We get an airlift outta here?' asked Kipper, sidling over to Simmo and staring hungrily at the The Sarge's cigar.

Simmo glared at him. 'Fuck off with that hungry look, Kipper. You proper fish-kipper, me thinking, when you go and leave all your own stash at home.'

'Aww, come on Sarge, you know I'd buy one off you but I've run out of money.'

'Yar, you lose it to me playing poker. Dumb ass. Find your own cigars.'

'Maybe I'll steal some from you when you're asleep!' laughed Kipper. Then he saw the look on Simmo's face. Stealing The Sergeant's cigars was not an option.

The TankComm rattled again. Simmo accessed it and strode away from the tank, trailing the bobbing curly umbilical cable behind him. Puffing on his cigar, he barked, 'Yeah? Simmo here.'

'Mongrel.'

'The Sarge was just thinking of you, lad.'

'Me? Why?'

'I was shelling a bunch of Nex, watching them burn in their tanks.'

'That supposed to be symbolic or something?'

'No, just little Sarge's death wish. What I do you for, Mongrel?'

'You heard about the sitrep on Durell, the fucker who almost brought the world to its knees with the QIII?'

'No. Fill me in.'

'We need help, Sarge. We need tanks – lots of your lovely tanks. Carter has gone ahead alone, to bring down this Durell, the Spiral betrayer. That mad Nex fucker is playing at being God again . . . he can control earthquakes all over the world and this is where the very big shit pie is going to hit the razor-fucking-bladed fan. You want to be at the heart of the battle? The big one? Then this is where it's going to be.'

'Simmo interested. Give me your coordinates.'

'Austria, target 226.443.223.457.'

'I've got a few hours to fill,' growled Simmo, realising that he had to be seen to be doing *something*, or Spiral might notice the fact that he had attacked two installations without actual permission. 'You leave it with The Sarge, lad. He see what he can do.'

The MiG 8-40 barrelled through the skies. It sped up past Slovenia's west coast, tipping slightly inland and cruising above the Austrian City of Klagenfurt, in Kärnten. Carter glanced down and saw weak autumn sunshine sparkling on the Glan river. Peering up ahead, he could make out the dark towering peaks of the Karawanken Mountains.

Carter started to decelerate, flashing over countryside, rivers, scatterings of trees. Checking his ECube, he began to visualise the coordinates against the landscape and plan his descent.

Where to land? he mused.

511

Passing over the stunning Niedere Tauern Alps, huge jagged teeth rising sheer and vast from the maw of the ground, he banked the MiG and realised that the place he wanted, the direct coordinates being fed through his tracking system, was an actual castle near to the village of Sankt Nikolai im Sölktal, high up in the Alps. Not the easiest of places to reach by fighter jet. Or by any other mode of transport . . .

Oak, hornbeam and pine lay scattered below Carter and he felt a strange calmness descend on him once more. The pain in his skull receded – as if it had simply been his brain's own warning jab. He licked his lips and composed himself.

Below, a narrow river snaked past a wide stretch of field carved unevenly from the mountainside. Along the opposite edge of the field meandered a long dirt track. Bracing himself, Carter turned the MiG and released the undercarriage; engines whining with deceleration, he lined up with the distant dirt track and watched his half-reflection glinting back at him from the cockpit interior.

'This is gonna be *real* fun,' he muttered.

The MiG came in, nose slightly raised. Carter touched down, gritting his teeth as the rear wheels impacted with the trail and the jolt almost threw him through the cockpit canopy. The whole fighter juddered with awesome violence, then its engines howled as they powered the plane into a frantic deceleration. Thundering down the rough trail, Carter's hands shook wildly on the controls and his teeth rattled in his pounding head. He could hear the shrieking stresses of tortured metal and the thuds of thumping wheels and battered suspension.

Carter watched a wall of trees rushing towards him and the hackles rose on the back of his neck.

Whining in protest, the throttled-back engines kicked

the fighter's speed down by degrees. Carter's sweat dripped into his eyes as the trail narrowed. He fought the weaving plane and watched the trees, a swathe of wide-boled oaks, growing ever closer.

The MiG slammed to a halt scant metres from the trees and there came a soft whine of exhaust. Carter lifted the cockpit canopy, worked his way down the first few rungs of the alloy ladder recessed in the fuselage and then leapt the final twelve feet to the ground.

He stared up at the dull grey flanks, sucking in the cold Austrian air. His breath emerged as smoke and he grinned, ears hammering, head pounding, eyes watering, and rolled his neck to ease the tension. Thought I was going through the mincer, he mused, and took a few steps back, his field of view widening . . .

Austria opened up before him.

Beautiful and serene.

A wide valley lay scattered with evergreens, undulating away and then sloping violently upwards towards and into the Niedere Tauern Alps. The mountains created a huge tunnel in front of Carter's awe-struck gaze, a giant's tunnel. The walls were sheer, unforgiving, blue-grey and wholly dominant, oak and pine scattered the lower slopes and Carter could make out a few distant streams and wider waterways. A couple of narrow roads and trails zig-zagged off to Carter's left, and he moved quickly beneath the wall of trees as he checked his ECube.

Blue digits glowed softly.

Carter matched the coordinates and realised that he was four kilometres from the bug planted in Durell's hel-icopter. He relayed the coordinates back to Mongrel and then, as an afterthought, to Spiral, with a short encoded digital transcript:

```
Have found Durell vb447. Will attempt to
halt his insanity.
By  whatever  means.  Coordinates  to
follow.
Request immediate back-up.
```

Carter attached his vb codes and the coordinates, and
sent the blip on the WarChannel. He had no idea if the
channels and the ECubes had been compromised by the
Nex – they had done it successfully once before. Carter
had to assume the worst: a total digital breakdown.

Carter had to assume he was on his own.

He took a deep cold breath, checked his weapons, and
looked up through the trees. How many Nex between me
and Jam? he thought. How many Nex between gaining
the Avelach and finding Durell? And getting the fuck out
alive?

Carter checked his pack, freshly stocked with ammo,
grenades and HighJ explosive from when he had hastily
dropped Mongrel at the Comanche. Then Carter
checked himself, prodding warily at various bruised and
battered parts of his flesh. Pulling free a PlasGrip™ bandage, he wound it tightly around one wrist and felt it pull
tight, electronically adjusting to offer maximum support
to injured limbs. He could still feel the staples pulling
tight in his back where the bullet had entered, and before
that where glass had sliced his flesh back in Switzerland.
Reaching into the pack he popped five K5 combo
painkillers and antibiotics, then pulled free a tiny vial.
Taking the yellow safety tag from the needle, he injected
his arm, needle slipping easily into the barely visible vein –
felt the kick as the small slow-release capsule entered his
circulatory system, being carried to lodge in his spinal
column where it would effect a slow and steady release of

514

chemicals. He would pay a high physiological price later . . .

But that was later.

Carter sighed, gazing around at the cold woodland. A fresh breeze made the trees hiss and sigh, and chilled the skin of his face. It was pleasant after the dry heat of Egypt, and he ran a blood-encrusted hand through his short hair, wondering how bad he looked: like a man who had been through the wars, probably.

Carter climbed wearily to his feet.

Nearly there, he thought.

One more burst, and then it will be over . . .

One way or another.

Carter moved up through the woods, slowly at first but speeding up as the chemicals kicked in. When he reached the edge of the trees he monitored for Nex activity.

Nothing local, but hostiles swarmed over the coordinate target on his ECube.

Settling his back against a tree, and pulling the straps tight, Carter secured his Browning and M24. He began a slow, loping jog.

He followed the rough stony trail for a while, then cut across fields scattered generously with hornbeam, their leaves rustling. Carter paused beneath one, breathing heavy now, and rested his hand against the smooth grey bark. He could see something ahead, the top of a grey – almost black – crenellated tower peering over the nearest hill.

Carter continued, reaching the crest of the slope and dropping to one knee beside the bole of another tree, eyes scanning. The castle came into view, built into the side of the mountain. Jagged uneven ground, rocky and scattered with a few pines led steeply up to the vertical grey walls of the castle. A slightly offset central tower rose from within, capped with dark red tiles. Another narrower tower rose from this central edifice. To the right the structure was more square in shape, like a vast cube of black, whilst to the left, leading away from the mountain, it fell in a series of small circular towers, each rising to a black or red spire. The building looked ancient, and very, very strong. Built to resist an attacking force. Built to rain down fire on the enemy. Built to resist an invasion . . .

A single wide dirt track swept up from the valley below, far to Carter's left, zigzagging through heavy woodland which thinned as it reached the castle's huge twin iron gates.

Carter could see a swarm of Nex activity by the gates, and up over the lower battlements he could make out more distant movement. His eyes narrowed, lips pursing in thought.

The whole castle was a massively imposing edifice, dominating the landscape below while in turn being over-shadowed by the magnificence of the vast mountains behind it.

Carter checked his ECube.

Durell's helicopter was there, somewhere in the castle.

Which meant that, logically, this was Durell's centre of operations – the heart from which he was controlling the earthquakes.

And this was where Durell had the Avelach. Guarded by Jam, Carter's oldest friend . . .

'*Let's do it*,' said Kade.

Carter said nothing.

He moved slowly, warily now that his target and desti-nation was in sight. The temperature was dropping as he moved higher from the valleys and up the vast steep slopes before him. His calves burned and offered him yet more pain. Despite the drugs, Carter felt far from OK. He felt a million fucking miles from fit, healthy, and ready to take on the greatest of his enemies . . .

'The Avelach.'

The word sounded strange, spoken out loud. And it felt bad on his tongue, like Carter was pinning his tentative hopes for Natasha's life on a machine that he did not understand, had never seen work, and that was the core of Durell's Nex creation.

It sat badly with him.

Carter moved forward, slowly, carefully, continually scanning for the enemy. If they know I'm coming, he thought, I don't want it to be because of carelessness. A disturbed bird, the crack of falling rock upon rock. Carter wandering aimlessly out into the open or silhouetting himself against a skyline like a shooting-range target . . .

Carter took his time. Used his eyes, and occasionally his Sniper Scope, which clicked and whined softly as a magnified and digitally enhanced landscape, castle and Nex came into Carter's field of vision. He noted the enemy's pattern of movement, and watched as a patrol of four tanks and two trucks growled through the gates, heavy steel tracks grinding the stone trail to dust.

Carter worked slowly, coming in from the south with the mountains to his right and hugging them, their sheer vast walls, almost as if for protection. The landscape was slowly changing as he gained height, long grasses scattered with more and more huge rocks which gave him plenty of cover.

'*They know you are coming,*' said Kade smugly.

'I don't care.'

'*You'll care when Jam shoots you in the face.*'

The sun was toiling across the sky, plunging behind towering clouds that sent vast rolling shadows tumbling across the valleys. The cold wind blew stronger, ruffling Carter's hair and chilling his fingers, nose and ears.

Reaching the base of the huge mound of rock on which the castle had been built, and with a sheer blue granite wall to his right, Carter started to clamber up the steep incline whose gradient steepened the further he went. Using his hands to help pull him forward, he found himself quickly sweating – sweat that was instantly chilled by the cold wind to leave him shivering almost uncontrollably.

A beautiful place, he thought.

But also a barren, deadly place.

A desolation.

After a half-hour of climbing, he reached the base of the castle wall. He crouched for a long time, searching for Nex, or cameras, or any other type of high-tech scanning devices. He could see nothing, and his ECube could see nothing . . . but Carter found it hard to believe.

Still, he couldn't exactly walk through the front gates.

He gazed up at the vast vertical expanse of stone ahead of him.

There were no windows, and no handholds that he could see.

Just stone . . . stretching high above his tilted head like some vast plain of rock, a towering wall of smooth sheer impossibility.

Breath coming in plumes, Carter pulled free his Sp_drag, his Skimmer, and reaching up he allowed the tiny alloy jaws to chew into the stone. With the aid of this digital crampon, Carter began the long long climb up the vast grey-black bulwark.

The climb was protracted, incredibly treacherous and an act of insanity. Wind smashed against Carter as he climbed; slowly, deliberately he moved upwards, and within minutes his hands were numb with cold and pain. Sweat ran and then chilled him, and he pressed himself tight against the flat wall, a limpet against a stone with the waves of cold air washing in violent crests up and over him.

Carter felt awesomely vulnerable. Perhaps more vulnerable than at any moment during his life. All it would take was a helicopter to spot him, or a sniper to sight him . . . and *bam*. Fish food. Dead meat.

Carter smiled grimly, and continued to climb.

Up, endlessly up, he travelled.

Carter did not look up. To do so might destroy his resolve, and so instead he focused on the grey wall to which he clung. The stone was rough, cold under his numb fingers. Pins and needles raced along his hands and arms, and cramps spiked his thighs and calves. The staples holding the bullet wound tight in his back moved and stretched his flesh, and he felt a little blood weep out, soaking into his torn battered dead Nex clothing.

Up, he climbed.

Eternally upwards.

Reaching for Heaven?

Or climbing to Hell in an ironic reversal?

Carter licked his lips, pausing, panting, and gazed out over the valley. He could hear distant noises, crashes and booms, the whines of engines and suddenly he brightened – when he realised that it sounded – *incredibly* – like Spiral TankSquad tanks being airlifted and fast-jetted to this location . . . backup?

I fucking hope so, he thought.

Squinting through the cold light, Carter could see nothing through the swathes of lowland forest. Then he heard a distant rattling and watched forty Nex tanks trundle onto the trails sweeping down from the castle and speed off, engines roaring. Something big was going down.

Something heavy—

But Carter had his own problems.

He continued to climb, and at one point broke his own rule and glanced up. The summit was tantalisingly close and the Sp_drag continued to eat stone, tiny spiral trails of grey stone dust whirling away down the face of the sheer castle wall and then, when he thought his endurance had finally reached its pain-filled limits, thought he could go on no longer, his aggrieved and screaming hands grasped the edge of the parapet and he hauled himself up onto a low crenellation, squatted, eyes quickly skimming the area before him as he drew his Browning with stumps of numbness and clumsily flicked free the safety.

The wind howled, a soft moaning, blowing eerily through the castle.

Below him spread a broad platform of uneven and time-worn stone flags. It measured perhaps forty or fifty metres square, was bordered on the left by a high stone wall leading to a tower and whose only feature was a narrow arched doorway. Ahead squatted another battlement that dropped away to what Carter assumed was the castle's central courtyard. To the right stood a high stone wall with three ancient doorways, all shrouded in gloom.

The sun disappeared behind towering black clouds. Carter glanced back at the dizzying fall, at the sheer wall he had ascended and the vast slopes beyond, dropping through to distant valleys. It was a fucking awesome drop.

Carter hopped down to the rough-worn stone flags and something moved in the shadows of the narrow doorway leading to the tower. Dropping to a crouch Carter sighted along the Browning's barrel, finger tightening on the trigger and eyes narrowing as Jam stepped into view.

Jam had changed since his last encounter with Carter. He seemed less . . . deformed.

Jam moved forward, triangular head swaying, and stopped a short distance away. He carried no weapons, only a silver box in black claws that had once been hands.

'Hello, Carter,' he rumbled softly.

Carter stared into those slitted copper eyes and his words caught in his throat. This was his oldest and greatest friend, and they had fucked with him, turned him into a Nex and now Carter would have to . . .

'*Kill him*,' supplied Kade.

Carter uncoiled slowly, lowered the Browning and slid his pack from his back, allowing it to drop to the stone flags. Clouds whirled across the bleak grey sky and the wind stung his face with its cold sharp needles.

'You knew I was coming?'

Jam nodded and stooped, placing the small silver box on the ground at the base of the tower. Then he smiled, his once twisted jaws now aligned and straight, his stance more powerful, more erect. The copper eyes looked at Carter coldly: calculating and appraising.

'Of course,' said Jam. 'You told me yourself that you wanted the Avelach. To save Natasha . . . and here it is. The prize you seek. The gift you would wish to steal. Our power, and our source for the creation of the Nex . . . it is in the silver box which protects it, encodes it, and yet haunts it.'

Carter licked his lips, glancing down at the box.

'You have changed,' said Carter.

'Yes. You misunderstand the process of creating a Nex. When I was created, at first I was horribly disfigured, deformed if you will. The ScorpNex always are – it is the

521

price of the more complex blending, the more complex and savage inhibitors used. But then the subject refines itself, heals itself, becomes more stable, more *beautiful*. To become a ScorpNex, Carter – it is a symmetry . . . it is celestial. It is an act of perfection, of healing, of evolution. You would not believe the way I feel; it is sublime. You could never understand unless you yourself became Nex.'

'And why the fuck would I want to do that?' snarled Carter.

'Because it is your future,' said Jam softly. He took several steps forward, and Carter found himself backing away involuntarily. Jam's movements were precise, controlled, and awesomely powerful. Carter felt a deep fear gnaw at him from the depths of his belly . . .

'I don't fucking think so,' said Carter. 'You have betrayed your race, Jam. Betrayed mankind . . . You have become something you are not – yeah, you never volunteered for it, but now you are part of Durell's fucking insanity.' Carter's eyes stared fiercely into Jam's copper slits. 'What do you want from me?' he said, his voice a hoarse whisper.

'Durell wants to turn you into a Nex – like me. A ScorpNex – the ruling elite. The all-powerful. As close to God as God.' Jam chuckled, a deep-throated rumble. 'He says you would make the perfect ScorpNex . . . and if you do this, then we will let you take the Avelach, we will let you heal Natasha. Everything you desire will be yours. Your life will be complete.'

'Fuck you.'

'Come on, Carter.' Jam moved forward again, armoured claws scraping the stone as his huge muscles coiled under black chitinous armour. Jam stared at the man in front of him. 'You can save Natasha's life – and we can be friends again, comrades – you can join our army,

522

you can rule the world with us, Carter, with Durell and I, you can be a part of this first great step to power and glory – when we overthrow Spiral, smash and control the world governments . . .'

'You want to rule the fucking world?' snarled Carter. 'Have you fucking heard yourself? It's like a dictator's wet fucking dream . . .'

'You do not understand, truly you do not.' Jam halted. Behind him, Carter could see the glitter of the silver box – a tease, he realised. Clouds broiled overhead, carried on the fury of the gathering storm. 'And if you do not wish to save Natasha, if you do not want to join us, then there is only one thing I require from you.' His head tilted. Slitted copper eyes surveyed Carter coolly.

'My telephone number?' Carter smiled as his whole body tensed for the battle and he slowly brought the Browning up.

'I want your *death*.'

Jam leapt forward and Carter started firing, the Browning slamming in his fist. One bullet took Jam in the leg, one grazed his armour, another passed over his shoulder, a fourth sliced a line across his throat and then—

The claw lashed out.

Carter's Browning skidded across the stone and he stumbled back.

Kade rattled against the bars of his mind but Carter ignored him. He would not allow him life.

Jam lashed out again. Carter ducked, smashed a right hook against Jam's triangular head and heard one of his own knuckles crack under the impact. Jam's armoured elbow crashed into Carter's sternum, slamming him back, and Jam's leg powered out, armoured foot catching Carter under the jaw and lifting the Spiral agent from his feet. He flailed backwards to roll against the battlements.

Carter slumped against the stone.

Stars danced in his head and he breathed in deeply. Rolling swiftly to his feet, he spat out blood and worked his jaw – but felt no pain.

Fuck pain, he thought.

I am beyond pain.

'Is that all you have to offer? Your future fucking wife could do better.'

Jam's copper-eyed stare fixed on Carter, who charged – and Jam leapt to meet him. Carter spun and whirled, dancing under Jam's heavy blows and then jumped, boots striking Jam's chest. Jam took a step back. Carter delivered a kick to Jam's throat, then another to his groin. Leaping up, Carter came down with his elbow smashing into Jam's broad head. Carter dodged a swipe from the glistening black claw and another kick to Jam's throat sent the huge ScorpNex stumbling towards the battlement wall above the cold square expanse of black cobbled courtyard below . . .

Snow started to fall, gentle swirls of flakes that danced on flurries of cold bitter wind from the mountains and landed, making the battlements slick and slippery. *Deadly.*

'*Go on, one more,*' hissed Kade.

Carter braced himself. He had hurt Jam, amazingly; could see it in the ScorpNex's face – in his eyes. His blows, although devastating to his own frame, had smashed through Jam's armour—

Carter sprinted and leapt, his boots aiming for Jam's head and a deep long tumbling fall for the ScorpNex into oblivion . . . and beyond.

Jam twisted with a blur of speed, caught Carter and smashed a heavy punch to the Spiral agent's forehead. Then another to Carter's nose, then a third to his jaw. He dropped Carter on the flags with a dull slapping sound and as Carter looked up Jam kicked him savagely in the face, snarling with contempt.

Jam paced around Carter in a wide circle.

He seemed agitated.

Filled with unease.

Carter rolled in a world of agony, his nose broken, pain screaming through his face. Through scattered flickerings of bright light he gazed up through the soft falling snow. It settled gently over him, a veil of pity.

Distantly, he heard the smash and crump of tank shells. Screams of metal filtered through the swirling snow to his ears. And with a deep dark thankfulness he realised that a battle – *the* battle? – had at last begun . . .

'Come back to us, Jam,' said Carter hoarsely, forcing himself into a sitting position and trying to stem the flow of blood from his nose. 'Come back to the real fucking world.'

'I *am* in the real fucking world,' hissed Jam. 'To be Nex, it is awesome, it is perfect, it is immortality.'

'You are living a lie,' croaked Carter. 'What about your friends back at Spiral? What about your comrades, men you fought with, men who fucking died for you? What about Nicky? Remember her, fucker? You would deny yourself this? You would cast your life away? Piss away your fucking *humanity*?'

'Fuck them all,' growled Jam. 'I do not need them. I am whole like this; I am perfect; I am *evolved*.'

'You are a fucking genetic mess.' Carter laughed weakly, through strings of blood and saliva. He dragged himself to his feet and despite the powerful drugs pain was screaming through him. 'Well then, fucker, come on, come and finish it. You're such a supreme fucking being, you think you are so fucking hard . . .'

'*Let me*,' whispered Kade.

The sounds of the tank battle were coming closer.

Below in the courtyard Carter heard the bustle of activity: the stomp of boots, the rattle of weapons.

Here comes the war, he thought, and watched idly as Jam leapt towards him, as if in slow motion, claws held wide and face an insanity of anger. Jam was finally ready, accepting the inevitability of Carter's death.

Casting off his inhibitions.

At last the ScorpNex was ready to murder those he had loved.

Simmo stared around at the tanks surrounding him on the Austrian valley floor. The last few to be airlifted were being freed of their chains, and the Chinooks were taking off, veering away to the south.

'Things are getting mad,' observed Rogowski.

'They always do,' growled Simmo.

Readying their vehicles, engines revving and tracks straining against the crushed-stone trails, Simmo was just about to close the HTank's hold when the scream of engines swept down to him from the mountains.

Five or six tanks swivelled their turrets, guns elevating towards this new threat, but Simmo shouted for the TankSquads to hold their fire. A battered Comanche leapt into view, slewing sideways and touching down on bobbing suspension beside Simmo's HTank.

The rotors were still whirling as Mongrel jumped free and moved towards the huge sergeant. Their gazes met, and over the noise of the machines Mongrel shouted, 'Carter's up there.'

Simmo shrugged. 'Do you know what's happening? With the LVA?'

'Have you been briefed?'

'We only know that Durell is commanding the earthquakes. What you tell us.'

'Yeah.' Mongrel nodded. 'He's doing it through the LVA. The Nex drop shafts to mine LVA, and while they are down there they plant Foundation Stones – control devices. Under the ground there is a whole massive worldwide fucking network of LVA running in underground streams, rivers, lakes . . . the fucking shite is a conductor of some kind – I know this sound crazy but it true – and through this natural grid network of LVA Durell control the quakes. He using a machine called a QuakeHub. If we can destroy it and Durell, we can stop the Earth being torn apart . . .'

'Let's just shell the fucking place,' growled Simmo.

Mongrel shook his head. 'Not so simple, Sarge. This LVA grid, this liquid network under the earth – Durell is playing game with what he shouldn't. If he fuck with it too bad, too *wrong*, then whole fucking world go up! God only know what will happen . . . maybe quakes across the whole globe. Maybe this underground sea of fuel ignite. Spiral not know and this simple squaddie not know, but Spiral say we not just blow everything up, we need to take control . . .'

Simmo rubbed at his chin.

'Easier said than done, Sarge thinking.'

'Sarge, they've spotted us.'

'Shit.'

Up the valley, the gates to the castle had opened. Dark grey Nex tanks poured out, tracks grinding, dust pluming behind them.

'At least in this battle we keep the shells away from castle,' said Mongrel, a weak smile crossing his grey drained features. 'Now you understand me, don't you, Sarge? No fucking bombing the castle . . . Spiral say we not risk it yet, they don't know what happen . . . we got a whole shitload of back-up on its way . . .'

'Yes, yes, I understand. You going to give us some air support?'

Mongrel glanced back at the Comanche, which he had nearly crashed three times on his journey to this rendezvous. He shuddered. 'I do my best. I hope they not got helicopters . . .'

Simmo pointed to where a swarm of ten machines had taken to the air from further down the valley. Mongrel cursed again, and Simmo laughed, slapping him on the back. The Sergeant's eyes were wild, and the stump of a cigar squatted between his teeth.

'You not worry, Mongrel, you give us support from air, and *we* give you support from ground.'

'*Cheers*,' snapped Mongrel as the heavy steel hatch of Simmo's HTank slammed shut and Mongrel ran back towards the Comanche. He could hear the roar of tank engines now, and the thumping of distant rotors slamming down the valley.

Above, heavy clouds rolled, and darkness and gloom tumbled across the land.

It's going to snow, he thought as he climbed into the Comanche and stared in horror at the controls. Tentatively, Mongrel squeezed the HIDSS back onto his head.

- `Battle data initiated`, came a soft smooth female voice in his skull.

- `All weapon systems primed.`

- `Targeting sequences aligned.`

- `Your Comanche is ready for battle. Please insert the correct Battle Disk labelled BattleDisk 2.`

Disk? What fucking disk?

Mongrel cast about frantically as a tiny drawer in the console slid out, awaiting its battle data.

'You got be fucking kidding!' he howled.

And then he spotted the rack, located the disk and slammed it into the console.

```
- Thank you.
- Your Comanche Battle 'Copter is now
fully on-line.
```

Mongrel stared up at the rolling clouds. He took a deep breath, watching as Simmo's tanks spread out into formation and two groups turned, disappearing through the trees to either side of the trail with their stealth motors engaged.

'Here we go.'

He eased the Comanche into the air, wobbling slightly, and watched in horror as the rotors cut the top neatly from a pine tree, sending ragged torn branches and a flurry of mashed pine needles mushrooming into the cold wind.

'I wish I never born!' he wailed.

The columns of tanks joined battle in a deafening metal thunder. Shells exploded in close-quarter heavy-tracked combat, and on both sides the rear tanks spat fire into the sky. Turrets whirred, and Simmo's HTank wreaked havoc among the Nex, its camouflage cloak making it an almost invisible target and its superior engines and turning capabilities giving it an all-important edge . . .

Spiral men and women burned in their metal coffins.

Nex screamed, melting in theirs . . .

'No way to die,' thought Simmo grimly, sweat stinging his eyes as his HTank powered up a slope impossible for a normal tank to climb and appeared behind the enemy. His turret whirled and its gun fired. For just a second his HTank was visible, and an enemy TK79 was kicked flaming from the trail and into a small valley beside the road. Flames billowed, the hatch opened and two Nex clambered out, their clothing burning, their mouths eerily silent . . . Rogowski used the HTank's 28mm machine gun to cut them mercilessly in half.

'We're winning,' said Rogowski, a humourless grin twisting his lips.

Something glinted on the scanner, then was gone.

Simmo threw open the HTank's hatch. Snow was falling, and the HTank's armour was slick beneath him as it became totally visible when the CamCloak powered down. He watched the remaining tanks fight it out on the trail and in the woods, where his TankSquad had come from three sides, crushing the advancing Nex column in a surprise encirclement.

Something caught his eye again, through the ever-thickening fall of snow.

Simmo whirled.

'What fuck is that?'

And then they materialised. They were HTanks, but not like any HTank Simmo had ever seen. They were a dull grey, and quite obviously belonged to the enemy. They squatted side by side on the trail, engines idling, matrix fission hissing cold chemical fumes. Simmo's eyes went wide in disbelief.

'You see them, Sarge?'

'Is fucking *impossible*! Spiral hold blueprints!'

'Sarge? I think we'd better fucking move . . .'

The five HTanks were huddled in a close formation on the trail – as if taunting Simmo with their very existence. Simmo's face darkened, blacker than the broiling clouds cloaking the summits of mountains above him. His fists clenched as a hatch opened in the hull of one of the enemy HTanks. A man climbed up, eyes blood-red and scarred, hiding their copper Nex origins. His head was heavily scarred from his run-in with drug purifiers many years earlier, and he smiled savagely at Sergeant Simmo as their gazes met.

'You!' exclaimed Simmo, pointing.

Kattenheim nodded, then without a word dropped into the tank's interior. The grey Nex HTanks instantly cloaked and all five dropped off the edges of the trail to disappear in the sloped ditches bordering the road . . .

Simmo dropped inside his own tank as Rogowski screwed the engines and the beast, now invisible, powered down the steep pine-strewn trail after the Nex tanks. Behind them, the rest of the Spiral SP57s gathered into a tight unit and started to advance—

'That *fucker*,' growled Simmo, scowling.

Behind him, behind his HTank, one of the SP57s was suddenly kicked into the air by a shell arrowing through the falling snow. Fire erupted and the metal carcass was catapulted into the air, trailing black smoke. The tank sailed in an arc to vanish flaming into a copse of pine trees, setting them on fire with its hellish descent.

'We have to do something *fast* . . .' snapped Rogowski.

Simmo nodded, his mind whirling.

Five HTanks!

Five fucking HTanks!

Five fucking HTanks *just like his*!

'Those bastards!'

Growling, Simmo spread his hands over the panel controls and his shaggy eyebrows met in a furrow of concentration as tracks pounded the ground. The HTank whirled around.

'Fuck you, Kattenheim,' he muttered. 'Why you not die?'

Carter watched the sparkling snowflakes, cascading and dancing around him on their wind-blown descent. Jam leapt towards him but Carter moved easily to one side and

531

slammed the heel of his hand against Jam's neck. As Jam doubled over, Carter brought his left knee up hard into Jam's face and then grasped the ScorpNex's head between both hands. He rammed Jam's face down against his knee once, twice, three times . . . and then again, and again and again. Something snapped and blood poured down over Carter's legs as he kicked Jam away. He crunched back through the snow and watched snarling as Jam stumbled to his armoured knees with blood pooling into his clawed hands—

Reality slammed into focus.

Carter blinked, cold breath smoking, snowflakes settling against his face and hair and shoulders. Jam raised his head up, eyes narrowing, and then he was back up. He attacked in a blur through the snow.

They exchanged blows, backed away, circled.

Engaging again, Jam struck time after time and Carter blocked each punch with his pain-ravaged forearms, returning blows that Jam blocked in his turn. Carter delivered a combination of punches and kicks, but Jam backed away, still blocking, and then, snarling, heaved himself onto Carter, smashing the smaller man to the ground. Jam's claws lashed down, pounding Carter's head. He was left stunned and bleeding heavily onto the snow.

Carter's world spun.

'*Let me*,' came Kade's confident soothing whisper again. '*I can take this fucker – you know I can.*'

Jam hoisted Carter up by the throat, dangling him in powerful muscled arms. Carter's knee slammed up again, but Jam blocked. Their stares met and understanding passed between them. Jam's claw smashed at Carter's head, releasing the man – and Carter reeled in screeching white-hot agony, slipping suddenly on the snow and sliding blindly back to flip neatly over the battlements . . .

For a horrible moment Carter hung suspended. He spun, his hands grasping nothing but air. He fell, twisting, fingers lashing out . . . his left hand grasped the icy lip of the battlements and he whirled round to slam against the stone wall. Below, a hundred Nex looked up with their copper eyes – and lifted their JK49s.

'Fuck.'

Carter scrabbled against the stone.

Time seemed to slow and the cold wind nipped his face. Kade's voice whispered messages in his head and Carter saw a bullet fly towards him, glancing from the stonework by his face. He swung around, boots scrabbling against the icy stone and his free hand reaching up to find a hold. Jam reared above him, leaping up to the crenellation and standing broad and tall and bleeding, staring down with triumph lurking deep within those seemingly emotionless copper slits.

In the valley, tanks blasted one another.

Carter saw a distant tank hull, within a globe of roaring flames, spat up above the tree line to trail dark black smoke into a trench further down the valley.

Carter glanced down, at where the waiting Nex were pointing their guns.

And up at Jam, who had lifted his glistening claws wide as if accepting acclaim from the audience of upturned Nex faces below him. He smiled down at Carter, blood dripping from his fangs onto Carter's face.

'Until the next time, my brother,' Jam breathed and lifted his heavy armoured foot into the air above Carter's face – above Carter's grimace of hatred and anger. And sudden understanding—

Around them, the snow continued to fall gently.

CHAPTER 19

ENDGAME

The cold wind bit into Carter. He watched Jam's armoured foot and knew that there was no mercy there, no forgiveness. They had done Belfast together. Crossed the desert after the Battle of Cairo 7. Suffered the horrors of the TankerRuns after the designer plague GreyDeath had slaughtered fifty-eight million people. And, ultimately, none of it mattered because Jam was a different person . . . Jam was a different *creature* . . . Jam was Nex, no longer human: and for Carter that meant death.

Carter could see Jam's eyes.

Copper slits.

'Wait.'

The words were a low melancholic growl, echoing through the snow. Jam obeyed instantly. He glanced down into Carter's eyes with a look he failed to read, then disappeared from view. Carter flexed his fingers, trying to get a better hold. One hand slipped, and for precious moments he was dangling . . . but he regained his grip and through all his waves of pain and pounding agony he focused his mind: to hold, not to fall; to live, not to die . . .

because to live meant that Natasha still had a chance at life, to live meant that Durell could still be stopped.

Carter glanced down, nervously, at the gathered Nex.

Distantly, more shells were exploding. And then there came silence. The Nex in the courtyard received a sharp barked order, and they filed from the gates in small groups, JK49s held in black-gloved hands, their balaclavas sprinkled with snowflakes. Carter looked back up—

Into the dark slitted gaze of Durell.

His hood was thrown back, his horribly deformed features exposed to the snow and the cold biting wind. He smiled – if his expression *was* a smile – down at Carter.

'Funny how these things turn out,' he said softly. Durell edged closer, boots now so close to Carter's fingers that he could have reached and touched him . . . if he had been able. If he had possessed the strength.

Carter said nothing.

'I hated you, Carter, for a long time I hated you. Yes, I admit I would ultimately like you to join our cause . . . I think you would make the most powerful ScorpNex ever. I think you would be a truly awesome killing machine. After all, look how well you kill with your, shall we say, *pure* blood.' Durell laughed softly, eyes twinkling with some inner humour, some inner irony, as the snow fell thicker now and Carter listened out for more gunfire.

Was Spiral nearly there? At the gates?

Or did they have their own fucking problems?

Kade? He thought. Kade? Where the fuck are you?

But Kade had gone . . .

Carter breathed deeply, fingers cramping. He glanced down. It was a damned long way to fall – and, unlike a Hollywood action film, there was no convenient tent, hay cart or series of balcony awnings to provide a soft landing for the hero. If indeed he *was* the hero. He smiled grimly at that. Have I ever behaved like a hero? he mused idly.

'If you were ScorpNex then I could study you. Examine how and why the military processor, the QIV, the QuakeHub – why it cannot see you and predict your actions. Your future.'

Something went cold and hard in Carter's soul.

'I destroyed the QIII processor,' said Carter softly, staring up.

Durell nodded. 'Yes, you did. But as in most cases of hardware development, as one project is finishing so the next project begins. The QIV was started two years before the completion of the QIII – we had already mapped out the QIII's successor, its superior, the next model. The next generation. And all it took was a further year of development. It was the QIV that decoded the ancient scripts, located the LVA fuel, told us where to mine . . . it was the QIV processor that designed and created the Foundation Stones that we use to control the quakes. But like the chip you destroyed, it is blind to you, Carter. It is as if you do not exist. As if your timeline, your world runs parallel with that of every other living creature on this planet – but they never intertwine.'

Durell was silent then.

Carter squirmed uncomfortably.

Again, his hand slipped. His fingers were too numb to hold on.

'I hope you enjoy your fucking kingship, arsehole,' snapped Carter. 'I hope it burns you into an early grave. Running the world can be so fucking *tiresome* these days, I believe.'

'Kingship? Ruling the world?' Durell laughed with genuine humour. His stare locked to Carter. 'Your schemes are so petty, so small,' he mocked. 'Your vision is so tame – it lacks, shall we say, true imagination, true ambition. Why would I want to rule the fucking world? To rule the world in itself is no great aim, no, no, vision goes much, much further than that – as far as the sun and the stars!' He laughed again, but this time it was a cold laugh. The humour of the dead.

'What do you *want?*' asked Carter, his breath pluming like dragon smoke.

'It is simple. I want everybody to be Nex. We are the Pure, Carter. And if people will not become Nex and experience the purity, the power, the *immortality* that we can offer . . . then those people will die. To be a Nex – you misunderstand the feelings and sensations involved. It is evolution, my friend. The way we are supposed to be. The way we *will* all be. A *controlled* evolution. An *obedient* evolution. A Blending that removes greed, and lust, and hatred . . . it will remove war, and famine, and terrorism.' He laughed. 'If everybody was Nex – evolved to the next stage of humanity . . . then the world would be a much better place. A new Eden.'

Durell sighed.

He glanced back at Jam.

'Now, Jam. Kill him.'

Durell disappeared from view.

'Kade? Where the fuck are you, Kade?' Carter tiptoed along the tightrope of panic.

'*You called, sir?*'

Jam reared into view, slitted copper eyes gazing down at Carter. Beyond the castle more explosions echoed. Carter could feel his grip slipping. Within seconds he wouldn't need Jam's help to find his way to the next life.

Jam lifted Carter's Browning.

You fucker, thought Carter. You'd shoot me with my own fucking gun?

'*Do you require a little assistance, Mr Carter?*'

'You think you're so fucking good, Kade . . . well, *you* fucking kill him!'

Carter felt Kade smile within him.

Felt Kade's *pride* burn him.

Jam's copper eyes narrowed. He aimed the Browning at Carter's face.

'*O sir, your wish is my command*,' said Kade. The world spun around and around and *down* into a flashing glittering knife-edge of razor-sharp shots: all filmed in a glossy and static sequential black and white.

The grey Nex HTank crawled along the gulley and stopped. Its turret rotated slowly, still cloaked and practically invisible to any but the specifically trained and practised eye. Tracks rocked against gravel and above, on the lip of the gulley, a cluster of Spiral SP57 tanks gathered, their engines roaring, their large guns constantly tracking on their hydraulics.

The Nex HTank's gun lifted. The air around it shimmered as it moved.

Time seemed to shift, to displace.

And Simmo's tank appeared with a whine of CamCloak – directly behind the Nex HTank and with its gun pointing straight at the weakest part of the enemy vehicle's structure – the base plate behind the rear tracks. Simmo growled and fired the gun.

There was a concussive *boom* and the gun recoiled. The enemy HTank in front of him was kicked high into the air, one track ripped free with a grinding shriek of steel; purple fire billowed and the tank, trailing smoke and fire, disappeared over the SP57s and the ridge beyond. There came a distant echoing impact.

'Fucked severely up ass,' grinned Simmo, cloaking his tank once more.

'Well done, Sarge,' came the voice of Mo over the comm. 'There's another in the woods to our right – spec co-ords 52.33.53. I got the eyes of an eagle . . .'

'If only you had good looks! I hear you . . . I'm on it,' growled Simmo, lighting another cigar.

The Spiral HTank crawled across the forest floor, tracks grinding through pine needles and patches of snow. Matrix hissed, cold and bright, and the HTank halted in the shadows and uncloaked. Simmo lifted the hatch and poked out his head, breathing deeply the dense damp vegetative stench of the forest and revelling in the rich fragrance.

'They're here,' came Rogowski's growl.

Simmo nodded, and smoked his cigar, eyes scanning the forest. Smoke trailed down past his throat tattoos and up past his shaved head. It curled through the branches above him.

In the distance, another SP57 blew up. Another two Spiral operatives died . . .

Simmo ground his teeth in frustration.

The fuckers were picking off his men . . .

One by painful one . . .

The first of two Nex HTanks came creeping through the forest. Simmo caught the disturbance of branches, the gentle displacement of pine needles and – trained to read the signs of the CamCloak – he smiled to himself and pretended to look in the opposite direction.

'You picked your spot well. The other tank is coming from the other side, directly opposite.'

'The Sarge know good gig when he see one. He know how to play fucking game.'

The two enemy HTanks halted. Now they were totally invisible. Simmo tilted his head and fancied that he could

539

hear the whine of their CamCloaks. Below, Rogowski readied the engines and flicked free the stealth switch. Like all stealth systems, a stealth mode was always a compromise between noise and power. Without the stealth mode activated the awesome matrix engine came truly into its own.

'Here we go . . .' Simmo felt himself tense; he forced himself to take a huge drag on the cigar, pretending to scan the undergrowth away from the enemy HTanks.

The enemy tanks both fired—

But with a burst of exhaust fumes, Simmo's HTank was no longer there. Engines roared, followed by the twin detonations of the enemy tanks. Trees were splattered with hot liquid metal and twin craters, glowing with fire, appeared in the soft forest floor. Simmo's tank skidded around and demolished three trees, its weight snapping thick trunks with ease. Simmo, who had almost been thrown from his perch halfway through the hatch by the sudden insane acceleration, glared down into the darkness at Rogowski.

'Fucking lunatic!'

'That went smoothly, I think,' said Rogowski.

'Yeah, except for mad-arse driving! You need take test again, lad! You need learn three-point turn and how to parallel park fucking big tank!'

'Sorry, Sarge! But we got 'em!'

Simmo suddenly grinned. 'Aye. We got 'em, lad.'

Simmo hammered the cloaked HTank up the trail, tracks crushing rocks as they went. Below, the remaining SP57s were moving up through the woods towards the castle. Groups of Nex soldiers had emerged with machine guns. Gunfire rattled and shells started to explode . . .

Suddenly, the HTank uncloaked—

540

And picked up a lot of speed.

'Nearly there,' grunted Rogowski.

Simmo watched his scanners, eyes fierce, cigar clamped between his teeth. Then, as the HTank roared along the rising trail, it suddenly grated against stone and veered right – ploughing through trees with crunches of tearing wood as it sailed inelegantly through the air and heavily falling snow . . .

Simmo held his breath.

They landed with a mighty jolt and a terrible crunch of battered steel. Simmo's HTank seemed to perch on nothingness, and then slowly it crunched its way down the invisible enemy HTank's hull and onto the trail. Tracks squealed and the HTank whirled. The enemy's CamCloak flickered, stuttering like a faulty strip light, and its engine revved but the tank could not move. Its turret groaned as Simmo slowly lined up the crushed enemy tank in his sights and paused, finger over the trigger panel.

'Poor fuckers,' mouthed Rogowski. Simmo glanced at him. 'Trapped in there, just waiting to die. It is every TankSquad's worst nightmare. Bad bad dreams, Sarge.'

Simmo caressed the trigger.

And, grunting, he fired.

The shell shot from one of the HTank's guns and impacted with a terrifying scream against the wounded enemy HTank. Fire flickered out to engulf and swallow it – and then, as if on the end of a piece of elastic, the tank was jerked from the trail and flung into the sky. It spun slowly, awesomely bright flames melting its hull and leaving a stream of molten metal. The HTank struck the stone wall of the rising trail from which Simmo's tank had just jumped, and left a metal smear like dark silver blood against the rock. Then it veered off onto the slope below, bouncing against several large boulders. It came to a final rest as a smoking wreck. Simmo stared, but the hatch did not open. Flames continued to burn and he could make out the almost perfectly drilled hole where the shell had entered the enemy tank and fucked it severely from within.

Simmo stared down at Rogowski.

'Fuck them,' he said slowly, and placed his cigar back between his teeth.

'Sarge?'

'Hm?'

'Look!'

Simmo turned. In the distance, facing them and with CamCloak deactivated, squatted the last Nex HTank. It looked subtly different to his own machine and Simmo bared his teeth in the parody of a grin.

'Kattenheim,' he said.

The enemy HTank revved its engine and cold fumes coughed from its exhausts. Simmo dropped to his seat and settled himself. He pulled tight his harness, buckling himself in, and stared into Rogowski's eyes.

'No,' said Rogowski.

'Yes,' said Simmo, and nodded, his eyes shining.

'No! You can't be fucking serious!'

'The Sarge always fucking serious.'

He throttled up the engines of the HTank to the max and the two machines lurched towards one another across the stone trail, pulping gravel into dust. Above, Mongrel's Comanche spun gleaming through the snow, its guns eating through three black Nex helicopters which plunged into the forest, setting a stand of trees on fire . . . But all this was as nothing to Simmo as he focused on the HTank roaring towards him from directly ahead—

542

The distance closed rapidly.

Tracks thundered and smashed at the stone trail.

Engines roared, billowing cold exhaust.

And Simmo's head dropped against his bull neck, shoulders widening out as his teeth gripped his cigar so hard that he bit it in half, and the glowing tip disappeared unnoticed . . .

'Come on, you piece of Nex shit.'

The tanks powered towards one another, pulping the snow.

The battle seemed to have paused to witness this insane predestined collision: two juggernauts heading towards each other for a final apocalyptic impact – a head-on crash between two of the most ferocious machines of war ever created.

Rogowski, covering his head with his arms, screamed like a baby.

But Sergeant Simmo did not falter, did not take his intense fixed stare from the scanners and the suddenly expanding hull of the enemy HTank . . . At the last moment Kattenheim's tank veered suddenly to the right in a last-ditch attempt to avoid collision.

With a growl, Simmo veered his own tank to the left, grinding tracks skidding over loose stones, to make sure that the impact took place.

The noise was indescribable.

The tanks collided, seemed to fold in on themselves and then rose up, whirling tracks crunching against one another and eating through steel. With engines howling and smoke pluming, sparks and shards of metal fired off in all directions like shrapnel as the two HTanks joined like nightmarish glittering steel lovers, *melded* in a dark ironic complimentary parody of the joining of the Nex with insect . . .

543

Metal-bred thunder rolled out.

And together the two HTanks flipped and rolled off the trail, fire and sparks glowing around their chassis and tracks and bent distorted guns. The conjoined beast rolled and smashed down a steep slope of trees and boulders, demolishing trunks, crushing rocks, and came finally to rest on its merged single side, rocking slowly.

Snow fell, melting against the hot flanks.

Flames flickered along one hull on a stream of arcing matrix fuel.

Silence reigned for perhaps a minute.

Then came a distant hammering. There was a heavy clang as Simmo's boots smashed open the hatch, and a deformed hunk of elliptical metal toppled into the snow. He squeezed his frame out – battered, bruised and bleeding from his reopened head wound and several slashes to his face, but with eyes still intent and focused. His groin smoked softly from the fallen cigar-tip, and he carried something in one fist – a package wrapped tight in blue plastic. Reaching back, he dragged a moaning and grumbling Rogowski from the remains of the Spiral HTank and dumped him unceremoniously in the snow where he nursed a broken shoulder; then calmly patted out his burning genitalia.

Simmo stretched his back and glanced up the slope where the SP57s were battling Nex soldiers on foot. Mongrel's Comanche flashed overhead, MiniGun roaring. Another black Nex helicopter trailing fire disappeared over the mountains and exploded. Simmo nodded in appreciation, then turned his attention to the fused steel mess in front of him.

Rogowski had crawled to his knees and vomited before glancing up. Simmo moved around the twisted steel carcass and started tugging at the Nex HTank's hatchway.

'What are you doing?' Rogowski shrieked.

Simmo ignored him. There was a crunch and something moved.

'It's fucking on *fire*! It's going to fucking *explode*!'

Simmo whirled. 'You fuck off up trail away from blast zone, there's a good lad,' he snarled, his mouth full of spittle mixed with blood. Rogowski paled, and started to drag himself away from the battered tanks.

More shells exploded in the distance.

The fight seemed to be going well.

Simmo yanked on the hatch, which finally came free in his battered bleeding hand. He staggered back, caught off balance for a moment, then dropped it in the snow.

Simmo squinted into the HTank's interior gloom—

Snarling, Kattenheim launched himself from the innards of the HTank and Simmo stumbled back, shocked. But Kattenheim was wedged in the opening, cursing and spitting, fighting to drag his body free—

The opening had been crushed.

It was too narrow for the Nex to squeeze through.

Simmo picked up his blue package. Kattenheim was raging insanely, scarred red eyes wide with anger and hatred. He stopped suddenly, his gaze meeting Simmo's.

Simmo smiled.

'You are a lucky, lucky man,' said Kattenheim softly.

Simmo shrugged, initiating the ignition sequence on the package of HighJ explosive. Red digits started to flicker across the tiny digital display.

Kattenheim watched him impassively.

Simmo tossed the HighJ package to the ground beneath Kattenheim's protruding upper body. Kattenheim glanced down, and gave The Sarge a sickly sweet smile.

When his stare met Simmo's his anger vanished, to be replaced by a kind of deep sadness. A melancholy, or nostalgia; a realisation that his time had come.

'I will save you a place in Hell – at my feet,' he said, a blood-slick grimace twisting his lips.

'The Nex don't earn a place in Hell,' snarled Simmo, and turning, started to sprint up the slope, injured body listing to one side, blood pouring over his face and into his eyes, making him almost blind. He dived behind a low wall of rocks—

And heard the click of detonation . . .

Whirling, falling to lie on his back on the slope, Simmo, half screened, watched a column of flame flare skywards. A deep concussive blast rolled out. Superheated air washed over him and he watched droplets of liquid metal start to rain down, setting fire to the trees around the blast zone.

Flames roared—

And then slowly died.

Wearily, Simmo dragged himself back to his feet and continued up the steep slope under the gaze of Rogowski, who was nursing his shoulder.

Reaching the top, Simmo slumped to the ground and stared back down at the purple fires.

'You OK, Sarge?'

'Aye, lad.'

'That fucker had it coming.'

Simmo cocked his head at Rogowski and saw the look of hatred there. 'Yeah, a fucking Nex, eh, lad? I suppose they all have it coming?' he said sardonically.

'*All* the fuckers should burn.'

Simmo sighed, lying back on the hard trail. Tiny stones pressed into his back, into his hands, into his skull, and he could feel the flow of fresh blood running into his eyes.

546

And a terrible deep sadness filled him, flowed through his body and ate like acid through his soul.

What a fucking world we live in, he thought sombrely. What a world.

Carter's pain fled. Was forced aside. Kade's hand was hanging limp. It dived into Carter's pocket and pulled free the MercG. In the blink of an eye it activated, humming softly, and Kade whipped it above his head where it sliced cleanly through ten inches of ancient parapet, carving a neat arc of stone that dropped silently away towards the distant courtyard below. The high-tech garrotte swung on into Jam's leg, producing a spray of thick dark blood. A shot from the Browning echoed across the courtyard as Jam stumbled back howling and Kade felt something nick his ear. He frowned. 'Untidy,' he whispered.

Scrabbling against the ice, Kade was forced to drop the MercG. He grunted, cursing as it disappeared into the white expanse below. He dragged himself up onto the parapet and glanced over at Jam, who was lying on his back, a huge slice carved from his leg, the wound pumping blood into the snow. Kade leapt down and moved forward as Jam dragged himself to his feet. With a roar, he charged . . .

Kade moved in a blur and they met, fists crashing against heads, Jam's claws striking against Kade's chest. Then they whirled away from each other in sprays of blood.

They circled, leaving vivid trails through the snow.

'That hurt, did it, fucker?' mocked Kade, grinning.

'Shut up.'

'You'll walk like a fucking donkey tomorrow . . . if you walk at all –' Kade launched himself at Jam and again they crashed into one another, claws and fists beating and pounding. Jam slipped on the ice and fell backwards with Kade diving atop him, fists slamming. Jam's knee came up but Kade twisted, head-butting Jam's face twice before rolling free. Jam rolled, lightning-swift, armoured leg lashing out and knocking Kade's feet from under him . . . and for long moments they scrabbled on the snow until Kade's stare fixed on the Browning.

He leapt for the weapon, fingers curling around the familiar solid stock and as it came around in a blur of dark metal Jam bludgeoned down with all the might of both locked claws—

There was a sickening crack . . .

And Kade's arm hung limp as the Browning skittered through the snow.

Kade danced back, twisting to keep the injured and obviously broken arm away from Jam. He glanced down and saw bone protruding from flesh and cloth. He winced, but channelled away the pain for later use.

Jam nodded.

'You cannot win.'

'Ha!' said Kade. 'I'll fuck you from behind and then piss on your mother!'

Jam launched himself at Kade, who stumbled back, blood pumping from his broken arm. Kade slipped on the ice, went down hard, head smashing against the parapet. Stars flashed bright in his mind and Jam placed his heavy armoured foot against Kade's throat – against *Carter*'s throat . . .

They halted briefly, sprinkled with white, like frozen sculptures in ice. Then Jam pressed down, using his heavy weight and his bulk. Kade choked, and with his good arm beat against Jam's injured blood-pumping leg. But Jam did not flinch and did not cry out in pain. He ignored the beating like a man ignores the ineffectual slap of a child.

'Fuck you, fuck you!' screamed Kade, face red with impotent fury.

Calmly, Carter took control from Kade and colour flooded back into his vision. With it came pain, smashing up from the broken arm and the pressure in his throat and he looked up at Jam, at those evil slitted eyes. Tears streamed down his face.

'You cry?' Jam lessened the pressure a little and stooped, staring hard into Carter's face. 'You've changed, Carter. What happened then? It was as if you were a different person.'

'It wasn't me,' choked Carter. 'It was Kade. The fucker always claims he will get the job done, get the killing done . . . but he fucked up this time, didn't he? He has left us both to die . . .'

'Kade?' whispered Jam, copper eyes hooded.

Carter could hear the distant roar of engines – and something else, a distant growling like that of a—

Quake.

'Jam, you and me – we'll both die,' snarled Carter through blood and saliva, his tears hot against his cheeks. 'Durell is betraying you even as he has you do his dirty work. I didn't realise you had stooped so low, Jam, I didn't realise your past and your friendships meant so little.'

Jam's head tilted. He removed the pressure from Carter's throat and moved across the snow, to where the small silver box nestled against the stone flags.

Carter watched him warily.

Beneath him, the castle began to vibrate.

'*The quake's coming*,' hissed Kade. '*Run!*'

'Fuck off, *pussy*. I don't need *your* advice.'

Jam returned and dropped to a stoop beside Carter.

549

He pushed the box out, held clumsily in his dark claws. His eyes were narrowed copper slits and Carter scowled in confusion.

'What are you doing?'

'Take it. Go. Save Natasha.'

'*What?*'

Jam stood, rearing to his full height. And then he *roared*, a terrifying sound that mingled with the cacophony of the approaching earthquake. It echoed around the bleak walls of the castle, filled with anger, hatred and pure frustration . . .

Carter scrambled to his feet, clutching the ornate box. He flicked it open, and within nestled the dark disc – the Avelach. The healing machine that he could use to bring Natasha back from the brink of death . . .

Jam dropped to a crouch, then stood once more. He was breathing deeply, panting, his stare fixed on Carter as he wrestled with inner demons.

'Why, Jam?'

'A present. From an old friend.'

The castle started to groan, and the walls began to sway. Parts of the battlements suddenly fell away, dropping to the distant courtyard where they impacted and exploded, showering the courtyard with stone shrapnel.

'Go, Carter. Go now.'

'I need to know why.'

Jam smiled then, and for just an instant Carter caught a glimpse of his old friend, a glint of the man who had been Jam – imprisoned within the shell of the ScorpNex.

'We all have our internal battles,' said Jam softly. 'Yours is Kade. Mine is – a different kind.'

Carter started to back away, towards the stairwell. The whole castle was shaking now as the quake took it and the mountains in its fist. Distant avalanches rocked the steep sides of the valleys, millions of tonnes of rock and ice and snow tumbling from high reaches and crushing the world beneath—

'You know what Kade is? You *know* him?' said Carter.

'Yes.'

'Tell me!'

But the world was descending into insanity . . .

'Go!' screamed Jam.

Carter turned to run, pain and panic driving him.

'And Carter?'

'Yeah?'

'Tell Nicky I love her.'

Carter nodded, and disappeared into the darkness of the winding stairwell. Through the falling snow Jam stared long and hard at the spot where Carter had been – and then turned towards the tower, the tower containing Durell and the QuakeHub and the core of all Jam's misery, pain, confusion, frustration and loss.

Evolution, he had said.

An evolution of the body – but a regression of the mind.

With a grim look, Jam stalked across the buckling stone flags of the battlements towards the dark confines of the tower and his mentor within.

The quake was rumbling, smashing across the Austrian landscape, shaking the mountains in the fury of its clenched and threatening fists. On the slope leading to the castle stood Simmo, Mongrel, Rogowski, Mo, Haggis, Remic, Fegs, Oz, Kavanagh, Root Beer and Samasuwo. Bob Bob was rubbing at the custard stains on his combats and muttering about detergents; everybody else was staring at the SP57 tanks, their engines roaring as their guns pounded the occasional shell into the shuddering castle.

The whine of abused engines howled through the sky. The gathered men cocked weapons in weary hands and turned to watch the Comanche settle into the snow-slush on the trail, its suspension bobbing.

The Priest stepped out, sandals slopping in the snow and robes whipping madly in the down draught of the war machine's rotors. He was followed by a woman, tall and slim and pale-skinned, with a long fan of brown hair worn loose across her shoulders and with piercing green eyes set in a pretty oval face. She was dressed all in black and carried a sub-machine gun. The Priest carried nothing except his Bible.

'You here for the party?' asked Mongrel, his face grey with exhaustion.

'Bless you, my son. I am here for Carter . . .'

Mongrel stared darkly into The Priest's eyes. And he remembered The Priest's words back on Crete. '*Don't make me come looking for you, Carter. Don't make me hunt you down – it would be a waste of a good man. One of the best we have.*'

With a sudden snarl Mongrel went for his M24 machine carbine, barrel lifting and finger squeezing the trigger. Simmo grabbed the gun, wrenching it skywards as a spray of bullets lifted on trajectories of fire.

'Whoa, lad,' snapped Simmo, easing the weapon away from Mongrel's paws.

Mongrel scowled at The Priest, who held his hands in the air, apart, a soft smile on his lips.

'You misunderstand my intentions,' said The Priest gently. Behind him, Roxi was pointing her Heckler & Koch MP5 at Mongrel. He glared at her, noting the determination and strength in her piercing green eyes.

'You've come to kill Carter,' snarled Mongrel, spraying spittle. 'Yeah, lads, he's come to kill Carter!'

552

There was a rumbling of defiance and unrest.

The Priest swallowed. He was facing a potential lynch squad. A mutiny. 'No, no, lads, I am here to find out what the hell is going on! The Lord has guided me, and yes, I do need to find Carter. He has disobeyed orders. He has disobeyed *Spiral*.'

'You try and kill Carter, and we fuck you bad,' said Mongrel angrily.

'Where is he?'

'In there.' Mongrel pointed at the shaking castle. Walls were toppling even as they watched. The rest of the TankSquad operatives were shooting any stray Nex who made a run for it from the gates. 'He beyond your wrath now, Priest. He beyond your fiery revenge . . . you fucking bureaucrats, everything in black and white – there no middle ground, no *compromise*. Carter – he in there, he trying to save Natasha, yeah, but he trying to take down Durell, he trying to smash the QuakeHub. He trying to save the world, Priest . . . with or without Spiral's permission; with or without divine fucking intervention. You, Priest – you need God. But Carter is alone, and he ask favour of no man. You understand?'

The Priest scowled. 'I am not here to murder the man,' he rumbled.

Mongrel grinned a shark-grin. 'Not unless he not follow orders, yeah? Carter has own guidance, own morals. He will do what right. If you not see that, then you just as blind as every other fucking bureaucrat in the universe.'

'He is confronting Durell?'

'Yes.'

The Priest took a deep breath. 'Maybe he needs a helping hand, then? We are standing here talking whilst the whole world is crumbling around our ears! We've got to help him . . . to stop Durell . . . to stop the quakes . . .'

'What about your God sending thunderbolts from the heavens to save us?' interjected Remic, his M24 held loosely in battle-scarred fingers. 'You seem to be an expert in that field, Priest. Maybe you could ask for a bit of celestial help?'

'God helps those who help themselves,' said The Priest primly. 'Now . . . gentlemen? Shall we go to Mr Carter's aid? Or wait for him to be served in slices on a cold meat platter?'

Mongrel grabbed his weapon from Simmo's battered hands and stalked towards his Comanche. 'We'll take my chopper,' he said, squinting at The Priest. 'And you can leave your fucking girlfriend behind.'

'As you wish,' said The Priest, fingering his rosary beads.

'Simmo?'

'Aye, lad?'

'Fancy giving me a bit of a hand?'

Simmo prodded the Sig P7 9mm into the small of The Priest's back. 'Don't mind if I do,' he snarled through a demonic mask of drying blood.

'That will be unnecessary,' soothed The Priest, his dark eyes hard, mouth a grim line. 'My mission is not to kill Carter; my mission is to stop the destruction of the Earth.'

'We'll be the judge of that,' said Simmo sombrely.

The castle was crumbling.

Jam squeezed his bulk through the corridors, up the steep steps and into the tower room where Durell stood, facing the rippling liquid screen. Images flickered through it like gun-bursts, flashes of destruction from across the globe; scenes of his Nex armies warring with soldiers of every nation . . .

554

'I don't understand,' screamed Durell suddenly, without turning. 'Why has the quake come here? What the fuck did I do wrong? What the fuck is the QIV *thinking* of?'

He reached down, grasped the black cube and yanked it free of its housing. But nothing changed – the castle still rocked, pitching violently . . . and now there came the whistle and crump of shells from Spiral's few remaining tanks. They exploded in the courtyard down below, adding to the cacophony of insane noise and the rocking, heaving insanity that had become the world.

'Maybe the processor is betraying you,' said Jam softly.

Durell whirled. 'Come on, we'll take the helicopter on the roof. It does not matter – the quakes are in progress, the world's armies are weakened, the Nex are strong! We cannot fail now, we must return to Egypt, from there we can—'

'Maybe it is the LVA, returning to haunt you.'

Durell stopped then and fixed his stare on the towering figure of Jam. He licked his lips with a small dark tongue. His eyes narrowed. 'What is wrong with you?'

'By making me Nex you promised me Heaven.'

Durell nodded, smiling, moving as if to push past Jam—

'But you delivered me into a waking Hell.'

Jam's claw lashed out, hammering against Durell and throwing him back across the narrow tower room. He struck the bench on which the dark screen rested and it toppled to the ground, smashing with a flare of obsidian fire. Black fluid poured over the stonework, eating into it like acid and burning with dark flames.

'What the fuck are you doing?' said Durell calmly.

'Give me the processor.'

'Come and take it.' Durell shrugged himself free of his

555

robes and beneath them huge coils of distorted muscle tensed. Between the two men – the two Nex – the dark fire from the smashed screen flared up and danced violently, silently, a barrier forcing them apart, a wall through which neither could pass . . .

They waited patiently, slitted copper eyes staring at one another.

'If we do not leave here, the quake will tear down this castle,' said Durell as the flames started to die down. Holes appeared in the stone flags from the powerful black screen acid, expanding circular portals showing a distant drop to the hall below. 'We will both die.'

'Then we both die. Give me the processor.'

Durell said nothing.

The quake was ripping through the Austrian mountainside. Both Nex stumbled as the tower swayed, and more shells could be heard raining down. Outside the tower they heard the whine of helicopter rotors.

Durell leapt suddenly at Jam and they smashed into one another—

As the quake tore the castle apart.

The tower collapsed and millions of tonnes of ancient stone fell. The castle buckled and heaved, was taken in the mouth of the quake and pulverised by mammoth jaws of rock and iron.

Stone sprayed out from the huge crater into which the castle sank and was swallowed, was consumed – as if in some ritual slaughter, some titanic revenge.

The mountains reclaiming their own.

The Alps taking back what was rightfully theirs: quarried and stripped and hewn and now absorbed – once again – into nature.

The roaring of the quake's gradual settling lasted for hours, slowly rumbling to a halt and returning peace and tranquillity to this quiet corner of Austria. It left behind a heavy cloud of stone dust, as well as torn earth, swallowed rock and a crater of war in the landscape. Gradually, the stone dust settled.

The castle had gone.

Nothing moved in the stillness.

The snow continued to fall . . . and soon covered everything in a blanket of virgin white.

Carter stood next to Mongrel on the mountainside. Below, in the valley, the tanks were retreating.

'They died together,' said Mongrel softly. 'We saw them both go down.'

Carter nodded. 'Swallowed by the quake that they created.'

'Spiral will send PopBots to scan for traces . . . when things finally return to normal.'

'What's happening with the Nex?'

'There's been wholesale slaughter worldwide. Human casualties numbering many hundreds of thousands, maybe even millions, I imagine – both civilian and military. Who can foresee the damage of the quake? Not me! But the soldiers of the world are beating the Nex back . . . and without the QIV's influence world military systems are slowly coming back on-line. According to ECube reports coming in every few seconds from different sources – tanks and fighters, satellite comms and weapons systems – the whole fucking WarGrid is self-repairing. Once everything's up and running we'll wipe those fucking Nex out once and for all.'

Carter nodded, his face grey with exhaustion and pain; haunted.

'I've learned one thing from all this,' Mongrel went on.

'What's that?'

'You do not fuck with Nature.' Mongrel reached over, placed his hand on Carter's shoulder. 'You OK, mate?'

Carter stared at Mongrel with war-torn eyes, filled with the horror of a thousand battles he never wished to relive. He took a deep breath of crisp cold mountain air, and with shaking blood-crusted fingers lit a cigarette thoughtfully provided by Mongrel. His broken arm was in a tight sling, and he clasped the silver box containing the Avelach to his chest as if it might bring *him* strength.

'Yeah, I'll fucking live. But we need to move, and we need to move *now*. Are you on for sharing a flight back to London? To Natasha and Nicky?'

'Be my fucking pleasure, mate,' said Mongrel, nodding.

They climbed into the Comanche and, as the sun was setting behind the mountains and withdrawing its light from a snowy landscape of incredible white clean beauty, the machine leapt into the air. With engines thrumming, it slewed sideways through the valley and was joined by a second Comanche piloted by Heneghan and containing The Priest, Roxi and Simmo. The two machines turned smoothly and suddenly accelerated, rotors thumping over the Austrian snow.

CHAPTER 20

NATASHA

The two Comanche war machines powered across Europe. Carter squatted in the back of one helicopter, face drawn, pain enfolding his awareness as he clutched the silver box to his chest and gazed out over the sprawling chaos below.

Occasionally the world would shake, accompanied by sounds of thunder. Carter stared out with bleak eyes, his soul calm for the moment and at least thankful that Durell had been halted in his quest for control . . . but in the same heartbeat he felt terrified at the state in which he might find Natasha when he finally arrived back in London.

It had been a long, hard flight.

And it was far from over.

As they flew, Mongrel ensconced in the HIDSS helmet and the bullet-riddled Comanche juddering around them, rapid-fire messages and comms flashed through on the ECubes – rattling with intel from the Spiral mainframes at a colossal rate.

According to the messages received, the earthquakes were gradually subsiding. Spiral HQs were collating data

559

from agencies, Spiral operatives and governments on a global scale – sorting information and sending it out to their teams. Somehow, the QIV had infiltrated many of Spiral's comms networks, including many of the ECube's functions – distorting information and corrupting the Spiral databases. Spiral were relaying messages through the temporary AnComm Posts, analogue transmitters and receivers that acted as ECube data bridges and had at least managed to slow the QIV's digital assault.

Carter toyed with his ECube, idly watching flashes of information. The world was in the process of getting its shit together after this act of global terrorism under the stomping boots of the earthquakes – finally. Whole armies were on the move, fighter jets were securing and patrolling airspace, navies were steaming ahead, submarines patrolling cold deep waters.

Carter shook his head in disbelief.

He remembered casting the schematics for the QIII military processor into the dark sea, and being thankful that the processor was better off dead. Instead, unbeknown to him, the QIII's successor had been almost complete, almost operational and destroying the QIII had been merely a stalling tactic on his part.

Carter gazed down at the silver box against his chest, running his battered fingers over the finely carved dull silver surface. His fingers fumbled for a moment, and with a tiny click the box opened. He stared down at the simple black disc. His finger moved forward to touch it . . . and he paused.

Something seemed to whine within him, as if some sixth sense was warning him of the dangers of playing with this awesome and terribly powerful machine. The Avelach. Carter frowned, and placed his finger against the surface—

560

White light pierced his mind, a fan of sparkling laser fingers that circled, and then disappeared to a needle point. The metal was cold and preternaturally smooth under his touch.

And then—

His pain soothed away. He felt the white light spread through his mind and with a shiver he felt it *examining* him. A tiny itching of flesh came from his bullet wound, and then he felt something moving through him, something hard and metallic gliding between his ribs. He wriggled in discomfort – the metal object moved under and *through* his flesh, and then dropped out onto the fabric of the Comanche's seat. He felt his arm straighten, forcing its way through the bindings that held it strapped tightly in place – there came the tiniest of clicks and he *felt* the bone knit together, the swelling around the damaged bone and flesh reducing in swelling.

Carter shivered again – and realised that his eyes were closed against the white light. He opened them, breathed deeply, and his weariness had gone. Not with any great jolt – but gently, as if drugs had just soothed away his troubles as he reclined in a hot bath.

Carter withdrew his finger from the Avelach and, reaching behind him, lifted the flattened stub of metal that had been resting inside him. He stared at it – the flattened sliver of bullet – in wonder at first, and then with a sudden, growing *hope*.

He flexed his arm, and noticed that the loss of skin from the motorbike crash had gone – to be replaced by a perfect sheen of pale newborn skin. His breathing came in shallow, panting gasps.

'Can this thing go any faster?'

'It's going as fast as it can, Carter.'

'Well, push it *harder*.'

'I *am* fucking pushing, Carter.'

Carter slumped back and slowly, with care and respect, closed the silver box. He stared at the finely carved inscriptions. The whorls were infinitely delicate, and peering close he could see that the work was truly magnificent even to his untrained eye.

Carter licked his lips.

Fear suddenly leapt into his mind . . .

'What if I am too late?' he muttered.

'Eh?'

'Nothing, Mongrel. Just fly.'

'Weather's getting bad.'

'Is The Priest still with us?'

'*Da*, Carter, he is. We keep close eye on him, good buddy, not you worry. Simmo keep Sig in The Priest's back, make sure he not on special mission from Spiral.'

Carter shrugged, grinning sourly, and gazed down over the insanity of a crumbled, *crushed* world.

Night had fallen. And with it had come the rain.

The Comanche helicopters flew in over the English Channel, crossing near Dover with the distant streak of white cliffs shimmering through the gloom. Carter watched them flash by in a blur and turned, gazing back over the rain-hammered expanse of sea.

As they approached the hospital in a whine of deceleration, The Priest's voice rattled over the comm. 'There's something going on down there . . .'

Mongrel squinted. 'What?'

'Shit,' hissed Carter, flicking free the safety on his Browning and gazing down with a look of horror. Shapes were sprinting across the wet tarmac, black shells glistening. Several halted, triangular heads turning to examine the helicopter—

562

'MiniGun?' requested Mongrel, grinning wickedly.

'MiniGun,' agreed Carter as the Comanche's engines howled and the machine veered, nose dipping. There came a heavy whirring as the General Electric MiniGun started to spin, hitting five thousand revs as Mongrel's sights locked on to six of the Nex creatures, one standing atop a roof-dented ambulance, illuminated by the flashing blue lights.

Mongrel pulled the trigger.

The gun fired and thousands of heavy-calibre rounds ploughed through the tarmac of the hospital car park and cut the Sleeper Nex into bloody strips. Bullets punched the ambulance with metal fists and the Sleeper on top of the vehicle, staring with slitted copper eyes, was hurled backwards against the brick wall and smashed into smears of gore. The MiniGun whined down and Mongrel landed the Comanche, its suspension groaning. Rain swirled through the blood and pulped sarcocarp of Nex flesh strewn across the tarmac.

Carter stowed the silver box in his pack, grabbed his M24 and leapt from the war chopper. The violent wind from the rotors smashed against him. Mongrel was right there behind him. They were only half aware of the second Comanche touching down . . . and of Simmo and The Priest leaping into the car park with their own weapons. Roxi followed, smoothly, calmly, her watchful gaze fixed on The Priest's back.

There were more of the strange big catlike creatures, and they had retreated into the hospital under the onslaught of the Comanche's MiniGun. They had disappeared far inside, leaving only blood streaks against sterile white tiles to mark their passage.

Carter sprinted forward.

'A panic burst has just come through on the ECube – request for heavy artillery,' called The Priest. Carter whirled, his stare meeting The Priest's gold-flecked gaze.

'From here?'

The Priest nodded.

'Shit.'

Carter sprinted into the Accident & Emergency foyer of the hospital, then into the triage waiting area. Bodies littered the plastic-themed waiting room; some were lying dead, streams of blood leaking from wide wounds in belly and groin, glassy eyes staring impassively at the strip-light squares above. Some had been tossed like toys over the plastic chairs to lie at irregular twisted angles. Some lay scattered in several separate torn pieces.

Carter stepped over a torn-off arm and heard a growl – his Browning jerked up as the Sleeper Nex attacked from the wide white corridor, claws leaving tracks of blood against the smashed tiles . . . it leapt, and the Browning boomed in Carter's fist. Behind him the other Spiral operatives opened fire.

The Sleeper seemed to dance in mid-air, twitching as if controlled by wires like some demonic marionette. It slammed to the floor and its head lifted, copper eyes staring at Carter. A growl rattled from its punctured lungs . . . then it slumped down, blood flowing in a wide pool. Without a further sound it died.

Carter swallowed hard, replacing the mag in his Browning. He had used all thirteen bullets.

Glancing behind him he saw the others nodding at him to take the lead. Carter sprinted forward through the hospital corridors. Twice more they came across Sleeper Nex – and twice more a hail of bullets felled them as they leapt, punching them to the floor and drilling them into a state of mangled death.

'Where the fuck did these come from?' growled Mongrel, wiping alien blood from his face.

'And more importantly, what *are* they?' said Carter.

'One of Durell's best-kept secrets,' said The Priest softly. The others turned to look at him and he shrugged. 'The Sleepers are part-breeds, not Nex but the original template for the Nex: a genetic master from which the Nex evolved. They are older than any of us can imagine, and far too savage and unpredictable to use as an army – hence Durell developing the Nex who are more, shall we say, *obedient*. Durell has been working on the Nex Project for longer than Spiral even *dares* to dream. The Nex you normally see – they are refined, a distillation of the pure hard-core terror, the pure bestial nature of the Sleepers. The Sleepers are *old*. And the Sleepers are pure evil. One avenue of Spiral scientific exploration even considers the possibility that Durell didn't actually create the Nex. Rather, the Nex discovered him. *He* is *their* tool. A reversal of what we believe to be true. Whatever, the fact remains that the Sleepers are Durell's wolves, his hunters, and if they scent you they will never allow you to escape. They will pursue you to the ends of the earth and eat your soul.'

'I think we need a *long* talk when this shit is over,' growled Carter, frowning.

'If it ever is over,' said The Priest calmly, closing his eyes.

Turning, Carter moved forward, down another wide corridor. They came across a few people who were still alive and had barricaded themselves into rooms: doctors and patients, some armed with fire axes and peering through glass with blood-speckled faces. One group of doctors had cornered a Sleeper Nex and between them had hacked it to bits with a collection of axes and kitchen knives. They came across another group of patients, one of whom had a sawn-off shotgun. Again, between them

565

they had managed to severely wound a Sleeper and it lay in a pool of glistening slick blood while they tried to kick it to death.

Carter moved on, his face grim.

The small Spiral group emerged into a corridor and a Sleeper stood, peering in through the small glass window of a door halfway down the passageway. Even as the group arrived bullets slammed through the glass and the Sleeper flipped to one side to dodge the assault, then whirled low and with incredible agility reared and slammed against the door, which crashed inwards on long shards of splintered timber.

Carter opened fire, sprinting down the corridor with his Browning bucking in his fist. His boots ate the distance, grim stare locked on the Sleeper's head which swung towards him. It suddenly charged, huge muscles writhing as its claws smashed the tiles beneath them into powder. Carter's gun clicked on an empty magazine and he pulled around his M24, firing a hail of bullets from the hammering weapon – and as he and the creature were about to collide he flipped himself right, sliding along the tiles as the Sleeper tried to suddenly twist. The carbine's bullets ate a long line across its underbelly. The Nex grunted and hit the ground in a gush of blood and Carter was past the creature as Simmo's and Mongrel's bullets tore into its thrashing carcass. Carter spun around into the small hospital room, gaze turning first to Nicky and her shocked face, her gun held in loose hands—

His eyes focused swiftly on Natasha's bedside . . .

And the flat lines on the monitor screens.

Nicky turned, confusion twisting across her face.

Carter dropped his gun and dragged his pack from his back. He fell beside Natasha, his hand smoothing back her hair, gazing down into the serenity of her cold still features. He pulled free the silver box, dropping it with a discordant clash on the tiles. The Avelach was cool to his touch—

'Place it against her breast,' came Nicky's voice. Carter turned, stared into her eyes, then turned back to Natasha and carefully placed the disc against her soft skin.

He stood and pushed himself back from the bed, his brow furrowed in panic.

Nothing seemed to happen . . .

He heard a commotion behind him. More distant gunshots, and the heavy blast of a shotgun followed by the splatter of its impacting shells. He did not move. His stare was fixed on Natasha's face—

The constant and eerily steady *beeee . . . eeeeep* of the monitor finally intruded on his senses.

'It's not working,' he whispered.

Nicky moved forward, checked Natasha's pulse – her *lack* of pulse. Lack of life. Natasha's heart was not beating. Nicky looked up into Carter's eyes, bit her lip, but could not bring herself to say the words – the words that she knew to be true. She whirled on a surprised Mongrel and Simmo and the two battle-stained warriors took a step back.

'Get a fucking *doctor*!' she hissed.

Carter placed his hand against Natasha's brow. Nicky placed her hand on his arm then, and he turned slowly and looked down into her eyes. She took a deep breath.

'What is it?'

'She's dead, Carter.'

'But . . . the machine . . . the *Avelach* . . .'

'It *heals*, Carter. It does not bring back the dead.'

The room whirled, smashed into him, slammed his face against a wall of chaos. It invaded him, ripped into his throat and tore out his insides. Carter fell to his knees, his hands sliding across Natasha's dead body to rest by his sides.

Mongrel and Simmo appeared, dragging two doctors with them. The men looked confused, traumatised by their violent encounter with a Sleeper Nex.

They stared from Carter to Nicky and then back.

Nicky said, 'This is my friend, Natasha. She is carrying a child – I think you need to work fast, gentlemen.' They moved forward and Carter scrambled back, was helped to his feet where he stood, swaying numbly, watching but unable to watch. His gaze was fixed on the shining silver instruments as the doctors applied their skills despite the shock of their own harrowing and horrifying experiences . . .

Blood splashed and dripped from the bed.

Stained the tiles.

Natasha's blood.

Mongrel's hand was there, right on Carter's shoulder.

There came a cry, the ragged squawk of a premature newborn. Nicky wrapped the babe in a blanket as the umbilical cord was tied off and cut and Carter looked hard at the doctors who stood confused, instruments dripping blood, returning his stare.

'Save her!' he cried, straining to get forward. Mongrel held him back and Simmo moved forward to help Mongrel to restrain the distraught Spiral man. 'Fucking *do something*!' screamed Carter.

But the men did not move.

They looked towards Nicky, confused . . .

And the blood-filled world spiralled down into an insanity of darkness . . .

Of *greys* . . .

Of *black and white*.

★

It was late.

Smoke hung heavy in the small room of The Gunmaker's Arms public house. Against the bar leant three men, clothes ragged and torn, smeared with dried blood. The locals in the pub on the outskirts of London avoided them – had been doing so all night as the three steadily drank themselves into oblivion.

Glasses lay scattered, stools overturned; the atmosphere was one of despair and fear.

'They tried to bring her back for an hour,' said The Priest, savouring his pint of Guinness and leaving a frothy moustache against his beard. He shook his head sadly. 'They should have left her . . . God had claimed her soul. They could never have brought it back from the other side.'

'Did you see Carter's eyes?' rumbled Simmo.

Mongrel nodded. 'He could not understand why the machine did not work.'

'Like Nicky said, it is a machine to heal. It was never designed to bring back the dead. It was never designed to work *miracles*. It is no God Machine.' The Priest tasted the words with a sour grimace.

'It worked miracles when it created the fucking *Nex*,' said Mongrel, eyeing the large barrel-chested man and resting his back against the bar. The pub had nearly emptied now – business was quiet, due to the earthquakes – and it was far past closing time. But the landlord did not have the heart, nor the courage, to demand that these three men should leave.

'That was different,' said The Priest softly. 'Natasha was badly wounded. In reality, she should never have lasted as long as she did . . . Carter should be thankful that the child survived – it was extremely premature.'

'Well, I let *you* pass on those sentiments when you see him next,' snapped Mongrel.

569

'How is he?' rumbled Simmo. 'They pump him with enough drugs to halt a rhino!'

Mongrel shrugged. 'I think they keep him sedated for a few days. He had look of insanity about him when they could not revive Natasha – damn near tried to kill those two doctors and eight JT8s who arrived to sort out the Sleeper Nex. Fuck, I've never seen a man fight like that . . .'

They all nodded.

'What was that he said?' asked Simmo. 'About . . . *Kade*?'

'He was delirious,' said Mongrel, nodding into his Green King beer. 'Fucker had just lost his woman. Man's allowed to get a little fucked up in the head when something like that happens.'

'It is a great shame that we petty mortals lead such weak and fragile lives,' said The Priest softly, his voice filled with great melancholy. 'Like glass, we shatter. Like pottery, we break. *Yea, though I walk through the valley of the shadow of death, I will fear no evil: for thou art with me.*' He paused. The Priest had his Bible on the bar, and it had become stained with beer. '*Surely goodness and mercy shall follow me all the days of my life: and I will dwell in the house of the LORD for ever.*' He glanced around, tears in his great brown eyes. 'Sometimes, my friends, I find death a very hard pill to swallow.'

'Well,' whispered Mongrel sombrely, finishing his beer and pulling on his heavy combat jacket. Live rounds rattled in his pockets. 'It's just the fucking law of the jungle, ain't it?' he said bitterly.

SIU Transcript

Due to a combination of the reduction of earthquakes and return of global military and electronic control by the QIV processor upon its [*suspected*] destruction, world powers were able to quickly organise and disseminate armies, air forces and naval forces in order to push back the Nex infiltrators and retake control.

Several pitched battles were fought, most notably in China, Siberia, the UK, Thailand, Germany, France, Norway, Nigeria, Peru, Iran and the central United States. It is ironic that Durell spread most heavy forces of Nex numbers around the globe at strategic positions needed to pull off his scheme, leaving his own central (if somewhat mobile) headquarters relatively unprotected. He was relying more on secrecy and speed of execution and it is acknowledged that if subject CARTER had not been involved in Durell's pursuit, it is unlikely his HQ in Austria would have been discovered – and destroyed – so easily (although it is currently unexplained why an earthquake struck at that exact location when Durell was supposedly in control).

Currently, world affairs dictate an AMBER state of emergency. The Nex forces are retreating or have been destroyed. The enemy's situation can best be described as *disintegrating*. The World Investigations Committee (WIC) has been commended and applauded on its excellent handling of the situation. General Hiamito Kassambra, spokesperson for the WIC said, 'Yes, our priority was action and speed of reaction – and without our decisiveness and ability to operate immediately and effectively on a true global scale, this state of world emergency would have been much more serious, and the traitor Durell probably successful in his machinations. We are to be congratulated, I think'.

Little is known of the LVA channels used to direct the earthquakes at the control impulses of the QIV processor. If this can be understood correctly, then the LVA channels are a freak geological occurrence that has a future potential to make the actual world plates unstable. Several research centres are being set up – even now before the war is truly over – to investigate this phenomenon.

Little is known of the QIV processor, other than it is based on existing QIII technology – all known examples of which were destroyed just over a year ago, again in events concerning Durell. The QIV's base architecture was put in place by Count Feuchter [*deceased*] and the lead designers on the QIV were Jessica Rade at Spiral_Q, and Tademo Svdenska and Suzy Pagan at Spiral_R in Tibet. This processor and all relative computing developments are now under investigation by Spiral Tac and the Spiral SIU.

To conclude:

Spiral has once again been integral in halting a plot for world domination. Further investigations are needed to determine exactly what Durell's ultimate goals were, and we still need to work hard to discover what actually happened to him - or his corpse. The file is far from closed. The game is far from over.

Search >>

Keywords: LVA, FEUCHTER, DURELL, NEX, DEMOL, QII, QIII, QIV, Spiral_Q, Spiral_R, LVA, WIC

ADVERTISING FEATURE

The TV sparkled into life with a digital buzz of electro-hum, diamond-sharp images spinning and morphing into the jewelled liquid logo of [newly formed x35 scale] *Firestarter Fuels!*

Do you despair at fuel companies always trying to rip you off? Do you tear out your hair at dictators trying to ram their overrated products down your throat with the Maximum in Hardcore? Do you WEEP when other fuel companies try and kill you with their earthquakes because their technology is so DEVOLVED that they cannot control their own drilling rigs? YOU can stop this . . . YOU can change the world. YOU can make a whole big difference . . .

Scene pans: from the ravaged cities of London, New York and Paris, bodies pulped and smashed and bleeding under devastation, people screaming, pulling their hair, fighting and looting in the streets . . .
Scene morphs: into a crystalline metropolis, glittering skyscrapers, the world being rebuilt by happy smiling workmen in gleaming yellow hardhats, sharing jokes, slapping one another on the back, a mix of races, creeds, colours. The site is powered by *Firestarter Fuels* [LARGE x50scale PRODUCT PLACEMENT HERE]

Firestarter Fuels proudly present Premium Grade good ol' Petrol, Oil and Natural Gas – just the way you know it and love it, and without the hassle of genetically altered warmongering dictators using their terrible power to take over the Globe. Go on, use *Firestarter*, because you know your children deserve a better future . . .

SCENE DISSOLVES TO ETERNITY

some photographs of a summer's day
a little boy's lifetime away
is all I've left of everything we've done
like a pale moon in a sunny sky
death gazes down as I pass by
to remind me that I'm but my father's son

i offer up to you
this tribute

Tank Park Salute
Billy Bragg

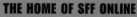